KENNEDY MUST BE KILLED

KENNEDY MUST BE KILLED

Chuck Helppie

iUniverse, Inc.
New York Bloomington

Copyright © 2009 by Chuck Helppie

All rights reserved. No part of this book may be used or reproduced by any means, graphic, electronic, or mechanical, including photocopying, recording, taping or by any information storage retrieval system without the written permission of the publisher except in the case of brief quotations embodied in critical articles and reviews.

Certain characters in this work are historical figures, and certain events portrayed did take place. However, this is a work of fiction. All of the other characters, names, and events as well as all places, incidents, organizations, and dialogue in this novel are either the products of the author's imagination or are used fictitiously.

iUniverse books may be ordered through booksellers or by contacting:

iUniverse
1663 Liberty Drive
Bloomington, IN 47403
www.iuniverse.com
1-800-Authors (1-800-288-4677)

Because of the dynamic nature of the Internet, any Web addresses or links contained in this book may have changed since publication and may no longer be valid. The views expressed in this work are solely those of the author and do not necessarily reflect the views of the publisher, and the publisher hereby disclaims any responsibility for them.

ISBN: 978-1-4401-8518-2 (sc)
ISBN: 978-1-4401-8520-5 (dj)
ISBN: 978-1-4401-8519-9 (ebook)

Library of Congress Control Number: 2009912011

Printed in the United States of America

iUniverse rev. date: 01/21/10

Author's Note

Many of the characters in *Kennedy Must Be Killed* may be recognizable to the reader while other characters may puzzle the reader as to whether or not they are fictional or real-life personages. As a fact-based story, I deliberately intended to perplex the reader as to what is historically true and what isn't. The fascination with the story will allow the reader to come to his own conclusion.

I can assure the reader that I have taken the utmost care in researching the historical settings, places, characters, and dialogue to remain as accurate as possible to the known facts. As one example, the reader may be interested to know that the dialogue of J. Edgar Hoover was based on research from his actual writings and speeches and was carefully crafted in order to present a point of view that reflected his stance on whether a leader of men must also be a moral man.

These historical facts are not disputed:

On November 22, 1963, President John F. Kennedy was shot and killed on the streets of Dallas, Texas.

On September 24, 1964, the United States government emphatically pronounced Lee Harvey Oswald to be the "lone gunman" with no evidence of a conspiracy in the president's murder. *"On the basis of the evidence before the Commission it concludes that, Oswald acted alone."*

On March 29, 1979, the United States government declared *"...on the basis of the evidence available to it, that President John F. Kennedy was probably assassinated as a result of a conspiracy. The committee is unable to identify the other gunman or the extent of the conspiracy."*

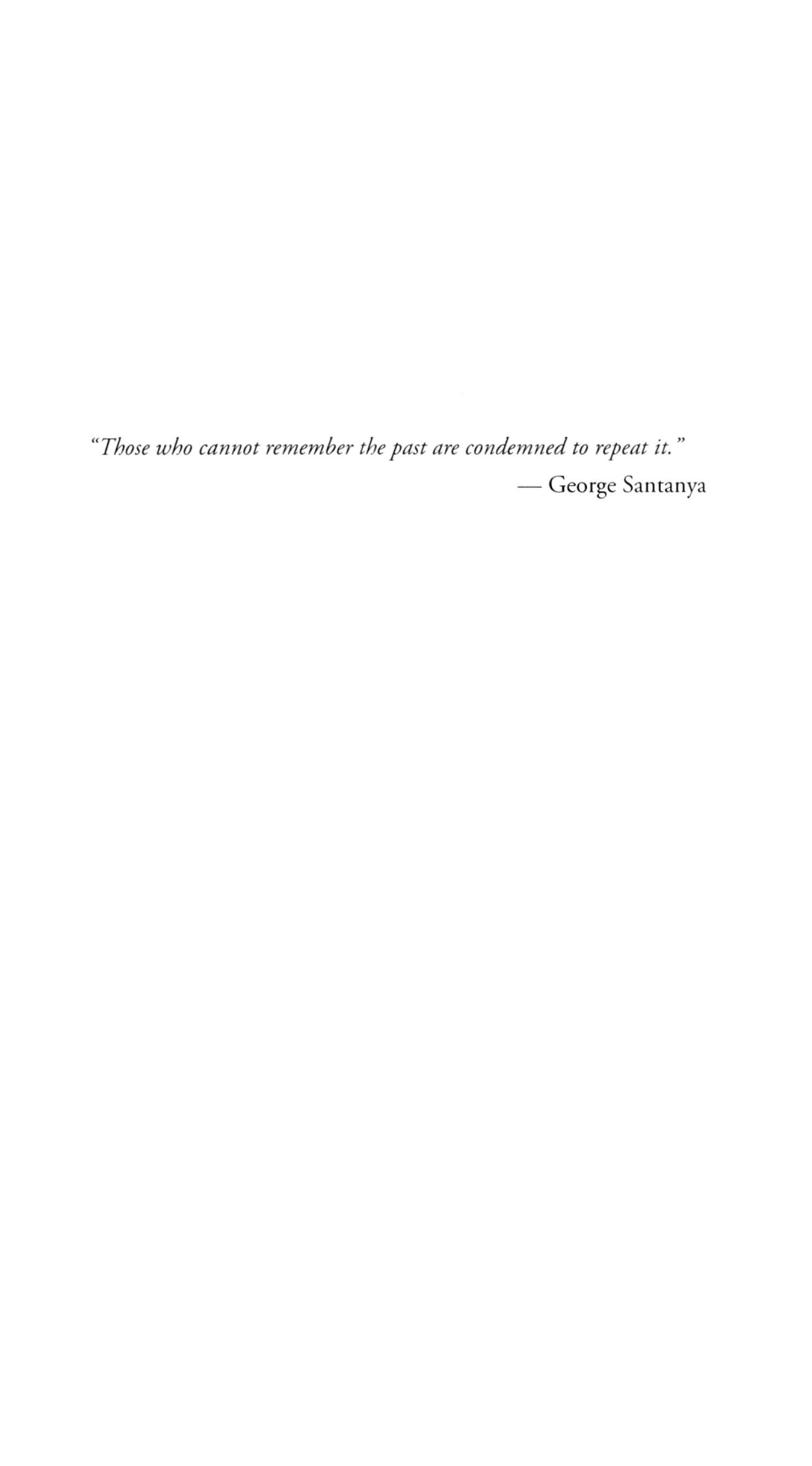

"Those who cannot remember the past are condemned to repeat it."
— George Santanya

November 22, 1963
12:30 PM

I knew the moment I squeezed the trigger that something had gone wrong.

The recoil of the rifle didn't deliver the customary hard, crisp jolt to my shoulder. The sound was dirty and muffled. I immediately knew from all the hours I had spent practicing that something wasn't right.

A fraction of a second later, I saw what I had just felt.

Damn it.

He was still alive.

The voice in my radio earpiece screamed, "Green light! Green light!" Out of the lower left corner of my non-shooting eye, I could see the motion down on the curb. The open, black umbrella mechanically pumped up and down in our prearranged signal.

He was still alive.

Through my telescopic sight, I saw both of his hands turn into fists as his arms flew up to protect his throat—my bullet's errant trajectory apparently caught him in the Adam's apple. A range of emotions swept over his face—he didn't know what the hell had hit him.

His survival instinct kicked into motion. He was having trouble breathing. He was alive for now, but he was doomed.

I calmly and quickly racked another round into the bolt-action chamber of my rifle. I again reacquired my target through the precision gun-sight. The head of the man sitting in front briefly blocked my view when he turned toward the commotion in the backseat. Instantly, a fusillade of bullets from Lucien and Ruger cut down the momentary obstruction—flinging him into his wife's lap and out of my way.

I heard the anxious "Green light! Green light!" as I searched to place my target's face in my crosshairs.

I felt a reassuring pat on my shoulder by my spotter, who kept his eyes pealed for anyone who might have observed us. He undoubtedly felt time was running out, but for me, time was standing still. My target was still alive—I had a job to finish.

The first shot I squeezed off had to have been a misfire. It wasn't my aim; I knew that. The sabot must have had a bad powder charge or had been incorrectly loaded in its firing sleeve. I knew that such an error wouldn't occur again—the second bullet in my chamber was a full-charge cartridge without a sabot.

I had meticulously used Lucien's jewelers saw to cut a small 'x' into the tip of all my bullets. That tiny 'x' would insure that the bullets would fragment immediately upon impact. The result would be a devastating wound.

It had to be. We were to kill him.

I watched through the optical precision of the expensive Zeiss gun-sight as the big 1961 Lincoln convertible parade limousine came to a halt directly in front of me. I brought my crosshairs to bear, centering upon his right eye in my sight. He was barely ninety feet away—so close that I felt I could reach out and touch him. I smiled to myself and thought: Jesus, he's no farther away than the first baseman would be if I were throwing a double-play ball from second base. Instead, I was delivering a bullet at over 2,000 feet per second at a distance of ninety feet. It would get there pretty damn fast and pretty damn hard.

I paused to study the familiar face in my sight. Fear had clearly taken hold of him. He knew he was helpless—sheer panic enveloped his face. I had prepared myself for any possible equipment failure or operational disruption—but I had never thought about how I would feel as I completed my assigned task.

"Green light! Green light!" The voice in my earpiece persistently chanted. That was fine—it was his job to call out as long as our man was still alive. It was an annoying reminder of my team's combined failure up to this point.

Roscoe's breath panted in my ear. "Come on, Patrick. You can do it." His voice rose at the end with coiled tension. The crowd below had begun to panic, but I was completely at ease.

His eyes wildly swept his surroundings; then, they locked onto mine through the telescopic gun-sight. I felt my adrenaline surge. Experienced shooters had warned me that seeing the eyes of my victim would shock the hell out of me.

I'd never shot a man before.

I knew that he couldn't see my eyes, but I sure couldn't miss his. His eyes frantically searched for answers.

"Goodbye, Jack!" I whispered, squeezing the trigger gently a second time. This time the rifle's recoil felt crisp and firm as it kicked back into my braced right shoulder. I saw my bullet's impact instantly. I was so close to where he sat—upright, wounded, vulnerable, and frozen in shock.

The full force of my shot took off the top of his head. I saw it explode in a pink cloud of blood, brain matter, scalp, vaporized skull bone, and gristle. There was no question about it. He was dead now.

The voice in my earpiece shouted, "Red Light! Red Light! Red Light! Red Light! Red!" I tore the annoyance out of my ear. The umbrella man on the sidewalk signaled that the President was dead. Our ambush had worked as planned.

I withdrew the rifle from the top of the slats of the white picket fencing and handed it to my spotter, Roscoe. He threw it into the open trunk of the sedan parked directly behind me.

I saw Jackie desperately try to crawl across the Lincoln's broad trunk only to be shoved back into her seat by a Secret Service agent who threw himself on top of her to protect her as he was trained to do. It hadn't registered with me that she had been sitting next to Jack the entire time

I solemnly watched the big Presidential limousine accelerate out of Dealey Plaza—its wounded occupants slumped in their seats. I turned away as the rest of the presidential motorcade raced underneath the triple underpass in a panicked pursuit of the President's car.

Roscoe adjusted his Dallas police uniform and drew his service revolver out of his holster. I pulled my fake Secret Service credentials out of my pocket and held them in my clenched fist, ready for display.

We descended into the horrified crowd, pretending to be just as shocked and alarmed.

It was how we had planned our escape.

It was hard, however, not to be too elated—our plan had worked.

President John Fitzgerald Kennedy was dead.

SEPTEMBER 6, 1978
6:07 p.m.

*"Welcome to my nightmare.
I know you're gonna like it.
I know you're gonna feel like you belong."*

The ominous tone of Alice Cooper's song struck me to my core. The irony of the lyrics sent goose bumps up and down my arms. Welcome to my nightmare, I thought to myself.

The crackling static from speakers in the dirty dashboard almost ruined the song. I wanted to sing out loud, but I didn't think my cab driver would appreciate my vocal styling. What the hell—I'm paying for the ride. The name on his cabbie license read Waylon Thibodeaux.

"Hey, Waylon, can you turn up that song?" I asked.

He cut his eyes at me in the rear view mirror, nodded and complied. He bristled just a little when I said his name. Most cab drivers are pretty talkative, but this one hadn't said a word the whole way from the airport.

His black, short-brimmed cowboy hat steadfastly pointed straight ahead. His dark beard was closely cropped, but his black hair hung in a wild tangled mess down past the blue collar of his shirt. An earring, a tiny silver cross with two tiny feathers, hung from his right ear. Most men would look kind of effeminate dressed like that, but on this guy, it actually looked good.

Mardi Gras beads and trinkets hung from his rear-view mirror and the plastic Jesus on the dashboard competed with a gris-gris bag, sundry voodoo feathers and bones. A family picture was fastened to the driver's sun visor by multiple and multi-colored rubber bands—probably his wife and kids. The wife was a pretty brunette, and the two kids were equally good-looking. It appeared that they had posed for the picture in front of their local church.

"I didn't pronounce it right, did I?"

I saw his dark eyes shift from the road ahead to the rear view mirror. "No sir, ya d'ent," he softly verified.

"Hey, I'm a Yankee. What do you expect?" I joked.

His eyes cracked a smile. "That's OK, sir. It's not an easy name to pronounce for y'all, anyway."

"I apologize, Waylon." I pronounced his name *WAY-lynn*, just like the country singer, Waylon Jennings. "I have to remember that whenever I get back down here to *N'Awlins, Loozeeanna*, I've got to be careful to speak properly."

My pronunciation of *New Orleans, Louisiana* broke the ice. Most out-of-towners ignorantly and blithely butchered the pronunciation as *New Ore-Leenz, Lou-wee-zee-Anna*. It must sound like fingernails on a chalkboard to the locals. A good friend had once corrected me, "The state is named after King Louis of France—not King Lou-wee-zee. Pronounce it right, *bon ami*."

A big grin split his face as he turned to look at me. "Now," he sighed, "dat sounds a lot better."

I decided to make amends, "I'm sorry I didn't pronounce your name right. Can I try again? How do you pronounce your name?"

Now I could see the brilliant white of his teeth, framed impressively by his dark black beard. "It's pronounced *Way-LAWN, Way-LAWN Tib-a-DOE*." The rich French accent gave a lilt to his voice that was marvelous to hear, reflecting a deep Cajun family background.

I repeated it as carefully as I could back to him, "WAY-LONE TIB-A-DOE."

This time, he didn't wince, but nodded his satisfaction with a big smile. Like any good cab driver, he dutifully asked, "Why ya here?"

"*Laissez les bon temps rouler,*" I replied. My French sucked, but I loved the way that particular phrase rolled off my tongue. It's the motto of this old city and it means, "Let the good times roll." *Laissez les bon temps rouler.*

He bobbed his head in a sort of rhythm as if he were both agreeing with me and getting into the mood himself. "Ya got that right! What's ya name?"

"It's an old Irish name, Waylon," I replied. "It's Patrick, Patrick McCarthy." As soon as I blurted it out, I winced. Damn it! I had just violated one of my long-time safety tenets. But it didn't matter. Nothing really mattered now.

"Nice to meet ya, Patrick," he smiled broadly once more. "Well, when ya get ready to leave, ya call me and I come pick ya up." He reached over the back seat and gave me a slip of paper with his telephone number.

I tried to mask my sudden nervousness by smiling. "Sure thing," I murmured. I hoped he wouldn't try too hard to remember me.

His entire mood had lifted dramatically in just the past few minutes. "Hey, Patrick, ya mind if I change the music? I's got's ta git cha in the groove for ya visit." His *patois* deepened just for me.

My song had long since ended. Some sickening song played instead. "Please—be my guest. I've never liked disco."

He fooled with the radio dial until he found a suitable station. I recognized the distinctive fiddle and washboard percussion of a familiar Cajun tune.

"Is that *Ce N'Est Pas Comme D'Habitude?*" I asked.

Waylon spun around in his seat to look at me, "Ah, this one ya know?"

"Yeah," I said wistfully, "I do. In English, it means *It's Not Like It Used To Be*—right?"

"Datz right." He sang along with the song as I sat back and enjoyed the ride. His voice was beautiful rich baritone.

"You've got a good voice—you ought to sing in a band."

He gave me yet another big grin, "Ah do—Ah've got a band, me."

"Where did you learn to play?"

"Ah grew up down the bayou in Houma."

He pronounced "bayou" *By-OH*, not *By-YOU* like the tourists did.

"My Paw-Paw taught me to fiddle when Ah's real little. Fiddlin's my real job; taxi drivin' is my hobby," he laughed at his joke. "Ya see me fiddle on Fr'day and Sat'day nights—some little clubs down in the Quarter."

"I should come see you play."

"Ya should. I'll play ya that tune there, the one ya know."

"I'd like that."

"Ya call me—have a good time, two-step, hear good music…"

"Thanks."

Waylon chattered away in the front seat. I suddenly felt overwhelmed with sadness—I hadn't come to New Orleans to party. I had quite possibly come here to die. The Big Easy attracted those people weak in character like moths to a flame, and I was, sadly, no exception.

I inhaled the distinctive aroma of the city as we rolled into the French Quarter, heading toward the warehouse district down by the river. The air was uncomfortably hot and thick—it poured through the open windows, humid and heavy with a mixture of odors that I think is unique to the French Quarter. The air had a sour smell—human sweat tinged with beer and alcohol— mold and moss—and sewage. New Orleans' sewage had fermented for about two hundred years just below the surface of the dirty and sticky pavement around Bourbon Street. On hot, sultry days, it's close enough to the surface to evaporate into the near-tropical air. There, it lingers and clings to all those who breathe it in. I've been in the jungles of Southeast Asia and some of the worst hovels of Iran, Guatemala, Cuba—I've never quite smelled the same combination of odors.

The taxi deftly maneuvered its way through the crowded and narrow streets until it braked to a halt in front of a dirty brown three-story building, tucked in among some larger boarded-up edifices. A sloppily hand-painted white sign with big blue faded letters announced *Little Rose Perpetual Mission and Salvation Hall.*

"Dis? De place?" Waylon looked in the rearview mirror. I nodded.

The taxi scraped the curb close to where a slightly built man slowly and meticulously swept the sidewalk. A black beret sat atop his grayish hair, covered in pins, feathers, and small voodoo trinkets, and a small ponytail peeked coyly out of the back. His blue denim work shirt had the sleeves rolled up. His khaki-colored trousers hung well over his worn reddish-brown Red Wing work boots.

Waylon leaped from the driver's seat deftly moving to retrieve my olive green duffel bag from the trunk. I saw that my driver was smaller in stature than I had realized, but he was stout and broad with a combination of muscles and a sizeable paunch.

The man in the beret paused in his work to see who had stopped at his doorstep.

I knew my long-time friend, known locally as "The Preacher," would welcome me without question.

"Behold a pale horse," he murmured when recognizing me emerge from the back seat of the taxicab.

"And his name that sat on him was Death. And Hell followed with him."

SEPTEMBER 6, 1978
7:14 p.m.

My old friend was not happy to see me.

He stood, the broom propped under his chin, both hands tightly gripping its handle. He shifted his weight, pushed back his beret and cocked his head in my direction. He stood frozen as I approached him with my worn canvas duffel bag slung over my shoulder.

"This is bad ju-ju. I can just feel it."

"Why do you have to look at life so pessimistically?" I asked, extending my hand.

His face broke open into a broad smile, "Because you are a big factor in the reason why my life has turned out so miserably." He ignored my proffered hand and threw his arms around me in a big warm bear hug. "Patrick McCarthy! What the fuck are you doing here in the Big Easy? Why didn't you let me know you were coming?"

His worn and dirty black beret scratched my chin as he tightened his grip around my waist. His shirt smelled musty and felt damp from his sweat in the high heat and humidity of the late summer afternoon. His forearms were slick with beads of perspiration.

"I knew I would get a warm welcome from the Preacher." I returned his hug with a strong squeeze of my own.

He briefly grunted and howled in pain as I did so, "Hey, not so hard. These old bones cannot take that rough stuff no more," he complained in mock seriousness.

"Don't tell me you're getting old," I teased.

"Hell no, I ain't gittin' old. It's those damn mattresses here in the mission. They've got me down in my back."

I was skeptical of his excuse. "The mattresses are bad? Or is it all the mattress dancing that you've been doing with the ladies of the night?"

He shook his head and guffawed. "I do like my ladies," he admitted with a laugh.

I laughed in return, "And I bet they love your money."

His pale face turned serious for a moment. "I don't have to pay for that," he said.

"Yeah, I heard they've been giving it away for free recently. That's gonna make New Orleans pretty popular with the convention trade."

He cracked a big grin letting out a loud, growling laugh. "Hey! That's a good one!" He turned his palms skyward in a gesture of surrender and conceded, "I might tip them generously, but I never have to pay them."

"And I suppose that the money comes from your collection plate?"

"The Lord works in mysterious ways. You know that."

"Are you saving their souls with a little laying of the palms?"

"That's why they call me the Preacher."

I laughingly shook my head. "I'll bet that's not all they call you." I scanned the street in both directions, noting whether anyone was watching our reunion. I was beginning to feel uncomfortable standing out in the open. "Hey, can we take this inside?"

The Preacher's eyes narrowed slightly at my request. He, too, had sensed my growing unease. "What kind of a host am I? Let's get you out of this heat."

The heat inside the tired wooden building was hotter than the temperature outside. A lazy ceiling fan stirred the contents of the vestibule but didn't offer any significant relief. Two winos in dirty brown shirts and pants lay sleeping on the bare wooden floor against the wall, clutching their brown bag drinks against their chests. A dirty and faded red sofa, the stuffing coming out of various rents and tears, was shoved into the corner of the small room, opposite a set of stairs that disappeared into the darkness of the floor above. A small reception desk, built with plywood and a crooked level, crowded against the sofa. Its battered green paint was obviously military surplus in origin. The desk was heaped with papers and various notes, which were scotch-taped all over the front, back, and sides. The notes looked as old as the building. They were in all manner of inks and handwriting and offered assistance for everything from the phone number and address of the nearest liquor store and free food line to various promises of "For a good time, call…."

The Preacher moved behind the desk and extracted a room key from a series of hooks affixed to the wall. Nimbly pirouetting, he scampered back over to the staircase and beckoned me to follow him. Two flights of steps and a long, dingy hallway led me to my room at the back.

"The view stinks, the room stinks, and your neighbors stink, but you won't be bothered here," he assured me as he unlocked and opened the door. He motioned for me to hand him my duffel bag. He pitched it onto the bed, immediately shut and locked the door.

"Come on. Let's talk." He led me to yet another set of stairs which opened up onto the roof of the building. The outside heat actually felt cooler than the oven-like conditions of the building. The Preacher motioned me to take a seat on the edge of the roof, overlooking the street below. He turned to an old refrigerator that was padlocked with a heavy chain up against the chimney and after fiddling with the lock, released the chain and opened the door.

"Goddamn it. I'm a-gonna kill Eddie! That little shithead got into my beer again." He looked at me in exasperation. "Just about everyone that lives here is either an alcoholic or a drug addict, with a criminal background of some kind, which comes from supporting their habit. Goddamn Eddie happens to be both an alky and a pretty good burglar. The little peckerhead sneaks up here when he runs low on cash and rifles my private stash of beer. He'll go out, rob a house up in the rich section of town, fence some crap, get some money, and he'll buy his own damn beer. Then he'll replenish what he stole from me. That's because he knows that if he doesn't, there won't be a next time."

I laughed at the absurdity of the story as he handed me my long necked Lone Star beer.

"That first cold slug always tastes so damn good when you're hot."

"You are so right, *bon ami*," he agreed. We clinked our bottles together in a brief and silent toast. He then leaned toward me. "What brings you here, my friend?"

I grappled with how much to tell him. A long and uncomfortable silence ensued. He did nothing to ease the situation.

I took a deep breath. "It's all coming undone. Everything we put together is in danger of coming unraveled." I stopped there because I really didn't know how to tell him any more than that.

He lowered his head to look at his scruffy Red Wing work boots and didn't say a thing. We both sucked on our beers in silence as he went through the possibilities of my declaration. The very fact that I was now in front of him must have unsettled him deeply.

"How bad is it?" he finally inquired.

"Bad."

He nodded and fell silent once again.

"Real bad?"

"Worse than that," I assured him.

"Damn."

He upended his beer and guzzled the rest of the contents in a series of swallows and then retrieved two more.

He upended one and drank the entire contents without stopping for a single breath of air. He tossed the empty aside and chugged the second one without even offering it to me.

"Wait a second…," I started to protest, but he cut me off with a wave of his arm.

"I need to be drunk to hear what you're gonna tell me. You need to be sober to tell it to me."

He quickly drained that bottle and headed toward the refrigerator for another. I sat frozen, unable to make up my mind about telling him the story or joining him in his drunken binge. He pulled over an old milk crate, turned it upside down, and sat prepared for the worst. "Go on," he urged me. "I'm listening."

I took a deep breath and ran my hand through my hair. "They're closing in on all of us. The House Select Committee has begun to put all of the pieces together. Our days are numbered, and we all know it. The killings are beginning to bunch up. People are getting scared."

The Preacher's face crinkled up, "Who's dead? I thought all of that shit ended ten years ago with Garrison's defeat."

"It stopped for a while. Then they all got greedy. They killed Bobby and Martin Luther King—because they knew they could get away with it. And once they got away with those, they began to feel invincible. This new government investigation is starting to turn up some strong clues that can't be ignored or swept under the rug like before."

"What did they find out?"

"Among other things, someone found a bullet casing on top of the Dal-Tex Building a couple of years ago."

"Yeah, but a stray bullet could have come from anywhere," he injected hopefully.

I waved him off. "I said they found a bullet *casing*—a shell casing, not a bullet. The investigators know that a rifle was fired from that rooftop. It's unlikely that there are deer hunters in downtown Dallas shooting off the tops of the office buildings. Nope, I'm certain it was one of ours."

"Shit!" He shook his head in disgust.

"I understand that they've also got some scientists who dug up some old audio tapes. The tapes were put through some new kind of acoustical tests that reportedly show a 95 percent probability of a shot coming from the grassy knoll."

"Damn!"

"They're also calling Agency personnel in to testify about what was not provided to the Warren Commission the first time around. Because of that, they're getting real close to some real important names. That's why people are starting to die."

"Yeah, but who's dead?" he asked again.

"They took out Sam Giancana three years ago and Johnny Rosselli two summers ago. Giancana was murdered in his own kitchen. They found Rosselli's torso stuffed into an oil drum floating in Biscayne Bay. The bastards chopped his legs off. Last year, de Mohrenschildt had his head blown off by a shotgun in Florida just before he was to be questioned by one of the House investigators."

The sound of the beer bottle hitting the floor and shattering stopped my narrative.

"That's bad shit," the Preacher muttered.

We sat in pensive silence.

"Jesus," he swore softly. Then he gravely asked, "Is that why you're here?"

"I've got a subpoena in my bag."

"What are you going to do?" His face scrunched up in alarm.

I shrugged my shoulders. "I don't know. It's pretty easy to figure out that my former partners would want me dead as well. Hell, I'm probably next on the list."

Something was bothering him. "What's the matter?" I asked.

I could tell it was hard for him to ask me because he still couldn't formulate his question. I thought I knew what it was, so I answered it for him. "Don't worry about me. I can take care of myself," I assured him.

I was shocked when I realized that wasn't what he was thinking. "I'm not worried about you," he said. "I'm worried about me. Do you think he'll come after me, too?"

"Don't worry. Nobody knows who you are. The only people that knew have all passed away."

"What about my records?"

"Your records don't exist either. You don't exist. You never did. You're safe."

I lied.

SEPTEMBER 6, 1978
12:01 a.m.

I sat in the cramped and squalid room listening to the night sounds of the street. I could make out a far away electric guitar playing *The House of the Rising Sun* and the plaintive saxophone of a street musician. Closer was the raucous laughter of two men and someone yelling, "Awright" then "That's it, that's it man." A distant siren, a bottle shattering on the pavement, a door slamming—my heart beating—I was scared.

I caressed a worn green loose-leaf notebook. It was heavy, close to three inches thick, and contained within its battered cover was my recollection of the greatest murder mystery of the twentieth century—the story of the conspiracy to assassinate the President of the United States, and even more importantly, the story of how the conspirators, my associates, had gotten away with murder.

I thought once more about why I had written everything down. I had a tough time convincing myself that it was a good idea, but events had left me no choice. It didn't take a genius to figure out that I was a marked man. The head of the conspiracy, Grant Grantham, my former roommate and one-time friend, had sent his killer after many of my former associates. I was quite certain he was coming after me. It was just a matter of where and when.

I glanced at the subpoena that lay next to my pillow on the bed. I had read it and re-read it so many times it was dog-eared. No matter how much I wished it would just go away, the reality of its presence confirmed my worst nightmares.

Having worked for the Central Intelligence Agency for almost a quarter of a century, I knew how to cover my tracks. Hours after two federal marshals served me the subpoena, I packed and was out the door, determined to get lost and to get lost fast. False trails for a Caribbean jaunt and an Alaskan sprint might buy me time to drop out of sight. I left clues for Europe, South America, and Southeast Asia just to be safe.

I was confident that absolutely no one still alive knew of my prior relationship with the Preacher. I officially hadn't seen him or had any contact with him in a number of years. Unofficially, I sent him some money, clothes, and food for his *Little Rose Perpetual Mission and Salvation Hall* whenever I could do so clandestinely. The Preacher worked with the dregs of humanity—those poor souls who had lost their lives to alcohol, drugs, or mental illness. He ministered to the needs of the downtrodden, dispensed his own brand of spiritual salvation, and offered them a roof over their heads, a safe haven. I wryly laughed at the thought that I had joined the ranks of the downtrodden—but there was little hope for me.

The Preacher, according to the word on the street, was a good man who could be trusted. The authorities respected him—they pretty much left him alone. No cops came around to check ID's because the Preacher didn't allow any criminal mischief on his property. That didn't mean that his guests didn't go elsewhere to commit their crimes because they did. However, the New Orleans police never had to answer a single call at the mission. The Preacher enforced tight regulations—midnight curfew was one of them. If you weren't in your room by midnight, the front door was locked, and you were left out on the street. Do it twice, and you lost your room to the next person on the waiting list.

I heard my neighbors in the surrounding rooms coughing, sneezing, and snoring through the thin, decrepit walls. I was probably the only one on the top floor still awake. In all likelihood, I would still be awake at sunrise, too.

The contents of my green duffel bag lay strewn across the floor and the end of the bed. My clothes, heaped on the bare wooden floor, were far less important than what lay carefully arrayed on top of the threadbare blue woolen blanket. Five tiny bullets without their shell casings, two round silver tins with small spools from two home movie cameras, and some developed pictures along with the processed negatives. Altogether, it didn't look like much, but it could ruin careers—it could bring down a government full of powerful men—it could get me killed.

The single bulb in the ceiling light wasn't especially bright, but it would do. I ran my left hand over and around the notebook's cover, just as I had many, many times before. I glanced at the subpoena that bore the seal of the United States House of Representatives. It commanded me to appear in two days before the House Select Committee on Assassinations in D.C. to testify about my knowledge of the Agency activities before, during, and after the murder of John F. Kennedy. Committee investigators said they had evidence that I may have participated in some very important meetings that had a direct bearing on their investigation.

Well, of course I did. In more than a few instances, I was the one who called for those meetings; of course, they already knew that.

If I appeared before the Committee, I would have to be the most convincing liar that had ever been deposed under oath. Of course, they knew that, too. The ball was in my court.

I had a choice to make.

If I made it alive to the hearings, I could testify, lie, and go to jail. Or I could testify, lie, and go home scot-free. Or I could testify, tell the truth, and destroy the entire governmental structure of the greatest nation on earth—destroying what remained of my life as well—there is no statute of limitations on murder. My son would forever be branded as the son of a presidential assassin, and my ex-wife would be hounded for the rest of her life. Any remaining feelings she might have for me would be destroyed when she found out that I ruined not only her life but also her best friend's life.

I could run like hell for the rest of my life—and hope like hell that Derek Ruger and Grant Grantham never found me.

Or, I could give up, accept the inevitable and kill myself, saving everyone the grief of dealing with me.

I looked once more at the small pile of artifacts lying next to my leg. The small bullets caught my eye first. I was amazed that such tiny pieces of lead could wreak such destruction, not only to another human being, but also to an entire country. The Warren Commission's Magic Bullet—magic only because of how we managed to plant it on a stretcher in the corridor outside the Emergency Room at Parkland—was a stroke of genius. The camera film was another coup. Confiscating the cameras and film at Dealey Plaza kept a couple of especially damaging pictures out of the public eye. I picked up one picture marked "Moorman" that I knew would instantly destroy the case against Lee Harvey Oswald if it were ever seen.

But the two, crown jewels were the small tins containing short home movies. The film marked "Oliver" clearly showed the flash of my gun's muzzle within the shadows of the trees on the Grassy Knoll. I was sure that new technology, which hadn't existed in 1963, could now produce my face in those shadowy prints.

The other tin was the most important one of all. We kept the film away from the public while we selectively destroyed a few key frames—frames critical to the investigation. The film showed that there had been one, and only one killer—our patsy.

I picked up the tin in my right hand and gently tossed it in the air, watching it glint in the light as it rotated back down into my waiting hand. It wasn't much bigger than a hockey puck. Even a casual viewing would reveal how we had carefully edited the copies to change history, we thought, forever. I set down the priceless contents of the small film canister—the writing on its lid face up: Original negative (uncut)—Zapruder Film.

Opening the notebook's cover, I once again confronted the neatly written words of my story, some of the pages stained and dog-eared. I always liked the way my handwriting looked. I had been quite careful to capture all of my memories in these pages, and I had made very few mistakes—that is, very few mistakes in my writing. But I made many mistakes in my judgment—mistakes that would haunt me to my grave.

My notebook contained the untold story behind the murder of President John Fitzgerald Kennedy. Kennedy's destiny didn't begin when he was elected president, it began decades earlier—a clash of titans—a tragic hero—a tragic flaw—no catharsis. It's a difficult story to accept, but it's all here—easy to research and confirm. I wished I could say that we were heroic, but there are no heroes in this story. We were the worst kind of villains; we were cowards. We thought we were patriots, working to save our nation and the world from harm. We were wrong. The world did not become a better and safer place without Jack Kennedy.

On November 22, 1963, I made the biggest mistake of my life, and my country has suffered for it ever since. Not even a merciful God can forgive me for what I did.

On November 22, 1963, I helped to shoot and kill President John F. Kennedy.

I, Patrick Sean McCarthy, was the gunman on the Grassy Knoll.

I was the biggest patsy of all.

Should anyone ever get to read my notebook, my plan probably didn't work the way I had hoped—I am most likely dead. Perhaps I can take some people to Hell with me.

I certainly hope so.

1947

I WANTED TO fight in World War II, but I was too young to join the military. Instead, I enviously watched my neighbors and their sons go off to fight for our country and our freedom while they left the younger men like me behind. When those brave heroes returned home, it became my life's mission to repay them for their sacrifice and their bravery.

Jobs were readily available for young men who were eager to serve their country. I left my small farming town in Minnesota to accept a job as a congressional aide to Representative Harold Hagen from the 9th Congressional District. Postwar Washington was an exciting hub of activity to a Midwestern kid like me.

Through the help of a family acquaintance, I found an apartment in nearby Georgetown. My two new roommates soon became my best friends. An only child, I quickly bonded with both of these guys—they were the brothers that I had never had. Grant Grantham, the son of a successful Texas oil wildcatter, worked as a congressional aide for Lyndon Johnson, another Texan. Grant was about my age, but our other roommate was about ten years older.

Chase Newman, a reporter with the *Washington Times-Herald* and the son of a Wall Street financier from Massachusetts, had come to D.C. during the war after being turned down for military service due to his flat feet. I immediately liked Chase—he knew the ropes of D.C. and set out to tutor his wet-behind-the-ears roommates in the secrets of surviving in the nation's capital. Chase's philosophy was to work hard and to play just as hard.

Shortly before Valentine's Day, Chase took us over to his favorite

Georgetown neighborhood Irish saloon, Rosie O'Grady's. Rosie's was a place where Georgetown students, townies, and other young government workers congregated for cheap food, beer, political discussions, sports talk about the Washington Senators and the Washington Redskins, and the hope of meeting someone of the opposite sex. That Saturday night the place was packed. A haze of cigarette smoke already hovered in the air when we arrived. We had to shout to hear each other over the raucous laughter.

We elbowed our way through the crowd, muttering apologies. Chase wanted to nab a table near the women's restroom. His strategy was to position us there because, he said, sooner or later every woman in the bar had to pass by our table to use the facilities. He described it as "a walking show of femininity on display." Every once and awhile, Chase scrawled a note on a bar napkin and slipped it to a particularly comely young lady as she swept past us, pretending we didn't exist.

"Watch her face after she reads it in there and comes back out."

The girls smiled as they emerged from the powder room and made eye contact with Chase. Sometimes they stopped at our table and whispered in his ear. The flirtations would carry on for several minutes.

"Hey, what did you write?" Grant asked, anxious to get in on the action.

"My name and phone number," he chuckled, "but it won't work for you."

I was still a naïve, insecure virgin in 1947. Even if Chase had written the note for me, I would have been too shy to look at the girl much less talk to her.

Another little trick Chase taught us involved bumming a cigarette off of the ladies at the next booth. "Use this technique to flirt with any women you see. It never fails. She will always talk to you after you borrow a cigarette from her."

Grant looked at his pack of cigarettes on the table and immediately hid them inside his jacket pocket.

Our favorite waitress, Diane, had just delivered our pitcher of Hamm's beer along with three frosty mugs when suddenly the relative din of the bar was broken by a group of rowdy people crowding through the door. We swiveled in our seats. A cluster of men and women about Chase's age pushed their way over to the bar.

Chase looked up, shook his head, and said contemptuously, "Perfect timing—here comes our comic relief." Before Grant and I could even ask what he meant, the leader of the group hollered out, "Chase! Chase Newman!" A tall, thin, sallow young man with unkempt hair dressed in rumpled, mismatched clothes headed over to our table. I judged him to be at least ten years older than I was.

His eyes, dark and sunken, dominated his face until he smiled. His face became luminescent. He spoke in a pronounced New England accent, "Chase Newman, you old bed-wetter! How have you been?" He leaned over and stuck out his hand expectantly.

"Just fine, Jack. Excuse me if I don't shake your hand, but I have a pretty good idea that you haven't washed it recently."

Jack grinned and ran his fingers up underneath his nose. "Oh, that's just Annie's cooze." He inhaled in an exaggerated fashion and crooned, "Mmmm, just like a fine wine. Sure you won't have a smell?"

"Get that out of my face!" Chase yelped, and they both laughed uproariously. Chase pointed over to Jack's group, "Which one's Annie?"

"Oh, she's not here," he whispered wickedly. "I dropped her off a half-hour ago because I was meeting Mary here. Look, she's the tall brunette over there with the pearls." He sighed lewdly, "Isn't she stunning? I plan to pop her cherry in about an hour."

Grant asked, "Which one is she?"

Jack waved in her direction. When he caught her eye, she cutely waved back. She barely looked as old as I was. I didn't mind admitting that rather than admiring his overt display of masculinity, I was actually both sickened and disgusted by it. I thought it contemptible for an older man to prey upon such a young woman. I had a tough enough time finding women my age to date without some older guy poaching the best for himself. I sat there quietly seething as he continued to make an ass of himself.

"Jack, Jack, Jack, Jack, Jack...," Chase stammered, as if to convey that he didn't approve of what was going on either. "Tell me, what are you doing in here, Jack? Slumming?"

"Yes, Chase," he smirked, "that's exactly what I'm doing. My friends all wanted to see what the less-fortunate try to do to find happiness. Feel like clueing us in?"

Chase responded with a derisive snort. "It's easy. We find happiness by avoiding assholes like you and your friends."

Jack looked at Grant for a brief moment, and then he looked at me and burst into laughter. "You know if anyone else had told me that, I'd probably be gullible enough to believe them. But Chase and I go too far back for me to believe that line of bull crap."

He straightened up jovially. "Listen, we're in here celebrating my recent victory. Come on over, you old mucker, and join us for a drink."

"Maybe later, Jack. We're looking for the chance to get Patrick and Grant laid."

That mention of sex suddenly got his interest. "How long's it been since you boys got your nut off?"

Grant bragged, "Last night."

"By yourself, I bet," Jack joked, "How about you?"

"Never," I said truthfully.

"Oh, my God!" Jack shouted, "How do you keep your balls from exploding? Don't those poisonous juices give you a headache when they back up like that? I know it would give me one!"

"Frankly, you're giving us all one," Chase muttered.

Jack turned back to his group of friends. "Hey! Can you believe this? This guy over here is a virgin!" He swung back to face Chase, "You've really got to be a social misfit not to be able to get laid in this town."

My face burned with embarrassment as this complete stranger made fun of me in front of the entire bar. I could see people at nearby tables giggling and pointing my way as this jerk named Jack graphically boasted about how he personally needed to get laid every day, no matter what.

Chase saw my mortification and quickly intervened, "Hey, Jack, cut it out. You're being an asshole, as usual. The only social misfit I see in here is you." Jack's smile quickly disappeared. Chase defused the situation, "Jack, as you can plainly see, never really learned any manners at all, but I certainly did. Please forgive him. He doesn't know any better."

Jack didn't have a chance to respond to Chase's insult.

"Speaking of manners, where are mine? I should have introduced everybody already. I'm sorry. Jack, this is Grant Grantham and Patrick McCarthy. Pat…Grant…this is the newest Congressman from the great state of Massachusetts, and my *former* good friend, John Kennedy."

A wry smile crept over Kennedy's face. "I'm still your friend, Chase. You know that." His tone turned much more conciliatory as he bent across our table and reached over our beers to shake our hands. "My friends just call me Jack," he said. He looked directly at me. I thought that he might even be on the verge of apologizing to me. But he didn't.

"Well, listen, fellas, if you'd like to join us, you're all welcome. Maybe we can scare up a couple of horny little split-tails to join us, too." He pointed his finger at me, "Who knows? Maybe you'll get lucky."

Kennedy glanced over in the direction of his waiting friends and then became serious, "Hey, Chase, be sure and stop by before you go. There're a few things I want to talk to you about." He then waved, "Nice to meet you, fellas." He strolled into the crowd to return to his boisterous entourage.

Grant watched him go. Once he appeared to be out of hearing range, he turned to Chase, "Is that really Ambassador Kennedy's son?"

Chase nodded his head and flipped his thumb toward Jack's retreating figure. "Yes, it is, and if you want to talk about everything that is wrong with American politics today, there's the best reason why right there."

"Geez—what an arrogant asshole," I sneered glaring at his retreating figure.

"How well do you know that clod?" Grant frowned.

"We actually grew up together. We went to a private school called Choate and then on to Harvard together. That's how I know him. In addition to the charming personality you just saw, I know that Jack is a lazy, phony cheat. He possesses many other unpleasant character traits almost too numerous to list. Listen, you guys want to hear a good story about Jack Kennedy?"

Grant and I looked at each other and nodded.

Chase smiled and launched into his tale, "Jack's father was appointed Ambassador to England, or should I say, Ambassador to the Court of St. James," Chase embellished his words with a British accent. "Jack withdrew from his studies at Harvard and decided to travel around Europe just before the war broke out in 1939. During his trip, he supposedly wrote a paper for college credit that he turned into a book called *Why England Slept.*"

"Wait a minute," Grant interrupted, "He didn't write that book! Winston Churchill wrote that book."

"Are you sure?"

"I'm certain of it, because I read it more than a couple of times myself."

"Want to put your money where your mouth is?"

I was beginning to know Chase well enough that if he offered you a chance to bet him like that, then something was up. Grant turned out to be far more gullible than I was.

Grant smirked confidently, "Sure, I'll bet you that he didn't write that book."

"Next round of beer," Chase set the hook to reel in his fish.

"Next two rounds of beer!" Grant held up two fingers.

"Done, shake on it," Chase extended his hand, sealing the deal.

"Grant," he began slyly, "you're almost right, but you're also wrong enough to lose our bet." Grant laughed then looked to me for support. Seeing my sober expression, he stopped laughing. He knew he had been duped the moment he saw the Cheshire-like grin spread across Chase's face.

"Winston Churchill did indeed write *a* book, and I'm positive it's *the* very book that you believe you read, but the name of Churchill's book was.... Are you ready for this?" Chase paused very melodramatically to build the suspense. "The name of Winston Churchill's book was *While England Slept.* Kennedy called his book *Why England Slept,* big difference."

Chase chuckled while Grant grimaced, shaking his head in disgust. Grant pointed over to where Jack Kennedy was standing. "How can he get away with something like that? That's plagiarism. That's fraud," he sputtered indignantly. "Most of all, that's…that's…that's illegal!"

"Nah, it's not illegal," Chase laughed riotously, "It might be unethical, but it's not *illegal*. Besides the rumor is, our young author over there didn't really write the damn book in the first place. His father supposedly had his speechwriter write it for his son. Then Ambassador Kennedy got his good friend, Henry Luce, to publish it as a favor to him and his family."

"Who's Henry Luce?"

"Ah, he's the guy who owns *Life Magazine*," Grant sourly grumbled.

"Well, I guess it helps to have powerful friends."

"Yeah, it does," Chase agreed as he summoned the waitress over for some pretzels, "But I'll say this about that darned book of his—his timing was perfect. The damn thing came out just as the Nazis started to bomb Great Britain, so it quickly made it to the bestseller lists. Although…," and here Chase paused and turned to see if Kennedy was out of earshot.

"Rumor has it Ambassador Kennedy's personal purchase of over 40,000 copies facilitated the book's place on the bestseller list. I'm convinced it had a huge impact upon its success." Chase lit up one of Grant's Camel cigarettes and added, "Rumor also has it that almost every one of those 40,000 copies ended up at the Kennedy house, where they languish in boxes in the attic and the basement to this very day."

Grant snickered in ridicule.

"You know what guys," Chase paused to gulp down his beer, "I fear America is going to face a real crisis in the future from the growing threat of Communism. What our nation needs right now are creative and fearless men to become our next generation of leaders. What we don't need in Congress are brain-less, sex-obsessed, sycophants like young Jack Kennedy over there. If you ask me, he's an appeaser like his old man."

"He's an appeaser? What do you mean by that?" I was troubled by that accusation.

Grant butted in with some information of his own. He acted somewhat exasperated by either my question or my lack of knowledge on the subject. "Don't you know anything about Old Joe Kennedy?" he spat out with disgust. "Jack Kennedy's daddy happens to be one of the most notorious con men in the country. He's a real miserable son of a bitch. He's got a reputation as a stock market swindler, a philandering husband, and a former bootlegger who still does business with some of the biggest crime families in the country."

"Grant's right," Chase added. "Did you know this? President Roosevelt appointed Old Joe Kennedy as Ambassador to Great Britain just before the war. Roosevelt was humiliated when Kennedy publicly became known around the world as the highest-ranking Nazi sympathizer in the United States government."

I put my glass down so hard I almost spilled its contents, "How could any American who considered himself patriotic admire someone as loathsome as Hitler?"

Chase immediately sensed my disbelief, "Patrick, this is a true story." He held up one hand as if swearing on a Bible. Grant nodded in agreement.

"Kennedy basically believed that Hitler really wasn't a bad guy, and that the United States was headed into an unnecessary war. He felt we were backing a losing effort if we sided with Churchill and his cronies. Kennedy actually believed war with Hitler could have been avoided altogether if we had just sat down and negotiated with the man. He's on record as saying: 'Look, Adolph's not an unreasonable guy. Let's consider giving him what he wants. It's better than going to war over it.'"

Chase's story was hard to fathom.

"He blamed the Jews for starting the conflict in the first place. Everybody knows that Old Joe Kennedy hated the Jews. He still hates them. He blames them for most of what's wrong with society. My father told me the Ambassador is a raging anti-Semite behind closed doors. Anyway, Old Joe actually became so vocally obnoxious about his opinion, and his public comments were so contrary to our own government's stated position in support of our British allies, that Roosevelt was forced to recall Kennedy to Washington and demanded his resignation. Roosevelt felt Kennedy had embarrassed him pretty badly with his isolationist stance, his public support of Hitler, and his caustic anti-Semitic comments."

"Jeez, I'm amazed that Roosevelt didn't have him thrown in jail as a traitor," I remarked.

Chase poured the last of the pitcher of beer into his empty mug. Then, he hoisted it over his head to signal to our waitress that we needed a refill.

"I don't think that old bigot Kennedy really gave a damn by that point. He thought Roosevelt was dragging us into a war against Hitler he felt we couldn't win. I believe he was convinced that he could be our country's political savior if Roosevelt's decisions eventually led to a huge and costly defeat. Remember Kennedy, Charles Lindbergh, and Henry Ford were just a few of the powerful business people who all opposed Roosevelt's stance on the impending war. I think Old Joe figured that once the electorate figured out what he had already figured out, they would boot Roosevelt out of the White House, and he could be voted in. He actually planned to run against Roosevelt himself, you know."

I was more than a little surprised. As I was growing up back home, everyone had been very vocal in their unwavering support of the President and the war effort. I had never been exposed to any real opposition to our President's actions. Chase's story was quite an eye-opener for me.

When the fresh pitcher arrived, Chase refilled our mugs sloshing the beer onto the table.

Grant gulped down half a mug. "Isn't Jack some kind of a war hero? I read that somewhere."

I stopped myself in the middle of a swallow. "What do you mean he's a war hero? What in the hell did he ever do?"

Chase paused to elaborately rub his forehead with his hands. He grinned, "Oh my God, you guys will love this story, too. It's so ridiculous it's hilarious!" He took a deliberate drink of his beer, paused, and let out a deep breath. Grant rolled his eyes at Chase's theatrics.

"After Pearl Harbor, young Jack over there joined the Navy. He was assigned to a pretty cushy job here in D.C. in Naval Intelligence, which was as far as you could get from having to be near any danger. Now, during his tour of duty here, he met a female reporter from the *Times Herald* whose name was Inga Arvad. She was an absolutely stunningly gorgeous Danish blonde even though she was a few years older than Jack. Now that I think about it, she was also a former Miss Denmark. Anyway, she had been married twice before. It turns out that while she was dating young Jack Kennedy, she was also the mistress of a Swedish journalist who boasted of his prominent ties to the Nazis. Of course, Jack eagerly, and I might add stupidly, took her to bed."

"Oh come on! You've got to be kidding me," Grant exclaimed.

"Oh no, I'm not kidding. Now, you guys have to understand that, up until then, Jack's style had always been to love them and leave them. But this time, something was different. Now, I don't have a clue as to what 'ole Inga-Binga' did to him in bed, but she did something. Jack fell head over heels in love with her like some kind of a lovesick puppy. The only problem was Jack didn't know the FBI suspected his new girlfriend of being a Nazi spy."

Grant started laughing so hard he choked on the beer he had just swallowed. Beer came shooting out of his mouth and nose. He coughed and gasped for air. I reached over and pounded him on the back. When I saw the glint in Chase's eyes, I sensed that he was setting poor Grant up for more of the same.

Chase paused to tilt his head back and exhaled a puff of cigarette smoke rings, which drifted into the smoky air of the tavern. He watched them disperse. Then he continued.

"Yeah, the rumors around D.C. claimed the FBI had actual wiretaps of good ole 'Mattress Jack' Kennedy, as he was being called behind his back, spilling classified U.S. Naval secrets to his little Nazi spy girlfriend while they were in bed together. Now, can't you just imagine what a huge scandal that would have been? I know for a fact that some of the higher-ups at Naval Intelligence wanted him immediately thrown right out of the Navy. Mind you, not just thrown out of Naval Intelligence, but thrown out of the Navy itself. However, regrettably, it seems cooler heads prevailed. Given Ambassador Kennedy's prestige, it really would have been a major scandal to dismiss him like that. I think they all finally decided to transfer Jack out of town to get him far away from her."

"Wow, that's quite a story."

"Do you think I'm finished?" Chase challenged.

I shrugged my shoulders, "Well, yeah, I thought you were."

"Oh no, my foolish young friend. Now, I don't even pretend to know what kind of a pussy ole Inga-Binga had down between those long, gorgeous legs of hers, but I know Jack Kennedy. I know he's seen and been in hundreds, if not thousands of 'em, but little Miss Denmark had some kind of a hold on Jack. Jack Kennedy was like a hound dog that smelled a bitch in heat—you couldn't keep him away from her. He used every opportunity he had to go and see her. When he was finally restricted from traveling to her, she would travel to see him."

"The authorities couldn't keep them apart?"

"No one could. In fact, get this...," he motioned us to lean in closer so that he could lower his voice.

"Jack even had the audacity to personally approach J. Edgar Hoover and ask him to issue a public statement declaring little Miss Inga-Binga completely innocent of any charges of spying."

Grant literally jumped out of his seat and leaned over the table. "He went to Hoover and asked him to do *what*?"

Chase, pleased with himself at Grant's reaction, grinned, and slowly enunciated each word for effect. "He actually had the cojones to go to the Director of the FBI and ask him to publicly clear his girlfriend of spying," Chase waited for the words to sink in. "But Hoover refused. He had solid proof—wiretaps and pictures—that she was a Nazi spy."

"What an utter moron!" Grant searched about the room, trying to locate Kennedy.

I was disgusted by that Kennedy guy. I looked across the room and saw him standing firmly against some young woman, whispering in her ear. I thought that quite possibly he was the most despicable man I had ever met. "He's more than a moron. He's a dangerously stupid man. Hey, how weak and shallow can any man be who would risk the security of the United States of America during wartime over any piece of ass? How can anybody place his own personal needs ahead of the greater good of his own country?"

Chase shrugged his shoulders and went on with his story. "Anyway, since Mr. Hoover refused his request, Jack was forced to come up with another brilliant plan that would enable him to continue seeing her."

He paused until Grant had to say, "Go on."

"He asked her to marry him."

"WHAT?" Grant and I exclaimed simultaneously.

"You heard me. He decided to marry her. Can you even begin to imagine the hell that broke loose with that announcement? Let me put it this way. Imagine the son of a former United States Ambassador, who also happened to be Adolph Hitler's friend and was until recently the highest-ranking Nazi sympathizer in the United States government, wanting to marry a known Nazi spy while he was also currently serving as a high-ranking officer in the Office of United States Naval Intelligence. How well do you think that would have gone over with the military hierarchy? Or for that matter with the American public? Especially with all of those millions of American G.I.'s serving their country by laying their lives on the line while Jack was simply busy getting laid."

"That's a repugnant story," I said.

"Old Joe absolutely blew a gasket. I'm sure he was the one who arranged to have Jack transferred to active duty far out into the South Pacific theater in order to get him away from her."

"Active duty in the South Pacific? That would have made it tough on the lovebirds," Grant observed smugly.

"Yeah, and it worked. They isolated Jack from his love. But maybe it worked too well because Jack got pissed off. He knew how much his father hated the war, so Jack voluntarily got himself assigned to a PT boat squadron."

"What are PT boats?" I asked.

"They're kind of like floating fighter planes, big plywood speedboats with three motors that could race straight into a Japanese convoy, release a bunch of torpedoes, and then race away. They were quite popular with Ivy Leaguers who had yachting and boating experience, and especially anyone who wanted to command their own boats right away. The Navy was always looking for athletes to volunteer to be skippers of these things—it was a gutsy thing to do, romantic too. The image of brave young American guys on a little PT boat attacking huge and powerful Japanese battleships and aircraft carriers appealed to Jack. He knew those same images would appall his father and his family, and yet would impress Inga."

"Did it work?"

"Well, it might have in more competent hands, but Jack, truth be told, was actually an inept captain. In fact, he almost sank his boat once when he rammed his own dock way too hard while trying to make the darned thing stop."

"See, he is a moron," I interjected.

"It quickly became known throughout the Pacific fleet that Jack also had a tendency to avoid dangerous fighting action. He preferred to hover on the far outskirts safely out of harm's way."

"That sounds real heroic," Grant said sarcastically.

"You want a story about heroism? Okay, get ready because here comes the great part."

Chase snuck a glance over at his friend Jack and once again lowered his voice. He had us huddle in closer together at the table so we could hear. "You've got to understand the PT boat was the most maneuverable boat in the United States Navy. They were so fast they couldn't be hit with shells or torpedoes. You also have to know this important little fact. During the entire course of the war, the United States Navy only lost one PT boat to hostile enemy action where no shots were fired—just one boat out of hundreds of PT boats." Chase dramatically held up one finger in front of us to further drive home the point he was making. "Now, do you care to guess who the captain was of the one PT boat that our Navy did lose?"

"Let me guess," Grant said. "Was it Captain Shit-for-Brains over there?"

"Bingo! Now, do you care to guess how the Japanese managed to sink that one and only PT boat?" Chase smiled devilishly at us. "Remember, we're talking about Jack Kennedy here. Think real hard! What's the most unlikely thing that you can think of happening?"

Grant and I both looked at each other and shook our heads. We were at a loss to think of something. Chase grinned even wider.

"Okay, you guys know how big a destroyer is, right?"

"Yeah, they are immense," I answered.

"Well, they're not immense, but they are pretty big—maybe you're right, Patrick, maybe they are immense compared to a PT boat. I told you PT boats are highly maneuverable. They can literally start and stop on a dime, and they could evade any ship the Japanese made. I told you they were the closest things the Navy had to water-based fighter planes. Got all of that?"

"Yeah," we said.

"Still want to guess how Jack's boat was sunk?"

"No."

Chase smirked. "He got run over."

"What?" we groaned in unison.

"He got run over."

"Run over by what, another PT boat?"

"Nope, he got run over by a Japanese destroyer."

"Ah, come on, Chase. That's not possible!" Grant protested.

"Oh, it's possible all right because that's exactly what happened to Jack's boat. He got run over by a Japanese destroyer. And, believe it or not, no other PT boat in U.S. Naval history has ever been rammed before or since, just Jack Kennedy's PT boat."

"Now, how in the hell did the Japs manage to do that? Was it in the middle of a fog or a storm?"

Chase shook his head, "No, another nearby PT boat captain said they could see that Jap destroyer coming from over a mile away. He said he radioed Kennedy's boat to tell them the destroyer was headed right in their direction, but no one answered the radio."

"Why didn't they see it coming," I asked.

"Something that big would be awfully hard not to see," Grand added.

"Once again, the rumor I heard was that everyone on the boat was asleep—a direct violation of all of the Navy rules and regulations concerning conduct within a war zone. It's also against the rules to drink beer on board a Navy ship in a war zone. My sources tell me Jack and his crew had probably violated that regulation as well, which is most likely why they were all asleep. It was also a very strict Navy regulation that no U.S. Naval vessel was allowed to have its engines turned off while in a war zone. It looks like Kennedy's boat also may have violated that regulation, too."

Grant stopped chewing a pretzel long enough to add, "You were right, Patrick. He is a dangerous moron."

We took advantage of the lull in conversation to replenish our drinks.

"I can't believe anything could have happened like that," I remarked. "That's almost too incredible to imagine."

"Well, if you think that was hard to believe, listen to what happened next. The survivors spent about three days swimming around in the Pacific Ocean before they were finally rescued. The sinking of that single PT boat became a huge military scandal within the U.S. Pacific fleet. Jack Kennedy had been in the middle of the largest ocean in the world in the world's most maneuverable boat. Yet, he somehow managed to get his boat run over and sunk by a Japanese destroyer that didn't even waste a single bullet on him. Everyone—and I mean everyone—in the entire Pacific fleet laughed about the complete and utter absurdity of all of that."

"I'm surprised he wasn't charged with something like negligence," I volunteered.

"Actually, because some of his crewmen died, he was almost charged with something far worse, like manslaughter or negligent homicide. General Douglas MacArthur, the Supreme Allied Commander of the Pacific Theater, wanted Kennedy court-martialed and thrown in jail, or at the very least, his sorry ass thrown out of the Navy. Kennedy really got in a lot of hot water over the whole thing. Everybody on that PT boat was ashamed and humiliated over being made the laughingstock of the Navy. Jack later told me and a few of our other friends that it was touch and go as to whether or not the Navy would give him a medal or throw his incompetent ass right out of the service."

Grant and I burst into laughter. Chase once again held up his hand and waved us to be quiet. He wasn't done.

"Well, once again, Old Joe came to Jack's rescue and worked some more of his monetary magic. His father leaped in to control the damage to his son's career, and more importantly to him, his family's image. After all, it wouldn't do for his son Jack to become the poster boy for incompetence in the United States Navy."

Chase began to pat his shirt pocket for his cigarettes. "It turns out that the author John Hershey was a buddy of Jack's. Old Joe paid him to write an article for the *New Yorker* magazine about the PT boat's saga. The article was later reprinted and carried in *Reader's Digest*. In the process, he cleaned up the story and embellished it so that Jack was turned into a real American hero for saving the lives of his ten men."

"They whitewashed the story?" Grant asked.

"They whitewashed the story—the real story of a feckless and incompetent screw-up who exhibited reckless behavior, poor judgment, and a deadly disregard of the rules and regulations of the United States Navy. Believe it or not, Old Joe actually had the balls to demand that his son be awarded the Congressional Medal of Honor for his actions. It took the direct intervention of the Undersecretary of the Navy, James Forrestal, to get Jack a medal of any kind at all—it turned out to be a very minor Navy and Marine Corp's life-saving medal."

I shook my head at the absurdity of it all, "So, he's not really a war hero after all."

"Oh, he's probably a hero to the men on that boat, even though his actions got two of them killed."

Grant picked up his nearly empty beer mug and drained the final warm dregs with one big gulp. "How in the hell did this jack-ass ever get elected to the United States House of Representatives? This is beyond all rational belief."

Our waitress magically appeared with a fresh pitcher of beer.

"His father arranged for him to win. He decided he wanted Jack to run as a Congressman in the 11th Congressional District of Massachusetts, where both of Jack's grandfathers had gotten their political starts. The only problem was most of the old-line Boston politicians felt young Jack was nothing more than a carpetbagger. Hell, some of the braver ones even went so far as to say so publicly, calling for him to serve on something like the Boston City Council before having the audacity to run for the United States Congress as his first elected office. But all that talk succeeded in doing was to piss off Old Joe. His hot-tempered response was: 'You fellows are just angry that you don't have Jack's ambition and talent.' And get this—he then predicted: 'My son is going to be President in 1960!'"

Grant laughed hysterically. I joined in a split-second later, and Chase was slightly behind us. I caught Kennedy and his party out of the corner of my eye. They turned to look at us. Kennedy had a quizzical look on his face. I wondered if he realized he had been the butt of our jokes all evening. I laughed even harder.

Grant pointed toward Kennedy. "That guy's gonna be our President in fourteen years? That'll be the day!" Grant choked this out between tears, he was laughing so hard. For a brief moment, I thought he might topple over onto the dirty tavern floor in a convulsive fit.

"Let me tell you, Old Joe put his money where his mouth was. I went home to Boston to see my family a couple of times, and Jack's name was everywhere you looked. It was on posters, billboards, streetcar placards, pamphlets, leaflets, balloons, banners—you name it. He actually had five campaign offices open in the district, and his district is not that big. You couldn't go anywhere in Boston without seeing Jack Kennedy's name on something."

"Wow!" Grant exclaimed.

"Oh yeah, and remember that story I told you? The one about Jack's PT boat sinking and how John Hershey wrote an article for *Reader's Digest* about it? Old Joe paid to have 100,000 copies of that article reprinted and distributed for free all over the district the day before the election."

Grant was truly impressed, "I wonder how much all of that cost?"

"I was told that the Ambassador spent over a quarter of a million dollars…"

"What?" Grant was shocked.

"He spent at least $250,000 just on that part alone. He actually spent far more."

"I can't begin to fathom that," Grant objected, "That's too unbelievable for words. Nobody spends a quarter million dollars on an entire election campaign, let alone a cheap gimmick like that."

"I'm not done yet. If you hosted a cocktail party or an afternoon tea for congressional candidate John F. Kennedy, you were given at least one hundred dollars to help defray your costs."

Grant again choked on another mouthful of beer. At the rate we going, more beer was ending up on our shirts and on the table than was going down our gullets.

"What?" he cried out, "A hundred dollars to host a friggin' coffee klatch? That's almost a month's worth of wages!"

"So many families wanted to take advantage of the offer the campaign didn't have enough time to book them all. Of course, the campaign didn't want to disappoint any of Jack's supporters, so it simply paid fifty dollars in cash to a large number of families to 'help out' at the polls. They didn't have to do anything except put their greedy hands out. I personally heard the Ambassador brag once that with the dollars he had spent, he could have gotten his Negro chauffeur elected to Congress in Boston, and Boston happens to be as racist as any place in Mississippi."

"They were buying votes. That's all they were doing. They were paying to buy that seat," Grant groused. "That's utterly obscene."

"I know. That's my point. Believe it or not, it still got even worse. A former Boston City Councilman by the name of Joseph Russo decided to run against Jack in the Democratic primary. He was explicitly warned not to, but he decided that young and inexperienced Jack Kennedy would be quite easy to defeat. I think many of the old-time Boston politicians secretly agreed with him because Old Joe didn't have many friends in town. More than a few powerful people would have been quite happy to see the Ambassador and his family taken down a notch or two. So guess what that wily old bastard did in response to the unexpected challenge?"

"I give up," Grant said.

"Patrick? Care to guess?"

I didn't have a clue. This was a view of politics that I didn't even know existed. "I don't know, paid him off not to run?"

"Nope, Old Joe found someone else who lived in the district that was also named Joseph Russo. He got the guy to place his name on the same ballot, thereby reducing Councilman Russo's vote totals. Then, he got some of his people to go out and campaign for the fake Russo. When the voters got into the polls, no one knew who the real Russo was on the ballot. They ended up splitting the Russo vote between them. Jack handily won the Democratic primary."

Chase motioned to Grant for a cigarette. Grant fumbled through his jacket, took out a smoke, and handed it to Chase.

"After he won the primary, Jack took a six-week vacation and spent most of the time out in Hollywood screwing starlets. He stayed out of the voter's eyes letting his father and his people run his campaign. Then, he returned to Boston to score a huge election victory. Now, you need to remember this important point. The Republicans won huge victories all around the entire country, but Democratic candidate Jack Kennedy was THE largest Democratic victor in the entire state of Massachusetts. He got over 60,000 votes to his opponent's 26,000."

Grant whistled. I'm not sure if he was impressed by the number of votes Kennedy got or the number of weeks Kennedy spent screwing starlets.

"You mean to tell me that guy standing over there essentially won a United States Congressional seat on the basis of his father's shenanigans?" I said.

"Yeah, well it probably didn't hurt that Old Joe elevated the Kennedy name during the election by giving $600,000 to the archbishop of Boston for a new children's hospital that was planned for the city."

"His father probably spent a million dollars to buy that seat for his son," Grant murmured with a tone of whispered awe.

"Probably," Chase agreed, "easily."

Chase took a long draw on his cigarette flipping his thumb in Jack's direction. "Jack's a friend of mine, but Jack is in over his head. He treated the congressional race like a popularity contest. He's a screw-up, and he'll never outlive that. Jack doesn't have a clue as to what's going on in the world today, and I don't think he cares."

"His father will protect him, though," Grant countered.

"Of course he will. He'll be sure to surround Jack with highly paid experts who will formulate every serious thought that young Jack ever needs to have. I believe if Jack were to be left up to his own devices, D.C. would chew him up and spit him out. Jack Kennedy's Washington career will largely depend upon how devoted the Ambassador remains to his son. As far as Jack's concerned, now that he's been elected to office and his father is off his back, his major goal in life will simply be to get laid every day. I don't think Jack really has a higher priority once the sun comes up. He'll devote his life to introducing J.J. to the numerous sweet young ladies of Washington, D.C."

"Who's J.J.?" Grant and I said in unison.

Chase howled, "J.J. is his cock! I can't quite remember how the name came about, but I think the initials stood for something like 'Jack Junior.' Jack got circumcised when we were at Harvard. He loved to tease a buddy of ours about what great shape J.J. was in, and how well J.J. was doing. Jack used to write these absolutely filthy letters all of the time, bragging about how much pussy he was getting. It was Jack's way of being mean and picking on our friend because he knew our friend wasn't getting laid at all. Jack loved to rub it in that he was getting laid every day."

"Real nice guy," I observed sarcastically.

Two pretty blondes gave Chase a flirtatious look as they headed to the powder room. Chase grinned and winked at them. "It's funny. I just remembered that Jack also had this lovely little stunt he loved to pull on unsuspecting women. He would innocently invite them out on his boat to go sailing. When the boat was out of sight of land, he'd bring the boat to a stop and declare an SOS. Do you know what that stood for?"

"Maritime emergency," I asked hopefully. Grant shrugged his shoulders—he wasn't sure either.

"Jack's cagey little SOS stood for 'Suck or Swim.' He boasted to me that not one single girl ever wanted to swim."

"Man, this guy is unbelievable!" Grant sounded strangely impressed.

Chase pointed to his crotch, "Yeah, Jack Kennedy thinks more with his little head than he does with his big head."

"Oh, come on, we're all like that," Grant snickered. "Every guy thinks about sex all of the time. That's just being a guy."

"Grant—you don't understand what I'm telling you. Sex isn't just sex with Jack; it's a daily obsession. His own father actually ordered all of his sons to get laid as often as possible. Jack used to tell us that he couldn't get to sleep at night if he hadn't been laid that day. He was serious."

"So that's why he asked me if I was afraid of my balls exploding!" Now I understood the context of the question, even though I was still embarrassed by it. "Come on, Chase, aren't you exaggerating? No one is that shallow. You've got to have some kind of expression of love for a woman—you have to cherish…"

Chase cut me off with an emphatic wave of his right hand. "No, I don't think normal things like emotions have much influence on the direction of Jack's life. In fact, I think that if you were to spend any time with Jack, you'd find him to be emotionally immature. He might appear to be friendly and concerned about other people, but he's really superficial."

Grant got a crazy grin on his face, "The only thing in life that he cherishes is his relationship with J.J."

Someone shouted at us from across the crowded bar. Chase acknowledged the drunken cry with a slight wave.

"Hey, here is a valuable piece of advice for both of you. If you have any women with you when Jack's around, watch out. At some point, Jack will start to brag about his friend, J.J. When the women become really curious about Jack's great friend, he'll offer to introduce them to him. He doesn't care if you're his friend or not."

I was repulsed by what I had just heard. I had come to Washington to serve my country. Instead I encountered a dubious war hero and an elected fraud named Jack Kennedy. He and his bigoted father appeared to be such slaves to their own appetites and egos that they had no real regard for the rest of the world. It was shocking and eye opening. My education in the real world was just beginning.

As those two pretty blondes came out of the ladies room and passed our table, Grant growled at them, "Hey, do either of you know what SOS means?"

They completely ignored him and his crude comment as they sashayed past, but they once again winked at Chase.

Chase looked at the three empty pitchers on the table. "Listen, we've solved enough of the world's problems for one evening. I will say this for my old friend Jack over there. He sure knows how to throw a party for his friends. What do you say we go and join Congressman Elect John Fitzgerald Kennedy and wish him well? We'll drink his beer for the rest of the night. Look over there. The ladies are starting to arrive. Who knows, Patrick? Maybe we'll get you laid after all!"

Chase was wrong about only one thing that night—I didn't get laid.

"Things are not what they seem; or, to be more accurate, they are not only what they seem, but very much else besides."

— Aldous Huxley

SEPTEMBER 6, 1978
8:00 a.m.

"God damn it to hell!" he screamed in frustration at the top of his lungs. Grant Grantham's day couldn't have started any worse.

His executive secretary sat in her outer office and debated whether to open the closed door to Mr. Grantham's office to see if he was all right. A cacophony of abusive and vile language reverberated off the walls of the inner sanctum—she decided to mind her own business and continued typing. If her boss wanted her, he knew where to find her. His temper tantrums were legendary around Washington, D.C. She knew other people who had lost their jobs when he lost his temper. She closed her ears to the racket and concentrated on her work.

Inside the sprawling Watergate penthouse office, Grant's rage was barely held in check. Floor-to-ceiling glass windows provided a breathtaking panoramic view of the Potomac River and the Virginia shoreline with the Lincoln Memorial off to the left and Arlington Cemetery across the water. Ordinarily Grant admired the view, but today, all he wanted to do was slam his fist through the glass in anger.

"God damn it to hell!" he swore again, this time even louder. Of all the days for this shit to spill out; today was just not the day. He was pissed at his son for what he had done; pissed at his first wife for what she had done; pissed at his former roommate for what he might still do; and pissed at his secretary for not coming through the door so that he could get mad at her and fire her.

"Karen! Get your sorry ass in here!"

Karen decided it was a good time to take her morning coffee break. She literally ran for the stairs at the fire exit. The elevator was notoriously slow; she couldn't afford to get caught by Mr. Grantham. He would probably dismiss her on the spot.

"God damn it to HELL!" he bellowed. Acid rumbled up from his stomach. He opened a desk drawer for a roll of *TUMS*. The drawer was stuck. "God damn it!"

Why was all of this happening now? Deep down, he couldn't afford to acknowledge all of the events which had catapulted him to this very day and time.

He had been awakened at 4:30 a.m. by a telephone call from the Austin Police Department. His son, Lyndon, had been arrested for statutory rape of a minor. To make matters worse, the fifteen-year-old girl was the daughter of one of the other partners of the law firm where Lyndon worked as a gofer. The desk sergeant put his son on the phone so Lyndon could tell him what had happened. He had picked her up when he ran into her at a local restaurant where she was having dinner with some friends. They got in his car, bought some beer, and drove around in the country, stopping to drink and make out. At some point during the evening, Lyndon had decided that he was going to "go all the way." He said he had sex with her and then took her home. "Everything was fine when I left her, Daddy. You gotta believe me."

"Then why is she pressing charges against you for rape?"

"Ah, Daddy, her mama's just pissed because she got home after her curfew. It weren't no big thing."

"Well, apparently it was a big thing because you've been arrested for rape. What the hell were you thinking?"

"Well, I wasn't thinking, Daddy. I just went and did it. But she liked it. I know she did."

"Why, did she tell you that?" Grant sarcastically asked.

"Well, kind of."

"What do you mean *kind-of*?"

There was a long pause on the other end of the line.

"I said, what do you mean *kind of*?"

"Just what I said I meant."

"Did she say she wanted to do it?"

There was another long pause.

"Well, did she?"

"Well, no, but I knew she wanted to."

Grant didn't like where this was going. "What did she say that led you to believe she wanted to?"

He hesitated again and then blurted out, "She didn't actually say anything. It was what she wasn't saying."

Grant was growing impatient with his son's convoluted reasoning. "Son, either she said 'yes' or she said 'no.' which was it?"

The pause was almost a minute long, "Well, she said no, but she meant yes."

Oh my God! Grant's rage seethed. He struggled to keep his voice under control. "Did you hear her say 'no'?"

"Ah, yes sir, I did."

"Did you understand she meant 'no'?"

"Well, sir…yes sir, I did, sir."

"And you did it anyway?"

"Yes sir, I did."

The boy was screwed. "Son, let me talk to the desk sergeant—and Lyndon, do me a favor. Don't you fucking open your mouth again until I get there. Do you understand me?"

Lyndon had heard that tone in his father's voice on enough occasions to know that he better obey him. "Yes sir."

Fuck.

"Karen!"

Grant didn't bother to see if Karen was at her desk. Karen was still down in the coffee shop and in no hurry to return.

Grant looked at the newspaper sitting prominently in the middle of his desk. The headline that morning read *House Select Committee on Assassinations Begins Public Hearings Today*. The byline displayed the name of one of his old roommates, Chase Newman. Why in the hell were they dredging up this old news? Everyone knew who killed JFK. The Warren Commission Report said so. It was Lee Harvey Oswald. So why in the hell did we need to waste public money on something that had already been adequately examined? The public certainly wasn't going to believe anything else, were they?

That was his rational side thinking. The insecure side knew better. If people started picking apart the threads of the Warren Commission that didn't make sense, the whole conspiracy could easily unravel, and when it did, it could take him down with it.

And how ironic was it that his two former roommates and best friends held the keys to his destruction? Patrick McCarthy could directly implicate him, and Chase's reporting skills could uncover whatever had been long-since hidden. Either one could put an end to the career of Grant Grantham. That is, if Grant didn't put an end to them first. One thing was for sure. He didn't have much time to act. The House Select Committee was scheduled to hold sixteen days of public hearings. Grant knew that Patrick, a former high-ranking officer in the Central Intelligence Agency, had been subpoenaed to appear and testify. Grant had only two questions: would Patrick appear and what would he say?

"What would I say if I were in his shoes?" Grant mused aloud. "Hell, I know what I'd do. I'd lie my goddamn ass off. That's what I'd do. But is that what Patrick would do?"

He knew the answer. Patrick was too honest to lie. He'd tell the truth if he was asked. After all, he had nothing left to lose. His wife and son had already left him, and his career was in tatters. The only reason to remain quiet was the threat of eternal infamy. No one wants to be forever enshrined in American history books as a presidential assassin, a stigma that would haunt the McCarthy clan to the end of time. Patrick McCarthy would go to great lengths to avoid that legacy.

Grant's rage which had been red-hot began to subside until he remembered the reason he went to bed angry last night. His first wife, Amy, had served him legal papers requesting an increase in her alimony. It turned out she had run into his second wife, Trixie, and they had compared divorce settlements. Amy came away from the meeting convinced Grant had screwed her compared to Trixie's settlement. Grant's third wife, a former exotic dancer named Lola, found out how lucrative it was to be a former Mrs. Grantham and had declared her intent to file for divorce as well. Grant told her it would be over her dead body and right now, he meant it. He was in a murderous mood. It was time to make the one phone call he had not wanted to make.

He walked over to his desk and found a small black book written in a special code that only he could read. He nimbly thumbed through the entries until he found the one telephone number he couldn't live without.

Derek Ruger.

1948

MY FIRST MEETING with Congressman Kennedy soon faded into one of those memories good for an occasional laugh over a beer. Kennedy was nothing more than one of D.C.'s typically brash young men. I was also turning into a similarly brash young man in a city already brimming with brash young men. I loved Washington, D.C.

I worked in Congressman Hagen's office with his friend and campaign manager, Spencer Lewis, and a succession of secretaries who came and went about every six weeks or so—D.C. was a transient town. Everyone was from somewhere else, bound for some other place with D.C. a stopping-off point in between. The town was populated mostly by politicians, bureaucrats, and the military—and a whole subculture of young people who existed solely to meet their needs.

Between congressional elections, Mr. Lewis served as the congressman's chief aide. I reported to him as his assistant. In other words, I was the assistant's assistant—a lowly gofer who ranked below the secretaries. At least they could type, take dictation, answer the phone, and open the mail. My job was to make myself available to do whatever no one else had the time or the energy to do.

Spencer Lewis was a good boss. He taught me the number one rule for getting ahead in this town—brown-nosing. "It's all a matter of who you know. It's an old Capitol Hill recipe for success. Offer to do things for powerful people on Capitol Hill. For example, stop by Joseph Martin's office (Mr. Martin was the Speaker of the House) and ask if he has anything that needs to go to the laundry. Tell him you were planning to go that way for

Congressman Hagen and thought he might need some stuff dropped off or picked up there too. Remember, it doesn't have to be anything major. Just make yourself constantly available and always be eager to please, especially for people that are more powerful than you are. These people will get to know your face, and eventually they will even get to know you. Most importantly, they will come to realize you can be counted upon and can be trusted. That will open a lot of doors for you down the line. After all," he added, "D.C. is really just a small town where everybody knows everybody else, and everyone knows what everyone else is doing. There are no secrets in D.C.—remember that. The insiders live that motto, and the outsiders never learn it."

I vowed to make it my motto, too.

WHILE MY FRIENDS and I worked and played in D.C., the rest of the world tried to return to normal after almost six excruciatingly tough years of war. America was fortunate because other than the sneak attack on Pearl Harbor and a brief Japanese bombardment of Los Angeles, our nation had physically escaped the war almost untouched. The Europeans were still reeling from the destruction wrought by the war.

All of Europe was in danger of slipping into social chaos brought on by the daunting task of rebuilding. Major parts of the European continent lay in bomb-blasted, smoky ruins. London was a mess. Most of industrial Germany was battered, blasted, and blackened. Complicating the rebuilding effort were a myriad of logistical problems and dangers. Destroyed and abandoned trucks, trains, planes, buildings, bridges, and factories clogged the landscape. What do you do with a destroyed German Panzer tank that sits squarely in the middle of your family farmland? What do you do if, rather than just one immobile Panzer on your property, you have ten, or fifty, or one hundred of them?

Complicating the removal of all of that mechanical carnage was the threat of unexploded ordnance still lethal enough to be set off by a careless shovel or an unsuspecting farmer's plow. Put a shovel or a pick in the wrong place and you could set off an explosion lethal enough to kill you and your family. Consider the sheer cost of dealing with that problem when you and your family are broke, your friends are broke and your country is broke.

To make matters worse, the Soviet Union and Joseph Stalin were using Europe's economic chaos to jockey for power and influence. The Communists were determined to take advantage of all this tumult to expand and strengthen their hold outside of Soviet Russia's borders.

I WAS SITTING in the apartment one rainy afternoon smoking a Marlboro and sipping a cold Hamm's beer while reading *U.S. News and World Reports* about the growing Communist menace in Europe. Grant was wallowing on the sofa reading a Superman comic book. Both of us were wrapped in laziness when we heard Chase bust in. He kicked the apartment door shut and slung his briefcase across the room in a fit of frustration and rage.

"Can you believe those damn Russians?" he fumed. "The Czechoslovakian foreign minister was murdered last night…"

"I don't even know who the Czechoslovakian foreign minister is," Grant grumped, "so why should I even care?"

"Maybe if you read something other than a comic book, you might know this stuff. Right, Patrick?"

My lack of reaction made Chase cynically laugh. "You two really are morons. No wonder women find you obtuse. You need to bone up on your world history."

Grant flashed an idiotic grin and quipped, "Hey, Patrick! Did you hear that? If we bone up on our world history, it will help our boners!"

I wanted to hear what Chase was all worked up about so I ignored Grant. "Was that Jan Masaryk? The radio said he committed suicide."

"I've got a source in the State Department who told me the Soviets murdered him." Chase paced around the room, kicking the couch and stomping his feet. I could imagine the little old lady who lived in the apartment below us complaining to the building superintendent about the noise from our unit.

"Hey, Chase, take it easy," I warned. "Grab a beer, calm down, and tell me what you heard."

Chase nodded and ducked into the kitchen. I heard the frig door slam as he returned with a cold beer in one hand. "Where's the church key?"

"Patrick's got it," Grant yawned.

I handed him the bottle opener. He popped the cap off and slugged down half the bottle. He wiped his mouth with the back of his hand and offered up his story, "Jan Masaryk wanted the Russians to stop interfering with the local politics in Czechoslovakia. Masaryk was stirring up a lot of anti-Soviet public opinion, and I'm sure that pissed off Stalin. Our State Department thinks Stalin ordered Masaryk killed."

Grant put down his comic book. "If you ask me, Stalin's the one who's pissing off people. Lyndon said there are plenty of people up on the Hill and at the Pentagon who are pretty concerned about Stalin's actions. They all think we sacrificed too damn much in the war to allow this bullcrap to continue."

"That's what's got me so worked up," Chase conceded. "Stalin was once our strongest ally in fighting Hitler, and now he's turned into our biggest headache. I don't frickin' understand it. We joined forces to defeat the Nazis, and now he's pulling this crap on us. It doesn't make sense."

I added my two cents, "My boss told me Stalin was going to try and force us out of Berlin. He said that Stalin wants to make sure a strong Germany will never rise up to threaten Russia again."

"Hell, who can blame them?" Grant asked. "They've been invaded by Germany twice before. It makes sense to me that Stalin wouldn't want that to happen again."

"I know that," Chase responded. "I didn't mean I didn't understand their fear of Germany. What gets me is that Stalin doesn't trust anybody. How much of a threat is a country like Czechoslovakia?"

"It's not a threat at all," Grant answered.

"It's part of the buffer Stalin is trying to put between Russia and the West," Chase talked over Grant, "I don't understand why he can't trust us. That's all I'm saying."

It dawned on me, "So we benevolently help the Germans get back on their feet…maybe Stalin sees it differently. Maybe he sees us helping his old enemy instead? Could that be it?"

"Maybe," Chase nodded. "The man obviously doesn't want Germany saved. He wants Germany destroyed forever. Deep down, he wants the Germans punished for what they did to his country, and he probably resents our interference. Since he can't kick us around, he's kicking around anyone else who stands up to him and opposes his actions. That's undoubtedly what got Masaryk killed. I don't understand why he can't take us at our word—we don't want Germany rebuilt as a military power either."

"Ah, he's just got his panties in a wad," Grant interjected.

Chase said, "Patrick, I'm telling you guys—people don't understand how dangerous this situation is. And it's not just the damned Russians—the Chinese are also having problems with a communist uprising of their own. What's the name of that Chinese communist guerrilla leader? Mao Tse-Tung. That guy has managed to push General Chiang Kai-shek's Chinese army almost right into the ocean. Can you explain to me why we're not helping those poor people? I'm telling you, I don't understand why President Truman isn't doing anything about it."

Chase was as miserable, upset, and angry as I had ever seen him. I knew from experience his bad mood would lead to a night of heavy drinking. Grant and I would drink with him and listen to his rants no matter how emotional and incoherent he became.

"You know what, boys?" Chase screamed at the top of his lungs, "We've got ourselves the first real crisis of this so-called Cold War."

Grant egged Chase on, "Maybe we sided with the wrong allies to fight the wrong enemies and produced the wrong outcome. Wouldn't it be a bitch if it turned out that Old Joe Kennedy was right about Hitler? What if the greatest threat to the United States turned out not to be Nazism after all?"

We moaned aloud at that thought.

CHASE WASN'T THE only one upset about the growing Communist threat. The news of worldwide Communist-directed agitation caused great concern all around the country. Capitol Hill exploded in a torrent of disbelief when the House Un-American Activities Committee conducted hearings to ascertain whether Communists had infiltrated our government.

Allegations that our own government was riddled with Communist sympathizers seeking to bring about our nation's downfall at the behest of Joseph Stalin were seriously discussed around the water coolers and lunch counters of the city. I was just as concerned about the threat of Communism as the next guy, but I never imagined that I would find myself in the middle of the growing controversy that rocked our nation that year.

August 3, 1948 was a typical steamy, hot and horribly humid summer day in the nation's capital. I rushed to work early to ask Mr. Lewis about taking some personal time for vacation. I was surprised to see Congressman Hagen and Mr. Lewis conferencing so early in the morning. I sat down outside the door to wait and studied my scruffy looking wingtip shoes. I noticed the Venetian blinds were cock-eyed and got up to straighten them. I took out my pocketknife to clean my nails. I checked my watch as I daydreamed about the cooler Minnesota summer back home.

My reverie was broken when I heard Mr. Lewis and the Congressman embroiled in a heated discussion about some closed committee hearings that were being held to discuss banning the Communist party in America. They were discussing the existence of some kind of positive proof of a Communist "fifth column in our midst."

I tried to be as unobtrusive as possible as I shamelessly eavesdropped on the argument. Mr. Lewis heatedly denounced the proceedings. "Parnell Thomas doesn't have diddly-squat, Congressman! I don't understand why the chairman of the House Un-American Activities Committee is even wasting his time airing these charges. No one in his right mind seriously believes that we've got Communists entrenched in our own government. That's just insanity—pure madness."

Congressman Hagen was much calmer and far more reasoned. "Spence, look—what troubles me the most is that the Federal grand jury in New York felt sufficiently satisfied with what it heard to go and indict twelve American

Communist party leaders. They were charged with conspiracy to overthrow the government of the United States of America. I'd say that is a pretty damn serious allegation. Please understand, politically I can't afford to ignore what is going on if that testimony turns out to be true. If that grand jury did find considerable evidence about Soviet high-level espionage within the upper levels of my own government, my constituents would turn me out of office in a New York minute if I didn't do something about it. That's the sort of information that could take President Truman's administration down, and I'm not about to go down with him—especially over an issue as serious as this."

"Well, then, what are you going to do? Don't tell me you are planning to sit through those hearings yourself? I don't think that's a wise move, especially since you're not even on the committee."

I heard the Congressman sigh. I heard them mumble a few other words before he finally agreed with Mr. Lewis that he couldn't be seen at the hearing. Suddenly, the closed door to Mr. Lewis' office swung open.

Mr. Lewis wrinkled his brow when he saw me, and I saw the Congressman roll his eyes. I got ready to receive a verbal lambasting from Mr. Lewis, and just as I stood up to sputter an embarrassed apology, Mr. Lewis grinned and turned back to the Congressman.

"Hey, I've got an idea. Maybe it will solve our problem. Why don't we send young Patrick over to listen in on the hearings? We can have him take some notes and report back to us on the proceeding so that you and I don't have to be seen there."

"Spence, I like that idea." Congressman Hagen looked thoughtfully at me for a moment. "Patrick, I'd like you to go to these House hearings for me and assess the mood of the audience. Spence and I would especially like to know how the public in the gallery views those proceedings. Find out if you think they believe these allegations about Communists infiltrating our government."

Impressed with the importance of my first real legislative assignment, I forgot my vacation plans as I hustled over to the hearing room for the House Un-American Activities Committee. When I arrived, newspaper reporters, members of the public, and low-level Capitol Hill gofers like me filled almost every seat.

A senior editor of *Time* magazine named Whittaker Chambers spoke first. He started the proceedings off by dropping one heck of a bombshell. He disclosed he had been a member of the Communist Party in the United States from 1925 to 1938. He also revealed he had worked as a paid courier in a Soviet spy ring that had easily infiltrated the government of the United States of America!

His shocking testimony virtually took my breath away. Here was the verification, under oath, that all of the alleged rumors about Communist activity in America were really true. The Soviets had targeted us as their enemy and had taken action against us.

Chambers' story had me on the edge of my seat. He testified that by the end of his thirteen-year career as a spy, he had finally become convinced the Communists were the *"party of Satan."* He revealed he was so horrified by the brutality of Stalin's bloody purges against his very own Russian population that he decided he wanted to stop spying.

He dramatically described how he had been in fear for his life in the year after he quit in 1938. He testified he had "lived in hiding, sleeping by day and watching through the night with a gun or revolver within easy reach…I had sound reason for supposing that the Communists might try to kill me. For a number of years I had myself served in the underground, chiefly in Washington, D.C…I knew at its top level, a group of seven or so men…A member of this group…was Alger Hiss."

I heard a collective intake of breath all around me when the name Alger Hiss was mentioned. I didn't know who Alger Hiss was, but many people around me in the crowd did. Two men behind me whispered, "You know who he is, don't you? Hiss is the president of the Carnegie Endowment for International Peace."

The guy next to him had a deep, gravelly voice with a Brooklyn accent. "How does youse know that?" he asked.

The other man replied, "My brother knew him when Hiss clerked for Oliver Wendell Holmes. He graduated Phi Beta Kappa from Johns Hopkins University and was a member of the *Harvard Law Review* when he graduated from Harvard Law School."

I knew Oliver Wendell Holmes was the most famous United States Supreme Court Justice of all time. I confess I didn't know the rest of that stuff about Hiss.

"Jesus, I woulda thought any guy with credentials like his woulda been almost beyond reproach," Brooklyn admonished.

The first voice added, "I think Hiss joined our State Department around 1936 or so. I know he advanced pretty quickly through our State Department ranks until he became a trusted advisor at Yalta to President Roosevelt."

Mr. Gravel Voice sounded impressed. "No kidding? Da guy sounds pretty sharp."

"Oh, he's very sharp," the other man replied. "He was the executive secretary of the Dunbarton Oaks conference. Then he became Secretary General of the United Nations Charter Conference in San Francisco. Two years ago, he became president of the Carnegie Endowment for International Peace. Chambers' allegation is sure-fire dynamite! The man Chambers has accused of being a Soviet spy is pure upper-society, blue-blooded Episcopalian. He has a pedigree that is 100% Eastern Establishment. I refuse to believe that he is a Communist spy. Chambers has got to be off his rocker."

I had to agree with the two men sitting behind me. I couldn't believe it either. Why would someone with credentials like Alger Hiss want to be a Communist? Why would an American like that—heck, why would any American—willingly embrace Communism in the first place? It just didn't make any sense to me.

According to the rest of Whittaker Chambers' story, the two men first met in D.C. in 1934. He claimed they had collaborated in stealing U.S. government documents and then had transmitted them to their Soviet bosses. Several times during his testimony, Chambers emphasized the aim of their group was not espionage but the infiltration of the government. He said the Soviet's main objective was to place Communists in positions of influence high up in the United States government.

The newspapers went wild in covering the allegations. Over the course of the next few days, everyone in the country, including me, wondered how Alger Hiss would answer Whittaker Chambers' spectacular charges. The credibility of our government was on the line, as well as our national security. No one doubted that other surprises would be forthcoming, perhaps even more explosive in nature.

However, we were all in for a huge letdown. When Hiss finally took the witness stand, he testified that Whittaker Chambers was simply a liar. Dressed immaculately in an expensive tailored suit, he read his denial like a bored patrician with a haughty, regal, and cultured air. "I am not and have never been a member of the Communist party. I do not and have not adhered to the tenets of the Communist party…I have never followed the Communist party line…To the best of my knowledge I never heard of Whittaker Chambers until 1947, when two representatives of the Federal Bureau of Investigation asked me if I knew him…So far as I know I have never laid eyes on him, and I should like to have the opportunity to do so."

The very way Hiss conducted himself seemed to legitimize his denials. As I listened to Hiss, I realized two men couldn't have had less in common. What had started out as a big bombshell of a story dissipated with every minute that Alger Hiss was on the stand.

AFTER HISS' TESTIMONY, the hearings concluded for the day. I scurried over to Congressman Dick Nixon's office to meet up with his two secretaries, Carol and Connie. Grant and I had met the two House staffers one night at a keg party over off of Massachusetts Avenue. We had double-dated two or three times since then. When I saw Carol and Connie sitting on the sidelines near Nixon, who was helping to conduct the Hiss hearing, I invited them to grab a beer. Because Grant was down in Texas trying to get his boss, Congressman Lyndon Johnson, elected to a more prestigious seat in the United States Senate, I called up Chase instead. He jumped at the chance to take two gorgeous California girls out for a few beers.

I waited for Carol and Connie to close their office down for the evening. It only took a few minutes for them to straighten up their desks and close the various doors and windows. However, just as we were ready to close and lock the door, Congressman Nixon angrily stormed in.

"Was that ever a wretched disappointment," he grumbled. "Hiss blew us out of the water." Both Connie and Carol looked at me and frowned—we might not be going for a drink if the Congressman needed them to work on the proceedings.

He vented his anger, "Chambers was a laughingstock by the end of the day. I don't think anyone in the room believed him after Hiss was done."

The girls half-heartedly tried to disagree, but Nixon saw me nod my head in agreement. I agreed—the seriousness of the charges Chambers had leveled against Alger Hiss had been reduced almost to the status of a bad joke.

Connie sensed Nixon's agitation and jumped in, "Hey Boss, you remember my friend, Patrick McCarthy? He's been over here before. He works in Congressman Hagen's office."

Nixon eyed me warily. He gave no indication of either recognition or even interest in Connie's last remark.

I politely extended my hand. "It's good to see you again, sir. I'm sorry the hearings didn't go better for you today."

I had been raised with the conviction that a handshake made the man. I had assumed a politician like Dick Nixon would possess a firm, friendly and confident handshake. I was stunned that Nixon's handshake was more like holding a cold, limp fish. When I later mentioned this to Connie, she told me her boss hated meeting "ordinary people."

"Why, thank you young man," he snapped testily.

There was a brief awkward period of silence before I volunteered, "Alger Hiss is pretty tough to like."

Nixon's eyes flashed. "He's a lying son of a bitch. There's something about that man I just don't like. I don't trust him. I damn well know he's lying, but I don't know how to prove it."

Dick slammed his fist against the desktop so hard I thought a stack of papers was going to cascade off and over its edge. "Damn it! He's got the entire country bamboozled by his hoity-toity act. I want to nail his ass to the wall for everyone to see. But how? How the hell do you break someone as smooth and smarmy as that?"

It was only later that I realized he wasn't asking me for my advice, but at the time I thought he was. I innocently said something that probably changed the course of the proceedings.

"Sir, one of them is clearly lying. Back where I grew up, whenever you were caught telling a lie, you had to admit to being ashamed about what you had done. I think you need to have these two men face each other. Force them to confront each other. I'll bet Alger Hiss breaks down long before Whittaker Chambers does."

Now, to this day, I don't know if I really believed Hiss would break down first, but I instinctively knew it was what Nixon wanted to hear. Nixon was greatly irritated by everything having to do with Alger Hiss, and maybe I accidentally inspired him to take a whole new approach. My simple idea ultimately became the crux of Nixon's attempt to break Hiss. Flashing a rather devious smile, and without another word, he whirled out of the room.

Connie was flustered, "Good God, Patrick! Look at what you did to him!" She looked toward Carol and then to me, "I sure hope you're right about that confrontation thing."

None of us had any idea just how right I would turn out to be.

DICK NIXON'S CONGRESSIONAL investigators were able to establish that Chambers and Alger Hiss actually had been close friends during the period Chambers described. When confronted, Hiss conceded under oath that perhaps he had known Whittaker Chambers. "Maybe it was under another name other than Chambers?" Hiss then shocked everyone when he said that Chambers might possibly be a man he had known by the name of "George Crosley."

A loud buzz went through the assembled crowd in the gallery.

"This just doesn't make any sense whatsoever," one woman said loudly.

Someone else in the back retorted, "Who in the hell is George Crosley?"

The next time I saw Nixon, he greeted me effusively—but he also extended the same dead fish handshake. He once again asked my opinion about how I thought the Hiss hearings would proceed.

"I think Chambers has been telling the truth all along. He has a terrific story to tell."

I added that I didn't like how overly dramatic he was in his testimony, and I thought he was paranoid. Chambers had a lot of things working against him. He had bad teeth and wore rumpled suits—compared to Hiss, he was an unattractive witness. "I'll bet he proves to be unflappable in his testimony because he's been trying to tell this story for ten years now and no one's believed him. Hiss is clearly becoming rattled by your line of questioning. My guess is that Hiss will break and fall apart long before Chambers ever does."

Nixon nodded gravely. "I believe you're right. Hiss has already asked for his lawyer to be present next time. He's also asked for access to his transcripts prior to each session. He's already refused to consider taking a lie-detector test, which Chambers actually volunteered to take." He paused for a moment, "Yes, I agree with you."

He turned to walk away and then stopped to add, "I'll never forget this, Patrick. I owe you a big debt of gratitude. If I can ever repay you in some way, don't hesitate to ask, okay?"

I smirked to myself. Spencer Lewis had been right about Rule #1.

Alger Hiss' carefully fabricated façade soon crumbled. He was later accused of perjury and Whittaker Chambers was vindicated. Congressman Richard Nixon had successfully proved that the Communists had very likely infiltrated the highest levels of our government. According to Chase, many people admired Nixon's uncanny ability to ferret out the truth when almost no one else had believed in him or his cause.

His success in the Alger Hiss hearing elevated Nixon into national prominence. As a result, Congressman Nixon had now become one of our nation's best-known anti-Communists.

IN SPITE OF the scandals concerning Communism that now surrounded President Truman and his administration, Truman pulled off a miracle upset of the Republican challenger, Governor Thomas Dewey and was re-elected to a second term as president. Grant returned from Texas to our apartment after helping to get Lyndon Johnson elected to the Senate by a vote margin of just 87 votes out of almost a million cast. "We've got a new nickname for him," Grant joked, "We're gonna call him Landslide Lyndon!"

After the 1948 elections were over, we settled back into a normal daily routine staying busy with our jobs during the day. To keep busy in the evenings, we played poker. When Chase found out that Grant and I didn't know how to play, he took it upon himself to teach us the nuances of the game.

"Listen you guys, poker is the universal man's game. It is a simple enough game to learn, and yet it's complex beyond belief once you try to master its subtleties. It's a game all men play, especially here in D.C. If you really want to understand the nature of the power in this town, then this is the game you need to learn. I guarantee it can open as many doors for you as it has for me."

Grant did not have the patience to become a good poker player, but he was attracted to the social nature of the game. I eagerly listened to Chase's lectures and lessons—I became addicted to cards. By the second week of instruction, we could play all the way up to 10 p.m. without a beer break. By the third week, we were sitting up past 11 p.m., and by the fourth week, we were quitting at midnight. Through Chase's persistence, guidance, and patience, we actually became decent players.

"Listen you guys," Chase announced one evening, "I think it's time we started playing for money." Grant and I exchanged worried glances. Neither of us had much money to spare out of our meager paychecks.

"Hey, relax! I don't mean we play each other for money. Here's my idea. I think we should invite some other guys over for a regular game of penny-ante. I think you're both good enough to test your skills against some other players, so I'll set up some games here at the apartment. We'll provide the beer and some sandwiches, and we'll have the guests all chip in to help pay for it. The house, meaning us, will also be entitled to take a cut of the pot for hosting the event. We'll pool our winnings—whatever we make over and above our expenses we'll apply toward a nicer apartment in a better neighborhood."

In late autumn, we began hosting two poker games a week on Tuesday and Thursday nights. Chase set up our first few games with some guys who were terrible card players; we made over $10.00 in profits in only one night.

By the first of the year, we hosted card games six nights a week. Due to word-of-mouth, the quality of the players and the money just grew and grew. Our profits reached almost $40 a night. It wasn't long before Chase announced, "Gentlemen, I am proud to inform you that as of today, our poker kitty holds the magnificent sum of $3,026.37."

We were rich! Grant began to talk about all the women he could wine and dine. I had visions of buying a '49 Mercury.

Chase put a halt to our fantasies, "Guys, guys! Remember our original goal? We wanted to move out of here, right? Well, I've found a nice townhouse in a better part of Georgetown—in fact, it's in a very nice part of Georgetown. It's a corner property. That means we can arrange to have our guests come and go through a side entrance without disturbing our neighbors. I've checked—we've got some pretty classy neighbors."

Grant was immediately interested, "Some rich dames?"

"No, Grant, even better! Some rich, powerful gentlemen we don't want to offend. Remember the golden rule here in Washington—if you have money, and if you have power, you will also have women."

"So who are our neighbors?" I asked.

Chase slyly grinned, "One of our next-door neighbors just happens to be the Director of the Federal Bureau of Investigation. Yes, I am talking about the one and only J. Edgar Hoover. Around the block, behind Hoover's place is a young Senator from the great state of Texas, a friend of FDR's, and a confidante of the Speaker of the House, Sam Rayburn. I'm talking about..."

"Lyndon Johnson!" Grant's voice was at least two octaves higher. "We're gonna live right around the corner from my boss? Are you nuts? My daddy's gonna kill me if Lyndon tells him what I've been up to!"

Chase looked at Grant quizzically. "What does your daddy think you've been doing, besides working?"

Grant visibly reddened. "He thinks I'm in a local Shakespeare acting group."

Now I appreciate Shakespeare as much as the next guy—which is not at all. Grant in tights? Prancing around an imaginary stage? I tried to do my best impersonation of young Juliet and warbled in an obnoxiously falsetto voice, "Romeo, Romeo, wherefore art thou, Romeo?"

Soon Chase and I were out of control, our whooping and hollering interspersed with "To be or not to be" and "Out, out damn spot."

Grant, however, didn't share our joke. "You guys are real jerks, you know that?" Finally, he gave in and began to flourish his arms, shouting to the sky in a self-deprecating way, "Friends, Romans, countrymen, lend me your ears. We have come to bury Caesar, not to praise him. The evil men do lives after them...."

Our laughter spent, I finally asked, "How much is the rent?"

Chase wiped his eyes. "I have no idea how much the rent is because we are gonna buy the damn thing."

Buy it? Did he say we were going to buy it?

"Yep, that's right."

Grant and I sat in stunned silence.

"I suggest we buy the townhouse as an investment. We should also upgrade the quality of our game. By inviting a richer, older crowd, we can cut back to two or three nights a week and still clear the same amount of money, or more. What do you say?"

I spoke up, "Frankly, Chase, I think it sounds like a recipe for disaster. Don't you think a business like this will eventually attract the attention of the D.C. Vice Squad?"

Chase and Grant exchanged conspiratorial glances. Chase said, "I'll give you three reasons why that is unlikely to happen." He held up a hand and showed one finger. "Reason One: A nice house in a nice neighborhood isn't going to get raided. Reason Two: A nice house in a nice neighborhood filled with powerful and influential people playing poker is also not going to get raided. And Reason Three…" He held up a third finger and grinned broadly at me. "Do you have any idea who our Monday night poker crowd is, or what they do for a living?"

I naively shook my head. "All I know is that they are a bunch of your newspaper friends."

Chase and Grant erupted in laughter.

Puzzled I asked, "What's so funny, guys?"

Chase looked at Grant, "Should I tell him, or do you want to?"

Grant, laughing so hard he was almost choking, gestured to Chase to tell me.

"Patrick, brace yourself for a little surprise. Those six guys who show up unfailingly every Monday night for their regular game *are* the Washington D.C. Vice Squad!"

"Let us not be deceived—we are today in the midst of a cold war. Our enemies are to be found abroad and at home. Let us never forget this: Our unrest is the heart of their success. The peace of the world is the hope and the goal of our political system; it is the despair and defeat of those who stand against us."

— Bernard M. Baruch

"A shadow has fallen upon the scenes so lately lighted by the Allied victory…From Stettin in the Baltic to Trieste in the Adriatic, an iron curtain has descended across the Continent."

— Winston Churchill

September 6, 1978
9:37 a.m.

Grant looked up from the work on his desk and was momentarily shocked to see Derek Ruger casually saunter through the door. "How the hell did you get past my secretary?"

"She wasn't a problem. I told her I wanted to surprise you."

"Hell, that woman is useless. I've a mind to just fire her ass."

Ruger said nothing. He remembered a colloquial phrase that Texans liked to use: "He's got a wild hair up his ass" and decided that was a perfectly apt description of Grantham's mood.

Grant resumed his tirade. "Did you see the goddamn news this morning? It's all over everything! Everybody's yakkin' about reopening that goddamn Kennedy investigation! Have they lost their minds? There's nothing there to be found. We all know that." He paused and added, "Don't we?"

"We know what we know."

"What the hell does that mean?" It clearly wasn't the answer Grant wanted.

Ruger didn't elaborate. He stared back at Grant with a hollow look that made most men uncomfortable. It had the same intended effect on Grant.

"Jesus Christ, Ruger, you give me the creeps. Why don't you just tell me what's going on in that psycho brain of yours—instead of making me guess?"

Grant immediately realized he had crossed a line. Ruger's eyes momentarily flared when he used the term "psycho."

"Sorry…I didn't mean to imply anything…I mean, to offend you. I've just got my nuts in a vise this morning. I didn't mean to take it out on you."

Seeking to diminish the sudden tension in the room, Grant offered his other excuses. "My son's gone and put his pecker where he shouldn't have.

I've got some business associates in Austin who are gonna be watching me real close to see what I'm gonna do about it. My damn second wife has stirred up trouble with my first wife, and now my current wife is siding with my ex-wives. We've got this House Select Committee poking their noses into old finished business—who knows what they might turn up—and I can't seem to find Patrick McCarthy anywhere."

Ruger didn't give a shit about Grantham's yammering until he mentioned Patrick McCarthy. Ruger acutely alert asked, "What's going on with McCarthy?"

"McCarthy seems to have gone missing. He won't answer his phone."

"Maybe you're jumping to conclusions. Maybe he's out for a walk."

"Yeah, and maybe my son didn't rape the underage daughter of one of my law partners. Come on, I know Patrick. He's a fuckin' Boy Scout. He got a subpoena to appear before that House committee, and he doesn't know what to do. He's gone somewhere to figure out his next move."

Ruger quietly took in this information. He was intimately familiar with the new House probe because it was his job to know what was going on. Grant was probably right.

"Did you hear me?"

He cut his eyes toward Grant in a cold and calculating way. Grant once again realized he had crossed a dangerous line. This time he waited for Ruger to speak.

The delay felt like an eternity, but finally Ruger tilted his head slightly toward Grant. "What do you want me to do?"

Grant pounded his fists on the desk and leaped to his feet. "What the fuck do you think I want you to do? Find him! God damn it to hell, Ruger, we're talking about our lives here! I've loved Patrick like a brother, but he can't be allowed to bring us down. It'll ruin everything we've ever worked for."

Ruger smiled sardonically, "You love him like a brother? Like Cain and Abel, maybe?"

Grant froze at the allegation. "Since when did you become interested in religion?"

Another pause then Ruger slowly replied, "I'm not interested in religion. I am, however, an expert on other topics. Topics like Cain and Abel. You know that."

Grant slumped back down into his chair and whispered wearily, "Find him. He's got some things that belong to us that he can no longer be entrusted with. Hell, he can't be trusted. If he intends to talk to that goddamn committee, we need to find him and stop him. You understand?"

Ruger lingered for a few moments. He left the room as surreptitiously as he had entered.

1949

THE WHITTAKER CHAMBERS' allegations about high-level Communist infiltration of our government were easily the most disturbing development of the past year. The HUAC hearings gave us tangible proof our Communist enemies had indeed infiltrated many aspects of American society. They were trying to take over our society from within, without firing a single shot. They had to be stopped, and I was happy other Americans thought the same way. The New York State Legislature reacted to the increasing Communist menace by ordering that all Communists be dismissed from teaching at their schools. The Atomic Energy Commission saw an enormous controversy erupt over the FBI's loyalty check of AEC scientists. Enrico Fermi and the California Institute of Technology president claimed the FBI investigation of AEC researchers was a major step toward a police state.

I frankly didn't care if it was a major step toward a police state or not—I didn't want Commies anywhere near our atomic facilities. The thought of the Soviet Union getting its hands on our secrets for making an atomic bomb was too horrifying to even contemplate.

The Soviets were becoming more and more dangerous. The Berlin crisis of 1948-1949 took the concern over Communism's spread in Germany to new levels of anxiety. The crisis was precipitated by Joe Stalin's heavy-handed attempts to deliberately make life miserable for the free West Berliners trapped deep in the heart of the Soviet-occupied zone. After the war ended, the German capital of Berlin had been divided into four major zones, with each zone controlled by an Allied power. Berlin itself was deep within the part of the country controlled by the Soviet Union.

The Russians ruthlessly denied access to the parts of Berlin they didn't control. Western aid of any kind was completely shut off, and it didn't matter if it tried to enter either by rail or by road. The Soviets kept it from going through. The only way the free world could keep West Berlin from falling to the Communists was to supply it ourselves. America resorted to flying in virtually everything the West Berliners needed for subsistence, including coal to heat their homes and apartments. Our Allied military airlift became known as "LeMay's Feed and Coal Company," named after U.S. Air Force General Curtis LeMay who headed the operation. It flew in an average of 5,000 tons of supplies each and every day. At one point in the spring, our Allied air force was landing a cargo plane in West Berlin about every sixty seconds for twenty-four hours straight.

The Soviets used their fighter planes to buzz and harass our unarmed cargo planes. They also deliberately tethered giant weather balloons in the middle of the flight paths for the take-off and landings to make it as hard as possible for our pilots to complete their missions. About the only thing Stalin didn't try to do was shoot our planes down. Although his actions, combined with a heavy flight schedule and the extreme fatigue of our pilots, contributed to over forty crashes and seventy-eight deaths of Allied aircrews during the airlift.

After a diplomatic solution to the blockade failed to stop the Soviet harassment, President Truman finally moved some of our B-29 bombers to England. Since those planes happened to be the delivery platforms for our atomic bombs, Stalin guessed we meant business if we were willing to station them within striking distance of Moscow itself.

By May 12, the Russian oppression suddenly ceased. Frustrated and beaten, Stalin reluctantly re-opened the borders to Berlin traffic. I heard it cost us about $200 million dollars to save Berlin. It certainly cost the Soviets a whole lot more, for it inflicted a huge major blow to their worldwide prestige. They had tried to push the United States around, and we had forced them to back down and admit defeat.

The biggest positive consequence of the Berlin crisis was the establishment of the North Atlantic Treaty Organization (NATO) by all of the Western Allies. We created NATO as the cornerstone of our combined protection policy for all of free Europe. It would be the free world's first line of defense against further Soviet expansion.

After the Berlin crisis, the mood of our entire nation improved. We had shown the Soviets the futility of trying to challenge America and our military might, and the pervasive pessimism of 1948 was replaced with a spirit of optimism in 1949. I now believed the whole world could finally begin to settle into a much more peaceful place. After all, we had won World War II, and now we had forced Stalin to stop his aggression in Germany. I was very, very proud to be an American, and a lot of other people felt the same way.

Americans alone held the one key to world peace—the atomic bomb, the word's most terrible weapon. Our journalists bragged about the "American Century" and proclaimed the new period of peace as "Pax Americana." Many commentators talked about how it had taken our country less than 175 years to become the most powerful nation on the face of the earth. They marveled that Alexander the Great, the Holy Roman Empire, Napoleon, and even Great Britain at the height of its empire could not equal the power the United States of America held at this moment in time.

Our nation felt strong and confident. I was present at a small congressional gathering at the White House one day when even President Truman asserted "the Russians would soon be put in their places…the United States would then take the lead in running the world in the way the world ought to be run!"

Clearly, it was our atomic arsenal that infused our feelings of strength and righteousness.

OUR TOWNHOUSE PURCHASE turned out to be a good idea. Just as Chase predicted, our reputation for conducting poker games grew by leaps and bounds when we moved to our new address. Because we were known to accommodate unexpected guests, our games attracted a fascinating and ever changing cast of characters. Since D.C. was a boring place to be—with few decent restaurants and almost no venues for entertainment—many visiting dignitaries, "friends of friends," often stopped by our townhouse for a night of poker. Like Chase said, poker was a game with a universal language, a language that created immediate friendships and loyalties.

Our most distinguished special guest was, without question, General Dwight D. Eisenhower, former Supreme Allied Commander of our troops in Europe. He appeared at our door one evening with one of our regular players. Grant and I were thrilled, giddy, and tongue-tied. We were in awe. But once we calmed down, we realized that he was just a normal guy who only wanted to relax and play cards like everyone else.

General Eisenhower had a passion for poker. He played a disciplined game unlike Grant who was a wild, devil-may-care bettor, risking everything on unpredictable chances. In between bets, Eisenhower told about an old illiterate muskrat trapper by the name of Bob Davis who taught him to play the game back in his hometown of Abilene. I got a special kick out of the fact that Bob Davis had once served as a deputy sheriff to Abilene's most famous marshal, Wild Bill Hickock.

"I don't know if Hickock taught Bob how to play poker or if it was the other way around," the General explained. "Hickock was a great poker player and so was Bob. Wild Bill was shot dead during a poker game while holding a full house of aces and eights. That's why that hand is now known as 'the dead man's hand.'"

I had to pinch myself. Here was General Dwight D. Eisenhower, the Supreme Allied Commander of World War Two, sitting in my house and talking to me about poker. My parents wouldn't have believed it possible.

"Bob Davis was a very patient teacher. He taught me how to play the percentages. He showed me how to calculate the probability that a certain card or card suit might show up in my hand or my opponent's hand at any particular point in the game."

"That's something I try to do from time to time, sir."

"That's good, Patrick, that's very good. I learned the only way to consistently make money at poker is to do it *all* the time. For example, if I'm holding four cards in my hand that are all hearts—let's say the 8,9,10, Jack, and the fifth card is an Ace of Spades, what should I be doing?"

"That's pretty easy, sir. I should discard the Ace and draw another card."

"That's right, but why?"

"Because I could possibly get another 8,9,10, or Jack and at least have a pair of something."

The General smiled, "Okay, but what are the odds one of those four cards might come up?"

"Well, there are possibly three more of each suit out there, so that's twelve cards, and there were once fifty-two cards in the deck, so I'd guess 25% or so."

"And how many hands will a pair beat?"

"Not many," I replied.

"So a pair isn't necessarily a strong hand, is it?"

"Nope."

"How about a straight?"

"A straight would be much stronger, sir."

"What's your chance of completing that straight?"

"I would need to draw either a 7 or a queen of any suit, so I have a 17% chance there," I said.

"Good. Now, how about a flush? How strong a hand is that?"

"It's very strong, sir. Almost unbeatable, in fact."

"That's right. And what are your chances of drawing another heart?"

"There are four suits—so one-in-four, sir."

"That's right. You have a 25% chance of drawing an almost unbeatable hand, a 17% chance of drawing a very strong hand, and a 25% chance of completing a weak hand. So, how do you bet?"

I liked the thought of holding a flush by simply drawing one more card. "I'd go for the flush, sir."

"Good. Now you're starting to calculate odds. You have to know how to calculate the probabilities if you want to win at poker. That's why I finally stopped playing regularly. I calculated the probabilities and my playing companions didn't." He sighed, "I would always win and take home too much of my buddies' hard-earned cash. That's why I play bridge now instead."

He told us this was the first real poker game he had played in a long time, but it was clear to me his skills had not diminished. I was learning that you can tell a lot about a man's character by how he played his cards. General Eisenhower was controlled, thoughtful, and disciplined. I had a great deal of respect for him, and I hoped he respected me as well—although I suspect he deliberately played his cards so that I ended up winning $5 from him.

Our favorite regular player, hands-down, was Joseph P. McCarthy, the junior senator from Wisconsin. Joe typically showed up at our apartment on Thursday nights between 11 p.m. and midnight, a sack of hamburgers and a bottle of champagne in hand. He was loud, fun loving, extroverted, and hyperactive. He bragged he could spend the day on the floor of the Senate, work in the evening on district business, devote most of the night drinking and playing poker, catch a few hours of sleep on the couch in his office, and wake up ready to do it all over again the next day. I noticed that his suits were generally rumpled as though he had slept in them.

He drove Grant crazy with his incessant needling and bragging. Joe's pattern of play was simple: make a play, a move, an assertion, a challenge—anything that was liable to catch Grant off-guard. Then, he'd sit back to see what Grant would do. Grant, who tended to think that he was smarter than the next guy, always fell for Joe's tricks.

"Hey, Grantham, I'll bet you a quarter that the next card is the two of clubs." Joe often bet on cards face down and sight-unseen. This drove Grant nuts because he thought that he could easily beat Joe by playing the percentages. Grant never failed to take the bait.

"Make it fifty cents, Joe, and you've got yourself a bet. There's no way the next card is a two of clubs."

"Anyone else want in on this, or am I the only one getting Grantham's money?"

None of us—except Grant—was stupid enough to bet against Joe. His lucky prowess at the poker table had long ago caused Chase to grimly advise anyone playing against Joe to play only for table stakes. Joe would bet his last nickel on the longest of long shots, and more often than not, he would win. He raised his bets on the poorest of poker hands and always managed to come out the winner.

Grant yelled at me, "Turn over that card, Patrick, so that Joe can give me my money."

Honest to God, I turned over the two of clubs.

"Yahoo!" Joe yelled exuberantly.

"Son of a bitch," Grant slammed his hand on the table. "He fuckin' did it to me again. I don't believe it. That goddamn son of a bitch!" Grant stormed out of the room, kicking a chair as he went.

While scooping up his winnings, Joe asked, "Hey Patrick, you were a big stud athlete in high school. Did you ever play donkey baseball?"

"Joe, I have honestly never even heard of donkey baseball, let alone played it. What are you talking about?"

"Aw, hell, it's a great game! It's baseball, but everybody has to ride a donkey—all the infielders, the outfielders, and even the base runners. I remember this one game where I hit a long fly ball to the outfield, a sure home run, but my stupid son of a bitch jackass refused to move from home plate. He just flat-out wouldn't budge. I didn't want to waste that great hit. I sure as hell didn't want to be embarrassed by getting thrown out at first base. So you know what I did?"

I said I didn't have a clue. Most of the time with Joe, I really didn't have a clue.

"I picked that donkey up in my arms and carried his lazy ass all the way to first base. You should have heard that crowd roaring and cheering me on. It was a sight to behold."

"Yeah, I'll bet it was," Grant exclaimed sourly as he rejoined the game, "One big jackass carrying another jackass."

"Oooooohhh!" the other players chorused

Joe laughed, "That's pretty funny, Grantham. Pretty funny, wanna bet the next card is the five of diamonds?"

I decided to leave the table to get another beer. "Anybody want anything?"

No one answered because Grant was busy taking Joe's bet. "Make it a buck this time, Joe. I wanna win my money back."

I was in the kitchen when I heard Grant explode, "SON OF A BITCH! THERE'S NO POSSIBLE WAY IN HELL THAT YOU JUST DREW THE FIVE OF DIAMONDS."

"Read it and weep, Grantham."

As I walked back in with my beer, Joe asked me, "Were you ever in the Marine Corp, Patrick?"

Now, Joe knew the answer—he knew I had been too young to join the military. I guess I was selected to be his straight man this particular evening.

"I joined up when the war broke out. I was an intelligence officer. My primary responsibility was to interview our pilots when they returned from combat. Sometimes, if I played my cards right," he winked at Grant, "I would get to ride along on their combat missions. I tell ya, I loved to ride in that tail-gunner's seat. Sometimes I even got permission to shoot the guns. That's how I got to be known far and wide throughout the Pacific theater as Tail Gunner Joe."

It didn't take me long to figure out that Joe never let the truth get in the way of a good story. His own embellishment of his war record was a great example of how he could let things get out of hand.

"Middle of 1943, I found myself on a seaplane tender where I was to cross the equator for the very first time. This is always a big deal in the Navy, and as a U.S. Marine, I was determined to participate in the ritual. They had created some elaborate ceremony that was almost beyond control. Somehow, I found myself climbing down a ladder with a bucket tied to my right foot. Well wouldn't you know it, I slipped! My left foot caught on the rung of the damned ladder, and I fell backward, breaking my leg."

Grant snickered, but Joe continued with his story. "Later on, when I was having my cast removed, some stupid corpsman used the wrong kind of acid on me, which chemically burned my leg and left a large scar. Anyway, it was luckily the only injury that I sustained in the war. But you're gonna love this part. I wrote a letter in the name of my commanding officer describing my heroism in the Solomon Islands. Then I personally sent it up through all of the proper Navy channels until it ultimately got to Admiral Chester Nimitz himself. He read my letter and immediately awarded me a citation that lauded my 'indomitable devotion' to duty, despite a severe leg injury."

I laughed at Joe's sheer chutzpah.

Grant, however, wasn't impressed. "I don't believe you," he interjected.

Joe looked hurt at Grant's remark. "Why don't you believe me?" he asked.

"Because no corpsman would ever be stupid enough to use the wrong acid on someone," he said defiantly.

"This one was and he did," Joe replied.

Grant came right back, "Dollar says he didn't."

"Dollar it is."

Senator Joe McCarthy immediately stood up. Right there in the middle of our living room, he dropped his trousers to show us the scar. Sure enough, there it was.

"Son of a bitch!" Grant swore as he fished in his pocket for a dollar bill.

I saw a devilish glint in Joe's eyes. "Hey, Grant, you want to see the hickey that my date gave me last night?"

Grant froze and looked at Joe. If there was one thing that always held an abiding interest for Grant, it was anything having to do with sex. "You got a hickey?" he asked.

Joe nodded, "Yep, right here." He kind of pointed to the back of his right leg. Of course, the way he was standing, with his pants down around his ankles, we couldn't see anything.

Grant was skeptical. "No you don't."

"Betcha a dollar I do."

"Prove it."

"Come here and look if you don't believe me," Joe said innocently.

I couldn't believe Grant's gullibility. Whenever he was around a senator or any other high-ranking official, his behavior alternated between one-upmanship and sycophancy.

He crouched down behind Joe, "I don't see anything."

"Oh, it's there. Look closer."

Grant got down on one knee moving his face to within inches of Joe's behind. "Where is it?"

"Right about there," Joe said and proceeded to let the loudest, oiliest, and greasiest sounding fart that I had ever heard—right in Grant's face.

"SON OF A BITCH!" Grant was red with frustration and embarrassment. He stood up as straight as he could, glared at Joe, and flew out of the room. The rest of us laughed until we cried because it was the perfect set-up—and Grant had fallen for it.

I couldn't help but like Joe. He was coarse, but he was also unpretentious. He enjoyed being the clown, the jester. Surprisingly, he was also a very pious and religious Catholic, which I found to be a hilarious contradiction to his lifestyle. Here was a guy who had a passion for all forms of gambling—poker, horses, roulette, slot machines—and yet he told me he would say his rosary while speeding down the highway to his next party.

Joe's unsavory and outrageous reputation made him an outcast among Senate insiders on Capitol Hill. When the Democrats returned to control of the Senate in 1949, the new chairman of the Senate Banking Committee said he would refuse to serve if Joe McCarthy kept his seat on the committee. "He's a troublemaker; that's why I don't want him," he said. The truth was that Joe had once embarrassed him, the same way he always did Grant, in a game of poker at our place. To mollify him, the other members banished Joe to the Committee on the District of Columbia, a lowly and less prestigious assignment. The lesson was that to make it in Washington, you had to be careful not to piss off the wrong people.

But Joe got even with his stuffed-shirt colleagues by mocking the seriousness of the Senate. He flaunted his vulgarity. He frequently invited newspapermen like Chase to photograph him unshaven and in his shirtsleeves with a drink in his hand. He got a big kick out of the reaction those photos made up on the Hill. He insisted on informality, requiring his staff to call him "Joe" and not "Senator McCarthy," which further pissed off his colleagues. He even signed his mail Joe McCarthy, and the people back home loved him for it.

Joe McCarthy was the type of guy that people either loved or hated—but no one could dispute that Joe was dedicated to serving his county. He just did it in his own way.

IN SEPTEMBER OF 1949, the world as I knew it changed forever.

Washington was a town that thrived on news, rumor, innuendo, and gossip. A deep feeling of foreboding and fear began to permeate the cloakrooms and cocktail lounges of the city. Something was wrong. The grapevine spread spurious and not-so-spurious rumors daily, but this time an aura of dread and impending doom hovered in the air. No one in the know talked about *what* they really knew. Finally, one horrible rumor began to circulate the Hill—if it turned out to be true, it would have a devastating effect upon all of America.

Chase broke the news to me first. He returned home one evening ashen and trembling. He went straight to the cupboard where we kept the liquor, and he poured himself a very healthy glass of Jack Daniels whiskey. Chase Newman usually drank beer.

"Oh God! Oh God!" he muttered over and over to himself as he grimly slugged down the whiskey. He was pale and sweating profusely. I thought he might have lost his job, or maybe someone we knew had died.

"Jesus, Chase, what's wrong with you? What's going on?"

He wouldn't even turn to look at me at first. He held up his hand to ward off any more questions while he poured some more Jack Daniels. He downed another big slug. He then took a deep breath, let out a long sigh, and turned to face me.

I thought he might be deathly ill. His eyes had a tragic, haunted look.

Chase swallowed hard, "The Russians have the Bomb."

The impact of those five words hammered straight into the pit of my stomach—it literally knocked the wind out of me. "Chase, where in the hell did you hear that?"

He stared at me blankly. "I heard it from a source that was as upset as I've ever seen him. I know he'd never lie to me. At least, he never has before."

"This doesn't make any sense at all, Chase." I tried to appeal to his intellect to show him how ridiculous his story and his fears were. "My friends at the Pentagon have repeatedly assured me the Russians won't even be capable of making an atomic bomb for at least another five years, or maybe longer than that…"

Chase interrupted me defensively, "I know, I know…my contacts in the White House told me the same thing. Truman firmly believes the Soviets will never be smart enough to figure out how to put an atomic bomb together."

"Well, there you have it! Don't you think these guys know what they're talking about? Our Army thinks the Soviets can't develop an atomic bomb until at least 1960. And our Navy claims that the Reds can't do it before 1965. So if all of our military experts say the Soviets are that far away from having an atomic bomb, then why do you think that they've already got it?"

Chase paused to collect his thoughts. He picked up his bottle, moved over to our kitchen table, and reached for one of my Lucky Strikes. He let out a huge sigh. Then he lit a cigarette as if to create a momentary aura of composure for himself.

"Patrick, this is all very hush-hush, but I have it on very good authority that the rumors of a Soviet atomic bomb's existence are all true."

He told me about a friend of his who was a flight line mechanic at Almendorf Air Force Base in Alaska. The guy had called him in the middle of the night to see if anyone in Washington could verify what they had discovered on some aerial reconnaissance flights that were flown out of his base.

Chase puffed his cigarette with a hollow-eyed expression. "About two weeks ago, a routine Air Force weather reconnaissance plane, flying at 18,000 feet from Japan to Alaska, detected signs of intense radioactivity over the North Pacific. The source was believed to be just east of the Kamchatka Peninsula of the Soviet Union. The plane's air filters showed something like 85 clicks of radioactivity per minute. I guess anything over 50 clicks a minute automatically triggers an alarm on the plane. The flight crew checked a second air filter, and that one registered 153 clicks per minute on the Geiger counter.

"Two days later, another plane flying over the Pacific picked up a count of more than 1,000 clicks. That's twenty times more radioactivity than normal. The Air Force immediately flew all of the filters back to D.C., and some of our scientists found various fission isotopes in the samples…"

"What's a fission isotope?" I interrupted.

"It's the by-product of a nuclear explosion. It's like a fingerprint of an atomic bomb blast. It contains things like barium, cerium, and molybdenum that leave absolutely no doubt that it came from a nuclear explosion. The only thing they are unable to tell was whether it came from a nuclear accident or was the result of an intentionally exploded device."

"Anyway, the Air Force began tracking the radioactive cloud from the Pacific all the way across North America and over the Atlantic Ocean as far as the British Isles, where it was also picked up and tracked by the Royal Air Force, too."

"Hold on, Chase. You said they couldn't tell if it was a bomb or an accident? Maybe it was an accident of some kind. Maybe they really don't have a bomb," I offered hopefully.

Chase shook his head, "No, they've got it all right. Some other sources told me our scientists now believe the Soviets intentionally detonated an atomic bomb somewhere in Asia between August 26 and August 29."

"Jesus, Chase—that was almost a month ago. My God! Does the President know about this?" My mind raced with a thousand different thoughts, and none of them were good.

Chase took another long drag on his cigarette. "I know the president was finally told after the tests were verified, but I can't confirm it. My source said that President Truman was officially briefed about it on September 20. Here we are almost a week later and not a single word has been officially released. My White House source is stunned that the President still clings to the belief the Soviets are at least ten to fifteen years away from having it. He thinks our scientists must be wrong in their analysis."

"Jesus H. Christ!" I blasphemed. "This changes everything, doesn't it?"

"Yeah," he sighed again in resignation, "it does."

My view about the safety of our world literally changed in that instant. It was our worst national nightmare. Suddenly the world's most exclusive club—the atomic club—contained two members instead of just us. This was truly a frightening development.

The Russians had already tried to blockade Berlin, the Communist Chinese had taken over China, and now the Soviet Union possessed an atomic bomb. Atomic bombs were no longer just a benevolent enforcer of the worldwide peace process. Now I worried they were to become weapons of death and destruction that could be used to start the final battle of Armageddon.

I repeated again in disbelief, "Damn it, Chase, everything changes now, doesn't it?" I guess I was hoping Chase might reassure me that it really didn't have to change. But he didn't. In fact, he didn't even bother to point out I was repeating myself. We both sat there in a state of numbed shock.

He whispered, "Europe is dead. There's no way we'll be able to keep the Soviets from overrunning all of Europe now."

"Why hasn't anyone said anything about this publicly?"

"They're too afraid of what the public reaction might be."

Chase's last comment hit me again with stunning clarity—now I understood why Washington D.C. seemed paralyzed with fear. None of our top leaders, starting with the President of the United States of America, knew how to respond to this threat.

"Man, oh man, Chase, what's the President going to do?"

"I don't know, Patrick. My sources want the President to announce the news as soon as possible before the Soviets announce it, or before it leaks out on its own."

"But it's already leaked out," I protested. "You've got the story in your hands."

"But it's a story no one will go on record to officially discuss. Without official verification, the story is just an unsubstantiated rumor. The press has a moral responsibility not to print gossip or rumor. Printing rumors would be highly irresponsible and unprofessional. We'll just have to wait for an official word."

Two days later, President Truman announced the Soviet Union officially possessed the atomic bomb.

> *"If the radiance of a thousand suns*
> *Were to burst into the sky*
> *That would be like*
> *The splendor of the Mighty One.*
> *I am become Death, the shatterer of worlds."*
>
> — J. Robert Oppenheimer

•

September 6, 1978
10:02 a.m.

Grant picked up the phone, dialed the Washington Post switchboard, and demanded to be connected to Chase Newman. The phone rang six times before someone finally answered.

"Chase Newman."

"Chase, it's Grant. How have you been?"

There was a brief, pregnant pause at the other end before Newman replied, "Grant? Wow! Long time no see. How long has it been since I've heard from the most hated man in Washington? Five years?"

"Since when did I become the most hated man in D.C.?"

"Easy—ever since Richard Nixon resigned."

Grant's feelings were hurt. He had never been called that before. "Is that something you made up just to be hurtful?"

The laughter came booming across the phone line. "Are you really that out-of-touch with reality? You've screwed so many people in D.C. I'm surprised you don't have someone tasting your food before you touch it. Grant, no one likes you."

"Including you?"

"What do you want, Grant?"

"Why do you think I want anything?"

"Because you've become a user, Grant. You use people up, and then you discard them. You discarded me a long time ago. That's why. Now what do you want?"

"I want us to be friends again, like we used to be."

Grant heard Chase's cynical laughter.

"Grant, we were never best friends, even when we roomed together. There was too much of an age difference. Besides, I didn't like your choice of friends. I still don't. The one exception is Patrick."

Grant was relieved that Chase brought up their former roommate first. This would make it easier to find out what he had called about. "Yeah, Patrick's terrific. Hey, have you seen him lately? How's he doing?"

"Yeah, I saw him last week. The divorce still has him reeling. He misses Pam and Tim. He still doesn't understand why they had to move to Michigan."

Grant didn't know Pam and her son had moved. "He doesn't know how lucky he is. I wish my ex-wife would move out-of-state." Grant was pissed that he had mentioned his own problems. He needed to focus on getting information about Patrick. "Still, I know it's tough, divorce and all. How's Pam doing in all of this? She's still a good-looking woman."

"Grant, you are such a prick," Chase almost hung up.

"God, I'm awful, I know." Self-deprecation usually worked. "I'm serious though Chase, how is Pam?"

"I stay in touch. She calls me from time-to-time to find out how Patrick's doing. She says he shut down emotionally—something he did messed him up, but he won't talk about it. She left because he was bent on destroying himself and their family. She hopes maybe one day he'll come to his senses and come back to her."

To Grant, women were more trouble than they were worth. His motto was use them, use them up, throw them away and get another. Once they got too old, too fat, too needy, get rid of them. Hell, as of this morning, he decided that if he ever thought about getting married again, he'd be better off just finding someone he really hated and giving them a house. It would save a lot of money and grief.

"Well, hey, maybe we three should get together soon. Catch up on old times. What do you think?"

Chase's reply was scornful and brief. "What for, Grant? We don't have anything in common with you anymore."

"Did Patrick say that?"

"No, Patrick didn't say that. I'm saying that. Besides, Patrick's got his hands full right now."

"What do you mean?"

"When we had lunch last week, he said he expected to be subpoenaed by the House Select Committee on Assassinations. Obviously, he wasn't looking forward to that."

Grant was overjoyed to hear Chase confirm what he had heard through his own sources. "Did he know anything about the Kennedy assassination?"

"No, I don't think so. I mean, he probably knew the CIA and the FBI lied about Oswald being an employee of both at some time, but that doesn't mean they're implicated in anything more nefarious. I think the Agency and the FBI were embarrassed that they might have been connected in a peripheral way to what happened. My guess is that Patrick might have found that out and doesn't wish to cast aspersions back upon the Agency with his testimony. You know how loyal he is."

Grant's mind was racing. It sounded like Patrick hadn't told Chase anything about their little secret. That was good.

"You know, maybe I should give him a call. You know, see how he's doing. I didn't know about Pam leaving. I mean, I knew about the divorce—I just didn't know about the aftermath. Do you know how to reach him?"

"He's at home, Grant. He still lives in Arlington in that house he bought. Call him there. Hey listen, I've got to go. If my colleagues found out I was friends with you I'd never live it down."

"Oh come on, you don't really mean that, do you?"

"Grant, buddy, you need to get out more. You'd be surprised at what you'd learn. Just watch out for people spitting in your food."

1950

NOW THAT JOSEPH Stalin had the atomic bomb, America couldn't afford to let her guard down. I was angry and depressed for weeks thinking about our future. Even though the United States had stood up to Stalin and had faced him down in Berlin, we might not be so lucky next time. We couldn't afford to allow the Communists to push us around.

How did the Soviets get the atomic bomb in the first place?

Great Britain provided the answer—Dr. Klaus Fuchs. One of the top atomic scientists in the British government, Fuchs had been sent to the United States from 1943 to 1946 to work on our atomic bomb project. While Fuchs was in this country, he transmitted top secret atomic data to a Soviet spy. Fuch's crime represented the ultimate betrayal of our free world—he had given sensitive nuclear secrets to the world's most powerful enemy. The security of the free world had rested upon nuclear secrets staying with the United States. Our confident feeling of security was gone forever.

How many other Communist spies were out there? It was horrifying enough if, like Alger Hiss, they had infiltrated our State Department and were helping to create our foreign policy. It was far more ominous if they had also infiltrated our nuclear weapons program and were now giving our most valued security secrets away to our enemies.

At the end of January, President Truman issued a public statement that the United States had decided to build the hydrogen bomb, a thousand times more powerful than the atomic bomb. As soon as the announcement was made, scientists worldwide predicted that the Soviet Union would soon have the H-bomb as well. That was enough to prompt Albert Einstein to go on television to warn everyone that "general annihilation beckoned."

ON JANUARY 21, Alger Hiss was found guilty of perjury. Secretary of State Dean Acheson felt compelled to defend Hiss: "I should like to make it clear to you that I do not intend to turn my back on Alger Hiss."

Acheson's statement prompted a Congressman from Pennsylvania to retort, "I don't know if we have anybody working with Joe Stalin more than the Secretary of State!"

Meanwhile, Communism's aggressive advance mushroomed around the world. Mao Tse-Tung's Communist guerillas steam-rolled across mainland China so fast they literally drove the Nationalist Chinese government onto the tiny off-shore island of Taiwan. Three days later, our entire nation was shaken when President Truman issued a presidential order that barred any further military aid to the beleaguered and besieged Nationalist Chinese.

Senator Taft of Ohio was quick to take to the Senate floor to denounce Truman's actions: "The State Department has been guided by a left-wing group who obviously have wanted to get rid of Chiang Kai-Shek (the leader of the Nationalist Chinese) and were willing to turn China over to the Communists for that purpose."

California Senator Knowland reflected my feelings exactly when he stated, "If ever a government has had the rug pulled out from under it, if ever a non-Communist government in the world has reason to feel betrayed, that government is the Republic of China." Indiana Senator Capehart angrily agreed: "There are other spies, too, and there will continue to be as long as we have a President who refers to such matters as 'red herrings' and a Secretary of State who refuses to turn his back on the Alger Hisses."

Now I was worried about the far-reaching arm of Communism infiltrating our highest levels of government.

BELIEVE IT OR NOT, the turmoil created by all of those events set the stage for the creation of perhaps the most unlikely political media celebrity our country had ever seen. I knew Joe McCarthy loved attention, and he didn't seem to care if it was positive or negative—he simply enjoyed the spotlight. But, I believed he was completely unprepared for the relatively innocuous circumstances that soon catapulted him into worldwide fame.

Chase called me up on Friday, February 10, shortly before I left for work. Chase was one of those guys who could get by on four hours of sleep a night.

He usually left our townhouse at dawn and showed up at the office early so he could read all of the Associated Press wire stories from the night before.

"Hey roomie, how are you this morning?" he asked. I knew that Chase had something interesting to tell me, but I didn't jump at the bait.

"Tired, Chase, you know that, and why in the hell are you calling me so early?"

"I thought you'd enjoy some great gossip to start out this lovely Friday morning."

I could almost hear him grinning into the phone. "I think our good friend and poker buddy, ole Tailgunner Joe, stepped in a deep pile of doo-doo last night in West Virginia. He is all over the AP newswires this morning. He's probably going to be the lead story in the afternoon editions of all the newspapers across the country!"

It briefly occurred to me perhaps one of Joe's boorish party pranks had finally backfired on him.

Chase continued on, "Last night our good friend, the junior Senator from Wisconsin, flew to West Virginia to deliver what was supposed to be a relatively routine Lincoln Day speech to the Ohio County Republican Women's Club in Wheeling. When he left D.C., he was supposed to deliver a speech on housing. By the time he got to the McClure Hotel, the subject had switched to Communism…"

"But what's the news in that?" I interrupted.

"Yeah, but here's the good part. Apparently Joe's speech started out a kind of a mish-mash of ideas from different sources. He quoted a little bit from the *Congressional Record,* and he mentioned some things from recent congressional hearings. He borrowed a phrase or two from an article in last week's *Chicago Tribune,* and he rehashed some dirt on Alger Hiss…"

I was impatient and unimpressed. "Yeah, yeah, yeah—that's all typical Joe—so what?"

"So what?" Chase sounded wounded. "Here's so-what. I'm going to be quoting directly from the wire services, so be sure to listen carefully."

"Okay, but don't read too fast."

"Senator Joseph P. McCarthy stood up in front of the 275 members of the Ohio County Republican Women's Club in the Colonade Room of the august McClure Hotel in downtown Wheeling, West Virginia, and delivered this bombshell to the assembled audience: 'I have here in my hand a list of 205—a list of names that were made known to the Secretary of State as being members of the Communist Party and who nevertheless are still working and shaping policy in the State Department.'"

"He said he had what?" I screamed into the telephone receiver.

"Joe said he had a list of 205 Communists working in our State

Department, and Secretary of State Dean Acheson knows they are there and refuses to do anything about it, just as he had refused to abandon Alger Hiss."

I whistled into the phone, "Jesus, Chase, that's pure dynamite! This could bring down the Truman administration. How can the President expect to be able to stay in office after this? What's the White House got to say?"

"The White House hasn't said a thing. This town is going to be in an absolute uproar this morning," Chase predicted.

"What else did the article say? Did it name any names?"

"Nah—Joe said something like '…I cannot take the time to name all the men in the State Department who have been named as members of the Communist Party and members of a spy ring.' Patrick, this story is going to be really huge."

"Jesus, Chase, Joe's been telling everyone who would listen that the Democrats are soft on Communism. Now it turns out he has the facts to prove it? Wow! Think of the implications. Maybe China fell because of Soviet political and military help, but maybe our own country somehow assisted in that country's downfall."

"I know."

We both pondered the ramifications, so I threw out another opinion, "Maybe the problem is we've been subjected to both domestic and political subversion, and that subversion has been secretly tolerated and encouraged by the Democratic Party, and nobody realized it. Hell, maybe some conspiracy is happening right underneath our very noses—something that would explain why the world seems to be falling apart all around us. Maybe Joe's onto something—something really big."

"That's what I'm thinking, Patrick. I've been trying to reach our buddy Joe all morning. I'll get back to you with whatever I find out."

Chase was right. Ole Tailgunner Joe had just stepped into the biggest pile of doo-doo ever made.

MEANWHILE, COMMUNISM'S RELENTLESS march advanced around the globe. As General MacArthur later proclaimed, "North Korea struck like a cobra." On June 10, ninety thousand Communist North Korean troops stormed across the border to South Korea. Fighting started on Sunday, and by Thursday, over half of South Korea's army of 65,000 men had been killed, wounded, or taken prisoner.

Truman had no choice but to commit U.S. troops to stop the invasion. Any American President who refused to stop this fresh Communist aggression would have been immediately impeached. Six weeks after the

Korean fighting started, we landed U.S. troops in Korea, expecting the North Koreans to panic and flee. Instead, the North Koreans decimated our young and inexperienced American troops. When our troops became isolated and cut off from one another, many American divisions surrendered rather than fight—that was before our troops learned the North Koreans didn't take Caucasian prisoners. The North Koreans dealt with surrendering troops and their perceived cowardice by tying the hands of their captives behind their backs and bayoneting them to death. Once our soldiers learned of the North Koreans' brutality, they "bugged out" in the face of overwhelming odds. It became known as "bugout fever" in the U.S. Army.

Our whole country held its breath as General MacArthur was given the impossible task of stopping the advance. Ignoring all rational advice, he divided his forces in half and staged a daring amphibious assault at the port of Inchon, one hundred and twenty-five miles behind the North Korean lines. The surprise maneuver succeeded brilliantly, splitting the Communist forces and almost destroying them. The General confidently predicted the Korean War would be over by Thanksgiving.

Despite that prediction, the atmosphere around D.C. reverted to a wartime government. We hunkered down as a nation while our troops fought the Communist threat in Asia. We sat nervously atop a volatile powder keg in Europe, staring at an aggressive and seemingly unstoppable Russian foe now armed with atomic weapons.

BUT EVEN AS war tensions heightened, life in D.C. still had to go on. After all, if we let ourselves think about "the Bomb" and nuclear annihilation every waking moment, we would end up in the loony bin.

Our bi-weekly poker games gradually became more popular as more and more influential and powerful men began to attend. Once word got out that General Eisenhower and Senator Joseph McCarthy had played cards at our house, the gossip made us a recognized name around Capitol Hill. We were invited to some ritzy cocktail parties and dinner parties, which further broadened our network of social contacts. Even so, I was still completely unprepared for the telephone call I received one evening.

"Hello, Mr. McCarthy?" The voice was warm and unctuous. "This is Clyde Tolson, the Deputy Director of the Federal Bureau of Investigation. How are you this evening?"

How was I? How does "scared shitless" sound? What the hell was the Deputy Director of the FBI doing calling me? I was momentarily speechless—that's how I was this evening. A thousand thoughts ran through my mind in the space of a moment, and none of them felt good. What had I done? How much trouble was I in? I finally managed to speak, "I'm fine, sir. Thank you for asking. How are you?"

"I'm very well, thank you, and please, Mr. McCarthy, try to relax," he said soothingly. "This is not an official business call. It's of a social nature. The Director would like to extend an invitation to you and your two associates, Mr. Newman and Mr. Grantham, to join him and a few friends on Wednesday evening for a relaxed evening of cards and conversation. The honor of your presence is expected at 8 p.m. sharp. May we expect you to join us?"

What do you think my response was? J. Edgar Hoover himself, Public Hero Number One, the most famous lawman in the world, wanted to meet us. I was thrilled beyond belief, and of course, I accepted the invitation. When I told Chase and Grant the news, they were less than enthusiastic.

"He wants to check us out personally," Grant said.

Chase nodded, "Yeah, I doubt we're going to become regular Wednesday night poker buddies with those two guys. My guess is he's heard about us and wants to know who we are and what we're really doing. He wants to meet us because we live and operate so close to his own house."

Grant nodded in silent agreement and then added, "Let's be sure to be on our best behavior. I suggest we let our host do most all of the talking. There's less chance that we can get in any trouble that way." Since Grant had the biggest mouth of any of us, I enthusiastically embraced his strategy.

Wednesday night found the three of us at the doorway of J. Edgar Hoover's stately home on Thirtieth Place, N.W., at exactly eight o'clock sharp. Mr. Tolson opened the door, ushering us through the cluttered hallway of the old Georgetown mansion. We had to carefully navigate the crowded conditions. Every usable space contained an antique vase or piece of furniture. The house had an old and musty smell, tinged with mothballs, as if it was rarely opened up and adequately aired out. So many photographs of the Director and various notable persons adorned the walls that the pattern of the wallpaper beneath it was barely visible. I was so awestruck by my surroundings that I immersed myself in a rapid study of the pictures. "This could be a museum of recent American history," I whispered to Chase as I tried to identify all of the celebrities, sports stars, and politicians in the pictures with Mr. Hoover.

A few minutes later, Mr. Hoover entered the room, resplendent in a dark blue pinstriped suit and expensive Ben Silver maroon silk tie, offset by a crisply laundered white shirt with monogrammed cuffs.

"Gentlemen," he said, "I'm so glad I'm finally getting to meet you. I've heard so many good things about you I thought it was time we meet in person." He ambled around an expansive card table and warmly shook our hands.

"I've invited one of my neighbors to join us, but unfortunately he is not as prompt as you are. Let's make ourselves comfortable in the meantime. Clyde, would you please fix our guests a drink?"

It was a little bit spooky that Mr. Tolson served us our favorite drinks without even bothering to ask us what we wanted. Chase leaned over and whispered, "Someone's been doing his homework on us."

We heard the sound of the front door slamming and a deep Texas drawl yelling, "Edgar, where the hell are ya, you old goat fornicator!"

Mr. Tolson spun toward the hallway as Mr. Hoover dryly proclaimed, "Well, it appears Lyndon has arrived."

Moments later, a tall, jug-eared man with a large nose burst into the room, followed by a small entourage. It was Grant's boss, Senator Lyndon Johnson.

"Damnit, Edgar, I'm sorry we're late—me and the boys here ran into Allen as we were leaving the restaurant, and I twisted his arm to join us. I knew you wouldn't mind. Allen, you know Edgar, don't you?"

Mr. Hoover stiffened almost imperceptibly as Lyndon swiveled to allow Mr. Hoover to greet his guests. The gentleman named Allen was a man in his late fifties, wearing a tweed jacket and smoking a pipe. With his wire-rimmed glasses perched on his nose, he reminded me of a college professor. Mr. Hoover didn't seem to show the same enthusiasm for meeting Allen as he did in meeting us.

"Allen, let me introduce you to my guests, Mr. Patrick McCarthy, Mr. Chase Newman, Mr. Grant Grantham. Gentlemen, this is Mr. Allen Dulles. Mr. Dulles is also one of your neighbors."

Allen firmly shook our hands. His name sounded vaguely familiar to me—it was obvious Chase and Grant knew exactly who he was.

"It's truly an honor to meet you, sir," Chase said.

As Chase engaged Allen in small talk, Grant quietly informed me that Allen Dulles was the President of the Council on Foreign Relations, a successful lawyer and author, and the brother of John Foster Dulles, one of the leading Republican voices in the country. "He was a lawyer at the Nuremberg Trials and was also a top U.S. spy during World War II alongside 'Wild Bill' Donovan in the OSS."

"Hey Edgar," Lyndon bellowed, "I also brought along Billy and Bobby. Say hello to Edgar, boys," Lyndon motioned for the two men to join us.

I sidled over to Johnson's side and extended my hand. "Hello, sir. I'm Patrick McCarthy. It's so nice to make your acquaintance."

He gave me a hearty politician's handshake, "Patrick, it's damn good to know you, too. I'm Lyndon Johnson, and these here goat-humpers are my friends Billy Sol Estes and Bobby Baker. Say 'hi' to Patrick, boys!"

Mr. Tolson waited for the men to remove their coats. Baker's blue fedora, which looked very expensive, perfectly matched his topcoat. Baker was impeccably groomed, right down to his manicured nails. Lyndon threw his gray Stetson on a chair. Mr. Tolson, retrieving the hat, took the men's coats to the foyer.

Mr. Hoover said, "Lyndon, these are the three young men I was telling you about…"

"Damn glad to meet you all," Lyndon interrupted, reaching across the table to shake hands with Chase. "I'm Edgar's next-door neighbor, Lyndon Baines Johnson, YOU-NITED STATES SENATOR FROM THE GREAT STATE OF TEXAS. And I want to warn you, I've come here tonight to take your money. And, as soon as I've accomplished that, then I'm going out on the town, because I promised 'ole Jumbo' here I'm a gonna git him a workout tonight!" Lyndon grabbed his crotch in an obscene fashion.

Lyndon's voice boomed out once again when he saw Grant, his young Senate aide, standing with us. "Well, damn it, Grant, what in the hell are you doin' here? Don't tell me that you're with these two other reprobates?"

Grant smiled shyly, "Yes, sir, I am. These are my two roommates."

Lyndon barked, "Damn, boy, I didn't know you was a queer!" He spun around toward Billy and Bobby and hollered, "Hey, boys, had you noticed our boy Grant was a little 'light in the loafers'?"

Mr. Hoover's face flushed disapproval. Mr. Tolson scurried out of the room. Johnson winked, "Hey, I'm just funnin' with ya! No hard feelings, huh boys? It's good to meet y'all—I mean it." Lyndon gave Grant a hard slap on the back, "Now we're all gonna be friends." But then he grinned at Grant and theatrically whispered, "But I'm still gonna have to tell your mama and daddy."

As Mr. Tolson took drink orders, Chase motioned me to his side and unobtrusively whispered, "Billy Sol Estes is Lyndon's money man. He handles all of the campaign financing for the Senator. Bobby Baker is the chief telephone page for the Senate…"

"That's THE Bobby Baker?" I interrupted wide-eyed. "I've heard a lot about him."

"Yeah, twenty years old and he's already a legend around D.C. Everyone says he knows where all of the bodies are buried in the Senate."

"He's really got that much power?"

"Probably more than anyone wants to admit. That's undoubtedly why Lyndon likes him. Johnson's been heavily criticized back in Texas as a man of no principles whatsoever. Rumor has it he somehow stole his 1948 Senate election with the help of an illegally stuffed ballot box. No one could prove anything one way or another, but Lyndon ended up winning his Senate seat by just 87 votes."

Grant made a joking reference to that very fact a couple of years back, but he conveniently left out Chase's tidbit about an illegally stuffed ballot box. I looked over at Grant, busy chatting with Johnson. Our whispering caught Grant's attention. He nodded and waved as if he knew we were talking about him. He probably thought we were acknowledging his relationship with the inner circle of these powerful men.

I snuck a quick glance at Johnson as Chase continued the story in a low voice, "Anyway, when he arrived back here in Washington in December, right after that election, he heard rumors about this Senate page who was already being called a real hustler in this town. The story I heard is Johnson called upon Baker to help him out in the Senate. He wanted to know what the best committees were, who held the real power in the Senate, how you go about getting things done in D.C., and the scoop on certain senators—who knew whom and what they knew for sure. I heard he interrogated Baker for over two hours. In the end, it was Baker who came away the most impressed."

"Can he really help Johnson that much?"

"Hell, yes, he can! Lyndon sent a pretty clear message to the rest of the Senate he was a man to be reckoned with. Baker is the Senate's chief backroom tactician. He made sure Johnson's message spread to all the right people in the Senate offices."

I was quite intrigued that Bobby Baker, who was younger than I was, had accomplished so much already in D.C.

Before Chase could say another word, Lyndon herded us toward the table. "Come on, boys, let's play some cards. I got me a damned 'kitchen pass' for the evening and damnit, this night ain't gittin' any younger."

Allen and the rest of the group politely laughed at Lyndon's outrageous comments and uproarious behavior. Mr. Hoover rolled his eyes in obvious disapproval. As Johnson continued to entertain his entourage, Mr. Hoover informed us he and Lyndon had been neighbors for about ten years. Hoover often visited the Johnson house for dinner, and he sometimes babysat for Lyndon's two young daughters. In turn, the two girls helped him to keep track of his pet dogs when they strayed out of his yard. "I'm like an uncle to those two delightful little angels," he said. He bragged the Johnson house was a place "where you could get the best chili con carne and the best mint juleps in Washington."

"Enough with that girly bullshit, Edgar, I thought we was gonna play us some poker." Lyndon whined. "Remember, 'ole Jumbo' has his own game of poker to play later, and it's starting to git late!" He winked lecherously at us. Billy and Bobby suppressed their chortles at Lyndon's innuendoes after glancing toward Mr. Hoover.

We took our seats at the ornately carved mahogany table. Its octagonal shape was designed to give each player a modicum of privacy when viewing his cards. The felt playing surface was a dark burgundy which matched the leather on each of the armchairs. I'm sure this table was a priceless antique. Even though there were cup holders inset at each place, I said a silent prayer that I wouldn't spill my drink on the rich wood.

Because there were nine of us, Bobby and Billy elected to sit on bar stools behind us sipping their drinks. They yapped and guffawed whenever Lyndon played poorly and occasionally whispered jokes to each other. I took the seat next to Allen Dulles. He puffed his pipe sending billows of smoke in my direction as he studied each card in his hand. His quiet sense of humor added an element of refinement to the table. Lyndon sat next to Allen. His loud, raucous laugh reminded me of Joe McCarthy. I was beginning to wonder if obnoxious behavior was a prerequisite for being a U.S. Senator.

Clyde Tolson sat next to Lyndon. A gentlemanly card player, he exuded courtesy, saying please and thank-you whenever the cards were dealt. He expertly attended to our needs between hands, making sure each of our drinks was continually topped off. Most intimidating was Mr. Hoover who had an imposing presence at the card table. He was taciturn whenever he dealt the cards, but he had a feminine, prissy flourish to his hand when he folded. Grant and Chase completed the circle. Grant was unusually quiet, as was Chase, who surveyed the entire scenario with the observant eye of a reporter.

Our poker game was supposed to be a friendly game, but it was apparent that Hoover, Johnson, and Dulles all played to win. Lyndon used every advantage he could muster. One of his strongest weapons was the constant stream of invective directed at Mr. Hoover. Even so, Mr. Hoover won more than his fair share of the table stakes. Allen was, by far, the most genteel in either winning or losing.

While shuffling the cards before one hand, Lyndon leaned over the table and jeered, "Hey, Edgar, what's the FBI gonna do when they finish jailing all of the crooks in this country? Won't that put you out of a job?" Lyndon eyed Mr. Tolson and said, "Don't worry, Clyde, you can always come work under me."

Allen picked up on Lyndon's needling and added, "Why Edgar, I didn't realize that you had been doing such a wonderful job. Are the streets really becoming safer?"

Mr. Hoover's complexion turned a little red, "You gentlemen may try and ridicule my efforts, but my work is more important now than ever before.

Decent people are being corrupted. When we see moral failure occurring, we know criminality is the result."

"What are you saying, Edgar?" Lyndon asked as he dealt out the cards. "Are you saying moral corruption leads directly to crime?"

"That's exactly what I am saying," he replied. "A man's immoral values will lead him down the road to ruin faster than any other character flaw that he might have. The difference, as I see it, is not so much between the lawful and the lawless as it is between respectability and indecency. The law alone cannot keep people decent. It is the influence within themselves that makes their obedience to law voluntary. Crime multiplies not because people respect laws, but because they no longer respect respectability. Crime exists largely because of a lack of discipline."

As the players anted up, Allen leaned across the table and pointed his pipe toward Mr. Hoover. "Edgar, does that mean a man is a criminal because of the criminal acts he commits, or because of his lack of values?"

Mr. Hoover paused momentarily, leaned backward slightly, examined his cards, re-arranged two of them in his hand, and then he placed his bet. Only then did he respond to Allen's question. "I believe that a criminal's state of mind is the most important indicator of the criminal's acts. Remember, criminal law is as much a branch of ethics as it is a branch of justice. A good lawman has to hate immorality. A man who breaks the law is not only a criminal, but he is also a sinner."

I had a lousy hand so I folded my cards and paid closer attention to the discussion. Allen continued his line of questioning. "Can you be a sinner and not be a criminal?"

Mr. Hoover fixed him with a steely stare. After pausing for a moment, he said, "Absolutely not. If you are a sinner, then you possess demons which will eventually force you to break the law. It is inevitable! Remember, when you break the law, you are also breaking God's laws—his Ten Commandments. God ordered us not to steal, not to murder, not to commit adultery. Those laws of God's are also laws of man. If you sin, you're breaking the law, and if you're breaking the law, you are sinning."

Chase and Clyde dropped out of the hand as Grant, Lyndon, Allen, and Mr. Hoover all anted up and received another card.

"Edgar, are you telling me the Federal Bureau of Investigation is going to become our nation's moral guardian?" Lyndon asked. "I thought the churches were supposed to do that."

Allen and Lyndon tossed their cards down in disgust. Grant raised his bet and Mr. Hoover checked. Grant turned over three kings and two eights—a full house. Mr. Hoover dropped his cards in feigned disgust as Grant scooped up the pot from the center of the table. Grant shot me a look of superiority.

"Belief in God is paramount to our freedom, Lyndon, but the churches of America cannot do it alone. If the Bureau has to become the moral, as well as the legal, guardian of this nation, then we are entitled to take whatever action is necessary to neutralize and destroy enemies of the moral order, and yes, we will act to enforce that protection."

Allen interjected, "But Edgar, don't most experts on crime disagree with your views? Shouldn't we try to understand why a criminal's upbringing makes him turn to crime? Maybe he can't help it?"

"That's hogwash! I'm in a better position to free my fellow man with a clear conscience than any members of the 'cream-puff school of criminology'—whose efforts daily turn loose upon us the robber—the burglar—the arsonist—the killer—and the sex degenerate."

"Edgar," Allen asked incredulously, "are you equating a sexual degenerate to a murderer?"

"Yes I am. I think it's very important for you to understand the point that I am making. It all comes down to this."

The card playing came to a halt as we waited for Mr. Hoover to make his point.

"Any man who lacks sexual discipline displays to all a basic sign of weakness in character." Mr. Hoover over-stressed the words "sexual discipline" in such a way that the very words sounded unsavory. I noticed that Grant was shifting uncomfortably in his seat.

"Immoral acts lead to criminal acts. It is proven and it is inevitable. Just look at the criminals I have arrested. They were dressed as well as we are dressed, and in a few cases, even better. They live as we live, and often upon a better scale owing to the rich rewards of their so-called professions. But they think nothing of violating the covenants of their marriages, or the sanctity of their personal commitments. They shamelessly allow their sexual urges to violate all common bounds of decency by engaging in wanton acts of fornication with women of loose morals. These are men who can never be trusted! Their standards in life are those of pigs in wallow; their outlook that of vultures regurgitating their filth."

I stole a quick glance over at Lyndon, who had swaggered in the door bragging about his plans for later in the evening. Lyndon shuffled the cards, oblivious to Mr. Hoover's tirade, acting as though he had heard this particular lecture before and had decided that it didn't pertain to him. However, I could see Billy Sol Estes and Bobby Baker perched on their bar stools behind Lyndon, smirking at the irony of the situation.

I think Allen also enjoyed prodding Mr. Hoover and, by extension, needling Lyndon. "Do you think our leaders need to be moral men?"

"Absolutely, a leader of men must especially be a moral man. Without a solid foundation in morality, that leader cannot lead. America cannot elect, nor can it follow, an immoral man as president. A man whose mind is clouded with sexual thoughts cannot be expected to think clearly or rationally in times of crisis. This is especially important with the specter of atomic warfare hanging over our heads."

"Ah, hell Edgar," Lyndon drawled plaintively, "didn't FDR get a little pussy on the side now and then?"

"Yes he did, but I want to make an exception in his case. If you were trapped in a marriage to someone like Eleanor Roosevelt, wouldn't you want to experience some normal human comfort?" Everyone in the room burst out laughing at Mr. Hoover's double standard.

I decided to use this lull in the conversation to ask a question that I hoped would make me appear somewhat intelligent to the FBI Director. "Mr. Hoover, what about Alger Hiss? Is he really guilty?"

"Of course he's guilty!" Hoover exploded, and he slammed his hand down hard on the table for added emphasis. "He committed perjury, and he committed treason. He also committed other crimes against the Bible, which just goes to reinforce my theories."

"But does that mean he is a Communist spy?" Chase asked.

"I don't think there's any doubt about it. His conviction shows unequivocally that the Communist menace has been with us since at least 1919. It proves the Communist enemy is capable of treason, and that the Communist enemy has, in fact, committed treason. Any so-called 'theories' about treason in high places can no longer be dismissed as paranoid ranting. Our President made the mistake of betting the prestige and the power of his Presidency that the spy scare was a hoax, and now he has lost. He's lost his bet; he's lost his credibility; and, he's lost his power to lead."

Clyde Tolson finally spoke up, "Richard Nixon was right, God bless him, when he said the country must support Mr. Hoover and the Bureau. Edgar recognized the Communist threat long before any other top government officials did."

Mr. Hoover flashed a smile of approval at Tolson and then said, "I'll tell you something that does more to confirm his guilt than anything else in the world. But first, let me ask all of you a few simple questions. Are you ready?"

Though we had just placed our bets, Grant, Chase, and I put down our cards. Allen gingerly placed his cards face down on the table. Lyndon finally tapped his cards together and slapped them on the table.

Mr. Hoover asked, "Do you think the Soviets trust us?"

The consensus around the table was they certainly did not trust us.

"Do we trust the Soviets?"

Again, we concurred that we did not trust them either.

"Next question, have you ever known of any instance where the Soviet leadership would want the United States to be placed in a position to exert any influence of any kind over them?"

Our combined response once again was "No."

"Can you ever imagine any situation in the arena of international politics in which the Soviet Union would prefer to have an American appointed to a position of power over any other equally capable Communist?"

"Certainly not," we all agreed.

"Can you ever imagine a situation where the Soviet Union would nominate a United States citizen to head an international body of politics that could, in turn, extend its sphere of influence over the Soviet Union?"

Lyndon spoke right up, "No, that would not, in fact could not, ever happen unless that citizen was actually a Soviet sympathizer who was taking direct orders from Moscow in the first place."

Mr. Hoover surveyed everyone's reaction. "Do you agree with Lyndon's assessment?"

We nodded our heads and replied "Yes."

"Then here is a statement of fact that will absolutely shock you and your notions of what is going on in the world today. In the summer of 1945, the Soviet Ambassador to the United Nations, Andrei Gromyko, told a group of our diplomats visiting in Moscow he wouldn't object to seeing Alger Hiss appointed as the first Secretary General of the United Nations. Did you know that?" Mr. Hoover asked smugly.

"It's an absolutely true fact. You can look it up. Now, do you think for a minute the Soviet Union would have nominated a United States citizen to that influential position unless they were positive they could control him?"

I was stunned—so it was actually true. Alger Hiss must have been a Soviet agent. I was even more in awe of Mr. Hoover than ever before.

Lyndon spoke up, "Well, I can see why it's important for the public to defend J. Edgar Hoover and the Federal Bureau of Investigation against anyone who would want to compromise their independence as a crime-fighting organization. When our own President equates the 'Red Scare' to a bout of national insanity, it shows that he has totally lost touch with America. Edgar, I hope you'll always count me as being solidly in your corner."

"Thank you, Lyndon, I have always known of your loyalty to me and my mission, and I will always think of you as my strongest ally in Congress. It's important for me to know I have the backing of powerful people like yourself in order to be able to do my job. I'm going to tell all of you right now there is nothing more important to the future well-being of the United States of America than its domestic security. Communism is the most dangerous threat to that security that has ever existed. In fact, the greatest crime of the entire twentieth century is the existence of Communism itself."

Lyndon interrupted, "Let's see your cards boys. Come on, let's see the cards."

"Well, Edgar, I can't really disagree with you on that," said Allen turning his card face up. "If we don't begin to contain the Russians and their quest for territorial expansion, we'll have serious problems down the road."

"That's right," Mr. Hoover continued. "I see events taking place here in the late 1940's and early 1950's that seem to be almost a re-run of 1919. Bolshevism is spreading from Russia. Once again, I see American radicals and their friends giving support to Moscow. Once again, there will be pressure for a drive to suppress the American defenders of the Communist revolution. This time, however, I will not make the mistakes that defeated my first attack on the Communist Party in 1920. Those mistakes almost destroyed my career…"

"YAHOO! Thank you, boys!" Lyndon crowed at the top of his lungs as he swept up the pot of the hand he had just won. "You all just keep talkin', Edgar, 'cause the more you piss and moan, the luckier I seem to get at this here table tonight."

Mr. Tolson scowled at Lyndon's remark. Billy and Bobby sniggered. Grant, Chase, and I surveyed the crowd for reactions to be sure we were responding correctly. The entire table had become still.

Allen puffed his pipe and stared off into space, deep in thought. For the life of me, I don't know what prompted me to open my big mouth. I asked, "Is the Soviet threat to the United States real?"

Mr. Hoover looked at me rather sternly, as if I hadn't listened to his lecture so far. "Of course it's real, Patrick. American politicians have to wake up and understand that. I might be one of the few people in D.C. who takes the threat of a war with the Soviet Union seriously. Now that the Russians have an atomic weapon, any repeat of Pearl Harbor may mean the end of America as we know it. That's why the Bureau has devoted so much time and money to planning a detention program. We've been compiling lists of people who would need to be arrested, based upon their beliefs and associations. A major part of the Bureau's intelligence work, both now and into the future, will be devoted to monitoring those potential troublemakers and terrorists."

"Edgar, I'm amazed at the Bureau's level of planning," Allen said as he tapped the bowl of his pipe into the ashtray next to him. He scooped some fresh tobacco into the pipe from a small leather pouch he produced from the side pocket of his jacket. Chase fidgeted with his poker chips as Grant shuffled the cards for a new hand while Lyndon leaned back in his chair to whisper with Billy Sol and Bobby. Mr. Tolson and I sat still, waiting for Allen to continue. Finally, as he tamped the tobacco down just right and lit it with a Zippo lighter, he proceeded with the rest of his question.

"Militarily or politically, which do you think we have more to fear from the Communists?"

Mr. Hoover didn't even pause to consider the question. He launched right into his answer, "Communism, in reality, is not a political party—it is a way of life. It is an evil and malignant way of life. Our goal at the Bureau is to protect the American way of life. We are the ones who oversee the internal security of the United States of America. That is a struggle we as a nation cannot afford to lose. If we lose the battle for the minds of America, then we lose the war itself. We've been preparing educational material so that in the event of an emergency, we will have an informed public opinion. The Bureau is responsible for undercutting the flood of propaganda that will be unleashed upon us in the event of extensive arrests of Communists."

"Jesus, Edgar, you're one hell of a well-prepared man," Lyndon said with evident admiration. "Not only are you a moral leader, you're a national leader as well."

"Thank you for noticing, Lyndon, a national leader has to be a moral leader. If you are not a moral man, as I said before, you cannot command respect, and if you cannot command respect, you cannot lead other men. It's that simple. I strongly believe morality is the only thing that really separates the just from the unjust. So, yes, I am a moral leader as well as a national leader. That's why I believe we face a crisis of leadership with regard to our current President."

"That doesn't sound like a vote of confidence for the man in the White House," Allen remarked. "What's it like working for a man like Harry Truman?"

The color rose in Mr. Hoover's cheeks and neck as he visibly began to fume. "Let me just say he is not an FDR."

"What do you mean by that?" inquired Allen.

"Allow me to explain. One of the New Deal's greatest successes during the Great Depression was the creation of a strong sense of community. Reverence for internal security, in my opinion, has become a test of loyalty to the true citizen's idea of traditional Americanism. President Truman, on the other hand, has shown a complete lack of respect for the values of the anti-Communists in this country. That means he shows contempt for the millions of moral Americans who identify strongly with those same values. This is a man who dared to criticize my preparations for Pearl Harbor, and then had the audacity to reject the conclusions of the Robert's Commission, which absolved the Bureau of any and all blame. I refuse to allow my country to be placed in a position where we could see another sneak attack perpetrated upon us again, only this time using atomic weapons. That will never happen as long as I am the Director of the Federal Bureau of Investigation."

Mr. Hoover's tirade had noticeably affected his ability to concentrate on his cards. He and Mr. Tolson hadn't won a hand in quite a while. It was more important for him to get his point across to his audience. Lyndon was nonplussed because either he was bored or he strongly believed in what Mr. Hoover had said. Allen Dulles, however, seemed to be very intrigued by Mr. Hoover's beliefs.

"Edgar, excuse me, but you sound as if you feel that liberalism itself is a threat," he observed.

"Liberalism is most certainly a threat. We are currently engaged in a massive test of strength for two opposing ways of life. You're either going to be an American, or you're going to be un-American. Liberalism stands indicted for having failed to perform the most elementary function of government: It has failed to provide for the common defense. Liberalism stands for an abandonment of traditional American values."

"I don't know about that, Edgar," replied Allen. "Don't you think this sounds a little extreme?"

"Extreme?" Mr. Hoover was indignant. "How can you call this extreme? These Communist cases demonstrate this battle between Americanism and un-Americanism is a struggle for the very soul of our nation. It's as dangerous as a battle between God and Lucifer himself. We, as a nation, cannot afford to lose this battle. It must be won at all costs."

Mr. Hoover's proselytizing slowed down our poker game. He was so intent upon making his points he couldn't take the time to look at his cards or to place his bets in a timely fashion. Consequently, our game was gradually turning into a lecture series (of which neither Bobby nor Billy—nor Grant—had any interest). Only Allen and I were mesmerized by his words.

Mr. Hoover continued with his passionate diatribe, "Our problem is we, as an open society, cannot adequately defend ourselves against a closed, totalitarian society like the Soviet Union, without adopting some forms of defense. I believe we need to act more ruthlessly if we are to survive. Winston Churchill said it best when he said that '…in times of war, the truth is so precious that it must at all times be accompanied by a bodyguard of lies.'"

"Gentlemen, make no mistake about it," he gave each of us a penetrating stare to emphasize his point. "We are at war right now for our very lives—our very souls. Perhaps it is not a war of guns and armies yet, but the struggle is every bit as titanic, and we as a nation cannot afford to lose it."

Lyndon finally lost his patience, "Ah, hell, Edgar, calm down. You're gonna give yourself a heart attack. Jesus Christ, every time you get your panties in a wad, you fuck up a perfectly good card game. What you say we quit the bitchin' and start the bettin'—OK?"

Mr. Hoover glared at Lyndon. He opened his mouth to reply when Allen smoothly stepped in to defuse the situation. "Edgar, I agree with you. We are at war with the Soviets, and we need to take precautions to protect ourselves. I happen to see America the same way you do." Mr. Hoover nodded his head, accepting Allen's affirmation.

"You see America the same way all great men have seen America. We are a small community of like-minded neighbors who are justifiably proud of their achievements, who are resentful of criticism, and who are fiercely opposed to change. We know that as twentieth century standards of mass society sweep over this old-fashioned, traditional America, it starts to subvert our old, cherished values; it disrupts our old established customs, and it dislodges our old, experienced leaders. Americans, who are frightened by this loss of community, see in you a man who understands their concerns and shares their anger. I see in you a powerful defender who will guard against a world of alien forces, strange people, and dangerous ideas."

"Well, Ah see a terrible card player who still has some of my future winnings in his pocket. Can we please just get back to our game?" Lyndon beseeched us.

Mr. Hoover ignored Lyndon's pleadings as he had ignored his jibes all night long. Sensing a sympathetic audience who agreed with and shared his same viewpoint, he continued on.

"I'll tell you something else," he said. "A first strike by the Russians is the ultimate nightmare, make no mistake about it. But it's not the very worst thing that could happen. The worst thing that could happen is the threat of domestic subversion. The fact the American way of life could be taken away from us—taken out from right underneath us, by the actions of our own citizens. Can you even begin to imagine what would happen if we were betrayed by our own leaders? Our own President? We cannot afford to let down our guard—our constant vigil must be maintained at all costs."

I was energized by the intensity of the interchange. These men were thinkers. This was not idle conversation—this was the talk of warriors. I was very impressed with Allen Dulles. He took a tense situation and easily defused it by agreeing with Mr. Hoover. I was proud to be in their presence and felt confident that they were the right men to lead our country.

"Mr. Hoover?" I asked politely. "Should we be worried about what this means for our country?"

"Patrick, of course you should be concerned. However, we'll be the ones to do the worrying for you," Mr. Hoover said paternally.

"I think he's asking if we should have any qualms about the process...," Allen said.

"I know what he meant," Mr. Hoover snapped. He turned to me, "I don't think we can afford to have any moral qualms about what we do or how we do it. We cannot be sensitive to any questions about deceiving the American press or the American people. We find ourselves engaged in an apocalyptic struggle with Communism in which the moral rules of fair play cannot apply. Remember, a dictator runs the Soviet Union, and the government controls its newspapers. They have no free speech or public debate as it exists in the West. To allow any democratic scrutiny of clandestine operations in America puts our country at a considerable disadvantage."

Mr. Hoover leaned forward once more and paused as if to give added weight to his next statement. "What we need is a closed state of our own inside the appearance of an open state."

"Ya mean, just do away with the whole fuckin' Constitution?" Lyndon asked.

"To put it bluntly Lyndon, yes. I can tell you this right now—our American foreign policy is going to have to change. I see it doing so very quietly, with very little debate, because public debate is something that can only aid the enemy. The President and his top advisors must believe we are operating in a period that is a continuation of wartime. We are engaged in a titanic struggle against Soviet expansionism. Because our enemy is cruel and totalitarian, we are justified in responding in kind. In fact, our very survival depends upon it. There are no restraints on the other side; therefore, there should be no restraints on us." He paused here to see if there was any disagreement.

Allen puffed on his pipe. "Please continue, Edgar. I'm very interested in hearing some more of your thoughts."

"The men who will direct this strategy are from a generation that has been profoundly affected by foreign powers, as Pearl Harbor has proven. We should worry endlessly the very nature of a democracy makes this country vulnerable to a totalitarian adversary. Therefore, in order to combat the enemy, the leaders of the free world's democracies will have to sacrifice some of their nation's freedoms and emulate their adversary. Our national security apparatus here in Washington has to be created in such a way America can compete with the Communist world, and do so without the unwanted clumsy scrutiny of the Congress and the press."

"That's an interesting idea, Edgar. How would you carry it off?" Allen inquired.

"As I see it, given the nature of this silent war and its attendant domestic political anxieties, the national security organization should gradually grow richer and more powerful, operating under a separate set of laws…"

"Or perhaps no laws at all," Allen mused.

"Exactly. In any crisis, if there was an element of doubt about legality, it is best to press ahead, because that is exactly what the other side would do."

I could follow Mr. Hoover's reasoning pretty easily—the laws for this secret regime were really being set by our sworn adversaries who, we were sure, followed no such laws themselves.

"Well, Mr. Dulles, I've prattled on too long. I am interested in hearing your viewpoint."

"Aw hell, Edgar, let's cut the political bullshit and play us some cards," Lyndon pleaded. "These guys don't want to hear any more of this right-wing rigmarole."

"Lyndon's right," Allen responded. "Let's play some cards and while we do, I'll be happy to enunciate my position for all of you."

"Jesus Christ!" Lyndon muttered unhappily. He looked on impatiently as Mr. Tolson started to shuffle the deck of cards.

"Go on, please, Mr. Dulles," Mr. Hoover implored.

Allen took a sip of his whiskey, drew a deep breath through his pipe, and began to speak. "Although I agree the question of Soviet military aggression poses a large threat to us all, I do not believe it is our primary threat. I agree with you, Edgar, the bigger threat is Moscow's ideological and political aggressiveness. The Soviet Union doesn't want a war with the United States. No, their goal is far more insidious. The Russians, by any means short of war, will exert themselves into destroying the capitalist economic system in Europe—thus weakening our already fragile allies there. The war we will have to fight will not be fought by force of arms in battle, but instead it will be fought by maneuver and pressure. The Soviets will engage in political warfare. And yes, that will include the subversion of our political and governmental and bureaucratic process by any means possible."

"So how do you see us fighting that threat?" Mr. Hoover asked.

"I believe the more we know about our enemies, the better prepared we shall be. Our intelligence agencies will necessarily have to grow in stature and scope."

"We already have a department within the Bureau that gathers intelligence. We've been doing that successfully for years. We have that area more than adequately covered," Mr. Hoover asserted.

"That's good, Edgar, but intelligence is not merely intelligence that is gathered. The raw material of information has to be first verified and then appraised for its usefulness. It may be interesting, but it might also be inconsequential. Once subjected to thorough analysis, it may, however, display elements, though seemingly insignificant, that begin to associate in startling fashion with other bits of information. New evaluations should then follow. The readjustments of old elements would then become new syntheses that have significance. And that means usable intelligence has been produced for the policymaker."

This was a bit over my head, but I noticed that Grant's interest had been piqued when Mr. Dulles spoke of intelligence gathering.

"Isn't that how all intelligence gathering should be handled?" Lyndon asked.

"Yes it should, but often it's not. If the gathered intelligence information is to have any real value at all, it must come in a tightly forged chain from its source, public or secret, to a central headquarters, which receives all information and tests its accuracy. Then and only then should it go to the policy level, where discussions and decisions can be made based upon that information. Understand this…," Allen's eyes twinkled behind his wire-rimmed glasses, "…that no link in this chain is either simple or straightforward. The pitfalls of tradecraft and judgment abound at every turning point. For example, the surprise attack on Pearl Harbor in 1941 has been shown to illustrate some of the perils that arise when information available to one set of officials is not properly assessed in relation to other known information, and then properly disseminated."

Grant decided to speak up, "So if I understand what you are saying, you're telling us that we need to increase the number of secret agents we have running around the world. Say, Patrick, maybe you and I could become spies."

"Grant," I said barely concealing my disgust, "you couldn't keep your mouth shut long enough to do any spying. You'd be found out and shot in your first two days at work."

"Yeah, but think of the great places you could travel to and the great babes you would meet."

"I'm sorry to rain on your parade," Allen interrupted, "but I'm afraid you'd find spying isn't all it's supposed to be. I think you've seen too many bad Hollywood movies. That isn't really what intelligence gathering is all about. You see a glamorous and mysterious side because of Hollywood's overemphasis on what we call secret intelligence. Secret intelligence is intelligence obtained by secret means and by secret agents. Now the bulk of intelligence is gained through more easily obtained channels, like through our diplomatic and consular missions, and our military, naval, and air attachés in the normal and proper course of their work. But we also obtain it through other means, like the world press, the radio, and by interviewing the many thousands of

Americans, business and professional men, as well as American residents of foreign countries, who are naturally and normally brought into touch with what is going on in these countries."

"Can all of that be accurate?" I asked.

"Oh yes, surprisingly accurate, and it reduces the amount of work we depend upon 'secret agents' to collect for us. I would say a proper analysis of the intelligence obtainable by these overt, normal, and above board means will supply us with over 80%, I estimate, of the information required for the guidance of our national policy."

"Do you really believe it to be 80%?" Mr. Hoover asked.

"Actually," Allen replied, "I believe the figure to really be closer to 90%."

"Well, Ah got a number that is 100% without a doubt," Lyndon challenged. "And that is Ah am 100% bored with this, and Ah am 100% ready to leave." He turned to Billy Sol and Bobby and asked, "What do you say, boys?"

"Let's go," Bobby answered.

The three of them disengaged themselves from the furniture and began to file out. Lyndon shook hands all around, thanking Mr. Hoover for the invitation in the first place, and then they headed for the door. Lyndon turned and asked, "Hey, Allen? Are you comin' with us?"

"No, Lyndon, it's late and I'm tired. Clover's going to wonder where I've been all night. Edgar, thank you for a most stimulating evening. I learned quite a lot here tonight."

"Allen, I've got something to tell you," Mr. Hoover said. "I've always distrusted you and your brother—you could even say I've long suspected Communist leanings in both of you, especially Foster. However, if Truman dislikes you, then I will have to treat you as an ally. I wasn't at all prepared to do that until I heard you speak here tonight. You're all right. Isn't he, Clyde?"

"Quite alright," Tolson agreed.

"Why, thank you, Edgar. That's as nice a compliment as I've received in a while." Allen turned to the three of us. "Well, what did you gentlemen get out of this meeting tonight?"

Grant answered, "I've got a much greater appreciation for the danger we face if we as a nation are too complacent."

I said, "I've decided I would like to ask Mr. Hoover for a job." I turned to him and said, "Mr. Director, I'd like to become an FBI agent and join you in fighting the Communist menace. How do I sign up?"

I'll always remember the look of surprise and mild disdain that passed over Mr. Hoover's face. "I'm sorry son, but I'm afraid it would be impossible for you to be hired by the Bureau. You see, you need a college degree from a good university like Holy Cross in order to become a Bureau special agent. I'm afraid you do not have the credentials to serve with us."

His words crushed me to my core. I had idolized J. Edgar Hoover and his G-men, and after hearing him tonight, I could envision serving my country by helping to protect it. Instead, I felt humiliated and dispirited.

Allen draped an arm over my shoulder, "Patrick, here's my card. If you ever decide you'd like a job serving your country in intelligence work, you come and see me. OK?" With that, he said his good-byes and was out the door.

Mr. Hoover turned to Chase, "What about you, Mr. Newman? What did you get out of this evening?"

Chase smiled and bragged, "Oh, about $100 of everyone's money!"

Grant whistled, "Wow."

"Congratulations." Mr. Hoover smiled for the first time, "The evening was a nice success. Now before you leave, who would like a quick tour of my recreation room? I have to show you three interesting miniature paintings I received as a gift from Mr. W.C. Fields." Mr. Hoover laughed aloud as he continued. "They happen to be three special paintings of Eleanor Roosevelt. You'll find that if you turn them upside down, you'll see she resembles, in rather exaggerated anatomical detail, a fat woman's pussy."

"This should really be the highlight of the night," Grant excitedly whispered to me as we took the private tour through the home of one of the most powerful men in America.

THREE DAYS AFTER Thanksgiving, 300,000 Communist Chinese unexpectedly surged across the Chinese border, attacked, and overwhelmed the United Nations' police-keeping forces in Korea. General MacArthur was handed "the worst defeat the United States has ever suffered," according to the *New York Times*. MacArthur immediately requested the authority to attack China directly.

On December 30, 1950, the General recommended that President Truman consider "dropping from 30 to 50 atomic bombs on air bases and other sensitive points" in Manchuria. To prevent further Communist Chinese attacks, he advocated "laying down…a belt of radioactive cobalt all along the Yalu (River)" which separated North Korea from Communist China. MacArthur received the sweeping support of the American public. A Montana draft board even refused to draft any more of its boys unless MacArthur was given the right to use nuclear weapons.

A Soviet diplomat promptly assured Peking that Russia would enter the war if Manchuria were bombed.

We were on the very brink of a nuclear war.

"It seems strangely difficult for some to realize that here in Asia is where the Communist conspirators have elected to make their play for global conquest, and that we have joined the issue thus raised on the battlefield; that here we fight Europe's war with arms while the diplomats there fight it with words; that if we lose the war to communism in Asia the fall of Europe is inevitable, win it and Europe most probably will avoid war and yet preserve freedom...we must win. There is no substitute for victory."

— General Douglas MacArthur

September 6, 1978
11:04 a.m.

From the curb, the house seemed like any other house on the street. On closer inspection, it was obvious that its owner had neglected some basic maintenance. The windows needed a coat of paint, a gutter filled with leaves hung cock-eyed, and the porch was impassable with overgrown shrubbery. The lawn had not been cut in at least a week.

Ruger walked purposefully into the back yard. Several lawn chairs crusted with rust were propped against the garage. He looked into the windows of the garage—no car. He opened the screen door and easily popped the spring lock of the wooden door.

The kitchen was clean—no dirty dishes or pots on the stove. He opened the refrigerator—no milk—only bottles of ketchup, jars of mustard, pickles, mayonnaise.

The floors were swept. He found a pile of newspapers on the landing to the basement—the most recent was several days old.

He walked into the living room. The drapes were pulled. He took the stairs two at a time. The bed was neatly made. The alarm clock on the nightstand was not set. He opened drawers, looked into the closet—mostly men's clothing. The bathroom was clean. He opened the medicine cabinet—no razor, no toothbrush.

Ruger went downstairs and picked up the telephone—still had a dial tone.

"He's gone."

"Are you sure?"

"Of course I'm sure." Ruger tolerated Grant's second-guessing him for now.

"God damn it! Ruger, that's the worst news possible. You know what this means, don't you?"

"Of course I do."

"Then track him down. He's got to be found, and he's got to be found fast. Otherwise, we're all dead."

"No we're not. You might be, but I won't."

"Just find him," then he added, "please."

"I'm already working on it." Ruger remained silent. When Grant didn't speak up, he asked, "What's that 'dog' thing you always quote, 'Dogs at war'…mumbo jumbo."

"Cry Havoc and let slip the dogs of war?"

"That's it. I've always liked that. Who wrote it?"

"Nobody you'd know."

Ruger put the telephone receiver back into its cradle. One day he'd have to have a little talk with Grant about his attitude.

1951

AS COMMUNISM BEGAN to spread through Asia, America found herself deep in a growing war in Korea. We had to thwart the virulent advance of Communism in Asia, and we had to block Joseph Stalin from advancing Communism in Europe. We needed to stand and fight in Korea. We were left with no other choice—the entire free world would be doomed if we didn't.

General MacArthur's solution was simple: use the atomic bomb to end the conflict. Much to the ire of the General, saner heads prevailed. The Pentagon rushed 200,000 U.S. fighting men to the Korean battlefront. The Pentagon hoped an increase in troops would intimidate the Koreans and the Chinese, forcing them to back down. Instead on January 4, the Communist Chinese mounted a major assault and easily overran the U.S. Army. The "ChiCom" forces numbered over 400,000 men with another 250,000 troops in reserve north of the Korean border. Our enemy possessed a "bottomless well" of manpower.

Even though we couldn't match the ChiComs in terms of numbers, we sure could outdo them in terms of bravery. Every single day, newspapers and newsreels across the country reported the status of our Marines. The country was on pins and needles. The 1st Marine Division, which had been forty miles in front of the troops, were trapped behind enemy lines at the Chosin Reservoir by a massive Chinese counterattack. Marine Colonel Lewis B. "Chesty" Puller managed to rally his men in the face of overwhelming odds. The situation seemed hopeless, but Colonel bravely vowed, "The enemy is in front of us, behind us, to the left of us, and to the right of us. They won't escape this time!"

Over the next fourteen days, the Marines ferociously fought their way for two hundred miles through a terrain of thousand-foot gorges, blinding wintry blizzards, and numbing sub-zero cold. The entire country prayed. At one point, our men had to bury 117 Marines in one frozen mass grave. Throughout the grueling retreat, the Marines took 2,651 casualties. Knowing the brutality of the enemy, those magnificently brave men refused to leave a single living American soldier behind. They carried their wounded comrades on their backs to safety.

Those Marines were the epitome of what made America great.

AMBASSADOR JOSEPH KENNEDY tainted his own tarnished reputation even further by denigrating our Marines' bravery and courage. He protested the war effort and encouraged America to "mind our own business and interfere only when someone threatens…our homes." He vociferously exhorted us to bring our troops home at once. His demands were tinged with racism and bigotry: Why should we sacrifice our boys for a bunch of people who weren't even white?

After what Chase had told me about Old Joe's being the highest-ranking Nazi sympathizer in our government in World War II, I could easily see how he didn't have the moral strength or courage to put up any kind of a fight. "When the going gets tough, the Kennedys get out," I thought to myself. "What a miserable goddamned coward. God help us if man like Joe Kennedy ever became our President."

Kennedy's defeatist attitude thoroughly repulsed me. I thought his criticism of our war effort both dastardly and despicable, especially for a man who had personally avoided serving his country while making millions of dollars in the safety of the home front. Old Joe Kennedy would probably have "bugged out" and deserted his friends in order to save himself. Our fighting men needed and deserved the support of every one of us back home. The cowardly rants of Ambassador Kennedy insulted the memory of all the brave soldiers who gave their lives fighting against the Communist threat.

Real men like Chesty Puller stared death in the face with an unbelievable inner strength. Because of the Marines' bravery and patriotism for the cause of freedom, I felt it was time for me to stand up and do something. I needed my country, and now my country needed me. I certainly didn't want to be lumped in with the spineless Kennedys of the world. I wanted to help defend my country and its most cherished values. I had to find a way to serve my country in the face of this rising threat.

I decided to take Mr. Dulles up on his offer. I contacted him about getting a job in the intelligence field. He graciously remembered me and was kind enough to put me in touch with some people he knew at the Central Intelligence Agency. Thanks to the written recommendations from Senator Richard Nixon (he came through as he had promised he would) and Senator Joe McCarthy, along with some extra help from Mr. Dulles, I was finally hired. It was the happiest day of my life.

MY AGENCY TRAINING started at 2430 E Street within sight of the Capitol Building. I was transferred shortly afterward to a dilapidated office building, Building K, near the Reflecting Pool and the Lincoln Memorial. The Central Intelligence Agency had two buildings, labeled K and L, for the Clandestine Services Division. Many other government agencies crammed similar dilapidated buildings that squatted like ramshackle tenements up and down the mall. D.C. almost quadrupled in size when World War II broke out, so the government hurriedly constructed office buildings to house wartime government workers. Even though the war had been over for almost six years, the flimsy pre-fab structures still stood to accommodate the growing peacetime federal government.

No one could call the accommodations luxurious, especially after what I had left behind in the House of Representative offices on Capitol Hill. The lack of any kind of a cool-air system, combined with D.C.'s summer heat and humidity, made the buildings sweat boxes. In D.C., hot weather could often arrive by March and not leave until late October. In the winter, the buildings became unbearably frigid.

My first position at the Agency, the lowest of the low-level positions available, entailed reading an inexhaustible supply of mind-numbing reports about Europe and the Iron Curtain. I was supposed to condense them down into smaller, more succinct mind-numbing reports and then pass them on to our senior Agency analysts to review. I never imagined so many pages existed concerning agricultural crop estimates and chicken production. Every tedious day, I reminded myself that I was contributing directly to our country's security and defense for the first time in my life.

My two roommates also progressed with their careers. Chase was promoted off the newspaper's city desk and assigned to cover various legislative committee meetings on Capitol Hill. However, he was chagrined to admit that instead of reporting on burglaries and petty neighborhood D.C. crime, he was now witnessing what he called theft on a grand scale—watching the government allocate its budget to various pork barrel projects.

Ironically, Grant's boss was often the recipient of that pork. Senator Lyndon Johnson had created a power base for himself through his unwavering support of numerous New Deal spending programs. Grant bragged that he was having a ball helping to lay the groundwork for much of Johnson's legislative arm-twisting. He often gloated that he was going to get absolutely filthy rich with the contacts he was making. Grant had finally worked his way into what he called "high cotton," a very Southern phrase he loved to use. As he explained to us Yankees, "high cotton" is the cotton that is the quickest and the easiest to pick.

Both Chase and I found it hard to relate to Grant when he talked about money. I hadn't come from money, and even though Chase had, neither one of us was motivated by the need to make money. But then, we didn't come from Texas, where apparently everybody was obsessed with building fortunes.

Grant was in awe of Bobby Baker's mastery of the Senate rules and regulations, as well as his ability to grease the wheels to get things done. Grant was right there beside him learning the ropes and watching "where the bodies were buried." Knowing what scandals and peccadilloes were being covered up and hidden was a skill highly valued by some people up on the Hill. Bobby was the best practitioner in town. Grant was his eager and willing acolyte.

Grant was irresistibly drawn to anything that involved money and power. He flat out could not get enough of either one. That was the difference between my two friends. Chase understood the difference between money and power, and he understood the influence of money on power. Grant, however, saw money and power as synonymous. If you had one, you had the other. Grant had developed the ability to say and do anything he felt necessary to advance his own agenda or, in Grant's case, the agenda of his boss.

If I hadn't already known Grant, I probably would never have trusted him at all. But we had forged a close almost brotherly bond since we both arrived in D.C. "without a pot to piss in" as Grant so eloquently put it. I felt very secure that Grant would never try to hustle me.

But just because I trusted Grant didn't mean that I would let him one-up me. We constantly competed against each other and had been engaged in a test of our abilities from the day we first met. He was the type of guy that would bend the rules, or even break them altogether if he thought it would create an advantage for him. I just couldn't bring myself to go that far. Grant felt ethics were meant to be tested, while I felt ethical behavior meant the same thing all of the time. The bottom line simply was this: Grant would cheat if he felt he could get away with it.

My grandfather had taught me, "Patrick, you cheat somebody, you only cheat yourself," so I never quite understood what motivated Grant to cut corners the way that he did. I also applied my grandfather's other caveat to my dealings with Grant. "Never let a dishonest man get the upper hand. Always know where you stand—always."

I don't think Grant thought of himself as dishonest; he thought he was clever. He prided himself on his ability to be cleverer than the next guy. Grant never missed an opportunity to demonstrate his one-upmanship even in a simple game like "Five Hundred."

THE CHERRY TREES were just starting to bloom when the three of us headed over to the baseball fields near the Washington Monument to play catch and shag some fly balls. The area around the base of the Washington Monument was one of the few open areas in D.C. that gave us enough room to hit a baseball around. I usually let Grant do the hitting while I ran and fielded the balls. Our game of "Five Hundred" involved a point system for keeping track of how well you fielded the ball. Usually it required more than one fielder, but since Chase had no desire to run around and exercise with us, Grant and I modified the game. I got 50 points every time I caught a fly ball. Grant got 50 points every time he hit me a fly ball that I couldn't catch. If he hit me a fly ball that I dropped, I lost 50 points. The first one to reach five hundred points won.

I loved to hear the crack of the wooden bat as Grant bashed towering fly balls to the limits of the boundaries in left field. I would easily run the ball down and catch it before it could hit the ground. I would then throw the ball in to my relay man, Chase. It didn't matter how hard Grant tried to hit the baseball over my head, he was never able to hit it far enough that I couldn't catch it. Naturally, he resorted to cheating.

Every time Chase tossed the baseball in, Grant moved up a few steps to catch it. And then, instead of returning to the approximate area of home plate where he was supposed to be, he would slyly hit from the spot where he caught the ball. Though he would gradually creep up until he stood almost on the edge of the outfield grass at deep shortstop, I never challenged him on his cheating.

His cheating gave him the ability to hit fly balls into the tree line or into the street, which meant I had to dodge trees or cars to be able to catch them. If the baseball managed to hit the ground, he laughed hysterically about my inability to handle his "best stuff" and boasted about scoring 50 to 100 points. I could chase down and catch anything hit in the air to me, but dodging trees and wayward cars made my efforts a whole lot harder. Grant knew that, but it didn't stop him from gloating anyway.

Chase was the only smart one of the three of us. He had absolutely no enthusiasm for running about in the D.C. heat. He was more than content to look on as we raced around and finally crumpled into tired, sweat-sodden heaps.

When we were both exhausted to the point of dehydration, Chase called a beer break. We collapsed around the brown metal Sears ice chest filled with our favorite Washington brew, National Bohemian. Grant had his first beer drained before Chase even got his beer opened. Then we lay back in the cool grass underneath the trees to relax, smoke cigarettes, belch and talk.

Chase asked, "What are the Commies up to, Patrick?"

Grant griped, "What are you asking him for? He's a stupid file clerk, for God's sake. He doesn't know what Joe Stalin's up to any more than I do."

"I don't know what Joe Stalin is up to, but I do know I've seen a National Security Council memo that alleges someone on Lyndon Johnson's staff is taking Soviet money to help advance the Commie agenda here and in Texas."

Grant turned beet red and fumbled for a witty retort. Chase had a better knack for getting under Grant's skin than I did. He added an insult of his own. "Yeah, I heard the Senate Ethics Committee is gonna subpoena some stupid young Texan whose daddy made the mistake of sending his bastard son to D.C. instead of teaching him to steal cows like the rest of his family does."

"Screw you guys," Grant tried to laugh. Used to our taunting, Grant knew it was better to join us in laughter even when it was at his expense.

"How is the new job coming, buddy?" Chase asked again, this time expecting a serious answer while Grant tossed me another cold beer from the ice chest.

"Right now, it's tedious," I complained. "Apparently my superiors think my talents are best suited for reading reports, lots of reports, lots of really boring reports. But I have learned something interesting. It seems the Pentagon and our State Department each have their own ideas about how to collect and use intelligence data. Get this—our military refuses to share their intelligence reports with the State Department, and the State Department's intelligence is useless to the military."

"Useless? How is it useless?" Chase stifled a belch.

"It's the techniques they use. Even a mediocre reporter at your newspaper is better at gathering information than the State Department. Our State Department diplomats seem to believe intelligence gathering means going to cocktail parties with foreign ministers and other ambassadors, somehow hoping those drunken social contacts will give them some usable intelligence."

Chase cracked me up when he yelled, "Hey, Grant, look's like you've got a future with the State Department!"

Grant smiled sarcastically and gave him the finger.

"The bottom line is this: our military doesn't talk to the State Department, and our State Department doesn't talk to the military."

Chase shook his head in disgust, "Is that how we got blindsided in Korea?"

"Nope, that screw-up happened to be the Agency's fault. Six days before those ChiCom troops invaded South Korea, our senior Agency staff briefed the White House about the current state of Communist intentions. Nowhere in that voluminous report was there any warning whatsoever of an impending North Korean attack. No mention at all. I mean, we're talking five detailed appendices, plus footnotes."

Grant crushed his beer can with one hand.

"Boy, the shit really hit the fan on that one once everyone went back and looked at the report. Heads rolled," I added.

"The North Korean attack caught us with our pants down around our ankles," Grant lamented. "Do you know how pissed off they were in Texas about the possibility of our nation going through another Pearl Harbor-type attack? I'm telling you, if we ever get blindsided again, they'll march on D.C. with enough rope to string each and every damn bureaucrat from each and every light pole in this town." Grant let out a belch and took another swallow of beer. "I'm tellin' you, they'll run out of people to hang before they run out of rope. They're not going to stand for that mistake ever being made again. You know: fool me once, shame on you; fool me twice, shame on me."

Chase chipped in, "Oh, man, I really hate to admit this, but Grant's actually right about something. This country will never, ever tolerate another Pearl Harbor—never, ever. The President's life would certainly be in danger. He'd have to be surrounded by guards twenty-four hours a day if he ever allowed an attack like that to happen."

"Then this country has to do everything in its power to be sure we are never that vulnerable again," I said. Chase nodded his agreement while Grant sipped his beer.

The combination of heat, exercise, and beer had rapidly drained us of our energy. Grant looked like he was ready for a nap, but still had enough energy to ask, "Hey, you guys, tell me: do you think it could ever happen again?" Grant's tone was serious.

Chase began to toss the baseball from one hand to the other. Grant shrugged his shoulders, lay back onto the ground, and closed his eyes. I paused to think about it. I finally responded. "I hope not. We've got the atomic bomb, which should be a huge deterrent."

Chase put down the ball, "Mutually Assured Destruction Strategy."

I added, "Besides, our Agency is much more vigilant now, and so is the

FBI. I think it would take a massive breakdown of our intelligence defenses for that to ever happen again."

"Well, I sure hope you're right." Chase glanced at his watch. "Hey, listen, I've got to go. I'm meeting a girl from the Treasury Department for cocktails in about an hour. See you guys later." He jumped up and ambled across the Mall, heading for home. I watched him retreat and then turned toward Grant's sprawled-out form.

"Grant, you want another beer?"

He didn't answer me. He was sound asleep.

A TITANIC STRUGGLE against Communism engulfed America. Each and every American was on guard against the Communist onslaught silently infiltrating our government. Americans, worried about President Truman's weak handling of the war in Korea, rallied behind General MacArthur who was so passionate about fighting the Communist menace. On April 5, General MacArthur in a letter to House Minority Leader Joe Martin made the plea: "If we lose the war to Communism in Asia the fall of Europe is inevitable, win it and Europe most probably would avoid war and yet preserve freedom... There is no substitute for victory."

President Truman was incensed. Within days, Truman and his administration relieved General Douglas MacArthur of his duties as General of the Army. In a late night radio broadcast, the President's press secretary told the world of Truman's decision: "With deep regret I have concluded that General of the Army Douglas MacArthur is unable to give his wholehearted support to the policies of the U.S. Government and of the U.N. in matters pertaining to his official duties...I have, therefore, relieved General MacArthur of his command...."

The President's actions were indefensible. Not only was the man-on-the-street seething in anger, but the Senate and the House were also fuming in indignation. Richard Nixon readily realized that the Truman administration had given "MacArthur's scalp" to the "Communists and their stooges." Senator William Jenner of Indiana pronounced: "I charge that this country today is in the hands of a secret inner coterie which is directed by agents of the Soviet Union. We must cut this whole cancerous conspiracy out of our Government at once."

Telegrams flooded the government. Telephone calls jammed the lines. Americans were not happy with Truman. "Impeach the B who calls himself President; Impeach the Judas in the White House who sold us down the river to the left wingers and the UN; when an ex-national guard captain (Truman) fires a five-star General (MacArthur) impeachment of the National

Guard Captain is in order." To Americans, Harry Truman had crossed a line. "Impeach the Imbecile."

Congress showed its vehement dislike of Truman by inviting General MacArthur to address a joint session of Congress on April 19. Over 300,000 cheering people lined the streets to show their respect and support of MacArthur. The mood was somber as the military greeted the General with a seventeen-gun salute.

Crowds cheered MacArthur and interrupted his thirty-four minute speech thirty times for standing ovations

"I address you with neither rancor nor bitterness in the fading twilight of life, but with one purpose in mind: To serve my country…You cannot appease or otherwise surrender to Communism in Asia without simultaneously undermining our efforts to halt its advance in Europe…Why, my soldiers asked of me, surrender military advantages to an enemy in the field?" I got chills up and down my body when he paused and said, "I could not answer."

The people closest to the podium said he was in tears when he ended his speech.

"I am closing out my fifty-two years of military service. When I joined the Army, even before the turn of the century, it was the fulfillment of all of my boyish hopes and dreams. Since I took the oath at West Point, the hopes and dreams have all vanished. But I still remember the refrain of one of the most popular barracks ballads of that day, which proclaimed most proudly that old soldiers never die, they just fade away. And like the old soldier of that ballad, I now close my military career and just fade away, an old soldier who tried to do his duty as God gave him the right to see that duty. Good-bye."

I stood in the vast audience overcome with patriotism and sadness.

MOST FRIDAY NIGHTS we headed over to Rosie O'Grady's, our favorite Georgetown bar. I loved everything about Rosie's: the heavy wooden door with the broken stained glass inlay, the old-fashioned mottled mirror that lined the space behind the bar, and the blue smoke that hovered in the air making you gasp for breath by the end of the night. I especially enjoyed people watching at Rosie's.

Grant, however, went to Rosie's strictly to get laid. Grant was fascinated with the fact that I was still a virgin, something he loved to lewdly remind me about.

As we negotiated our way through the obstacle course of tables, Grant nudged me in the ribs. "This is the night, Patrick. This is the night you get to visit the Promised Land."

"Cut it out, Grant." I was in no mood for his needling.

"Come on, Buddy. Where I come from, life ain't worth livin' if you ain't gettin' laid. Remember that. Now let's go get us some pussy."

I glared at him.

"Hey, don't be nervous. Look at it this way, not everyone hits a homerun the first time at the plate." Feigning annoyance, Grant added, "But at least promise me you'll try to get to third base."

I mumbled that I wasn't even sure what third base was.

"Believe me, if you ever get there, you'll know immediately."

Guys like Grant who bragged about their conquests never failed to annoy me. And it really annoyed me that Grant usually left Rosie's with a cute girl on his arm. And sometimes, it wasn't a cute girl. We still teased him about the night he brought home a girl with a harelip. Of course, my mother would be mortified if she ever heard me making fun of the poor girl, and I admit she was the butt of our cruel joke.

I couldn't go up to a girl I didn't know and say, "Hi Darlin'" like Grant. I was from Minnesota, for God's sake. And I didn't have a way with women like Chase, who was truly a ladies' man. Chase had a way of charming women that was masterful. He could effortlessly start a conversation with any woman.

That night, Chase showed up at Rosie O'Grady's with three women in tow. He introduced us to Jackie Bouvier, Gwen Koch, and Pamela Leonard. Bouvier was the so-called "Inquiring Fotografer" of the *Washington Times-Herald*. Miss Bouvier was somewhat attractive in a rather plain way. She had frizzy black hair and bad skin, along with an overly large mouth and eyes that were set too far apart to make her truly beautiful. She also had a voice that was impossible to hear in the noise and strident din of our neighborhood bar. But she was nice, she was female, and she allowed Chase to bring her there to meet us, along with two of her girlfriends.

The girl Jackie brought for Grant to meet, Gwen Koch, was a somewhat plain redhead with crooked teeth and an annoying tone to her voice. Her enormous breasts almost threatened to spill out across the table and knock our drinks into our laps. Grant and Gwen flirted shamelessly, putting on quite a show in front of God and everybody, as my grandmother would say.

Grant started by saying, "Help me with the pronunciation of your name. Is it *Cook* or *Kock*?"

She smiled and said, "It's *Cook*."

"I see. Tell me, do you like *Kock*?" he grinned unabashedly while he stared at her chest.

She wagged her finger at him and said, "You're bad, you know that?"

"That's funny—all the other girls claim I'm really good!"

They finally announced they needed to step outside and get a breath of fresh air, which turned out to be the last we saw of them for the rest of the night.

Though Chase was doing a good job of making small talk with the other two girls, I sat wordlessly staring at Jackie's friend, Pam. I was embarrassingly shy. I was completely incapable of contributing anything worthwhile to the conversation. Pam took my breath away the moment I saw her. A tall blonde close to five foot eight inches tall, she was the most beautiful girl I had ever laid eyes upon. I found out from their conversation that she and Jackie had known each other since they were in boarding school together.

While the three of them joked and carried on, I smiled mutely. When I was out with the guys, I was usually very relaxed and enjoyed myself. But when we went out for the express purpose of picking up girls, I was a miserable social retard.

I liked women. I loved the way they looked, and I loved the way they dressed. I loved the way they smelled—that heady bouquet of perfume, soap, and shampoo. I loved the way they talked and the way they thought. I loved being around them—but I was tongue tied around women I found attractive. I was especially dumbstruck around Pam—week after week, it was the same story. I sat there a complete emotional mess.

Both Grant and Chase knew I was attracted to Pam. Neither of them could understand why I found it so difficult to talk to her. Chase said I looked like a lovesick puppy. Grant said I looked like some kind of a sexual pervert. "Just talk to her!" they pleaded. I actually think Grant felt sorry for me because he refrained from making any off-color jokes about my situation for the first time in my memory.

The following Friday night, I walked into Rosie's a little later than usual. Pam and Grant were sitting at the bar. She wore a navy blue pleated skirt and white open-toed heels. Her long wavy blond hair was pulled behind her ears, exposing delicate pearl earrings. I stood frozen in my tracks. She was laughing, and I could tell by Grant's expression that he enjoyed her company. I immediately felt a strong wave of jealousy wash over me. I looked around the bar and recognized my old friend Connie and some of her friends at a table in the back. Feeling miserable, I ordered a beer and moved to the back of the room to join them. I needed to summon up the courage to talk to Pam. As I pulled the chair from under the table to sit down, I felt a hand on my shoulder.

"Hi, Patrick, we've been waiting for you." The sound of Pam's voice sent chills up and down my spine. My heart was pounding so hard in my chest I was sure everyone in Rosie's could hear it. Grant stood behind Pam giving me the A-OK sign.

"Geez, Pam," I stammered. I didn't know what else to say.

"Why don't we move to that empty booth? Let's hurry before it gets taken." Pam picked up my beer, took me by the hand, and moved me toward the dimly lit booth.

I sat face to face with her, staring into the most incredibly blue eyes I had ever seen in my life. After a few awkward moments, I asked her if she enjoyed teaching—I knew she taught at Kate Waller Barrett Elementary School in nearby Arlington. Her eyes sparkled as she talked about the kids in her sixth grade class. She had such a contagious enthusiasm, she almost convinced me to forget about the CIA and join the teaching profession. She talked for quite some time before she stopped and apologized to me. "I'm sorry. I'm dominating the conversation, and that's rude of me. Tell me about you."

"No apologies needed," I responded. My shyness returned. I was at a complete loss of words.

She leaned across the table, "I'm actually a very shy person. I don't know what comes over me when I start talking about school. I was so petrified the first day I faced a classroom full of wiggly sixth graders. I felt their eyes boring into me as I stood in front of them. But I surprised myself. I soon discovered I wasn't shy in front of them. In fact, I loved it!" She paused, "When I was a little girl, I would make my cousins play school whenever they came to visit, so I guess that practice gave me a sort of false confidence. I just pretended... and all my shyness evaporated."

"You seem like you are very sure of yourself." Then hoping I had not offended her, I quickly added, "I mean you don't seem like a shy person to me." I felt myself putting my foot deeper and deeper into my mouth.

"Well, after a week of talking only to eleven and twelve year olds, I crave adult conversation." Pam looked down at the chalk dust that tinged her fingertips. She had beautiful hands with long fingers.

Grant interrupted us with Chase close behind putting on his coat. "Come on, Patrick. We've got to get going to that boxing match." Before I could say anything, the girls swooped in on Pam—they were in danger of losing their dinner reservation. Pam extended her hand, "It was nice talking to you, Patrick. Maybe..." she looked at her friends as they walked out the door. "Maybe I'll see you later." Then she was gone.

I couldn't stop thinking about her, and each day seemed longer than the next. When Friday finally arrived, I headed straight to Rosie's after work hoping to casually run into Pam. She didn't show up. And she didn't show up the week after that. Grant told me that some guy was wining and dining her. I was absolutely crushed.

Both Chase and Grant found an excuse not to go to Rosie's for the next couple of weeks—both of them were trying to avoid seeing Jackie and her friend Gwen. Chase told us Jackie Bouvier was looking for something he didn't have, which was mainly a huge bank account. Grant finally decided Gwen's annoying personality outweighed even her pendulous breasts, and he decided he didn't want to see her anymore. That meant, of course, that I would have no excuse to tag along to see Pam.

Five miserable weeks passed. Chase and Grant had grown disgusted with me. I shot them down every time they tried to get me out of my funk.

The night before Thanksgiving, the guys forced me to go to Rosie's with them.

"She won't even be there," Grant groaned. "Look, she's just like everyone else—she's gone home for the holiday. I guarantee you—she—won't—be there."

I finally relented. "Okay, okay. I'll go, but don't try to set me up with any of your girlfriends. I'm not in the mood."

We hadn't been at our table ten minutes when Pam walked in the door. I knew it was a set up. Chase and Grant looked at me and inclined their heads toward her. Grant pushed back his chair and shouted, "Pam, darlin', come over and join us."

As soon as she got to our table, Grant said that he needed to go to the men's room, and Chase suddenly needed to buy cigarettes.

"Haven't seen you around in a while," I said, trying to act casual. "We've missed you on Friday nights."

"Who's missed me? They've missed me? I don't believe that."

"No," I said quietly. "I've missed you."

"Then why didn't you pick up the phone and call me?"

I wasn't expecting her to ask me that so I stammered, "I heard you were dating someone."

"No, I'm not dating anyone. I had one dreadful dinner date with an absolutely boring guy—a blind date that a friend set up. When I got home, I was so depressed with my pathetic love life I found other things to do on Fridays."

I almost interrupted her to say "me, too" when she added, "I couldn't bring myself to come all the way to Georgetown on Friday nights because there was this guy I really liked, but he didn't seem interested enough to ask me out."

I remembered her conversation with Grant at the bar. Oh God, I quickly prayed to myself, please don't let it be Grant! PLEASE!

"Is it someone I know?"

She nodded, and then, she moved toward me so our faces were just inches apart. She looked deep into my eyes and whispered, "It's you, Patrick." She then very gently kissed me on the lips.

I cradled her face in my hands and gave her a long, passionate kiss in return. I never heard the thunderous catcalls that erupted around us.

From that point on, Pam and I were inseparable. We spent Thanksgiving together. And Christmas. And New Years. And Valentine's Day. And every other holiday and regular day on the calendar. I had finally found the girl of my dreams. I had also reached a "Promised Land" Grant knew nothing about.

I SOON DISCOVERED that when you got Pam, you also got her friend, Jackie Bouvier. One night cuddling on the sofa in Pam's apartment, I summoned the courage to ask her about Jackie.

"I've known Jackie off and on since we were in school together at Miss Porter's School in Farmington, Connecticut. We were the only two Catholic girls in a Protestant girls' boarding school. The other girls nicknamed us the 'Mackerel Snatchers' because we only ate fish on Fridays and went to Mass on Sundays. After I left Miss P's, I enrolled at Vassar, and the next year, Jackie arrived. But—we had different ideas about our college education."

"My only goal in life was to be a teacher. Once I got to Vassar, I was in awe of my professors. I didn't know women could be professors. They were so profound, so knowledgeable—I knew that I had found myself." Pam sighed, "Jackie, however, was more into the social scene. Going to classes was just a backdrop for her."

Pam shifted her weight and folded her knees beneath her on the sofa. "I don't want to sound judgmental—Jackie is immensely bright and really loves art, literature, and history. I just think she didn't apply herself because of her father."

"Was she close to her father? I mean, wouldn't he want her to apply herself?" I was confused.

"Jackie's father, 'Black Jack' Bouvier, was a joke. I personally found him to be kind of creepy. Jackie called him 'Black Jack.' Can you tell me where any father got a name like 'Black Jack' and why he ever would want his daughter to call him that?"

"Anyway, whatever their relationship was, Black Jack took it upon himself to educate his daughter about how she should treat men. He taught her how to play upon a man's ego—how to be," she struggled for just the right word, "a geisha, an American geisha."

"A geisha? He's not like any father I know. Most fathers try to teach their daughters self-respect and warn them about men who might take advantage of them."

"He did warn her about men. His favorite saying was 'All men are rats!' I once heard him screaming at Jackie, telling her: 'Remember: All Men Are Rats! Don't trust any of them.' He badgered her: 'Play hard to get, play hard to get!' I think Black Jack truly believed no man was good enough for his daughter."

She paused reaching for the silver cigarette case I gave her. She wrinkled her nose, rolling her eyes to decide if she should tell me more.

"He was the only male caller Jackie had at school. He'd show up in a shiny convertible loaded down with presents—not your typical presents, but things like silk stockings, movie magazines, and one time he even brought a bunch of gardenias!"

"He gave her stockings? That's an unusual gift," I tried to contain my sarcasm because Pam seemed so earnest.

"That's because they are. He actually made a big scene about laying the gardenias out in the snow beneath her dorm window, almost like he was her boyfriend." Pam scrunched up her face in disgust, "All of the girls in the dorm thought it was a disturbing way to act toward his daughter."

"I think it sounds perverted," I said as I lit her cigarette. She lightly cupped my hand with two gentle fingers to hold the flame steady. After slowly inhaling the first puff, she delicately exhaled, looked me in the eye and evidently decided to resume her story.

"He was almost a caricature of the typical dirty old man. I mean, he was decidedly repugnant—the worst lecher any of us had ever seen. But Jackie didn't seem to think anything was unusual. She flaunted her father at us. They looked like a couple of love-struck teenagers, tearing around in that convertible of his, showing off."

Pam tossed her blond hair back and wryly laughed. "You know something, Patrick? Now that I think about it, her father actually taught Jackie how to be irresistible to men. I'm amazed at how thoroughly she can capture any man she wants. Have you noticed how she talks with a soft, whispery kind of a voice, almost like a coo?" Pam paused for a moment and then whispered "Yesss" in a breathy little voice, imitating her friend perfectly. We had tears in our eyes from laughing so hard.

"Anyway, I was interested in getting a teaching degree while Jackie was only interested in getting a husband. She concentrated upon the men of Princeton, Yale, and Harvard. Once classes were over that year, she took off for a European vacation. She sent me lots of letters and postcards, bragging about all of the fabulous parties she attended. She was invited to numerous social events in London, Paris, the French Riviera, Italy, and Switzerland. She even attended a garden party at Buckingham Palace where she swooned over meeting her wartime hero, Winston Churchill."

"She met Churchill? How did she manage that?"

"Well, she was actually in a reception line the whole time. She admitted she stood in the reception line twice in order to shake his hand. She said she waited for over half an hour the first time, and then, immediately went to the back of the line and waited another half hour just to experience the thrill of shaking his hand all over again."

We both laughed once more, picturing Jackie in her gloves and hat waiting in that line.

"Anyway, while I was studying, Jackie was partying. I remember how envious I was that she was able to go to Paris and study at the Sorbonne her junior year. She lived with a French family that didn't speak English, so Jackie was forced to learn French, which she speaks quite fluently now. She also met some rich French aristocrat who started introducing her all around Paris society. She said she met celebrities like Orson Welles, Aly Khan and Rita Hayworth, Pamela Churchill, Jean Cocteau, and on and on."

We burst out laughing again, primarily because we were amazed at how Jackie always managed to meet such famous people. "So tell me—how did Jackie end up as the Inquiring Fotografer?"

"Pretty simple, she came to D.C. to study at George Washington University. She liked journalism, and she needed a job. So, she used her family connections to get hired into a fairly inconsequential position. She's the one who managed to build it up into something more prominent. Jackie's quite a smart girl. It's no wonder that the men fall in love with her."

"She doesn't do a thing for me," I said.

"Oh, come on," Pam teased me. "You want me to believe that you don't find Jackie Bouvier attractive?"

"That's right," I admitted. "I don't."

She stared at me incredulously. "I don't believe you." She then said breathlessly, "Every man finds Jackie irresistible."

"Well, I'm not *Everyman*," I said.

She stopped when she realized I was serious. "Wow," she whispered, "I didn't think there was a man alive that was able to resist her charms. Patrick McCarthy," she shook her head in disbelief, "you continue to amaze me the more I get to know you. Tell me: what don't you like about her?"

"She's not you."

Pam didn't have a smart-ass retort. As I gazed at her, I noticed her eyes were glistening.

"What's the matter?" I asked.

She grabbed my hand and pulled me to my feet and said, "I have never found you as attractive as you are right at this very moment." And with that remark, she dragged me toward her bedroom doorway.

"To be prepared for War is one of the most effectual means of preserving the peace."

— George Washington

September 6, 1978
12:35 p.m.

Karen knew from experience that Mr. Grantham's firecracker anger always erupted in a series of explosions. She needed to stay out of the range of fire. She tried to file down a nail that she had bitten into the quick. An incoming call lit up her phone. She glanced to see that Grantham's line was open so she buzzed him over the intercom.

"Mr. Grantham, Mr. Ed Clark is on the phone for you."

"God damn it to hell! You tell that son of a bitch I'm not here right now."

There was an uneasy silence, and then Karen admitted, "I...I can't do that, sir. He already asked if you were in, and I told him you were. I'm sorry."

"I'm up to my ass in alligators without having to talk to him."

When her boss didn't give her any further direction, Karen asked, "Should I tell him you'll call him back?"

"Ah, hell no. He'll know I'm lying. Shit, what line is he on?"

"Line one."

The last thing she heard before the intercom went dead was a string of expletives.

Grant picked up the phone and cooed, "Hey, Ed. What a pleasant surprise. How is everything down in Austin?"

"Cut the bullshit, Grantham." Grant could hear the anger through the slight lisp in his mentor's voice. "You know damn well how it is down here.

You wanna tell me what the fuck is going on right now? Tell me why your son's pecker was inside my fifteen year-old granddaughter's…well, you know."

"I'm really sorry about that, Ed. I'm just as pissed-off as you are, believe me."

"I don't think you realize how seriously I take this, Grant. This is my underage granddaughter we're talking about. Your son is a college graduate. There is nothing remotely right about that. I gotta tell you, I'm so goddamn mad right now I could kill him. And you, too, for that matter."

Grant knew he was on very thin ice. Ed Clark was probably the most powerful man in Texas. His standard rule was a simple one: you were either 100% with him or you were 100% against him. There was no in-between with Ed—once you entered into his inner circle of power brokers, you were privy to incriminating information. Ed valued loyalty and silence. Since 1960, Ed Clark had been in charge of the secret round table that ran all of Texas state politics. He had been Lyndon Johnson's law partner since 1937, and he knew where all of the bodies were buried, both figuratively and literally. Ed and LBJ came from the same background in the rough-and-tumble world of Texas business where lawlessness met frontier justice—the only concern was personal survival. Grant had been taught early that when both sides entered into an illegal agreement, who would dare complain? If everyone in the deal could go to jail if they opened their mouths, then they better damn well keep their mouths shut. If you couldn't keep your mouth shut, then a bullet could do it for you.

Grant's father had been a prominent Texas wildcatter oilman who relied on Ed Clark and his law firm for all of his legal work. When Grant was old enough, his daddy had him working in Clark's law office as a gofer. After graduating from college, Ed helped Grant get a job with Lyndon's political machine, which in turn took him to Washington, D.C. and eventually elevated him to a position as one of LBJ's most dependable aides. Even though Grant was now the most powerful lobbyist and powerbroker in D.C., he was still a subordinate to Ed Clark.

"I am so sorry about that, Ed. The boy should have known better. He was raised better than that, you know."

"Cut the bullshit, Grantham. I've a mind to take the boy down to the creek and hold his head under water till the thrashin' stops."

There was an ominous silence on the other end of the phone.

"Hell, I'll march him down there with you," Grant tried a little levity.

"I'll level with you, Grantham, if that boy were anyone else but your son, I'd have had him hauled off into the desert and castrated, then I would have personally put a bullet in that thick skull of his. In fact, I'll tell you something else: if I don't get some assurance from you to calm me down, I might still go ahead and do it anyway."

"Oh, Jesus, Ed, you know you don't really mean that." Actually, Grant knew he did mean it, but he needed to mollify him. Ed Clark was one mean son of a bitch when riled up.

"Shut the fuck up, Grant. You know I mean it. Besides, I've got another bone to pick with you. What the fuck is that House Committee stirring up old shit for? I thought you said you had this all under control years ago. We can't afford to have anyone poking around in Dallas anymore, you understand?"

Grant felt a line of sweat rolling down the back of his spine. Ed was the head of the Patriots, and Grant knew he didn't waste his words—he meant business. "I understand, Ed."

"Who do they think they're gonna hang this on? Oswald's dead. Who else they gonna go after? Lyndon? Hell, he's dead. Hoover? He's dead. Giancana? Roselli? They're dead. This is just a waste of time and money. It's political grandstanding."

"I know that, Ed. And I've taken steps to make sure nothing comes of it. We've got some witnesses that the committee will call who will turn into laughingstocks. It'll all blow over. Trust me."

"My problem is that I've trusted you too much, and you've fucked up. Maybe you're in over your head, Grant. Maybe you're the problem."

Oh God—that was exactly what Grant didn't want to hear. Ed continued with his behind-the-woodshed harangue.

"I think it's time we tied up that other loose end of yours. Patrick McCarthy has to go. What if he ends up testifying and spills his guts to save his ass? We can't afford that. Take him out. Have it done today. I know he's your friend, but he's got to go. It's too risky to keep him around with what he knows."

Grant didn't know what to say. He struggled over telling Ed that Patrick had apparently disappeared on the eve of the House hearings. He quickly concluded Ed didn't need to know that. "I'll see that it's taken care of immediately, Ed."

"Good. You know something, Grantham? I thought I made the right decision in making you my right-hand man. Now I'm not so sure. You need to convince me that you can be trusted with what you know. Understand?"

"Of course, sir, I understand."

"Good. Now figure out how your son is going to get my granddaughter's virginity back. Make it soon."

Before Grant could stammer a response, Ed Clark hung up.

1952

I PROPOSED TO Pam over a candlelit dinner at a tiny French restaurant named Chez Paree on New Year's Eve. I got down on one knee and presented her with a very modest ring. I was too poor to afford much of a diamond, but she told me in between her sobs that she didn't need a large diamond—she only needed me. We decided to get married in July. We called my parents that night to break the news, and then we traveled to Massachusetts the following weekend to meet her parents.

Pam's mother and father lived in a traditional two-story New England style home situated on ten acres of wooded terrain. Both were standing on the front porch by the time we opened the doors of the old Plymouth we borrowed from Chase for the weekend. Pam's mother, a petite silver-blonde, could barely contain her excitement at our arrival. Pam's father, tall and dignified, was dressed in a gray cardigan which gave him a professor-like charm. They met us with open arms, hugging and kissing Pam first and then turning to welcome me with a warm embrace. I had been nervous about meeting Pam's family, but by the time we had unpacked the car, I felt like part of the family.

After lunch, Pam's father suggested that he and I take a walk out back to check on the condition of some fencing. As we walked, we discussed the politics of Capitol Hill, my career, and most of all my relationship with his daughter. I assured him I loved Pam with all of my heart; then, I asked him if he would allow me to marry his daughter.

Mr. Leonard's face conveyed his mixed emotions. "I knew this day would come, Patrick," he said.

I followed him down the snow-covered woodland path. He motioned toward some boulders that nature had haphazardly strewn. He rested by propping his leg on the flat surface of one of the massive rocks and stared pensively ahead. Snow-encrusted evergreens towered around us.

"She was the cutest little girl imaginable. I still have a picture of her in my mind. It was Easter Sunday, and she was only four years old. She had on a frilly little pink dress, white patent leather shoes and matching lace gloves. That girl refused to take off those gloves for a week."

He took in a cold breath of air and exhaled its icy smoke.

"I look forward to seeing Pam in her white lace wedding gown standing before the congregation in our church."

He was silent for what seemed like an eternity. "A father never gives up his daughter willingly even though he knows he eventually has to. This is an increasingly dangerous world we live in. I'm entrusting her to you from now on, Patrick. Promise me you'll take care of my daughter forever."

I swallowed hard to suppress the lump forming in my throat. "I promise."

Mr. Leonard wiped away a tear when he thought I wasn't looking. "Now, let's get back and break the news to her mother. I'm sure Martha will immediately want to start making preparations for the wedding."

Most of Pam's friends were overjoyed when Pam broke the news to them—that is everyone but Jackie. Pam said that Jackie whispered, "That's nice" and seemed to be lost in a fog for the rest of their conversation.

"Now that Jackie sees most of her friends settling down, she realizes that she doesn't have any prospect of getting married. I think that depresses her."

"It's not like she'll become a spinster," I cajoled.

"But she feels like a spinster. All through college, everyone's favorite saying was 'Get the ring by spring!' We were expected to have a fiancé lined up by the end of our senior year and to get married immediately after graduation. If you waited beyond the age of twenty-five, you were considered to be too old to marry respectfully."

"Maybe Jackie's problem is she has set her standards so high she can't realistically fulfill them. Chase told me that she didn't seem interested in anyone who didn't have a pile of money. He said that he felt he was being interviewed for a job every time they went out."

"You are exactly right," Pam sighed in exasperation. "Jackie wants Prince Charming, the white horse, and the palace. I think that is why she is so impressed with celebrities. She needs to be married to someone with lots of real money. She never said so, but I know she was embarrassed to have to get a job, and her job pays her so little money she isn't able to live the grand style she desires. Her family certainly doesn't have that kind of money—and even if they did, her sister Lee would expect equal treatment. There just isn't enough money to go around for both of them. She's caught in the middle of a major dilemma—love or money."

Not long after our announcement, Pam received a phone call from Jackie who had unexpected news.

"Oh, my God!" I overheard Pam scream. "Are you pulling my leg?" The two of them chatted briefly. When Pam hung up the phone, she was shaking her head in astonishment.

"You're not going to believe this—Jackie just got engaged!"

"What did you just say?"

"I said, Jackie's engaged. She told me her stepfather introduced her to a Yale-educated, Wall Street investment banker named John Hustad, and the next thing she knew, he asked her to marry him. Isn't that the nuttiest thing you've ever heard?"

"I might ordinarily say 'yes', but since we're talking about Jackie Bouvier, I guess it sounds like something she would do. Did she say if he got down on his knee to propose to her?" I hoped Pam's marriage proposal was more romantic than Jackie's.

"If he did, it must have been in a telephone booth," she quipped. "He proposed to her over the telephone. She's going to New York to formally accept his marriage proposal."

"Now that sounds more like the Jackie I know," I laughed.

The more I thought about it, the more it seemed that Jackie had deliberately upstaged her friends' wedding plans with her sudden announcement. I thought it was selfish, but Pam was more forgiving and understanding.

The New York Times carried a sizeable announcement of the Hustad-Bouvier engagement in its January 20th edition, inferring the wedding would take place in June. Miss Bouvier sent all of her friends a copy of the newspaper announcement.

Jackie's engagement to John Hustad was barely a month old when her mother, Janet Auchincloss, told Pam she had started an investigation into Hustad's background. She didn't like what she found out. From what Jackie told us and from everything we had read, I thought Hustad had an impeccable WASP background. He had attended a high-level prep school in England before going to Yale. He had a spotless war record. He was a member of the Yale Club and the Racquet & Tennis Club, both top-notch social clubs.

Apparently his credentials were not enough to suit Mrs. Auchincloss who was mortified to learn that Hustad earned only seventeen thousand dollars a year. I thought that was an extremely impressive income when you consider the national average was only $3,515 a year. But it was far from what Mrs. Auchincloss thought her daughter was worth. Pam told me Mrs. Auchincloss felt Jackie's future husband, whoever he might be, ought to be worth at least another decimal point in annual income—in order to care for her daughter in the style to which she was accustomed. She wanted her daughter to begin her life at the top rung of the social and economic ladder. In March, Jackie told Pam that she had started to date again. Mrs. Auchincloss had finally convinced Jackie to cut her losses and to look elsewhere for true happiness.

Just before our wedding in June, Jackie managed to surprise us once again. This time, I didn't laugh at the news. I became flat-out, pissed-off angry.

Jackie arrived at Pam's apartment one evening to breathlessly tell us that she was dating Congressman John F. Kennedy. The news rendered me momentarily speechless.

I looked at Jackie and Pam as they sat at the kitchen table drinking hot tea. Jackie's head was in the clouds, and Pam was sitting beside her, "oo-ing" and "ah-ing" at Jackie's every word.

"Ladies," I tried to sound calm when I asked, "How could any intelligent woman," I paused for effect, "possibly find even a tiny shred of redeeming value," I paused again to let them consider my words, "in that arrogant jerk?"

Pam's upper lip immediately disappeared. She glared at me—if looks could kill, I would have been reduced to a simmering pile of ash.

"Shut up, Patrick! Get out of here and leave us alone."

Jackie started to whimper. Pam shot me a parting glance that she would deal with me later. I slunk out of the apartment.

When I got back about an hour later, Jackie was gone. I had expected Pam to be furious with me, but instead she filled me in on the story.

"I made a few telephone calls, and I got the rest of the story Jackie didn't tell me. Please do us both a favor and try not to come unglued when I tell you what's going on."

"I'll do my best," I promised.

"Okay, here it is in a nutshell. Jackie said she was introduced to Congressman Kennedy at a dinner party in Georgetown arranged by a married family friend. Jackie claimed this friend had always had the hots for her."

Pam's girlfriends told her Charles Bartlett and his wife, Martha, had invited Jackie to dinner. Both had their reasons for inviting her. "I guess what Jackie told me was true—Bartlett's been openly smitten with her for a long time and has been trying to set her up with one of his friends—hoping to keep her around in his social circle. On the other hand, his wife—who is pretty perceptive about what her sleazy husband has been up to—has been trying equally hard to get her set up with anyone but her husband's friends.

She wanted to get Jackie out of her husband's life and as far away from him as possible."

"Pam, number one, I don't understand why women seem to be so attracted to Kennedy. And two, I don't want him hanging around with us."

Pam rolled her eyes, "God, Patrick, you are a clod! Jack Kennedy was just voted 'America's Most Eligible Bachelor.' He even defeated Rock Hudson, the movie star. That easily answers your first question. And as for number two—if Jackie sees something in him she likes, then maybe we should try and look for that same good quality in him, too."

I wasn't at all convinced by that argument. "Listen, I never have admired Jackie's decision-making prowess. Besides, Kennedy's got to be at least forty-years old…"

"He's thirty-five," Pam quickly corrected me.

"Okay, he's thirty-five years old, which makes him at least thirteen years older than Jackie. That means he's 50% older than she is. What do you think that age difference really means? For God's sake, it means he was graduating from college when she was entering the second grade. So you tell me: What do they have in common?"

Pam listened to me rant like a lunatic for the very first time in our relationship.

"What kind of a pervert preys upon women so much younger than he is? Can you tell me that? I think it's both indecent and immoral for someone as innocent as Jackie to be taken advantage of by someone like Kennedy. He's depraved! In fact, that whole family of his is depraved. They are cowards, con-men, shysters, liars…" I started counting off the fingers on my left hand, "…cheats, predators…"

"Hey, calm down a minute, Jimmy Stewart. Why are you so darned touchy about the subject of John Kennedy?"

We sat down on the sofa as I told her about my face-to-face meeting with Kennedy about five years ago at Rosie O'Grady's. I told her about how I knew he was a dubious war hero, as well as how his disgraced father had carefully manipulated Kennedy's life for the benefit of his own warped political goals. Nobody I knew admired Kennedy. Pam listened to me—there wasn't much she could say to change my mind about Jack Kennedy.

Chase Newman came down even harder on the subject of Congressman John F. Kennedy when he stopped by Pam's apartment one evening. The conversation turned to Jackie Bouvier and her screwed-up life.

"I'll never forget what Jack once told me," Chase said. "I ran into him alone late one night at a Georgetown bar. Since I was his old school chum, he let his hair down. He was trying to impress me by how worldly he was. He bragged ad nauseum about the women he had fucked."

Chase glanced toward Pam and grinned, "Excuse my French."

"Jesus, Patrick, by his own calculations, there must have been thousands. And I'm talking hookers and call girls to secretaries and movie stars. Their background, their age—hell—even their race—none of that mattered. They all had a pussy between their legs, and his only goal was to get in it. He bragged he had screwed Lana Turner, Joan Crawford, Susan Hayward, Sonja Henie, Gene Tierney, and the list just went on and on."

I saw Pam's upper lip disappear with disapproval when Chase used the word "pussy."

As a red-blooded American male, I was impressed by the quality if not the sheer quantity of the list Chase rattled off. The women were all sexy actresses. Any man would have been envious of Kennedy.

"Yeah, but that's not all," Chase smirked. "Get a load of this! This is an actual, God-be-damned quote of his. You won't believe it when you hear it."

"Try me."

"I'm telling you, you won't believe any decent man would say something like this. It is unbelievably vile."

Pam rolled her eyes imploring me to make Chase stop. But Chase had my attention, "I give up. What did he say?"

Chase smirked, "He told me: 'I'm never finished with a girl until I've had her three ways.' Can you believe he actually bragged about that? A United States Congressman? And then he started laughing in a very sick way, as if he expected me to admire him for that. I felt nauseated listening to him."

I looked over at Pam—she actually looked pale. "I think I'm going to be sick," she said as she scurried to the bathroom. I was grateful Grant wasn't here because he would want all the details.

"That might be the most perverted thing I've ever heard," I shuddered. "It is more than vile. It is repugnant, reprehensible, repulsive, loathsome…"

"All right, all right, Mr. Thesaurus, I get the picture. You're preaching to the choir."

"Did he really say something that vile?"

"Oh, yeah, he said it all right. And what's worse is he meant it. He said his favorite phrase had become 'Wham, bam, thank you, ma'am.'"

I started to get up from the sofa to go check on Pam.

"Oh, I'm not done yet with my Jack Kennedy stories. Believe me. I've got hundreds of them. Listen to this one: Jack spent the summer of 1939 in Europe, traveling and living off his father's fortune. I asked him what kinds of sights he had seen, expecting him to mention cultural sights like the *Louvre* in Paris or the antiquities and art of Florence, Italy. Instead, he told me about a girl he had met in his travels who had shown him a cigarette case that had an engraving of a naked Snow White, lying down on her back with her legs spread. Standing around her were the Seven Dwarfs, with their cocks in their hands, waiting in line to gang-bang her. That is Jack Kennedy's idea of culture."

It was hard to believe any respectable man could act so reprehensibly. Chase described a man who had little respect for women. I wondered how he would feel if someone treated his sisters the same way he treated young women. I worried that Jackie Bouvier was getting herself into something that was way over her head.

"You know, I remember something Jackie told Pam and me over dinner one night. She said, 'I can't get over how vain this guy is: You know, he goes to a hairdresser almost every day to have his hair done so that it will always look bushy and fluffy.' Isn't that something?"

Chase raised his eyebrows, "I'm sure she told Pam a lot more than that."

"Well, actually, she did. She also told us: 'When we go out to a party or reception or something where nobody recognizes him or no photographer takes his picture, he sulks afterward for hours.' I almost fell off my chair laughing when she added, 'Really, he's so vain you can't believe it.'"

At that very moment, Pam rejoined us in the living room, wiping her face with a wet washcloth. "You feeling better, honey?" I asked.

She nodded, sighing in resignation, and plopped down next to me on the sofa. "I've got to tell you guys this story. Jackie and I stopped by Jack's apartment last week so that she could see how he was doing. Did you know that he lives with his sister?"

No, we didn't.

"Anyway, Jackie knocked on the door and when it opened, Jack was standing there wearing only his underwear!"

"Aw, no—he wasn't," Chase protested.

"Oh yes, he was," Pam laughed. "I squealed and turned my head in embarrassment. Jackie chastised him for his vulgarity, but she later told me he was always practically naked whenever he opened up the front door to greet her or anyone else."

"I guess Jack is still as sick in the head as when I knew him."

"Well, believe it or not, it got even worse," Pam laughed, "I…I probably shouldn't even be telling you guys this."

Chase encouraged her—just to give him more ammunition for his own stories. "Of course you should. Come on. Tell us. Tell us everything," he cajoled.

Pam looked at me for the go-ahead. When I shrugged my shoulders, she bashfully continued. "When Jackie ordered Jack to go get dressed, we followed him into the Georgetown townhouse he shares with his sister, Eunice. Honest to God, Chase, I never knew two intelligent people could live in such filth. That place was an absolute wreck! There were dirty clothes and dirty towels just slung all over the place—on the floors and all over the furniture. I went into the kitchen to get myself a glass of water, since no one offered me anything to drink, and I couldn't even find a clean glass." She shuttered, "It wouldn't have mattered anyway—the sink was so full of old, dirty dishes I couldn't get to the faucet anyway."

Pam grimaced, "There were old newspapers piled everywhere—some with dates that were almost a year old. I went into the library and found a place to sit that wasn't too creepy, and as I reached for a book to peruse, I accidentally grabbed someone's old sandwich. It was half-eaten and looked as if it had been there at least a few months."

"Oh, my God!" I exclaimed in mock disgust. Pam punched me in the shoulder. I redeemed myself by saying, "That's awful. How anyone can be that much of a slob?"

"Oh, wait—the story gets even better. Jack came downstairs wearing a horribly wrinkled shirt with a frayed collar, an ill-fitting, rumpled suit that looked like he had slept in it, mismatched socks, and one black shoe and one brown shoe. Can you believe it? He had made no effort to dress up for his girlfriend and her best friend. I wanted to haul Jackie out of there by the scruff of her neck when she turned to me and sighed, 'What I want more than anything else in the world is to be married to him.' I thought she had absolutely lost her mind."

"Can someone please tell me what the hell she sees in him?" I asked. "He's one seriously mixed-up guy."

"Money—she sees money," Pam stated simply.

"Yeah, but you wouldn't know it to spend any time around him," Chase observed.

"You're right. She told me once Jack never carries any money whatsoever, he just expects someone else to pick up the check wherever they go. In fact, he expects her to pay the dinner tabs and to pay for the movies and the cab fares. She claims he's just helpless when it comes to managing money."

"So that's how he got to be a millionaire," I joked.

Chase retorted, "No, he got to be a millionaire by being the son of Joe Kennedy. He gets to stay a millionaire by never spending a penny of his own money when he has friends surrounding him he can mooch off of instead."

"Well, I hope Jackie comes to her senses and drops this guy before he ends up hurting her," I said.

"Patrick, you're such a dope."

Chase shrugged his shoulders and shook his head at me.

Pam explained, "The other reason she puts up with his crude behavior is maternal. He needs someone to take care of him and that brings out Jackie's maternal instinct. Remember Black Jack taught her to be an American geisha."

I thought that was the dumbest thing I had ever heard.

OUR OWN WEDDING that July was a modest affair. We traveled up to the family cottage on Cape Cod where the Leonards, a small tight-knit family, met each summer for a family reunion. We were married in a picturesque little church with our family and friends present. Chase was my best man, and Grant served as our usher. Jackie was Pam's Maid of Honor, and another friend from Vassar named Letitia was her bridesmaid. Jackie invited Jack Kennedy, but I was thankful that he did not bother to attend. My parents came all the way from Minnesota, and although they seemed to enjoy themselves, they left to return home before the wedding reception was even over.

Like all newlyweds, we did the obligatory honeymoon in Niagara Falls, and then we returned to an apartment in Georgetown, which was a thirty-minute bus ride for Pam to school in Arlington. Our apartment was more convenient for me because of my long work hours. Pam never complained; she used the time on the bus to do her lesson plans and to grade papers. Pam had a short bout with the "flu" when school started in September. She finally visited her doctor who gave us the happy news that she was pregnant. We were both ecstatic.

Meanwhile, my career slowly plodded along. Every morning, I headed to the bus stop for the ride to my office while Pam headed over to nearby Arlington, Virginia, to Kate Waller Barrett Elementary School. The same familiar, weary faces waited at every bus stop. Some read the newspaper; some stared blankly out the bus windows. The bus slowly filled up, block by block at every stop, as we headed into D.C. Finally, the bus deposited me a half-block around the corner from my Agency's front door.

When I arrived home every day around six o'clock, Pam would greet me with a kiss and lead me into the kitchen where dinner waited on the table. At every meal, she excitedly relayed the details of her day—what lessons they had worked on and who had misbehaved and who had excelled. At every meal, I sat and patiently listened. I never grew tired of her stories. She never asked how my day had gone because she knew she wasn't allowed to know. I was forbidden to tell her anything—the Agency's mandate—out of concern for national security.

Pam was the perfect Agency wife in that regard. She accepted that she could never be a part of my career. While she graded papers and prepared lesson plans after dinner, I read the newspaper. We splurged on a purchase of a tiny black-and-white Hallicrafter television, so some evenings we quietly sat and read together until Pam's favorite program, *Texaco Star Theater*, came on. Pam loved Milton Berle, "Mr. Television."

I preferred to read a good book—especially anything written by Mickey Spillane. His hero was a tough private eye named Mike Hammer whose main job was killing Communists. My favorite was his 1951 book, *One Lonely Night*, which ended with Hammer gloating: "I killed more people tonight than I have fingers on my hands. I shot them in cold blood and enjoyed every minute of it…They were Commies, Lee. They were Red sons-of-bitches who should have died long ago…They never thought that there were people like me in this country. They figured us all to be soft as horse manure and just as stupid."

Well, we weren't soft, and we weren't stupid. I knew that, and I was glad that others knew that as well—others like my friend, Senator Joe McCarthy. Joe was anything but soft on Communism—or on Communist sympathizers.

He had gotten involved in an ugly scandal when he beat up columnist Drew Pearson in the men's room of the Sulgrave Club in D.C. Grant called me and told me Joe was drunk when he ran into Pearson, who was there celebrating his birthday.

"Dick Nixon happened to wander into the men's room after attending a different function at the club and encountered Joe beating the living crap out of that commie-lover, Pearson. Apparently, Joe screamed when he saw Dick, 'This one's for you, Dick!' and then belted Pearson repeatedly in the chops."

"Since when did Joe turn into a mean drunk?"

"Oh, I don't know, but get this. He told Dick, 'I'm going to prove a theory. If you knee a man in the balls hard enough, blood'll come out of his eyeballs.' Then he kicked him in the balls as hard as he could," Grant laughed hysterically.

"Jesus, Pearson's lucky Joe didn't kill him."

"Yeah, Pearson should be thanking God Dick Nixon walked in when he did. I mean, he's damn lucky Nixon intervened. I guess Dick grabbed Joe by the arm and told him, 'Let a Quaker stop this fight,' and he tried to steer Joe out of there. Joe got huffy and mad and yelled, 'No, not till he goes first. I'm not going to turn my back on that son of a bitch.' Dick wrestled him out of there anyway."

Although beating a man is despicable, I could relate to Joe's anger. I hoped the stress and strain of tracking down Communists wasn't getting to Joe. I hated to think what would happen if it weren't for Joe's perseverance in exposing Communists. Communist sympathizers would find it easier and easier to get away with their subtle brand of subversion. Because of Joe McCarthy, our nation had become committed to its war against Communism.

Mr. Hoover's FBI agents had become even more vigilant—conducting security checks on our college campuses to insure that Communist ideas are not being taught. At least now, everyone is on the look out—even a housewife in San Antonio, Texas, created a list of suspected authors and demanded the local library do something about it. She suggested that any suspicious book be branded on the inside cover with a bright red stamp specifying the writer's Communist affiliations and sympathies so the reader "will realize that in many instances he is reading Communist propaganda."

I was clued in to how dangerous and devious the Commies could be when the Agency released an internal report to all employees that the Russians planned to spike the cocktails of our overseas American diplomats with a drug called lysergic acid diethylamide, known as LSD, a drug that could cause some very strange behavior. Reputedly, the more unstable an individual's personality was, the greater his potential sensitivity to its properties. The Agency made the decision to test it on volunteers to see if we could both detect it and control it ourselves. I thought the possibility of some kind of a mind-control drug was almost as threatening as an atomic bomb.

However, since my job involved reading and condensing reports, I could only daydream about what our other departments did and what their experiments might prove.

MEANWHILE LIFE AROUND D.C. focused on the 1952 Presidential Election. Republicans hurled angry accusations at Democrats, and Democrats hurled hateful accusations back at the Republicans. The atmosphere was charged with the type of partisan electricity that energized Capitol Hill.

I met Grant and Chase at Rosie O'Grady's one night after work. Chase couldn't wait for the beer to arrive before he started needling Grant. "Hey, three Missouri cronies of President Truman look like they're up to their necks in various misdeeds involving improper loans from the Reconstruction Finance Corporation." He sarcastically added, "That should help the Democrats this year."

I thought it was shameful that these men, the President's right-hand men, had lined their pockets at taxpayer expense, "I heard that as many as nine of the president's men, including his appointments secretary, may be going to prison."

"One guy received a $9500 mink coat as a gift for his wife from a company he had helped—that's gonna be a disaster for President Truman," Chase said.

Grant scoffed, "It wouldn't surprise me if the wives of every man who worked in the Truman administration had a mink coat in their closet. That's the way the system works. We all know that."

Chase shot a surly and disapproving look at Grant. "Who's teaching you your ethics? Bobby Baker? That is not how the system works."

"Sure it is, Chase. Get off your high and moral perch. The whole system needs to be lubricated to run right, and money is the grease that gets it done."

I could see Chase was about to lose his temper. I changed the subject before our evening was ruined.

"I think it's great that General Dwight D. Eisenhower has left his position as the president of Columbia University to run against Adlai Stevenson. I don't think an Illinois Governor has a chance in hell of beating the general, and I think the Democrats know it."

Grant grimaced at my remark, "The Dems will retain the White House. Trust me."

"I don't think so, Grant. Look, we've got Nixon as the Republican Vice-Presidential candidate—it's hard to believe that someone I know from my own generation might be qualified to be the leader of our nation. Pam and I are excited enough that we've spent considerable time canvassing our neighborhood. We've passed out fliers, set up some rallies, served a bunch of hot dogs…"

"Well, aren't you two just the perfect little Republican couple."

"Hey, jerk. Maybe we're just excited about changing the future of our country."

"Well, there's no doubt that President Truman's no longer an effective leader. Korea proved that last year. That was the final straw for this nation," Chase observed.

"President Truman wanted to negotiate a peace settlement, beginning with a cease fire. That was a good start," Grant countered. "What was he supposed to do? Listen to General MacArthur?"

I said, "Maybe he should have. General MacArthur had his own peace plan in mind."

"Yeah? His idea of negotiating was to annihilate first—and negotiate second."

"Truman never should have fired MacArthur," I stated.

"The President claimed he was left with no choice but to fire the general. The guy's crazy as a Texas hoot owl."

"I'm not the only one who feels that way. There are plenty of Americans who are still plenty angry about MacArthur's dismissal," I retorted.

"They burned Truman in effigy in San Gabriel, California, and Worcester

Massachusetts," Chase pointed out. "Hell, it's not uncommon to see the stars and stripes flying at half-staff or even upside down in support of him."

"Yeah, well, if my party goes down to defeat in November, we'll all know who to blame," Grant said.

Chase needled Grant, "Listen to this joke the Republicans are spreading around the Capitol: 'I'm going to have a Truman beer—just like any other beer except it hasn't got a head.'"

I ventured, "America wants the President to know, in no uncertain terms that they consider it the President's job and duty to stand up to the threat and the spread of Communism." I glanced at Grant whose sullen expression deepened the more I said. "General MacArthur was ultimately fired because of politics."

Grant interjected, "Thank God."

I ignored him, "But he responded to the insulting end of his distinguished military career with great class."

"I agree," Chased added. "I covered the story. I loved his line: 'The only politics I have is contained in a single phrase known to all of you—God bless America!'"

Grant pushed himself away from the table and downed the last of his beer as he stood. "I need to go." He glowered as he fished a couple of dollars out of his pocket.

Chase and I shrugged, exchanged "So what?" looks and continued our conversation.

DURING THE CLOSING weeks of the presidential election, Republican Vice-Presidential candidate Nixon predicted a Democratic victory would mean "more Alger Hisses, more atomic spies, more crises." He reminded American voters the Soviets had received hundreds of secret American documents "from Hiss and other members of the ring" and "the lives of American boys were endangered and probably lost because of the activities of a spy ring."

Dick Nixon was a street fighter of a politician, and the Democrats knew it. So it was quite suspicious when an allegation of a secret slush fund broke in the papers—a secret fund set up by his millionaire pals and supposedly devoted to providing financial comfort to Senator Nixon and his immediate family. The damage to Dick's reputation actually threatened his place on the Republican ticket. The true facts proved to be quite different. Contributions had been raised to pay for the speeches, travel vouchers, postage, and mail to publicize Dick's views. Every penny of it was legal and fully accounted for, and none of it was secret. Most importantly, none of it had ever gone to Dick or his family.

Dick was compelled to go before the nation on television to explain himself and his role in this fund. "My fellow Americans, I come before you tonight as a candidate for the vice-presidency and as a man whose honesty and integrity has been questioned." He detailed his campaign expenses, as well as every thing he owned and the debts that came with them. I was glad he made reference to the mink coat scandals that had plagued the outgoing Truman administration. "I should say this—that Pat doesn't have a mink coat. But she does have a respectable Republican cloth coat."

But what brought the house down was his one and only admission of a gift. His daughters had been given a small puppy by a man down in Texas. "It was a little cocker spaniel dog…black and white, spotted, and our little girl Tricia, the six-year-old, named it Checkers. And you know, the kids, like all kids, love that dog, and I just want to say this, right now, that regardless of what they say about it, we're going to keep it!"

The public reaction to the "Checkers" speech was overwhelmingly positive. It not only saved Dick's spot on the national ticket with General Eisenhower, it helped propel them to their November victory.

As the year 1952 closed out, Pam and I were expectant parents, my friend Dick Nixon was in the White House, and my career with the Central Intelligence Agency was on track.

Life was terrific.

"I know that the Lord is always on the side of the right. But it is my constant anxiety and prayer that I and this nation should be on the Lord's side."

— President Abraham Lincoln

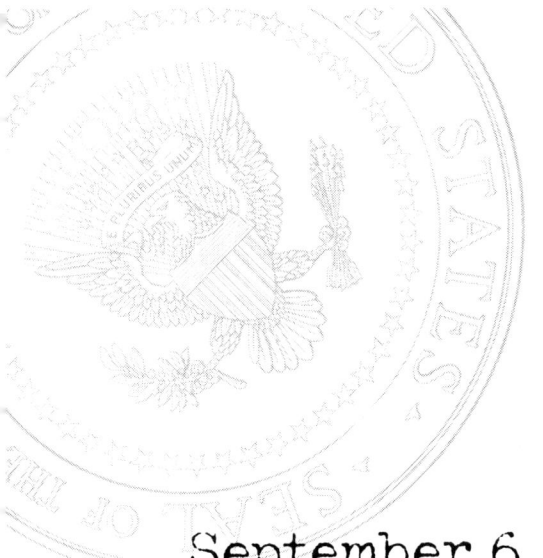

September 6, 1978
12:51 p.m.

Karen should have gone to lunch at noon, but she decided it would be better to sneak a snack at her desk. Mr. Grantham demanded that his secretaries be professional at all times—and that included no eating or drinking at the front desk. She looked at her nail. Her manicure was ruined. That was another thing that Mr. Grantham insisted on—nails had to be perfectly manicured. She would keep her hand hidden if he called her into his office.

The phone line lit up again, but this time it was Mr. Grantham's private line. She hoped he wouldn't go into another rage. She wanted to lay low for the rest of the day.

Grant picked up the second the light on his phone indicated he had a call. It was Ruger.

"I've put out an 'All Points Bulletin' on the law enforcement channels for the make, model, and license number of McCarthy's car. If he's driving, he'll be picked up. My bet is he's stashed the car somewhere and is using some other form of transportation. I've got men scouring the train stations, the bus stops, and the three major airports: Washington National, Dulles, and Baltimore. If he used any of those, we'll find him. If he's hitchhiking or riding the rails, he's likely gone for now. There's no way to track that stuff."

Ruger's news depressed Grant. He had hoped Patrick would be easier to find than that.

"Do you have enough men to do this?"

"Plenty, I'll contact you if I need more. I've got my resources."

Grant shuddered. The Patriots could not have accomplished all that they had if it weren't for the help they had received from organized crime.

"My guys are better than the Feds. When I combine their talents and resources with the Feds resources, there's nobody that can get away. I'll find him."

Grant felt a slight sense of relief. He moved his head in a circular motion to release the tightness in his neck. He had one more stipulation, "We also need what he took with him. It doesn't do any of us any good if we find him and we don't find our stuff. I want our stuff returned—all of it."

Ruger churlishly chuckled, "I can be extremely persuasive. Patrick already knows that. Don't worry. When I find him, you'll get it all back."

1953

I LOVED MY job at the Agency. I'll admit there were days I dragged myself out of bed wishing that it were Saturday. But, on the whole, I approached each workday with enthusiasm, probably because I was the new kid on the block. I had been assigned to the Directorate of Intelligence, the division best known for its analysis of intelligence data. Everyone reported directly to the Deputy Director of Intelligence (also referred to as the DDI). There were two other Deputy Directors at the Agency, the D.D. of Plans (DDP), and the D.D. of Support (DDS). My mentor, Allen Dulles, was the DDI, and shortly after the new Eisenhower administration took office, he was promoted to Director of the entire Agency.

Eight departments were contained within the DDI. They were the National Photographic Interpretation Center, the Office of Central Reference, the Office of Research and Reports, the Office of National Estimates, the Office of Current Intelligence, the Office of Scientific Intelligence, the Office of Basic Intelligence, and the Office of Operations.

For the past two years, I had been routinely shuttled back and forth between all eight departments, serving about ninety days or so in each one. Just as I became familiar with the routine and the workload of one, I was abruptly transferred to another. My assignments were structured to teach me a little bit about a lot in a very short period of time. Mr. Dulles had placed me on a specially designed career fast track. If my talents warranted, I would be groomed for a position in the upper levels of the Agency. It was strictly up to me to prove I had the talent and temperament to handle whatever challenges my superiors decided to throw at me.

I worked and socialized with Agency people. Most of the top brass at the Agency lived with their families in Georgetown. As the youngest couple in the neighborhood, Pam and I were virtually adopted by the other Georgetown wives, who unanimously had taken a great liking to Pam. The other wives in the group were mother hens—doting on Pam and offering lots of advice on what to eat, when to rest, and how to exercise during her pregnancy. I believe I advanced in my career in part due to the good nature and good will of the Georgetown wives. Their husbands took a slightly different tactic with me. They deliberately dumped massive amounts of work on me to see if they could break me under the pressure. So while Pam was being pampered, I was getting my balls busted. Both of us could not have been happier.

My directorate job was to help our policy makers make the best decisions they possibly could with the best and most up-to-date information available. When I started reviewing data, Mr. Dulles told me: "The most important thing was not whether we were right or wrong about the occurrence of events, but to help the people making policy decisions by giving them background information. Sometimes you give them information that is right, and they make the wrong decisions. Sometimes you give them information that is wrong, and they make the right decisions for different reasons. Sometimes you give them information that is right and they make the right decisions. Sometimes you make a prediction on something coming up, and the policymakers take an action which, in effect, makes your prediction wrong, but it was the right thing to do based upon your prediction. So do the best job you possibly can."

Day in and day out, I tried to do just that. My impending fatherhood had further sharpened my desire to make the United States safe from any threat. I wasn't just working a job anymore. I was soon going to have a family of my own to protect.

In March, the United States finally caught a break in our growing and unrelenting struggle with the Soviet Union. Joseph Stalin suffered a massive stroke and died. The hierarchy of the Soviet Union was soon engaged in a power struggle to fill the vacuum created by his death. We hoped for the best—moderates who were prepared to ratchet down the tension with the West. But we prepared for the worst—hard-liners who were prepared to press on even more aggressively.

ON THE HOME front, life was uneventful—except for Pam and her involvement in Jackie's life. Jackie's love life drove me nuts. Because Jackie confided in Pam and Pam confided in me, I became an unwitting participant in Jackie's affairs of the heart. After a particularly long phone conversation with Jackie one evening, Pam confessed Jackie had seen that jerk, Kennedy, a few times prior to her broken engagement to her stockbroker. Jackie told her she had listened to Chase and Grant mocking Kennedy one night at Rosie's, and she was embarrassed about us finding out she was seeing him.

"She should have been embarrassed about it," I fumed.

I knew for a fact Kennedy was still up to his sleazy ways by cheating on Jackie while she believed they were seeing each other exclusively. Audrey Hepburn, the movie actress, had been seen sneaking out of Kennedy's Georgetown townhouse early one morning by one of my secretaries. Grant said it was common knowledge all over Capitol Hill that Hepburn was seeing Kennedy.

God, did that ever piss me off. I hadn't liked Kennedy the first time I met him, and I still had no reason to change my opinion of him.

Ever since meeting Pam, I had come to like her many girlfriends, and as flighty as Jackie was, I felt protective of her. I certainly didn't want her to get hurt by some arrogant asshole of a millionaire playboy who was over a decade older than she was. I had hoped Jackie would realize what a sleaze he was and dump him.

Unfortunately, it became evident that Jackie was willing to overlook a lot in order to get a ring on her finger. Jackie had been on a mission to get married ever since her younger sister, Lee, became engaged and showed off her engagement ring to the family. According to Pam, Jackie and Lee had always been fiercely competitive when it came to men. Jackie was an emotional mess by the time Lee's wedding rolled around in April.

I sat in our kitchen, angrily nursing a beer as I listened to Pam consoling Jackie in the other room.

"Jack hasn't called in days," she cried. "I'm going to call him."

"Jackie, a woman doesn't call a man," Pam counseled her.

"But I need to talk to him," she whined. "Jack's got to ask me to marry him."

"That's not the right thing to do. Remember the advice your father gave you back at school. Don't be so available to him. If you look too anxious or too eager, you will scare him off."

I wanted her to run him off—it would be the best thing that could ever happen to Jackie.

Of course, that's why I was sitting in the kitchen by myself. Neither one of them wanted my advice.

IN THE SPRING, Tracy Barnes, my immediate superior, approached me with some exciting news. I was being assigned to work with Kim Roosevelt on a Special Operations project.

Kermit "Kim" Roosevelt, a political heavyweight around D.C., was a grandson of Teddy Roosevelt, a cousin to FDR, and a cousin to the noted national columnist, Joseph Alsop, who also happened to be one of the leaders of our little Georgetown group.

I hustled over to the Special Operations building and met with Roosevelt. He was brief and to the point. "I want you to study up on Iran. Cram your brain with as much information on that damn country as it will hold. I need you to be so intimately familiar with the history of that entire region that if I ask you what time the Prime Minister wipes his butt, you'll be able to describe the toilet paper he uses."

I spent hours and hours over the following days and weeks in the archives and the library. Iran was part of the vast, but aging, British Empire. Oil was first discovered in Iran in 1909, and literally from the time the first barrel was pumped, the British treated that Iranian oil as if it were their own oil. I was aghast to discover that in 1950, Great Britain had collected over 50 million pounds—in taxes alone—on Iranian oil production while the Iranian government barely earned 16 million pounds in total profits. The British gouged the Iranians unmercifully.

The Iranians desired a more equitable relationship with Great Britain, but the British were quite happy with things the way they were. Frustrated by the lack of any meaningful progress in those negotiations, the Iranians moved to nationalize the oil companies. In October 1951, the Iranian Prime Minister Mohammed Mossadegh sent Iranian troops to occupy the huge British oil refinery at Albadan. He then officially kicked Great Britain out of the country. The British, who had previously rejected a 50/50 equitable split in oil profits, now found out that they owned 100% of exactly nothing at all.

The British retaliated by trying to break Iran with a Western boycott of its oil. Mossadegh retaliated by breaking diplomatic relations with Britain. Now the United States faced a real problem. The British actions were driving Iran right into the Soviet's welcoming arms. With an almost fanatical hatred of the British, Mossadegh became more and more determined to expel them from his country forever, no matter what the cost.

British Intelligence had contacted Kim Roosevelt with a detailed game plan for a coup against Mossadegh in November 1952. Roosevelt encouraged the British to hold off until Truman had left office. He believed the new Eisenhower administration would have a more favorable policy toward covert operations.

After a few weeks, Roosevelt called me into his office to review my research. His office was a standard, utilitarian government office. A picture of President Eisenhower hung on the wall behind his desk as well as numerous plaques and photographs of various politicians and world leaders. Partially opened Venetian blinds cast a striated shadow over the floor. Two gray metal armchairs faced the front of the desk. I selected the one nearest the window.

"Patrick, President Eisenhower's right-hand man, Beetle Smith, called me this morning. He specifically asked me, 'When are those fucking British coming to talk to us?' and 'When is our goddamned operation going to get underway?' He is especially anxious that we proceed with the idea of an Iranian coup. He feels it is imperative we get this operation underway immediately."

"Yes sir."

"I believe the key to the success of the Iranian coup, or any coup for that matter, is the Iranian army. To whom are they loyal? Now, we know Mossadegh is popular with the people, but real support for him within the Iranian army is very thin. What can you tell me about the Shah of Iran?"

"I know that he is a young man who is the hereditary leader of the country. My research shows he is considered to be so weak and ineffectual that he has been labeled the 'Boy Scout' by our own intelligence people here at the Agency," I answered.

"Even though the Shah is immature in nature and very young in age, he still represents a connection to Iran's past—that's awfully tough for the Iranian army generals to ignore." Roosevelt opened the manila folder containing my research and looked through its contents.

"I have a few reservations about this idea of the United States either starting a coup or supporting one." He paused as he perused a document. "I still feel the British and the United States have two different agendas. The British simply want to get their Iranian oil fields back. They also want to punish Mossadegh and send a message to any future Mossadegh's of the world. That's fine—that's their right to feel that way." He closed the folder and looked over to me.

"However, we Americans have an entirely different reason to act," he informed me. "We have our own large domestic oil deposits in Texas, as well as very tight connections to the Saudis, so we don't need more oil of our own. Instead, we must be concerned about keeping Iran out of the Soviet orbit and denying them access to the oil fields in the Middle East. Do you agree?"

"Yes, sir, from what I've been able to glean from the available research, you're right."

Roosevelt rose out of his chair, handed me back my folder, and patted me on the back. "Good work, Patrick."

Unfortunately for everyone concerned, the Soviets were every bit as smart as we were. They also realized what was at stake in Iran. It now was a race between the Soviets and the West. In early spring, the Soviets dispatched their ambassador to Tehran. We ominously observed that he was the very same man who had been in charge of the Soviet embassy in Prague in 1949 when Jan Masaryk had been assassinated.

My superiors decided to accelerate Operation AJAX. Our plans for a coup began to take final shape.

MY CONCENTRATION ON Iran was interrupted by the second most momentous event of my life. On June 2 after ten hours of labor, Pam gave birth to our son, Timothy Patrick McCarthy. I was thrilled and proud to be his father. I happily passed out cigars to everyone I knew, as well as a bunch of people I didn't know. Even getting up with Pam for the late night feedings didn't wear me down because I felt so blessed.

Our elation at the birth of our son was immediately tempered by a telegram Pam received from Jackie, who was in London attending the coronation of the new queen, Elizabeth, to the throne of England. First, she congratulated us on the birth of our son; and then, she announced that Kennedy had proposed to her by telegram.

"What's with her? One guy proposes over the telephone and another proposes by telegram."

"Shhhhh, you'll wake the baby," Pam said in a whisper. "Not every man is as romantic as you are, honey. Jackie is happy, so let's try and be happy for her, too."

"I am happy. I'm happy about loving you, and I'm happy about my new son. I'm even happy that Jackie is finally getting married. I'm just very unhappy she is marrying an asshole like Jack Kennedy."

"I wish her the best—even though I don't think she and Jack are a good match—by any stretch of the imagination."

"Well, I think Jackie is marrying beneath herself."

Pam and I felt Jackie was marrying for the money. Kennedy was marrying for—hell—I don't know why Kennedy was getting married. I remembered Chase's story about Inga-Binga and how hard Kennedy had chased after her. I sure hadn't seen that same kind of behavior in his relationship with Jackie.

Chase cleared up the mystery when he stopped over at our apartment after work one evening looking for a beer and someone to drink it with. Chase always included Pam in our conversations unlike Grant who dismissed her as "the little wife." Pam had just cleared the dinner dishes. She came into the living room, wiping her hands on her apron.

"Chase, let me make you a plate. It's no trouble at all," Pam said.

"The beer is fine—I had a late lunch. Come join us," he looked at Pam, who was a little flushed, as she tucked a wayward strand of hair in place. "You know, Patrick, you are one lucky guy."

Pam stood beside my chair and patted my shoulder.

"Look at you two—you really are an old married couple now that you have a baby," Chase looked wistfully and then immediately checked himself. "Speaking of marriage, do you want to know why Jack Kennedy is finally getting married?" he smirked and sipped his Pabst Blue Ribbon.

"Because he finally found the love of his life?" Pam optimistically guessed.

"Oh, hell, no!" he spit out, laughing. "Kennedy's secretary, Evelyn Lincoln, told me confidentially that Old Joe told Jack he'd better get married, or people would think he was a faggot."

"Has it ever occurred to either of you that Jack may have fallen in love with Jackie?"

"So you still believe in Cupid and his little arrow?" he teased her.

"The only little arrow I've ever heard about is yours," she said as she retreated to the kitchen to heat Tim's bottle on the stove.

"Damn, Patrick, she's quick!" He started to raise his bottle to his lips and then paused, "I love that about her! I'll tell you what—when she finally comes to her senses and realizes she's too good for you, I'll marry her."

"Not even if you were the last man on Earth!" she shouted from the other room.

"Hey, Pam, I'm sorry. Come on back in here, and I'll tell you about a conversation I had yesterday with Jack over on the Hill."

Pam returned carrying my son and his bottle. She plopped down on the sofa. Once she was settled in and comfortable, Chase started in on his story.

"I ran into Jack at the Senate Dining Room yesterday. I bought him a bowl of Senate bean soup, and we talked about our friend Jackie. I asked him, 'Why her?' and you know what he told me?"

I thought I knew the answer, but Pam answered, "No."

"He said, 'I don't want to marry a girl who's an experienced voyager.'"

Pam's face contorted in confusion. "What does he mean by that? Jackie travels all the time. He knows that. She just made her umpteenth trip to Europe."

Chase dramatically shook his head side to side, "He said, 'I'm not referring to travel on land and sea. I mean, I don't want to marry a girl who's traveled sexually—who's sexually experienced. There are too many complications with a girl who's an experienced voyager. They make comparisons between you and other men. I want someone young and fresh. I want to marry a virgin.'"

"Now, that's just disgusting," Pam retorted as she retreated into the nursery.

IN EARLY JUNE, the *Saturday Evening Post* ran a profile of Jack Kennedy. Beneath the headline, "Jack Kennedy—the Senate's Gay Young Bachelor," was a cover photograph of Jack. Two weeks later on June 25, the Kennedy-Bouvier engagement was officially announced. Jackie insisted the public announcement follow the publication of the *Post* story, thus enhancing her status with her mother, who was critical of every man Jackie dated.

The potential nuptials created an unexpected controversy in the upper echelons of East Coast society. The Kennedys were regarded as *noveau-riche* upstarts in society. They were coarse, loud, vulgar and Irish. The East Coast WASP society looked down their collective noses at the entire family. It certainly didn't help that Jack's innumerable sexual liaisons were well known throughout the entire country. His escapades had been the spice of many a newspaper gossip column and popular fodder in the scandal rags on the newsstand. Proper families of good breeding and manners clearly looked down upon "Mattress Jack" and his exploits.

Jackie laughed it all off. She reminded people that her own father was just as notorious. But as I pointed out to Pam, on a scale from 1-10, Black Jack Bouvier was a relative piker at a "2" or a "3" while Jack Kennedy was a solid "10" adulterer. No doubt about it.

Pam felt Jackie was blinded by the immense wealth of the Kennedy clan. She was incapable of listening to reason from any of her friends. The simple fact was—Jack had more money than anyone else who pursued her.

To me, that was a sad reason for getting married.

SHORTLY AFTER TIM'S birth, Tracy Barnes came into my office with details of my new assignment. "Patrick," he said, "have you ever been to Tehran?"

"I've never even been to Tulsa," I replied.

"We've got the go-ahead for AJAX. Roosevelt has requested that you be included. He wants you in."

I liked to think I was recruited because of my promising career potential and my proven analytical prowess. But I suspected that I was essentially just expendable cannon fodder if something went wrong—so much for my indispensable abilities.

Roosevelt ordered me to spend the last full week in June lounging around the swimming pool at nearby Fort Myers in Arlington. I took Tim with me every day and kept him protected from the sun with some strategically draped towels around his bassinet. Within a week, I had developed a deep tan that might help to convince a casual observer I was of Middle-Eastern heritage.

It was difficult to leave my wife and son. Because of the nature of my job,

I couldn't even tell Pam where I was going—or when I would return. Luckily, the other wives in the Georgetown group had been through this drill many times before. They rallied around Pam to help her out in my absence.

I had no input in the actual planning of Operation Ajax. I assumed that others more skilled than I had carefully considered the details of the plan. Our strike force consisted of exactly five American agents. None of us spoke Farsi, the local language in Iran. We had $1 million in Iranian currency to buy whatever we needed, and we had the talents of a handful of Iranian organizers at our disposal. The plan had all the characteristics of a Hollywood screwball comedy.

Looking back on it now, we were lucky we weren't all caught and shot.

Our small group was smuggled into Iran in the sweltering heat of the July summer. A series of planes and trains finally got us into Tehran by mid-month. Our journey consisted of hitching uncomfortably long rides in the back of various cargo trucks, alternating with cramped and sweltering busses crammed full of sweaty, dirty, and smelly Iranian peasants. I crossed the border in the guise of an itinerant laborer. I pretended to be suffering from a flu-like illness, too miserably uncomfortable to speak. My Iranian companions shepherded me to our safehouse.

Roosevelt arrived a few days after we had with the carefully smuggled cache of $1 million in Iranian currency. He handed me $25,000 and put me in charge of recruiting a mob that would be willing to participate in a protest. I passed out money at various wrestling and boxing clubs, as well as seedy bars throughout the area. I discovered the dregs of humanity were quick to give me their undivided attention and loyalty if I gave them enough "moolah," a lesson I carried with me for the rest of my life.

Our first attempt at staging the overthrow of a foreign government bordered on calamity. We had no system for communication—messages were not delivered on time and those that got through were garbled. On August 16 when the coup was scheduled to start, nothing happened. Tehran radio was supposed to announce the Shah had fired Mossadegh. Instead, Mossadegh announced the Shah, aided by foreign elements (I guess that meant us) had tried to oust him as Prime Minister. He proclaimed that he was immediately seizing all government power for himself. For a couple of days, it appeared that our coup would fail.

Roosevelt, a little bit testy over this development demanded an explanation—what had been my contribution to the failed insurrection? After threatening to abandon me in a Tehran jail if I couldn't get the job done, Roosevelt sent me back out to the gyms, wrestling clubs, and bars to find out what was going on. I discovered my rented mobs of angry rioters were waiting for me to come back and tell them what to do and how to do it. It was up to me to organize some simple slogans and help letter some banners, and then get my guys pepped up ready to go.

On August 19, my mob took to the streets chanting anti-Mossadegh slogans—the tide turned in our favor. Mossadegh saw the pro-Shah forces assemble, and he saw that the army remained loyal to the Shah. To my amazement, he quickly fled the country. Our coup was a complete success.

That night, with a handful of our Iranian organizers, we smoked victory cigars and polished off a healthy assortment of liquor. We had succeeded in removing Mossadegh from office—we had accomplished our mission. We hadn't known at the time, but Roosevelt had received a telegram from Beetle Smith with a succinct five-word order: "Give up and get out" dated August 18, the day before our success.

Roosevelt cabled his reply back to D.C.: "Happy to report the Shah will be returning to Tehran in triumph shortly." He said he signed it, "Love and kisses from the team."

"Think about what we just did!" Roosevelt boasted. "We managed to topple a government hostile to the West with only five guys." Roosevelt held up his hand, "Oh, there's one more thing—we still have $900,000 left over. Washington's gonna love this. We're all going home first class, fellas!"

We felt absolutely invincible.

I COULDN'T WAIT to get home to see my wife and son. I was home only twenty-four hours when Pam and I had to hightail it to Jackie's wedding. According to all of the newspapers and magazines, the Kennedy nuptials were the most important social event of 1953. Pam and I left Tim with Pam's mom and dad and then traveled on to Newport, Massachusetts. Because Pam was one of Jackie's bridesmaids, I had graciously been included in the festivities.

Things were already starting on rocky ground. The entire family knew Jack had flown to Europe in August with a male buddy to take full advantage of his last days of freedom—to indulge in every sexual liaison possible. Janet Auchincloss, Jackie's mother, was furious with him. "What kind of a man does this sort of thing? A man who is about to be married wants to be with the woman he loves." She demanded answers to questions that couldn't be answered, let alone explained.

Jackie told Pam she hoped Jack had been able to "get it out of his system." Pam and I were dubious Jack Kennedy could ever change his ways. I believed deep down Jackie probably felt that way as well.

The wedding turned out to be a test of power between two proud families. Even though Jackie Bouvier had been raised a Catholic, her mother had married into one of the oldest Protestant families on the East Coast. The

Auchinclosses were solidly old money WASPs. Jackie's mother and stepfather wanted a tasteful wedding and had their own ideas for planning the wedding. However, Old Joe Kennedy was determined to make his son's wedding THE social event of the year. So even though the Auchinclosses were paying for the wedding, Old Joe Kennedy submitted a guest list of over fourteen hundred people.

Two days before the wedding, Jackie's stepfather, Hugh Auchincloss, hosted a small bachelor party at an exclusive Newport restaurant known as the Clambake Club. Since I was with the bridal party, I accompanied Hugh to the party as his guest. Hugh was a gracious host. He insisted upon bringing some Auchincloss family heirlooms to the dinner party—glasses and china that had been in his family for generations and had been lovingly preserved and passed down to each successive generation.

Before we left to go, he showed me the antique glassware. He caressed a glass saying, "My grandfather toasted my father's nuptials with these very glasses, and my father proudly toasted my marriage with them as well. It's my fondest wish in life that the magnificent good luck these glasses have represented will some day be passed down to my grandchildren's grandchildren."

He beamed with obvious sentiment as he handed me one of the crystal goblets. I am certainly not an expert on antique glassware, but even I could admire how the impossibly thin crystal had been very delicately etched years before by some master craftsman. The thin band of gold leaf that encircled the rim of the crystal stemware was absolutely unblemished. There wasn't a nick or a scratch to be seen anywhere on its fragile surface. I also became a little emotional just thinking about the history of this precious heirloom.

"Hugh, I'm going to give this back to you right now," I said as I carefully handed it to him. "I'm afraid I'm so nervous holding it I might somehow manage to break it, and I wouldn't want that to happen."

"Nonsense, Patrick. You're doing just fine," he reassured me. Nonetheless, I could detect a sense of relief in his eyes when he removed the crystal from my nervous grip. He planned to use these priceless heirlooms as a generous gesture to his new son-in-law.

There were eighteen of us at the small dinner that night. Hugh sat at the head table with his future son-in-law while I sat with some of Jack's buddies, Senator George Smathers and Red Fay. Hugh's crystal heirlooms, filled with champagne, were set in the center of each table.

During dinner, Jack stood up. "Gentlemen, I want you all to rise and drink a toast to my lovely bride." One by one, each man pushed back his chair and stood to make the toast. Hugh beamed with pride as we raised our glasses toward the ceiling, the crystal sparkling and reflecting the light of the room.

Jack moved to the fireplace. "To my lovely bride," he drained the champagne and tossed his crystal glass into the fire. Before Hugh could raise either his hand or his voice in protest, Jack bellowed, "Into the fireplace! We will not drink out of these glasses again!"

Jack's friends did not hesitate to follow his lead—they began to hurl the priceless crystal into the stone fireplace. The glasses tinkled and shattered into hundreds of pieces. Hugh looked positively ashen—his precious Auchincloss family heirlooms—in chards. I could see he was physically pained as he, too, reluctantly pitched his crystal in with the others.

I saw Red elbow George Smathers to get his attention. "You know," he said confidentially, "Jack asked me before dinner what the proper protocol was for the toast. I told him there was really only one thing to keep in mind. That is for you to be sure to offer the first toast to the bride. And when the glasses are drained, no one should drink out of them ever again. They should be thrown into the fireplace." He smiled proudly, "That was a grand toast!"

I could see a visibly shaken Hugh calling and motioning to the waiters to replace the crystal ware and the champagne. I knew Hugh brought along enough extra stemware to allow the wait staff to remove the dirty glasses and to replace them with fresh, clean stemware after dessert. I'm sure Hugh never dreamed that his precious crystal would be destroyed.

I'm equally certain he never imagined what would happen next. I know I never saw it coming.

As soon as the fresh crystal was set on the tables and filled with champagne, Jack rose from his seat once again. "Maybe this isn't the accepted custom," he admitted, "but I want to again express my love for this girl I'm going to marry—a toast to the bride."

All raised their glasses to the heavens, affirmed the toast, drained their champagne, and once again followed Jack's lead by smashing the irreplaceable and expensive crystal into the fireplace. Too much of a gentleman to protest, Hugh politely followed suit. Once again, cheers erupted. "That a boy, Jack," shouted Red as he slapped Kennedy on the back.

After the dinner was over, the groom and his friends fled into the night. I sat on the floor next to the fireplace as an emotionally shattered Hugh picked through the broken pieces of crystal, looking for some piece that might have miraculously escaped the carnage. Since no one was around to see his grief but me, the tears flowed quite openly.

"Was that an Irish custom?" he moaned. "All my family's crystal—gone. Why?" He looked at me, his eyes red with emotion. "Why? Can you tell me why, Patrick?"

I felt as crushed as he was. I bent down and put an arm around his shoulders to comfort him. "I don't know, Hugh. All I can tell you is that some people just don't care about the feelings of others."

He picked up a partially broken glass and after lovingly examining it, allowed it to gently tumble from his fingers and break along with the rest. His misery, on what should have been a very joyous occasion, was heartbreaking.

I helped him to his feet and gently whispered to him, "I've got something for you. Stay here." I went back over to my table and retrieved my suit coat and my linen napkin. "I'm sorry it's not more," I said as I handed it to him.

He looked at me quizzically and then carefully unwrapped the napkin. Nestled inside was my crystal stemware, pristine and unblemished. He looked at it and then up at me in astonishment without saying a word.

"I couldn't bear to break such a thing of beauty," I murmured. "I'm sorry I didn't have the strength of character not to break the first one."

"God bless you, Patrick," he said gratefully. "You're a good man."

ON SEPTEMBER 12, two thousand onlookers crowded the sidewalks and the streets outside of St. Mary's Catholic Church in Newport hoping to get a glimpse of the nuptials. Inside the church, every pew was filled with the nation's political, social, and economic elite.

The wedding party was huge. Jack had eighteen ushers alone. Jackie's bridal party was stunning. Pam was one of the attendants (the prettiest one, I'm proud to brag) while Jackie's sister Lee was the matron of honor and Jack's brother, Bobby, was the best man. The Archbishop from Boston, Richard J. Cushing, presided over the Mass and even read a special papal blessing from the Vatican.

Jackie was frantic with emotion when it was time to walk down the aisle. "Where is he? Where is he?" Jackie's father should have been anxiously waiting to escort his daughter down the aisle—but he was nowhere to be seen.

Pam said that Jackie's mother appeared triumphant. "It's just like him, not to show up." When pressed, however, she admitted that she had dispatched Lee's husband to Bouvier's hotel to inform him "he could of course come to the church and give away the bride but he could not come to the reception." Obviously humiliated, Black Jack apparently headed straight to the bar instead. Pam told me Mrs. Auchincloss was surely aware of the impact this would have on Jackie.

All eyes were on Jackie as she walked down the aisle. Jackie was calm, composed, and radiant even though moments earlier she had been at the brink of tears. I'm not sure how many people even noticed that Hugh Auchincloss was a stand-in for Black Jack Bouvier. And I wondered how many people saw what I did at the end of the ceremony—Jack surreptitiously removed his wedding band from his finger before he even left the church. (Many weeks later, Pam showed me several of the wedding pictures. They all showed what I already knew—Jack was not wearing a ring.)

Twelve hundred guests attended the wedding reception at the Auchincloss estate, Hammersmith Farm, overlooking Narragansett Bay. An elegant buffet was served in the house, on the many terraces, and on the carefully manicured lawns outside. The newlyweds cut the five-tiered, four-foot-tall wedding cake as white-jacketed waiters slipped among the vast crowd, distributing trays of champagne to the guests.

At one point, I sat by myself at a table on the terrace, enjoying the magnificent view. I saw Pam approaching arm-in-arm with Jack's younger brother, Bobby, on one side of her and Jack's father on the other side.

"There you are," she cried out. "We've been looking all over for you. Are you having a good time?"

I was having a miserable time. I knew few people, and I was too shy to mingle like a good guest should. "I'm having a great time," I lied.

"Good," Pam sighed. "I told Bobby and Joe I was worried about you, and they offered to help me find you and here you are!" Pam had obviously been partaking of the free champagne. She was both giddy and a little unsteady on her feet.

Bobby self-consciously removed his arm from around my wife's waist when I met his eye. The Ambassador moved closer to Pam in a private challenge of his own. Before I could say anything, Pam said, "Listen, I've got to find the ladies room, now. Will you gentlemen stay here with Patrick and keep him company until I get back?"

Bobby looked uncomfortable, but before either one of them could voice a reason not to comply, Pam planted a kiss on their cheeks, yelled, "Thanks!" and disappeared toward the house. We each stood awkwardly, watching her go.

"Why don't you join me? I'm sure she'll be back soon."

Joe Kennedy sat down next to me while Bobby plopped down in a chair across from me just as a waiter came by with champagne flutes. I motioned the waiter over, and he placed three full glasses in front of us on the white linen tablecloth. The sun overhead was warm, the breeze was cool, and the conversation was cold.

"That's quite a wife you have there," Joe grinned. "I'll bet she's a wild one, isn't she?"

I was a little nonplussed by his question. It seemed to be a double entendre, but I couldn't be sure. Surely he wasn't brazen enough to make a sexual comment about my own wife to my face?

Bobby jumped in to get his father off the hook. "He means she seems like she can dance all night long."

We both knew that wasn't what he meant, but there wasn't any sense in starting an argument on a day like this.

"Yes," I responded. "She loves weddings. You married?"

"Yeah, three years, Ethel and I have got one kid and one on the way."

"Good for you."

Joe Kennedy was distracted by a lovely young woman who sashayed past us. He seemed particularly interested as she bent down to take off her shoe. He stopped looking around and suddenly asked, "You work for Allen Dulles, don't you?" I was flabbergasted that he would know that.

"Ah, yes—yes, I do," I stammered. "How'd you know that?"

"We Kennedys know everything," he said cryptically. "How do you like it?"

"I love it," I admitted. "I really feel like I'm doing my part to make America safe against Communism. That's a very satisfying feeling."

Bobby, who had been politely bored, now registered some interest. "I know what you mean. I'm working on a government case for Senator McCarthy's committee right now. We're about to indict a real shit-bird for taking American money under false pretenses." Bobby put his champagne glass down. He looked at me seriously as if he was considering whether he should elaborate. "We've got American troops fighting Red Chinese in Korea, and we've got this Greek shipping asshole busy making money while trading with our enemies. It's 'blood trade.' I'm out to bust his balls over it."

"Bobby's pretty damn tough and pretty damn smart," Joe said smugly. "That Greek greaseball doesn't stand a chance of getting away with anything."

"It just doesn't make sense that people who are supposed to be our allies—who we are aiding financially—should be trading with the very Communists who are killing our GI's. Am I right?"

"You're right," I agreed. I was pleasantly surprised that Bobby seemed nothing like his brother. "What's the story?"

For a moment he looked reluctant to say anything else, but he seemed to relax when I added, "Hey, I'm with the Agency, remember?"

"This guy is nothing but trouble. He first came to Jack's attention at the Office of Naval Intelligence when he was caught running an insurance scam during the war. The greasy bastard was spraying bales of tobacco with salt water during their stay in Genoa and declaring the bales "undeliverable" due to sea damage in transit. He would collect the insurance money from the insurance companies and then he would dry the bales out and deliver them to the buyer as promised. He was thus able to collect for both the shipping and the transit 'loss.' At least he did until he was caught, and we made him stop. After the war, this same guy bought ten surplus T2 tankers from the United States under false pretenses. You have to understand that, due to their size and strategic significance, the sale of these ships to any foreigner is illegal. But at a cost of as little as $1.5 million each, the price was too low to resist, and so this guy set up a dummy U.S. corporation with three American citizens as the so-called buyers so he could illegally grab them."

Bobby paused and motioned to another waiter for three more fresh glasses of champagne. His father's attention was again occupied by the pretty young ladies who were fluttering past us on the terrace. "Now, if I can get this federal indictment, every time one of his ships pulls into an American port, we'll be able to seize it and impound all of its cargo. That ought to make the bastard sit up and take notice that you can't fuck around with the United States. He should also know he can't fuck around with the Kennedys, either."

"Amen to that," Joe brutishly chipped in. "Punish the bastards and make them pay. No one screws with us and gets away with it."

Now I was really paying attention. This apparently was a deeply personal vendetta, too. "What else has this guy done?"

Bobby stopped momentarily while the waiter served the champagne. Taking a glass from the tray, Bobby continued, "Ah, the guy is fifty-three years old and married, and he's making an ass of himself chasing after a long-time lady friend of my family. He told Pamela," he saw my face and quickly added, "Not your Pamela—Pamela Churchill. He told Pamela Churchill, 'I approach every woman as a potential mistress. Beautiful women cannot bear moderation; they need an inexhaustible supply of excess.' Have you ever heard such utter horsecrap in your life?"

"No—no, I haven't," I admitted. Just at that moment, my Pam reappeared at the table.

"Hey you guys, I'm sorry to break this up, but Jackie wants all of us back at the head table for some pictures or something. You want to join me?"

I didn't need any of that misery. "I think I'll just stay here, if it's OK with you," I said.

"Sure! I'll know where to find you." She grabbed Bobby and pulled him to his feet. "Come on, Robert. The bride and groom await us."

Bobby reached over and extended his hand to me. "It was nice chatting with you, Patrick."

"It was nice chatting with you, too, Bobby. By the way, what's the name of the Greek scumbag you're going after? Maybe I'll see the announcement of the indictment in the newspaper."

"His name's Onassis," he replied. "Aristotle Socrates Onassis."

"I hope you get him."

"Count on it. I will."

Joe made no attempt to get up and leave. He sat with me, sipping champagne. I was fascinated to find myself in such infamous company, the disgrace of the diplomatic corps. It didn't take long for Joe to prove the rumors were all true.

"I've taught my boys you can't let people push you around or take advantage of you because if they do it once, they'll never stop. I remember when I ran RKO Studios out in Hollywood. Everyone out there was a Sheenie rag trader. Louis B. Mayer was nothing but a kike junkman. They all thought they could push this Irishman around and I had to prove them wrong."

He drained his glass and looked around for a waiter. "You can never find a Sambo when you need him. Am I right?" I was becoming repulsed by his anti-Semitism and racism, but because it was his son's wedding day, I just shrugged my shoulders as if I agreed with him.

I was relieved when he abruptly rose from his chair, "I've got to get back to the family. Nice meeting you." He didn't offer to shake my hand.

"Nice meeting you, too, Mr. Ambassador."

I now had a story to tell Chase when I saw him.

FOR HER HONEYMOON, Jackie had selected a quiet, pink-painted house on a cliff in Acapulco, overlooking the ocean as a romantic retreat. However, it was too quiet to suit her new husband. After a few days, they headed to Beverly Hills, where they stayed in a home owned by Marion Davies, the former mistress of William Randolph Hearst. Jack spent most of his time calling and visiting old friends. Eventually, the newlyweds met up with one of Jack's old Navy buddies and his wife. The couple accompanied Jack and Jackie on a drive up to San Francisco. On the last day of their honeymoon, the men took off to a pro football game leaving the girls to fend for themselves.

Jackie was crushed by Jack's lack of attention. It certainly hadn't been the romantic getaway she had dreamed about.

Pam told me she could tell their marriage was already in trouble.

ON SEPTEMBER 23, 1953, President Eisenhower pinned the National Security Medal on Kim Roosevelt. He later noted, "Our agent there, a member of the CIA, worked intelligently, courageously, and tirelessly. I listened to his detailed report and it seemed more like a dime novel than a historical fact."

The surprising success of the coup in Iran led the Eisenhower administration to believe in the power of covert operations and the integrity of the CIA. Although the Cold War was at an impasse in Europe, Communism was aggressively expanding into Asia. The United States was prepared to take covert action against the spread of Communism outside European borders. Looking back, I felt that it had been too easy to overthrow the government of a country.

My career at the CIA took off as well. Kim Roosevelt was positively effusive in giving me credit for my role in organizing the pro-Shah mob. My credentials were now gold-plated. When the Agency expanded my responsibilities, I almost burst with pride that they had such faith in my abilities. Plus, I was a happy new father, and now I had time to be at home with the two loves of my life—my wife and my tiny son.

I was surprised that Bobby Kennedy turned out to be a man of his word. One month later a federal grand jury handed down a sealed indictment against a Greek shipping magnate named Aristotle Onassis.

"Our country! In her intercourse with foreign nations, may she always be in the right; but our country, right or wrong."

— Stephen Decatur (1848)

September 6, 1978
1:10 p.m.

The phone call from Ed Clark left Grant emotionally drained. Everything he had worked so hard to achieve in life was on the line. His son could get killed for thinking with his little head and not his big head. Grant could get killed for thinking he could keep the truth buried. He felt tired, old, and scared.

He flopped back down in his chair and stared out the window at the Virginia shoreline. He could see the Custice-Lee Mansion up on the hillside overlooking Arlington Cemetery and the Kennedy gravesite. The trees blocked the eternal flame from his view, but he knew where it was. He also knew what it stood for.

That flame was a symbol of an American *coup d'etat*. The Patriots had been mistrustful of Jack Kennedy ever since his old man helped him steal the presidency from Dick Nixon.

Kennedy was a fuck-up—he had brought the country to the brink of nuclear war. Hell, his little Cuban Missile Crisis could have annihilated all of Texas. The Patriots did what they had to do. Did it hurt that their native son, Lyndon Johnson, may have benefited from the assassination? Not at all. Did it hurt that the Patriots benefited from the assassination as well? Not according to Grant.

The federal government had been close to figuring out Lyndon's relationship with the various scams of Bobby Baker and Billy Sol Estes. Kennedy had already told Senator Smathers that LBJ would be dropped from the ticket in 1964. Hell, he might have gone to jail. Instead, he went straight into the White House.

J. Edgar Hoover benefited. Kennedy probably would have fired him after he won a second term. Hoover got to stay on years after he should have gone.

The generals got back control of the Pentagon. The war in Vietnam kept them from obsessing over Cuba. It was win-win.

Dick Nixon got into the White House, too. It was ironic that the Watergate burglary was over the Patriot's role in the assassination. That thirteen-minute gap in the tape had to go, or they would've all gone to jail as murdering traitors.

Grant closed his eyes and remembered that fateful party at Clint Murchison's mansion on November 21, 1963 when the Patriots made the final decision to go ahead with the planned ambush in Dealey Plaza the next morning. Emotions had run high that night, and everyone had left with the feeling that the country would be in safe hands in twelve hours time. Sixteen years later—was it all worth it?

Grant let out heavy sigh. His ass was in a sling—too late for regrets now.

1954

AFTER THE SUCCESS of Operation AJAX, I received a promotion and a modest pay raise. I assumed it was because of my bravery, but Pam let it slip that some of the Georgetown wives pestered their husbands to get me some more money so I could take better care of my growing family. Tim had literally been adopted by all of the other mothers in the Georgetown dinner group. They constantly fawned over him and offered to baby-sit for us. I didn't think any young man had as many women fighting over him for attention as that cute little guy did. His white-blonde hair and ready smile charmed every woman that looked his way. I often caught Pam beaming with pride at her little boy. She was a doting mother, and Tim was her adoring son. I couldn't have been prouder myself.

Meanwhile, the Agency sent me to Quantico, Virginia, which was just outside Washington for specialized schooling. The base was a training station for the U.S. Marine Corps, but the FBI also had a school there. Because of my connections to Mr. Hoover, I was included in a very small CIA class that studied with the FBI.

I had unlimited access to the Quantico rifle range, one of the few perks of training. I had quite a bit of spare time, and though I had never been one for hobbies, I soon found I enjoyed the rifle range. I was captivated by the discipline necessary to be a good marksman. Learning how to accurately shoot at various targets from various distances with various guns was both a mental and physical challenge.

The gunnery sergeant at the range let me borrow rifles from the Marine Corps Armory. I had two favorite guns—a 1903 Springfield and a modified

.30 caliber M-1, called the M-1D. The M-1D was a specially modified sniper rifle. I actually preferred to use the '03 whenever it was available. It had a more powerful 8X Unertl scope, a cleaner bolt-action design, and increased accuracy at long range. I felt more comfortable and confident using the '03, which translated into more satisfying time on the range.

I savored the challenge and the solitude of long-range gunning, shooting at targets that were 500 to 700 yards away, all the way out to about 1,000 yards. I spent hours at a time sighting in on a target the size of a silver dollar from a distance of about ½ mile away. It took patience, a steadiness of nerves, and absolute muscle control coordinated with my breathing to hit a target. Nervousness and excitement were my two worst enemies when trying to concentrate on the target's center.

No one else on the base enjoyed the long-range practice as much as I did. I was virtually alone most days, with one notable exception, an older Marine in his mid-forties who was often on the range when I arrived.

We both preferred the '03 Springfield and thus enjoyed a little of competitive one-upmanship. Since there was only one in the armory, whoever got to the range first had the advantage of using the best rifle. Some days it was me, and other days he was the one who luckily arrived first. In the beginning, we rarely exchanged words but gave the early bird who held the prize a silent salutatory nod of respect.

One day, while lying on my stomach and sighting in the Springfield, I looked up to see the older officer standing near my position.

"I've been observing your groupings, son," he said. "You've got a nice, smooth technique."

"Thank you, sir. I've been admiring your targets as well. I've tried to use them as a benchmark for my own shooting," I replied.

He grinned and offered his hand to me, "I'm Lt. Colonel Claude Harris."

"I'm Patrick McCarthy, sir." His handshake was firm and strong as he helped me rise to my feet.

"Are you Bureau, Patrick?"

"No sir, Agency, sir. How about you?"

"American by birth—Marine by choice!" he proclaimed proudly. "I've been admiring your dedication. You've been putting in long hours here. Who taught you your techniques?"

"I'm afraid no one, sir. I'm self-taught," I confessed. "I haven't had the benefit of any formal weapons training. Why, did you notice I was doing something wrong?"

"Oh no, not at all. I usually find it's only the boys out of Kentucky or West Virginia, or off a farm, who can shoot as well as you do. You know, kids that have grown up with guns all of their lives. Where did you grow up, Patrick?"

"Minnesota, sir, I'm a town kid. I had a BB gun once—until my mother took it away from me for shooting holes in the side of the shed. I've never even handled a rifle until I got to school here. I guess that makes me a lot less experienced than most shooters you've seen."

"Well, Patrick, you've been doing extremely well for someone who has no experience with long guns. Would you like some professional pointers?"

Lieutenant Colonel Claude N. Harris was the epitome of the career military man. His hair was cut in a flattop, his shoes were highly polished, and his trousers were pressed with a razor-sharp crease. He was the retired commander of the first Marine Corps Scout and Sniper School, which was formed in 1943 at Green's Farm and located north of San Diego in the hills of California. His school became the model for other Marine and Army sniper schools during the Korean War.

I had a rare opportunity to learn from a man who had more than book knowledge under his belt. Lt. Col. Harris understood the art and science of shooting as well as every style of warfare in existence. He believed a corps of snipers could single-handedly win a war. Harris knew whenever a supremely competent marksman appeared, it was a foregone conclusion someone was going to die. He often repeated a brief slogan to me: "Remember—one determined sniper can change the course of a war—hell, he can even change history! Snipers can save a country."

He remarked he had seen very few students who possessed such an unquenchable desire to learn as I had. I was pleased and honored when he made me his student. As a result, plenty of afternoons at the rifle range turned into late evenings at the Officer's Mess where he instructed me in the intricacies and nuances of the professional sniper.

Lt. Colonel Harris immersed me in lessons passed down from previous marksmen as far back as the American Revolutionary War. We studied the trajectory of bullets, and how wind, humidity, and temperature affected them. He taught me that weather conditions were very critical on the bullet's flight as modern technology increased the distance over which a bullet could travel.

I learned if the wind was blowing *toward* me, my bullets would have a tendency to *rise*, while if the wind was from *behind* me, my bullets would have a tendency to *drop*. Temperatures also became as critical as the wind at distances of six hundred yards or more. My bullet would react differently on a warm, bright morning than it would on a cool, overcast evening.

The Lt. Colonel fervently believed it wasn't enough for a sniper to be able to hit a stationary target at four or five hundred yards. A sniper had to be a human weapon who could not only shoot well, but could also find his way around on the battlefield and survive. My personal course involved training in map reading, sketching, aerial photo reading, the use of a compass, camouflage techniques, individual concealment, the construction of sniper hides, stalking, and my personal favorite, long-range shooting. Over a period of three months, whenever I could find the time away from my other CIA studies, Lt. Col. Harris was there as my constant companion. His enthusiasm and devotion to his craft were without equal.

"First of all, it takes incredible patience and perseverance to be a successful sniper. You have to be still and remain still for hours at a time. The first thing a hunter or its prey looks for is movement. Movement will tip off the wary to danger well before the danger manifests itself. A dedicated shooter must be prepared to dig into a spider hole for days at a time, even shitting in his pants if necessary, in order to get that one necessary shot."

We did a lot of silent walking or scouting over the terrain of Quantico, Virginia. In the early morning or late at night, the two of us would shadow various Marine platoons out training. One of my tests was to lie in the total darkness and estimate the number of men in a passing patrol by the sound of their footsteps alone.

"The terrain is your friend," he repeatedly lectured me. "You can use it to your advantage. In fact, you can make it a distinct advantage. Have you ever heard of Captain Herbert W. McBride?"

"No, sir, I have not."

"Captain McBride was an American who enlisted with the Canadians to fight for the British in France in World War I. He is the man I would credit with formulating the sniper's skills into a science."

The static trench warfare of World War I allowed sharpshooting to evolve to a higher level, as snipers found it the only way to pick off the enemy without being picked off in return. McBride wrote a textbook on the subject after the war based upon a logbook he kept on his combat experiences in the trenches. He was extremely meticulous in his record keeping. His remarkable and insightful diary conveyed the seriousness of killing and became the core of my training by Lt. Colonel Harris. McBride kept voluminous notes on how the ballistics of his special Ross rifle and telescopic sight were affected by external variances like temperature, humidity, wind, and other changes in lighting conditions and the weather. He improved upon various known techniques of camouflage and concealment.

"But the one principle that will keep you alive more than any other was his use of the terrain in order to fool the enemy about a sniper's exact location. If there is only one lesson to be learned from all of Captain McBride's work, it would be this one. Remember it well, Patrick, because it could be the one lesson that saves your life one day."

I determined to commit this to memory. I was mesmerized by Lt. Col. Harris' knowledge and expertise.

"Captain McBride learned that a rifle bullet fired past a tree, a rock, or a building will make a sonic 'crack' in passing that will totally confuse the enemy. It will sound as though it came from that location instead of from the sniper's true hiding place. In other words, if you use the terrain as your ally, it can help to confuse the enemy and to further conceal and protect you."

"A tree can do that?" I asked.

"That's right. An obstacle of any kind—a tree, a large boulder, a deep ditch, a creek, a building of some kind, can all be used to make that rifle shot appear to originate from there instead of from its true location. I personally witnessed that phenomenon a number of times. During the war, I took a shot at a group of Japs that had just passed a small stand of trees with a larger tree just off to the side. I missed my shot, but I was fascinated by the Jap reaction. They literally carved up that tree and that small stand of vegetation with their bullets, but they did not send a single shot in my direction."

He stressed the importance of staying on the move once you have hit your human target. "Know your location. Once you've succeeded in getting a shot off, move to another location as soon as you can. It will help to keep you alive. The one mistake, the one truly deadly mistake inferior shooters will make, time and time again, is that they will fall in love with a hiding place. You have to remember you are the hunter until that first shot is fired. Once it's fired, you become the hunted. Your life expectancy stands to be shortened considerably if you forget that one maxim."

He taught me a rifle range gives a marksman the opportunity to create and to hone a skill. Shooting a gun is really no different than practicing a musical instrument or playing a sport like baseball. You could be talented enough to be the next Joe DiMaggio, but if you don't practice or try to develop your skills, you'll never make it to the big leagues, let alone play for the Yankees or the Dodgers. To become a great shooter takes skill and constant practice to hone your talents. You don't just pick up a rifle, use it a few times at a range, and then stay proficient at it. You have to know what you're doing and practice it over and over again, just to stay sharp.

"Poor shooting can be attributed to a lack of practice," he told me, "but a lot more of those poor shootings are also due to a lack of knowledge about marksmanship. Most of our soldiers today don't know or even understand why they should 'zero-in' their rifles. Some don't even know how to zero-in their sights, and a few will never be able to zero-in their sights because of the poor maintenance of their rifles in the first place. I've examined rifles where the front sights were rusted beyond adjustment, and some actually had worn-out gun barrels. Believe it or not, a few rifles had no front sights whatsoever."

Everyday was a new lesson in warfare and marksmanship.

"Patrick, do you have any idea of how hard it is to actually kill an enemy soldier out on the battlefield? Of course you don't—because you've never been to war. But try and tell me: How many bullets does the average soldier have to fire in order to kill another enemy soldier? Take a guess."

I didn't have a clue, "Three to five?"

He shook his head.

"Listen to these statistics: During World War II, Allied troops fired an average of 25,000 bullets for each and every enemy soldier that they killed!"

I was astounded at that statistic.

"Korea was even worse. Our United Nations troops fired an average of 50,000 rounds of ammo for every one enemy soldier that they killed."

I had read about a similar Civil War statistic and assumed that modern weaponry would have reduced the number of rounds a soldier used. "How do you account for that," I asked.

"There are some major obstacles that will have to be surmounted if military marksmanship is to be saved. One of the biggest problems is that most Marine officers and NCO's think they know rifle marksmanship. They do not. For example, here in the Marine Corps, we have three levels of proficiency a Marine can grade out at. The top is 'Expert.' These soldiers know their weapons and what can be done with them. Unfortunately, there are damn few of them in the Corps. The next level is 'Sharpshooter.' These soldiers are pretty good, but their skills will deteriorate if they don't put some time in to stay somewhat sharp. The lowest class is 'Marksman,' and this is a badge everyone gets, regardless of how bad they really are."

"Why do they call them 'Marksman' if they're so bad?" I asked.

"It's a political thing. The Marines have an image to uphold. We have to make people think we are the best out there—even if we have some soldiers that are so bad it's a wonder that they don't blow the toes off their own feet. If you're ever going to be a casualty of 'friendly fire,' these are the guys that will most likely be responsible. For them, a shovel is as much a tool as a rifle is. But there is one fact no one can ignore: if you don't practice, you can't become proficient. Look around you. How many Marines do you see out here practicing—the way we are practicing?"

"None," but then I had to ask, "Can they really be that bad?"

"Patrick, if you're ever out here on the range with a group of Marine Marksmen, you'd think that they were practicing for a parade with all the red flags waving. Our Marines call this Maggie's Drawers. During shooting qualifications, if a shooter fails to hit the target itself, a spotter waves a bright red flag which indicates a clean miss. Everyone up and down the firing range knows he not only missed the bull's eye—he missed the whole friggin' target. The mere act of breathing wrong, or trying to hurry a shot, will result in a complete miss of the entire target."

As I considered that, he said, "Let me ask you this question, son. If your job was to hunt and kill other men before they had a chance to hunt and kill you, wouldn't you want some kind of an unfair advantage?"

"Yes sir, I would."

"So would I, and that's what I teach my men. If it comes down to two men squaring off against each other—two of the best in the world—then I want my man to be the one who wins. I'll give him all the tools he needs, but it's up to him to utilize them. We're all on this earth as a God-given right to life. But if our enemy is prepared to send us to our holy reward a little too early, then we have to rely on our own man-made skill in order to survive. The best shooters will develop a much higher level of discipline and concentration than the average soldier in the field will. They have to—because they have to be the best there is. They must possess a total awareness of their surroundings, focused by a remarkable one-ness of purpose. Patrick, you cannot afford to be careless. Second-place trophy in this competition is a casket."

His steely eyes met mine. "You have to be disciplined. I don't want any heavy smokers working for me. Heavy tobacco users become nervous and fidgety whenever they can't light up a smoke, and that's going to be most of the time they are in the field. Cigarette smoking can also get you killed. A simple waft of smoke could betray the shooter's position by its telltale trail, giving away a camouflaged hiding place. Even the odor could give you away out in the field. I don't want a man who can't give up the pleasures of a smoke for the few days he might be working. For that matter, you must have complete control over your own body for the job at hand. You have to have complete mastery over the 'Three B's'—your brain, your balls, and your bowels. You have to put physical discomfort out of your mind. You have to forget about sex. You have to forget about food and water. You have to be willing to piss and crap in your pants rather than move and reveal your position at the wrong time.

"I want my shooters to be right-handed. Rifles are built for right-handed shooters, with their bolts on the right-hand side. You can't wear glasses either. Glasses can become lost or broken, and they can fog up at a critical time which can obscure your sight. They can even betray your position by catching a glint of sunlight and reflecting it back at your target, thus exposing you.

"Let's try and sum up the whole package. What does it take, emotionally and mentally, for a man to coolly take aim and calculatedly blast another man out of this world and into the next? What kind of man does it take to be a sniper and not be destroyed by it? As I said before, it takes a very special kind of man—a man who has the courage to be alone with those fears, and alone with his doubts, yet be able to overcome them to perform at the very highest levels of efficiency. No one can teach you that strength. It has to come from within."

I was an avid student. These lessons appealed directly to the warrior spirit deep within me. All Americans could feel the looming threat of a nuclear war with the Communists hovering over us. I fervently hoped that someday I would be able to put my newly acquired knowledge to work on behalf of my country. Harris knew my inner fire burned hot, but he also knew there was one more lesson that I had to learn. And although he could prepare me for it, the ability to pass that final test was on my shoulders alone.

I had listened eagerly to all of Harris' combat stories, but now it was time to address his ultimate question: Could I actually do it? Was I the kind of man that could kill another man? Harris knew I was ready to ask it, and he was finally ready to talk about it as well.

"It takes a very special kind of courage to be alone with your fears, alone with your doubts. You'll never know what you'll do until you have your first enemy in your sights. The first thing you'll notice through your scope will be the man's face. It will probably be a young and healthy face. He might even be laughing, or saying something to the person next to him. The next thing you'll see will be his eyes. That's when it will hit you—that you are looking eye-to-eye with a man you're about to kill. Killing someone, seeing him die, is a tough thing to do. It takes a special man—a very special man—to be able to do that. I've trained many a shooter who graded out with top honors on the gun range, only to be unable to pull the trigger on the battlefield."

"I find that hard to believe," I said solemnly. "If you're trained to do a job, that training should just automatically take over for you."

"Yes, it should, and you would think it would, but it's hard to overcome your other life-long training." He paused for a moment and then asked me, "How often did you go to church as a boy?"

"Catechism every Wednesday, and Church every Sunday."

"A good Catholic boy. Tell me, were you taught the Ten Commandments?"

"We weren't just taught them. We were expected to live them."

"Of course you were. Religion is an integral part of all of our lives. All good children are taught the Ten Commandments. Now you tell me: What is the greatest of those ten laws?"

I had to pause to think about that one. "As a child, the two that guided my life more than any others were *Thou Shalt Not Steal* and *Thou Shalt Not Lie."*

"I'll bet that *Thou Shalt Not Covet Thy Neighbor's Wife* and *Thou Shalt Not Worship Craven Images* were two you felt you really didn't need," he joked, "because you either didn't really understand them, or you felt they really didn't apply to you."

I smiled and nodded in agreement. He was right.

"What about: *Thou Shalt Not Kill?"*

Before I could even formulate an answer, Harris picked up my train of thought.

"When a Catholic breaks one of the Ten Commandments, it's a Mortal Sin, isn't it?"

"Yes sir, it is."

"And if you die with a Mortal Sin on your soul, you've been taught that you'll go to Hell, haven't you?"

Chagrined, I again nodded.

"So tell me, Patrick. As you look through your scope into the very eyes of the man that you are about to murder, aren't you about to break one of God's most sacred laws?"

He was correct. "You're right. I would be."

"Would that cause you to pause and reflect on what you're about to do?"

"Yes sir, I guess it would."

"Well, you're not alone. It affects all of us. As good Christians, we can't help it. But let's examine those four powerful words: *Thou Shalt Not Kill.* Does it literally mean you should not kill? Period? Or does it mean: *Thou Shalt Not MURDER?* His steely eyes once again closely examined me. "Is there a difference? I think that there is."

"I am not a murderer. But if I don't kill my enemy, he is bound and determined to kill me. That's just the very nature of war itself. If I don't kill my enemy, he'll kill me, or my fellow soldiers, or even my friends and family. That's why we fight. It's your job, your duty, to kill each other until one side gets sick and tired of being killed, or until they run out of people to be killed. Remember, they are also hunting you. They want to kill you, perhaps more than you ever thought you wanted to kill them. You have to want to kill them in return. You have to be able to take comfort from the fact that this man in your sights will have to pay with his life for trying to take your life, or the lives of your fellow soldiers. That is the very creed you have to live by, the very moral defining force that will allow you to pull that trigger, time and time again."

Lt. Col. Harris was passionate, "To stay alive, you've got to be able to kill when the time comes. You can't have any compunction against killing, but you do have to have compassion. You also have to have a conscience. If you're killing wantonly, then you're worthless to me as an asset. I don't want a man who will kill just for the sake of killing. You have to be able to kill for a purpose."

"I hope I am never put in that situation, sir."

He slowly exhaled, winding down to his conclusion. "I sense in you the makings of a great shooter, Patrick. Not just a good shooter, a great shooter. We've spent a lot of time together over the past few months, and I've seen a lot of things I like and admire about you. In all my years of teaching, I can't ever recall a brighter or more willing student than you have been. It's too bad you're not a Marine with a war to fight because I would have liked to turn you loose in the field to see how well you'd do."

His compliment made my chest puff with pride.

"One last secret, Patrick—there were days out here on that rifle range when I was deliberately late, just so that you could enjoy the '03 Springfield a little while extra." He smiled in self-satisfaction, turned and walked away.

WHEN I RETURNED home from Quantico, Pam brought me up-to-date on all of the news. I was amazed to see how fast Tim was growing. I realized I had missed his first steps, his first words, his first everything. I didn't mind the personal sacrifice because I knew that I was making the world a safer place for my wife and my son. But, I was a little sad, and I regretted that Pam had to spend so much time alone.

In my absence, Pam had allowed herself to be drawn deeper into Jackie's family problems. Jackie had stopped by one day to deliver a cute sweater outfit for Tim then had unburdened herself to Pam over more than a few cups of Nescafe. Pam was distraught that Jackie was upset and despondent over how Jack's family treated her.

"I don't think she'll ever be accepted into the Kennedy family. Jackie said they are a very overbearing bunch, even obnoxious. They have their own private jokes, she said, and they smugly tell them in such a way to make it clear she is not part of their group."

I bit my tongue and refrained from comment as Pam continued. "I hate girls that gang up on someone to simply make fun of them for the sport of it. And that's what they're doing, Patrick. Jackie said they are all loud and boisterous roughnecks. They called her 'the Debutante' or 'the Deb' right to her face—and even made fun of how she talked by trying to imitate her wispy little-girl voice."

Pam was so incensed at the Kennedy girls' treatment of Jackie that I tried to gently intercede. "Pam, honey, Jackie has to fight her own battles."

"But she won't. That's not her way. She's too refined, too sensitive. Jackie told me she was at one of the Kennedy family gatherings and had happened to mention in passing she had always dreamed of being a ballet dancer. One of the girls blurted out, 'With those clodhoppers of yours? You'd be better off going out for soccer!' Patrick, Jackie was mortified—they snickered about what they called her 'over-sized manly-looking' hands and feet."

I tried to commiserate, "You can't fight her battles for her."

Pam glared at me. "I know that, Patrick. But it just pisses me off she's treated that way. She doesn't deserve that."

"Well, all I can say is, whenever she gets tired of it, she'll do something about it."

AS MUCH AS I enjoyed Quantico, I was glad to be back at my desk at the Agency. I was pouring over a stack of reports trying to decide which one to read first when Tracy Barnes slapped me on the back. "Patrick, get ready to pack your bags."

Before I could even reply, he said, "You did a great job for us in Iran. We need to have you on our team for the next project. Are you interested?"

"Yes sir. Of course I am, sir!" I replied.

He saw me shuffling through the reports which had managed to topple over. "Read the report on Guatemala. We'll have a briefing this week."

The report discussed our easy success in Tehran which led Allen Dulles and the top brass at the Agency to conclude that the CIA could, through covert political action, easily change the politics of almost any country in the world. The report said that our job, and probably our job alone, would be to make the world a safer place. Best of all, because we weren't United States military, whatever we did was deniable by the President.

Our coup in Iran started over oil. Our coup in Guatemala started over bananas. Guatemala was one of the poorest places in the Western Hemisphere, if not the entire world. In 1936, John Foster Dulles set up a banana monopoly in Guatemala for his United States client, the United Fruit Company. By 1950, United Fruit virtually ran the tiny country. The company owned most of the land, almost all of the railroad tracks, the telephone and the telegraph companies, and it owned the most important Atlantic seaport. Anything modern belonged to United Fruit. Anything else, old or broken down, belonged to the nation of Guatemala—the term, "Banana Republic," aptly described Guatemala.

The trouble started in 1952 when Jacobo Arbenz, an ardent land reformer, took control of the Guatemalan government. That summer, the National Assembly of Guatemala eagerly passed a radical land reform bill—passionately championed by Arbenz—allowing about 234,000 acres of United Fruit land along the Pacific coast to be seized by February 1953.

And to make matters worse, the Congress of Guatemala stood for one minute of silence on March 12, 1953, to honor the late Joseph Stalin. To Allen Dulles and the rest of the Agency hierarchy, Guatemala's actions assumed ominous worldwide significance—providing us with the rationale to intervene in Guatemala. Guatemala was the only country in the entire Western Hemisphere to pay homage to the deceased Communist dictator. The report concluded that the United States could not allow a beachhead of Soviet influence to be established in Central America within easy reach of the Panama Canal.

Because of my experience in Iran, Mr. Dulles called me into a conference with my CIA superiors. Our meeting laid the groundwork for a program called Operation PBSuccess, which we later shortened to Operation Success. Tracy Barnes suggested we essentially pull out our Iranian playbook and simply tweak it a little. Instead of hiring local mobs, he suggested we create a fictional liberation army, populated by Guatemalan exiles. The exiles could launch an invasion of their homeland from neighboring Honduras in order to simulate a broad popular uprising against Arbenz. We hoped Arbenz would think that a revolution was starting and flee the country, just the way Mossadegh did in Iran.

I was assigned to act as the Agency's eyes-and-ears on the ground in Guatemala. I was responsible for coordinating all facets of the ground operation and keeping my superiors posted about our progress. In plain English, it meant I would be told what to do while everyone else was safely out of harm's way back in D.C. Once again I suspected I was simply cannon fodder, but this time I had a Top Secret security clearance badge.

Two other Agency operatives, E. Howard Hunt and David Atlee Phillips were under my direct supervision. David Atlee Phillips, a charming though unsuccessful actor from Broadway, was recruited for his good looks and his ability to speak Spanish. Hunt, our logistics expert, had been with the Agency for about five years and was a loud-mouthed braggart with a flair for the dramatic. He wrote trashy dime novels of imaginary daring-do, with spy thrillers as his chosen genre. He became so combative, argumentative, and hard to control that I finally forced him to stay back in Opa Locka, Florida at our secondary command center.

On June 15, I accompanied Mr. Dulles, Frank Wisner, Tracy Barnes, and Richard Bissell to the White House. Mr. Dulles needed the President's final approval for the mission. The President's secretary seated us on a divan to await Mr. Eisenhower. I wondered how many important people had once sat in this very same place—I was overcome by the majesty of the Oval Office. Soon, a door opened and the President entered. We immediately stood.

"Please be seated, gentlemen. Mr. Bissell and Mr. Barnes have briefed me on Operation Success. I was impressed with their clear, concise synopsis of the plan."

I slowly let out my breath. I hadn't realized I had been holding it in.

"But, a word of warning—I want you all to be damn good and sure that you succeed."

Mr. Bissell spoke, "We will succeed, sir."

"This is very important to the future well-being of our nation. I've placed great faith in the ability of the Agency to carry out these tasks. This will be your greatest test yet. The security of our country rests, in part, in your hands. Be confident in your plans, and be confident in your ultimate success."

He stood up. It was our cue that the meeting was over. The President was an imposing man. His demeanor was stern when he looked each of us in the eye and said, "Remember this above all else! When you commit the flag, you commit it to win!"

The gravity of his words hit me squarely in the stomach.

As we shook hands to leave, President Eisenhower spoke directly to me, "Patrick, I'm glad to see you again, son. Mr. Barnes told me of your heroic exploits in Iran. Good work."

"Thank you, Mr. President," I stammered. "It was an operation that went as well as we planned it to. I was fortunate to serve with other brave and talented individuals."

"So you were, Patrick. When I heard that you were taking part in the planning of Operation Success, I told Allen I felt a little more confident about giving permission to proceed. Keep up the good work. I'll be keeping my eye on you!"

"Yes sir, I will, sir."

As the President firmly shook my hand, he leaned in and whispered, "By the way, when are you going to invite me back over to play some poker at your place?"

"Anytime you wish, sir. Anytime you wish."

My heart pounded with pride as I left the Oval Office. I was overwhelmed with the knowledge that I, an ordinary American, had personally met with the President about a mission that involved protecting the security of the United States of America.

I don't even remember my feet touching the ground until we were outside the White House gates.

ON JUNE 17, we found the news of our secret invasion had somehow slipped out in Guatemala. Ironically, it was the school-age son of Ambassador Peurifoy who broke the news. It seems the training camp mercenaries had widely boasted to their friends and families that they were going to liberate Guatemala. When Ambassador Peurifoy's son came home early from school, he told his father that school had been cancelled for the afternoon because the revolution was scheduled to begin at 5 p.m.

On the morning of June 18, I followed through on my orders and gave the signal for the invasion to get underway. Tracy Barnes' handpicked rebel leader, Castillo Armas, led the charge. Wearing a checkered shirt instead of a standard military uniform, Armas drove a beat-up old station wagon across the Honduras border into Guatemala followed by two hundred of his trained troops. Armas' mission was to capture two important strategic points in Guatemala: a rail junction at Zacapa and the main port of Puerto Barrios. Unfortunately, his troops had other ideas. They marched six miles into Guatemala from Honduras and then refused to budge, preferring to take a siesta instead. No one fired a single shot.

Once the land invasion had begun, our rebel air force took control of the skies. One of our crack pilots, a former American skywriter, flew over Guatemala City and dropped leaflets announcing the upcoming revolution. Our second pilot flew over the military installation in Puerto Barrios in an antique Cessna, dropping Coke bottles filled with gasoline on the targets below. The bombs made lots of loud noises but caused almost no real damage. Our third pilot was assigned to knock out the government's radio station, but he actually ended up destroying the radio transmitter belonging to some American holy-roller missionaries. Two of our Cessnas were shot out of the sky by pistol and rifle fire on the ground. Another crash-landed just over the border into Mexico because he forgot, in all of his excitement, to put fuel in his plane's gas tank.

I directed our Agency station chief in Guatemala City to send a cable to D.C. advising them our bombing effort was "absolutely pathetic." Needless to say, the Guatemalan people did not rise up to join their liberators. By the morning of June 19, the invasion looked laughably inept—so much so that Mr. Dulles, when interviewed, stated that the reports of unmarked planes bombing Guatemala City were a hoax.

By June 20, I sent another cable warning everyone in our planning group "the outcome of the efforts to overthrow the regime of President Arbenz of Guatemala remains very much in doubt. The controlling factor in the situation is…the position of the Guatemalan armed forces, and thus far, this group has not given any clear indication of whether it will move, and if so, in which way. If the effort does not succeed in arousing the other latent forces of resistance within the next period of approximately 24 hours, it will probably begin to lose strength."

I grew concerned about our central command in D.C. It was readily apparent in the many cables I received that their morale was fading. Mr. Bissell suggested we call the whole thing off. It reminded me of how Beetle Smith had lost confidence in us while we were in the middle of the Iranian coup. I remembered President Eisenhower's rousing pep talk in which he told us: "Remember this above all else! When you commit the flag, you commit it to win!" I personally did not want to stand in front of President Eisenhower and admit we had failed in our mission.

I redirected our method of attack from a land invasion to an invasion of the airwaves.

FROM THE ROOF of the American Embassy in Guatemala City, David Atlee Phillips broadcast phony war bulletins—giving minute by minute reports of the invasion through his *Voice of Liberation* radio. Phillips became more and more creative with each passing hour, breathlessly reporting heavy government casualties in a variety of fictional pitched battles. He called upon the Guatemalan people to rise up against their Communist bosses. He employed classic disinformation techniques to start rumors and to spread fear. One broadcast began: "It is *not* true that the waters of Lake Atitlan have been poisoned." Another stated: "At our command post here in the jungle, we are unable to confirm or deny the report that Castillo Armas [the rebel leader] has an army of 5,000 men."

Phillip's reports helped to inflate the level of the imaginary enemy. Phillips warned the Guatemalan army that Arbenz planned to betray them and arm the peasants. Suddenly, the Guatamelan officers were listening—and one air force colonel attracted our attention when he unexpectedly defected. Phillips sent his men to persuade the colonel to broadcast an appeal to his fellow officers—to encourage them to throw down their arms and join him. But the colonel was too scared. Someone offered him a drink. Soon the colonel was absolutely stinking drunk and began to rant about the necessity of rising up against Arbenz. His fiery and drunken harangue against the government was secretly taped, and while the colonel slept off his hangover the next day, Phillips broadcast his rousing speech on the *Voice of Liberation* radio to the entire Guatemalan nation.

Our Agency radio station jammed the real government radio station. The message was incessant—the government troops faltered and refused to fight—the liberation troops relentlessly moved toward Guatemala City— Guatemala City prepared for capture. Over the course of three days, our

P-51's made "bombing runs" over the capital city. The planes really didn't do much more damage than the Coca-Cola bottle bombs of our little Cessnas, but it was enough to frighten the Guatemalan army officers, who feared that the rebel army was backed by the United States.

The *Voice of Liberation* radio continued to broadcast—two huge columns of rebel soldiers were almost on top of Guatemala City—the final battle was about to take place. Thinking they were defeated, the Guatemalan officers pressured Arbenz to step aside for a military junta. Arbenz promptly resigned, obviously convinced that a full-scale American intervention was imminent.

AFTER THE TRIUMPH of Operation Success, I was awarded the Distinguished Intelligence Medal, the Agency's second highest honor. (The highest honor was always awarded posthumously.) I also received another nice promotion, and my pay grade was increased significantly, commensurate with my higher-level security clearance.

Gratified and proud, President Eisenhower summoned the members of Operation Success to the White House for a formal briefing. "Gentlemen, I'm proud of you, and the country owes you its gratitude. The odds were always against you, but you managed to pull off an operation that was beyond the ability of the State Department and the Pentagon."

We left the Oval Office that day thinking we had learned a valuable lesson for our nation's future. Once again, this operation reminded us of our success in Iran. And, just like Iran, this operation had also proved too easy.

Our hubris would come back to haunt us all later.

WHILE I SAVED the Western Hemisphere's supply of bananas, Pam raised our son and worried about Jackie who was deeply concerned over her husband's health. I had been home only a few days and was looking forward to a little rest and relaxation. I knew that Pam wanted to bring me up-to-date on Jack's condition, but I had been avoiding the topic.

I was listening to a radio broadcast of the Washington Senators baseball game—the score was 6-4 in the top of the ninth inning and the Senators were at bat. Grant had bet me a steak dinner that the Senators would lose. So far the season had been dismal for the Senators—they had more losses than wins—but I was a diehard fan. I kept my fingers crossed that they could beat the Red Sox, hoping it would be Grant, not me, buying the steak dinner. Just as the pitcher wound up and released the ball to the batter, Pam came into the room.

"Hey honey, I looked up Addison's disease in a medical dictionary."

I leaned into the radio so that Pam would take the hint that I was listening to the game.

"Do you have any idea how serious Jack's condition actually is?"

"Nope," then feeling a little guilty, I added, "Isn't it that shaking condition?"

"No, that's Parkinson's disease. Addison's is completely different."

"Oh."

"It's actually life-threatening. The dictionary said it affects the adrenal glands."

The Senators were two runs ahead. They had a good chance of winning, so I turned my attention to Pam.

"According to this, our adrenal glands produce steroid hormones, and they affect the function of virtually every organ system in the body. When you get Addison's disease, the adrenal glands fail to produce enough steroid hormones."

"So what does that mean?"

"It means that Jack's entire immune system has been severely compromised by the disease. He's very susceptible to infection. In fact, his life expectancy may be severely shortened because of it. Now, I understand why Jackie is so worried."

I suddenly felt sorry for the poor guy. I didn't like Jack at all, but he didn't deserve to die. "What's the prognosis?"

Pam's eyes were misty with tears. "Jackie told me Jack has to take cortisone pills orally every day of his life, just to stay alive. He also has a massive dose of cortisone pellets implanted underneath his skin every three months to boost his protection."

"That sounds pretty serious."

"It is serious. I guess his father is so worried about him that he has secretly stashed cortisone tablets in bank safety deposit boxes all over the world—just in case Jack needs emergency access on one of his trips away from home."

"Geez Pam, that sounds truly awful."

"I know. Jackie is so worried about him she's almost sick herself. Jack's spine has deteriorated so much—he's desperate for relief from his back pain. He needs surgery, but no reputable surgeon in Boston will even consider taking him as a patient. They all know that Addison patients are too easily susceptible to infection after any operation, and the possible resulting infection could easily kill him. Jackie said she's afraid that he is willing to risk dying to stop the pain. He's been secretly shopping around for any doctors to perform the surgery."

"What's he going to do?"

"I don't know." Pam leaned over and kissed me, "I'm glad we're both healthy." She looked at the clock, "I've got to get Tim to bed. You stay here and finish your game. Later, you can join me upstairs for a little game of our own."

When I returned to the game, the Red Sox had managed to score three runs in the bottom of the ninth to win the game seven to six. Damn.

ON OCTOBER 21, 1954, Jack underwent a double spinal fusion to remove a metal disc Naval surgeons had implanted in his spine in 1944 after the wreck of PT-109. Three days after the operation, Kennedy contracted a staph infection of his urinary tract and hovered near death. He was placed on the critical list and shortly thereafter, lapsed into a coma, from which the doctors told the family he would probably not wake up. The hospital twice summoned the family for what might have been his final hours and twice a priest administered the last rites.

Jack finally emerged from the coma in mid-November and was able to feebly sit up in bed. He had defied the odds and lived to tell about it, but he still faced a long period of recuperation.

Obviously, Jack was unable to perform any of his legislative duties. Everyone in the Senate wished him well in his recovery. Grant told me he had never heard Dick Nixon so emotionally distraught before. Grant, a natural mimic, lowered his chin, slightly shaking his head and in a gruff voice imitated Dick's distress. "Poor brave Jack is going to die. Oh God, don't let him die!" Nixon even sent a note to Jack's hospital bed pledging he would never, ever, use his vice presidential power as President of the Senate to break a tie vote until Jack was well enough to cast his own vote.

Jack, however, was about to become the center of attention in a vote to censure Senator Joseph McCarthy.

Joe McCarthy, who had become effective in ferreting out the Communist menace in our own government and who had been described as the second most powerful man in the country at the start of the New Year, now faced growing opposition. Though I had admired Joe, now I just felt bad for him. He had finally gone overboard with his intimidating tactics, accusations, and character assassinations.

Joe's heavy-handed tactics had worn out even his staunchest supporters when he lambasted a genuine war hero, Brigadier General Ralph W. Zwicker, in front of his Senate committee hearing. Joe made a huge blunder when he decided to take on the Army after one of his young legislative aides had been erroneously drafted. Incensed, Joe claimed the gentlemen's agreement protecting congressional aides from the draft had been intentionally violated.

Joe lambasted Zwicker: he was "not fit to wear that uniform"—he should be "removed from any command"—he did not have "the brains of a five-year-old child." The Pentagon brass protested Zwicker's treatment. He countered with a bold accusation: "beyond any shadow of a doubt…certain individuals in the Army have been promoting, covering up, and honorably discharging known Communists." He accused the Army of attempting to "blackmail" him into calling off his "exposure of Communists" by holding his former legislative aide as a "hostage."

People on both sides of the Army-McCarthy hearings placed a great deal of political pressure on Jack Kennedy to take a stand on McCarthy. Jack stubbornly refused to reveal what he planned to do. Jackie later told Pam that Jack had written out two speeches for the occasion—one speech explained why he was voting against the censure of McCarthy, and the other explained why he was voting for it.

Kennedy had three real problems voting against the rabid anti-Communist. Number one: Tailgunner Joe had been a longtime ally of the Kennedy family, and Jack's father was one of McCarthy's biggest political contributors. Number two: Two of Jack's own sisters, Pat and Eunice, had at one time dated the Wisconsin senator. Number three: Jack was enough of a political realist that he understood the idea of one Roman Catholic Senator (Kennedy) voting to humiliate another Roman Catholic Senator (McCarthy) would not sit very well with the Catholic voters of his state who were staunchly pro-McCarthy.

In the end, Jack did exactly what Jack always did when the going got rough: he ducked the issue altogether. He became the *only* Senator not to cast a vote on McCarthy. He didn't even bother to cast an absentee vote.

He avoided any potential controversy—by simply not voting at all.

"A nation that can not preserve itself ought to die, and it will die— die in the grasp of the evils it is too feeble to overthrow."

— Senator Morris Sheppard

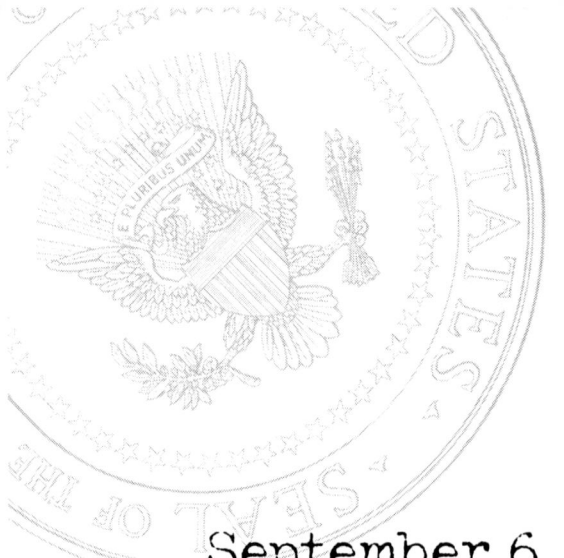

September 6, 1978
1:36 p.m.

Grant folded his hands to stop their quivering. He had barked and snapped at his secretary so much that morning that she finally went home early with an upset stomach. Fine. She was only getting in the way.

The phone rang on the private line Grant had given Ruger. He didn't want to pick it up.

"Tell me you've got some good news, Ruger."

"I've got good news alright, but only for McCarthy. We haven't found him yet."

Grant could feel the heavy ball in the pit of his stomach growing. "What do you know?"

"Nothing. Every man I have is out scouring the area, and no one has turned up anything as of yet."

"Goddamn it, Derek, McCarthy couldn't have just disappeared—just like that. Have you checked to see if his passport has been used?"

Disdainfully Ruger replied, "I doubt if he would travel on his own passport. I'm checking for aliases now."

"How could you possibly find that out?" Grant waited for a response and was ready to launch into another tirade when he realized Ruger had hung up on him again.

Goddamn it.

1955

FOR LESS THAN $20 million, we drove Communism out of the Western Hemisphere in our Guatemala operation. Unfortunately, we lost one man in the process. One of our couriers infiltrated Guatemala prior to the invasion and tried to join a partisan group—they thought he was an Arbenz spy, so they shot him.

President Eisenhower found it incredible that we had accomplished the overthrow of a foreign government for so little cost. I actually felt just the opposite. The overthrow of Mossadegh in Iran only cost $100,000. The overthrow of Arbenz was two hundred times more expensive just one year later—a trend that was disturbing to me.

We now focused our attention on the Panamanian President Jose Antonio Remon who we perceived as a threat to our country. Unlike Iran and Guatemala, our game plan of creating civilian unrest or agitating the military wasn't feasible in Panama. The Agency introduced a new plan for regime change—Executive Action.

Executive Action was a euphemism for the assassination of a foreign leader. It was the most economical way to effect foreign policy change—if it could be done without leaving any trace of our involvement.

The idea of assassinating the leader of another country didn't bother the Soviets. In our intensifying war against Communism, we felt compelled to employ whatever means necessary to stop the Soviet threat. If that meant we had to do what they did, then so be it. However, our role in any assassination had to be so thoroughly disguised that if our mechanics were caught, any involvement on the part of the United States could be denied.

On January 1, 1955, I flew to a meeting in Honduras with Vice President Nixon where we were briefed on the plan to assassinate President Remon. The security of the Panama Canal, and by extension, the security of the United States, was at stake. The protection of the nation, and the protection of my own family, was more important than the life of one crazy Latin American Communist-leaning dictator. I remembered the lessons of Lt. Col. Harris as the hit team gave us the details of the mission. I felt rather emotionally detached as the various aspects of killing a man in cold blood were discussed.

The following day, President Remon was machine-gunned to death at a racetrack outside of Panama City.

SHORTLY AFTER I returned from Honduras, Richard Bissell summoned me to his office. We met in a conference room which was little more than a long table surrounded by several mismatched chairs. Frank Wisner and Tracy Barnes were sorting through documents and files that were strewn across the table. Barnes made an attempt to straighten the mess when he saw me walk through the door. Both Frank and Tracy stood, extended their hands, and alternately congratulated me for my work in Panama.

"You're the man of the hour," Tracy said, "Good job, Patrick."

Frank added, "You've passed another Agency test with flying colors." I had not known that I was under such scrutiny. Before I could respond, Mr. Bissell entered.

"Take your seats, gentlemen." Bissell surveyed the disorder on the table. I saw a slight glimmer of annoyance cross his face.

"Patrick. First let me congratulate you on your work in Panama."

"Thank you, sir."

"We were lucky. The execution of the mission was pristine. Nonetheless, we have to be more concerned about blowback in the future."

"I'm not familiar with that term, sir."

"Any Executive Action is risky. Blowback occurs when the assassination of a foreign leader blows back into our faces. Ideally, we would like to make the death look like a natural occurrence though that is not always possible. What would happen if our operative were captured, or worse yet, if he revealed the origin of the mission? We also have to consider what would happen if our man was stricken by conscience and was unable to complete his mission."

Frank spoke, "We have to cover all the bases."

Mr. Bissell continued, "I called you, Patrick, because it is now time for you to spend some time on our Technical Services Staff."

Technical Services Staff was a think tank made up of intelligence officers and mad scientists. Bissell continued, "Both Wisner and Barnes have been working on surveillance and electronic eavesdropping. You need to familiarize yourself with their techniques and procedures."

"Our task is to oversee the development of special cameras, recorders, and telephone taps," Tracy added. "TSS has come up with some ingenious bugging devices."

"TSS has an even more important task: to research and develop weapons," Bissell paused, "weapons that would dumbfound even the imagination of the Pentagon."

"The more sophisticated we are in gathering data, the less likely there will be blowback," Tracy explained. "Ultimately, we would like to execute an Executive Action without leaving any trace of our involvement."

Frank interjected, "We're considering how we could develop a weapon that could be aimed at a particular target from a very long distance without being traced back to us."

I think Mr. Bissell hoped that TSS could invent some sort of a death ray, an undetectable beam that could be aimed at a target from long distances. TSS had worked long and hard on the concept, but never came close to achieving success.

I considered what Lt. Colonel Harris had taught me about snipers. "That's a very interesting proposition," I said.

Though I was excited about my new assignment, I was leery about working with TSS. TSS, a division cloaked in even more secrecy than normal, had a reputation for conducting bizarre experiments. Bissell initially assigned me to work with the surveillance and eavesdropping division. One of my first tasks involved a strange experiment that turned an animal into a walking bomb. Scientists surgically implanted a battery-driven guidance system inside a cat, using its tail as the antenna. On our very first remote-controlled outing, the addled cat wandered off the sidewalk where it was promptly run over and squished by a taxicab, thus ending the experiment.

After a brief stint in surveillance and electronic gadgets, I was assigned to work directly with Dr. Sydney Gottlieb, Assistant for Scientific Matters to the Clandestine Services Chief. The Agency knew the Soviets were experimenting with mind control weapons, and to the Agency, a Soviet mind control weapon was as threatening as an atomic weapon. The Agency ordered Dr. Gottlieb to conduct experiments that would allow us to detect and control any mind control substance.

Dr. Gottlieb began his study by experimenting with *Lysergic acid diethylamide*, an obscure drug rumored to lead to odd physiological activity. In 1952, the Agency had been warned that the Soviets planned to spike the cocktails of our American diplomats with LSD. An American military attaché in Switzerland reported that the Swiss chemical firm Sandoz, the only producer of LSD in the West, was preparing to sell the Russians 10 kilos (22 pounds) of LSD, enough for 100 million doses. The Agency feared the Soviet Union was attempting to buy up the world's supply of LSD.

Our military attaché made a grave mathematical error in his report—he confused a *milligram*, 1/1000 of a gram, with a *kilogram*, 1000 grams. According to the Sandoz chemists, their entire inventory of LSD was never more than 40 grams, which was about 1.5 ounces. Our informant's calculations were off by a factor of about one million-to-one.

His careless math error directly led to our high-priority involvement in LSD research.

ON APRIL 4, Frank Wisner's deputy in clandestine services, Richard Helms, sent an urgent proposal to Allen Dulles to expand our mind-control experiments. Helms wanted approval "to develop a capability in the covert use of biological and chemical materials." Helms referred to the project as MKULTRA.

Mr. Dulles finally approved it—but demanded that all work be done with the utmost secrecy.

All MKULTRA research would be done in-house. Mr. Dulles was concerned about the highly sensitive nature of the experiments. Everyone present acknowledged that the experiments could be construed to be unethical and perhaps illegal—which could lead to serious repercussions for the Agency if political and diplomatic circles discovered the true nature of the project. Neither the President nor Congress was to be informed of the existence of MKULTRA, and for obvious reasons, the American public had to be kept in the dark forever.

Just as Richard Bissell wanted to develop a long-range death ray to prevent blowback, the Agency feared the Russians would develop and perfect a new technology for controlling men's minds before we did. In the late 1940's, the Soviets held various "show trials" in Eastern Europe in which defendants with glazed eyes confessed to crimes they hadn't committed. In the Korean War, we intercepted reports of brainwashed captive U.S. soldiers acting like robots. In 1951, the Agency and the State Department suspected that our own ambassador to the Soviet Union, George Kennan, had somehow been drugged or had his mind altered. Kennan had appeared at a press conference in Berlin and made such inexplicably undiplomatic remarks that the Kremlin declared him persona non grata. What if he had been the victim of a Soviet mind control experiment? Could our political leaders and generals be similarly victimized down the road?

The Agency assigned me to the MKULTRA as an observer. I was to read all of the reports generated from the project and report directly back to Mr. Dulles. He privately told me to keep my eyes and ears open—and to speak only to him about my findings.

LSD was a terrifying drug. Virtually all of the experiments tested the effects and after effects of lysergic acid on personality and behavior—in unsuspecting victims. In November 1953, one of Dr. Gottlieb's top assistants, an Army civilian scientist named Frank Olson, was found dead under a broken tenth-floor window of the Statler Hotel in New York City. The unsuspecting Olson had been given 70 micrograms of LSD in a glass of Cointreau, by one of his Agency colleagues, as they sat discussing their research in New York.

Olson's colleagues closely observed his behavior after ingesting the drug. They noted Olson was intermittently boisterous and cheerful, then morose. At 2:30 a.m. on Saturday morning, the Agency officer sharing Olson's room reported he was awakened by a loud crash of glass and discovered that his roommate had jumped to his death. Olson died never knowing that the directors of MKULTRA had sealed his fate when they concluded "an unwitting experiment (victim) would be desirable." However, an unexpected suicide was not desirable.

Mr. Dulles severely reprimanded the Technical Services Staff. Although he was personally distressed over Olson's death, he rationalized that this was the price we often had to pay to maintain national security. The Agency went to great lengths to ensure that no one—especially Olson's family—knew the circumstances of his death or our involvement in his death. We were determined to cover it up forever.

The Agency continued with the covert LSD experiments—only they restricted the experiments to unwitting subjects outside the Agency. The Agency had a perfect venue for future experiments—whorehouses in Greenwich Village and San Francisco. Jokingly called Operation Midnight Climax, agents slipped mickeys into the drinks of the johns, who they then observed through two-way mirrors. The Agency also used drug addicts from the Addiction Research Center in Lexington, Kentucky. Seven Negroes were kept on LSD for seventy-seven straight days. None of them ever recovered from that experiment.

The experiments were a dismal failure. LSD was not a mind control drug—it was a mind-altering drug. Dr. Gottlieb and his behavioral research teams soon abandoned their LSD experiments and began to explore hypnosis. The program, code-named ARTICHOKE, promised to be the "ultimate experiment in hypnosis."

I was briefly assigned to monitor this program which involved the creation of a programmed assassin who could be manipulated with hypnotic suggestions. Mr. Dulles felt that the use of hypnosis could possibly be used in our Executive Action program.

On February 19, 1954, one of Dr. Gottlieb's researchers put an Agency secretary into a deep trance; then, he hypnotized a second Agency secretary. The second subject had been specifically selected because of her adamant fear of firearms. The second subject was instructed to try to wake her friend from a deep sleep. If she could not wake her up, she was instructed that she would feel rage, and "her rage would be so great that she would not hesitate to 'kill' her friend." Despite her known fear of guns, she picked up an unloaded handgun the scientist had planted in the room. Astonishingly, she coldly pulled the trigger on her sleeping friend when she was unable to wake her.

Once the scientist brought the secretary out of her trance, she vehemently denied having shot her friend—she exhibited total amnesia about the incident. According to the file, she maintained that she would never under any circumstances shoot anyone. The results were promising—the Agency might be able to control an assassin through hypnotic suggestion.

There were times that I was conflicted about the ethics of the Agency's experiments—especially when the Agency placed itself outside the law in order to protect the safety of America. I remembered what Mr. Hoover said to me in 1950: *"This battle between Americanism and un-Americanism is a struggle for the very soul of our nation. It's as dangerous as a battle between God and Lucifer himself."* Sometimes lives of the subjects were clearly placed in jeopardy, and sometimes various laws of the United States of America were clearly violated and ignored.

National security always had to come first—the ends truly did justify the means.

TWO MONTHS AFTER Jack Kennedy's operation, he was still in poor health. Jack weighed less than one hundred and twenty pounds and suffered with a surgical wound that would not heal. By February, the tissue around the new metal plate used in his spinal fusion had become infected; doctors suggested a bone graft. On February 15, 1955, Jack underwent a third operation—once again a Catholic priest administered the last rites. His family stayed at his bedside where he hovered between life and death.

Jack struggled to recover from his latest brush with death at his father's house in Palm Beach, Florida. He spent most of his time lying on his stomach in bed. Jackie did everything she could to keep his spirits up—she read him poetry, played his favorite records, told him the latest jokes, and kept him apprised of the latest gossip from D.C. During his ordeal, Jackie blossomed into the perfect wife. Jackie learned to change the dressings on his incision even though the ghastly eight-inch wound constantly oozed pus.

Though I had no respect for Jack Kennedy, I admired his fortitude and decided to cut him some slack. I hoped the bastard would change his ways and start treating Jackie with the respect and love Pam and I both felt she deserved.

During his recuperation, Jack authored a book on the political courage of eight United States Senators who had been forced to take unpopular but morally correct stands. When Jackie told me about it, I immediately thought he was going to feature Joe McCarthy. Then I recalled Jack had cut and run from his former friend in his greatest hour of need.

With the assistance from a small army of researchers and editors, Jackie helped Jack assemble the research material and even scribbled down dictation as Jack drafted ideas of his own. All of the material was then turned over to Jack's young assistant, Ted Sorensen, who did most of the actual writing of the book. When I heard that Jack intended to call his book, *Profiles in Courage*, I was quick to joke to Pam, "Obviously, it's not about him or his father." She didn't laugh.

Jackie's sister Lee took the finished book to her father-in-law at Harper and Brothers. The publisher's comments were so positively flattering that Jack boasted to his friends that he was a writer at heart, and he would "rather win a Pulitzer" than be elected president of the United States. I thought that was welcome news for the American electorate.

Though the pain in his back was horrendous, Jack returned to the floor of the Senate on May 24. Gingerly walking without crutches, he was warmly greeted by the leaders of both parties. Two days later, Jackie told Pam he visited Dr. Janet Travell, who prescribed a regimen of hot baths, massages, and exercises to strengthen his back muscles. Dr. Travell regularly began to inject his back with Novocaine, which provided instant but temporary relief. She suggested something more potent that would eliminate the pain in his back altogether—but the side effects of the drug would leave him numb from the waist down. Jack completely rejected that idea.

Jack had a litany of medical concerns. Tests had shown he was lactose intolerant; he had an unbelievably high cholesterol count; and, his thyroid was virtually inactive. Most devastating was sterility—the lingering effect of a genital disease he had contracted in college.

Jackie was crushed. She desperately wanted children and was anxious to start a family.

ON JULY 1, 1955, Richard Bissell summoned me to his office. I was looking forward to receiving a new assignment since my tenure with MKULTRA was drawing to a close.

Bissell's office conveyed his growing power with the agency. He was sitting behind a large mahogany desk in a comfortable leather chair when I entered. A few brief moments of pleasantries ensued before he got down to business.

"I've chosen you to be part of the new Development Projects Staff or DPS. I think you have the skills and background necessary to enhance the team."

"Thank you, sir." I tried to contain my enthusiasm as he presented the proposal.

"If you are agreeable to undertake this project, you are in. It will require your undivided attention for an extended period of time."

I knew that Pam would not be excited about me being away from home. I hadn't been around as much as she wanted me to be. I felt guilty that my family was second to the demands of my job; yet as far as Mr. Bissell was concerned, any concerns about my family would be the kiss of death to my career. I had to be careful about how I broke the news to Pam.

"We're drawing $22 million from the CIA's reserve fund for a special program. We won't need congressional oversight on this project. The project is extremely important to our national security—we don't need the extra scrutiny from congressmen, or senators for that matter, who know nothing about us."

"I see, sir." He now had my full attention.

"It's been designated Project Aquatone. If you perform as well as I think you will, it's going to be the next stepping stone of your career."

"Thank you for your confidence in me, sir."

"I assume you want in," he asked.

"It would be an honor to be part of the team," I answered. I knew that the Agency had been carefully watching my performance. There was no way that I was going to turn down this opportunity. I asked, "Just what is Project Aquatone?"

"We are building a state-of-the-art spy plane," he smiled.

"Mr. Bissell, I have no background in aeronautics. I don't know anything about airplanes or even how to build them."

"That's OK—neither do I," he dismissed my concern. "We've already got a group of twenty-nine talented engineers at Lockheed working on the project. What's important is that we get this spy plane in the air as soon as possible. The Agency is alarmed about the complete lack of information on Soviet military progress. The Pentagon believes the Soviets are planning a future atomic attack. We just don't know how and when it might occur. Millions of innocent Americans could be killed. We have to know what the Soviets are up to—and we need to know now."

"I agree, sir. I've read numerous reports about German scientists who had been detained by the Soviets at the end of the war. They left the Soviet Union with disturbing stories of Soviet research into surface-to-surface missile technology."

"I believe the threat is even greater than that, Patrick. We have reliable reports that before his death, Stalin had ordered the development of long range nuclear bombers which were capable of striking the United States."

"That is a terrifying thought, sir."

"Yes it is—considering the Iron Curtain is virtually impregnable to our traditional espionage techniques. It is far easier for the Soviets to collect information on us than it is for us to collect information on them."

"We live in an open democracy while they live in a closed totalitarian society," I added.

"And that's the crux of the problem. To date, we have failed miserably at collecting information from deep behind the Iron Curtain. What information we have obtained has been at great cost—a number of very good agents have been killed in the process."

Bissell resumed, "You may recall that President Eisenhower said that 'Modern weapons (have) made it easier for a hostile nation with a closed society to plan an attack in secrecy and thus gain an advantage denied to the nation with an open society.' We need accurate information, and we need it soon. We need to understand the size of the Soviet military threat in order to insure the safety of our nation. After all, our own bombers are useless if they don't know what to bomb, or where to bomb."

"Will the spy plane be a state-of-the art bomber?"

"Nope. It will actually be an unarmed photo-reconnaissance aircraft. The most valuable means of securing the vital and useful information we need is through photographs."

"Yes, but how are we going to do that? The Soviets will never allow us to come in and take pictures."

"That's why we need this spy plane. We need military aerial reconnaissance. I don't need to tell you that such reconnaissance would be considered an act of military aggression—if we are detected. Overflights of another country's sovereign territory are highly illegal—but it's only a problem if they are detected."

Overflights occur when a government aircraft, expressly on the direction of a head of state, traverses the territory of another country in peacetime without that other country's permission. Theoretically, a head of state must ask permission to enter sovereign airspace of another country. No leader in his right mind would allow his enemy to fly military aircraft over his sovereign borders and boundaries. Such overflights are considered highly illegal, and are actually considered to be an act of war.

"I'm not sure I am following…"

Bissell tilted slightly back in his chair and continued, "Our own Air Force has conducted overflights all along the borders of the Soviet Union and its satellite states since 1946. We have been able to collect some information on the disposition of Soviet forces behind the Iron Curtain."

I waited for him to pause and then interjected, "Yes, but the Soviet Foreign Ministry has always vigorously protested the intrusion of American bombers over Soviet territorial waters."

"True. Our previous techniques always involved the deliberate provocation of the Soviets."

I was familiar with the technique. One of our planes would make a hostile pass, while our second plane would follow to observe the Soviets' defensive countermeasures. By 1952, the Soviets had gotten good enough with their MIG-15's to intercept and photograph us. At that point, our air force together with theirs made a tacit gentlemen's agreement not to initiate hostile actions.

"You will also remember that the Soviets finally lost patience with us and simply began shooting our airplanes down without warning. Many brave American fliers were lost and killed. That's where Project Aquatone comes in," Bissell paused, "and you come in."

I anxiously waited for the details.

"The congressional sub-panel on intelligence has accepted our proposal to create a reconnaissance airplane capable of flying completely undetected over the entire length of the Soviet Union to take surveillance photographs. In order to do that, we have enlisted the aid of Clarence "Kelly" Johnson of Lockheed Aviation to join our secret Agency team to help us design and build just such a unique, one-of-a-kind airplane," Bissell leaned back in his chair. "It will be the most remarkable spy plane ever developed."

The most remarkable spy plane ever developed? I couldn't imagine what my role would be.

"Acknowledging the urgency of this mission—to the national security of America—Kelly Johnson has pledged his Lockheed's resources for the creation of our super spy plane. Johnson also pledges that this plane of ours will be in the air and flying within eight months of us giving him the go-ahead."

I realized I was sitting on the edge of my chair. To create a super spy plane in less than eight months would be a real testament to the American "can-do" spirit.

"Patrick, I need you to help me supervise Project Aquatone. I can't be out there all the time, so you will act as my eyes and ears at Lockheed. Say goodbye to your family for a while and prepare to help us make history."

Lockheed's legendary "Skunk Works," which had created the first

American jet fighter in 1943, was about to add another impressive accomplishment to its history,

I couldn't wait to leave for California.

SHORTLY AFTER THE Fourth of July, I arrived at Burbank Airport outside of Los Angeles and headed to Building 82, a dilapidated old bomber production facility left over from World War II.

The Skunk Works was a ramshackle facility. The windows were painted black; a bluish-white fog of cigarette and cigar smoke hung in the air. Every square inch of space was crammed with drafting tables, drill presses, and metal lathes. Bird poop and feathers dotted the floors and furniture. Whenever the old hangar doors were occasionally opened to let in some fresh air, birds flew up the stairwell to the small balcony area where they swooped around the drawing boards. The birds knocked themselves out flying into the blacked-out windows.

I understood the significance of the Skunk Works name after touring the facility. The name was taken from the 'Lil Abner comic strip which featured an eccentric character who stirred up a mysterious brew that consisted of old shoes and miscellaneous pieces of junk and was flavored with dead skunk. Since our shop was right next to Lockheed's plastics area, it smelled just like the imaginary cartoon strip site must have smelled, and so Skunk Works became its new name.

Since security concerns prohibited outsiders like janitors or secretaries from coming in, the Skunk Works was like an out-of-control frat house. We hung framed centerfolds of gorgeous babes in swimsuits that could be quickly flipped around to reveal reproductions of waterfowl on the other side. On the rare occasions when a high-level visitor like Mr. Bissell was shown through the offices, someone would yell out "Present Ducks!" We'd quickly flip over our framed pictures of full-breasted beauties to reveal a different kind of breasted beauty.

Everyone who worked there had a nickname or a secret code name. Mr. Bissell became known as "Mr. B." One engineer named Ben Rich chose the nickname "Ben Dover" for himself, although everyone else called him "Broad Butt" after he won a contest in the office to see who had the biggest behind as measured by a set of calipers. I was nicknamed "Casper" for the Friendly Ghost of comic-book fame. That nickname puzzled me, and I finally had to ask them how they arrived at the name "Casper." The head test pilot, Tony LeVier, replied, "Well, you are a spook, aren't ya?"

The young guys who worked with us were dedicated engineers who lived to design and build airplanes—they were brainy, witty, and high-spirited.

Their airplane was the strangest and most unusual aircraft I had ever laid eyes on. The fuselage was not even fifty feet long, but the wings spanned more than eighty feet.

The plane was essentially a jet-powered glider. The emphasis in its design and construction was on weight savings. Each pound of weight cost our plane one foot of altitude. The engineers even eliminated the normal landing gear to reduce the weight. Kelly loved to say he would "trade his grandma" for several pounds of weight saving. Thus, every time the engineers saved a pound, it was known as a "grandma."

The goal was to design a spy plane which could fly at an altitude of over 70,000 feet, putting it three miles out of the reach of the very best Soviet fighter plane. The unique aluminum skin of the plane was roughly comparable to Reynold's Wrap, only two one-hundredths of an inch thick. Three 5/8-inch bolts held the entire tail section of the plane together.

Besides the specially modified Pratt & Whitney J57 jet engine, the rest of the airplane was essentially one big fuel tank. Because our plane was designed to fly at altitudes in excess of 70,000 feet, standard military JP-4 jet fuel couldn't be used because it would freeze in the minus 70 degree centigrade temperatures of high altitude. Mr. B convinced the Shell Oil Company to concoct a special jet fuel for us without even knowing what it was for. It smelled very similar to the Ronson fluid used in our Zippo cigarette lighters, but a match wouldn't ignite it—it was chemically similar to FLIT, a popular bug-spray. Once our airplane became operational during the summer of 1955, Shell diverted tens of thousands of gallons of FLIT fuel for our airplane, inadvertently triggering a nationwide shortage of mosquito repellent.

The most prized part of our spy plane was the pressurized area of the fuselage ahead of the engine. This was the payload area containing the cameras and other delicate reconnaissance gear. The cameras were loaded with two rolls of film especially created by Eastman Kodak, each nine-inches wide and five thousand feet long, which was enough film for an eight-hour flight. The resolution of the cameras was so precise that objects on the ground as small as two-and-a-half feet could clearly be identified from almost thirteen miles up in the air.

This new aircraft could fly directly over the Soviet Union, well above all of the Russian air defenses. There was no way for them to hide from our cameras, and no way for them to shoot us down and stop us. Even their radar couldn't detect us at an operating height of 70,000 feet. Mr. B's enigmatic and repetitive phrase, "if detected" was clearly starting to make sense.

On July 15, the plane was finished. Mr. B praised everyone at the dedication. "Your expertise and dedication is going to save the lives of hundreds of brave Air Force pilots who have previously defied Soviet airspace and have been shot at, shot down, killed and or captured in order to help get us the information that we need. You've designed and built an airplane that can fly for nine hours without refueling or landing. On a single mission it can, in clear weather, photograph a strip of mother Russia two hundred miles wide and twenty-five hundred miles long, producing four thousand crystal-clear pictures. We'll see air bases, missile test sites, shipyards, industrial centers, nuclear plants, power grids, railroad lines, and highways. Any target of strategic value will be seen and photographed to be plotted and mapped for possible targeting later." He paused to let those remarks sink in; then, he added, "If we are successful, this might prove to be the greatest intelligence coup in the history of this country. Thank you so very much for a job well done!"

Though I had been involved with many of our nation's most clandestine activities, from Iran to Guatemala to MKULTRA, the magnitude of this particular secret project took my breath away. I felt incredibly proud to be part of our nation's defense against Communism.

IT WAS IMPOSSIBLE to test our airplane at either Lockheed's Palmdale facility or Muroc, the Air Force's California desert airbase. We required a remote location shielded from any and all spying eyes. After an extensive and exhaustive search, the Agency selected a deserted, dry lakebed out beyond Death Valley for our test flights. Our only neighbor was the Atomic Energy Commission Proving Ground; the atomic fall-out from their frequent tests scared everyone else away. The site was known locally as Groom Lake, but we referred to it as The Ranch.

Kelly Johnson was in charge of disassembling and transporting our plane to Groom Lake. Once the plane was reassembled, our first test was scheduled for the morning of August 2. The tension was palpable. The mission was so top secret that we could not even refer to our plane as an airplane so we referred to it as "The Article." It was decided "The Article" would fly directly off the dry lakebed at Groom Lake rather than using a runway.

Test pilot Tony LeVier climbed up into the cockpit. Kelly instructed him to go no faster than fifty knots for the first taxi down the lakebed. Tony gave him a thumbs-up and off he went with a cloud of dust in his trail. The rest of us piled in a pickup truck and followed. He accelerated to fifty knots then dutifully slowed the plane down to a complete stop.

Kelly next told him to go east and take it up to sixty knots. We chased after him again getting covered in dust from his wake. Two miles later he coasted gently to a stop.

We pulled up alongside once more, and Kelly ordered, "Go back to the barn and take it up to seventy." Off he went, again with us in grimy pursuit.

Kelly screamed, "Oh Shit!" as The Article rose up above its dust cloud. "Goddamn it. It wasn't supposed to be airborne!"

Horrified, we watched the plane stall and slam back down onto the ground, blowing out both tires and setting its brake lines on fire. Luckily, we had fire extinguishers ready as we rolled to a stop. Jumping from the truck, we doused the fire.

Tony rolled his cockpit open. Kelly wailed, "Goddamn it, LeVier, what in the hell happened?"

Tony was shaken. "It fuckin' caught me by surprise! It was the same routine as before, Kelly, only at seventy knots. But this time, when I looked out at the wings, I saw that they were lifting. So I rolled the plane a little from side to side, but the goddamned thing was in the air. None of our other planes can get airborne before you hit one hundred knots, or even two hundred, and here I was in the air at seventy. Who'd have guessed an airplane would take off going only seventy knots? That's how light it is, Kelly. The son of a bitch took off and I didn't even know it."

It took a couple of days to repair the minor damage. By August 4, we were ready to try again. The day dawned with rare thunderheads hovering over the flats—Kelly wanted us to adhere to his rigid testing schedule. We prepared The Article for its first official test flight at a low altitude of 8,000 feet and a speed of 150 knots. This allowed the designers to check the airplane's low-speed control. Tony's orders were to keep the plane over the Groom Lake area, close to its landing site. Kelly boarded a T-33 chase plane to fly alongside The Article to more closely observe how it handled in the air.

At 4 p.m., Tony took off. Within thirty seconds, he was in the air. He circled the lakebed as he retracted the landing gear. Using the call sign, Angel One, he began to expand his circles around Groom Lake, testing the various control surfaces of the plane. He operated the speed brakes and made about six stall checks by deliberately re-deploying the flaps and landing gear to see how the airplane reacted. He radioed it "flies like a baby buggy."

I stood in awe on the ground. The shiny metal finish of the craft glistened against the backdrop of the darkening sky.

After about twenty minutes, Tony radioed, "This is Angel One. I'm starting to get a light rain up here, so it's time to come home—over."

Tony skillfully brought The Article in low and slow, with partial flaps down, fuselage speed brakes fully extended, and the engine almost idling. The plane had such a flat glide angle that as Tony came in at a slow speed of barely 90 knots, the plane got down into the "ground effect"—the area where the ground's proximity to the plane actually added to the lift of the wings—The Article floated back up into the air. Tony immediately applied power to gain altitude for another attempt at landing.

By this time, the sky had turned black, and the wind and rain were racing in. Tony tried again and again to land, and each time he was forced to pull up.

Tempers were growing short. The thunderstorm was almost upon us. We had to get that plane down onto the ground. The violence of a simple thunderstorm could tear off the plane's fragile wings. We began to panic.

Kelly radioed Tony to crash-land the plane, "Bring it in on the belly."

Tony refused, "Kelly, I'm not gonna do that!"

On his fourth attempt, Tony brought the plane in. Just before touching down, he pulled the nose up. The plane settled down toward the ground tail-first and bounced slightly a couple of times. Tony allowed it to stall onto the ground in a perfect two-point landing. At 4:34 p.m., The Article's first flight came to a stop.

The moment Tony touched down, the sky opened up on us full bore, flooding the dry lakebed under nearly two inches of water. Kelly's T-33 chase plane landed right next to Tony.

Tony struggled to get out of the cockpit as Kelly did the same from his airplane. Tony emerged first and was mad as hell—the veins were popping on his forehead. He made a bee-line for Kelly's chase plane and before Kelly was barely out of his cockpit, Tony was inches from his face screaming, "WHAT THE HELL WERE YOU TRYING TO DO, KILL ME?" He thrust his finger into Kelly's chest, "WELL, FUCK YOU!"

Kelly was equally angry—and just as red in the face. He gave Tony the familiar one-fingered salute and screamed back in his face, "AND FUCK YOU, TOO!"

With the conclusion of the emotionally charged exchange, our airplane was bestowed with its new name: the *U-2*.

On August 8, Mr. B and several other high-level government and Air Force representatives gathered at the Ranch to watch the official flight of our U-2. The plane performed spectacularly. The takeoff took but a few hundred feet of runway, starting a steep climb almost immediately. Tony flew one low-level pass over the spectator spot, and then accelerated almost vertically up toward 30,000 feet while the T-33 chase plane that followed behind struggled in vain to keep up.

Mr. B was both impressed and happy. "Sweet Jesus," he said, "if the cameras work as well as the rest of the plane, we've got an unqualified success on our hands!"

AFTER THE FIRST successful test flight, Mr. B sent me home for some rest and relaxation with my family. I hadn't been home in two months, and I was amazed at how much my son had grown in that short a period of time. Pam had spent the better part of two months redecorating our living room. She had changed our style from "frightfully outdated" to "Danish Modern." She told me not to even think about putting my feet on the coffee table. I discovered that she had relegated my comfortable yet worn brown armchair to the basement. She removed my favorite painting, an English landscape, from above the fireplace and replaced it with a mirror that "picked up the light." We now had two matching ceramic lamps on either side of the sofa and a floor lamp positioned strategically next to one of the new chairs. Although it was my firm belief that a living room was for "living-in," I discovered it was Pam's belief that a living room was for "looking-at."

Later that evening, Pam gave me the most recent update on Jack and Jackie's marriage. "Jack's feeling much better. They've gone off to Europe for a working vacation."

"I think Jack's definition of work might be different than Jackie's definition of work," I teased.

"I know, I know." Pam didn't laugh. She sensed something else was going on. "Actually, Jack's planning to go to Sweden with a male buddy, and Jackie's going to meet her sister in England."

"That doesn't sound good."

"I talked to Jackie, and it sounds like she's thinking of leaving him. She didn't seem too upset about all of the joking rumors about Jack's 'fucking vacation' in Sweden." Pam actually blushed at the double meaning of the words.

"Pam, it might be a little harder for Jackie to extricate herself from that marriage than she thinks. Old Joe has major political ambitions for Jack. Any divorce would be the kiss of death to those plans. The Roman Catholic Church would never sanction a divorce, and the voters wouldn't want a divorced man in the White House," I warned her.

"But Patrick, Jackie deserves to be happy."

"Hey, let's not talk about Jack and Jackie anymore. Come here." I took Pam in my arms, "Have I told you I'm the luckiest guy on the face of the earth to have a wife like you?"

"Mmmm, not in the last couple of hours," she murmured.

ON AUGUST 18, Jack traveled to Cap d'Antibes to join Jackie on their vacation. Then they joined a traveling caravan of friends with Jackie's sister,

Lee, and her husband, Michael Canfield. Pam read me a letter from Jackie with all the details.

"She says here they stayed at the home of the Aga Khan. His house overlooks the sea east of Cannes," Pam sounded wistful. "I imagine that was incredibly beautiful. And she says she met Gianni Agnelli, the young heir to the Fiat fortune. He picked her up to go water-skiing. I guess Jack stayed behind sitting in the garden."

"Sounds like Jackie may be using some of Jack's old tricks."

Pam continued on without taking my bait, "And she's met some wealthy Greek shipping magnates who have monstrous yachts. I can't read her writing here. I think she says she was introduced to Stavros Niarchos and Aristotle Onassis. Anyway, they are incredibly rich and famous."

I stopped her at that point and asked, "Did you say Aristotle Onassis?"

Pam looked at the letter again and said, "Yes, that's what it says. Why, do you know him?"

"No, I don't know him, but I know of him." I remembered my conversation with Bobby and Joe Kennedy at Jack and Jackie's wedding. I wondered if Onassis knew it was Bobby Kennedy's tenacious legal work back in 1953 that had cost him so much money in legal fees and cancelled bookings.

"She's included a newspaper clipping about a party on board Onassis' yacht, *Christina*, which was anchored off the Cote d'Azur. The party was to pay tribute to Winston Churchill, the Man of the Century."

"Imagine meeting Winston Churchill," I said. Now it was my turn to sound wistful.

"Oh, this is funny," Pam read on, "Jack wore a white dinner jacket and looked very handsome. Jackie said Jack was the only one besides the waiters who had on a white tuxedo jacket," Pam giggled. "It seems that Churchill thought Jack was a waiter. Churchill wouldn't even acknowledge him. Jackie said Jack became quieter and quieter as the evening wore on."

"Well, what did he expect," I began.

"Serves him right for all the times he's ignored Jackie."

"No, no…listen, Pam, I think it's more than that. I don't imagine Churchill was happy to see Jack Kennedy there. Remember, Ambassador Kennedy supported Adolph Hitler, and Churchill reviled Kennedy for his public support of appeasement toward the Nazis. I recently read somewhere that Old Joe rented a mansion outside of London during the Blitz. He fled London nightly while he left his entire Embassy staff there every night to face the blitz. The British people thought Old Joe was a coward. I'm sure Churchill definitely made the connection between young Senator Kennedy and Old Joe Kennedy."

"Maybe," Pam replied in a non-committal tone that indicated she didn't agree with me.

But I continued on, "Churchill probably remembers how Old Joe acted and what he said in the newspapers."

"What did he say?" Pam asked.

"Ambassador Kennedy delivered a scathing diatribe in a newspaper interview predicting that democracy in Britain was finished."

"Did he really?"

"He sure did. Plus, he's an avowed anti-Semitic—and that made him a social pariah in some circles. Not to mention the fact that he predicted the King of England would be among the first to make peace with Hitler."

I was a little piqued Pam didn't know this history. "For God's sakes, Pam, President Roosevelt had to recall Ambassador Kennedy to Washington because of his pro-Nazi leanings. You think Churchill will ever forget that?"

"Patrick, there's no need to raise your voice." Pam ended the discussion by walking out of the room, leaving me alone to fume once again over the Kennedys.

IT DIDN'T TAKE long for the rumors about the Kennedy marriage to start flying. I think that Pam was more distressed than Jackie was. Pam had a network of friends who kept her informed about the state of Jackie's affairs. Pam called it her "gossip circle." Out of loyalty to Jackie, Pam rarely divulged secrets; she always tried to be non-committal when friends pumped her for information. Unfortunately, Pam would fret about Jackie, and when Pam needed an outlet, I became her sounding board. I learned to listen—which meant not making any comments about the current state of Jackie's affairs.

Jackie's British friends were smart enough to recognize the signs of trouble. One friend told Pam that Churchill's snub of Jack at the yacht party was deliberate. He didn't approve of the way Jack had been treating his wife in public. It was evident Churchill knew all about Jack's personal life. Another one of their mutual friends told Pam that Jack had arranged to meet some old girlfriend in Sweden and had told her he wanted to leave Jackie and marry her—Jack actually had the brass balls to call his father and tell him the same thing. Jack later told Chase his father became absolutely livid at that idea. Jack complained his father "…doesn't even want to hear about my troubles with my wife—because she likes him and he responds to that…."

Now it was Jackie's turn to show Jack that she could live without him. She wrote to Pam about the interesting people she had met and the great time that she was having. She told Pam, "I'm never going back," referring to Jack and their life together. She didn't seem the least bit upset over the rampant rumors of their marital discord. In fact, Pam said she actually sounded happy, for the first time in a long time. Pam was convinced the marriage was on the verge of dissolving.

Shortly after the yacht party incident, Jackie and Jack did split up. Jackie sought refuge with her sister and her husband in London while Jack sought out young women on the beaches with a buddy. Jack found a Swedish girlfriend and asked her to accompany him to Poland for a fact-finding mission on behalf of the Senate Foreign Relations Committee—he tried to convince her that he could not go on without her and wanted to end his marriage to Jackie.

Of course, Old Joe Kennedy was predictably livid when he found out what his son was up to. "You're out of your mind! You're going to be President someday. This would ruin everything. Divorce is impossible." Joe called Jackie and ordered her to go to Warsaw as fast as she could get there. Upon her arrival, Jack dropped his plans to meet his Swedish lover. Instead, Jack and Jackie traveled to Rome to meet the Pope. Then, they had dinner with the French Premier Georges Bidault—Jackie's fluency in French enabled her to act as the translator for Jack. Things must have reverted to sanity, for when Jack and Jackie finally returned to the United States, Jackie was pregnant.

The "happy" couple returned to D.C. where they immediately went house hunting. They bought an old farmhouse called Hickory Hill which was once General George McClellan's headquarters during the Civil War. The house was an eye-popping $125,000 purchase in McLean, Virginia, and Jackie couldn't have been prouder. Our house cost $16,000, and I never felt richer in my life by comparison.

Meanwhile, I found out from Grant that Jack had rented a suite at the Mayflower Hotel in D.C., where he and George Smathers invited the likes of Judy Garland, Audrey Hepburn, Lee Remick, and the stripper Tempest Storm to party with them, as well as sundry other starlets, stewardesses, female congressional staffers, and even the occasional prostitute. It seemed to me Jack Kennedy was out to make up for his near brush with death in a big way.

Even though Pam and I had a few tense days while I was on leave, we were both upset when I got the news that I was to resume my duties at Groom Lake. Pam wanted another baby. We both knew that expanding our family was not practical at this time. It would be unfair to leave Pam to care for an infant and a toddler by herself. And as much as I loved our son, I had to admit I had not been much of a father for him. I had missed his first words and his first steps. If we decided to have another child, I didn't want to miss those things again.

When I walked out the door with my bags, both of us were silent with disappointment.

I RETURNED TO the desolation of Groom Lake. There wasn't much to occupy my free time except target shooting, reading, and thinking. I looked forward to Pam's letters—she never received a letter from me because of the nature of my job. Occasionally, I was able to telephone her, but our conversations were limited to mundane topics. She did tell me that Jackie had a miscarriage after three months of pregnancy. I sensed Pam was depressed, but there was little that I could do to comfort her.

Like my time at Quantico, I spent the days shooting targets and improving my rifle skills. I got so good with a .22 rifle I could throw an aspirin up in the air and shoot it down in flight. To pass the time in the evening, I read. I found a tattered volume of the complete works of Shakespeare. I read *Macbeth* and *Othello*—Grant and Pam would be proud—and although some parts were difficult to understand, I still enjoyed them.

I liked *Macbeth* better than *Othello*. I thought about *Macbeth* for days wondering what would motivate a man like Macbeth to kill his King. Both Macbeth and Lady Macbeth were ambitious—I was struck by how their selfish actions destroyed their country. Essentially both plays were about betrayal. Othello was betrayed by a man who he thought was his friend. I didn't understand how Othello, who was supposed to be such a great leader of men, could allow himself to be so duped by Iago. I couldn't fathom Othello's reaction—Othello cries O! O! O!—when he realizes he murdered his own wife based on the lies of his so-called friend.

After reading two tragedies, I occupied myself with newspapers and magazines until I found a small hardbound copy of *The Prince* by Machiavelli. Niccolo Machiavelli, who lived in Florence, Italy during the 1500's, was a political philosopher who wrote about the principles of warfare. These readings so inspired me that I began to formulate an intelligence operation to pass the time.

I knew from intelligence reports that Soviet agents were here in the United States collecting as much information as they could get their hands on. They literally loaded boxcars full of telephone books, class yearbooks, newspapers, social registers, and corporate annual reports and shipped tons of material to Moscow for cataloguing. They were harvesting a treasure trove of information from our society, while we knew absolutely nothing about theirs. In Moscow, even the telephone books are classified as Top Secret.

I reasoned that we needed to get more involved in the lives of the average Soviet citizen to better understand our enemy. Our new U-2 spy plane would be able to take pictures of newspapers from 13 miles up in the sky, but those same airplanes couldn't read the thoughts of the average Soviet citizen. We needed people behind the Iron Curtain.

After many weeks of deliberation, I came up with an idea I thought could work. I typed up my thesis and sent it on to Mr. B and Allen Dulles at Agency headquarters.

Early in December, Mr. B summoned me back to D.C. When I arrived, I was ushered into a meeting with him and Allen Dulles. I discovered the topic of the meeting was the paper I had written. It seemed that more than a few people were impressed.

"Patrick, Richard tells me you've been working on an idea to get us inside the minds of the average Soviet man-on-the-street. We've been thinking along the same lines. We'd like to hear your ideas."

I related the report about the Soviets shipping boxcars full of Americana back to Moscow for study and why we needed to do the same here. Mr. B interrupted me, "But Patrick, the USSR is a closed society to foreigners. How would you expect to accomplish that task?"

"We get our agent into Russia posing as a defector. A defector from the United States of America into the USSR would have tremendous propaganda value to the Soviets. They would welcome any U.S. citizen wanting to trade life in America for life in a Communist society. The Soviets would milk the defector for propaganda value and then exile him into Soviet society. The Soviets would view the defector as a potential spy and wouldn't let him near a military target, but that would be OK because that's not why we sent him there. We need to get into the minds of the average Soviet citizen to see if they wholeheartedly support the aims of their government and its actions."

Dulles and Mr. B listened impassively to me. I couldn't tell whether they bought into it or not, but I kept explaining my rationale. Finally, Mr. Dulles stopped me, "OK, Patrick, let's assume we can get these defectors of yours into the USSR—then what?"

"We have him assimilate into regular Soviet or Russian society. He needs to act, and react, with regular Russian citizens. We make sure he's accepted as a regular Russian 'Ivan.' We lull the KGB into boredom with the regular nature of his routine—because it's the daily routine we're really after. We need to know and understand how Russian and Soviet society functions. How does the average man or woman in the street live, and what do they think of life in Russia? What do they think of the Kremlin leadership? Do they support the Kremlin or do they simply put up with them out of necessity? Most importantly, would the population rise up in revolt if given the chance? And if they did revolt, how might the Soviet leadership react?"

They sat still for a few moments pondering my idea. Finally Mr. B asked, "OK, let's say you get your defector behind the Iron Curtain, and he collects data for us. How does he get his information out of the country, and better yet, how does he get himself out?"

"I think the best way to get him out is to have him get thrown out for doing something they don't like," I said.

"Homesickness," Mr. B suggested.

"What did you say?" Dulles asked.

"Homesickness—he can pretend to be homesick. He misses his family. He's changed his mind, and now he wants to go back home…"

"Or his mother is sick, and he's needed back home to take care of her," I added.

Dulles slowly nodded, thoughtfully rubbing his chin. "That might work. We've got to be able to get him out of the USSR at some point. Getting him back here on humanitarian grounds might work. How long does he need to stay behind enemy lines?"

"I think it's got to be at least a few years. Any time less than that and they might refuse to let him leave—any longer than that and the information might not be of any value to us. If a nuclear war starts before then, his information won't be worth anything anyway," Mr. B projected.

We stared at each other in silence, lost in thought. Finally, Dulles said, "Patrick, you've given us a lot to think about. This idea has been floating around the Agency, but no one has elucidated the concept better than you have."

Dulles stopped, stared at Mr. B, and after a few moments, Bissell nodded slightly to him. Dulles then said, "If it ends up going forward from here, we'll put you in charge of this project. I want you to begin to refine the operational details for me and tell me how it should be handled strategically. I will then be able to assess what type of budget needs you might have. We'll continually evaluate it to see if a project title is warranted. Until then, keep working with Bissell on the U-2."

Their reaction was beyond anything I expected.

"I cannot forecast to you the action of Russia. It is a riddle wrapped in a mystery inside an enigma; but perhaps there is a key. That key is Russian national interest."

— Winston Churchill

September 6, 1978
2:01 p.m.

Grant weighed what to do about his son's predicament. His private line lit up. Grant anxiously picked up the phone, "What do you have?"

"I have a splitting headache is what I have," Amy complained. "What are you going to do about Lyndon?"

For God's sake! Grant didn't have the time or energy to hold his ex-wife's hand.

"I thought I told you to never use this line," Grant said angrily.

"Well, if you had hired a secretary for her brains and not her breasts, I would have used the other line. No one answered the phone. You didn't answer my question. What are you going to do about Lyndon?"

"I'm working on it now. I'm waiting for a phone call," Grant partially lied. He was working on it, and he was expecting a phone call. He needed to get Amy off the line.

"Well, I called my lawyer. He's going to look into it."

"Amy, he's a divorce lawyer—not a criminal lawyer," Grant berated. "Do you want Lyndon to go to jail?"

"No," Amy cried, "I do not. I'm trying my best to do something."

"Well, asking advice on a criminal case from a divorce lawyer is asking for trouble. I don't have time to talk to you Amy. I'm hanging up. And don't you ever use this line again," Grant warned.

"Or what? What are you going to do, Grant? I'll use this line any damn time I please." Amy slammed down the phone so hard, she hurt her hand. "Take that, you son of a bitch," she muttered.

Grant's ear was still ringing when the light lit up again.

"What the fuck do you want now," Grant bellowed into the phone. Grant realized from the silence on the other end that it was not Amy, it was Ruger.

"Ruger?"

"Dulles airport is clean. No car and no sign of him. We passed his picture around to all of the ticket agents and no one matching his description was there recently."

"Do you believe them?"

"No reason not to."

"What's next?"

"I'm following a lead that he might already be out of the country."

Now, it was Grant's turn to be quiet. If Patrick got away, Ed Clark might march Grant himself down to the creek. He couldn't think about that now. Grant finally summoned enough energy to ask, "Where?"

"Maybe the Caribbean. I'm waiting for the other teams to check in."

1956

I HAD RETURNED to the Agency temporarily to update my superiors on the U-2 and also to work with Mr. Dulles about the details of my intelligence project. Anxious to get started on my new project, I immediately got back into my old routine. I looked forward to spending a few days of family time with Pam and Tim, but first I had to see to the success of Project Aquatone.

When I arrived home for dinner, Pam and Tim were in the kitchen. Tim was playing with some toy soldiers on the kitchen table. Pam was singing happily to him while she was stirring some soup on the stove.

"You sound happy tonight. What's up?" I asked as I walked straight into a trap of my own making.

"Jackie's pregnant again—isn't that great?" Pam was reopening an old wound and she knew it. We had not spoken of having another baby since I had returned from Groom Lake.

I smiled and lied sweetly to her face, "Yeah, that is good news."

Pam swung around from the stove to face me. "I'm telling you, hon, she is just overjoyed. I don't think I've ever seen her so happy in all of the years I've known her. She stopped by about an hour ago and brought Tim some belated Christmas presents, and she brought me this good news."

Again, I affected a smile, but she saw through me. "Aren't you happy?"

I was forced to lie to her again. "Oh, yeah, that's terrific." I knew she wanted me to say we should get started on expanding our family, but I had too many projects on my plate to do that. I had left the responsibility of raising Tim solely in Pam's hands. How could I, in good conscience, agree to have another child at this time?

My wife studied me to discern if I was sincere, and then she added, "Jack has also finished his book. Jackie thinks it's going to win a boatload of awards, it's that good."

I tried—I mean, I really, really tried not to be too sarcastic, but I couldn't help myself. "I'm sure that if his father has anything to do about it, he'll probably win the Pulitzer."

She shot me the look—you know the one that all wives possess—to let me know I had just crossed a line.

I ARRIVED BACK at the Skunk Works in Burbank in time to accompany six newly hired Air Force pilots out to the Ranch. We had deliberately kept them in the dark about the nature of the plane they were to pilot for obvious security reasons. After completing their flight training, two of them commented that they had visions of flying some kind of top-secret rocket ship or high-speed fighter plane. The joke turned out to be on us.

Our C-54 cargo plane landed on the dry lakebed of Groom Lake and taxied to a stop next to the U-2. Mr. B had the hangar door open. He stood back proudly waiting for an enthusiastic reaction of approval from our new hotshot pilots.

"What the fuck is that?"

"Is that a fucking glider? I ain't flying no fucking glider!"

Four of the pilots got off the transport to get a better look at the U-2. The other two pilots refused to even so much as get up out of their seats. "I didn't sign on to fly that piece of shit," one shouted then stubbornly stared out the window until one of his buddies stuck his head back in the door and said, "Come on, Marty, you've come this far—at least come out and get a better look at this thing." Grudgingly, Marty and the other pilot disembarked and joined the other four pilots for a close-up look. The six walked up to the side of the cockpit—what they saw horrified them all even more.

"This fucking glider doesn't even have a *stick*! It's got a goddamned *yoke*, for chrissakes."

Mr. B and I had been completely ignorant of the bias all fighter pilots had toward bomber pilots—the fighter pilots believed that bomber pilots were well beneath them in terms of skill and bravado. We had made a huge blunder in the design and construction of the U-2, at least as far as our Air Force hotshots were concerned. The Skunk Works had adapted the control yoke out of a P-38 instead of using the traditional stick control these guys were so used to. So when these six macho guys saw a wheel where a stick was supposed to be, they lost their composure. They climbed back on board the C-54 muttering, "Thanks, but no thanks!"

I was ready to panic. But Mr. B was not fazed—he reminded them they had signed contracts and that he was prepared to let them sit on that "goddamned C-54" for the next sixteen months if he had to. He would not change his airplane to suit them, and he would not allow them to quit on him without even giving our plane a chance—my job was to convince them to change their minds.

It took all night (and about six cases of booze) to persuade them to give the U-2 a chance. The next morning we met with Mr. B for a briefing. Sparks began to fly, once again, when they realized that they would be flying the "flimsy unarmed glider" over "goddamned Russia" in order to take "fucking pictures" of secret Soviet military installations. They didn't sign on to spend the rest of their "goddamn lives" living in some "shit hole Soviet prison!" Were we "crazy"—because they sure "as hell weren't crazy enough" to sign on for a death march across Siberia.

This time, it took several days, several rounds of poker, in which I lost my shirt, and twelve cases of booze to get them to calm down and consider the mission.

To complicate matters further, the U-2's Pratt & Whitney engine continued to give us problems with its tendency toward high-altitude flameouts—a flameout is when the jet engine unexpectedly shuts off. In early testing, we averaged seven flameouts per flight. Since the engine could not be restarted in the oxygen-deprived environment of 65,000 feet, the re-start procedure forced the pilots to descend below 35,000 feet in order to re-ignite the engine. This is where things got very dangerous. At 70,000 feet, our plane and our pilot were safe from any danger from Soviet fighter planes or missiles. At 35,000 feet, however, they would easily become a sitting duck, probably more like a dead duck.

On one of the first flights with an Agency pilot at the controls, we experienced a now-predictable flameout at an altitude of 65,000 feet over Arizona above the Grand Canyon. The pilot radioed he could see Nellis Air Force Base just eighty miles away and that he had already pointed the nose of the plane in that direction. He said it looked close enough to touch—from that altitude the pilots could see from the Monterey Peninsula south of San Francisco all the way down to Baja, California. He also had plenty of time to look—we calculated that from 65,000 feet our plane could glide for up to 70 minutes and travel as far as 240 miles.

Since the U-2 was designed to fly above 70,000 feet, it was necessary to design a survival suit for the extreme altitude. We found out if the pilot lost air pressure above 60,000 feet, his bodily fluids would literally boil away in about a minute, killing him so fast he wouldn't have time to do anything about it. Our pilots had to wear a special helmet and a pressure suit which tended to make them look like some kind of spaceman, just like in those popular science fiction movies.

On our final test flight on April 14, one of our pilots was forced to make an unscheduled landing at an unsecured military air base. He experienced a flame out at 65,000 feet over Memphis, Tennessee, and although he was able to re-start the engine as he passed over the Mississippi River, it flamed out again over Arkansas. We had planned for this type of emergency, and previously had sent sealed orders to every military air base around the country with instructions on the procedures to be followed in the event of an unexpected landing. When we asked the pilot how far he thought he could glide, he indicated a distance we calculated to be as far as New Mexico. We decided to have him try to land at Kirtland Air Force Base outside Albuquerque, New Mexico, which was a Strategic Air Command base. The base commander was alerted to the emergency and was directed to open the sealed orders that resided in the safe in his security office. He was instructed to have his base police get the U-2 into an available hangar as fast as possible and to keep all onlookers away. We told him to expect our top-secret airplane to land within half an hour.

Thirty minutes came and went as the base hurriedly prepared for the high-security arrival. Perplexed, the base commander called the Pentagon back to inquire where the airplane was. While he was on the phone, the U-2 began to glide in for a landing on the short and narrow taxiway next to an open hangar.

He sputtered into the receiver, "That's not a plane, it's a *glider*!"

The base police were in for an even bigger shock when our pilot emerged from the surrounded aircraft. He opened the canopy and stepped out wearing his green partial-pressure survival suit and white helmet—with no identifying insignia visible anywhere.

"Lordy be, it's a man from Mars," one of the shocked onlookers exclaimed.

ON MAY 7, 1956, we publicly acknowledged the existence of the U-2. Project Aquatone needed a legitimate cover story. The National Advisory Committee for Aeronautics (NACA) sent out a press release announcing a data-gathering research program—the U-2 would collect data in the upper atmosphere to help us understand and study the jet stream, the ozone layer, clear air turbulence, cloud formations, cosmic radiation, and air quality. This data would assist us in the design and manufacture of future jet aircraft. The data collection would not be limited to the United States but would also extend into the United Kingdom and other parts of the world.

We deliberately lied about the U-2's top ceiling of 50,000 feet and other performance characteristics.

Carrying the designation Weather Reconnaissance Squadron (Provisional)-1 or WRSP-1, we flew to the USAF's Lakenheath base in East Anglia, England. Our real tactical designation was Detachment A or Det-A for short.

We swiftly unpacked then assembled the four U-2's. Our pilots began to fly some shakedown sorties as the Royal Air Force fighter pilots practiced intercepts against us. The Brits were absolutely amazed—they couldn't get anywhere near the altitude of our U-2's.

Before we were even settled into our new home at Lakenheath, we were asked to leave the country.

The British had narrowly avoided a major escalation of tensions with the Soviets in April when Premier Khrushchev made an official state visit to England aboard the Soviet naval cruiser, Sverdlov. While docked in Portsmouth, the British Secret Intelligence Service (SIS) sent a diver to inspect the Sverdlov's sonar and any other equipment below the waterline, despite explicit orders from the British government to leave the Sverdlov alone. Incensed, the Soviets protested the underwater spying incident to the world's press. The British Prime Minister Anthony Eden, embarrassed by the incident, had to fire the head of SIS, Sir John Sinclair. Prime Minister Eden swore before the British Parliament that the covert operation had been conducted without the knowledge or authority of his government. This incident hit pretty close to home—we hadn't planned to tell the British government what we were doing covertly either.

Meanwhile, our secret aircraft wasn't much of a secret in Britain. Our U-2's made numerous check flights and rapidly attracted the attention of amateur civilian British aircraft spotters. Fearing another unpleasant episode with the Soviets, Prime Minister Eden called President Eisenhower and withdrew all permission for us to operate from British soil. We were given twenty-four hours to get the hell out of Dodge.

On June 11, we moved to Wiesbaden, West Germany. Mr. B was eager to begin our operational overflights. Weather experts had predicted a twenty-day window of ideal, cloud free weather over the western part of the USSR between June 20 and July 10. We counted the days, but we still had not received President Eisenhower's official approval for any overflights.

We assured the President that the U-2 would be invisible to Soviet air defenses; naturally, as a former general, he was skeptical of the claims. President Eisenhower delayed approving the overflights—he was well aware of the U-2's propensity to flame out at high altitude and understood quite well how risky it was to fly the plane. The President had another overriding concern: The United States had carefully cultivated an international image as a country that would never break the law, especially when it came to stooping low enough to spy on another country. Soviet spies were known to break international law, but not the United States of America—we were the good guys.

The clock ticked away as we watched our precious weather window rapidly closing. Mr. B decided rather than waiting for outright Presidential approval that he would invoke his own. He had Allen Dulles and Air Force Chief of Staff General Twining deliver a prepared paper to the President, titled the Aquatone Operational Plan. Mr. B informed the President that since President Truman had previously granted permission to the Air Force to conduct illegal overflights of Eastern Europe, he was going to use this previously existing presidential permission to begin U-2 overflights of the Soviet bloc in Eastern Europe. I thought such an action took really big balls on Mr. B's part, but he managed to pull it off. Project Aquatone was officially renamed Project Chalice.

The weather was good and holding. Mr. B ordered up a flight over several Soviet satellite countries. The first flight plan took our pilot over Czechoslovakia, then routed him far west to Warsaw, Poland. Our U-2 took photos continuously. Once Warsaw had been reached, the pilot turned west for Berlin and Potsdam, East Germany. He managed to photograph every major Polish city before he landed back in Germany.

Incredibly, there was no screw-up. The U-2's engine worked flawlessly. The cameras did exactly what they were designed to do—the image quality surpassed anything previously seen. The photo resolution was so good that an object the size of a basketball could be clearly discerned on film from an altitude of 13 miles.

Our first mission was a total success.

I HAD LITERALLY just popped the cork on a bottle of champagne to celebrate when I received orders to return to Washington for a meeting with the Agency's leadership. Arriving on June 26, I was immediately taken to the White House and ushered into the Oval Office filled with my Agency brass and senior military brass. President Eisenhower cordially acknowledged me as we moved to our seats.

"Patrick, you're here today at the specific request of your superiors, who feel you're the best man for this particular job," the President said. "I've known you and your work for a few years now, and I happen to agree you are valuable to us all. I think you already know the Air Force Chief of Staff,

General Twining. Let me introduce General Power and my personal assistant, General Goodpaster."

I shook hands around the room.

The President continued, "We have received a very unique invitation from the Soviet Union. Heck, it might even be called unprecedented, don't you gentlemen agree?" There were knowing nods all around the room.

"Chairman Khrushchev has personally invited an American military delegation to join a group of international military chiefs in Moscow for Soviet Aviation Day. We're here today to discuss the acceptance of that invitation. Your role in all of this will become clear in just a moment. General Twining, would you care to continue?"

The General rose to his feet to address us in a formal fashion. "Gentlemen, I think it is clear that Khrushchev is becoming highly agitated over our existing overflight programs. The Russians are pissed, and they want us to know it. Premier Khrushchev wants to demonstrate to us that he possesses the ability to not only stop our overflights, but to prepare us for his own overflights of American soil if we persist. I expect this to be a powerful demonstration of Soviet air power."

"If he's agitated now, imagine his reaction if and when he finds out about our pending U-2 overflights. He'll really have a reason to be agitated. But why is he inviting us on an official visit?" Richard Bissell asked. "Wouldn't he accomplish the same thing just by having the world's press cover the event with our Ambassador present?"

"No, Richard, that's just the point," Allen Dulles calmly interrupted. "He's planning on publicly taunting us. He wants our military to be front and center for that spectacle."

"Allen's right," General Twining interjected. "Let's face facts. General LeMay has been overly pugnacious in provoking the Soviets. He has conducted numerous broad daylight overflights of Soviet border regions with those RC-47 spy planes of his. I've tried very hard to rein him in, but as you all know, the General is both thickheaded and stubborn. He believes what he is doing is helping our country's security, and I have to admit, we have gathered some vital intelligence data from his methods."

"But those methods may end up starting a war. Will they be worth it then?" Richard asked.

The President held up a hand to stop the conversation from veering in a wrong direction. "Listen," he said, "I'll deal with General LeMay if he crosses a line. Until then, let's stick to the subject at hand. General Twining, I think you should go to Moscow for Soviet Aviation Day. You'll get a chance to meet your opposite in the Soviet military hierarchy so that, in and of itself, could be worth the trip."

The President turned directly toward me, "Patrick, you're here for two reasons. Number one: Allen wants someone from the Agency included on the trip. I don't think this trip will yield a lot of new intelligence information, but I could be wrong. So I am ordering you to accompany General Twining and General Power to Moscow."

The President paused for a moment to observe my reaction. I was stunned to be going to Moscow, the very center of the Communist world. I was apprehensive—and excited. It dawned on me that this might be another career test. Did my intelligence project hinge on my performance in Moscow? I stopped myself from jumping to conclusions until I knew the second reason.

Before I could even ask, the President smiled and said, "What's the second reason? It seems Mr. Bissell here is a little too enamored with his new toy to wait for official orders from me as to when he can fly it and where. I personally don't believe it to be very prudent for us to send one of our U-2's over Soviet airspace while a high-ranking American delegation is on Russian soil. General Twining has, in fact, specifically asked me that no overflights even be attempted while he is over there. Therefore, I want you to accompany our generals to Moscow in the hopes your presence will act as a deterrent to temper any rash behavior on Mr. Bissell's part."

I glanced over at Mr. B who was noticeably flushed and embarrassed. It looked like the President's message had gotten through. At least, I hoped it had. I sure didn't want to end up in a Siberian gulag due to his stubbornness.

The President concluded, "Patrick, this is your first official diplomatic mission. Keep your eyes and ears open. I expect you to learn a lot about the Russians on this trip." He shook my hand and warmly said, "Good luck and have a good time." Then he turned back to his desk as his secretary ushered us from the room.

THE NEXT FEW days were consumed with getting my passport, travel documents and any security clearances needed to make the trip. I also spent one full day being briefed on protocol by the State Department. I still did not have a clear concept of what my responsibilities were as a member of an official delegation. My role was to play a military attaché to our generals. I was given a uniform and a rank as a commissioned officer as part of my cover.

Even flying non-stop, the trip lasted almost an entire day. Our Boeing 707 flew much higher than the prop-jet airliners. We were high above the clouds and couldn't see much ground detail as we traversed northern Europe on our way to Moscow. I tried to imagine what the view from a U-2 would be like since it would be flying three times higher than we were flying. Up in the air, I had an even greater appreciation for our mission. Our camera technology was unprecedented—it not only could accurately capture a newspaper on the ground at 30,000 feet, it could also accurately photograph it at the 90,000 foot altitude of the U-2.

Upon arrival, we were taken by military vehicles to Tushino Airfield outside of Moscow for the military aerial demonstrations. A small squad of Russian soldiers in full dress regalia formally led us across the tarmac. I tried not to show my discomfort as we marched behind the ominous sickle and hammer of the Soviet flag. We took our seats on a set of bleachers along with the Soviet delegation. General Twining quietly pointed out Red Air Force Commander General Mikhailov and Soviet Defense Minister, Marshal Georgi Zhukov. As I sat in the bleachers, I began to feel a little homesick for America. I wanted to feel the comfort of the Stars and Stripes waving in the breeze—I wanted to hear a military band play our national anthem. I struggled with my strange feelings as I looked in the faces of the Soviet soldiers and officers. It was difficult for me to reconcile the fact that these men were equally proud to be Communists.

Once seated, the air suddenly thundered with what must have been at least a hundred fighter planes, Mig-19's and Yak-25's. Next came sixteen different kinds of Russian bombers, known variously as Bears, Bison, and Badgers, all flying in low formation directly above our heads. Our hosts saved the best for last, displaying their newest fighter prototypes. General Power pointed out a new version of a Yak-25 fighter, followed by a three delta-winged aircraft made by Sukhoi, and the latest two MiG's the staple of the Soviet Air Force. It was an impressive display of air power. Just as suddenly as they had appeared, the planes disappeared into the clear blue sky, leaving behind only contrails.

It was then that I realized Chairman Khrushchev himself had joined us on the podium. Khrushchev looked exactly as he did in all of the pictures that I had seen of him—but the camera could not capture the intensity of his demeanor. He exuded a kind of combative power. His eyes sparkled, but not with humor—with intimidation. His very presence as the First Secretary of the Communist Party emphasized the importance of the air show to the Soviets—but the real exhibition began after the demonstration of Soviet air power.

Chairman Khrushchev sought out General Twining, personally inviting him to a near-by park for a private reception just for us. Hundreds of dancing children in traditional Russian dress met us when we arrived. Our escort led us through a gauntlet of bright red Russian flags, which fluttered against a brilliant blue summer sky, to tables overflowing with platters of food and bottles of vodka. I was at a picnic deep behind enemy lines—I had to suppress a wry smile.

Once we were seated, pretty Slavic waitresses handed everyone in the entire American and Soviet delegation tall, narrow glasses of vodka. Chairman Khrushchev stood behind a small podium and welcomed us with a traditional Russian toast. We stood, tossed our heads back, and drank down the vodka. My throat was on fire as the vodka burned its way into my stomach. We had no sooner taken our seats than Chairman Khrushchev began another toast—an exceptionally long toast "in defense of peace"—and we stood once more.

His tone careened from boastful and intemperate; saber rattling to cajoling. In the middle of his tribute, Chairman Khrushchev turned to General Twining warning, "Stop sending intruders into our airspace! We will shoot down uninvited guests. We will get all of your *Canberras*. They are nothing but flying coffins."

Seeing how distressed Khrushchev was over our illegal RC-47 overflights of Soviet border territory, I could only imagine how he would react if our U-2 was ever detected flying over the heart of Russia and Moscow itself.

"As far as we are concerned, this sort of espionage is war—war waged by other means," he shouted. Premier Khrushchev's face turned red as he harangued our military. He pounded his fist on the podium to emphasize his points. I stood stiffly by my seat, afraid to even make any eye contact with him.

Even though he was stating the need for peace, I could see how his volatile nature could set the tone for American-Soviet relations for many years to come. Khrushchev was a hard-liner—he wanted us to take his message back to Washington. It sure made a hell of an impression on me. It would be a mistake to underestimate the man.

As Chairman Khrushchev continued speaking, I began to feel a little ill. I had never drunk vodka straight up—or any alcohol for that matter—on an empty stomach. Combined with my weariness, the vodka had made me queasy. I covered my glass with my fist and tried to unobtrusively pour the contents on the ground.

To my complete horror, my movement happened to catch Chairman Khrushchev's eye. He stopped mid-sentence, stared directly at me—his eyes bored holes in me. Just as quickly, his look changed to wide-eyed amazement.

He turned to our ambassador, Charles Bohlen, "Here—I am speaking about peace and friendship—what does your military attaché do? He insults me! He pours out his drink."

All eyes turned to me. General Twining looked at me in disapproval.

General Power looked at me in disgust. Ambassador Bohlen just looked at me and slightly shook his head. I felt my head swim; I thought I could feel my blood run cold. My *faux pas* could ignite an international incident. Never in my life have I ever wished to be somewhere else as much as I wanted to at that very minute—I wanted to hide from this nightmare. As my legs started to buckle beneath me, I struggled to stand tall.

Mr. Bohlen then sternly admonished me, "Mr. McCarthy, would you please step up to the podium?" The entire group parted as I struggled to make my way up to the front of the crowd, but the speakers waved me to come over by them. I stood face-to-face with Comrade Nikita Khrushchev. The Chairman draped his arm around my shoulder as he turned me to face the assembled group.

"What is your name?"

"My name is Air Force Captain Patrick McCarthy, sir," I replied.

"Well, Air Force Captain Patrick McCarthy, why will you not drink to peace with me? Why do you insult me by pouring my vodka on the ground? Do you not believe in peace between our countries? Or do you not like me?"

My cheeks burned hot. I could feel sweat rolling down my back as I tried to figure out a safe answer to the Chairman's inquiry. I didn't have an answer—so I made one up. Sheepishly, I replied, "A bug flew into my glass and I didn't want to swallow it by mistake!"

Chairman Khrushchev smiled sardonically, shrugged his shoulders elaborately, and then said, "Well, we are very aware of how much our American friends do not like bugs." And with that remark, the entire group erupted into laughter. (I was so lightheaded that I didn't get the joke at the time.)

He continued on, putting his arm strongly around my shoulder, "Air Force Captain Patrick McCarthy, tell me: do you believe in peace between our nations?"

I nodded, "Yes sir, I do."

"Good! Air Force Captain Patrick McCarthy, will you drink with me to that dream of peace?" He held up his glass in a magnanimous gesture.

I nodded, "Yes sir, I will, sir."

He smiled. He had a noticeable gap between his upper teeth. "Good boy! Bring me a glass for Air Force Captain Patrick McCarthy." Someone handed him a vodka glass and he said, "Nyet, a proper glass is necessary for Air Force Captain Patrick McCarthy to toast to peace." Someone then produced a much larger water glass to the delight of the assembled crowd. Chairman Khrushchev grabbed a nearby bottle of vodka and filled the glass up to the brim.

"Air Force Captain Patrick MCarthy. Nyet! Comrade Patrick McCarthy! I want you to drink a toast to our mutual friendship. This toast will celebrate this new friendship between you and me and will further symbolize the friendship that should exist between my country and your country. Let us all recognize accidents happen, and accidents can be repaired. This toast will repair your previous accident and allow everyone to see there are no hard feelings between us, just as there are no hard feelings between our nations. Are you ready?" His eyes devilishly twinkled as we raised our glasses, touched them for luck, and began to drink.

The vodka seared my esophagus in a trail of fire all the way down to my stomach. I was afraid it was going to come right back up. I squeezed my eyes and clinched my jaws. I strongly fought back the urge to retch—Khrushchev was standing so near to me that he would be covered—I could not vomit I told myself. I would not vomit!

My eyes were crossed and blurred as I finished. When I had emptied my glass, Chairman Khrushchev grabbed it and turned it upside-down on the table. He embraced me in a bear hug—then kissed me on both cheeks as the crowd thundered its approval applauding us both. "Peace be with you, Comrade Patrick McCarthy," he roared into my face.

"And, with you, as well sir," I stammered in reply.

"*Dos vedanya!*" he yelled to the group. He turned on his heels, followed by his retinue of security and advisors.

I was very thankful for the steady hand that led me back to our waiting cars. It didn't take long before my legs became rubbery and vomit drooled out of my mouth onto my uniform. I babbled incoherently as we headed back to the consulate for the evening. General Twining and Ambassador Bohlen were both upset over the initial tone of Chairman Khrushchev's abrupt and threatening speech, but I could hear them agree that I had inadvertently defused the situation instead of allowing it to escalate into something much uglier. After that, I passed out.

Khrushchev, who had been bombastic when we first arrived, was a cordial host during the rest of our stay. Fortunately, I didn't have the opportunity to speak directly with him again. On our last night as our delegation was saying its farewell, he looked at me, gave me a broad Cheshire-cat grin, and a slight wave of his hand.

ON JULY 1, our group left Moscow. We received a warm send-off from the commander in chief of the Soviet Air Force, Chief Marshal of Aviation P.F. Zhigarev, and other senior Soviet military officials.

Exhausted from the long flight, I was grateful to see Tracy Barnes waiting for me as I disembarked the plane. I reeked of vodka—its smell seemed to emanate from my pores. I was a little unsteady on my feet, I assumed, from sitting so long during the flight.

Tracy smiled his characteristic insolent grin, "Hey," he said, "I understand you're quite the expert on Russian vodka now, Comrade McCarthy." Apparently, my exploits were already legendary in the diplomatic community.

Tracy filled me in on what had happened while I was gone. After the debacle in Great Britain, President Eisenhower notified West German Chancellor Konrad Adenauer of our overflight plans "before deep operations are initiated." Richard Bissell flew to Bonn to meet with the Chancellor who surprised him by saying, "This is a wonderful idea. It's just what ought to be done!"

Now that General Twining's visit to Moscow was over and Chancellor Adenauer had been briefed, the political restrictions on the start of our U-2 surveillance flights over the Soviet Union itself should have been removed. The President was still ambivalent about issuing the ultimate order. General Goodpaster finally sent word to Mr. B that the President had authorized limited overflights of the USSR for a ten-day period.

When Mr. B asked if this meant ten days of good weather, Goodpastor replied, "It means ten days from when you start. And let me remind you of something the President told you early last year when he first approved this program: He believes the country needs this information, and he's going to approve the flights. But he also believes that one day one of these machines is going to be caught, and we're going to have a hell of a storm to pay. I hope you have contingencies ready for the day that happens."

Mr. B assured him he did, but in reality we had never discussed a contingency plan. I truly believe he didn't think we'd need a contingency plan because we didn't plan on being caught. Mr. B, while not a true risk-taker, was an opportunist. "Let's go for the big one straight away. We're safer the first time than we'll ever be again."

I immediately boarded the first available Agency plane back to West Germany to monitor the planned July 4 operation. I only had time to phone Pam to let her know that I was back in the country. I had looked forward to telling her what I could about my trip over a home-cooked meal. But instead of a warm greeting, she was curt with me. "Fine, Patrick, do what you need to do."

I put our conversation on the back burner and tried to concentrate on my orders. The first strategic target for our first mission was the Soviet capital itself—Moscow. Not only was this an important target for our bombers, but the surrounding area was rich with Soviet research and development facilities. As early as July 1953, Western observers had spotted an unusual, herringboned network of roads being constructed around Moscow. These sites were about twelve in number by 1956. They were about eight to nine miles apart and arranged in two circles about twenty-five and forty-five miles from the center of the city.

We had reports of "missile-like" objects at some of these sites. NATO had given us a specific report describing the missiles as about three feet in diameter and about thirty feet long. NATO designated them as SA-1 missiles, which we simply referred to as SAM's, Surface-To-Air Missiles. There was a chance that the Soviet air defense network might have operational surface-to-air missiles that could possibly endanger our mission. Our U-2 would have to fly through the potential danger areas twice—coming and going.

Our pilot was Carmine Vito. I liked Carmine—he was levelheaded and professional. He began the first flight by crossing over East Germany which was enveloped with considerable cloud cover. He then flew over Krakow, Poland continuing into the Ukraine region of the USSR itself where some suspected *Bison* bomber bases were supposed to be located. The weather began to clear as Carmine followed the railroad line from Minsk directly up to Moscow. For miles below him, he could see the mosaic pattern of the collective farm fields spread out to the horizon.

I monitored the overflight at a SIGINT, Signals Intelligence ground station, in West Germany. I was on edge as we closely monitored the Soviet radio frequencies. My anxiety peaked when we began to hear all manner of hell break out on the Soviet radio frequencies. Soviet radar had picked up Carmine's movements as soon as he penetrated the border and Soviet airspace. The Soviet high frequency radio transmissions from their ground controllers were frantic in nature.

At first, our guys were puzzled by the text of the transmissions. It sounded as if the Soviets were trying to direct fighter planes to intercept an aircraft flying at over 20,000 meters and at a speed of 800 kilometers per hour. Our SIGINT guys knew that no aircraft could operate at altitudes of 66,000 feet or higher—or so they thought. They didn't possess a high-enough security clearance for me to tell them about the U-2. I kept my mouth zipped shut and listened to the utter confusion on both sides of the border. Moscow air control grounded all air traffic and sent everything they had up against Carmine, who was blithely soaring far above their heads. He later told me he monitored the activity below as one-by-one, various MiG's tried and failed to get enough altitude to shoot at him. He actually saw two jets collide, nose-diving to a huge crash on the ground below him.

Later in a debriefing, Carmine told me that he did experience one very close call—his ground crew mistakenly put his cyanide pill in the wrong pocket of his flight suit. It was supposed to be kept in an inside pocket, but it was placed in his outside right front pocket by mistake. He told me that breathing pure oxygen makes your mouth very dry. All of the pilots carried cough lozenges to suck on when their mouths became too parched. Carmine was unaware that the cyanide pill was in his right front pocket when he dropped a fist-full of lemon-flavored cough drops into that same pocket. Feeling his throat go dry as he approached Moscow, he reached into his pocket and popped the cyanide pill into his mouth. He said he almost shit his pants when he started to suck on it and realized what it was—in a split-second, he spit it out. If he had bitten down on it, he would have died instantly and probably would have crashed in the middle of Red Square.

As soon as the U-2 landed and the film canisters were removed, I hopped on a plane back to D.C. to get the film developed. Our Photo-Intelligence Division, PID, was set up in Washington in the Steuart Building at 5th Street and New York Avenue, which was a rundown Ford dealership in the middle of the ghetto. PID occupied the fourth through the seventh floors. This squalid little setup had no air conditioning, no parking, and no cafeteria. Known as Operation Automat, it could provide any level of photoanalysis services at any time, day or night—photointerpretation, photogrammetry, graphic arts, collateral research, data processing, and analytical research—but, it had mainly been set up just to process the U-2's canisters.

After the first photos were developed, I accompanied Allen Dulles to the White House where the President and Allen spread the pictures out on the floor of the Oval Office. Mr. B shrewdly organized the pictures so that the first photos he showed to Mr. Eisenhower were detailed photographs of the courtyards of the Kremlin and the Winter Palace in Leningrad. These pictures represented the innermost secret sanctum of the Soviet government and its leaders. No Western observer had ever seen this before. He then pulled out the operational photos of the bomber bases so that Ike could count the actual number of visible planes himself. The President marveled at the photographs. He and Mr. Dulles looked like a couple of kids playing with a model train set on Christmas Day.

The President was stunned by the clarity of the photos themselves; the pictures were bigger, better, and clearer than anything ever seen before. I think he was excited about our gigantic breakthrough in intelligence gathering. It was truly astounding to realize that the photos were taken from almost fourteen miles up in the sky. Not only could he clearly see every feature of every item at an air base, he could almost count the very blades of grass on the lawn next to the tarmac.

Through the aerial photographs, we learned that our own military analysts were wrong. The United States did not have a so-called "bomber gap" with the Soviet Union—the Soviets did not possess massive numbers of bombers capable of overwhelming us. The U-2 flights proved that if a bomber gap did actually exist, it was ironically to our advantage, not theirs. The President was especially pleased because he could make more informed decisions about our national defense budget and the looming Soviet threat. The previous guesswork and bias which had shaped our foreign policy was now removed from the equation.

The Soviets formally presented a protest note to our embassy in Moscow concerning the July 4 overflight. The note was very specific as to the actual route and time that our plane violated their airspace. A Russian attaché told our intelligence source at the American embassy that our overflight deeply angered not only the Ministry of Air Defense, the entire Soviet armed forces and the entire Soviet government, but also Khruschev and Bulgarin themselves. I guess I was able to put it into perspective later when I thought about what our government would have done if a Russian plane had flown over Washington D.C. I'm sure we would have felt angry and helpless if we had been unable to stop it—what would we do if it came back to drop a nuclear bomb?

As soon as the note was officially received by the White House, General Goodpaster called Mr. B and canceled all further flights. By July 19, the President told Allen he had "lost his enthusiasm" for U-2 operations. His feelings were based upon the need to maintain the trust of the American people. He was worried that the American public would be shocked to find out the overflights of the USSR had violated international law. He said, "Soviet protests were one thing, any loss of confidence by our own people would be quite another." He also worried the Soviets would retaliate with overflights of the United States. If that happened, "the reaction would be drastic."

I didn't believe the Soviets had the technological ability to pull that off.

A COUPLE OF days later, I had a beer with Chase and Grant over at Rosie's. One of the subjects that came up after we were done talking about baseball and the Washington Senators was Jack Kennedy and his newly published book.

Chase laughed and rolled his eyes, "Old Joe's been up to his old tricks again. The Ambassador aggressively lobbied all of his powerful friends in the press to provide favorable reviews for Jack's book. He spent well over $100,000 on ads promoting the book. He even tried to use those ads to push it onto the bestseller lists. My editor at the paper told me that Joe approached a member of the Pulitzer committee to get the book reviewed for the award."

"It didn't work, did it?" I couldn't get over the arrogance of Joe Kennedy. He had to have some really big balls to try to manipulate the Pulitzer Prize Committee.

"Apparently it did. My editor was disgusted because the Pulitzer jury had not even deemed the book worthy of review for their nominating process. But Old Joe got his friend, Arthur Krock, to get the advisory board to actually overrule the Pulitzer jury decision and award the Pulitzer Prize to Jack."

"I guess it is all in who you know," Grant said.

Chase continued, "Get this: Jack started calling his friends to let them know he had won the Pulitzer Prize before the advisory board had even met to render its decision. The fix was in."

Grant chipped in, "It figures. Jack needs that book to be successful. Everyone, and I mean everyone, in the Senate leadership knows Jack hates to work hard. How else can he distinguish himself from all the other anonymous faces in the Senate? So now, he's pretending to be some kind of a multi-talented genius—who's much better than his lowly seniority status in the Senate might indicate—because he's won the Pulitzer Prize. You know, shit like that just annoys the hell out of Lyndon and the other guys. Kennedy just pisses them off with his lackadaisical attitude and his lack of a work ethic."

"Speaking of Lyndon, he's really become the King of the Hill, hasn't he?" I said. "How does it feel to be working for the Majority Leader of the Senate?"

"It feels damned good," Grant admitted. "I'm learning a lot about the real way politics works."

Chase gave me a knowing look. "I'll bet that's been an eye-opener," he said sarcastically.

Grant cut his eyes at Chase, "Lyndon's looking ahead to the White House. Eisenhower's unbeatable this year, but the Democratic nominee could easily be the front-runner for the 1960 nomination. That's what Lyndon plans to be."

"I'm happy for you, Grant," I said. "You've worked hard for Lyndon."

Grant looked at his watch, "Buddy, I have to get going. I've got a meeting to attend." He got up, straightened his tie, and buttoned his suit coat. After shaking hands with us, he threw a twenty-dollar bill down to cover a $2 bar bill.

I was astonished because Grant had, up until now, always exhibited what we used to call his "alligator arms"—arms that are too short to reach for the bill when it is time to pay. In fact, I couldn't ever remember him being generous when it came time to pick up the check.

"What's going on?" I asked Chase suspiciously as Grant jostled his way to the door through the crowded bar.

"I'm starting to get concerned about our old roommate," he confessed.

I didn't like the tone in Chase's voice. "What's he up to?"

"Oh, I'm hearing stories that Grant and Bobby Baker are bagmen for Lyndon, and it doesn't sound good. I'm almost afraid to look into the gossip because I'm afraid of what I might find."

I was confused. "Why?"

Chase sighed in exasperation. "Money is power in D.C., Patrick, and Lyndon is rapidly becoming the most powerful man in the Senate. Here's how this works. Businessmen give Lyndon money, and then Lyndon gets things done for them. He also gives money to other politicians who can't raise money as easily as he can. I've heard stories of brown shopping bags stuffed with thousands of dollars being handled so casually they were sometimes accidentally forgotten after being delivered. Johnson's got a five-room suite in the Munsey Building over on E Street leased as his collection office, just so he isn't in violation of the federal rules regarding receiving contributions on federal property."

"Is that what Grant's doing?"

"I suspect so. I haven't asked him because, like I said, I don't really want to know. But Bobby Baker's involved, so I wouldn't be surprised at anything that might be going on."

I didn't like the sound of this. "What do they hope to accomplish?"

"Come on, Patrick, it's the oldest story in Washington. It's a quid pro quo. You give me something; I'll give you something back. Political contributions are one of the surest ways to get money back from the government. Make a political contribution to the right person and you are on your way to becoming wealthy. And—a contribution insures that you'll also receive help from the government in the future in protecting your wealth. It's a proven system—it works—until you get caught. I hope Grant doesn't get in over his head."

As I stared at that twenty-dollar bill lying on the bar in front of me, I had a sinking feeling it might already be too late.

NOT LONG AFTER our meeting at Rosie's, Jack Kennedy won the Pulitzer Prize for *Profiles in Courage*. However, columnist Drew Pearson publicly insinuated on ABC's television show, *The Mike Wallace Show*, that it was really Theodore Sorensen, not Kennedy, who had actually written the book. Jack had Washington attorney Clark Clifford threaten to sue ABC and Pearson over the allegation. When Sorensen issued a sworn statement that Jack was the author, the network issued an embarrassing retraction.

Chase called me up gloating, "What did I tell you? I was right, wasn't I?"

Chase passed on the surprising rumor that Jack might be named a possible vice-presidential candidate. When I ran into Grant a few weeks later, I decided to pump him for a little information.

"Hey, I hear that Jack Kennedy's name is being bandied about as a possible vice-presidential candidate. How does Lyndon feel about that?"

Grant replied with an air of nonchalance, "Yeah, says who? Chase?"

"Chase usually has impeccable sources," I countered.

"Sometimes he has impeccable sources. Patrick you ought to know by now Chase says things just to test the waters." Grant checked his watch to indicate he was in a hurry.

"So, is Lyndon going to endorse Kennedy for the nomination?" I pushed.

"Hell no," Grant spit out with disgust. My goading worked. Suddenly Grant was more forthcoming with information. "There are rumors that Jack told Adlai's people that he wasn't interested in being Stevenson's running mate. But I heard that Jack's family is working feverishly behind the scenes to secure the coveted nomination for their boy."

"So, where does that leave you and Lyndon? I thought all you southern good ole boys stuck together."

"We do stick together. There are a number of prominent Democrats that flat out don't like Jack. And while I can't speak for Lyndon, I heard Sam Rayburn, the Speaker of the House, refer to Jack as 'that little piss-ant Kennedy.' That ought to tell you what his chances are."

"Chase said the Kennedys sent autographed copies of *Profiles in Courage* to all of the Democratic Party leaders along with a letter urging them to tune into a television re-creation of Jack's heroic PT-109 story." I added with sarcasm, "Did Lyndon get his autographed copy?"

"That's the biggest bunch of bull-crap ever invented," Grant exploded. "I'm sure Jack's wartime heroics, along with his youthful, clean cut appearance, might fool some ignorant people, but I've got to think the Democratic party leaders are a little bit more savvy than to be taken in by it."

With that, Grant impatiently checked his watch. "I've got to get going—I'll be late for an important meeting. See you around, buddy. Oh, yeah, do me a favor and tell that beautiful wife of yours I love her."

As he left, I couldn't help but notice Grant was quite a bit more guarded, especially in speaking for Lyndon, than he had been in the past. In prior conversations, it had always been "Lyndon thinks this" or "Lyndon thinks that." I also noticed Grant had an air of authority about himself he had never possessed before. Maybe it was the expensive suit he was wearing or the expensive watch he flamboyantly consulted that had added to his self-confidence.

I was seeing a whole different side to Grant's character. He had apparently learned to hold his cards closer to his vest than I had ever seen him do before.

I HOPED THE rumor of Jack's pursuit of the vice-presidential nomination was untrue. I harkened back to that evening of poker in 1950 where Mr. Hoover had lectured us about the importance of morality in our leaders. *"A leader of men must especially be a moral man. America cannot elect, nor can it follow, an immoral man as President."* In my opinion, that pretty much ruled out John Fitzgerald Kennedy as a vice-presidential candidate.

That August, the Democratic Party chose Jack to narrate the twenty-minute convention film, *Pursuit of Happiness*, on the opening day of the convention. His narration of the party's film made him a popular figure with the convention delegates. The media immediately promoted him as a serious contender for inclusion on the presidential ticket. When Adlai Stevenson won the nomination and then turned to the convention to select his running mate, the Kennedy clan aggressively swung into action. Jack's wartime heroics, along with what Grant had described as his youthful appearance and clean-cut image, made him stand out from the other Democratic officeholders.

The problems facing Jack, however, were almost insurmountable. The country certainly wasn't ready to have a Catholic as either a president or a vice president. The Kennedy machine went into action giving Ted Sorenson the task of defusing the issue. He urged journalist-author Fletcher Knebel to write a *Look* magazine article called "Can a Catholic Become Vice President?" which concluded it would be good for America if a Catholic were elected to such a high office. Of course, it would be even better if that Catholic also happened to be named "Kennedy."

The number of prominent Democrats who didn't support Jack also presented a problem. Eleanor Roosevelt, FDR's venerated widow, disliked Jack and publicly declared that the Democratic Party should never nominate for the presidency "someone who understands what courage is and admires it, but has not quite the independence to have it." It was a scathing indictment both of Jack and of Old Joe's influence on Jack. Arthur Schlesinger, Jr. was hurriedly dispatched to try to change Mrs. Roosevelt's mind—but to her everlasting credit, she absolutely refused to change her mind or her public statement. Jack even made a personal appeal to Eleanor Roosevelt for her support, but that backfired when she once again publicly berated and belittled him in front of a room full of people for not taking a firmer stand against Joe McCarthy and his tactics.

Aware of Jack Kennedy's numerous liabilities, Candidate Stevenson rejected Jack's personal entreaty to place him on the ballot. Instead, he asked Jack to be the person to nominate him for the presidency at the convention the next night—a clear sign that he had no intention of choosing Kennedy as his running mate. The convention vote for the vice presidential slot came down to a contest between Jack and Senator Estes Kefauver—Senator Kefauver won.

Grant, who was in the Texas delegation, said they were mystified by the convention's endorsement of Jack. "I don't know what to say, Patrick. We're all surprised. Lyndon even complained to a few us after the convention was over that he was still really confused by how the convention had reacted to Jack."

Grant imitated what Lyndon had said complete with his Texas drawl. "It was the god-damnedest thing—here was a young whippersnapper, malaria-ridden and yellah, sickly, sickly. He never said a word of importance in the Senate and he never did a thing. But somehow, with his books and Pulitzer prizes he managed to create the image of himself as a shining intellectual, a youthful leader who would change the face of the country. Now, I will admit that he had a good sense of humor and that he looked awfully good on the goddamn television screen…but his growing hold on the American people was simply a mystery to me."

Grant resumed his normal voice, "I think we were sandbagged by how ignorant the convention was. Lyndon was obviously a far better choice than Kennedy could ever hope to be. They should have drafted Lyndon instead of Kennedy."

THE CONVENTION'S ACTIONS were a mystery to me as well—as they were to anyone who actually knew Jack. I was surprised, I don't know why, about Jack's reaction to his defeat at the convention. Anyone in politics knew that it was rare for first term senator, a senator with very little experience, to be put on the presidential ticket. I had assumed that Jack knew he had dues to pay and would accept his defeat graciously. But Jack took his defeat personally with a sense of entitlement and arrogance. He bitterly complained—vowed to hold grudges against many of the people who failed to back him in full, including presidential candidate Stevenson. He refused to acknowledge that it was his own voting record in the Senate, especially his many votes against farm supports earlier in the year, which had cost him crucial support in the Midwest. He was oblivious to his own long list of shortcomings. The Governor of Oklahoma said it best when he remarked, "He's not our kind of folks."

The day after the convention, Jack and Jackie flew to New York, where Jack promptly boarded a flight to France—Jackie was not invited to go along. Jack planned to spend his vacation sailing the Mediterranean with his friends. Jackie, devastated and exhausted, returned home to Virginia.

Six days after the convention, Jackie lost the baby. She had not been home long when she was rushed to the hospital hemorrhaging and in excruciating pain. Jackie, undergoing an emergency caesarian section, hovered between life and death. Finally preparations were made to call in a priest to administer the last rites.

Pam was full of anger and grief.

"I blame it all on the Kennedys," she stormed. "They knew she was eight months pregnant, and they forced her—virtually strong-armed her into attending the convention." Pam slammed a pot into the sink, filled it with water, and slammed it down on the stove. "She was on her feet night and day. She attended almost every single function—and she never even saw Jack!"

"Honey, calm down. Take a breath."

"Don't tell me to calm down," she said as she emptied a package of macaroni into the boiling water. "He didn't even care—did not even care—that she was there. He only wanted her on the podium with him when he lost the ballot for vice president. And then, all she could do was cry—she was so physically and mentally drained."

I watched Pam furiously move to the refrigerator for a carton of milk. She moved to the cupboard, opening and slamming the doors.

"What kind of husband is he? What kind of husband leaves his pregnant wife at home so he can go on a vacation with his friends? What kind of husband abandons—discards—his wife so callously—a wife that stood by his side even though she was exhausted? Her mother is right—she should leave him. As soon as she gets better, I'm going to tell her so myself."

"Pam, you need to stay out of Jackie's affairs," I tried to warn, but she cut me off mid-sentence.

"She almost bled to death! Where was he? Where was he, Patrick? He was off—off carousing with his friend—God knows where. Why wasn't he at home? Tell me that?"

I sat at the kitchen table waiting for the next heated blast.

"It was Bobby that sat by her side—Bobby that held her hand—Bobby that told her she lost the baby…," she gasped as tears streamed down her face.

The pot began to boil over on the stove.

"Damn," cried Pam, "Damn. Damn. Damn," she sobbed. She tried to wipe her eyes on her apron and then collapsed onto the floor, overcome with sorrow and fury. I turned off the stove and bent down next to her. I held her while she cried—and sobbed—and cried.

Pam knew how much Jackie wanted the baby. She was crying for Jackie and her loss. A part of me knew that she was also crying for herself—and the child she wanted. I held her tight. I felt guilty. As much as I hated to admit it, I had caused Pam pain by not being there for her as much as she needed me to be.

It took three days to track down Jack. No one knew where he was. *The Washington Post* carried a front-page story that was picked up by wire services all around the world: *Senator Kennedy on Mediterranean Trip Unaware That His Wife Has Lost Baby.* Jack was finally located when his chartered forty-foot yacht docked for re-supply in Genoa, Italy. He had blithely called home to talk with his wife and discovered the tragedy that had transpired. He was in the company of Senator George Smathers, his youngest brother, Teddy—and a boat full of prostitutes and girlfriends. To everyone's absolute shock, Jack told his grieving wife that he saw no reason to cut his vacation short to come home—he had already missed the burial of Baby Arabella in Newport.

Old Joe was so mad that he ordered Jack home at once. The message finally got through to Jack that he needed to head home to be at the side of his shattered wife.

Pam was mollified when she learned that Jackie had decided to ask for a divorce. But she became upset once more when she found out that Jackie had changed her mind—for when Jackie approached her father-in-law with the news that she wanted to end her marriage, he offered her a million dollars not to divorce Jack. Jackie shrewdly accepted Old Joe's offer. She understood that she now held Jack's future political aspirations in her hand.

After all, a divorced Roman Catholic would stand zero chance of ever being elected President of the United States.

LATE IN AUGUST, we trained a second group of U-2 pilots for deployment. We decided to set up a second base of operations in Incirlik, Turkey. By having two separate bases of U-2 operations, we could formulate even longer flights. We wouldn't have to worry about making it back to Wiesbaden. Though as we began to settle in and become operational, we became increasingly concerned about two threats to world peace in Egypt and Hungary.

In July, Egyptian president Gamal Abdel Nasser nationalized the Suez Canal Company from the British in retaliation for the British and the Americans withdrawing support for the Aswan Dam project. The British began to build troop concentrations on the islands of Cyprus and Malta in preparation for an intended invasion of Egypt to overthrow Nasser and regain control of the strategically vital canal.

In October, the Hungarian Revolution occurred. What began as a student protest in Bucharest to demand free elections and the removal of Soviet troops from Hungarian soil erupted into 250,000 Hungarian citizens spilling out into the streets in support of those demands. On November 4, the Soviets attacked Budapest with 200,000 troops and 4,000 tanks. The Hungarian people put up a valiant fight, but the superior Russian forces overwhelmed them. The Soviets justified their actions by claiming that they acted "to help the Hungarian people crush the black forces of reaction and counter-revolution."

Despite frantic requests to assist the Hungarian people, President Eisenhower refused to extend any help. The Soviet Union warned everyone they possessed long-range ballistic missiles armed with nuclear weapons which they were not afraid to deploy. Eisenhower believed their threat and considered our option—if the Soviets attacked the Allies, the United States would have to retaliate. His only option was restraint. As Americans went to the polls on November 6, 1956, the President was pointedly worried about the possibility of World War III breaking out.

President Eisenhower began to change his mind about the value of the data he received from the U-2's after the events in Hungary and the Suez. The President's desire to maintain a "correct and moral" position was tempered by the need to adequately defend the United States from any Soviet threat. Thus, he decided to allow overflights to continue, as long as the planes stayed "as close to the border as possible" and didn't venture deep into "denied areas." By "denied areas," he meant the USSR itself.

President Eisenhower was elected to a second term in a landslide over Stevenson. At Thanksgiving, the Kennedy family assembled in Hyannis Port, along with a few close friends. At Jackie's firm insistence, Pam, Tim, and I were invited to join them. During the weekend, Jack and his father retired to the privacy of a small study off the living room. Upon emerging hours later, Jack announced to the entire family he was going to be a candidate for the presidency in 1960. Jack pointed out that he had managed to come within thirty-three and a half votes of winning the vice presidential nomination. "If I work hard for four years, I ought to be able to pick up all the marbles."

Yeah, just keep dreaming, Jack, I thought. There's not a chance of that ever happening.

"Whether you like it or not, history is on our side. We will bury you."
— Nikita Khrushchev

September 6, 1978
2:22 p.m.

Grant lay down on the leather Bauhaus sofa in his office, something he rarely did. He knew his blood pressure was elevated. His doctor had warned him that he had to get his pressure under control, or he could have a massive coronary. He suspected that he had an ulcer—his stomach hurt most of the time.

"Hell, I'm gonna fix me a drink," he sat up.

Standing before his bar, an antique armoire with rosewood and maple inlays, refreshed his resolve. It was one of the first purchases that he made when he "hit the big time." He reached for one of matching glasses to a heavy cut-crystal bar set.

Grant poured himself three fingers of Chivas and sat down in the wing chair next to the sofa. That was another one of his purchases, an antique wing chair. His office was elegant and understated.

He honestly didn't know what to do about his son. The legalities were easy—he could take care of that. But Lyndon had defiled Ed Clark's granddaughter. That wasn't so easy to fix. Lyndon could marry the girl, but fifteen years old was awful young. Grant suspected that it was going to cost him a lot to get out of this one. And if he didn't take care of Patrick, well, he didn't want to think about that.

Grant's private line lit up. He answered the phone that was next to his chair.

"I'm listening," he said morosely.

"We're following a lead about a guy matching Patrick's description who got a cruise ship for Puerto Rico. Also, the name is one that Patrick has used before. I'll have someone there when the ship docks."

"Any other leads?"

"Baltimore airport was clean."

"What about his car?"

"We haven't found it yet."

"Do you think he's on his way to Puerto Rico?" Grant wanted Ruger to say yes.

"It would be good for us if that's where he's headed. I've got a number of reliable people who could help us out. We'll wait and watch."

"Thanks," Grant said. And for the first time that day, Ruger didn't hang up on him.

"We'll get him. Don't worry."

Wait and watch. Or wait and worry. Either way, he had to depend on Ruger.

1957

OVER A YEAR had passed since I first presented my intelligence project to Mr. Dulles and Mr. B about collecting information from inside the closed borders of the Soviet Union. Since then, I had drafted a formal proposal and had presented it to the DDI for review by the strategic planning committee. I was contacted twice to elaborate and answer questions about my idea, but nothing further had developed. I felt, now more than ever, we needed human intelligence to go with our new U-2 photographs. "Humint" would enable us to better quantify our enemy's ability to wage a war against us. I had about lost hope of ever seeing my proposal implemented. Now suddenly, I was told not only was my idea viable, upper management had even come up with a possible candidate for me to interview.

I met A.J. a few days later at a safehouse in Georgetown. I had already read his dossier, so I knew he was born in Riga, Latvia. He and his parents escaped from behind the Iron Curtain in 1946 by way of Helsinki, Finland. I was excited about A.J. because he was fluent in Russian. Although his parents didn't speak English, his English language proficiency and his use of American slang made him appear to be a typical teenager raised in a typical American household.

A.J. was about twenty years old. He had thin, wispy brown hair cut short to his head, just slightly longer than a brush cut. His eyes were gray and clear, almost penetrating in their gaze. His facial features, aside from a cleft in his chin, were really rather bland, as many people of Slavic descent seemed to be. I guessed that he stood about five foot eight and weighed no more than 130 pounds. He certainly wasn't handsome in a Nordic or Scandinavian sense.

He was exactly what I had envisioned—his features would not stand out in anyone's memory, which would allow him to easily blend in with the Russian populace.

I found him to be intelligent and very self-assured. He had been recruited by the Agency at the University of Wisconsin, where he attended classes. The Agency had a number of professors in major universities under contract to assist us in finding promising young men who might have a talent for espionage. A.J. was a political science major, who according to his professor "had a burning desire to bring the Soviet Union down and restore freedom to the oppressed Soviet people." I discovered over the course of our two-hour interview that he indeed had a deep and abiding hatred of the Soviet Union. His older brother and two of his uncles had been taken away in the middle of the night by the KGB, imprisoned, and later executed for simply expressing unhappiness with the Soviet government.

A.J. had a natural gift of mimicry. He reminded me of Grant in that respect. He had been active in the drama school and was astute at people watching. He briefly demonstrated how easily he could take in speech patterns, dialects, and the mannerisms of even the most casual acquaintance by imitating the southern agent who had set up this interview for us. I was excited about the possibilities. A.J. seemed to be the perfect candidate—he had a non-descript appearance, and like a chameleon, he could easily assimilate into his immediate surroundings.

By the time our interview was over, I was convinced he represented the best possible candidate for my project. I got the go-ahead to start training him as a low-level Agency analyst here in D.C. We decided to put him through a thorough orientation and training course while we subtly subjected him to a battery of tests to determine whether or not he had the aptitude to become a field agent.

I CONTINUED MY work with Project Chalice. Each U-2 flight over the Soviet Union advanced our knowledge of the USSR's strengths and weaknesses. We were, however, slightly disturbed by how easily the Soviets tracked our overflights—they knew where we were flying to and from, and they knew the approximate height at which we operated. We knew it was only a matter of time before they figured out how to stop us.

They had already positioned people outside of our West German and Turkish airbases who diligently called the Soviet air defense network every time they saw one of our U-2's take off. On one night flight out of Turkey, the Russians scrambled fifty-seven fighter planes to try intercepting one of our U-2's. They also developed a technique for flying squadrons of airplanes directly below our plane hoping their planes might block our view of the ground and facilities below. I remember Kelly Johnson referred to them as "aluminum clouds."

We continued to collect intelligence data. On one flight, the pilot spotted a railroad track in the middle of nowhere and followed it to its terminus. After developing the film, we discovered stunning new pictures of a Soviet missile launcher at a site we hadn't even known existed. Richard Helms was impressed. He said it was "as if we in the intelligence community had cataracts removed, because previous to these splendid U-2 missions our ability to pierce the Iron Curtain was uncertain and the results were often murky."

IN MID-MARCH, I was sent to the Naval Air Station at Atsugi, Japan just west of Tokyo to set up our third U-2 detachment and to supervise the Agency side of the operation. My superiors were giving me more and more responsibility; I was on an Agency fast track. As pleased as I was with my career, I could not convey those feelings to Pam.

Originally built by Emperor Hirohito in 1938 for the Japanese Imperial Army, the Atsugi base had an impressive history. The Japanese conducted their air defense from this base—Zero and Gekko fighter planes—Kamikazes. General MacArthur flew to Atsugi to accept the Emperor Hirohito's formal surrender on August 30, 1945. By 1950, the facility was in a state of total disrepair. Even though there were three rail lines—Odakyu, Fujisawa, and Jinchu line—the place was secluded and forlorn. Situated in the heart of the Kantu plain, the base was surrounded by farmland or pine forests. I knew that the United States government had dumped a great deal of money in refurbishing the facility.

I was pleasantly surprised to find comfortable accommodations when I arrived. After living in the crude lodgings of The Ranch at Groom Lake in Nevada and the drafty, noisy rooms above the local pub in Lakenheath, I was prepared for the worse. I was bivouacked at BOQ—Base Officers Quarters. The base was a home away from home for all those stationed there. It had a bowling center, theater, outdoor pool, basketball and volleyball courts, a supermarket, and all different types of social clubs—entertainment was limitless. The men would not have to resort to just eating, drinking, and gambling to pass the time—or to setting off homemade rockets, firing them into sky and almost hitting a C-124 transport plane which was attempting to land at Groom Lake. The men also had their families here at Atsugi. I wondered if Pam and Tim would be happy here.

The Agency had selected Atsugi because of the vast improvements in other areas—a new photo lab, control tower, updated telephone lines—and the accommodations for high performance aircraft like the F3H, F4H, F8U, FJ-4, and the F11F. It was the perfect site for our U-2.

I spent the first few days in operational details, planning out various routes for our flights. Having worked three 12-hour days in a row, I decided to go over to the basketball court to blow off a little steam. Several guys were already on the floor. Hoping to join in on a game, I sat down on a bench to change my shoes. I had just pulled the laces tight when I heard, "Mr. McCarthy, over here."

"Mr. B?"

"I just got in this morning." He extended his hand, "How are you doing, Patrick?"

I knew something was up if Bissell had traveled all the way from Washington to see me. "Let's go over to the Officer's Club. Even though this is Japan, you'd think you were at home—the food's actually good," I said.

I waited until he was on his second cup of coffee to ask why he was in Atsugi.

"We may have a problem with our U-2 program. It seems we're not the only ones to have a supersonic aircraft."

I felt like I had been sucker-punched. Had the Soviets been able to develop a similar plane? All the reports had been emphatic that they were years behind in their technology.

"The Soviets?" I asked.

"No. The Canadians."

I blinked in wide-eyed amazement. The Canadians?

"The Canadian aerospace industry is about to announce the Avro Arrow C-105. They've been secretly working on a high-speed, high altitude interceptor for the past four years."

"Is it comparable to the U-2?"

"It is better. The Royal Canadian Air Force jet is a supersonic jet capable of operating at a combat ceiling of not less than 60,000 feet with a maximum speed at the altitude of Mach 2."

I thought the United States possessed the most advanced aeronautical expertise in the world. We obviously didn't have a plane like that on our drawing board; otherwise, we would have built the U-2 with those superior specifications. Our U-2 flew 180 knots at 70,000 feet. This new Canadian jet could fly somewhere around 1400 knots at that same altitude.

"We have a massive problem on our hands," I pushed my coffee cup aside. We had given ourselves two years to make our U-2 program work—after that, we felt the Soviets would probably be able to finally intercept and stop us.

"What makes this so highly unusual is the Canadians have never been known as front-line international aerospace manufacturers or builders, and yet they've somehow managed to design and manufacture what might be the world's most powerful and potentially fastest fighter aircraft," Mr. B said.

I shook my head. "I know the Agency has kept a careful eye on everything the Soviets, the French, and the British were up to, but who would have thought to keep an eye on the damned Canadians?"

"Sweet Jesus, I sure didn't. When I investigated the first rumors, I found out they have been working with our own Air Force and some of our American manufacturers on this for the last five years or so."

"Well, one thing's for sure," I said, "it appears their Skunk Works is as good as ours. I'd like to know why our guys didn't say anything. They must have known we would have been interested in that information."

"I don't know. Maybe this is General LeMay's way of getting back at us for starting our own air force." He paused to collect his thoughts. "I guess I believed we had a solid monopoly on genius here in the United States. I now have to re-evaluate our position."

"How could this have happened?"

"Complacency. Arrogance?"

"We should have been actively engaged in developing an airplane with these specifications. So, should have the Brits."

"The Canadians were smart enough to see an opportunity while our attention was focused elsewhere. Actually, it is a remarkable achievement. They've already hinted Mach 3 capability might soon be within their plane's reach."

I laughed in surprise, "This immediately renders our U-2 obsolete—because if the Canadians can design and build something like this, surely the Soviets can too."

"Probably, although I suspect the Soviets will be as surprised as we were when they find out what our northern neighbors have been up to. My most immediate concern is the possibility the Soviets will get their hands on one of these Avros and use it to make a quantum leap forward in their own designs."

"Are we going to buy some of these ourselves?"

"You've come to know Kelly Johnson pretty well. What do you think his reaction would be if we suddenly announced we were going to start buying airplanes from Canada that were significantly better than anything he has ever produced?"

"He'd be damn pissed off."

"Well, just multiply that reaction by the number of Congressmen that would be equally upset. No, I don't think we'll be buying any Avro Arrows."

"Then what's going to happen to them? The Canadians obviously have an attractive product to export worldwide. The Israelis, the Egyptians, and the Chinese, at the very least, will all be lined up to buy these planes if they're as good as you say they are."

"I'm worried," he sighed, "that they might actually be even better than we think they are. I've got it on good authority that these planes might be the finest fighter planes the world has ever seen."

With the state of the world as it was, it would be dangerous for the Egyptians, the Chinese, or the Soviets to get their hands on these planes.

Mr. B could see my apprehension. I patted my pocket for a cigarette.

"Patrick," he looked at me directly and lowered his voice, "that is, *IF* the world ever gets to see them."

"What do you mean?"

"I mean, we're going to put a halt to their manufacture."

"Sabotage?"

"Only the political kind. I prefer to think of it as a form of moral-suasion, as they say on Wall Street. Allen's already talked to his brother—Foster said he's going to put significant and powerful political pressure on the Canadian government to pull the plug on this project."

"Do you think that will work?"

"I expect it will. Foster can be persuasive when he has to be."

As it turned out, the Canadian government later killed the Avro Arrow project. The decision was so extremely controversial it almost destroyed the Canadian aerospace industry, the Canadian economy, and nearly brought down the sitting Canadian government.

The Canadians dealt with ripple effect of the Avro debacle for many years afterward.

PAM AND I resumed our practice of Friday night date-night whenever I returned home. Even when we were newly married, we always reserved Friday evening as our special evening. I turned down many an invitation to play poker with my buddies, go to a ballgame, or just to go to the bar, in order to spend time with Pam.

Grant criticized me unmercifully about this practice, claiming Pam was going to get the upper hand and start calling the shots in our marriage. He protested I was too predictable and women didn't like predictable men. He made it a project of his to get me to go out with him and "the guys" on Friday night.

That was one area where Grant and I didn't see eye-to-eye. Everything was an issue of control with Grant. Pam derisively referred to him as "The

Grand Puppeteer," and she had a point. He was constantly orchestrating, always trying to manage the strings of his life and those of the other people around him. He never understood that I actually looked forward to my Friday nights with my wife, and I never once considered giving them up—especially to spend time with him.

On my first Friday night home, Pam arranged to take Tim for a sleepover with one of his friends. I could not believe how much he had grown. He was now almost five years old and could actually engage me in conversation. He also had some impressive powers of observation. He told me the color and the make of every car in the neighborhood by showing me the pictures he had drawn. In the center of one was a bright blue sedan with the sun shining above it. Down at the very bottom of the picture was our car, which he had colored a muddy shade of green. I could tell he thought our old Ford was substandard.

The rest of his childishly drawn picture almost brought me to tears. Tim had drawn himself with his mother, hand in hand, standing by the old car. The words *mommy* and *me* were carefully printed above their heads. I wasn't in the picture at all. I asked, "Where's Daddy? Do you have a picture with Daddy in it?" He simply said, "Nope." His picture was worth more than a thousand words because I had seen into my son's world—a world that didn't have a Daddy.

Pam tried to brighten my mood by handing me a picnic hamper. "Come on. We're going down to the park. The Arlington Forest Civic Band is holding an evening concert at the band shell. I thought it would be fun, and I thought maybe you could get to know some of our neighbors." It struck me that I couldn't remember meeting a single neighbor in the two years that we had lived in our house.

We had purchased our home on Edison Street within walking distance of Kate Waller Barrett Elementary School. Across the street from our house was a deep ravine leading down into Lubber Run Park. The park consisted of a secluded area of thick woods split by Lubber Run Creek, deep in the heart of tiny Arlington. When we bought the house, we had imagined what fun Tim would have playing there. It was a little boy's paradise. We also imagined what fun we would have there as a family—taking walks and temporarily escaping from our busy lives.

Navigating the steep incline down to the center of the park was a little precarious since I was carrying a huge hamper and Pam was carrying lawn chairs. We laughed as I tripped and almost fell down the path. "You should have worn your tennis shoes instead of your slick-soled work shoes," Pam teased me. "I don't want to have to wait on you hand and foot because you're in bed with a broken leg."

"I don't think waiting on me in bed is such a bad idea," I countered. I was ready to make a little more suggestive comment when I saw a dark cloud descend over Pam's face. We walked a little farther in silence. I could tell by Pam's worried expression that she was upset about something.

"Honey, what is it?" I didn't expect Pam to answer. She had become adept at keeping her thoughts to herself. Both of us had begun to feel the distance in our relationship.

"I don't want us to end up like Jackie and Jack," she confessed to me. "There are all kinds of rumors up and down the East Coast that Jack and Jackie are splitting up, and that bothers me as much as it bothers her."

"How's she doing with this latest pregnancy?" I asked. Jackie was now pregnant for the third time. I knew Pam had her fingers crossed every day that Jackie wouldn't lose this baby the same way she had lost her other two.

"She's having a tough time. Black Jack Bouvier passed away this summer and was buried in the family plot up in East Hampton. I went to the funeral, and there weren't any more than two dozen mourners present. I truly felt sad for her. Jack wasn't even there. He was off doing, well you know, what he was probably doing. I hate it that he leaves Jackie alone for such long stretches at a time. I know it bothers her as much as it bothers me—probably more."

What really bothered me was she was describing our relationship, but without the serial philandering. I silently vowed to try to cut down on the amount of traveling that I was doing. Both my son and my wife had painted a very dreary picture for me. I clearly needed to start paying more attention to my own lovely wife and her needs.

In early September 1957, I reluctantly returned to Atsugi, even though in my heart I wanted to stay in D.C. I had an assignment to complete, and it was an unfortunate stroke of bad luck that it involved traveling halfway around the world to complete it. I knew it was important to the future safety and well-being of my country and my family.

Pam tried to be supportive and understanding when I packed my bags to leave, but I knew that it was an act. I was sad when I tried to say good-bye to Tim this time—he continued coloring and only slightly raised his head to say "Good-bye again, Daddy."

I WAS WALKING through the radar room at the base at Atsugi when I almost ran headfirst into my new protégé, A.J., who was wearing a Marine uniform. I was momentarily speechless, for here was my low-level Agency trainee, working at a radar console in a highly classified area where he was monitoring our top-secret U-2 surveillance flights.

I was shocked when he looked right at me and acted as if he didn't even know who I was—this guy was a great actor. I was shaking inside. How in the hell did A.J. get in here without me knowing about it? I convinced myself this must have been a test of our operational security.

I approached his radar console. "Hey, A.J., what are you doing here?"

Instead of a reply, I received a startled glance as A.J. looked me in the eyes—then turned to look over his shoulder.

"A.J.?" I said again.

He straightened up in his chair and said, "Sir, are you speaking to me, sir?"

I gawked at him. He had even managed to disguise his voice with a little bit of a southern accent.

"Yes, soldier, I am speaking to you."

He quickly stood up and assumed a more formal stance as any good Marine would do when in the presence of a senior officer. "Sir—I'm sorry, sir—for not properly acknowledging you—sir. But I wasn't sure you were addressing me, sir."

Even though the Agency hadn't inducted me into the armed forces, those men working in the operation knew my status at Atsugi around the U-2 program. I was treated with the same respect and dignity by the enlisted men that the Marine Corps afforded all of its officers.

I looked at his nametag to be sure I was reading it right. I stared directly back into his eyes. "Is that your real name, soldier?" I asked.

"Yes sir, but my friends all call me Ozzie, sir."

"Ozzie?"

"Yes, sir, like Ozzie Rabbit, sir," he acted as if I was supposed to know who "Ozzie Rabbit" was. There was still not a single sign of recognition flickering in his eyes. I had to admit he was playing the part extremely well; he thought I was testing him.

"At ease, Marine. That's all. Return to your station."

He nodded and sat back down to concentrate on the glowing radar screen in front of him. I walked down the hall to find the unit commander. Colonel Stan Beerli was on the telephone at this desk. I waited outside the door until he acknowledged me.

"Colonel, I just met one of the young radar operators." I gave him the name from the nametag. The colonel turned to retrieve his personnel jacket from a file cabinet directly behind him.

"Did he give you any problems," he asked.

"No, no problems. I'm just curious about him. He reminds me of someone I know. What can you tell me about him?"

The colonel began going through the file. "There's not much here—standard material, that's all."

"Is it all right if I look at the file, Colonel?" I was anxious to determine if A.J. was here under an assumed name.

"Sure thing, here it is."

According to the file, his birthday was October 18, 1939, and his birthplace was New Orleans. That had to be wrong. A.J. wasn't born in New Orleans—he was born in Riga, Latvia.

"Colonel," I asked, "what do you know about this guy?"

"Not much—at all. Coffee Mill has 117 men in it, and they just don't stand out unless they're incompetent or they're troublemakers. I've never had any complaints about him. Why, is there a problem?"

I shook my head. "No, there's no problem, thank you, Colonel."

So this wasn't A.J. after all. What surprised me was how much the two men looked alike—weight, height, eye color, hair. Ozzie was virtually a dead ringer for A.J.—except A.J. had a pronounced cleft in his chin.

The almost identical appearance of the two men had completely fooled me.

I HURRIED BACK to my office and sent a teletype to D.C. to access Ozzie's service record. Unfortunately, it was the middle of the night back in the States, so I had to wait a day or two for my answer. I began to run scenarios through my head, and they all involved Ozzie. I was excited—what were the chances that the man I selected to infiltrate Russian society would have a double? I did not know exactly how I would use Ozzie, but I instinctively knew that he would play a key role in my project. And once I reviewed his service record, I realized that it would be easy to switch Ozzie's identity with A.J.'s in Project Cocoon.

Ozzie enlisted in the Marine Corps in July 1956 and was sworn in on October 24. He was sent to San Diego for ten weeks of boot camp. He almost flunked out of the Corp, not because he could not endure the rigorous training of boot camp, but because he couldn't shoot. He had barely qualified for *Marksman*, the lowest designation that the Corps awards. If he'd had one more miss, he would have been out. After finishing boot camp, he was sent to the Infantry Training Regiment at Camp Pendleton, California on January 20, 1957. On March 18, he was transferred to the Naval Air Technical Training Center in Jacksonville, Florida; on May 3, he was promoted to "Private-First Class" and was given security clearance to handle confidential material. The Marines sent him to Kessler Air Force Base in Biloxi, Mississippi, where they trained him to be an aircraft radar and warning operator. He was designated as an aviation electronics operator in June after he finished seventh in his class of thirty. He was classified with the Military Occupation Specialty Code of 6741, and then he was assigned to the Marine Air Control Squadron One (MACS-1) here in Atsugi. He joined his unit here on August 23, 1957.

I wondered what led Ozzie to enlist in the Marine Corp and not some other branch of the military. The warrior mystique of the Marine Corp has always had a certain appeal to young men. The Marines have been regarded as an elite brotherhood of warriors ever since Captain William Jones first advertised for "a few good men" in 1779 to help staff a naval base outside of Boston. They also have the reputation of "first to fight," but I think their values of honor, courage, and commitment have been most responsible for igniting the flame of patriotism in hundreds of thousands of soldiers. I can only imagine how many men have joined the Marine brotherhood because of those simple values. I know that General MacArthur's praise of the Marines' courage in Korea moved me—I was also moved (and still am) by the Code of Conduct approved by President Eisenhower in 1955: *"I am an American, fighting in the armed forces which guard my country and our way of life. I am prepared to give my life in their defense...I will never forget that I am an American, responsible for my actions, and dedicated to the principles which made my country free. I will trust in my God and in the United States of America."*

I needed to talk to Ozzie to find out if he was also moved by honor, courage, and commitment.

I first approached Ozzie when he was taking a cigarette-break outside the building. After we got past his initial nervousness and his need to punctuate every response with "sir," he began to tell me about his family.

"My father died of a heart attack two months before I was born, so I never knew my father at all. I have a stepbrother, John, and another older brother named Robert—my mom was married before. I didn't know them too well though. After my father died, my mother put John and Robert in a Catholic boarding school. She had to go out and find work. She was a telephone operator."

"That must have been rough on you, not having your mother around much."

"Well, we lived with my mother's sister, Aunt Lil, and her husband, Uncle Dutch."

"Where did you live? I mean, what part of the country are you from?" Of course, I already knew the answer to the question.

"New Orleans." He reached for another cigarette, pointed the package in my direction, "You smoke?"

"We lived with my aunt and uncle until my mom remarried," he said. He stopped as if he had a bad memory, "But that didn't work out. They got divorced. I think I was about ten years old."

Ozzie seemed to have had a turbulent childhood. He changed schools five times before fifth grade. He lived for a time in New York when his brother John got married, but he was miserable there.

"I can hear a trace of New Orleans in your accent," I said.

"Yeah—that got me in lots of fights, I can tell you. Every time I opened my mouth, some kid tried to shut it for me. After a while, I stopped going to school. I got tired of having black eyes, skinned knuckles, sore ribs—you name it."

"What did your mother do? Didn't she make you go to school?"

"She tried. I got in trouble with the city juvenile authorities for truancy. I spent six weeks at the New York Youth House—that was a juvenile detention facility."

"I can't imagine being locked up at that age. How did you handle it?"

"I don't know. I just did. I can tell you that it made school look like a vacation. I did real good in eighth grade—I was even voted president of my class. But that didn't last long."

"Why? What happened?"

"Oh, I screwed up, and my probation got extended for an extra two months. That made mom mad. So, we packed up and moved back to New Orleans."

"Now you are in Japan. You are a Marine. You have discipline. You've come a long way, Ozzie."

"Yeah, but I've had a tough time fitting in and finding friends. I guess that's why I love the Marines. I always wanted to become a Marine because they're the toughest fighting outfit that Uncle Sam has. I love my country and the only thing I ever wanted to do was to join the armed forces like my two older brothers."

"What do you think you'd be doing if you weren't in the Marines?"

"I don't know. I've never thought about it."

"Okay. Think about it this way—what would you like to do after you leave the Marines?"

"That's easy. I'd be a spy—like Herbert Philbrick."

Ozzie could tell that I had no idea what he was talking about.

"The TV program—*I Led Three Lives*. You never heard of it?"

"I don't get to watch much television," I replied.

"It was my favorite program as a kid. There's this FBI informant—Herbert Philbrick—he posed as a Communist—in order to bring down the Communist spy outfits operating in the United States. I always wanted to be just like Philbrick, and live undercover and root out Commie traitors like he did."

This was too easy. I thought that I would have to spend a great deal of time with Ozzie to convince him to be a part of Operation Cocoon. I decided to end the conversation. I needed time to further investigate Ozzie. On the surface, it appeared that he was just a kid who wanted to serve his country. Before I made him a part of a top-secret operation, I needed to know more about him.

"I've kept you too long, Ozzie. Your break has been over for a least a half an hour. I'll tell your commanding officer you were with me so you don't get into trouble."

Ozzie stood and straightened his uniform. "Nice talking to you, sir, I mean, Patrick," he smiled a crooked smile, and I understood how much it took for him to open up to me as a potential friend.

THERE WASN'T MUCH more to find out about Ozzie. Over the course of the next few weeks, I made some subtle inquiries, but everyone said the same thing: "Nice kid—works hard—doesn't talk much." I asked the Agency to launch some clandestine investigations on Ozzie's family—they didn't find anything.

I called down to the radar room and advised the sergeant on duty that I needed to see Ozzie. Within minutes, he was standing in my office. I thought he looked like a kid who had been called to the principal's office. I decided to get right to the point.

"Ozzie, this is a long story, most of which I cannot tell you for reasons of national security. But you've convinced me you're the right man for a job we have planned. I work for the Central Intelligence Agency out of Washington, and I need your help."

Ozzie looked unsteady on his feet. "Sit down, Ozzie. There's no need for you to stand."

"Yes sir."

I ignored his use of "sir"—after all I would be his boss. I liked that about Ozzie. He understood his place in the scheme of things. "You told me that you've always wanted to be a spy. Were you serious?"

He nodded, "I haven't told anybody this, but I tried to get into the FBI..."

I continued on without giving him a chance to elaborate. "This country's best spies are employed by the CIA not the FBI—which really doesn't matter—I want you to come work for us."

"Am I qualified? The FBI said that I wasn't."

"Ozzie, you are qualified if I say you are qualified."

Ozzie let out a deep breath and shook his head a little.

"I know—this is a lot to take in." I gave him a moment. "I am currently in charge of a top-secret program that can use your help. You told me you've always wanted to serve your country in a heroic way. Well, this could be as valuable to your country as Herbert Philbrick's work. Would you be willing to look into this with me?"

For the first time, I saw a spark of excitement in Ozzie's eyes.

"I have to go back to D.C. and review a few details with my superiors. This conversation is top secret—that means that you cannot say anything about your meeting with me—not even to your sergeant, should he ask about our meeting. If you tell anyone about what I've just told you, I'll be forced to revoke my offer. Understood?"

He nodded and replied, "Understood."

OUR ELATION OVER the success of the U-2 program suddenly evaporated. On October 4, the Soviet Union launched the world's first orbiting satellite. Called *Sputnik*, which meant "fellow traveler" in Russian, it represented a huge psychological victory for our enemy and significantly raised the level of threat to the United States, especially in the age of atomic weapons. A French journalist wrote, "The Russian people can…see in the sky a brilliant star which carries above the world the light of Soviet power."

Senator Henry Jackson of Washington wanted President Eisenhower to declare "a week of shame and danger" while Senator Lyndon Johnson stood on the floor of the Senate and warned, "The Roman Empire controlled the world because it could build roads…the British Empire was dominant because it had ships. Now the Communists have established a foothold in outer space."

As we examined data, we uncovered some disturbing facts. The Russian rocket that put *Sputnik* in orbit had a calculated thrust that was roughly ten times greater than our most powerful rocket, and the Soviet scientists had achieved an earth orbit that was extraordinarily precise. These two facts, when put together, indicated they also had the ability to deliver a weapons payload with considerable precision anywhere in the world—which most likely, meant anywhere in the United States.

That damned little satellite also broadcast a continuous "beep-beep"—the whole world could tune a simple radio to hear it. The tone oscillated between 20 and 40 megacycles, which seemed to indicate it was sending some kind of a code back to the Russians from outer space. Our Agency assigned teams of our best cryptographers to work in shifts to break the code.

In the blink of an eye, Soviet satellite technology had suddenly and completely rendered our U-2 obsolete. We felt as helpless as the Soviets must have felt when we started flying our U-2's so high over their heads and out of their reach. The obvious success of their Sputnik created a sense of insecurity throughout America. We heard over and over again "the nation is in grave danger" and that we were falling behind the Soviets in the technology race.

One night I stood out on the front lawn of our house with my family as we scanned the evening sky for the sight of the bright light that represented *Sputnik's* presence. I could clearly see the stress and strain reflected in Pam's eyes as she contemplated the reality of this new threat.

"The Russians are really up there, watching us?" She held Tim tight against her, "Patrick?"

I didn't want to unnecessarily alarm Tim, so I said, "It's only a satellite; it's just another light in the sky."

"I don't see it, Daddy."

"I guess that makes your job even more important now."

Pam had never commented on my job. But I agreed, "Yes, it does."

WHILE I WAS in Washington working on the details for the next phase of Project Cocoon, I got an urgent wire from Colonel Beerli. On October 27, Ozzie had been involved in a shooting accident at the base. He faced a possible court-martial for the offense. I jumped the next military plane heading for Atsugi.

In the Navy hospital at Yokosuka, Ozzie was being treated for a self-inflicted gunshot in his left arm just above the elbow. He told medical personnel he had been wounded when he accidentally dropped his military-issue .45 caliber pistol on the ground; it had discharged, hitting him in the arm. The medical staff was extremely skeptical because the bullet hole was a lot smaller than a .45. It was more like the wound that a .22 caliber bullet would make. That meant Ozzie was in serious trouble, for it was against all regulations for any enlisted men to own private firearms. He looked embarrassed when he recognized me as I walked into his hospital ward.

"Do you want to tell me what happened?"

"What, no flowers or even a simple, 'Hi, how are you doing?'" he weakly joked.

I didn't laugh. I repeated my question, "Ozzie, what happened?"

He averted his eyes and took a deep breath. "I don't know. I panicked I guess. Especially when I received orders sending me to the Philippines."

I knew that several units had been deployed to the Philippines because of a growing civil war in Indonesia. "I don't understand, Ozzie."

"I had to do something. It was stupid—I know that now. But I was worried that I would lose the chance to work on your project if I wasn't here in Atsugi."

"So, you shot yourself?"

"I had a little two-shot derringer tucked away. I've had it for years."

"Ozzie," I angrily stopped him. "Do you realize that you now face a court martial? Do you understand the gravity of what you have done? Do you understand how your actions have potentially compromised the project?"

I had to calm down so I left his room and fumed in the hallway. My entire project could be jeopardized by Ozzie's stupidity. I needed to clean up this mess. Although I wasn't a Marine, my position in the Agency gave me some influence in the matter. After several minutes, I re-entered his room.

Ozzie had his eyes closed, but he wasn't asleep. I moved next to his bed. He opened his eyes—his expression conveyed sadness, shame, and dread.

"Listen, Ozzie, I'm not sure if you are right for my project."

Ozzie groaned, "God—I've screwed up again—just like when I was a kid." He kicked at the footboard of his bed. "Patrick, I really want this. I love the Corp, but I'm not officer material. I don't have what it takes," he said with a self-deprecating sigh. "Patrick, I am so sorry I let you down."

I felt bad for Ozzie. Here was a kid whose heart was in the right place. He loved his country. My anger began to diminish; I could feel the tension leave my face.

"I will do anything—anything—to get back on track again."

"It's almost out of my hands—it all depends on your commanding officer. You're going to have to take your medicine like a man. You're going to be punished for what you did. How you accept that punishment will go a long ways toward helping me determine whether or not you're the right man for this project."

He perked up. "I will do whatever I have to do to restore your faith in me," and soberly adding, "You can count on me—this time."

"Just get well, report back to duty, and keep your nose clean. I'll come get you when I need you. If you are successful in staying out of trouble from this point on, I think I can still use you."

Ozzie's eyes teared up with relief. "Thanks, Patrick," he choked out. "I'll never let you down ever again. I promise."

I looked at him and said quietly, "I hope not, Ozzie. I hope not."

THE WEEK BEFORE Thanksgiving, Pam and I made preparations to go to Texas to attend Grant's wedding. If Grant had not phoned me to personally ask us to attend, I think we would have begged off. Grant promised me that this was going to be one "Texas Extravaganza" we wouldn't want to miss. He and his fiancée, Amy, planned a weekend of special activities and revelry for their guests. The nuptial invitation arrived in a package which, when opened, revealed an embossed leather envelope. Inside the envelope were several parchment-like sheets that detailed the events on an hourly basis. Pam and I were to be picked up at the airport by a driver and transported to the ranch. We would have an afternoon barbecue lunch followed by private time at the guesthouse. The invitation read: *Friday Night—Western Wear Required. Gentlemen, please wear a white hat.* Pam was not too thrilled with the idea of western wear, and I didn't have a white hat. I told Grant I didn't think I'd be able to find a white hat suitable for the party. He asked for my hat size and told me not to worry.

We arrived in Houston and were met by a Texas good ol' boy by the name of Mitchell. "Where are y'all from?" he asked as he led us to a brand-new Cadillac. He had a cooler filled with longneck bottles of Pearl beer on ice. About 30 miles or so outside of Austin, we pulled off the main highway in what seemed like the middle of nowhere and drove through a set of fences with lengths of pipe laid in a trench perpendicular to the road. Mitchell explained we would cross four more "cattle guards" just like this one before we reached the main entrance to the house. The cattle guards were designed to allow a car or truck to drive over the pipe, but cattle wouldn't walk through the opening because they didn't like putting their hooves between the pipes. We saw numerous Longhorn cattle grazing along the mile long drive as we approached the house. Cadillacs parked end to end lined both sides of the drive.

"I don't think I have ever seen so many white Cadillacs in my life," Pam observed. "Doesn't anyone drive a Ford or a Chevrolet?"

"No, ma'am, everybody drives Cadillacs," Mitchell answered politely.

The sight of Grant's palatial home caught us both by surprise. Two large Spanish wooden doors with elaborate iron handles opened into a magnificent terrazzo tiled foyer leading to other wings of the house on either side. Our house was a small two-story suburban home barely nine hundred square feet in size with three bedrooms and a bath—it probably would fit entirely inside Grant's foyer. Standing at the front door, we could see a large fountain in the center of an outdoor terrace. A massive Mexican credenza lined one side of the foyer, and two huge Mexican chairs defined an informal seating area. Carved French doors opened into the living room/library of the east wing. Private living quarters were in the west wing.

Mitchell announced, "Y'all are going be stayin' in the guest house. You can follow me. I'll bring in your suitcases."

When Pam and I returned to the main house after our afternoon "private time," the other guests were already milling about the fountain area. A large bar had been set up in the shade of a jacaranda tree, its branches filled with clusters of purple blossoms. The waiters, wearing traditional Mexican wedding garb, circulated among the guests refilling their glasses with Sangria.

Grant and Amy, both beaming, greeted their guests on the terrace. Amy was incredibly petite and beautiful. Her long, shiny dark hair set off her flawless skin. She wore a delicate white lace Mexican peasant dress with a silver and turquoise concha belt encircling her tiny waist.

When we sauntered in, Grant and Amy were busy encouraging their guests to move to the barn for dinner. The inside of the barn had been transformed into a gorgeous Mexican ballroom. A strolling Mariachi band serenaded the guests as they found their tables, the center of each graced with white luminarias surrounded by a wreath of yellow Texas roses. Chandeliers with enormous white candles hung from the rafters. Large urns of flowers were placed strategically throughout the room. Everything glistened, even the highly polished hardwood floor, hardly the type of floor found in a typical barn.

Pam was wide-eyed with the beauty of the room, and I was wide-eyed with the beauty of my wife. Even though she was challenged to find suitable western wear in D.C., Pam had put together a stunning outfit. She had found a full organza skirt in a rich brown color in a resale shop. She had paired it with a tailored white blouse and wore a western style sash around her waist. A heavy amber necklace, which she said was just plain gaudy, hung around her neck and matched the bracelet on her wrist. I noticed quite a few men turn to glance her way as we took our seats.

We were seated with Chase and his date, a sophisticated and likable redhead from Georgia. I later found out Deanna was an editor for *Vanity Fair* magazine. She and Pam became fast friends and engaged in animated conversation throughout the evening.

It was obvious Grant and Amy had spared no expense for the event. We were treated to a lavish six-course meal with a different wine served for every course. Grant later bragged he had flown in the head chef from the famous Commander's Palace in New Orleans to prepare the meal. After dinner, we men were encouraged to go out to the terrace for cigars. I didn't want to leave Pam alone, but for the first time in quite a while, she was immersed in adult conversation and didn't seem to mind. I reached down and kissed her, promising to be back shortly.

Chase and I meandered down to the terrace. As we arrived, a waiter stopped us and opened a highly polished wooden box which contained cigars for us to select. Another waiter brought over a tray of short crystal tumblers, a decanter of aged whiskey, and a small pitcher of water.

Grant met us enthusiastically directing us to a ring of comfortable chairs where several men were seated with their cigars and whiskey.

"Patrick! Chase! Man, I'm glad you boys could make it." Turning to introduce us, Grant exclaimed, "Gentlemen, I'd like to introduce you to my closest friends. We were roommates in Georgetown, drinking buddies at Rosie O'Grady's, and poker players on the side," Grant laughed. "Lyndon, you remember Patrick, don't you?"

Senator Lyndon Johnson extended his hand in greeting, "Of course, I do. And if you want to get a little poker game started, I'd be happy to take your money—again." Everyone laughed as Grant continued to move me through the crowd, making the appropriate introductions. His guest list was the *Who's Who* of power brokers. I recognized Sam Rayburn, the Speaker of the House of Representatives. I was introduced to Clint Murchison, a wealthy Texas oilman, along with H. L. Hunt, his noted rival. J. Edgar Hoover and Clyde Tolson had flown in from D.C. to attend this little shindig. I saw Bobby Baker and a number of other influential Texas businessmen. There were some gentlemen there from Brown & Root, a Texas construction company, long-time political supporters of both Johnson and Rayburn.

Chase was by my side for most of these introductions, but he moved away when Grant started making introductions to a couple of swarthy Italian businessmen named Sam Giancana and Carlos Marcello. When I turned around, I glimpsed Chase heading back to the barn.

I was all set to follow him when Grant caught me.

"Hey Patrick! Some of us are going to sit around the fire about midnight. I hope you'll join us." I could see Chase slowing down to wait for me. Grant sensing my hesitation, "Hey, listen—go on back to your lovely wife. Spend some time dancing with her. Then, when she gets tired, take her back to the guesthouse. If you like, you can join us when Pam turns in for the night." He patted me on the back and returned to his guests on the terrace. I noticed he hadn't mentioned Chase.

"Hey, wait up. Why are you leaving?"

He stopped to let me catch up. "Patrick, I didn't think it was a good idea to stick around. That's some group of 'friends' Grant has back there. Do you even know who half those guys really are?"

"Some. Some I've never met before."

"Well, *some* of them are mobsters, Patrick. And I personally don't want to be around them."

"You're kidding me! Mobsters? At Grant's wedding?"

"And that's not all. Clint Murchison. H. L. Hunt. Bobby Baker. All of them buddy-buddy with J. Edgar Hoover? That doesn't make sense to me."

Chase must have expected me to make a connection. When I didn't, he shook his head in disgust and stated, "I'm going back to the girls. You should come too, if you know what's good for you."

I didn't like the tone of Chase's voice, but I tagged along anyway.

Around 11:30, Pam squeezed my hand, our signal that she was ready to turn in. We said our goodnights and walked out into the cool Texas night. We were both in awe of the black Texas sky. "I guess the stars do burn bright, deep in the heart of Texas," Pam sighed as we looked at the twinkling above. I took her in my arms and gave her a kiss. "That seemed like a goodnight kiss to me," she teased, "Not a let's go-to-bed kiss, but a you-go-to-bed kiss." She knew me so well.

"Honey, Grant wants me to join some of his friends around the fire. I'd like to go, but I'll stay here, if you want."

"You go on. I am tired," she pecked me on the cheek. "But stay out of trouble—you know Grant."

I followed the stone walkway around the house until I could see the silhouette of a dozen men seated around the flickering campfire. As diverse as the group seemed to be, there was camaraderie among them judging from the sound of the banter.

As I approached the group, Grant stood up. "Patrick!" Several others stood as well. LBJ almost knocked over a small table that held his ashtray and glass of whiskey. He shook my hand, "We were just talkin' about you. You've got quite a reputation in D. C. Allen Dulles and Richard Bissell both have been braggin' about you and your talents."

"So, this is the young man that might be running the CIA one day," Sam Rayburn wheezed as he stood and extended his hand. Grant paused to bend over and grab his cigar from the ashtray in front of him.

I was a little unnerved by their greeting. I looked to Grant, hoping to see some explanation in his eyes.

Mr. Rayburn continued with his greeting, "Edgar, Lyndon, and Bobby have all commented about your skill as a poker player, and they hope we can get a card game going later this weekend. What do you say, son? Do you feel like playing a game?" Laughter rippled among the group. I felt everyone was in on the same little joke.

"Let me introduce you to Ed Clark. He's my Daddy's lawyer." At first, I thought Grant said "liar," but then I accounted for his Texas drawl and knew he said "lawyer." I extended my hand, "It's good to meet you sir."

"Patrick, these gentlemen here have been anxious to meet you. Both Allen and Richard told us your love of country is strong and admirable, as is your dedication to duty. Your exploits have greatly impressed all of us." Grant's praise was effusive.

While I had always known Grant as a sex-crazed, beer-drinking buddy who was sometimes full of crap, tonight he presented a smooth, well spoken persona. These men clearly respected him and regarded him as some kind of an up and coming power broker.

If what Chase had said was right, there was a powerful connection between all of these men—perhaps some kind of a connection I should look into. I was in unfamiliar territory. I scanned the eyes of the crowd seated around me. All eyes were on me and me alone. I shook off my distracting doubts and focused on Grant's performance.

Grant paused to take a long pull off his cigar, but I also think he did it to allow me to absorb the compliments he had made in front of the group. After exhaling a big cloud of smoke, he continued. "This rather motley collection of gentlemen, and I do use that term loosely…"

"Oh, fuck you, Grantham," Lyndon said, giving Grant "the bird" and turning to his friends for a laugh.

"…represents some of the most powerful and influential men in the country," Grant continued, ignoring Lyndon's rather raw outburst. I got the distinct impression that this type of repartee was par for the course, a cross between the serious and the bawdy.

Grant continued, "We are a group of like-minded individuals—a select group, an exclusive group, if you will. We all believe in the same principles, and we have pledged to advance and protect the ideals upon which this great nation was conceived and built."

I saw nods of approval among the shadows from the fire. "Here, here," the men raised their glasses in a toast. I was still standing and felt uncomfortable. I didn't know how I should respond. Mr. Hoover motioned for me to sit down in the empty chair next to him.

Grant attempted to make me feel comfortable, "What do you think of your cigar?"

"It's the best Cuban cigar Havana produces," Carlos Marcello boasted.

"Carlos brought these with him after his last visit to Havana," Grant said.

"Hey, Carlos, how's that Cuban pussy?" Lyndon chortled. "I hear it's the best there is! I'll bet 'ole Jumbo' here could really get a workout down there," he lewdly massaged his crotch, "couldn't he?"

"Oh hell, Lyndon, they've got some niggers down there with cocks the size of your arm. They'd make 'ole Jumbo' look like a cocktail weenie," Sam Giancana snickered. Everyone in the group, except Mr. Hoover, laughed.

Lyndon asked in exaggerated disbelief, "You mean to tell me that you've got some nigger down there with a cock bigger than mine? That big?" He comically held his hands about two feet apart. "I gotta see that!" That brought a loud round of laughter from everyone.

"Hell, Lyndon, you just won't believe your eyes. They've got this fuckin' guy they call 'Superman' with the biggest cock you've ever seen. He gets up on stage and fucks women right in front of your eyes! American tourists pack the place every single night—they can't get enough of him," Giancana chuckled. "The first time I saw him, I turned to Carlos here and said 'Damn! Does that thing come in *white*? I've never seen anything like it. The dames in the audience love it."

"Well, damn, that's just great for Superman. But that won't help 'ole Jumbo' get his nut off tonight, now will it?"

I glanced at Mr. Hoover. It was obvious that he did not approve of the conversation. He motioned to Clyde Tolson. Grant saw that Mr. Hoover was planning to leave.

"Lyndon, just calm down," Grant said. Then, he added bawdily, "Just as soon as we get done here, Sam will introduce you to a little gal who can suck the chrome clean off a trailer hitch."

"Ah, Edgar, sit down. Don't get your panties in a wad." Lyndon held up a hand, either in acknowledgement or resignation, I wasn't sure. Lyndon motioned to Grant, "Go on."

Grant resumed his host persona, "Patrick, we're all here tonight because we share a common vision for our country, and all of us have managed to find a way to work together to see that common vision realized. We come together from the worlds of business, politics, and government. We're always looking for bright new people, and you come with the highest of recommendations. That's why I'm proud to introduce you tonight to this group that we call *The Patriots*."

Mr. Hoover added solemnly, "We represent only a small part of a larger hierarchy. We try to help develop and nurture the careers of select individuals, individuals whom we consider to be the brightest and the best that the United States has to offer. We can provide guidance to you, open doors for you, and help make your life, and the lives of those in your family, much more comfortable."

Grant elaborated, "Think of us as a social organization with great ties to the business world and to government and politics."

Mr. Murchison then added, "Our influence on your behalf can help you realize your career goals and thereby eliminate any and all of your future financial concerns."

I looked at the men surrounding me. Some of them I knew, and some of them I admired. Each of these men was highly successful and respected. And all of them were united in the fight against Communism. They seemed to be sincere in their praise and acceptance of me. I didn't know how to respond. This could be one of my life's turning points, but Chase's cynical comments gnawed at me uneasily.

Lyndon blurted out, "Hell, Grant, let's get this show on the road. Ole Jumbo wants to get going."

Grant stood up and the rest of the group stood up. Our meeting was over. I was left with the feeling they had other business to discuss without me around until I heard Grant say, "Gentlemen, we're going to move our little soiree. We have several limousines to transport you to another location, not far from here. I'll join you soon."

I began to walk toward the stone path when Grant called to me. I stopped and waited for him to approach. Grant took me in a big bear hug, "Congratulations."

Unsure of myself, I asked, "Why are congratulations in order?"

"You're in. Do I have to explain to you what just happened?" he looked toward the men who were making their way to the front of the house. "Come over here and sit down," he motioned to the terrace wall. Grant oriented himself so that he could see me and simultaneously keep an eye on his guests.

"I hope you're not offended I didn't include you in the invitation to continue our little soiree," he began. Grant was both giddy and on edge.

"Patrick, we've always been the best of friends. I've perhaps been luckier than you in accumulating wealth, but you've done substantially better in proving what an asset you are to our country. I also wanted to go to war and fight Nazis and Japs, but I was too young to go. However, I wasn't immune to hard work, and with many able-bodied young men at war, there was a distinct need for bodies in the oil fields of Texas, so I went to work instead. I was getting my own education in the 'school of hard knocks,' and it was hard, almost too hard."

Grant's demeanor had changed. I was tempted to taunt him, to remind him who he was talking to, but something told me to remain quiet. This evening was a test of him and his judgment. He was being sized up as much as I was.

"There were more than a few days when I felt my resolve being tested and my back giving out, but I persevered. Every single day, I got up out of bed and went out to face my world, and every single day I crawled back into bed having learned a new lesson in life. That's the same thing I sense in you—that every single day you learn something that will only help you later in life. I like that and these men like that too."

I noticed Chase watching us from the shadows of the barn—Chase stood there alone, smoking a cigarette. I glanced at my watch; it was past 1:00 in the morning.

"None of us had anything handed to us—we all went out and earned what we have today. We all worked our asses off to achieve whatever success we are now able to enjoy. The Patriots were founded many, many years ago in order to provide a helping hand to those who were in need and might benefit from a nudge or a hand extended in friendship at just the right time.

For example, we provided financial help to Richard Nixon long before he was vice president in order to help him get elected because we liked what he stood for. You know Nixon is a good man, and our group likes to help good men like him."

He had a point. I recalled Chase telling me about how Nixon had received financial help from some wealthy Texans in some of his earlier elections.

"In fact, when Ike almost dumped Dick from the national ticket, members of our group helped to persuade him how foolish that might be. We turned out to be right, for not only has Dick made a great vice president, he'll be an excellent president in 1960 when he's elected to continue Eisenhower's legacy."

Grant paused in his story to wave to a new carload of guests who had just arrived. The party appeared to be picking up steam, not winding down.

"Let me tell you a little about the men who joined us here tonight. I know that you can keep a confidence. Let me tell you why these men get along so well. Let's start with my boss, Lyndon Johnson. Lyndon's sole ambition is to be the most powerful, most admired, most feared, most beloved, most revered man in the entire world."

I looked at Grant and wondered if he understood the humor in his hyperbole. Grant must have sensed my cynicism because he jokingly added, "Since he's not Catholic—and because he seems to have a very tough time obeying the Ten Commandments anyway—he had to rule out Pope. But seriously, President of the United States of America is very much within his grasp."

Was Grant being groomed to be a future President's right-hand man? Now, I understood his transformation.

"Lyndon has cultivated the patronage of Sam Rayburn, and Sam's shown Lyndon the ropes of political life. Around here you've heard us facetiously refer to him as 'Landslide Lyndon' for his ability to win some very close elections. Were those elections completely on the up-and-up, you might ask? Maybe, and maybe not, but Lyndon always managed to find a friendly voting box when he needed it. He's also learned how to dispense largesse to his friends and allies. He's become so good at taking money back to Washington that we also teasingly call him 'The Bagman' for the amount of loot he distributes."

Grant did not seem to have any ethical qualms about what he just told me. I now understood why Chase had decided not to investigate any further into Grant's sudden prosperity.

"But make no mistake, despite his cornpone routine, Lyndon is as shrewd and ruthless as they come, He surrounds himself with people just like himself who understand that—like Bobbie Baker over there. Lyndon's the one who gets firms like Brown & Root interested enough in the political process to support him, and then Lyndon repays their support with help securing government contracts for construction projects the world over. Lyndon's good for business, and business is good for Lyndon."

He pointed over to where the two swarthy gentlemen were sitting and drinking. "Carlos Marcello and Sam Giancana are businessmen who also have a world view of capitalism and how it works. Both are successful businessmen with vast interests in real estate and a myriad of other companies. Sam's a genius at making money. He handles money like a Jew—and better than most Jews, as a matter of fact. And when Sam makes money, everybody makes money. He also sees the whole picture better than anyone I've ever met, perhaps except for Foster Dulles. He has extended himself into alliances in Lebanon, Egypt, Guatemala, Cuba, the Far East, and virtually everywhere. He's more far-flung than the United States government. It wouldn't surprise me if he ended up running a country some day, he's that good."

I decided to needle Grant, "I think I recognize his name. Isn't he that crime guy from Chicago?"

"Shhh," Grant warned, as he suddenly looked around to see if anyone overheard my question. He leaned closer to my chair and lowered his voice. "Listen, Sam Giancana may have some business ventures which are reputed to be somewhat illegal, but so what? He's as patriotic as you or me, and he has the balls to prove it. He's always ready to lend a hand to us when we see an opportunity to strike back at communism. I happen to like him. I know that there are many rumors about him, but I've always found him to be a real stand-up guy."

"What about Mr. Hoover? What's he doing hanging out with these criminals?"

"See, that's exactly what I mean. If Mr. Hoover doesn't see anything wrong with Mr. Giancana and his business, then why should we?" Grant had a good point.

I thought about that for a minute. Though I didn't agree with Grant, I assured him, "You're probably right. If there were something wrong, I'm sure Mr. Hoover would arrest him, not go drinking with him."

"That's right, that's right," Grant stammered. "Besides, Mr. Murchison and Mr. Hunt have really taken to developing a friendship with Mr. Hoover. They're all great friends. All these guys are good guys. Look at the way Clint and Sam take care of Edgar. Clint makes sure that Edgar and Clyde Tolson get to stay at the nice hotels that he owns, and Sam helps to augment Edgar's government salary while providing tips on the horses for Edgar to play. I've never failed to see Edgar cash in big on a tip that Sam has given him. Some of those tips have paid 20-1 odds! I've personally seen Edgar walk into a track with $10,000 and walk out with $200,000 after getting some advice from Sam."

"Don't the bettors at the windows get a little nervous when they see Mr. Hoover cash in?" I didn't bet on the horses and really didn't understand horseracing, but I was certain that the sight of America's most famous G-man winning big at the horse track might appear unseemly to some.

"Oh, Edgar and Clyde take precautions about that. Edgar will go to the $1 window and bet $10, while he sends an agent to the $100 window to place the bigger bets. That way there's no suspicion aroused. It works like a charm." Grant paused and reconsidered what he had just told me, "You understand that I am talking off the record here."

I nodded.

"The one thing that we all have in common and share with you is our deep and unwavering love of country. We truly are patriots in every sense of the word. We admire and help anyone else that is also a true patriot—like yourself, Patrick. Listen, I have to get back to my guests so they don't wonder what's happened to me. I'm so goddamned happy that you were able to make it down here this weekend. It really means a lot to me." He stood up, preparing to rejoin the party. "If there's anything else you need, don't hesitate to ask."

I sat in the darkness for several minutes. Grant had always cut corners ethically, and he had always been cunning. I was torn. On one hand, I found it satisfying to know there were other people who had the same vision for America as I did. I was also grateful that The Patriots recognized my patriotism and my dedication to my country. I was strangely comforted that there seemed to be a "shadow government" of powerful men that moved America forward—no matter the party affiliation of Republican or Democrat. On the other hand, I was troubled by Chase's warning, and I was troubled by Grant's seeming lack of ethics when money was concerned.

IN NOVEMBER, JACKIE successfully gave birth to a baby girl whom she named Caroline. Mother and daughter returned to a new townhouse at 3307 N Street in Georgetown, which had been purchased by Old Joe specifically for them. Jackie had refused to return to her home in Hickory Hill, Virginia, after the death of her second baby—the property had been sold to Bobby and Ethel Kennedy at cost.

Jackie described Caroline's birth as "the very happiest day of her life." Jackie had felt inferior to the other Kennedy women who so easily gave birth—now she was ecstatic over the new daughter. She told Pam she couldn't wait for Tim to be able to play with Caroline, and Pam was sensitive enough to Jackie's joy not to remind her that Tim was over five years older than Caroline and was unlikely to be her playmate.

> *"Who saves his country, saves himself, saves all things, and all things saved do bless him. Who lets his country die, lets all things die, dies himself ignobly, and all things dying curse him!"*
>
> — Senator Benjamin H. Hill

September 6, 1978
4:39 p.m.

Grant glanced at the crystal clock on his desk and was startled to realize it was almost five o'clock. He hadn't had anything to eat all day. He was even more surprised to realize he wasn't hungry.

His private line bleeped.

"Well, the bus stations and the train stations are clear. No sign of him. Still can't find his car. No police agency has seen it either."

Grant's mind raced, "What about the cruise ship?"

"I should know in about an hour if it's him or not. I also have someone checking out flights to Canada that might be flying on to London or Paris. Patrick's not stupid."

"Maybe he's simply staying out of sight and hiding."

"Is that what you believe or what you want to believe?"

"It's probably what I want to believe," he admitted.

Grant had had several drinks. He was feeling relaxed for the first time all day. "Tell me, Derek, do you think he could be dead?"

"Nope. If he had offed himself, we would know by now. He's gone. Plain and simple."

"Do you know that for a fact?"

"Let's just say I probably have more experience in this than you do."

Grant thought a moment then conceded, "You're right."

Grant couldn't argue because he had no experience in tracking a man down. He was good at stalking a good-looking woman, but that was different. His goal was to get laid.

He shook his head at the grim irony. *This time I'm the one who might get fucked.*

1958

I CONTINUED PLANNING the details of Project Cocoon. Ozzie returned to his MACS-1 unit in November 1957 and was immediately deployed to the Philippines where he was stationed until March 1958. He returned to Atsugi to face court martial on the gun charges scheduled for April 11. I had less than a month to determine if Ozzie was the right man for the project. He had a positive attitude when I met with him at the officer's club at the base. We sat at a small table at the back of the room that offered us some privacy.

"Ozzie, this mission is for your country's national security. It's also for another brave young man, just like yourself, who wants to do whatever he can to fight the spread of Communism worldwide. I have to make sure you understand that. The stakes are extremely high for everyone involved."

He folded his hands prayerfully and rested them on the table. His eyes met mine—he was ready for me to continue.

"I know your patriotism and your love of country run pretty deep throughout your character, but I also sense your frustration in proving that to the people around you. Am I right?"

Ozzie blinked, "Yes, sir, you are right. The military made very good men out of my two brothers. I want to prove to them and to my family I can be just as good."

I paused, exhaling slowly. Ozzie would have to give up life as he knew it to work on Project Cocoon. I knew I was asking him to make a supreme sacrifice. "Oz, this is a top secret project. If you agree to help us out, you may become the most hated man in America."

Ozzie shifted uncomfortably in his chair—he stared blankly for the longest time. "Okay, go on Patrick," he said tentatively.

"Oz, listen to me and listen carefully. What I am going to ask of you will go down in history as one of the most selfless acts of bravery and patriotism ever committed for our country. Remember Nathan Hale, the Revolutionary War hero? He said, 'I only regret that…'"

"'…that I have but one life to lose for my country,'" Ozzie finished for me. "I know it by heart. It's one of my favorites."

"You will have to give up your life—your identity—for your country." I held my hand up—Ozzie sat still so I could finish. "You will not be in any physical danger. We want to use your name and your life story to infiltrate the Soviet Union."

"Just like Philbrick," Ozzie whispered.

"Yes it is. But, your friends and family will come to hate you. And I guarantee you won't be able to tell anyone what you've done until this war is over. You'll have to trust me that we will do everything in our power to clear your name when the project is completed. Do you understand what I'm telling you?"

"I understand." Ozzie paused thoughtfully, "I know this sounds kind of corny. As a kid, I would listen to guys with the big tattoos on their arms talking about battle. I know that war is horrible. That's not what I am trying to say. It's just," Ozzie paused again to find the right words, "I've never been to war. I haven't had the opportunity to give my life for my country in a war…like D-Day. This is a different kind of war—I understand how the Communists are fighting a war with us. So, this is my chance—my chance to fight for my country." Ozzie put his hands on his head, running his fingers across his buzz-cut, and bowed down over the table. After several minutes, he looked up. "I'll do it. I'll do it for my country. I'll do it for you, Patrick."

For a moment, I sat in silence with Ozzie. We both realized the seriousness of the commitment he had just made. Ozzie was the first to break the silence, "Okay, tell me what I have to do."

"We have an agent who was actually born in Russia, and we need to get him back inside to do some important work for the United States. The problem is, he can't return using his real name. He would be arrested and probably shot. The only way we can convincingly get him across the Russian border would be to use your name and identity."

"I don't see how that can work," Ozzie said.

"Remember when I first met you? I thought you were someone else?"

Ozzie nodded.

"You look just like the agent who was born in Russia. You could be twins. He's a little bit taller than you, and he has a slight cleft in his chin—but otherwise, he looks exactly like you."

Ozzie's jaw dropped, "Exactly like me? I've always heard that everyone has a double, but this is kind of weird. Can I meet him?"

"No, not yet."

Ozzie looked crestfallen.

"Ozzie, you have to trust me. Do you trust me?"

"Of course I do—I wouldn't be here today."

"Then, you have to believe that I will look out for you."

Ozzie motioned for me to continue.

"The government is prepared to give you a whole new identity, a whole new start in a new life in the United States in exchange for the use of your name and your credentials. Only a few select people in our government will ever know the truth about what you've done until the agent safely returns. You have to be secure with that knowledge in order to make this work. There might be other rewards for you somewhere down the road, but right now I can't guarantee you anything."

"Yes, sir, I understand." Through the simple use of the word "sir," Ozzie sealed his fate. "I promised you I'd never let you down again."

"Then if I've got your word, and you've got my word, are you ready to hear what we've got planned?"

He nodded once again—we firmly shook hands. Project Cocoon was ready to go.

AGENCY WORK WAS stressful. We not only felt the stress of the worldwide struggle, but we also felt the daily stress of living with secrets. Unlike most people, we couldn't let off steam at home or at the bar with co-workers after work. We learned to live with it. But sometimes people who couldn't handle the stress cracked—it was becoming apparent around headquarters that DD/P Frank Wisner was going through a mental crisis.

Tracy Barnes was the first to clue me in. "Listen, Patrick, I want to warn you that if Frank says some things to you that seem to go against the grain, please don't take it personally. He's been having a rather rough time. If you have any problems dealing with Frank, do me a favor—come see me."

The Frank Wisner I encountered shortly thereafter was not the same Frank Wisner I had worked with. As we discussed ongoing operations, his eyes glazed over, and he rambled about topics not even pertinent to the discussion. People whispered that Frank was having a nervous breakdown. I had no experience dealing with mental illness, so I didn't really know if he was or not. I do know the more I came in contact with Frank, the more I appreciated Tracy's warning.

The Hungarian Revolution in 1956 had filled Frank with optimism when it appeared Communism was on the verge of collapse. Mr. B told me Frank had been "profoundly moved, distressed, depressed" when the Hungarian people reached out to the United States for help, but President Eisenhower ordered us not to respond in any way.

"Patrick, he felt we were witnessing the first big break of the Cold War. I think he saw it was so close to breaking apart that he became incredibly excited. He believed the Agency was created to eliminate the Communist threat through our covert operations. Frank's spirit was crushed first when we were ordered not to interfere, and second, when he visited the Austro-Hungarian border and saw the thousands of refugees attempting to flee their country."

"Why did that crush him?"

"He had previously met with the men who led the anti-Communist resistance. He had pledged our nation's total support to their fight. When they asked for our help, Frank had to personally turn down the very people he had promised to support. It became an intensely emotional time for him. He felt the United States was responsible for inspiring and encouraging the rebellion. He was given presidential orders to turn his back on the brave people who precipitated the event. He had given his word and had gone back on his word; he felt angry, personally betrayed, and even disgraced. I think Frank had a real crisis of confidence because he saw the Soviets were ripe for the picking, and yet our country refused to act. Everything in which he had passionately become invested had come to nothing. His daughter said he felt we were losing the Cold War."

"Why are you telling me all this, Mr. B?"

"Because I think we'll see a shake-up around here. I want you to know that whatever happens, you'll be all right. Allen loves to see boldness and panache in his people—you've embodied that in every assignment you've ever been given. He likes that, and I like that. Keep your nose to the grindstone. Everything will work out for you."

"Thanks."

"Good," he said. "There's also an important lesson in this. Do you know what it is?"

I replied that I didn't.

He smiled, "Whatever happens, don't take it personally. Frank did, and it's ruined him."

ON MARCH 27, I sent A.J. to the El Toro Marine Corps station near Santa Ana, California, to have him checked out physically. His teeth were cleaned and X-rayed. I made sure that any Iron Curtain dentistry that might have been performed in his youth was removed and replaced. I put his dental records in Ozzie's file as the first step in switching his identity with Ozzie. He was fingerprinted, given a clean bill of health, and sent to me.

On April 11, Ozzie was court-martialed and found guilty of illegal possession of that stupid derringer. I arranged for leniency in his sentencing. He received twenty days at hard labor (suspended); a fine of fifty dollars (which I paid); and a reduction in rank to private. He was also given six months probation and ordered to keep his nose clean.

HAVING RESOLVED OZZIE'S legal problems, I rushed back to D.C. for a new assignment. Mr. B felt that I was wasting my time in Atsugi primarily because the President was reluctant to authorize overflights of the USSR. Although I assured him that I was making progress on Project Cocoon, he was not interested. Instead, he wanted me to direct my energies toward Cuba, a potential new trouble spot in our war against Communism.

"Patrick, there's growing concern over a rather charismatic, but violent young revolutionary named Fidel Castro and the support he seems to garner with the Cuban people."

He handed me a magazine. "Here's the February issue of *Coronet*. Read the article "Why We Fight." Castro thinks that an armed revolution is, in his words, the path to true liberal democracy. As you know, General Batista and the current government of Cuba have been good economic and political partners to the United States."

"Does that mean that Castro is anti-Communist?"

"We don't know. There are rumblings that Castro is behind a movement to overthrow Batista—as of now, I don't give Castro much of a chance—but we need better information. I want you to fly down to Havana, meet with Batista, and seek out Fidel Castro. I need to know what you think of the situation and report back on the stability of the government."

"Don't we get reports from the State Department? It would seem they're much more qualified than I am in analyzing this."

Mr. B's response was terse. "You should know by now we don't listen to the State Department around here. The only person over at State that I trust is Foster Dulles, and he even admits he doesn't trust the information he's getting from his own people."

He opened a folder and began to rifle through its contents. "No, you're my man. You've been to both pre-revolution Iran and Guatemala. I want you to use your experience to tell me whether there is any possibility that Castro might succeed in his revolution. I trust your judgment and your insight." He handed me a paper containing several handwritten names and phone numbers. "Here, contact these people. They'll assist you once you land."

Mr. B reached for an envelope at the bottom of the pile—a rather thick unmarked letter-sized packet. "When you finally sit down with Fidel, please give this to him." And with that, I was dismissed.

Before leaving for Havana, I pulled our files on Cuba. I wanted to get a picture of what had been happening in the country—it wasn't a pretty picture. Fulgencio Batista had ruled Cuba since 1940. While still a sergeant in the Cuban army, he took over the Cuban government in a surprise coup of his own.

According to the file, Cuba had evolved into a country of extreme contrasts. Three factions vied for nominal control of the country. The first faction was the ruling class which consisted of the large plantation owners, who, ironically, were supported by our old friends from the Guatemala coup, the United Fruit Company, and the casino owners who were mostly controlled by American organized crime families. The ruling class supported President Batista almost without question. Business was good, profits were huge—all of them were getting rich.

The second faction consisted of an extremely large and extremely poor lower class. These people were systematically overtaxed, overworked, and underpaid by the ruling class. They were extremely unhappy with the Batista regime.

The third faction was an increasingly sophisticated urban middle class, which benefited from advances in communications with the outside world and also increasingly understood the foul power of the corrupt Batista government. None of the three factions trusted the others.

Cuba was an ugly and decadent place of two extremes. The outlying areas were poor and getting poorer while gambling had transformed the seaside resorts within the capital of Havana into a playground for the rich and famous from America. In fact, gambling was Havana's biggest industry. Or, I should say, sex and gambling. Under Batista, Havana had gained a reputation as a place where "anything goes"—gambling, drinking, prostitution, and live sex shows were the major attractions—I now understood the significance of the crude comments Sam Giancana made at Grant's wedding about the Negro sex performer named Superman.

Various crime families from the United States ran the gambling casinos in Havana. They paid a large percentage of their profits back to President Batista himself. Batista, in turn, paid out the bribes and kickbacks to the police and military, which kept the system running and kept it loyal to Batista. The major American-owned business interests in Cuba, such as United Fruit Company, also paid off Batista. Everyone got what they wanted out of this arrangement. Everyone, that is, but the impoverished. They were the ones getting screwed. The heavy-handed brutality of Batista's regime offended almost everyone except those who directly profited from its kickbacks.

It was clear from reading the various reports that the United States didn't quite know what to do with Cuba. How concerned should the United States be about the problems of a small country within ninety miles of our border? Was Batista losing his grip on the country? What would happen if Batista did lose control of the country? How important were American business interests outside the U.S. to business interests inside the U.S.? Did Fidel Castro offer a viable alternative to Batista's government? Was there some other problem lurking out there that we had yet to recognize?

Those were the questions that Allen and Richard wanted me to research in person.

I ENTERED CUBA with a wallet full of U.S. dollars. My papers identified me as an employee of a Miami firm looking to export sugar out of Cuba and import industrial equipment back into the country. A number of businesses routinely took advantage of the cheaper cost of labor in Cuba.

My plane landed at José Marti International Airport a few miles outside of Havana. Havana's close proximity to the United States had falsely lulled me into believing that I was going down to visit a twin sister of Miami—it wasn't even close. I remembered watching the Steve Allen show with Pam in January when it was broadcast from Meyer Lansky's new Riviera Hotel. Pam had been shocked by all of the sexual innuendoes in the show, and I was surprised by all of the references to gambling. While we usually enjoyed "Steverino" and his guests, it seemed that the Cuban show strayed from the wholesome comedy which we had enjoyed in the past. Still, the ambience and luxury of the hotel was captivating. Pam even commented that perhaps we could go there one day for a vacation. I thought that Havana would be a beautiful tropical paradise, but I found it to be a hellhole—the heat and humidity were oppressive—and the cab ride into the city exposed Havana's seamy underbelly.

I had selected one of several dusty taxis that waited for patrons outside the airport. I regretted my decision as soon as I slid into the back seat. The cab reeked of stale cigar smoke. The taxi's bad exhaust coupled with the hot sticky air gave me an instant headache. As we drove through Havana, I tried to breathe through my mouth—I had not expected to see, much less smell, puddles of raw sewage in the streets.

Traffic, everything from cars, trucks, and busses to horse-drawn carts, motor bikes, and wagons, clogged the streets. Shoulder-to-shoulder crowds—not the well-dressed crowds you would find on the sidewalks of

New York or Chicago—jammed the walkways and spilled out into the streets. Beggars—blind beggars, one-armed beggars, child beggars—clustered at every intersection. Each time my cab slowed to a stop, they converged upon it, thrusting their dirty, sweaty arms and hands into the open windows, imploring me to give them money. Some of the more aggressive young boys yelled, "Want to screw, mister? My sister is very beautiful!" Some offered to shine my shoes; others offered drugs. Everyone had an angle.

Once my taxi entered the gated grounds of the beachfront hotels, the poor and squalid world outside ceased to exist—now I was barraged by a new set of sensations. Grandiose exhibitions of wealth—art deco architecture, manicured landscapes, garden sculptures, marble fountains—were juxtaposed next to billboards advertising the risqué. The stage shows at the casinos competed to see who could offer the most lavish and lurid shows on the strip. Naked men and women cavorted across the stage, simulating almost every sex act the mind could conceive. For the more adventurous among the guests, if the simulations seemed too tame, the real thing could be ordered up at various discreet clubs nearby.

The American crime families raked in money hand-over-fist. Sam Giancana had ownership in the Hotel Nacionale while Meyer Lansky ran the Riviera Hotel—his brother Jake ran the nearby International Casino. Santo "Sam" Trafficante out of Miami ran the gaming rooms at the Deauville, the Seville-Biltmore, and the Sans-Souci. The Captril was a favorite hangout for Hollywood celebrities; actor George Raft was paid big bucks by Charles "The Blade" Tourine and Nicholas Di Constanzo to meet and greet wealthy guests at the front door.

Prostitution was a thriving business in Cuba—twelve thousand prostitutes did business in the city alone. Cheaper brothels had sprung up along the side streets and alleys that ringed the beachfront resorts. Legitimate Havana merchants regularly conspired to attract their own share of the vast visiting Yankee wealth. For the price of a $4,000 under-the-table payoff, merchants could arrange to have a bus-stop sign erected right in front of their stores—but stop sign fees were just the tip of the proverbial iceberg.

Government corruption was rife throughout Cuba. The crime families paid Batista $1.3 million a month for the privilege of operating in Havana. Each army regimental commander in the various outlying provinces was required to pay Batista $15,000 a month in order to keep his job, and that put another $1 million a year into Batista's pockets. Additional money was raised from "voluntary contributions" made by the various businesses operating within their regional borders. Even Batista's chief of staff, a pot-bellied man named Tabernilla, received a fee from each bottle of Scotch imported into

Cuba. Street-wise smart-asses around town had come to refer to Scotch by a new name, "Old Tabernilla."

AN ASSOCIATE OF Meyer Lansky arranged for me to have dinner with Batista and his second wife, Marta, at the Presidential Palace. I was unprepared for the grandeur of the building. The palace, designed by Cuban architect Carlos Maruri, faced the sea in Old Havana. The reception area was lavish by American standards with a high domed ceiling and a grand marble staircase dominating the space. I was led to a formal dining room that had been ornately decorated with crystal chandeliers and candles—Batista pointed out that Tiffany's of New York was largely responsible for the decorations throughout the palace.

Mrs. Batista greeted me with an ostentatious flourish of her out-stretched arm. I believe she expected me to kiss her hand, but I politely shook it instead. Mrs. Batista, a pretty young woman, was over-dressed, over-jeweled, and over-perfumed. Her social mannerisms evoked an air of snobbish pretentiousness. As far as high society goes, she was clearly out of her element. But, for that matter, so was President Batista himself. Both he and his wife had developed a reputation as world-class fashion plates. Even I recognized that they tried too hard.

Once we were seated for dinner, Batista made a grandiose display of carefully decanting and sniffing the wine. I knew almost nothing about wine, so his actions were clearly wasted on me. Although there were only three of us for dinner, at least nine waiters attended us throughout the meal. At one point, Mrs. Batista merely raised her little finger and a waiter appeared with a finger bowl. The meal was extremely lavish. I also knew nothing about Cuban food, but I had heard that it was heavy with garlic and onions. I was surprised that Mrs. Batista had planned a dinner based more on French cuisine rather than Cuban. *El Presidente* wolfishly devoured every morsel on his plate while Mrs. Batista delicately picked at her platter. I had read that once Batista gorged himself, he would excuse himself, go to the men's room and vomit. Then he would return to the table and resume feasting. Darned if he didn't do just that—excusing himself numerous times, leaving me to engage in small talk with Mrs. Batista, who was as limited in her command of the English language as I was in Spanish.

Our dinner conversation was restrained primarily because of the ritual of the meal. At one point, Batista asked me if I liked Boris Karloff and began to retell the plot of his favorite horror movie. Since there was little I could contribute, I was reduced to nodding my head at the appropriate points. Our entire interchange consisted mainly of Batista bragging while I quietly listened. He bragged about the wealth he had accumulated—sugar plantations, cattle ranches, and even his own airline. He bragged about his plans to accumulate even more wealth—the burgeoning casino business, gambling, slot machines. He bragged amount his business alliances—his good friend, Meyer Lansky, the U.S. ambassador, Earl E. T. Smith, and his contacts with other businessmen in America. His self-absorption was overwhelming.

I could easily see the problem for the United States. He never once mentioned what he planned to do for the people of Cuba. I had seen with my own eyes the massive social problems that plagued the city of Havana—I could only imagine the dire conditions out in the countryside.

When the waiters had cleared our plates, he dismissed Mrs. Batista with a slight wave of his hand. She obediently disappeared. He ushered me into ornate sitting room surrounded by mahogany bookshelves filled with leather-bound books. He pointed to a massive overstuffed leather chair. As I settled deep into its plush cushions, a servant brought out cigars—and in a pretentious ritual similar to the wine decanting—the waiter opened the highly lacquered wooden humidor. I selected a cigar, held it up to my nose and inhaled its deep aroma. Satisfied, I handed it to the waiter who held the cigar nimbly in his hand expertly snipping the tip with a gold cigar cutter. A second servant stood in front of me with a small chalice containing a flame for me to light my cigar. A third servant handed me a brandy snifter containing cognac.

I savored the cigar and cognac while Batista leaned back comfortably in his chair, carefully blowing smoke rings above his head. Perhaps he was waiting for me to request something of him. He reminded me of Khrushchev—a bully at heart—I knew that he would pounce if I made a false move or comment. He was every bit as good as Khrushchev was in proselytizing—he believed the key to his survival was the unwavering support of the United States government and the various businessmen who traded in Cuba. As I left, I remembered one of Grant's favorite sayings—I felt like "he was pissing on my shoes and trying to convince me it was raining."

Back in my hotel room, I collected my thoughts on the meeting. Our State Department had been concerned about developments in Cuba for years and had even recommended the United States cease our unconditional support of Batista. I could clearly see why the State Department was apprehensive about Batista's leadership and why they were troubled with the revolutionary message being promoted by the guerilla leader Fidel Castro. A Castro government was certain to have a fresh appeal to the Cuban people's burgeoning discontent with *El Presidente's* corrupt and indulgent government.

KENNEDY MUST BE KILLED

FIDEL CASTRO'S DOSSIER read like something out of a Hollywood farce, but with disturbingly sinister undertones. While in college in Cuba, he received a monthly allowance of $500 from his father, a huge sum of money for anyone in 1947, yet he actively cultivated an indifference to clean clothes and personal hygiene. His nickname around campus was *bola de churre*, Spanish for "dirtball." Somehow, he managed to get elected president of the University Students Federation. He succeeded in arousing students to take to the streets of Havana to protest a slight government increase in bus fares. The small group of protestors drew the attention of the police, who showed up in large numbers and proceeded to beat them. Fidel escaped from the fracas unscathed, but he later appeared at various radio stations and newspaper offices with his head bandaged in white gauze to protest the brutality of the government's response to his demonstration.

When Fidel publicly threatened to lead another even larger demonstration, the Cuban president, Dr. Ramon Grau San Martin, invited the student delegation to his office at the Presidential Palace to discuss the planned rise in bus fares. After being escorted into a conference room overlooking a courtyard on the fifth floor, the president briefly excused himself to attend to an urgent matter. While he was gone, Fidel suggested to the assembled students, "I know how to take power and get rid of that old son of a bitch. When he comes back into the room, let's pitch him off the balcony. When's he's dead, we'll proclaim the student revolution and speak to the people on the radio."

The students were horrified. They were invited guests of their nation's president, and a filthy, bushy-headed, wild-eyed nutball with fake bandages still rapped around his head was proposing a political assassination. At least they had the common sense, if not courage, to say, "We came here to discuss lowering bus fares, not to commit murder!"

Shortly thereafter, Fidel became maniacally concerned about a high school student who wasn't even enrolled in college. Seeing him as a threat, he ambushed the poor kid and shot him in the chest. The kid recovered, but Fidel was forced to flee to the Dominican Republic.

A year later, Fidel surfaced in Bogota, Columbia, where representatives from twenty-one nations assembled to discuss mutual problems at the Inter-American Conference. On April 8, 1948, a bloody series of riots exploded upon the streets of Bogota, precipitated by several shadowy clandestine groups dedicated to disrupting the conference. The revolutionaries had hoped to overthrow the duly elected government of Columbia and, just for good measure, assassinate visiting United States Secretary of State George Marshall, who was scheduled to address the delegates at the conference. The rioters succeeded in trashing Bogota by firebombing, looting, and sacking the city. Hundreds of people were wounded or killed. Thanks to intelligence data gained by U.S. secret agents, the government and Secretary Marshall were spared. The Columbians suspected Fidel Castro had something to do with the carnage.

On July 26, 1953, Fidel and his brother, Raul, led an inept attack against a well-fortified army installation known as Moncada Barracks. Their aim was to capture arms and ammunition; in the end, they were the ones captured. Those rebels who weren't wiped out were put in jail, of course, that included Fidel and Raul. After a short show trial, Fidel received a fifteen-year jail sentence and Raul, thirteen years. Once again, Fidel's string of luck continued, for in the biggest blunder of his political life, President Batista released the two brothers in a general prisoner amnesty in May 1955.

Almost immediately, Fidel began running bombastic tirades in two Cuban newspapers. President Batista had little patience with his crazy rhetoric. Fidel was tipped off that there was a price on his head and that Havana police had prepared a bullet-riddled car for his body to be found in while "resisting" arrest by the authorities. Fidel immediately fled to Mexico City to raise money and support for his planned revolution. Though his *26th of July* movement championed the poor common man, in private, he begged and cajoled money from wealthy benefactors, especially the anti-Batista Cuban exiles.

By early 1957, his rag-tag revolutionary army numbered eighteen men. Calling his followers "The Apostles," he encouraged them to let their hair and beards grow unkempt to more closely resemble the original Apostles. He also began cultivating the image of a brave, idealistic leader to whom the disillusioned and the disaffected could flock. It was time to talk to America—to sell himself to a wider audience.

Through a series of contacts, Fidel convinced an editor of the *New York Times* to travel to his rebel camp in the Sierra Maestra Mountains and do a story about him and his army. The reporter wrote three glowing articles about the rebel leader which appeared on the front page of *The New York Times*. The story said: "Here was quite a man…(his) personality…is overpowering…It's easy to see that his men adored him and also to see why he has caught the imagination of the youth of Cuba all over the island."

The New York Times articles had a worldwide impact. Fidel Castro had become an object of media attention from all parts of the globe. Reporters trekked to the Sierra Maestra Mountains to interview him.

It was in the midst of this media frenzy that I made my way to Fidel's rebel camp.

I MET MY next contact in La Habana Vieja, Old Havana, which is east of the Malecón, an eight-kilometer seawall that stretches along the coast of Havana. Once there, I was to follow the Prado, a pedestrian walk, to the Calle Obispo which I would then follow to The Hotel Ambos Mundos. I recognized the name of the hotel as one of Ernest Hemingway's haunts. I seemed to remember that he wrote the last part of *For Whom the Bell Tolls* in Havana at this same hotel. Once I arrived, I waited for my contact who, I was told, would find me. I waited for over an hour and had begun to think that he would not show up when I noticed a young man staring intently at me. Finally, he approached me and insisted that we walk to La Bodequita del Medio. La Bodequita was a very small bar which could barely seat five people. My contact, who had not told me his name, ordered a mojito. He then rubbed his fingers with his thumb indicating that I was to pay, sat down, and began to sip his drink. Soon a burly man walked in, dismissed the young man, turned to me, and asked my name in Spanish. I was somewhat limited by the fact that I did not speak Spanish very well. I was tempted to respond by saying, "Dónde está la biblioteca?" which was one of the only questions I remembered from my high school Spanish class, but instead I simply nodded my head and followed him out the door to an old truck parked in the alley.

Another man was in the front seat—his name was Emilio—he was to be my guide for the next day or so. Emilio spoke no English, but he did smile frequently. We rode in silence until we reached the train station. The burly man heaved some heavy bags from the truck, giving instructions to Emilio. I helped him to carry the bags to the platform where he produced our tickets and we boarded the train. I suspected that we were headed to Castro's command center in the Sierra Maestra Mountains—I was seriously unprepared for a long trek. Emilio had on heavy boots and pants suitable for a jungle hike.

After a rail trip of several hundred miles, we finally arrived in a small town. Emilio motioned for me to follow him in boarding a rickety bus for a bone-crushing ride to our final destination—or so I thought. A peasant with a mule-drawn wagon met us and helped Emilio with the bags—Emilio took the reins and indicated that I was to ride in the hay-strewn wagon bed. We begin a slow journey to the foothills of the Sierra Maestra Mountains. Finally arriving, Emilio strapped his bundles onto a donkey and led us both up a steep mountain incline. It was an arduous hike in the hot, humid Caribbean air.

Comandancia de la Plata was a rustic, bare to the bones encampment of several crude buildings made of sticks and palm fronds. We stopped at a guard post which contained some radio equipment. Once we were cleared to enter, Emilio found his friends and disappeared. A soldier finally took me to Castro's lodgings. Only two rooms, it was simply furnished with a writing desk, crudely made wooden bookshelves, and a bed. I noticed a copy of Machiavelli's *El Principe* on the shelf. The other room was a simple kitchen containing a table and refrigerator run by kerosene. The soldier left me by the doorway while he tried to locate Castro. I walked over to a babbling creek just beyond the hut. I was so thirsty that I decided to take a drink—I found out later that only Fidel himself was allowed to drink from the creek. I was exhausted and wanted nothing more than to lie down and sleep—but I didn't relish the idea of sleeping on the soggy ground with the rest of Fidel's men.

Fidel warmly greeted me. He had a commanding presence, but I sensed he could turn his charisma on and off at will. He was a con man—slick and charming, a snake-oil salesman—if Fidel ever became disenchanted with starting revolutions, he could become a public relations shill on Madison Avenue. I even thought that he might have an uncanny knack for show biz. He must have nurtured a flair for the dramatic ever since he threw his first temper tantrum as a child and discovered how easy it was to get what he wanted—a lesson that seemed to set the pattern for his life. Here was a guy who had a $100,000 bounty placed on his head by Batista; yet, the very people, whose poverty should have been motive enough to turn him in, were charmed and mesmerized by him.

Castro's eloquent line of drivel was as patently absurd as anything Batista had told me—it was just told from a different point of view. He was clearly disappointed I was not a journalist. Although he recognized how important it was to win over the support of the Miami business community, he kept looking over my shoulder as if he were looking for someone more important to talk with instead of me.

His speech was a canned sales pitch, designed to lure me into investing my money into his daring quest for justice. I didn't see any of the vaunted "Christ-like" qualities of compassion and boundless wisdom to which many journalists had breathlessly alluded. Instead, I saw a pragmatic, self-serving rogue with aspirations of grandeur and power.

We spoke for about an hour; or should I say, Fidel droned on monotonously for about an hour while I quietly sat and listened. I think that about three-quarters of the way through, he began to realize I wasn't buying into his bullshit. When he was finished, I pulled the unmarked envelope out of my jacket that Mr. B had given me, "I was told to deliver this to you."

Castro smiled slyly, "Why didn't you give this to me an hour ago? It would have saved us both a lot of wasted time."

I could see that Batista and Castro were quite similar in a number of ways. Money was the common denominator for both. Batista squandered his wealth on ostentatious displays while Castro squandered his on advertising his revolution. I got the impression that like Batista, Fidel cared little about the poor citizens of Cuba. Castro was every bit as capable of oppressing the masses as the Batista regime.

To my utter amazement, Fidel opened the envelope in front of me. I was stunned to see a thick packet of bills—he began to count his bounty. Smirking he said, "It takes a lot of money to run a revolution. This $50,000 will go a long way toward insuring our success. Be sure to thank my benefactors for me."

With that, he got to his feet—leaving me to get back to Havana on my own.

I RETURNED FROM Cuba just in time for Tim's fifth birthday. Pam planned a birthday party for him with all of the neighborhood children and their mothers in attendance. She had decorated the dining room with streamers and balloons. A large birthday cake was placed in the center of the dining room table. Tim, sitting at the head of the table, wore a golden King's crown and beamed from ear to ear as everyone sang "Happy Birthday" to him.

I could see Tim was truly a happy little boy. I had to give Pam a lot of credit. She was a firm believer in gentle discipline. She preached children will rise to the level of expectation. She also stressed children must have routine and order. I knew that was the teacher in her speaking. I believed children would be children—they will take advantage of any situation to run amok. I knew that from experience. I always had taken advantage every chance I got whenever the adults weren't paying attention. I fully expected the party to be chaos with little boys terrorizing little girls and little girls screaming and crying. But to my surprise, the children at the party were all well behaved. Several were playing with their party favors, some were playing party games supervised by other mothers, and some were just eating cake and ice cream.

After the party, Tim was worn out. I tucked him into bed and took out his favorite book.

"Don't read that story, Daddy. That's a baby book." He jumped out of bed and selected a better book for me to read. It was book called *What Do You Want To Be When You Grow Up?* Halfway through reading, Tim announced he wanted to be a teacher like Mommy.

"When I go to kindergarten this year, my mommy's going with me." I didn't think much about his statement because most mothers do accompany their children to school on the first day. "And I can see her at recess, so I don't have to worry about the big kids."

I decided I should gently tell Tim mommies don't go to recess when he added, "But, I have to call her Mrs. McCarthy, not mommy, because she's only mommy here, not at school."

I gave Tim a kiss, tucked him in one last time, and made sure his circus nightlight was on.

"Goodnight, little guy. I love you."

"I'm not a little guy—I'm a big guy," Tim dutifully explained, "I'm a big guy because I'm five."

"Goodnight, big guy." And with that, I quietly shut the door.

Pam was in kitchen, cleaning up the rest of the party dishes. I stood behind her. I wanted to put my arms around her waist, but I put my hands on her shoulders instead. "So, Mrs. McCarthy, when were you going to tell me?"

"Tell you what?" Pam asked nonchalantly.

"Tell me you're going back to work. I think that's an important decision for our family. I think I deserve to be in on that decision." I was trying hard not to sound angry. Pam turned on me, and I could see a spark of her own anger waiting to be ignited.

"Patrick, I have to have more in my life than waiting for you to come home for one or two weeks between assignments. We have one child, and he is starting school in September. What am I supposed to do with myself?" She turned back to the sink of dishes.

"Okay, now I understand. Is this about you wanting to have more children?" I regretted asking the question the moment it came out of my mouth, but I continued on. "Is this a way to blackmail me so you get your way?"

"How dare you talk to me about getting my way. It's always your way, Patrick! Tim and I are second in your life. The agency, your assignments, and God knows what else, are first in your life." Pam started to raise her voice, but reconsidered and shouted at me in a whisper. "I knew when I married you there would be secrets. And I was willing to live with that. From talking to the other wives, I knew you would be on assignment, sometimes for weeks and months at a time. I was willing to live with that. But, I am not willing to live a life of solitude any longer. If you can have your career, I can have mine. Now, you live with that!"

When Pam and I got married, her father told me the secret to a good marriage was to never go to bed mad. He should have also told his daughter that because I slept on the sofa that night—and the next night—and the night after that. Finally, the last night before I was scheduled to leave to go back to Japan, I was reluctantly allowed back into my marital bed. Pam and I talked. And we made up.

ONCE I WAS back in Japan, I made arrangements for Ozzie and A.J., the main players in Project Cocoon, to meet. I needed to get Ozzie away from the prying eyes of his unit, so I had him provoke a fight with a non-commissioned officer, which resulted in the military police filing a formal complaint against him, a clear violation of his April probation. He was ordered to serve the original penalty of his first twenty-day jail sentence in addition to a new sentence of twenty-eight days in jail and a fifty-five dollar fine. I arranged for the location to be at my discretion where I sequestered him for forty-eight days beginning June 27, 1958.

I was apprehensive when, two days later, I brought Ozzie and A.J. together outside of Tokyo. I hoped they would like each other and get along well. I was stunned that they looked so much alike. Both had a lean physical build and weighed around one hundred and thirty pounds though A.J. was two inches taller than Ozzie. Their facial structure was also very similar: Ozzie's chin was pointed while A.J.'s was square with a slight cleft. Even their smiles were similar though I thought Ozzie's smile seemed more sincere than the smirk that A.J. generally had on his face. It surprised me that A.J. did not think he looked like Ozzie; Ozzie agreed, but he thought that A.J. might look like his brother, but certainly not a twin. My job was to make them so much alike that they could fool their friends and families.

They spent several days together. Ozzie, surprisingly the more gregarious of the two, spent much of the time teaching A.J. about his background and coaching A.J. in his mannerisms. A.J. was a quick study, and by the end of the first day, he had mastered Ozzie's speech patterns. By the end of the second day, A.J. had acquired most of Ozzie's mannerisms—now he could walk and talk like Ozzie. I realized that I could not afford to slip up by calling A.J. by his real name. So, we decided that I would continue to call Ozzie, Ozzie—and I would begin to address A.J. as Lee.

Lee's first task was to pass himself off to Ozzie's unit. Ozzie's sentence was to be completed on August 13, so I planned to have Lee return to Ozzie's unit in his place. Most of the guys in the radar unit were on rotation, so they never really got to know the men they worked with on a daily basis. I instructed Lee to act brusque and withdrawn, like he was coming out of prison with a big chip on his shoulder.

"You mean like James Dean?" he asked.

"Yeah like James Dean, but without being likeable. I don't want you to startup any new friendships. We need to sever Ozzie's existing friendships. The only way to do that is to portray Ozzie as a jerk—he's pissed to be back, he's pissed about being punished, in general, he's pissed about everything. And you have to be believable—can you do that?"

Lee gave me his sardonic little smile, "Watch and wonder. I'll turn Ozzie into the most despicable guy on the base if you want me to."

"Throw in some anti-American rants if you can," I suggested.

"I'll take care of it."

Each time Ozzie got a weekend pass, Lee would exchange places with him when it was time for Ozzie to return to duty. Lee virtually antagonized everyone; Ozzie was taken aback how much his unit was beginning to dislike him.

Project Cocoon was almost ready to be launched.

WASHINGTON, D. C. is hot and humid in the summer. Most of the Congress leaves Capitol Hill after the Fourth of July to work in their home districts and don't return until after Labor Day. Only the bureaucrats and their minions who are responsible for the day to day operation of the government remain. When I finally returned home, I was not surprised to find Pam packing up to take Tim to Hyannis Port for the summer. Jackie had begged Pam to come and stay with her and the new baby—Jackie was a new mother and was overly worried about properly caring for Caroline. She had seen how comfortable Pam had been with Tim when he was an infant and wanted Pam to help her learn how to be a good mother. Pam thought Jackie really needed her to act as a buffer to all of the other Kennedy girls. I didn't have much room to object to Pam's plans. After all, I had been flying back and forth between Cuba and Japan leaving my family alone. Even if I was in D.C., I would be working everyday. There would be little opportunity for me to spend much time with my family, so I gave Pam my blessing. We made plans to see each other on our anniversary, during the middle of the month.

Since Pam was away, I tried to have a decent lunch each day—that way, I could just have a snack for dinner. I called Chase and asked him to meet me at the Capitol—I had a craving for Senate Bean Soup. We discussed the usual—politics and sports. It was about time for me to return to work when he put a large manila envelope on the table.

"Want to see a picture of Pam Turnure?"

"Who's Pam Turnure?"

"Jack's new mistress. There's been a lot of talk about Jack and his extra-curricular activities." Chase opened up the envelope, pulling out several letters, pictures, and small spools of recording tape.

"Here's the story. Pam Turnure started out as a receptionist at the Belgian Embassy. She first caught Jack's attention at Nina Auchincloss' wedding last summer."

He handed me a photograph. Turnure was slim, dark-haired, green-eyed, and very, very pretty. I was immediately struck by how much she resembled Jackie and said so.

"Yeah, she's Jackie in miniature. You know she once dated Aly Khan?"

"The international playboy?"

"Yup—same notorious scoundrel. Anyway," Chase continued, "once Jack got his hooks into her, he actually had the balls to hire her as a receptionist in his Senate office."

"Oh, come on! You're making that up. There's no way Jackie would stand for that."

"Jackie never goes to Jack's office, and even if she did, I'm sure the kid would be hustled out of sight as soon as she showed up."

I thought for a moment, "You're probably right."

"I know I'm right. Apparently one night not too long ago, Turnure's landlords, Mr. and Mrs. Leonard Kater, were awakened around 1 a.m. by the sound of someone lobbing pebbles at their tenant's second floor window. When they peeked out, they were shocked to see Senator John F. Kennedy himself standing in the midst of their garden and yelling, 'If you don't come down, I'll climb up by your balcony!'"

Chase sorted through several letters on the table. "Look at these—it's only a sample of the letters Mrs. Kater has written to the paper. She was pretty pissed that a married congressman would be carrying on so indiscreetly."

"Well, *discreet* isn't a word I would use to describe Jack," I said.

"Mr. and Mrs. Kater are both deeply devout Roman Catholics. I mean, daily Church and everything. Well, when they figured out what was going on, they installed tape recorders in their own house to pick up the sounds from the bedroom. Can you believe that?"

I had to ask the question, "Did they pick up anything with the recordings?"

"See, these spools—it's all right here. Mrs. Kater told me, and I am quoting her directly: I can assure you that he was not a very loquacious lover."

Chase started laughing and I joined in. After a few raucous moments, he resumed his story. "Anyway, I guess that was when the Katers decided to ruin Jack's life. At 1 a.m. on July 11, 1958, the Katers successfully photographed Jack coming out of Miss Turnure's apartment. They immediately made copies of the photographs and sent them to all of the newspapers, magazines, and television stations in the area. They launched this publicity campaign to embarrass Jack with—if you'll excuse the pun—firm evidence of his adultery."

"How did you end up with all of this stuff?"

"They sent it to the paper. Mrs. Kater launched a writing letter campaign as well—I don't know how many she sent—these are just a few. She also wrote to Eleanor Roosevelt, Joe Kennedy, and some officials of the Catholic Church—she was so morally indignant."

"This is pretty scandalous. I can't believe that Jack would continue seeing his mistress."

"Well, you know Jack—water off a duck's back. He simply moved Miss Turnure out of her apartment." Chase brushed his hands palm to palm, "End of landlord problem."

"Where did he move her? Wouldn't she have the same problem in another apartment?"

"Not in Mary Meyer's apartment, she wouldn't."

"Mary Pinchot Meyer? Cord Meyer's ex-wife? Pam and I have known them since we got married—we were both upset when they separated."

"Keep this to yourself—I heard that she and Jack might have something going on."

"Cord Meyer works at the Agency. It would be pretty risky to screw his wife."

"Maybe Jack likes the danger of it all. Who knows?"

"But, Chase, why hasn't this story been in the paper? Why haven't you written a story?"

"I would have it if it were up to me. But, it's hands-off—no one wants to print this story in this town. My paper refuses to print it. My editor gave me the song and dance that we don't print stories about a politician's sex life—it's journalistic etiquette—it's tradition. As long as a politician is not incompetent or doesn't exhibit a clear lack of integrity, my paper won't print it."

"I think Jack's lack of integrity is something the entire world should know about," I protested.

"I agree. The *Washington Star* ran the only item about it, and it was small—buried deep within the paper."

"Who is protecting him—his father? Does Old Joe know what's been going on?"

"All I can say is that there are some powerful people who own the newspapers in this town who intend to cover for him. There's no doubt about it—they are protecting their golden boy."

Chase returned the evidence to the envelope. "I'm supposed to give this to my editor for safe-keeping. I'll tell you, Patrick—nothing, I mean, nothing in the way of a scandal is going to derail Jack Kennedy or his father's train to the White House. Mark my words."

THINGS IN CUBA began to dangerously escalate—Raul Castro, Fidel's brother, started kidnapping foreign nationals and holding them for cash ransom. Various U.S. and Canadian citizens who worked for United Fruit Company, various sugar mills, and some mining companies became pawns in the game of international blackmail. Fidel upped the ante by kidnapping thirty unarmed U.S. Marines at gunpoint while they were in civilian clothes on a local bus with weekend passes. He made three demands for their release: first, the United States government must stop all aid of military equipment to Batista; second, the U.S. must end the practice of supplying fuel from Guantanamo Naval Base to Batista's air force; and third, Batista must pledge that he would never use any military weapons already supplied by Washington against Fidel's guerrillas.

The U.S. State Department branded this a clear violation of international law. Secretary of State John Foster Dulles warned Castro the United States could not be blackmailed. The United States Senate promised "effective help (would) be given to Batista" if the hostages weren't released within forty-eight hours. The U.S. Navy wanted its Marines back and favored armed intervention if necessary. Ambassador Smith concurred with the Navy that force was both justified and necessary.

In the midst of this uproar, the United States made a strategic blunder. Our State Department, John Foster Dulles not withstanding, urged a total capitulation to Castro's demands. The hacks, who ran the State Department's Caribbean affairs area, argued that an armed intervention might cause the rebels to kill the hostages, so they pushed for a diplomatic settlement to the crisis. We sent the U.S. consul to Sierra Cristol to negotiate with Raul. Once again he demanded that the United States stop supporting Batista because it was that support, and only that support, which was keeping Batista in power. Raul exacted a pledge from the beleaguered consul that we would not supply the air force training planes which Batista had already ordered and paid for. In exchange, the captured Americans would be released. The consul agreed, and Castro freed the prisoners.

The rebels then stepped up their campaign against Batista, turning it into a surge of terror. Anything that smacked of Batista's power or prestige was a target for bombs planted by the guerrillas. Government buildings, casinos, movie theaters, and banks were the most common targets. Batista retaliated by indiscriminately torturing and killing suspected members and sympathizers of Castro's movement and dumping their bodies on busy street corners as a warning not to cooperate with Fidel.

On July 31, 1958, Ambassador Smith's car was stopped in Santiago by forty women dressed in black mourning garments, who unfurled a large banner in front of his windshield which implored in English "STOP

KILLING OUR SONS." The entire stunt had been staged to get instant worldwide publicity by scores of newspapers and television crews who had been notified in advance. When Batista's police belatedly showed up on the scene, they turned fire hoses on the assembled "mothers" while the news media of the whole world watched. It became a huge propaganda victory for the *26th of July Movement*—and huge black eye for Batista.

OUR ANNIVERSARY CAME and went. I had been unable to leave the city. Pam said she was disappointed but understood. I could sense she wasn't having a good time. It was obvious she had something she could not tell me about over the phone. I could hear tears in Pam's voice, but she didn't cry to me. Maybe it was just the lack of privacy. I knew that the Kennedys could be a demanding family. Maybe Tim had endured some childish insult. Whatever it was, I was sure Pam could work it out.

A week later, I returned home earlier than usual to find Pam and Tim upstairs unpacking.

"Dad-deeeee," Tim screamed enthusiastically grabbing me around the waist.

"Hey, big guy, you're home early!" I returned his hug and put him on my back, piggyback style.

"Honey, why didn't you call?" I asked Pam. She was unfolding clothes and putting them in Tim's chest of drawers. She concentrated on folding each of his shirts just so.

"Oh, we just got tired of being away from home. And I guess I felt a little guilty, leaving you in the city." I could tell something was wrong, but Tim was in the room so I didn't press her. I noticed she had an ugly bruise on her forearm.

"How did you get that? Let me see." As I touched her, she pulled back.

"It's nothing. It's a bruise, probably from playing a little too rough with Tim," she dismissed my concern. Tim started to say something, but Pam cut him short. "Why don't you go out to the car, Tim, and bring in those cookies. They're in the back seat."

For the rest of the evening, Pam was overly emotional. As she was washing the dishes and I was drying them, she broke down and cried. I took her in my arms, "Honey, this isn't like you. What's wrong?"

"I don't want to talk about it. You have enough to worry about. I'll handle it," she answered with an air of finality. "Go upstairs and read Tim a story, will you?"

Later that evening, she spent a very long time in the bathroom. When I tried to go in, the door was locked.

She apologized, "Sorry, I guess I'm just used to living in someone else's house. The Kennedys they just barge in—you know. I'll be out in a minute."

For several weeks, Pam was fragile. I just assumed she had been insulted in some way. Either that or she'd become too emotionally invested in Jackie and Jack's marital problems. So, I didn't bring up the issue.

I should have pressed her for an explanation.

IN SEPTEMBER, OZZIE'S unit was transferred to Formosa to set up a radar position at Pingtung. The Communist Chinese were shelling the islands of Matsu and Quemoy where the nationalist government of Chung Kai-shek was located. The Communist Chinese had block-aided all naval traffic—war looked imminent. I couldn't afford to lose either man to a freak accident or a war-related injury, so I ordered Ozzie to get himself thrown in the brig again.

Around October 2, Ozzie while on guard duty staged an incident by firing his rifle at some intruders. Strangely, he then collapsed weeping against a tree. I would have expected something that dramatic from Lee not Ozzie. The next day Ozzie was flown back to Atsugi for medical reasons—Ozzie was starting to crack up. Whether it was the pressure of creating a disruption or the realization of his irrevocable commitment to give up his identity, I don't know. I couldn't afford to have Ozzie undermine the project—it was time for a permanent switch. I sent Ozzie home to the States for some R & R. On November 15, I greeted Ozzie as his ship arrived at the port facilities in San Francisco. He had a thirty-day furlough to visit his mother and brother, Robert, in Texas.

In the meantime, I sent Lee to Iwakuni to take Ozzie's place. At Iwakuni, Lee ran into a Marine named Owen Dejanovich who had attended radar training school with Ozzie at Kessler AFB. Happy to see Ozzie, Dejanovich tried to re-establish their previous friendship, but Lee successfully brushed him off. Lee said that Dejanovich ended up calling him an asshole—Lee bragged that it was his best performance ever. Shortly thereafter, Lee was assigned to a new radar unit, MACS-9, in Santa Ana, California.

Phase two of Project Cocoon had begun.

OZZIE WASN'T THE only one I knew who was having mental problems. Frank Wisner's mental state had completely crumbled; he was clearly in need of urgent help. He even looked different—physically, he looked gaunt, and his skin had a pale grayish tint. Frank checked himself into a private psychiatric hospital near Baltimore called the Sheppard-Pratt Institute, where he was diagnosed as suffering from psychotic mania. The doctors thought a six-month stay with full treatment might help his condition, and he reluctantly consented. Frank was more afraid of letting Allen Dulles down than he was of the horrendous therapy the doctors recommended. Even in his diminished mental state, he didn't want Allen to fire him. The doctors prescribed a combination of psychoanalysis and electroconvulsive shock therapy. The electrically stimulated convulsions were a painful, barbaric procedure and would not prevent the reoccurrence of the mania. Six months later, Frank was released from the hospital a completely broken man.

Richard Helms was the logical and popular choice to succeed Frank as Deputy Director of Plans. Everyone in the Agency was stunned when Allen named Richard Bissell as the new DD/P instead of Helms. Even though Mr. B had no experience as a spy or had never run a covert ground operation, his experience in running the U-2 spyplane program had convinced Allen that he was the best candidate to fill Wisner's shoes. As one of Mr. B's right-hand men, I agreed, as did Tracy Barnes, who also happened to be Allen's regular golf partner.

Despite that, I think Mr. Dulles made a serious mistake, a mistake that would come back to haunt us in the future. For although Allen loved take-charge kind of guys, I don't think he realized that Bissell was an in-charge type of guy. Mr. B thought that he could run everything at the Agency without any help. He took charge and attempted to do just that, which pissed off Richard Helms.

Allen liked Mr. B because he didn't mind rocking the boat, while Helms hated to have the boat rocked. Actually, Helms should have been a perfect compliment to Bissell, but both men couldn't get past their pride. It was bad enough that Helms was passed over for the position, but then Bissell wouldn't consult him about his knowledge of operations which offended Helms who was still Chief of Operations at the Agency. To further rub salt in the wounds, Bissell barely spoke to Helms outside of the daily briefing meetings each morning.

Richard Helms, who had a restrained and quiet personality, was not a likeable man. Helms responded to Bissell's treatment by freezing Mr. B out of what he needed to know. If Bissell wasn't going to consult with Helms, then Helms wasn't going to consult with Bissell. This became rather sticky, for Richard Helms was still in charge of the DD/P espionage operations. If a particularly dangerous covert operation came up at a morning meeting, Helms simply kept his mouth shut tight.

The rest of us kept our feelings to ourselves—including me. Even though, I felt that Mr. B was my friend, he was still my boss. I received a promotion to Assistant Head of Operations, which made me Richard Bissell's right-hand man. If he ever became Allen Dulles' replacement, I was in line to become the future head of the Central Intelligence Agency.

I was proud of what I had accomplished in my career.

JACK KENNEDY WAS re-elected to the Senate that fall—he received 73.6 percent of the vote in Massachusetts. It was the largest number of votes ever cast for any single candidate in the entire history of the state. It also represented the largest majority of votes racked up by any Senate winner in the entire country that year. Surprisingly, the Kennedy clan was disappointed by the small size of their landslide. They received a victory margin of 874,608 votes, but they had expected to win by over a million.

After Jack's re-election, Jackie spent more time in Jack's office helping out with the correspondence while sitting at a huge secretary's desk in the middle of his Senate office.

THE SITUATION IN Cuba deteriorated rapidly. Presidente Fulgencio Bastista and guerilla leader Fidel Castro each vied for control of Cuba. While President Batistia professed the importance of free and impartial elections, Castro gathered a revolutionary army to overthrow the leadership of Cuba.

Batista masterfully rigged the ballot box to insure that his hand picked successor would win the election. The Batista government printed the ballots under the supervision of honest and impartial election officials in Camp Columbia. After the officials left for the evening, a second set of ballots was printed—using the same presses and paper as the first run ballots. The second set of ballots was then marked by hand for Batista's candidate, Rivero Aguero, who ended up with twice as many votes than the other three candidates combined.

It was a race against time to get Aguero into office by the scheduled inauguration date of February 24, 1959. Fidel Castro was beginning to lead his men down from the mountains in preparation for his final advance against Batista in Havana. His rebel radio stations continuously broadcast propaganda to the people of Cuba. Batista was powerless to stop the onslaught.

Raul Castro ordered Ernesto "Che" Guevara to take his force of a few hundred men and attack the city of Santa Clara, which was defended by 3,200 troops loyal to Batista. The garrison barely put up a fight—the city of 150,000 fell to the rebel forces. Batista had sent a trainload of soldiers to reinforce the beleaguered garrison. None of the soldiers even set foot off of the train.

Batista was disturbed by the defeat of his army at Santa Clara. He had a tremendous advantage, controlling 40,000 soldiers and 30,000 policemen—Castro's rebels numbered in the range of 3,000 men, yet Castro had Batista's men on the run. At one time it had been inconceivable that Castro could force out Batista; now, it was a sobering reality. The news of the rebel victory and the subsequent refusal of his troops to fight all signaled the end of Batista's dictatorship.

THE DAY FOLLOWING Christmas, Richard Bissell called me into his office. After exchanging some minor courtesies concerning my family and our holiday celebration, Mr. B gave me an unexpected assignment.

"Have you read the new Graham Greene book?"

"*Our Man in Havana*? I haven't had time, but Pam read it and loved it. She teased me about it one night while I was fixing the vacuum cleaner."

"What did she say?"

"She asked me if I was selling vacuum cleaner diagrams to my bosses."

Mr. B smirked, "Well, are you?"

"Of course not, I told her I don't have anything in common with that guy in the book."

Mr. B smiled again, "Well, now you do. You're going to be *our man* in Havana. We need you to get down there as quickly as possible. That country is disintegrating right before our eyes. You need to let Batista know he's got to hang on."

"Isn't that the role of the State Department?" I didn't want to leave my family during the holidays. I had promised Tim that I would help him build a town using his new Lincoln logs.

"We do some things better than the State Department. You know that."

The next day, I boarded an almost empty Pan Am airliner out of Miami flying into the eye of a political storm.

HAVANA WAS IN turmoil on December 31, 1958. Most of the gala dinner reservations at the major casinos had been canceled. A climate of fear gripped the population—and the Batista administration as well. Our State Department had been invited to a New Year's Eve gala outside of Havana, and I was asked to tag along. I found myself in a caravan of black Cadillac limousines that transported President Batista and his chief supporters to Camp Columbia, an army base outside Havana, for an elaborate New Year's Eve dinner party. About sixty guests from the government and military mingled with their wives at a formal buffet. The Cuban military officers were in full uniform, with ribbons and medals gleaming. The civilian leaders were in tuxedoes; their wives wore the designer fashions—and jewels—from Paris, London, and New York. The mood, however, was funereal and oppressively somber. The buffet was barely touched. Though the band played, no one felt like dancing.

When the clock chimed midnight, I looked up at the head table as President Fulgencio Batista rose from his chair, *"Felicidades!"* he called out to the crowd.

Then General Eulogio Cantillo stood up and stunned everyone present: "For the salvation of the republic, the military forces have decided that it is necessary for General Batista to withdraw from power."

I was stunned by the sudden announcement. I hadn't even had time to meet with the president to deliver Mr. B's message of encouragement.

The crowd was silent as General Batista announced, "I will not leave before handing over power. A plausible successor must be named."

I gaped open-mouthed as Andres Rivero Aguero was given the oath of office in the middle of the ballroom. "Is this really happening?" I asked my State Department escorts. They shrugged their shoulders in bewilderment— they were just as shocked as I was.

President Batista then abruptly bolted from the dining hall. He led a mad dash to the airport with his guests and their families rushing to keep up. We scrambled for our Cadillac and took off in pursuit of the fleeing group.

Standing on the airport tarmac, I watched Batista and his wife flee to the Dominican Republic with a reputed $40 million worth of money and valuables crammed into their suitcases. He was frightened to death of Fidel Castro and his revolution. Andres Rivero Aguero, after just two hours as President of Cuba, fled as well. He had the distinction of serving the shortest presidential tenure in the history of the Cuban republic.

When the Cuban people woke up on New Year's Day, they discovered that the entire national government had fled between midnight and sun-up, taking everything they could carry and vanishing into the night.

"Every act alters the soul of the doer."
— Oswald Spengler

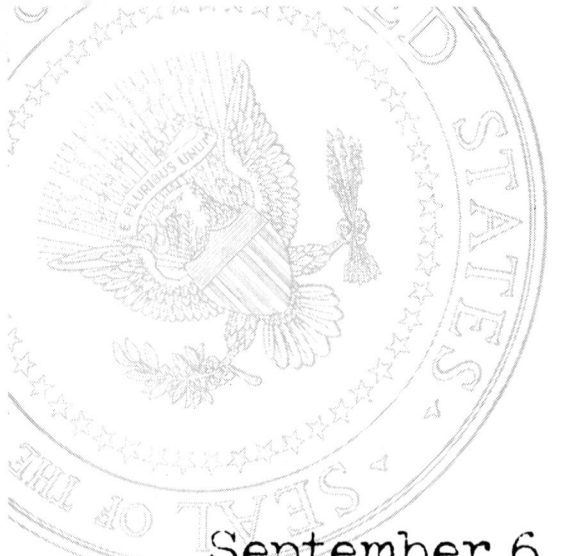

September 6, 1978
6:12 p.m.

Grant felt exhausted. He decided he would go home once Ruger checked in. He called his housekeeper and asked her to keep his supper warm. Grant was alone now—he liked it that way. He didn't have to make small talk over dinner. Or grovel to get sex. If he wanted sex, he paid for it. It was actually easier that way; both parties knew what they were getting—there were no hidden agendas. Maybe he should get laid tonight—that was a thought.

Grant had been staring out his window, his back to his desk. He turned around and was horrified to see the light blinking on his phone. He anxiously picked up.

"We found his car."

This was the first piece of encouraging news he had heard all day long. "Where was it?"

"Less than a couple of miles from his house. Found it tucked into a parking space in a parking garage on Glebe Road in Arlington. It's part of a shopping mall."

Grant knew where that was. It was short walking distance from the elementary school where Pam McCarthy used to teach. He and Patrick had occasionally killed time there waiting for Pam to get off work.

"Where do you think he is?"

There was a pause and then Ruger said, "My guess is that he hopped a city bus to Washington National. The Glebe Road bus runs down to the Pentagon and over to the airport."

"So he could be anywhere by now?"

"Maybe. But we also know where he isn't. That's a good sign."

"Does that mean that he isn't in Puerto Rico?"

"It wasn't him. It could have been a false lead that he deliberately set."

"What do we do now?"

"I'm headed to Washington National with everyone I've got. We'll flood the ticket concourse with questions until we find the person with the right answer."

"Make it quick. We're running out of time."

Ruger sneered as he hung up.

1959

AFTER A FITFUL night, I was awakened by screaming crowds in the streets surrounding my hotel. I looked down from the window of my room to see hundreds of Havana University students triumphantly waving the flags of the *26th of July Movement*. Havana was gripped in bedlam.

The students surged through the streets, picking up passersby and momentum as they headed for the center of the city. Their emotions ran high and pent-up frustrations boiled over. The celebration degenerated into a riot, complete with all the ugliness a riot brings. The crowds sacked two newspaper offices, smashed the gambling casinos, and looted and burned the homes of loyal Batista supporters. When even that wasn't enough to satisfy their urges, the killings began. The howling mobs hunted down Batista's policemen and publicly executed them in the streets they had once patrolled.

As the news of the rioting spread, the *Batistianos* became desperate to escape the carnage with their lives—and whatever possessions they could carry. Men, women, and children, all frantic to leave Cuba as quickly as possible, jammed the airports and seaports. Taxi drivers returning to the hotel from the airports told me that all airplanes were packed to capacity, and private aircraft were barely able to lift off due to the extra weight jammed on board. They didn't care where they were going as long as they could leave Cuba. Hundreds of airplanes headed to West Palm Beach, Miami, Ocala, the Florida Keys—you name it, it didn't matter. The local radio reported a Cuban Airlines plane was hijacked at gunpoint and forced to fly to New York City with ninety-six frightened "immigrants."

Late in the day, the Apostles, Che Guevara and Camilo Cienfuegos, rode into Havana atop two captured tanks. As I wandered the streets, a large crowd advanced toward me pushing to stay in front of two large captured battle tanks. Che Guevara and Camilo Cienfuegos straddled the turrets like two of Hannibal's warriors astride their elephants. They waved to the crowd; the crowd enthusiastically cheered and waved in return.

After innumerable attempts to place a phone call out of Havana, I finally got through to the Agency. Mr. B told me that Meyer Lansky, Santo Trafficante, and Charles "The Blade" Tourine, three prominent American mobsters, had chartered planes to fly them, their wives, their girlfriends, and their suitcases stuffed with money and loot to the safety of Jacksonville, Florida.

There wasn't any reasonable way to get me out of the country. "Be our eyes on the ground, Patrick. We need to know what is really going on. Fidel's on his way to Havana and he's making all kinds of promises: free elections, free speech, a free press, and, oh, most importantly, free land to all the peasants. He claims not to want anything for himself. See if he holds to that pledge."

IT TOOK CASTRO nearly a week to reach the capital because he insisted upon stopping to deliver a string of rambling, incoherent speeches every time a group of people streamed out of their homes or businesses along the way to cheer for him. By the time he actually arrived in Havana on January 8, the crowds were screaming that he was the messiah. I saw hundreds, if not thousands, of Cubans jamming the streets, cramming the balconies, and hanging over the rooftops chanting *"Fi-del! Fi-del!"* and *"He's coming! He's coming!"*

After several days in the safety of my hotel, I decided to venture into the streets with the Cuban people. I was immediately swept up in a swift current of a frenzied mob and was helpless to do anything but march along with them as they made their way to the Presidential Palace to welcome the conquering hero. When we arrived, I was butted and nudged by rebel soldiers using their rifles to clear a path open enough through the adoring crowds to allow Fidel's jeep to ease its way by. Castro was close enough to see me, but he didn't recognize my face from our previous visit.

I momentarily lost sight of Fidel until he mounted the steps of the Presidential Palace and turned to address the vast crowd. He assured the people of Cuba that he had no interest in assuming power himself. "Power does not interest me and I will not take it! From now on, the people are entirely free!" He piously vowed to restore Cuban constitutional law and pledged to form a new government based upon the tenets of "Peace with Liberty, Peace with Justice, Peace with Individual Rights!"

Within hours of taking over the Presidential Palace, Fidel's *26th of July Movement* contacted the State Department and demanded the immediate firing of American Ambassador Smith who was "openly showing his hostility to Dr. Fidel Castro, the national hero of the Cuban people."

The public image of the benevolent leader clashed with his ruthlessness behind the scenes. After I left the demonstrations at the palace, I headed over to our embassy where they had just received a tip that Castro's people planned to kidnap Ambassador Smith with the key members of his staff and hold them on the top floor of the embassy until the United States government formally recognized the legitimacy of the Castro regime. If the United States failed to comply, the rebels planned to drop one man after the other to his death from the top balcony, starting with Ambassador Smith. Combat-trained U.S. Marines swiftly fortified the embassy grounds and even installed listening devices in the Ambassador's bedroom to monitor his safety around the clock.

Over the next few days, the pressure on American interests in Cuba continued to grow. Castro had cultivated many friends and fans in the United States. As shocking as it was to me, newspaper and magazine journalists continued to fawn over Castro and his revolutionary army. A fiery and controversial congressman from Harlem, Adam Clayton Powell, demanded that Ambassador Smith be sent packing and offered to introduce a bill which would provide $200 million in U.S. taxpayers' money to the new Castro government. Other similarly smitten officials in Washington bombarded the State Department with their own demands for Smith's removal; the Eisenhower administration finally caved into their insistent demands. Ambassador Smith was recalled to Washington and relieved of his duties. To add insult to injury, Smith had one last official obligation; he had to deliver our country's formal note of recognition of the Castro government to the Cuban Foreign Ministry. The note expressed the hope that Castro would "comply with the international obligations and agreements of Cuba." Smith privately told me he believed he had just handed over Cuba to the Communists.

When I spoke by telephone to Mr. B, he said Allen Dulles had concerns similar to those expressed by the ambassador. He was not convinced that Cuba would stay in the Western camp should there be any showdown with the Soviet Union. He believed the people of Cuba had done nothing but exchange "one bad apple for another" and predicted "blood would flow in the streets of Havana." He was also apprehensive about the "…possibility that the land reform (Castro) was insisting upon may adversely affect certain (U.S.) properties in Cuba…."

Unfortunately, it didn't take long for Allen Dulles' prediction to come to pass.

EARLY IN THE morning of January 11, the Castro regime tried and swiftly executed sixty former Batista supporters. On January 12, Fidel made headlines around the world when he threatened that "two hundred thousand Yankee gringos will die if the United States sends Marines to Cuba." Other than the Marines still guarding our embassy, there were no plans to send more. I chose that time to exit the island and return home.

Shortly after I left, the Castro regime accelerated the pace of executions. By the end of February, 392 people who had been sentenced to death were killed—Raul and Fidel Castro ruled as murderous thugs. Tribunals arbitrarily condemned to death anyone the brothers identified as enemies of the state. On February 16, 1959, Fidel appointed himself Premier and named his brother, Raul, Commander of the Cuban armed forces. The ideals of free speech and a free press which Fidel had espoused quickly withered and died. Fidel postponed free elections for the next two years and sanctioned the Communist Party.

A reign of terror descended over the entire country.

PROJECT COCOON WAS scheduled to launch before the end of the year, but the uproar in Cuba almost derailed my participation in the project. I was shocked when I found out that the Agency wanted to reassign Project Cocoon to someone else so that I could focus solely on Cuba. I had never questioned my superiors about my assignments; I always accepted whatever I was given. This time, I strenuously objected to being reassigned. Cocoon had been my idea from the beginning. I had recruited A.J. and Ozzie, and I wanted to see it carried through to its launch. I appealed to Richard Helms and Allen Dulles. After considerable discussion (and some unexpected support from Helms), I was permitted to continue supervising Cocoon, but my work on the project would terminate at the end of the year regardless. As long as Cuba didn't interfere with Cocoon, and vice-versa, I was free to shepherd the project to its launch. It wasn't going to be an easy balancing act.

On February 25, Lee took the Marine Corps proficiency exam in Russian language skills. I reminded him that although he was fluent in the Russian, it was highly unlikely Ozzie would have the same mastery of the language as he did. "You've got to pass, but barely. I want you to get through this as poorly as you can. But don't fail the exam or you will wash out of their language program."

"I have it covered, don't worry."

He scored a plus-four on his reading (he got four more answers right than he got wrong), a minus-five on his speaking, and a minus-three on his writing—he passed the test.

Lee also applied for admission to *Albert Schweitzer College* in Switzerland. His acceptance would provide the perfect cover for him to officially leave the United States.

ON APRIL 17, Castro accepted an invitation to fly to the United States to address the annual convention of the American Society of Newspaper Editors in Washington. I left Agency headquarters and headed over to Washington National Airport to catch his arrival. The newspapers had been touting his visit, so I wasn't surprised to run into Chase once I got there. What did surprise me were the thousands of Americans who crammed the tarmac at Washington National Airport to cheer Castro's arrival—they were almost as frantic to touch him and express their adulation over him as the Cuban people.

I was growing disgusted by the sheer number of people who had fallen for Castro's propaganda. Even more disgusting was the number of reporters bamboozled by Castro. Chase shared my sentiments. He had been assigned to cover Castro's American visit and was not looking forward to the assignment.

"I ran into a fellow reporter who was working on Castro's flight up here. He said Castro spent the entire flight reading comic books. Can you even imagine that? What kind of an intellectual lightweight is this guy?"

"Chase, don't underestimate him," I warned. "There are hundreds, if not thousands of dead bodies in Cuba that once represented people who underestimated this creep. He's charming, and he's deadly. That's not a good combination."

"Patrick, I've covered Mafia trials, corruption cases, rapes, murders, you name it. He doesn't scare me."

"Hey buddy, none of those guys had diplomatic immunity, and none of them ran their own country—with their own army and their own secret police force. Let someone else stoke the fires. You keep an eye on the aftermath."

Chase considered what I said, "I've always been the one to give you advice. Now you're advising me—I guess we're growing older."

I smiled ruefully. "Whenever anyone mentions getting older, I think about something Grant liked to say: You are only young once, but you can be immature forever. Then I remember your story about the old bull and the young bull standing on top of a ridge looking down on a pasture full of heifers. The young bull gets excited about his prospects and says, 'Let's *run* down there and make love to one of those girls.' The old bull says, 'Take it easy. We'll *stroll* down there and make love to all of them.'"

Chase and I chuckled.

"Chase you've taught me a lot over the years. I have appreciated your take on things, your viewpoint. But, I want us both to be old bulls someday, standing around and reminiscing about our past together. I can't look forward to that if you do or say something stupid."

"Okay," he grinned. "I'll watch what I say. Listen, I have to get going. Castro's on some sort of a public relations blitz, much to the chagrin of the Eisenhower administration staffers that I've talked to. His first official appearance is before the Senate Foreign Relations Committee, where I'm told he'll pledge that he has no intention of confiscating United States property in Cuba. He'll probably secure the support of Congress if he attests that he has no connection with the Communist Party."

That's exactly what happened later that afternoon. Congress foolishly resolved to assist the Castro regime in his fight to free the Cuban people from oppression. I knew from firsthand experience that the Cuban people would never be free of oppression as long as Fidel Castro was in power.

THE MEDIA CLAMORED to interview Castro—he was an instant celebrity. Reporters listened attentively as Fidel spewed his propaganda. On *Meet the Press*, Fidel assured the American people that he was a friend of the United States—he vehemently opposed Communism, and in any showdown with the Soviet Union, he would side only with the United States. He later told a group of students he stood for "Cubanism," not Communism.

Of course, we at the Agency knew differently. We closely monitored Fidel's nightly telephone calls from his brother back in Havana. Raul was furious—the Cuban people thought Fidel was selling out to the Yankees. Fidel dismissed Raul concerns—he swore that he was not a puppet of the United States of America.

President Eisenhower certainly had no intention of greeting or being seen with Castro. He arranged to play golf in Augusta, Georgia while Castro was in town. Eisenhower did not wish to extend any further recognition to Castro. Dick Nixon was to meet Fidel instead, and he asked me to sit in on the meeting. Their meeting was a quiet and secluded one, held in the vice president's office in the Capitol Building, far from the prying eyes of reporters.

Nixon bluntly asked Fidel about his views on free elections and on Communism. Fidel told Nixon the people of Cuba didn't want free elections because free elections "only result in bad government." When asked about the tribunals in Cuba—in which 521 people had been executed—Fidel replied, "the people don't want fair trials; they want them shot as soon as possible." The Vice President queried Castro about whether or not he was concerned the Communists in his government might attempt to seize control; the Maximum Leader confidently responded, "I am not afraid of the Communists. I can handle them."

Nixon was bothered by Fidel's demeanor. "Castro is either incredibly naïve about Communism or is under Communist discipline." I remembered my trip to visit Castro in the mountains where I saw that copy of Machiavelli's book, *The Prince*. I knew that he wasn't naïve.

The next afternoon, the American Society of Newspaper Editors' convention opened in the ballroom of the Statler Hilton Hotel. Over a thousand news executives had vied for tickets to attend the event. Chase was on the ticket committee and had managed to get me a pass and a seat next to him.

"What do you think we'll hear?" I asked him.

"Probably the same old bombastic crap he's been spouting since he got here. I've been reading up on him since our talk yesterday. I'll admit I wasn't prepared for the dichotomy between his clownish act here and the deadly nature of his actions in his country. The problem is, will any of these knuckleheads realize that or will they just swoon in his presence?" He added, "This guy's as dangerous as they come. He's gonna piss on their shoes and convince them it's raining."

"You've been hanging around with Grant again, haven't you?" I laughed remembering that I had the exact same reaction when I first met Castro.

"Hey, what can I say? He rubs off on you."

"That won't be all that rubs off…" I was interrupted by the start of the show.

Fidel, dressed in green Army combat fatigues, told the newspaper editors that he was a staunch advocate of a free press because "The first thing dictators do is to finish the free press and establish censorship. There is no doubt that the free press is the first enemy of dictatorship."

When asked about free elections, Fidel described a scenario that was pure hogwash—the newspaper editors, the best and the brightest in the business, accepted his propaganda. He maintained that four years would have to elapse before his government could "establish conditions for free elections." Asked why, he simply said, "Real democracy is not possible for hungry people."

He went on to say: "We want that when elections come…that everybody will be working here, that the agrarian reform be a reality…that all children have a school…that all families have access to hospitals…that every Cuban know his rights and his duties, that every Cuban know how to read and write…Then, we can have truly democratic elections!" In other words, he advocated revolution first and democracy later.

In the question and answer period, they repeatedly raised the topic of Communism, and Fidel repeatedly replied, "We are not Communists." He told the assembled press that he did not agree with Communism—if there were any Communists in his government, "their influence is nothing."

Blatantly lying, he told the journalists what they wanted to hear, and they gave him what he wanted to hear—a thunderous standing ovation. *The New York Times* turned him into an immediate hero. They eagerly painted Fidel Castro as the "Caribbean George Washington." The rest of the American press dutifully followed *The Times* lead. It was truly an insult to the memory of Washington, who was undoubtedly turning over in his grave just fourteen miles away at Mount Vernon.

I had a beer with Chase at Rosie O'Grady's when he returned a few weeks later. After the usual jokes about our beloved Washington Senators and their pennant chances for 1959—"Washington: First in war; first in peace; and last in the American League"—Chase opened up about covering Castro's visit.

"This country has lost its mind," Chase shook his head disgustedly. "Our first stop after we left D.C. was at Princeton University where Castro was invited by the university president to speak. Mobs of students cheered and waved Cuban flags in his honor."

"Where did they get the flags?" I wondered aloud. It sounded like a staged rally.

"Who knows?" Chase shrugged his shoulders. "He spoke for two hours to an audience of adoring fans. He was carried bodily from the auditorium on the shoulders of a bunch of exuberant college kids."

I was speechless over the insanity of it all.

"Oh yeah, but you should have seen his arrival in New York. I talked to a New York City police officer who estimated a crowd of at least ten thousand people who turned out at Grand Central Station. They mobbed his limousine and his motorcade everywhere they went. New Yorkers—cynical New Yorkers caught up in an idiotic frenzy. I don't understand it."

"Me either. I've met the guy. He's a con man pure and simple."

"People are so gullible. No one questioned him. Throughout his entire New York stay, he professed his love for freedom and his friendship for the American people. It was the same way in Boston. The crowds treated him like he was Elvis Presley."

"What's the fascination for this guy?"

Chase sipped his beer and paused to think. "I think it's a Robin Hood type of thing. The American public likes to root for the underdog."

"But that's not the real Fidel Castro. I know what he's done—I know what he's capable of doing. He's no one to admire."

"Hey, I know that now. It's too bad my esteemed colleagues in the press don't know it. Reporters that I respect just aren't asking any hard questions."

"Then you've got to tell them."

"Patrick, you've still got a lot to learn about not rocking the boat. Right now I have a cushy job and a liberal expense account with a great newspaper. I'm not about to jeopardize that and end up writing pet obituaries in Podunk, Pennsylvania. I'm going to write what my editors want me to write."

I finished my beer and poured another from our pitcher. "I thought you were the idealistic, probing reporter who vowed to keep the world honest. What happened?"

"I'm in my early forties, unmarried, and suddenly thinking about a gold watch and a pension someday. That's what happened. If my editors want to jerk-off over my stories about Castro, then I'm gonna give them the best pornography I can write."

"That's pretty cynical."

He stopped his mug in mid-air and slowly lowered it from his mouth. "You're calling me cynical? You work for the CIA and Allen Dulles—and you call me cynical? Are you out of your mind?"

When I didn't answer right away, he sat his mug down and said, "I've got a long day tomorrow. I'll call you next week." He was out the door before I could think to apologize.

A few days later, Tracy Barnes dropped a report on my desk. "We thought you'd like to see what the Caribbean George Washington has been up to," he smirked before walking away.

The report was precise about Castro's true intentions. On April 27, Castro arrived in Houston. On the 28th, he met with Robert Ray (Dick) McKeown, a Bashore, Texas gunrunner who had been supplying Castro with arms over the years. Fidel offered McKeown a post in his government. McKeown, on five-year probation with the U.S. government over his gunrunning activities, could not leave the country but was more than willing to broker a deal. McKeown had been paid $25,000 by Jack Ruby, a mob contact in the Trafficante crime syndicate, to set up a meeting with Castro.

Even though Jack Ruby had never personally met Fidel, Ruby was well known to him. Ruby had been running guns and ammunition to Fidel Castro's revolution since 1957 under an ingenious moneymaking scheme that also included Jimmy Hoffa of the Teamsters. Hoffa and Trafficante had a good business relationship since Teamster Local 320 operated in Santos Trafficante's Miami territory. Our Agency wiretaps revealed Hoffa had been active in supplying arms for both sides of the Cuban revolution, profiting from both Batista and Fidel during the conflict.

Even after Castro took control of Cuba, Hoffa came up with a way to invest $300,000 of Teamster money. Hoffa's idea was to use a $300,000 loan from the Teamsters to buy and sell a fleet of war-surplus C-74 Globemaster airplanes and weapons to Castro in the hopes of scoring points with the new leader. Trafficante liked the idea and added mob money to sweeten the deal. At the same time, Trafficante and the mob pursued plans to assassinate Castro if he made any move to restrict their casino and moneymaking operations.

However, Castro must have gotten wind of the potential double-cross and threw Trafficante in jail as soon as he returned to Havana. The mob sent Ruby to Havana to secure Trafficante's release along with three other Americans from Cuban jails. Whatever Jack Ruby offered Castro must have worked. On July 8, the Castro cabinet decided to expel Santos Trafficante, Jr. from Cuba.

PROJECT COCOON was finally ready to launch. I was more and more comfortable with Lee's ability to pull off the deception. Lee easily fooled old Ozzie acquaintances like Sherman Cooley, Owen Dejanovich, and Edward Murphy who had been with Ozzie at MACS-1. Lee even made friends with another Marine named Kerry Thornley. They spent hours discussing everything from socialism to atheism. I have to admit that I had my doubts, but Lee continued to surprise me with his improvisational abilities when confronted with unusual circumstances—like when Lee met a stewardess named Rosaleen Quinn, who had been studying Russian for a year with a Berlitz tutor. He decided to show off his mastery of the Russian language. His mistake was he was too good—she actually believed he was from Russia. He quickly made up a story about how he learned Russian from listening to Radio Moscow.

I think Lee sometimes tried too hard to fit in. Lee tried playing football on the MACS-9 team, but he was so bad the team couldn't even keep him around for practice fodder—although he did get to impress the coach with his knowledge of international politics and economics. Lee tended to be cocky and somewhat of a know-it-all. He had one of those personalities that tended to irritate people after a while,

Ozzie, on the other hand, was unpretentious. He was a likeable kid with a desire to please. While Lee viewed Project Cocoon as an opportunity to make his mark on the world, Ozzie had a much nobler goal. He took simple pride that he was doing his patriotic duty for his country. I was determined to do everything possible to repay him and protect him in the years ahead.

I had tremendous respect for both men and their willingness to sacrifice themselves for their country.

IN JULY, ALLEN Dulles called me to his office.

"Patrick, I've got another assignment for you. You're going to Moscow with Dick Nixon—after all, you and Chairman Khrushchev got along so well at your last meeting, Listen, do me a favor this time and drink the vodka—don't pour it out." His eyes flashed at his little joke.

"I had to pull a lot of strings to finagle a spot in the entourage for the Agency. I don't need to tell you that irritated the State Department no end. This is the State Department's show. Be discreet and invisible."

The *American National Exhibition* had been the talk of Washington for over a year, but I had been so busy with Cuba and Project Cocoon that I missed the obvious excitement the exhibition had generated within the city. Officially, the exhibition would be held in Moscow from July 24-September 4, 1959. Everyone who was anyone wanted an invitation. Even Pam had told me that Dior was holding fashion week in Moscow—a tidbit that I admit I scoffed at. Everyone seemed to understand the importance of the event long before I did. Vice President Richard Nixon, who would open this landmark cultural exchange, was taking a huge entourage with him. He would be accompanied by his wife, his office staff, the president's brother, Milton Eisenhower, as well as people from the State Department, the military, various academics from Harvard and other institutions, and seventy members of the press. I couldn't begin to imagine the logistics involved.

I remembered that President Eisenhower had first presented the idea to the American people in his State of the Union address in January 1958. Eisenhower felt that the Cold War was not just a war about military might, but it was also "a massive economic offensive that has been mounted by the communist imperialists against free nations." Eisenhower saw the danger in regarding the Soviets only in military terms—we needed to fight the spread of Communism by promoting our economy. He concluded that a "cultural exchange program would be the path to genuine peace." We needed to show the Russian people how their lives could be improved through a free-market economy.

On the whole, it was a noble endeavor to improve U.S.-Soviet relations and to lay the groundwork for a reciprocal Khrushchev trip to New York in the fall. I agreed with the concept of promoting world peace, but at the same time, I disagreed that a cultural exchange program would diminish the likelihood of war.

Hadn't anyone at the State Department ever heard of the Hatfields and McCoys?

OUR CONTINGENT ARRIVED in Moscow after flying eleven hours non-stop from New York in a new Boeing 707. The Boeing 707 was the United States' first production jet airliner. It was an imposing looking aircraft standing 42 feet tall with a wingspan of 130 feet and a length of 144 feet. I was impressed with its cruising speed of almost 600 mph at an altitude of 25,000-40,000 feet. No country in the world, not even the British, had a jet like the Boeing 707.

As I disembarked with the reporters and dignitaries, I was surprised at the size of the welcoming committee. I had expected to see a ceremonial display—children dressed in traditional Russian regalia, a military band, bleachers filled with excited crowds—for the arrival of the Vice President of the United States of America, the second most powerful man in the free world. But there were only a half dozen Soviet dignitaries standing soberly on the tarmac in a makeshift receiving line. The Soviet Deputy Premier extended a welcoming hand to Dick, handed Mrs. Nixon a bouquet of flowers, and gave a brief welcoming speech. It was a chilly reception, especially after all of the hoopla about the historical significance of the event.

I was asked to join Nixon's personal entourage which was departing to Ambassador Llewellyn Thompson's residence, Spaso House, located about a mile from the Kremlin. The press and other non-governmental dignitaries were escorted to two hotels nearby. Spaso House was a residence of magnificent grandeur. We entered a red-carpeted main hall, which I guessed to be over 75 feet long. Overhead was a domed ceiling, much grander than Batista's El Presidente's Palace, from which a colossal crystal chandelier hung. Built in 1914 for a wealthy textile merchant, the neoclassical structure had molded ceilings, carved doors and woodwork, elaborate columns and archways, balconies, numerous chandeliers, a grand staircase, sitting rooms, a library, a music room, and a State Dining Room. A ballroom was added by the Embassy in the 1930's.

While the staff took our luggage to our rooms, we were led to the library, where an informal buffet had been laid out. It had been a long day. All of us were tired and hungry. I helped myself to a cup of tea. Dick Nixon motioned me to the divan where he was seated.

"Not much of a welcome, was it?" Nixon said.

"Certainly not like the last time I was here. I'm a little surprised actually."

"The Ambassador relayed to me that the Soviets are insulted, in fact, they are extremely offended by The Captive Nations Resolution."

It seems that every year since 1953, Congress had passed a resolution referred to as the "Captive Nations Resolution." This resolution required the President to proclaim one week of the year as Captive Nations Week—during which the American people were urged to pray for all of the people living under Communist tyranny throughout the world. This year Americans were to pray for a change of government for the people in the Soviet Union, even if it meant a full-fledged revolution against the Russian government to aid the Russian populace.

"It certainly is bad timing," I concurred.

"I'm sure we'll hear more about this. Premier Khrushchev won't easily overlook our faux pas. Bad timing, that's all."

We were soon interrupted by several others who brought over their tea and sandwiches. Before Nixon excused himself, he off-handedly said, "See you in the morning, Patrick."

I didn't think much of the comment until I arrived at my room. On the bed was an official itinerary—I would accompany Nixon and his delegation the next day.

AS PREDICTED BY Nixon, Chairman Khrushchev was spoiling for a fight when the Vice-President arrived at the Kremlin the next morning. The delegation awoke at dawn, and by 6:00 a.m., we were touring the Chaikovsky Street Farmers' Market. Khrushchev escorted us through the market proudly pointing out the vast array of food available to the Russian housewife. Khrushchev definitely played to the cameras—he smiled, he laughed, he jovially patted Nixon on the shoulder. Publicly, he couldn't have been more cordial, telling us he welcomed peaceful competition. But once we were behind closed doors, Khrushchev was a blustering bully.

After a group portrait, Nixon took his seat next to Khrushchev behind a large mahogany conference table surrounded by reporters and photographers. Khrushchev was holding what looked like a baseball in his hands. As he turned it over and over, I could see that it was really a model of the Russian satellite, Lunik. Khrushchev ordered the press to leave then stared belligerently at Nixon.

"Senator McCarthy might be dead, but apparently his spirit lives on," he baited, catching Nixon and our delegation completely off-guard. He rocketed into a spirited attack on the Captive Nations Resolution. "People should not go to the toilet where they eat!" he yelled. "This resolution stinks! It stinks like fresh horse shit, and nothing smells worse than that!"

Dick, stunned by the ferocity of the tirade, stared face-to-face with the Soviet leader. A master of debate, he retorted, "I am afraid the Chairman is mistaken. There is something that smells worse than horse shit," he paused for effect and finished, "and that is pig shit!" It was Khrushchev's turn to look stunned. He shrewdly smiled and changed the subject. Dick Nixon was not to be bullied—his parry caught Khrushchev off guard—Nikita Khrushchev had started in life as a pig farmer.

After his heated tirade, punctuated with much pounding of his fists on the table, Chairman Khrushchev stood, straightened his jacket, and left the room. Ambassador Thompson took Nixon aside. I guessed that Nixon was somewhat unsure of how to proceed with the afternoon's activities since he was to give Khrushchev a private tour of the American Pavilion before it opened to the public. The afternoon's itinerary was scheduled to begin at noon at Sokolniki Park.

The park was the site of the American Pavilion which had been designed around the theme of capitalism and its triumphs—it would show the Russian people how free enterprise, unlike Communism, could help everyone live a more prosperous and luxurious life. The pavilion, one of three exhibition areas, was actually a huge Buckminster Fuller geodesic dome standing over 80 feet tall. The gold anodized aluminum structure looked almost otherworldly and made a strong statement about American ingenuity and our vision for the future. Visitors were met by RAMAC 305, an electronic brain created by IBM. It had been programmed in Russian to answer 3000 questions about American life. There were seven huge screens placed about the pavilion which projected films—Disney produced a film called *Circarama* about the Family of Man—and slide shows about American life. One of the slide shows, *Glimpses of the USA*, showed the inside of an American supermarket. I was sure that Khrushchev would have something to say about that.

I was tense about the prospect of another Khrushchev tirade, but I knew Dick could hold his own. Dick graciously greeted Khrushchev—we were surrounded by cameras using the new Ampex color videotape for color television broadcasts back home—I knew that Khrushchev would play to the cameras. Nixon and the diplomatic staff were dressed in black suits, white shirts, and black ties. Khrushchev had on a rather unflattering light brown suit and wore a white fedora with a matching brown hatband. Nixon, together with Milt Eisenhower, led Khrushchev to the Pepsi kiosk.

The Soviet Union prohibited western consumer goods from coming into the country so many American businesses felt that it was fruitless to have a display at the exhibition. Donald Kendall, the head of Pepsi-Cola, went out on a limb to bring over the ingredients and the machines needed to make Pepsi on the spot in Moscow. Kendall offered Khrushchev a cup of Pepsi made in Moscow and a cup of Pepsi made in the United States. Khrushchev drank at least six cups, and encouraging others in his entourage to sample the product, postured aggressively and said, "Drink the Pepsi-Cola made in Moscow. It's much better than the Pepsi made in the U.S."

Khrushchev imperiously moved through the pavilion. He frowned at the displays of consumer goods and began to berate Nixon on American trade policies. Playing to the cameras, Khrushchev criticized the United States again for the Captive Nations Resolution. Khrushchev poked and prodded. When Nixon didn't take his bait, he launched a fresh assault of insults.

Nixon's anger simmered, undetectable to most of those around us. "There must be a free exchange of ideas," he told Nikita.

"What about this tape?" He challenged Nixon to guarantee that whatever he said, it would be shown in America with a full English translation. Nixon said it would be. Now the games began.

"How long has America been in existence? Three hundred years?" Khrushchev demanded.

Nixon replied that it was over one hundred and fifty years.

Khrushchev screwed up his face. "One hundred and fifty years? Well, then, we will say America has been in existence for one hundred and fifty years and this is the level she had reached. We have existed not quite forty-two years, and in another seven years we will be on the same level as America. When we catch you up, in passing you by, we will wave to you." He made an exaggerated waving motion to an imaginary future America. "Then, if you wish, we can stop and say: 'Please follow up.'"

Dick tried to change the subject, but he made the mistake of saying to Nikita, "You don't know everything…"

Before he could finish his thought, Khrushchev intervened, "If I don't know everything, you don't know anything about communism except fear of it!"

The show went downhill from there as far as diplomacy was concerned, but it made for great television. Nikita was a natural performer, far more demonstrative in his comments and gestures than Dick. The situation soon deteriorated into a boasting competition between the two men. Whenever Richard Nixon tried to point out what America did well, Khrushchev countered that Russia did them better.

The tour moved into a model American home constructed within the exhibit. Nixon focused on the American standard of living. Nixon tried to be magnanimous and conceded that the Russians were ahead of the Americans in rockets and space, but pointed out that America was ahead in other areas, like "color television, for instance."

"No, you're not," Khrushchev replied, "we are up with you on this, too. We have bested you in one technique and also in the other."

Nixon was combative, "You see, you never concede anything."

Khrushchev merely replied, "I do not give up."

When they walked into the General Electric kitchen, Dick pointed out the latest laborsaving devices that filled the room. Khrushchev wasn't the least bit impressed—I almost expected him to begin kicking the appliances. He alleged many of the devices didn't even work and were probably out of order;

others were merely worthless. "Don't you have a machine that puts food in your mouth and pushes it down?" he mocked.

Nixon sensed Khrushchev was turning the televised tour into a filibustering attack upon America. "You do all the talking and you do not let anyone talk. I want to make one point. We don't think this fair will astound the Russian people, but it will interest them…To us, diversity, the right to choose, the fact that we have a thousand different builders, that's the spice of life. We don't want to have a decision made at the top by one government official saying that we will have one type of house. That's the difference."

Khrushchev immediately countered by saying only the rich could own such a kitchen. Nixon resisted Khrushchev's invective by directing his focus to the washing machines. Once again, the Soviet leader contrarily argued that it was inefficient to produce so many types of washing machines or houses. Once more, he sermonized about the superiority of Soviet products.

Nixon retorted, "Isn't it better to be talking about the relative merits of our washing machines than of the relative strength of our rockets? Isn't this the kind of competition you want?"

Khrushchev quickly answered, "Yes, but your generals say, 'We want to compete in rockets. We can beat you.'"

Nixon once again acknowledged both sides were strong, and for that reason, "neither one should put the other in a position where he faces an ultimatum."

"Who is giving an ultimatum?" Khrushchev challenged.

"We will discuss that at another time," Nixon replied.

"Well, since you raised the question, why not when people are listening! We know something about politics, too. Let your correspondents compare watches and see who is filibustering. What do you mean, giving me an ultimatum?" he shouted.

"I'll be very direct," Nixon said. "I'm talking about it in the international scene…"

'That sounds like a threat to us!" Khrushchev yelled. He jabbed his thumb into Nixon's chest for emphasis. "We too are giant! You want to threaten us? We will answer threat with threat!"

Nixon jabbed right back with his finger. "Who wants to threaten? I'm not threatening. We will never engage in threats!"

And back and forth they went, standing toe to toe, each getting more heated and brazen in his assertions.

While the journalists enjoyed the spirited repartee, the State Department people were mortified. I stood behind Ambassador Thompson and Milton Eisenhower, who openly moaned—why didn't someone pull the plug on the fiasco. Khrushchev undoubtedly enjoyed himself. He had engaged in a good, solid debate with another politician, and he reveled in the give-and-take aspect of the confrontation. Nixon had stood his ground, demonstrating that we were not going to be pushed around.

Like a chameleon, Khrushchev beamed as they ultimately emerged from their kitchen debate. William Randolph Hearst called out to Nixon, "Hey Dick!" Khrushchev, who had been interviewed by Hearst earlier, pushed Nixon aside to grasp both of Hearst's hands in his. He enthusiastically shouted, "My capitalist, monopolist, journalist friend! Do you ever publish anything in your papers that you don't agree with?"

"Oh, boy, do I ever!" Hearst exclaimed.

Nixon chirped, "You should see what some papers print about me." Everyone laughed at the break in the tension. Khrushchev wasn't entirely buying it, so Nixon told him, "If there is one idea you must get out of your head, it is that the American press is a kept press." Since the Russian press was a kept press, Khrushchev was dubious and seemed to be on the verge of another harangue—then he saw me.

"Is that Patrick McCarthy? My great drinking friend, how are you?" And before I could say a word, Nikita exuberantly threw his arms around me in a massive bear hug.

"I'm fine, Mr. Chairman," I stammered, "and you?"

Grinning, he winked, "I am much better now that I know I have a worthy drinking partner to join us at dinner tonight! *Dos vedanya!*" and he was off into the crowd.

An embassy aide approached me moments later—my credentials had been extended to the rest of the events, courtesy of Chairman Khrushchev.

WHILE NIXON TOURED Moscow the following day, I spent a few extra hours in bed sleeping before visiting the Agency offices on the seventh floor of the Embassy located on Chaikovsky Street. Sure that I could easily retrace yesterday's route, I wanted to get a map of Sokolniki Park and check out the Hotel Metropol as a possible place for Lee to stay once we got him into the Soviet Union. I needed to get the lay of the land.

While in the Ambassador's residence, I felt I was being watched. Soviet surveillance had always been problematic. I had read a report on how Ambassador George Kennan found Spaso House to be a veritable fortress when he arrived in 1952. Kennan said that while he was in his study, he had become "acutely conscious of the unseen presence in the room of a third person...he could almost hear his breathing." Technicians scoured the room but could find nothing. Finally, they instructed Keenan to go about his daily business while they searched the room—they found a highly developed microphone that could only be detected when activated. The microphone was cleverly concealed in the replica of the Great Seal which hung on the wall of the Ambassador's study.

After a day filled with ceremonial functions, Nixon returned to Spaso House where the Ambassador planned a private dinner with Khrushchev later in the evening. Spaso House had become a center for American and Soviet social relations. Just a few years back, it was unlikely that many Soviet officials would attend functions put on by the Embassy. Former Ambassador Bohlen and now Ambassador Thompson encouraged gatherings that allowed Soviets and Americans to mingle. Khrushchev had been a frequent visitor to Spaso House—he even showed up unannounced one year on the Fourth of July.

After the tensions of the last couple of days, I was hoping that the dinner would be pleasant. But I was on my guard. While at the Agency's offices, I had been confidentially informed that a new Soviet bug was found just prior to our arrival in a chandelier near the Ambassador's office.

KHRUSHCHEV SURPRISED US all with an invitation to spend the night at his dacha about thirty miles just outside of Moscow. Immediately after dinner, we packed our bags and loaded into cars for a midnight ride. Khrushchev's tone seemed to have changed after two tense days. Affably, he told us he looked forward to visiting with us on a more personal level the next day.

After a leisurely breakfast, we were escorted to dock where we were met by a flotilla of boats for a cruise down the Moskva River. I learned that Moscow was named after the river which means "dark" and "turbid" in the ancient Finnic language—dark and turbid was an apt description for our relationship with the Soviets.

I joined the Nixons in Chairman Khrushchev's boat, the lead vessel for the trip. All along the river's edge, people swam and cheered our boat as we floated by. Some of the heartier swimmers even came up to the boat to shake hands with their leader. Khrushchev made it a point to exploit the photographic opportunity for the reporters accompanying us in another boat. He bellowed to the people on shore, "Do you feel like captive people?" They enthusiastically answered, "Nyet! Nyet!"

Dick Nixon sardonically laughed, "You never miss a chance to make propaganda, do you?"

Nikita grinned widely exposing the gap in his front teeth, "I don't make propaganda! I tell the truth!"

Milton Eisenhower later told me that the pilot of his boat mentioned that the swimmers were all high-ranking members of the Politburo—that particular stretch of river had always been off limits to ordinary Russian citizens.

At one point, our lead boat accidentally ran aground and became briefly stuck in the mud. Everyone felt the tension. Khrushchev looked like an angry jack-o-lantern—I was afraid he would shoot the captain on the spot. Dick tried to make a joke by mentioning that his good friend Bebe Rebozo often did the same thing when they went sailing, and "he was a very experienced boatman." When the boat proved to be too tightly jammed in the mud to be freed, we were forced to transfer to another boat. As we were disembarking, Dick nudged me to turn and look at the boat captain. "That might just be," he said, "the most forlorn, hopeless-looking individual I'll see on my entire visit to the Soviet Union."

While I couldn't say that we liked Khrushchev, Dick and I certainly were beginning to understand Nikita Khrushchev. We respected him. Beneath his bluster was a man who was fascinating to behold in public and in private. He was a colorful show-off who possessed a quick-hitting sense of humor. Highly intelligent, he took the offensive in almost every situation—he alternately tested and pressed his advantage whenever it suited him. Khrushchev's steely tenacity would decimate anyone who showed signs of timidity or weakness. Khrushchev, after all, had successfully survived Stalin's frequent and deadly political purges.

Dick felt Khrushchev was "particularly effective in debate because of his resourcefulness, his ability to twist and turn, to change the subject when he is forced into a corner or an untenable position." He wasn't the type of man that you could charm with bullshit because he would see through that in a minute. No, to earn his respect, you had to prove to him you could stand up to him on his terms, both intellectually as well as pragmatically. If you weren't man enough to defend your position in front of him, then he was going to bulldoze you into the ground.

I was proud of Dick Nixon's performance with Khrushchev. With President Eisenhower's term in office ending in January 1961, I knew I would feel comfortable with Dick Nixon in the Oval Office as Ike's successor. I had the distinct impression that Khrushchev felt that way as well. These were two political war-horses who knew where the other man stood, and they respected each other because of it.

Our press corps was impressed with Dick's composure under fire. James Reston of *The New York Times* mentioned to me that he thought Nixon had chosen "the perfect way to launch a campaign for the U.S. Presidency." I agreed.

My admiration for Nixon grew day-by-day. He had decisively stood up to Khrushchev every time the Soviet Premier tried to badger or bully him. Khrushchev was tenacious in trying to uncover any faults a man might bring to the negotiating table. I also understood that Khrushchev's conviction about the long-term supremacy of the Communist system over capitalism would not be swayed by any type of reasoning. Chairman Khrushchev respected only one thing—a show of force to match his own.

Woe to the United States if we faltered at any time in expressing our resolve.

ON AUGUST 17 Lee, who had now officially taken over the identity of Ozzie, filed for a hardship discharge from the Marine Corps, citing the need to return to Fort Worth, Texas, to take care of his ailing mother. Using Ozzie's birth certificate, he applied for a passport so that he could attend college in Switzerland. Lee was issued his passport on September 10; the next day Ozzie was officially discharged from service.

Lee went home to Fort Worth to visit Ozzie's family. This was an important test—we wanted to see if Lee could fool Ozzie's own mother. I was certain that if he was successful, he would be capable of fooling the Soviets. Lee spent two days with Ozzie's mother in her apartment—she accepted Lee as her son Ozzie. Ozzie had apparently grown up while in the Marines—his family didn't notice any change in his behavior, or if they did, they did not press him for details. We hustled Lee onto a bus on the morning of September 16. He boarded a freighter named the *Marion Lykes* in New Orleans, which was scheduled to depart for France on September 20.

The *Marion Lykes* arrived in port on October 8 at Le Havre, where Lee disembarked and headed for Southampton, England. He told emigration authorities that he planned to stay in England for seven days before heading for school in Switzerland. As it turned out, we advanced the timetable for the trip. Lee flew out of London for Helsinki on October 10.

I met him when he arrived at the Helsinki airport about 11:30 that night. We spent the next week in a variety of hotels and safe houses—I gave Lee his final briefings before sending him on his way. He departed for Stockholm, Sweden to initially apply for his visa into Russia. I received word from one of our sources that the KGB was making it much harder to cross the border with a Swedish-issued pass than they were from Finland, so at the last minute, I recalled him. He obtained his visitor's visa through the Soviet consulate in Helsinki without any problems. On October 15, Lee was set to leave Helsinki for the USSR.

We had a brief going away dinner at a small restaurant outside of the capital. The meeting was tough for both of us because we realized what was at stake. I had never been personally responsible for another's man life in any of my missions. Daunting images of what could go wrong for Lee weighed heavily on me.

Lee, on the other hand, was ready to brazenly infiltrate the most secretive and closed society in the entire world while using another man's identity.

One slip-up anywhere in his story and he would be a dead man. He was incredibly brave.

"You know something, Lee? This is your last chance to back out of this whole deal. Nobody will blame you if you got cold feet," I said.

He let out a huge sigh of relief or maybe it was resignation, I really wasn't sure. He shook his head. "Nope," he replied simply, "I'm going in." He reached for his drink—vodka straight up. "I gave it a lot of thought on the trip over. This is too important to the safety of our country for me to be pissing my pants right now. I won't shit you, Patrick, I am fucking scared to death about what might happen to me, but I'm also determined to see it through." He then downed his vodka in two big gulps.

I was respectfully silent for a minute. "Is there anything that I can do for you?"

He smiled a sardonic smile, "Nah, I'm OK. Just don't forget I'm over there. Promise to bring me home, no matter what."

"I don't know how I'll ever get a good night's sleep again until you're safely out of there."

I detected a slight welling of tears in his eyes. "That's really good to know," he whispered softly.

I changed the subject before we both started bawling and had the entire restaurant staring at us. "You've got the mailing addresses that you are supposed to use?"

He nodded and patted his shirt pocket, "Got them right here."

"Good. Address the letters to your mom and your brother. We will intercept them…"

He held up his hand to stop me from going on any further. "Patrick—a week of continuous briefings has drilled that into my brain. I know what to do."

I was embarrassed about my mistake. Of course he knew what to do—he didn't need a reminder from me. He quickly recognized my discomfort and assured me, "Hey, I'm going to send you guys more information on the average life of the average Soviet citizen than you could ever imagine. You're gonna think that I am writing articles for *National Geographic*. The Russkies won't have a clue as to what's really going on."

"It's not the Russkies I'm worried about. It's the KGB. I don't want you to get a one-way ticket to Lubyanka prison, that's all."

"Wait a second!" Lee said, looking suddenly concerned. He dramatically whipped his travel itinerary out of his pocket and made a show of closely examining it before exclaiming triumphantly, "Guess what? There's no Lubyanka prison showing anywhere on my itinerary, so I guess your concerns are groundless."

He flashed a smile once again then became serious, "There is one thing."

"Of course, what is it?"

"Can you tell me what's going to happen to Ozzie?"

"We've given him a whole new name and identity. He's off to a new life."

"Will he ever see his family again?"

"I don't know, Lee. Once the news of your defection gets published all over the world, they'll be humiliated. They may never want to see him again. But don't worry—Ozzie is a strong little shit. He's going to be just fine."

A look of sadness appeared in A.J., "Before I go, will you say my real name one last time? It may be the very last time I'll ever get to hear it." He clenched his jaw in an effort to hold back his emotions.

"Sure I will, A.J. In fact, it would be my honor to be the last one to say your name. *Alek James Hidell*, I am extremely proud of what you are about to do to help make America safe from the threat of attack. I greatly appreciate your sacrifice, and I know that Ozzie, I mean, *Lee Harvey Oswald*, is equally proud of what you will accomplish in his name." I fought back my own tears, "God bless you and be with you, Lee."

Lee Harvey Oswald left Helsinki that night with some other students who were also traveling to the USSR. They all arrived at the train station in Moscow the next day. We had booked another agent, posing as a student in Lee's group, to let us know that Lee had made it safely into the country. Their *Intourist* guide was a woman named Rima Shirokova, who spoke English and was almost certainly KGB as well. Virtually upon meeting her, Lee passionately declared his deep sympathy for all things Communist and how he was convinced that Capitalism was the root of evil in the world.

Our shadow agent thought he was laying the baloney on a little too thick. The agent was right—the Soviets didn't believe Lee's story either. After a week in the Soviet Union, our agent reported Lee Oswald was informed he would not be allowed to extend his stay; he must leave the next day. Goodbye Project Cocoon.

Knowing what was at stake, Lee did something extraordinarily brave. He attempted to take his own life by slitting his wrists in his *Hotel Berlin* room. Miss Shirokova found him on the floor of that room, bleeding heavily. She rushed him to the hospital, where Lee claimed that he would rather die than be forced to leave the Soviet Union. Miss Shirokova told the other tour group members that Lee had been stitched up and then put in the psychiatric ward of the Botkin Hospital, where doctors evaluated his mental condition for two days. He then spent another five days in the regular ward of the hospital before the doctors finally released him.

Our next report showed that upon his release from the hospital, Lee marched over to the American Embassy and informed Consul Richard E. Snyder that he wished to relinquish his American rights. He submitted a written note that proclaimed:

I, Lee Harvey Oswald, do hereby request that my present citizenship in the United States of America be revoked.

I have entered the Soviet Union for the express purpose of applying for citizenship in the Soviet Union, through the means of naturalization.

My request for citizenship is now pending before Supreme Soviet of the USSR.

I take these steps for political reasons. My request for the revoking of my American citizenship is made only after the longest and most serious considerations.

I affirm that my allegiance is to the Union of Soviet Socialist Republics.

(signed) *Lee Harvey Oswald*

It took the Soviets about three months to finally accept Lee's story. They suspected him of being a spy, so we had given him the okay to sweeten his story with some juicy facts about our U-2. Little did they know, we had another plane already on the drawing board which would render the information on the U-2 obsolete. Unlike the U-2, which was a high-flying, slow speed glider, our new plane was capable of outrunning any Russian airplane or missile, flying three times the speed of sound. The U-2 had outlived its usefulness to us—but, the Soviets didn't know that.

On January 4, 1960, Lee Harvey Oswald was granted a "stateless" residence permit and banished to Minsk, which was as far from any strategic Soviet military installations as possible, 450 miles southwest of Moscow. They gave him a rent-free apartment and 5,700 rubles a month living expenses. I was absolutely amazed at his audacity when in one of his early letters he revealed that his new Soviet friends found his *Lee Harvey Oswald* name too difficult to pronounce so he told them to simply call him "Alek."

Like I said before, the kid had balls.

"True patriotism sometimes requires of men to act exactly contrary, at one period, to that which it does at another, and the motive which impels them—the desire to do right—is precisely the same."

— General Robert E. Lee

September 6, 1978
7:00 p.m.

Grant called for his driver to pick him up.

"Good evening, Mr. Grantham, going straight home?"

"Yes." Grant disliked talking to the help. He paid them well—he didn't need to engage in chit-chat. Ordinarily, Grant would have gone to the club for a drink for a little glad-handing. He'd shake everyone's hand, tell 'em how good it was to see 'em and that they'd get together soon. You never knew when you might need a favor. But tonight, he just wanted to get home.

He'd barely stripped off his stiff shirt and tie when the phone rang in his bedroom. He'd told Miz Ezzie that he would pick up the phone if it rang. He had hurried her out the door, "You deserve to take off a little early. I can take care of myself. You go on home and rest." His housekeeper loved him.

Ruger didn't even wait for him to say hello. "We're canvassing the ticket counters. I've got men going out and tracking down ticket agents who have gone home to show them pictures. It shouldn't be long now." Ruger wasted no more words and hung up.

The optimism in Ruger's voice reassured Grant. Maybe they would find him after all. Grant felt a moment of relief until it occurred to him what finding Patrick meant.

Better him than me, he snorted.

He opened his little black book. It had been a long day. He deserved some rest and relaxation.

1960

ON JANUARY 2, 1960, Jack Kennedy formally announced his intention to run for President of the United States of America. Stories, which raved about young Senator Jack Kennedy, appeared in the nation's best political journals. Magazines and newspapers ran a constant string of articles promoting Jack's candidacy. It was no surprise that Joe Kennedy had been shamelessly pitching his son as a candidate since Jack's failed bid for the vice-presidency in 1959. Many of Joe Kennedy's friends were powerful members of an elite circle of media moguls.

I couldn't think of anyone more unsuited for the Presidency than Jack Kennedy—unless, of course, it was Old Joe himself. I feared that Chase might be right—it would be hard to derail Kennedy's ride to the White House. I ran into Jack just after his formal announcement of his candidacy—I halfheartedly congratulated him and wished him luck. He slapped me on the back and thanked me for my support. He felt confident that he would receive the nomination, but said that if the Democrats didn't have the common sense to give him the nomination, he would vote for his old friend, Republican Dick Nixon.

He was deadly serious when he told me that.

BACK IN D.C., the Agency grappled with how to handle Castro's regime in Cuba. Castro's revolutionary government had gained control of Cuba through violent means though Castro championed democracy when touring the U.S. Neither Raul nor Fidel were the type to bend to the will of the people. Handling Cuba would require finesse. As one of Allen Dulles' new assistant deputy directors, I would be in on all strategy sessions.

On January 18, Dulles convened a meeting with Richard Bissell, Tracy Barnes, and J.C. King to discuss a Presidential Directive which would impact our operations in Cuba. We took our seats around the conference table. Each of us had a thick folder of briefing materials which we perused while we waited for Dulles to begin the agenda.

"Gentlemen," he announced, "you have been selected to serve on a new presidential task-force, which will become the fourth branch of DDP King's Western Hemisphere division. From this point on, the task force—designated WH/4—has one goal. And that is to focus solely on Cuba."

Each of us shifted in our seats as a current of excitement coursed around the table. All of us had been frustrated, and now we were finally going to get serious about Cuba.

"If I may, please let me give you a little background on how this decision was reached," Dulles said. "Almost six years ago, on March 15, 1954, President Eisenhower approved a paper entitled "National Security Council Directive on Covert Operations." The directive, entitled NSC-5412, created a staff and a chain of command for managing secret warfare," he paused for effect, "which empowers this group to make national security decisions. Are you with me so far?"

We nodded that we were.

"Good. One year after that on March 12, 1955, NSC-5412 was revised to include a Planning Coordination Group. However, nothing was put into place until December 28, 1955, when a senior group of advisors—direct designees of the President, the Pentagon, the State Department, and the Agency—were named to positions on that Planning Coordination Group. They adopted the name 5412 Group. The 5412 Group was a strictly need-to-know group."

Mr. B slightly raised his hand. He waited until Dulles gave him the go-ahead to speak. "I am assuming that the President was not directly involved in any of the 5412 Group's activities or meetings, thus preserving 'deniability' for him in all of the Group's actions. Is that a correct assumption?"

Dulles nodded his head. "Yes, the President designated his special assistant for national security affairs as his personal representative in the Group."

Dulles paused and looked around the table to be sure we were paying attention. He then picked up a folder marked "Top Secret—For Eyes Only" and pulled a few sheets out of it.

"I want to read to you the most important part of that directive because it is vital to what I am about to tell you. I am sorry that you cannot have a copy to read, so please listen carefully. NSC-5412/2 says:

> "The NSC has determined that such covert operations shall to the greatest extent practicable, in light of U.S. and Soviet capabilities and taking into account the risk of war, be designed to: Create and exploit troublesome problems for International Communism, impair relations between the USSR and Communist China and between them and their satellites, complicate control within the USSR, Communist China, and their satellites, and retard the growth of the military and economic potential of the Soviet bloc.
>
> a. Discredit the prestige and ideology of International Communism, and reduce the strength of its parties and other elements.
>
> b. Counter any threat of a party or individuals directly or indirectly responsive to Communist control to achieve dominant power in a free world country.
>
> c. Reduce International Communist control over any areas of the world.
>
> d. Strengthen the orientation toward the United States of the peoples and nations of the free world, accentuate, wherever possible, the identity of interest between such peoples and nations and the United States as well as favoring, where appropriate, those groups genuinely advocating or believing in the advancement of such mutual interests, and increase the capacity and will of such peoples and nations to resist International Communism.
>
> e. In accordance with established policies and to the extent practicable in areas dominated or threatened by International Communism, develop underground resistance and facilitate covert and guerrilla operations and ensure availability of those forces in the event of war, including wherever practicable provision of a base upon which the military may expand these forces in time of war within active theaters of operations as well as provide for stay-behind assets and escape and evasion facilities."

Allen finished reading the directive and looked up at us, "What do you think?"

Barnes was quick to speak up. "It sounds to me that it gives us *carte blanche* to do whatever is deemed necessary to defeat our enemies."

Dulles nodded his head, "That's exactly right. That's exactly what the directive was designed to do."

King spoke up, "That means that we can take off the gloves to actually fight against Communism."

Dulles agreed, "As such, we've had Operation Success at work in the Far East, and we've provided help to the French in Viet Nam, as well as the Israelis in Suez and Egypt. We should have done more for the Hungarians in 1956, as we all know."

We all conceded that we dropped the ball in Hungary. After we dissected the handling of the revolution, Dulles redirected our focus.

"Well, gentlemen—this initiative empowers the Agency to confront Communism head-on. I am pleased to tell you that on January 13, the 5412 Group decided that it could not, that it would not, tolerate the Castro regime in Cuba."

I could feel the hair stand up on the back of my neck.

"We, WH/4, are meeting here today to make specific recommendations on how to carry out the directive. My question to you is: Are you up to that challenge?"

Once again, our discussion overtook the agenda. We were definitely up to the challenge and committed to doing whatever was necessary to insure national security.

Over the next several hours, we reviewed the material in our briefing packets—we appraised, reappraised, scrutinized, critiqued, and assessed the options—finally, we agreed on three strategies. One, we would train 20-30 Cubans who would act as guerilla leaders for our cause; two, we would work to sabotage the sugar refineries and disrupt the Cuban economy; and three, we would employ Executive Action—kill Fidel Castro, Raul Castro, and Che Guevara.

At the end of the day, we felt encouraged about the direction of the task force. The Agency was now allowed to do whatever was necessary, including military action, to protect the interests of the United States. I had seen how a charismatic dictator like Castro could execute his enemies without remorse or conscience, and at the same time, bluff the United States Congress into supporting his revolution.

Castro was a dangerous man only ninety miles south of our borders—we could not allow him to operate a Communist regime.

ON JANUARY 13, we began to implement our plan. Logistically, we had to be careful not to step on each other's feet and inadvertently create any blowback which could undermine the entire project. Our first priority was to identify and support any existing rebel insurgents who might be capable of inciting a revolution against Castro. Once identified, the insurgents would need weapons—I was put in charge of that operation.

We had more than enough resources to get money and munitions successfully smuggled onto Cuban soil especially since we combined our fledgling gunrunning operation with that of Sam Giancana, Carlos Marcello, and Santos Trafficante. We were fully functional in a reasonably short period of time. The Agency also received the mob's joint cooperation in setting up guerrilla training camps in Florida, Louisiana, and Guatemala.

We were on target for a possible invasion of Cuba by the end of the year.

TRACY BARNES PULLED me aside one day at headquarters and asked if I liked Frank Sinatra.

"I've always liked his music. Pam and I listen to Sinatra records all of the time."

"Sinatra is playing in Las Vegas—we want to send you out there next week. I've cleared it with Allen and Richard—they think it would be a good idea to let you go and enjoy yourself."

"Enjoy myself? What are you talking about? Am I taking Pam?"

"This is essentially a business trip, Patrick. Sam Giancana would like to meet you. He's very happy with how you've been running the Cuban operation."

Even though I had once met Sam Giancana at Grant's wedding a couple years ago, I didn't know him. I assumed that as a fellow Patriot, I could trust him. Giancana had been a tremendous help to the Agency's efforts in Cuba. Whenever I needed something, all I had to do was ask—he always came through. He had contacts, like Jack Ruby, who had been invaluable to our efforts.

Tracy added, "Frank Sinatra and Giancana are very close friends—Giancana pays Sinatra huge sums of money to perform at his hotel in Vegas. I'm sure that you'll personally meet Frank while you're out there."

I wished that I could tell Pam about the trip—she would love to hear the details—but I couldn't.

"Sam asked permission to invite you out for a few days—so go have a good time. Just remember to write up a full report when you return."

He started to walk away, then stopped and turned.

"Oh, I almost forgot. Any gambling that you do is not covered by our budget or your expense account. *Capisce?*"

"*Capisce*," I grinned. I wondered what the poker tables were like.

JOHNNY ROSELLI, ONE of Giancana's right-hand men, met me at the airport with a warm smile and a firm handshake, "Patrick, we're so glad you were able to join us. Sam is especially pleased he'll be able to spend some time with you."

"Geez, Johnny, thanks for inviting me. I value any time that I get to spend with you and Sam—it only makes our jobs easier to do. What's the agenda?"

"We're heading over to the Sands to get you settled in."

As the air-conditioned Cadillac limousine cruised out of the airport, Johnny casually pointed out the sights of the Las Vegas Strip. I spotted the marquee for the hotel, "Sands—A Place In The Sun," long before I saw the hotel itself. What really caught my eye was the billboard below the Sand's name—in letters six-feet tall, it announced:

Frank Sinatra
Dean Martin
Sammy Davis, Jr.
Peter Lawford
Joey Bishop

Johnny saw me staring at the sign. "Yeah, Frank and the boys are here. They're filming some kind of movie about a casino heist here in Vegas. They're shooting the movie during the day—I think they are calling it Ocean's Eleven—and performing here at Sam's casino every night."

"That sounds like fun. I'd love to see a show."

He smiled at me, "That's already been arranged. Did you bring your tuxedo?" He paused, "That's okay if you didn't. I'll round one up for you. Sam wants you to join him at his table tonight for the midnight show. Listen, these guys stay up all night long. With the time difference and everything, I recommend that you catch some shuteye. You don't want to miss anything—these guys are crazy."

Johnny took a puff of his cigarette. "Listen, Patrick, you'll get in the door because of Sam Giancana, but you'll only be allowed to stay inside the door if Frank likes you." He then went over the ground rules. "Frank and the boys live to have a good time. That's their credo. You're automatically expected to jump in and have a good time, too. But don't ever act like a 'Clyde' or a 'Harvey,' because if that happens, you'll be gone so fast you won't know what happened."

Johnny noticed my confusion and grinned slyly. "Sorry. You don't know what a Clyde is or a Harvey. Clydes and Harveys are part of the boys' secret language. A 'Clyde' is a bum—strictly a brown-shoed loser. Clydes come from the province of no-where, a place where all losers dwell. These 'denizens of loserville' are also known as Harveys."

As soon as he opened the door to my room, Johnny went over to the small set-up on the dresser and poured himself a shot of scotch, neat. "These guys live to party, although they call it by a myriad of names, and they do that because they're cool and 'hep cats.' They like to have their F-U-N, as Frank spells it, or their 'ring-a-ding' or their 'hey-hey!' Their smokers are referred to as 'gassers.'

Johnny poured himself another shot, swallowed it in one clean gulp, and continued his lesson.

"They will do anything as long as they think its fun. They'll do it over and over again to excess. If it has to do with women, alcohol, joking, laughing, singing, low-grade explosives—they'll do it. They will generously accept you into their group; then, they'll test you to see if you deserve to stay. If you pass the test, whatever it might be, you're in for the time of your life. If you fail the test, you'll have had a brief glimpse of the good life—then you'll be gone forever."

I was already becoming concerned. Johnny read it in my face.

"Listen, Patrick, Sam vouched for you to get you in the door—that carries a lot of weight with Frank. Once you're in the door, you're on your own. Don't make Sam look bad. And don't ever try to upstage Frank. You'll get crucified. Nobody cares about how witty and clever you might be—they only care about how witty and clever Frank is supposed to be. Don't ever forget that."

He opened the door to leave, "I'll make sure the bell captain brings your bags right up. I'll pick you up around ten."

WHEN I WOKE up a few hours later, I found the tuxedo draped on the sofa. It fit like it was custom made—Pam would have been impressed—I looked pretty good. Johnny arrived promptly at ten—we grabbed a late dinner at the casino before heading over to the Copa Room for the midnight show.

The Copa Room at the Sands held over 800 people. Not only was every single seat taken, but there must have been several hundred more people outside also trying desperately to bribe their way in. It was a madhouse of excitement and energy.

I caught Johnny's eye and nodded at the mob in the outer hallway. "Harveys?" I asked.

"Mr. and Mrs. Harveys."

Johnny caught the eye of the maitre'd who immediately took us down to the booth in front of the center of the stage. Johnny handed him a fifty-dollar bill, "How was the eight o'clock show?"

"It was wild, Johnny—just unbelievable! They fractured the joint. Frank came out after the show and joined some friends of his at a table way up in the back." He pointed to the back corner where a raucous crowd was milling around, smoking, drinking, and carrying on. "He's still up there."

Johnny and I sat down, ordered our drinks, and took in the energy that filled the room. There was a palpable feeling of excitement like none I had ever experienced. I was startled by a hand grabbing my shoulder from behind. A familiar-sounding voice asked, "Patrick McCarthy? Let me personally welcome you to the show."

I swiveled in my seat to face Frank Sinatra himself.

"It's a pleasure to meet you. Sam's told me lots of great things about you—I'm Frank Sinatra."

I was awestruck—Frank Sinatra had come down from his party to personally say hello. I slid out of the booth to shake his hand—his handshake was firm and confident. There was a mischievous glint in his eyes, "Sit down, man, and enjoy your drink. In fact, slide over and I'll join ya."

A waiter immediately brought him a drink, "Two fingers of Jack Daniels—just the way you like it, Mr. Sinatra."

I was impressed by Frank Sinatra's effortless charm. He talked to me like he had known me for years, "What are you doing hangin' out with this guy? Roselli's such a pussyhound I'd be afraid of gettin' a dose of the clap just from breathin' the same air he's breathin'. Hey, how's your *bird*, John?"

"My bird's just fine, Frank. In fact, I'm lookin' forward to my bird doin' a little singin' after the show."

They both chuckled at their inside joke, and then Frank asked me, "Patrick? How's your bird? Is it up for a good time tonight?"

I figured out that Frank's concern was anatomical by the way Frank and Johnny were smirking and leering, and even though I tended to be reserved in situations like these, I said, "My bird is up for a good time too, Mr. Sinatra."

Frank grinned and slapped me on the back. "Call me Frank, Patrick. Mr. Sinatra is my old man, and he ain't here tonight."

The house lights dimmed and the band began to strike up a song. Frank checked his watch, "I guess it's time for a little *F-U-N!* If you two guys don't mind, I think I'll screw with the boys and start the show from right here in the booth with you."

Holy cow! Of course that was all right with us.

Loud, sustained applause broke out as Dean Martin and Sammy Davis, Jr. walked on stage and launched into a song about friendship. As they sang, it was obvious that they were looking for Frank. When he didn't walk on stage at his cue, they peered through the glare of the stage lights—they thought he was still at the party up at the top of the room. Of course, everyone in the room knew exactly where Frank was seated and were waiting for the hi-jinks to begin.

Frank quietly summoned a waiter to our table and whispered something to him. A few minutes later, he returned with a cylindrical foot-long object wrapped in a white towel. Frank discreetly took it and slid it into the booth between us as Dean and Sammy continued to sing.

Frank leaned close to me. "Patrick, do you have a lighter handy?"

I nodded and pulled my Zippo out, handing it to him.

"No, no—I don't want it. Here, you take these." He pulled two cherry-bomb firecrackers from the pocket of his tuxedo jacket. "When I give you the signal, light these and toss them up on stage behind Sammy."

He grinned slyly, "Good! Get ready."

I lit the two fuses and tossed the cherry bombs up on stage behind Sammy. Neither Dean nor Sammy saw them coming, but the boys in the band sure did. Three or four of them dove for cover just as they exploded with two thunderous bangs.

Dean and Sammy jumped a mile high. Dean's drink went flying across the stage—Dino clasped his heart. Sammy leaped so high his knees almost touched his chest—then, he crouched down to catch his breath.

Frank suddenly appeared—dashing through the cloud of smoke—carrying the seltzer bottle the waiter had brought him. He sprayed Dean, Sammy, and anyone else he could reach on stage, all the while yelling, "Don't worry, boys! I'll save ya! I'll save ya!"

The entire room roared in laughter. Dean bent over laughing so hard he almost fell on the floor, and Sammy staggered around with his eyes crossed, acting completely discombobulated. Frank pointed the seltzer bottle in the direction of anyone in the crowd he could hit. None of the women even seemed to mind getting their outfits wet. The crowd was laughing, screaming and clapping while hysterical pandemonium engulfed the room.

"What an entrance!" Johnny Roselli screamed in my ear. "Didn't I tell you? This is what everyone comes to see every night. Isn't it wild?"

It was wild. And it got wilder. As the house finally began to settle down, Dean asked Frank where the hell he had been hiding the whole time. "I didn't see where you came from. I thought you were up-top with the boys."

"Naw," Frank replied, "I was right down in front, you big Dago. I was sitting with my good friend, Patrick McCarthy. Yeah, that Patrick is a firecracker!" Again, everyone erupted in laughter.

"Hey everyone! Say hello to Patrick. Patrick, stand up and take a bow for the crowd."

A single bright spotlight scanned the crowd. As I stood, it landed on me, illuminating the entire booth. Everyone wildly applauded. Frank motioned for me to come forward near the stage and accept the ovation. As I moved toward the stage, several people patted me on the back. I heard Sammy say, "Crazy man." I overheard someone else say, "You're a cool cat, man." I shamelessly loved every second of the attention.

The rest of the show was nothing but a blur to me. My body was running on so much adrenaline that the songs, the jokes, and the music all overwhelmed me. I can say, however, I've never seen five guys have so much fun working in my life.

Before I knew it, the show was over. Three encores later, the house lights came up; the show was officially over. However, to my surprise, the night was just getting started. One of Frank's buddies, Jilly Rizzo, came by our seats and told us Frank wanted us to join him for a party afterward. Johnny and I followed him directly to Frank's suite in the casino's hotel—the party was already in high gear.

"Patrick, this is the most happening spot on the planet. Man—it's Mardi Gras and the Playboy Club all rolled into one." Jilly accepted a drink from a buxom young woman, and motioned for her to give me one too. "See what I mean. You don't even get in the door and some broad meets you with a drink and a smile."

Jilly immediately disappeared into the crowd. I took my drink and tried to be nonchalant—it was a little hard for me, a guy from Minnesota, not to gawk.

Sheer madhouse enveloped us the moment we entered Sinatra's suite. The rooms were filled with Hollywood actors, famous people, gorgeous women of all kinds, and lots and lots of laughter. At one point, I made small talk with Henry Silva, one of Frank's friends in the movie.

"Man, I'm amazed I'm even here. Get this, a year ago, Frank chased *me* down on Sunset Boulevard just to tell *me* how much he liked *my* movies. I thought, 'Holy shit! That's Frank Sinatra. And he's telling *me* how much he liked *my* movies.' And look at me now—here I am in a movie alongside *him*."

Silva waved to someone coming through the door. His attention lagged as he scanned the room, then he said, "I've got one piece of advice for you while you're here—live it up! Nobody sleeps for fear of missing something. There's all the booze you could ever want—not that I drink. There's all the cigarettes you could ever smoke—not that I smoke. And there's all the women you could ever fuck—okay, I do that. Man, Patrick, the women are all over us. I am falling out of bed every morning laughing with some girl I just met. There's something so surreal about this that sometimes I feel like I'm dreaming. And if I'm dreaming, please, God, don't let me ever wake up!"

Sinatra's suite was filled with gorgeous women—blondes, brunettes, and redheads. I recognized some famous faces milling about—actor Tony Curtis was standing by a buffet table. I wandered over to help myself to some hors d'oeuvres. "Try the shrimp," he said and then he recognized me. "Hey, I really liked what you and Frank did to open the show. That was jazzy, man." We traded small talk, and I asked if he was in the movie. "Yeah, I've got a cameo as a blackjack dealer, but to tell you the truth, I'm here for the party and the pussy. This is a table-pussy buffet, if you ask me. You getting any of it?"

I avoided the question and commented that Frank's reputation as a womanizer was apparently well deserved. Tony smiled and shook his head to disagree with me. "Listen here, Frank's not a womanizer—he's being *womanized*! There's a big difference. He doesn't have to throw himself at the ladies—they're throwing themselves at him. And if they can't get him, they'll settle for anyone who has been next to him. So, I plan to just hang around and catch the ones who can't catch Frank. I'm tellin' ya, it's beautiful, man, just beautiful."

I saw actress Angie Dickinson who played Frank's wife in the movie. Johnny Roselli introduced me to Judith Campbell, a strikingly beautiful young woman in her mid-twenties. She looked so much like Elizabeth Taylor she could have been her sister—I was certain that she was an actress. We talked for about a half an hour. I was surprised that she was divorced—she readily told me that she had married an actor who was an alcoholic when she was only eighteen. Although she was young, she seemed comfortable around Frank and his friends.

Peter Lawford and Sammy Davis both spent a little time talking with me. I guess that I had preconceived notions that celebrities didn't talk to people like me. I was certainly in a different world. It was after 4:00 in the morning when I asked Johnny what time the party usually broke up. "I don't know—it hasn't stopped since it started a month ago."

"Don't these guys ever sleep?"

"Naw, sleep is overrated—they just pass out from time to time. We're taking bets as to who ends going home in a box. Right now, everybody's a candidate. Last week, Sammy passed out colder than a refrigerated mackerel from too much bubbly water, not enough sleep, and a hard day and night in front of the movie cameras and the Copa Room footlights. These guys are not only burning the candle at both ends, they've lit a fire in the middle just to be sure."

I hung out with everyone until the sun came up. Frank finally disappeared into a bedroom with a lady, so I quietly slipped out to my room.

THE NEXT EVENING, Johnny and I followed the same routine as the night before. We took naps until dark, enjoyed a late dinner (without alcohol), and got to the second show just before midnight. Like last night, it was pandemonium outside the Copa Room. But unlike last night, we didn't get the front-row seats—the maitre-d told us it went to a "Very Important Person" from out of town. I was, however, invited to join Frank's entourage at their tables in the back of the room.

The show started with Frank, Dean, and Sammy singing about friendship; then, Peter Lawford and Joey Bishop joined in. After the number was over, Frank took center stage.

"Get a load of this next one," Jilly Rizzo said as he nudged Johnny in the ribs.

Frank pointed to the same front row table that Johnny and I had sat at the previous night. "Ladies and gentlemen, we have in the audience tonight a very special guest."

"Thank you, Frank!" We heard a voice suddenly yell from over at the side of the room. It was Milton Berle, standing up, smiling, and waving to the audience.

Frank laughed and shook his head. "No, not you, Milt. I said it was a special guest."

Milton Berle put on his famously perplexed look and sat down to great applause.

"Ladies and gentlemen, let's have a big round of applause for the distinguished Senator from the great state of Massachusetts—and the next President of the United States of America, Senator John F. Kennedy and his brother, Teddy."

The orchestra began to play "High Hopes" as the spotlights illuminated the table. People stood up to get a look at Jack Kennedy. Judith Campbell and another girl I saw at the party last night were also seated at the table with them.

Jack stood up and waved to huge applause while Frank proclaimed, "I personally feel I'm gonna visit him in the White House one day very soon."

Dean quipped, "I personally feel I gotta visit the outhouse very soon."

"Stand up again, Mr. Future President! Your voters want to see you."

Dean turned to Frank and asked in mock seriousness, "What was his last name again?" Frank almost fell down convulsed in laughter. He goosed Dean for some more cheap slapstick laughs.

The party at Frank's suite that evening managed to surpass the previous evening's fun. Gorgeous women, handsome men, booze, food, music, loud laughter, dancing—everyone was there to have F-U-N. Some of the Sands showgirls were there, most in various states of undress. It was a bacchanalia.

It was an orgy. It was the epitome of Las Vegas sin. And it was the very last place on earth a candidate for the Presidency of the United States should have been found.

"Hey Patrick, come over here," I heard Frank shout above the crowd noise. "There's somebody here I want you to meet. He's from your hometown!"

It turned out that Frank meant D.C. The person he wanted me to meet was someone I already knew—the husband of my wife's best friend.

"Patrick, this is Jack, although he now has a new name, 'Chicky Baby!' Hey, Chicky Baby, say hello to Patrick."

With Judith Campbell draped all over his arm, Jack Kennedy looked as surprised to see me as I was disappointed to see him. But Jack was as cool as a cucumber. "We've met. What are you doing here?"

He shook my hand, but his handshake was not a firm, warm one—it was a bone crushing warning. I didn't flinch, but I got his subtle message. I returned his bone buster with one of my own—he wasn't going to intimidate me in any way.

Before I had a chance to reply, Jack glanced over toward a sofa where his brother Teddy was reclining—two nearly nude showgirls draped over him. He looked at Judith, "Do me a favor—go get me another drink and make sure Teddy is OK, will you?"

She smiled sweetly at him, made eye contact with him for just a moment too long, and left to fulfill his order. Jack and I watched her leave; then, he turned to confront me while Frank was distracted talking to someone else.

I now had a chance to answer his original question, "I could ask you the same thing, Jack. What are you doing here? You ought to know better than this."

"What do you mean?" he feigned innocence. 'I'm not doing anything wrong. I'm just here meeting the voters."

"Bullshit, Jack. I doubt there's a single registered voter in this room other than you and me, and I'm not even sure that you're registered. So don't tell me you're here to mingle with the voters." I shot a glance over at Judith. She had on a silky evening gown that accentuated her lovely back. "I know just what you're up to."

Jack's eyes met mine with a hardened gaze. "You're way out of your league, McCarthy," he whispered in a threatening tone. "You don't belong here—why don't *you* go back home—where *you* belong?"

"Jesus, that's funny, Jack. That's exactly what I was going to advise you to do. One month ago you publicly declared your intention to run for the Presidency of the United States of America. Isn't this a little reckless even for you? Do you really want to publicly confirm for the country what the pundits already suspect? You've already got a number of strikes against you—

you're Catholic, you're a daddy's boy, you're young and immature, and you've got a terrible work ethic. You've famously touted yourself as a loving family man. Do you want your morals to be called into question, too? You can't afford to make any mistakes and yet look at you. Go ahead—throw away your chances, I don't really care. I'm not gonna vote for you anyway. Nobody I know, who has any brains, will vote for you, either."

Jack's face turned red as his Irish temper threatened to explode. Before he could get in the last word, Frank turned back to us.

"Come on, Patrick. Stop hogging Senator Chicky Baby's time. There's other people that want a piece of him." And with that, Frank dragged Jack by the elbow into another crowded part of the room.

Later while making small talk with Sammy Davis, Jr., Peter Lawford joined us. "Hey Patrick, you having F-U-N yet?" he asked.

He surveyed the room, tipping his head in Frank and Jack's direction. Peter sighed and lit a cigarette with Sammy's lighter. He exhaled a deep plume of smoke and wearily confessed, "I've always been Frank's pimp, Sammy. Now I guess Frank is Jack's pimp."

Sammy shrugged and said, "It looks like the guy's doing alright to me."

Peter smirked, cautiously looked around, leaned in, and lowered his voice. We leaned in closer as well. "If you want to see what a million dollars in cash looks like, go into the next room. There's a brown leather satchel in the closet. Open it."

Sammy leaned away, shook his head, and said in all seriousness, "I'm not going anywhere near that."

Peter sensed Sammy's nervousness, "It's OK. Jack's got four of the wildest girls you've ever seen entertaining him as we speak. He'll never see you."

Sammy put his hands over his ears and protested, "I don't want to hear that either."

Peter laughed, "Oh, come on, Sammy. You know about these Kennedy men."

"No, I don't," he protested, "And I don't want to know! Leave it alone, man. Back where I come from, just knowing about shit like that can get you hurt."

With that, Sammy picked up his drink and left. Peter looked at me, shrugged his shoulders, and went back to join the party. From that day on, I had new respect for Sammy Davis, Jr.

Jack stuck around town another day or two. I saw him having breakfast with Judith Campbell on Frank's patio the next morning. I ran into her later down by the pool. She pulled up a chaise next to me and began chatting about Jack. She had stars in her eyes when she whispered that she had already fallen in love with him. I felt a twinge of anger that I quickly suppressed.

I thought back to Sammy's reaction from the night before, and I decided to just keep my mouth shut. She was a grown woman; she didn't need any advice from me, and I'm sure it didn't bother her that Jack was married.

I found out later Frank slipped Jack into a scene in his movie as an inside joke. I couldn't believe Jack was so cavalier. I didn't believe he had a chance in hell of ever getting elected president, so why should I care?

But I did care. I thought back to Pam and Jackie. I really felt bad for Jackie—she had married a man who was incapable of being faithful to her. She didn't deserve to be treated like this, especially with all she had previously been through for Jack and his career.

When my time in Vegas was up, Johnny Roselli drove me back to the airport. Not until I was on the plane, did it occur to me—I never saw Sam Giancana the whole time I was out there.

OUR TASK FORCE pushed ahead in developing a Cuban resistance force. Eisenhower felt it was a waste of time to concentrate on creating economic chaos for Cuba. According to Allen Dulles, Ike said, "Don't just fool around with sugar refineries. Let's get a program that will really do something about Castro." Following the President's directive, I helped write our memorandum entitled "A Program of Covert Action Against the Castro Regime."

We were confident that we could develop "an adequate paramilitary force outside of Cuba" and train a number of "paramilitary cadres… at secure locations outside of the United States." Concurrently, we developed a covert military action and intelligence organization inside of Cuba which would be "responsive to the orders and directions of the exile organization." Our plan, code-named Pluto, was vague enough to give us tremendous latitude to do whatever needed to be done.

Organizationally, Richard Bissell was in charge of planning; Tracy Barnes was in charge of operations; I was placed in charge of coordinating outside resources with our contacts in organized crime. David Atlee Phillips, who had served three years uncover in Cuba as a journalist during Batista's regime, was placed in charge of psychological warfare, having previously distinguished himself in that same capacity in Guatemala back in 1954. Phillips planned similar radio broadcasts of propaganda continuously using both long-wave and short-wave bands to be sure that the Cuban people received the messages.

E. Howard Hunt, who I had also worked with in Guatemala, was appointed as one of two political action chiefs in Miami. My experience with Hunt had not been positive—he wasn't a team player. I wasn't surprised when Hunt developed a hatred for Gerry Droller, the other political action chief. Droller's appointment was somewhat curious because he was from our European division, meaning he had no previous Latin American experience, and he didn't speak a single word of Spanish.

I WAS NOW juggling three major projects: Project Cocoon, the WH/4 task force, and the U-2 overflights. I had been fairly confident in the success of all three until my home telephone rang unexpectedly in early May.

"Patrick, Carmine Vito's on the phone for you," Pam called out. I was a little bit surprised to get a call from Carmine on a Sunday. I detected the tension in his voice the moment he started to apologize for disturbing me.

"Hey Carmine," I asked, "What's the matter?"

"We've got a missing Article."

"Which one," I asked.

"Grand Slam. It's long overdue."

This was my worst nightmare, and it couldn't have come at a worse time. One of our U-2 flights, Mission 4154, code-named Grand Slam, was the most ambitious overflight of the USSR we had ever attempted. Instead of a limited penetration of Soviet airspace, this particular mission would fly across the entire width of the USSR—a 3800 mile flight with 2900 miles over the Soviet Union. Grand Slam would be in the air for nine hours—it was to photograph operational Soviet intercontinental ballistic missile sites, as well as plutonium-production facilities and shipyards where Soviet nuclear subs were being built.

"What can you tell me?"

I could hear a heavy sigh coming from Carmine's end. "It took off from Peshawar, Pakistan. We lost it over Sverdlovsk."

There was silence on the other end of the phone. "As you know, there was absolutely no room for error. If the pilot didn't follow the planned altitude schedule and fuel schedule exactly…," Carmine trailed off.

We both knew what would happen—the plane would crash.

"Any evidence the plane was intercepted?"

"Patrick, we had this thing timed—there was no possibility of adding evasive maneuvers to the flight plan—even to engage in a zig-zag pattern."

The Soviet response would be a problem. We knew the Soviets had tracked every U-2 overflight since day one; they were adamant about ending them. They had beefed up their radar network to provide earlier warnings of our intrusions, their commanders had become better at vectoring interceptor jets loaded with air-to-air missiles closer and closer to our planes, and the

SAM missiles (Surface-to-Air) had been augmented with more powerful and more accurate SAM-II's.

"What about the SAM's?"

"Don't know. We're in a holding pattern. But the Soviet air defense ministers have been charting our overflights. They could probably guess our route."

I had a sick feeling in the pit of my stomach. The Soviets knew our missions originated in Pakistan and Iran. If they could guess our target, they could predict our flight path with accuracy.

We had been operating on borrowed time.

THAT AFTERNOON, I accompanied Allen Dulles to the White House to officially notify the President that the Article was missing—and had possibly been shot down. Dulles had guaranteed the President that it was virtually impossible for the Soviets to shoot down the U-2.

Eisenhower met us with a stony silence. He surprised me when he asked, "Who's the pilot?"

"Francis Gary Powers, sir," Dulles responded. "There's not a chance of his being alive."

"You're certain?" The air was thick with tension.

"Mr. President, our pilots have been instructed to blow up the plane before being captured. In a worse case scenario, our pilots have cyanide."

Eisenhower looked grim.

Mr. Dulles assured him, "They will never—ever—capture one of our pilots alive."

The President shook his head gravely. "I'm deeply distressed about the loss of this young man. You gave me assurances—now keep this from blowing up in our face," he said as he dismissed us. Then, he added, "Handle it."

THE NEXT DAY the Agency had NASA issue a press release from Incirlik, Turkey announcing that one of their unarmed Lockheed U-2 weather planes had vanished over the Lake Van area of Turkey. The pilot, a civilian employee of Lockheed on loan to NASA, had reported having trouble with his oxygen supply system before disappearing. In case the Soviets protested the violation of their airspace, the United States government could claim that the pilot blacked out, and the U-2, on autopilot, innocently strayed into Soviet airspace.

However, it wasn't that easy for us to get away with telling that lie—

especially after Khrushchev shocked the world on May 5 by announcing that a U.S. spy plane had boldly violated Soviet airspace on May Day, the greatest of all Soviet holidays. He claimed the Russian air defense system had shot down the illegal intruder. Khrushchev indignantly declared this "an aggressive provocation aimed at wrecking the (upcoming Moscow) Summit Conference" with President Eisenhower.

I was immediately called into a high-level meeting with Allen Dulles, Richard Bissell, Tracy Barnes, and Cord Meyer. We were apprehensive about how this would play out for the Agency and for the country. We didn't know quite what to do, but we had to do something.

Richard finally proposed something that seemed to make the most sense at the time. "Since no mention was made about the fate of our pilot, Frank Powers, we have to assume he's dead. If he's dead, the Russians can't claim he was actually engaged in any actual spy activity. I think our gambit can hold up to world scrutiny if the plane is destroyed, and the pilot is dead."

That seemed to be our best option. On May 6, after considerable debate with the upper levels of the Agency, we instructed our State Department to adamantly refute Khrushchev's allegation. They laid it on pretty thick when they said "There was no, N-O, no deliberate attempt to violate Soviet airspace, and there has never been. Any suggestion that the United States of America would try to deceive the entire world about the purpose of such a flight as other than a weather flight, was 'monstrous!'"

In our emergency meeting the next day, we all agreed that any further Soviet actions had been successfully quelled. "We're holding some strong cards, gentlemen," Mr. B reminded us. We were now in politically dangerous waters, but Allen and Mr. B thought we could get away with it as long as Frank Powers was dead.

On May 7, once again, we were proved wrong. Khrushchev was a better poker player than we were. He was holding a royal flush, essentially an unbeatable position. Premier Khrushchev announced not only did he have the wreckage of our plane, he also had the pilot plus the film recovered from our spy cameras!

The wily Communist leader had literally caught us red-handed and proved to the world that America had lied.

I GOT A CALL that night from Chase.

"Are you guys really that stupid?" he asked incredulously.

"Is this off the record?" I replied.

"Of course, I don't want you to get in trouble. But tell me, what the hell went wrong?"

"You know I can't tell you that," I protested.

"Yeah, I know. I'm just blowing off steam. There're a lot of scared people around D.C. right now."

"Yes, I know that. I also happen to know a lot of scared people."

There was a silence as if he expected me to elaborate. We both knew I couldn't.

"The shit's hit the fan up on Capitol Hill. You know that, don't you? Congress is in an uproar over this incident. The entire world thinks the Soviet anger is completely justified. The United States of America has been caught intentionally violating their sovereign airspace, which is technically an act of war. Patrick, both the U.S. and the Soviet Union possess hydrogen bombs, and those bombs happen to be held in check by the most fragile of trigger-happy fingers. This provocative trespass could have easily launched a nuclear war. In the very least, your 'spying and lying' has seriously damaged our national reputation and worldwide prestige. What in the hell are you guys gonna do about it?"

"Chase," I protested, "you know I can't tell you anything."

"Ah hell, Patrick, let me finish, will you? Those poor bastards over at NASA are going to be crucified over this fiasco. Weather plane, indeed! Their weak cover story makes them sound like a whorehouse piano player who claims not to know what actually goes on upstairs. Come on, Patrick. Everybody's worked up right now with rumors, accusations, and gossip—you name it. Everyone I talk to has an opinion on what has happened and what should be done. I corralled John Eisenhower, the President's son, and he is going to publicly demand that the President fire Allen Dulles."

"I hope he doesn't do that."

"Why not?"

"Because this country needs Allen Dulles right now more than ever."

Chase's laughter carried across the telephone lines. "You really have turned into a government brown-noser, haven't you?"

I was starting to lose my temper so I kept my mouth shut. I knew there was no sense in making it worse.

Chase continued needling me, "To make matters worse, Khrushchev alleges that perhaps President Eisenhower was unaware of the overflight. That would be a bombshell of an allegation if he's right. Any overflight is clearly an act of military aggression, but if our President admits he *wasn't* aware of the flight, then where in the chain of American military and intelligence bureaucracy did such a provocative order originate? Do you understand what that means? The next question then has to be, who is really running the show if the President wasn't in charge of an operation that had the potential to start a nuclear war? And if Eisenhower admits he authorized the flight, he goes on record as having lied to the American public and to the rest of the world about secretly authorizing an act of military aggression against our enemy. That would be a damning accusation with the potential of fueling a damaging political scandal."

"How so, Chase? He can't run again for another term."

"It could cost the Republican Party the November election. The voters won't stand for such a risky action by their leaders. They're liable to clean house and vote the Democrats in, just to be safe."

"That wouldn't be very smart."

"We'll see."

Chase was right about John Eisenhower. He did put pressure on his father to fire Allen Dulles. Though Dulles disagreed with the accusation that he had misled the President, he gallantly offered to resign and take the sole responsibility for the failure. Eisenhower was royally pissed off at all of us in the CIA. But true to his nature as a former General, he announced, "I am *not* going to shift the blame to my underlings!" rejecting Allen's resignation offer.

Chase was also right about the political pressure put on President Eisenhower. The poor guy took it squarely on the chin. The President flew to Paris for the long-planned Summit meeting with Premier Khrushchev, Prime Minister Harold MacMillan of Great Britain, and President Charles de Gaulle, with a good part of the Washington press corps in tow, Chase included. Chase's stories reported that as soon as the Paris Summit opened, Khrushchev demanded an apology and a promise from the President that the overflights would cease.

But President Eisenhower did not apologize. Instead, he did something that no other U.S. President had ever done. He publicly admitted that he had approved peacetime intelligence operations. He justified it by saying, "No one wants another Pearl Harbor. This means that we must have knowledge of military forces and preparations around the world, especially those capable of massive surprise attack…secrecy in the Soviet Union makes this essential. In most of the world, no large-scale attack could be prepared in secret, but in the Soviet Union there is a fetish of secrecy and concealment. This is a major cause of international tension and uneasiness today. Our deterrent must never be placed in jeopardy. The safety of the whole free world demands this." He further explained that intelligence gathering was distasteful but vital. From the beginning of his administration, he had instructed the Agency to adequately prepare for our national defense and "to gather, in every feasible way, the information required to protect the United States and the free world against surprise attack."

Not surprisingly, Soviet Premier Khrushchev denounced Eisenhower as both a "hypocrite" and a "liar." The Paris Summit collapsed after the Summit attendees were treated to the sight and sounds of a massive temper tantrum by the Soviet Premier.

Meanwhile, safely at home in America, Senator Jack Kennedy self-righteously implied that President Eisenhower was appeasing Khrushchev with his admission of our spy mission. I secretly laughed and thought it was a sign of political desperation to accuse Eisenhower of appeasement. What Eisenhower did wasn't even close to being in the same league of appeasement as the Kennedy family—Joe Kennedy was the clear champion there.

Though I believed the U-2 overflights had been justified and had made our country more secure, the revelations were incredibly damaging to our image around the world. The Turkish government, which had been friendly to us and our base at Incirlik, was rebuked by riots across the breadth of their country. Student riots in Korea similarly caused the pro-U.S. government of Syngman Rhee to publicly denounce us. President Eisenhower, who had planned a last good-will visit to Japan before he left office, was humiliated when 10,000 Japanese demonstrators demanded that our U-2's at Atsugi be immediately removed. In the end, the Japanese government withdrew its invitation to the President and he was told he was not welcomed to land on Japanese soil.

I admired Eisenhower. He was a strong commander in chief who fully assumed the responsibility for our botched intelligence-gathering actions. President Eisenhower's legacy was irrevocably tainted in the aftermath of the downing of our U-2. I could not ignore the fact that I might also bear some responsibility for the debacle. After all, I had provided Lee Harvey Oswald with the obsolete U-2 technical information he used as part of his cover story. I worried that my information may have helped to take down the U-2. Like everyone on the project, I felt responsible for the imprisonment of our pilot—the Soviets sentenced Francis Gary Powers to ten years of "deprivation of liberty" in a Soviet prison.

I let the President down—I did not sleep soundly for many, many months afterward.

IN EARLY JUNE, Mr. B, who rarely came out of his office, walked over to my desk and handed me a folder.

"Patrick, this FBI memo just came to our attention. We thought you should see it as soon as possible."

Before I could say anything, he turned and walked back toward his office.

The folder was non-descript—it had no markings of any kind on it.

Inside was a single typed page—a memorandum from the Director of the FBI dated June 3, 1960 regarding Lee Harvey Oswald. The memo was only a few lines, but it contained an ominous warning.

Open-mouthed, I read the following: "Since there is a possibility that an imposter is using (Lee Harvey) Oswald's birth certificate, any current information the Department of State may have concerning subject will be appreciated. (signed) J. Edgar Hoover."

Someone was using the identity, Lee Harvey Oswald, in the United States? What in the hell was going on? I reread the memo—it was clear—someone in the country was using the name Lee Harvey Oswald. I could feel the sweat rolling down my back as I tried to make sense of the Hoover memo.

A.J. Hidell was safely ensconced behind the Iron Curtain. I had switched the identities myself. This didn't make any sense. Had the Russians discovered our ruse? Were they screwing with us? Had Ozzie decided to unilaterally resurrect his prior life and forsake the new identity we had constructed for him?

I called in a few favors and found out an FBI agent by the name of John W. Fain had interviewed Lee's mother, Marguerite Oswald, in April. She had confided her suspicion that someone else was posing as her son. Since Lee Oswald had defected to the USSR from a high security position involved with the U-2 program, her suspicions were duly noted and passed on up the chain to where Hoover ultimately learned of the issue. I couldn't ascertain if Hoover suspected something more complex, or if he was simply passing on a worried mother's concerns about her missing traitor of a son.

Rather than risk exposing the truth behind Operation Cocoon, I decided to let the matter drop and hoped it didn't turn into something bigger down the road.

EVEN THOUGH GRANT, Chase, and I didn't work together or see each other often, we still had a close bond forged from our early years in D.C. We tried to get together every few months or so. We no longer met at Rosie O'Grady's; instead, we preferred a small, exclusive steak house near Capitol Hill. The restaurant was known for its privacy with its subdued lighting and enclosed booths. Politicians came here to make deals; adulterers came here for a secret rendezvous. It wasn't unusual to see a woman hide behind her scarf until she was seated.

After a couple of drinks, the topic of conversation moved to the upcoming presidential election. Chase had been assigned to follow and report on the upcoming campaign and was interested in what we thought of the candidates.

I knew President Eisenhower backed his own vice-president, Richard Nixon, but he also favored Lyndon Johnson as the Democratic nominee. Ike appreciated the Majority Leader's method of governing; he seemed to prefer working with him rather than the more conservative Republican leaders in his own party. Whatever the Democrats might think of LBJ, I knew Eisenhower liked him.

I shared that insight with Grant and Chase. "I was in the Oval Office with Mr. Dulles and Mr. B when Ike told Arthur Krock he couldn't understand how the Democrats could consider nominating an 'inexperienced boy' like Jack Kennedy. The President said that he felt 'Lyndon Johnson would be the best Democrat of them all as President from the standpoint of responsible management of the national interest.'"

Chase added his two cents, "Everyone I talk to on the Hill knows Kennedy lacks the experience to be able to handle the presidency, especially at this point in the Cold War."

Grant listened quietly, sipping his vodka martini. I briefly wondered when he started drinking martinis. I noticed Grant made a point of ordering only the best vodka for his drink. I should have pointed out he was wasting his money; it didn't make sense to order the best liquor for a mixed drink unless you were drinking it straight up. Or you were showing off.

Grant made eye contact with Chase as he leaned into the table. "This is all strictly off the record, Chase." Chase nodded that he understood, and Grant continued, "Lyndon told me and Bobby Baker he knows ten times more about running the country than Jack does. Lyndon says 'That kid needs a little gray in his hair…I don't think I'm absolutely qualified to be President, but when I look at the other boys, when I look at Jack, I think I'm better qualified than they are. I'm a doer; I've passed bills; I've minded the store.'"

Grant was dressed in very expensive looking suit—I'm sure his tie was pure silk. What we had once called his "shit-eating grin," had evolved into an arrogant smirk. Grant was riding high in D.C. and had begun to take on some unbecoming mannerisms. Grant continued with his appraisal, "Kennedy is just a playboy and a lightweight who is smart enough but hasn't shown any of the aptitude necessary for the hard work required of an effective leader, especially the President."

Grant made quote-marks with his fingers to indicate that those words were descriptions that Lyndon had used. "And, according to Lyndon, 'Jack was out kissing babies while I was passing bills, including his bills.'"

Chase agreed, "Your boss is right, Grant. The guy's run the Senate like a clock for the past six years or so. He ought to know what he's doing."

"I don't think Kennedy has a snowball's chance in hell of getting the nomination," Grant said with authority.

"It all comes down to experience and the ability to lead and govern effectively," Chase added.

"Lyndon plans to tell the Democratic Convention in Los Angeles that Communism will show (Grant mimicked Lyndon's Texas drawl) 'no mercy for innocence, no gallantry toward inexperience, no patience toward errors.'" Grant could be theatrical when he knew he had an audience.

"I hope Lyndon can win the nomination. You remember what happened in '56? Nobody thought Jack Kennedy was a viable vice-presidential candidate, but he sure managed to get the Democratic machine to take him seriously for a little while," I cynically replied.

"I don't think the American voters would like the idea of Joseph Kennedy *buying* his son the presidency," Chase added.

"Exactly!" Grant agreed. "Kennedy may be popular with the people, but you can't buy the presidency. You have to be worthy. Jack Kennedy's not worthy to be president—especially not at the age of just forty-two. Lyndon's the one who is the seasoned politician. Everybody will see Jack for what he is: (and he once more adopted Lyndon's Texas drawl) 'that scrawny fellow with the rickets—that sickly little shit—that spavined hunchback.'"

"I overheard Lyndon in the Senate cafeteria trying to persuade Tip O'Neill that Jack was barely a senator, let alone a legitimate presidential candidate," Chase said.

"How did you hear that?"

"I'm a professional reporter—I was in the right place at the right time, doing my job." Chase grinned and then gave us his best imitation of LBJ. "Tip, I want you with me on the second ballot. That boy is going to die on the vine. You and I know the boy can't win. He's just a flash in the pan. He has no record of substance."

Both Grant and I laughed at Chase's weak impression.

"Gentlemen, I personally think Lyndon's a shoe-in," Grant added confidently, "It's all a game, boys. You've seen Lyndon play poker. You know how it's done."

"Yeah, but I'm afraid your so-called 'Master of the Senate' is going to stubbornly cling to his belief that public service like his would ultimately be rewarded," Chase countered. "It's a strategy that could backfire on him."

"Right, Chase. You are always right," Grant said caustically.

"No, Grant. You should listen."

Grant rolled his eyes, "Continue, by all means."

Chase ignored Grant's sarcasm. "Senator Johnson's strategy for securing the nomination is strictly a convention-based, and not a primary-based, strategy. He needs to see the convention move into the smoke-filled back rooms where he can twist arms and make his point. I don't think that's going to happen. Many of us who are following this campaign feel that if Johnson succeeds in getting Kennedy into those back rooms, Jack would never emerge from them with the nomination. Johnson is too tough a political street fighter for Jack to beat."

Chase's observation made sense.

"I agree with Chase. The problem is, the Kennedy machine knows that too, and they will do everything they can to sew this up prior to the convention."

"Ah, that's not gonna happen," Grant dismissed. "He's not going to be able to defeat seasoned political opponents who are all far more qualified to be President than he is."

I reached for my drink—house gin and tonic—and added, "Well, all I can tell you is that Jack pissed us all off at the Agency when he accused President Eisenhower of equivocating on the U-2 incident. I was especially irritated at Jack's arrogance—which—he continues to effectively hide from the voting public. He can be charmingly cordial to anyone and everyone, but behind their backs he will denigrate even the greatest of men as hollow—and not worthy of his attentions."

"On the other hand, he can be unbelievably charming if he wants something from you," Chase pointed out. "Especially, if a man or woman possesses a quality of influence, eloquence, or intelligence that he either needs or admires. I think he displays a dangerous style of leadership—personal feelings count far more with him than cold-blooded assessment."

"Chase, if you don't think personal feelings enter into politics, then you're naïve," Grant said.

"Grant, a leader has to put personal feelings aside for the good of the country. A lot of good men, good thinkers, are alienated from the 'inner circle,' and a lot of flawed individuals are elevated into that same inner circle because they know how to play on a leader's feelings." Chase put quote marks of his own around the word *feelings*.

As always, Chase made a good point. I always thought it was relatively benign and harmless for Jack to surround himself with sycophants. He was shallow himself and surrounded himself with shallow people. That behavior could be dangerous especially if Jack miraculously became President.

"Well, I'm only comforted by the fact that a Jack Kennedy victory in November is very unlikely," Grant said.

"I will say this," Chase conceded, "Jack understands the grass roots of national politics better than a whole lot of other politicians. Since 1956, I've watched the whole Kennedy organization work to identify who the important people are in each state. He has put together intelligence files on the power structure of every single state Democratic Party, and he has memorized them.

By the time the primary elections are over, Jack might very well harvest all the political seeds he has sown."

Grant grew strangely silent as Chase's comments sunk in. I could see he was worried about his Johnson's strategy in light of the Chase's assessment.

"It's been real interesting following Jack around. In some cases, Jack has been both magnificent and humble; in other cases, he has been coldly arrogant and brutal. When he was in a receiving line, accepting the congratulations of some old-line Democratic Party bosses whom he had just outflanked and outmaneuvered, he could barely suppress his contempt. He was polite—but distant. If Jack defeats you," and here he paused to stare at Grant, "he also demeans you, just to rub it in. He has no use for the old and the weak, especially the old and weak that he has just outsmarted and no longer needs."

"But is that a probable strategic mistake for Jack?" I asked. "A political convention is usually comprised of older, serious men in their fifties, and in the case of the Democratic Party, many of those older delegates could probably boast of an unbroken string of attendance at the Presidential nominating conventions going all the way back to Woodrow Wilson. They are also usually wiser men than the common voters who sent them there. If the convention became deadlocked, they're not likely to be Kennedy allies, are they?"

"It's who you know," Grant interjected. "I wouldn't risk alienating any wise old power-broker. It might come back to bite you in the ass."

WHEN THE DEMOCRATIC Convention convened in Los Angeles, Chase's assessment proved to be right. The Kennedy political machine had thoroughly outmaneuvered LBJ and his supporters. Grant said Lyndon Johnson exploded in angry frustration right in front of the Washington state delegation when he compared his Senate record to Jack's. Then he blasted Joseph Kennedy for wanting to appease Hitler during World War II. "I wasn't any Chamberlain-umbrella policy man. I never thought Hitler was right." According to Grant, LBJ mostly groaned behind closed doors, "I can't stand to be pushed around by that forty-two-year-old kid."

Chase reported that the Democratic Party was caught off-guard just prior to the convention when former President Harry Truman resigned as a Democratic convention delegate. Chase interviewed Truman who said he was quitting because he was not going to participate in "a pre-arranged affair" that would result in nominating a candidate who was too young and inexperienced to be president. He also wanted to make it clear to Chase and his readers that he could not sanction the son of Joseph Kennedy as a candidate.

Chase said it was apparent former President Truman so disliked Joe Kennedy and his tainted influence in presidential politics that he either accidentally or purposefully referred to Jack as 'Joseph' throughout the interview. The insiders in D.C. understood the code—no friend of Harry Truman was to support Joe Kennedy or his son in this ill-advised venture.

In the end, it didn't matter. Jack went to the convention in Los Angeles with 600 firm votes out of the 760 necessary for nomination. He won those votes during a tough primary campaign. One by one, he had defeated Hubert Humphrey, Lyndon Johnson, Wayne Morse, Adlai Stevenson, and Stewart Symington—all seasoned politicians and all far more experienced than Jack.

The only exciting floor fight came from Texas delegate and Johnson supporter, John Connally who let the cat out of the bag to the American public—Jack Kennedy secretly suffered from Addison's disease, and Jack was intentionally hiding that truth from the voters. Lyndon Johnson's camp fervently hoped most voters would be hesitant to elect a man to our highest office who might not live out his term, or might even become incapacitated during it.

Kennedy couldn't duck the health rumors anymore, so his team took a different approach—they repeatedly denied the story and aggressively mocked Connally. The Kennedy machine put the health issue to rest—and put Lyndon Johnson on the ticket as his running mate. It was in the bag—John Fitzgerald Kennedy received the Democratic Party's nomination as their presidential candidate.

Grant later told me LBJ received a million dollars in cash from Joseph Kennedy to insure his loyalty on the ticket—the money greatly assuaged Lyndon Johnson's battered ego and wounded pride.

BEFORE THE 1960 Presidential Campaign could get started, the candidates had to complete a special summer session of Congress. For three hot and humid weeks in August, Jack, Lyndon, and the Republican Party Presidential nominee, Vice President Richard Nixon, were trapped in this special session to finish their legislative business.

Forty thousand curious tourists a day filed through the Capitol Building to gawk at the country's future leaders in the bowl of the Senate. Lyndon and Dick were squarely in the spotlight as the Majority Leader of the Senate and the Vice President. Jack Kennedy, however, was relegated to the back row of the Senate. He was powerless to lead or to even show off any discernable leadership skills. Jack was also chained to D.C. by Senate roll-call votes while Dick Nixon was free to leave whenever he wanted to roam the country campaigning. By the end of August, Dick led Jack 53% to 47% in the Gallup polls regarding voter preference.

Allen Dulles briefed the new Democratic Presidential nominee on a variety of matters concerning national security. NSC-5412/2 happened to be part of that presentation, but Allen refused to elaborate on many, if any, details. Allen shared the same viewpoint that many of us did—Jack Kennedy was not a serious threat to Richard Nixon in the upcoming election. We were wary about giving classified information to Kennedy. Old Joe Kennedy could never keep his damned mouth shut about anything, and his son was a "chip off the old block." Though Allen told Kennedy as little as possible—it didn't mean that someone else wouldn't divulge classified information to Kennedy later.

By September 1, the Senate had formally wrapped up its work, and Jack Kennedy confidently sprinted out onto the campaign trail. I had just left the Capitol building when I ran into Chase, who was looking bedraggled. Without even consulting Pam, I invited him over for dinner and a beer—he surprised me and accepted my invitation.

School hadn't started yet, so Pam was busy doing all the things around the house that she hadn't completed over the summer. Pam was always a Dr. Jekyll and Mr. Hyde at this time of the year, excited about the new school year but hating to give up her summer freedom.

"Honey, look who I brought home."

"Oh my God—Chase," Pam warmly greeted him.

Chase, always the gentleman, kissed her on the cheek. "Pam, you are as beautiful as ever. Patrick, you two are lucky—you know that?"

Pam put her arm around my waist and gave me a peck on the cheek. "You've got to stay for dinner—doesn't he Patrick? I'll put some burgers on. It'll be like old times."

I found some lawn chairs in the garage and took them into the backyard under the shade of tree. Our heavily wooded backyard was cool even in the Virginia heat. Pam brought out two cold beers. "You two make yourself comfortable. I'm going to run next door and see if Tim can have dinner with Donny and maybe sleep over."

Pam, ever the gracious hostess, put out the perfect late summer picnic—burgers, potato salad, watermelon, and homemade chocolate chip cookies. While I took everything into the house, Pam engaged Chase in conversation.

"Now, give me the scoop. Patrick never tells me anything. To be fair—he can't. But you can," she winked at Chase. "But first, tell me: when are you going to get married?"

Chase was always reluctant to talk about his personal life with me. But, when I returned, Pam must have gotten him to bear his soul because he looked embarrassed that I interrupted them. Pam easily moved into the next topic.

"Chase, do you think that a Catholic can win the election?"

"It's hard to tell. It's definitely an issue for Jack's campaign. Now, Pam, you tell me the scoop—do you want to see a Catholic in the White House?"

Pam blushed at getting caught in her own net. "I think Jackie would be a wonderful First Lady. I have mixed feelings—I certainly don't trust his father. And I know that the Kennedys don't do anything without consulting him."

"I think that's what the American people are worried about," I interrupted. "They don't want their President to be unduly influenced. I know there are people that don't trust Joe Kennedy either—but the vast majority of Americans haven't given that a thought. They worry more about the Pope and any influence he might have."

"There have been several editorials around the country examining that very same thing," Chase added. "Emotions are running pretty high. There are a lot of church-goers who are offended that Catholics consider it a sin to set foot in a place of worship for any other religion."

"I know. I was raised a Catholic girl. Even some of my Baptist friends, who know me well, think that Catholicism borders on Satanism. I remember going to dinner at a girlfriend's house when I was a senior in high school. Her mother asked me if I 'talked in tongues.' I didn't know what she meant at first. Then, she wanted me to recite something in Latin."

"Catholicism is still mysterious to many people—it involves incense and mysterious rituals—things that most Protestants are uncomfortable with. What do your sources say, Chase?"

"Reverend Norman Vincent Peale, who is influential with many Protestant pastors, has openly questioned who a Catholic president would be loyal to. He seriously questions the wisdom of choosing any man of Catholic faith for our nation's highest office."

"Well, maybe we should qualify that," I quipped, "to mean any *good* Catholic man. I imagine Jack has broken most of the tenets of the Catholic Church, and I can't imagine that he would honestly tell a priest what he's been up to in confession."

"Patrick!" Pam gave me a disapproving look. "Ignore him, Chase."

"Jack is supposed to go to Houston on September 12 to address 300 ministers at the Greater Houston Ministerial Association. I talked to Ted Sorenson, Jack's speechwriter, yesterday. He feels that Jack can win or lose the election right there."

The summer night descended around us. "Look at the fireflies," Pam said. "There must be hundreds and hundreds."

KENNEDY MUST BE KILLED 331

"The street lights are on. It's time for me to go," Chase said getting up out of his chair. "Thanks for your hospitality, Pam."

He extended his hand to me. "Good seeing you, buddy." We walked out to Chase's car. "Hey, don't you ever let her get away—she's a keeper."

Later that month, Pam and I read Chase's report in the *Washington Post*. The ministers asked Jack if he would accept the direction of his Church in public life. He replied, "If my Church attempted to influence me in a way which was improper or which affected adversely my responsibilities as a public servant, sworn to uphold the Constitution, then I would reply to them that this was an improper action on their part, that it was one to which I could not subscribe, that I was opposed to it, and that it would be an unfortunate breech—an interference with the American political system." Jack went on to say that if he found any conflict between his conscience and the responsibility of the Presidency, he would resign that office.

Knowing Jack as I did, I knew it was complete bullshit. Jack wouldn't listen to any Church official because he had absolutely no respect for either their advice or their judgment. Hell, he didn't even respect the senior members of his own party, let alone the Vatican. And as for that crap about resigning if his conscience called for it—well, that was never going to happen.

The Jack Kennedy I knew had no conscience.

EAST COAST POLITICAL pundits declared that the 1960 Presidential Election was in the bag on September 25, 1960. I thought it was extremely arrogant for the prognosticators to so authoritatively select the winner two months before Election Day in November. Jack Kennedy hadn't won the election that day.

But Dick Nixon sure lost to Kennedy.

Pam and I settled in with seventy million other Americans to view the first of four televised presidential debates that Sunday night on CBS.

"Tim, I made a big bowl of popcorn and some orange Kool-Aid. Come on into the living room with us and watch some television. It's history in the making!"

Pam, always the teacher, did her best to get Tim to join us. We had very few evenings together as a family, and Pam tried to make the most of our time together. Tim, however, was not interested in watching television quietly with his parents. He sat with us for a few minutes, ate some popcorn, and then he slipped off to his room to play with his toy soldiers. Pam and I were left to ourselves to watch a disaster unfold before our eyes.

Just before the debate began, Pam asked, "Don't you think Vice President Nixon has been successful so far in portraying Jack as inexperienced, young, and immature?" Her remark caught me by surprise because I had just assumed, in the end, she would support Jackie and Jack in the upcoming election.

"Yeah—Nixon definitely is a more seasoned politician. I think this debate will make that obvious—Nixon has eight years under his belt as Vice President. Look how Nixon handled Khrushchev. I don't think there is any comparison between the two as far as experience is concerned."

"What do you think will happen tonight?"

"Well, I think that because Jack is the challenger in the race, his strategy should be to come out on the attack. He'll probably make some grandiose promises and offer a far more aggressive view of the future than Dick will. I don't think it will work."

"Why not?"

"Nixon's too good a debater for Jack. He'll mop the floor with him. Just watch and see."

Sure enough, Jack began his remarks by stating, "I think it's time America started moving again." If we didn't move society ahead, he told the audience, we wouldn't be able to move the world ahead. I smirked at Pam to show how right I was in my assessment.

I was soon wiping the smirk off my face. As the debate began to unfold, not only did Jack appear to be the Vice President's equal, but to everyone's surprise, he even managed to look more commanding and presidential.

Jack shrewdly played to his audience of seventy million potential voters with his grand vision for America. I kept waiting for Dick to explain his own grand vision—but he didn't have one. It quickly became apparent Dick was actually trying to debate Jack. Jack not only didn't answer any of the questions he was asked, but he used the time instead to sell his ideas. And he sold them effectively.

What really hurt Dick the most was the eye of the television lens. The visual impression of the television cameras shattered any illusions that Jack wasn't the equal of the sitting vice president. Jack wore a dark suit with a light blue shirt that helped to soften the harsh contrast of black-and-white television under the bright white studio lights. The uncontrollable side effects of his Addison's disease had actually given his complexion the appearance of a healthy tan. Dick Nixon, on the other hand, looked haggard—he was suffering from an extremely painful infection in his knee. Prior to the debates, he had been bedridden for a few days, and he was taking pain medication. Upon arriving at the studio that afternoon, he banged his sore knee getting out of his car.

Chase later told me Nixon's aides had also not researched the studio lighting the way Jack's people had. Nixon had selected a light gray suit with a white shirt which heightened the pallor of his light skin. Dick also had a dark heavy beard, eyebrows, and hair, all of which added to the highlighted contrast of the black-and white TV broadcast.

"He looks tense and almost frightened," Pam observed as Nixon struggled to address the questions put to him. His expression alternated between glowering, haggard, and menacing. Sweat poured off his brow and jowls, his eyes conveyed discomfort and anger, and his shirt collar hung loosely around his neck.

"He looks more like a white-collar felon than the next President of the United States of America," I joked. But I was shocked by Dick's total collapse.

What the hell was going on? Where did his wimpy "me-too" debating style come from? Where was the decisive Richard Nixon I had known and admired since I saw him confront Alger Hiss so decisively? Where was the scrupulously honest Nixon of the "Checkers" television appearance in 1952? Where was the famously combative Vice President of those Moscow Kitchen Debates with Khrushchev? I was mystified.

When the debate was over, I expected Pam to be exuberant because Jack had clearly won.

"Patrick, Nixon is going to lose the election," Pam looked and sounded downcast.

"I thought you would be rooting for Jack. After all, if Jack wins, Jackie will be First Lady," I tried to sound upbeat.

"But I don't think Jack should win. There's a dark side to that whole family. Maybe they shouldn't be in the White House right now. Most people haven't seen what we've seen." Before I could question her further, she scooped up the popcorn bowl and rushed out of the room.

I figured Grant would be ecstatic that Kennedy had done so well in the debates. But he told me that both he and LBJ were surprised when they read the papers declaring Jack as the decisive winner. He and LBJ listened to the debate on their car radio, and both of them thought Nixon had won. In fact, Johnson was irritated that Jack hadn't faired better against Nixon and moaned over and over "the boy didn't win." His saw his political future sinking with the Kennedy ship.

Jack didn't fool me the way he fooled the public. After the debates, Jack was a celebrity—fawning fans vied for his touch and his autograph. The crowds at his campaign stops grew with exponential numbers and mounting enthusiasm. I knew the public never saw the real Jack Kennedy—he kept that part of himself hidden from view.

A few days later, Pam called Jackie to congratulate the two of them on Jack's successful debate.

"Guess what she told me."

"Jack's decided to concede the election to Nixon?"

"Noooo! Be serious—remember how good Jack looked? Do you want to know why he looked so healthy?"

"Okay, I'll bite. Gee, Pam, why did Jack look so healthy?"

"He had vitamin shots. Two days before the debate, Jack slipped away to see this 'doctor to the stars.' I think his name was Dr. Max Jacobson. Jackie said everyone from Eddie Fisher and Johnny Mathis to Zero Mostel and Alan Jay Lerner use vitamin regimens to help them feel and look better."

"Too bad Dick didn't know about this doctor," I sarcastically said.

"I know—Dick looked terrible."

I shook my head—sometimes my sarcasm just rolled off her—I loved that about my wife.

Knowing Jack and his reckless nature, I decided to investigate the mysterious Dr. Jacobson and his vitamin regimen. I called Johnny Roselli and found out Jacobson was known around Hollywood as "Dr. Feelgood." Johnny told me Jacobson injected his patients with a witch's brew of amphetamines, heavy on the Dexedrine. Johnny called him a "mad scientist"—he thought the good doctor had been testing far too many of his homemade concoctions on himself.

I used the Agency resources to find out more about these drugs. I knew that Jack had a host of health problems. I wanted to give him the benefit of the doubt that he was taking drugs for medical reasons. I was very troubled to find out how powerful the drugs were. According to the Agency expert I consulted, the drugs made a person feel powerful and created a pleasurable, but temporary sense of well-being. The downside was that amphetamines were highly addictive and could lead to periods of strong depression and could even trigger symptoms of paranoid schizophrenia.

God, didn't Jack possess any common sense?

MEANWHILE, OUR STRATEGY to free Cuba from Castro's iron grip was mired with problems. Our propaganda campaign failed—no armed uprising materialized. Castro had successfully eradicated any opposition when he took power. The Cuban people were now afraid to openly oppose Castro. David Atlee Phillips' radio broadcasts fell on deaf ears.

Mr. B's solution was to increase the size of Operation Pluto per our original directive—"to supply and train somewhere in central America a group of exiled Cubans who are preparing for a guerrilla invasion to overthrow Castro." The Agency secured a remote facility in Guatemala, a coffee plantation in the Sierra Madre Mountains near the Pacific coast which we called Camp Trax. This facility enabled us to train a few hundred men together rather than at piecemeal locations—I was ultimately responsible for logistics and training. By August 27, we were operational.

It was about this time that E. Howard Hunt resurrected the idea of killing Castro. Although part of our original three-part strategy, no one had actively pursued its implementation. Hunt sent Tracy Barnes a memo. Barnes deferred to Mr. B who decided that the Mafia was best suited in carrying out such an assignment—the syndicate wanted their Cuban investments restored. I contacted Johnny Roselli who assured me that the mob could take care of the assignment. By the end of September, Sam Giancana gave Roselli his approval to approach his old Havana boss, Santos Trafficante, Jr. about a Castro assassination. Once Trafficante became involved, the plan gained momentum. At that point, Vice President Richard Nixon was briefed on the planned assassination—he endorsed the plan.

At Camp Trax, our real training could not get underway until we received weapons. Sam Giancana provided us with untraceable guns to train 160 guerilla recruits. Additionally, we brought in twenty mercenaries from Mexico, Eastern Europe, China and the Philippines. Although Operation Pluto was a clandestine project designed to conceal any involvement of the United States government, total secrecy was impossible because of the number of operatives involved. Our fingerprints were all over the operation. Inevitably, Castro got wind of our plans and convinced a *New York Times'* reporter to investigate. Luckily, he contacted the State Department for confirmation, and they persuaded him not to publish the story.

We had to discontinue using the U.S. Air Force to deliver goods and personnel. Mr. B bought a faltering air transport company, Southern Air Transport, for a little over $300,000 to provide air cover for our invasion force. He enlisted our old friend, Colonel Stan Beerli of the grounded U-2 program, and put him in charge of Air America.

ON FRIDAY, OCTOBER 13, Nikita Khrushchev, having spent twenty-five consecutive days in the United States, left New York to return home. Having virtually camped out at the United Nations, he had alternately charmed and blustered—pounding his shoe in anger on the podium and declaring that he would bury us. He weighed in on the upcoming election by brusquely announcing that he was suspending his discussions with America until Americans decided upon a leader. Fidel Castro felt he needed to weigh in as well and derisively described the two presidential candidates as "beardless, ignorant kids."

KENNEDY'S "NEW FRONTIER" acceptance speech at the Democratic National Convention received accolades from everyone—there were few critics of his grand vision for the United States—except for those of us here at the Agency. His speech was a slap in the face to everyone in government who had worked so patriotically for the American people. It suggested that we were mediocre—it pissed off a lot of people.

Kennedy had said, "A New Frontier is here whether we seek it or not. Beyond the frontier are uncharted areas of science and space, unsolved problems of peace and war, unconquered problems of ignorance and prejudice, unanswered questions of poverty and surplus. It would be easier to shrink from the new frontier, to look to the safe mediocrity of the past, to be lulled by good intentions and high rhetoric....That is the choice our nation must make—a choice that lies between public interest and private comfort, between national greatness and national decline, between the fresh air of progress and the stale, dank atmosphere of 'normalcy,' between dedication or mediocrity. All mankind waits upon our decision. A whole world looks to see what we shall do. And we cannot fail that trust. And we can not fail to try...."

In a nutshell, Kennedy suggested that the military power of the United States was falling behind that of the Soviet Union.

"Why does he think that?" Tracy Barnes asked one day at our morning meeting. "Allen briefed him and explained that our U-2 surveillance proved the Soviets were the ones with the missile gap. They're the one's that should be scared, not the U.S."

Mr. B saw through the ruse. "Jack cleverly knows those facts are classified Top Secret. He also knows that while he might be able to talk about it, Vice President Nixon certainly cannot. As the sitting Vice President, as well as one of the integral members of President Eisenhower's team of security advisors, Nixon is bound by security restrictions that he cannot violate. Senator Kennedy, however, has no compunction about releasing classified information if it will help him win the election. So he did."

"That's certainly gutless," Cord Meyer said.

"That's also politics," Mr. B retorted.

"That's not all," Tracy added. "One of my friends over at State told me that Fidel has his own supporters at the State Department."

"There are supporters of Castro in the State Department?" I was shocked. This sounded like a "fifth column" to me. To think that there might be people in our own State Department whose support for Castro could undermine their own country appalled me.

"There's at least one—a fellow by the name of William Wieland."

"I know who he is," Cord said. "He's a troublemaker from way back."

"Well, I guess he's still up to no good," Tracy said under his breath.

Mr. B went on, "Wieland is a vocal Kennedy supporter. He knows that Kennedy's election would mean great things for him and his career, so he deliberately leaked classified State Department information to Jack. It seems he slyly introduced our anti-Fidel leaders to Jack at the Los Angeles Convention. Those guys were so impressed with Kennedy that they naively spilled their guts concerning the planned secret invasion of Cuba."

"So Kennedy's people then leaked the information to *The New York Times*?" Cord Meyer asked.

"Yes. We all remember when the front-page story broke on October 17—thank God Khrushchev had already left the country. The headline read: "KENNEDY ASKS AID FOR CUBAN REBELS TO DEFEAT CASTRO. URGES SUPPORT OF EXILES AND FIGHTERS FOR FREEDOM."

I was angry for hours after reading that headline. I couldn't believe that Jack would expose a national security operation designed to rid North America of a Communist dictator for a few points in the polls.

"The story puts Dick Nixon in a terrible position—he can't even respond to our official government line that the United States would not interfere in Cuban affairs," I said.

"Jack knows that Dick won't violate his security covenants, so Jack becomes free to declare that his 'patience with Castro was over; it was time to eradicate this 'cancer' from the American hemisphere to prevent further Soviet penetration.' It's a brilliant political move. It not only shows Jack to be a 'man of action', but also it appears that Dick is unwilling to commit to do anything about Cuba." Mr. B frowned each time he said "Jack."

Tracy asked, "What can Nixon do?"

"The only thing that Dick can do is to remind Jack that the Organization of American States has treaties and laws in place that we would be violating, breaking many of our long-time commitments in the process," Cord said.

"Dick did label Jack's idea '…the most shockingly reckless proposal ever made by a presidential candidate,'" Cord elaborated. He reminded Jack that we would also be risking the condemnation of the world community in the United Nations if we took such a tack. Dick flat out said, 'If the United States backed the Cuban freedom fighters, we'd be condemned in the United Nations.' He warned Jack that his position would be akin to '…an open invitation for Khrushchev to come into Latin America and engage us in … civil war or something else.'"

"We all know why Dick said the things he did. But unfortunately for Dick, his response is going to look weak in the eyes of the voters compared to Jack's seemingly creative and aggressive policy," Mr. B observed.

For the first time, I began to worry about what a Kennedy Presidency would mean for the Agency.

BY THE END of October, I had amassed thirty-two B-26 bombers, ten C-46 transport planes, and seven C-54 cargo planes. Now I needed to find enough qualified Cuban pilots to fly them all. I returned to D.C. to brief Tracy Barnes about Operation Pluto and to see if he had any ideas to handle our shortage of manpower.

Tracy politely listened to my report. "Patrick, you're doing a fine job. Everybody's noticed, and they are all impressed with what you have accomplished. Now I've thought about what you need and think I've got a solution that will work."

"What's that?"

"I'm going to call a friend of mine who's the commander of the Alabama Air National Guard. I'll see if they can help us out by loaning us some of their pilots."

"Whoa, Tracy, has the President changed his mind about that? The last I heard was that the President had issued express orders not to use any American forces."

"Hey, relax. I've got it covered. Give me a little time and I'll come up with something," he promised.

"As long as you're at it, we could use some ships to help move men and munitions into place. We've got too much gross tonnage to move it all by air. Besides, we could use ships and boats to help insert our guerilla forces into the Cuban countryside."

"What do you have in mind?" he asked.

"It would be terrific if we could get a couple of converted landing craft infantry ships. We could use them as mother ships. They could remain in international waters while our men go ashore in rubber rafts or speedboats."

He paused a few moments and thought about my request. "I know of a defunct company in the Florida Keys called Mineral Carriers. I'll see if they can give us a base to use, and I'll ask about the LCI's. I'm pretty sure they've got a few left over from World War II."

He started to dismiss me and then he added, "Oh, I almost forgot. We brought back one of your old buddies to help you out," he joked.

"Who's that?"

"It's old 'Rip' Robertson," he grinned.

"Not the Mad Coke Bottle Bomber of Guatemala!" I groaned. I heard he had been previously run out of the Agency during Operation Success in Guatemala after he accidentally bombed that innocent British freighter. How in the hell did he get back on board?" I was shocked that somehow he had been allowed to return to active status with us despite his previous record.

"I guess it's all in who you know," he laughed. I responded with a barrage of obscenities as I left his office.

On the diplomatic front, things were heating up. On October 14, Fidel nationalized the entire Cuban sugar industry. On October 19, President Eisenhower responded with an embargo on all trade to Cuba from the United States. While the administration worked publicly to castigate the Cuban government, the Agency worked secretly to overthrow the dictator.

MY WORST FEARS were realized on November 8, 1960. John Fitzgerald Kennedy was officially elected President of the United States of America by a scant margin of just 118,574 popular votes out of 68, 837,000 cast. In fact, if only 4,500 voters in Illinois and 28,000 voters in Texas had changed their minds, Richard Nixon would have been elected instead since the electoral votes of those two states would have swung into Nixon's column rather than Kennedy's. When Mayor Daley of Chicago reported that Illinois was in Kennedy's victory column even before the final tally came in, I was more than a little suspicious. I suspected that Sam Giancana might have had something to do with it.

The truly unthinkable had happened. We now had an immature, sickly, inexperienced playboy as the leader of our nation in a time of war. He was going to have to go head-to-head against the most powerful Communist leader in the world, Nikita Khrushchev of the Soviet Union. I looked back upon my two previous encounters with Khrushchev and knew immediately Jack Kennedy wasn't up to the task. The Jack Kennedy I knew was extraordinarily unprepared to be the commander in chief of the most powerful nation in the free world. He had certainly proved to be a gifted campaigner, but that didn't automatically make him a gifted leader.

The necessity to project an image of youthful health and vigor during the long campaign had also taken its toll on Jack's health. He was a mental and physical wreck when the election was over. At times, he was barely coherent in the month after the election. He was attended to by his personal physicians, who ministered to his needs with various injections of narcotics and amphetamines.

Jack was more promiscuous with his drugs than he was with women. He was being kept alive by daily injections of all manner of things. When Chase asked him in a news conference about the rumor that he had Addison's disease, known to be a fatal failure of the adrenal glands, Jack forcefully asserted, "I never had Addison's disease. In regard to my health, it was fully explained in a press statement in the middle of July, and my health is excellent." He had brazenly lied. Pam and I knew he had received the last rites of the Catholic Church on at least four occasions.

It had taken John Fitzgerald Kennedy just fourteen years to go from a freshman Congressman from Boston into holding the highest elected office in the land. His inner circle of advisors were mostly Ivy League graduates in their thirties and forties, and they would replace a generation of experienced leaders who were in their sixties and seventies, but who had helped to win World War II and had staved off World War III ever since 1945.

One of the dirty little secrets of the election was the large number of Jack's friends who voted for Dick Nixon instead of Jack. One of Jack's own Hyannis Port neighbors had become an acquaintance of mine when we visited the Kennedy compound. "Jack's a wonderful human being," he told me. "Don't get me wrong, I love the guy. But I just thought Nixon would make a better president."

The Auchincloss family, as well as the Bouvier family, also knew Jack very well—they all voted for Richard Nixon.

WASHINGTON D.C. was a city always on the brink of change. Elected officials could never get too comfortable in their positions—they were at the whim of the voters. The unelected officials were just as vulnerable—their jobs were at the mercy of the President. Now the city prepared to make the transition from a Republican White House to a Democratic White House.

The day after the election, Jack began the process by asking Allen Dulles and J. Edgar Hoover to remain on the job. I was pleased when I heard that Jack had asked Dulles to stay on at the Agency. Allen was an important figure in the fight against Communism

If I had been a betting man like Grant, I would have bet that Hoover would have been the first to be replaced by the new administration. It was even going around Washington that Jack said, "You don't fire God!" when a reporter asked him why he was keeping Hoover on as the Director of the FBI. While I was encouraged by Jack's decision to retain Hoover, I was also uneasy. Mr. Hoover had strong opinions about morality. I remembered what Mr. Hoover had said about an immoral man at the poker game at his home in 1950. It made an impression on me so much so that I immediately wrote down what he said when I got home. Young and impressible, I had the idea that I would write down everything that I thought might give me some moral guidance—somewhat like Benjamin Franklin. I had to laugh—I was really full of myself back then.

Hoover told us that night: *"Any man who lacks sexual discipline displays* to all a basic weakness in character. Immoral acts lead to criminal acts. It is proven and it is inevitable...they think nothing of violating the covenants of their marriages, or the sanctity of their personal commitments. These are men who can never be trusted!" I also remembered him saying, *"A man's immoral values will lead him down the road to ruin faster than any character flaw that he might have...a good lawman has to hate immorality."*

I wondered how Mr. Hoover would react while serving and taking orders from Jack Kennedy. Hoover had to know of Jack's sexual peccadilloes. He had repeated many times over *"A leader of men must especially be a moral man."* He even made the comment that he thought it was especially important to have a moral man as President in the age of the atomic bomb. Mr. Hoover had to be apoplectic at the idea of serving under Jack.

President Eisenhower, who had felt the sting of Jack's campaign attacks, had less than two months to prepare Jack to take over the country. Eisenhower still smarted over Nixon's loss of the election. The election results were a strong repudiation of his eight years in the White House even though the country had enjoyed prosperity and peace during his two terms in office. Tracy Barnes, who was upset that Nixon hadn't won the election, said that the press was responsible for Kennedy's win—they had made Kennedy seem messianic with his brilliant intelligence and exciting view of the future. Eisenhower even commented that the nation had sold itself "on the naïve belief that we have a new genius in our midst who is incapable of making any mistakes and therefore deserving of no criticism whatsoever!"

On December 7, I accompanied Allen and Richard to the White House to discuss Operation Pluto as well as the Agency's role in the Kennedy White House. Allen asked the President Eisenhower how his meeting with Kennedy had gone. The President told us that they talked for over an hour on the foreign affairs and national security. I thought it sounded like both leaders thinly veiled their contempt for the other.

"Most of President-elect Kennedy's questions centered around the decision-making process, and it quickly became apparent to me that young Mr. Kennedy thought the process was way too long and cumbersome, with too much being debated and decided outside of the President's reach. He seems to want to manage it all himself."

"That doesn't sound promising," Allen observed.

"Oh, I think it gets worse. I tried to subtly educate young Mr. Kennedy about the naiveté of that approach. After all, I've sort of had some experience in that regard."

Mr. B, aware of Eisenhower's tendency to be overly modest, pointed out, "Yes, let's see what kind of experience you've had. You once served as the former Supreme Allied Commander of Europe. You helped organize and presided over the greatest invasion the world had ever seen at Normandy. And you've served eight successful years as the President of the United States of America…"

Allen interjected, "Let's add that he skillfully guided the U.S. through a very difficult stretch of the Cold War with the Soviet Union."

The President seemed to be embarrassed by praise. He slowly shook his head and continued, "I tried to patiently explain to young Mr. Kennedy how and why I had built up the best intelligence apparatus the free world had ever conceived—which I feel methodically collected, analyzed, and fed this information in a very systematic fashion up the chain of command to the commander in chief. I explained that this system allowed me to filter my decisions back down the same military chain of command with alacrity. It also allowed me to implement and coordinate my decisions in a very precise fashion."

President Eisenhower was a leader who valued the chain of command and saw it not as an obstacle but as an important part of leadership.

"I specifically told him, 'No easy matters will ever come to you as President. If they are easy, they will be settled at a lower decision-making level.' But he said such an idea had no appeal whatsoever to him. Young Mr. Kennedy told me he wanted to be directly involved in every decision and to see it all happen. He said he had no use for my old-fashioned process. He wants to be in the center of all the action, making big decisions as well as small ones. He said he didn't want to sit atop an organizational chart—he planned to be at the center with all of the spokes radiating outward from him in all directions. That's going to be disastrous."

"Will he really do that?" Allen asked.

"He'll scrap my carefully designed and constructed national security organization as quickly as he can," the President replied.

President Eisenhower was convinced that Jack Kennedy not only was exceedingly naïve about the actual duties of the President, but he was also ill informed about how to be President. Jack said he believed the Presidency was simply about getting the right people in the right jobs.

It was evident that Jack dismissed much of Eisenhower's instructions. Within days of Jack's meeting with Eisenhower, everyone on Capitol Hill was gossiping about Jack's joke in which he comically mimicked Eisenhower and illustrated that he was not intimidated by the President. "The President greeted me like so: 'Good morning, Mister Ke-e-nnedy.' I bowed, removed my hat in a grandly exaggerated gesture in order to show the same respect to him that he had just shown to me and I said: 'Good morning, Mister Eeeeee-senhower!'"

Then he would grin and wait for the laughter to indicate how clever he was— Jack's disrespect for Eisenhower made me sick.

OPERATION PLUTO CONTINUED to be plagued with problems— which meant that I was plagued with problems. Our revolution plans which had called for a guerrilla infiltration force of 800 men had been modified to conventional amphibious landing force of two to three thousand men—we only had 420 men training in Guatemala. The Agency set up additional training sites in Lake Pontchartrain, Louisiana. Since we were still short of men, E. Howard Hunt, in an effort to recruit more Cubans in Miami, placed an ad in the Miami Herald newspaper—complete with pictures of the Trax training camp in Guatemala. Fidel got wind of our plans and published the pictures in the Havana papers. And to make matters worse, the exile community in Cuba had not been able to unify their leadership—so we had been unable to select a suitable replacement for Fidel.

The Pentagon was also a problem—they had been dragging their feet in releasing Special Forces personnel to train the exiles, and they decided that they no longer could support the Agency's plans for invasion. They directly lobbied the President for control in planning of the invasion—but the Agency prevailed. Finally, an approximate date for the invasion was set for March 1961. Though Ike approved the date, he unhappily remarked that he didn't want to be "in the position of turning over the government in the midst of a developing emergency."

DURING THE TIME between the election and the inauguration, Pam stayed busy helping Jackie prepare to move to the White House. I pitched in whenever I could to help out Pam. While packing dishes one Saturday afternoon in the Kennedy kitchen, I was interrupted when Jack waltzed in. We talked—or he talked and I listened for ten minutes or so—he never offered to help pack a single dish.

"Patrick, I'm going to entice only the best and the brightest young men in America to come to Washington and join my administration." Jack always talked down to me—he sounded elitist in how he phrased "only the best and the brightest."

"Do you know Robert McNamara?" he asked.

"The president of Ford Motor Company?" I shook my head, "No, I've never met him."

"I read about him in a *Time* magazine article in December," he said, "so

I called him up. He came to Washington six days later. I liked him. He had read my book, *Profiles in Courage*. He even asked me if I wrote it myself," Kennedy laughed.

We both knew his friend Teddy Sorenson wrote the book for Jack.

"I said, of course I did. Who else could have written it?"

Finding it difficult to talk one on one with Jack, I busied myself in properly wrapping the dishes in newspaper.

"I offered McNamara his choice of Cabinet seats—either Treasury or Defense."

"You did?" I was taken aback. What did the president of Ford Motor Company know about the Treasury Department—or the Defense Department for that matter?"

"The guy's a registered Republican, and he tried to protest that he didn't know anything about government. Isn't that ridiculous?"

I said it sounded that way to me.

"I said that's OK. I don't know how to be President, either."

That I knew.

Jack finished his story, "I grinned at him. Great, we can learn our jobs together!"

Jack was even more cavalier with many of his other appointments. Paul Nitze was approached to be either the Deputy Secretary of Defense or the National Security Advisor. Dean Rusk and I were in Jack's office when Paul called Jack back one afternoon. "Listen to this," Jack smirked as he put Paul on the telephone amplifier for us to listen in. They chatted for a few moments; then, Jack offered him the choice of the two positions. Nitze hesitated for a moment, "How long do I have to make up my mind?"

Jack quickly replied, "Thirty seconds."

"I choose Deputy Secretary of Defense," he firmly stated.

Jack alternately laughed and puffed his cigar, "See how easy this is?"

As it turned out, Jack had promised Robert McNamara that as the new Secretary of Defense he could personally approve everyone who worked under him. Instead, McNamara offered Nitze the position of Assistant Secretary of Defense. Pissed off, Nitze called Jack's private number in Palm Beach which was answered by a woman who didn't identify herself but said she would get Jack. When she came back a minute later, she abruptly informed him "Mr. Kennedy doesn't wish to speak with you" and hung up.

That was Jack's normal way of dealing with problems.

OLD JOE'S DREAM to see his son in the White House had finally been realized. But his dream was not complete—he wanted to see Bobby appointed as Attorney General and Teddy elected to the Senate. Pam and I had been at a Kennedy dinner party one night about a year before the presidential elections when Eunice Kennedy joked: "We'll make Bobby Attorney General so he can throw all the people Dad doesn't like in jail. Of course, they'll have to build a lot of new jails."

Now that Jack had won the election, Joe pushed Bobby's appointment. But Jack knew that it would be a difficult proposition to sell outside the Kennedy compound. In fact, Jack sent Clark Clifford to Hyannis Port to convince Joe that Bobby might not be the right choice for the post. Clark was known to have "very serious reservations" about Bobby's qualifications for supervising the thirty thousand employees of the Justice Department. Old Joe wouldn't budge: Bobby had to get the job. Bobby could protect Jack's political back by squashing any investigations into the Kennedy family's past business and campaign practices.

The New York Times blasted Jack's choice. "If Robert Kennedy was one of the outstanding lawyers of the country, a pre-eminent legal philosopher, a noted prosecutor or legal officer at federal or state level, the situation would have been different. But his experience is surely insufficient to warrant his present appointment." *The Wall Street Journal* concurred by saying that thirty-four-year-old Bobby would be "an unqualified disaster."

I especially liked what LBJ told Bobby Baker. Describing how upset Senator Richard Russell was about Bobby Kennedy's appointment, LBJ cackled that Russell was "absolutely shittin' a squealin' worm! He thinks it's a disgrace for a kid who's never practiced law to be appointed. I agree with him."

JACK EVEN MANAGED to show his disdain for the controversy and scandal raised by Mr. and Mrs. Kater over his infidelities. He found a place for his girlfriend, Pamela Turnure, in his new administration.

Jack appointed her as the new press secretary for his wife.

"John Fitzgerald Kennedy was considered to be a lightweight in D.C.—the sheltered son of a wealthy right-wing bigot."

— Gore Vidal

September 6, 1978
9:05 p.m.

Grant's stomach jumped when the phone rang.

"We got him!"

"Hold on a second." Grant put his hand over the receiver and spoke to the blonde who was lying nude on the bed. "Sugar, why don't you go fix us a bubble bath. I'll be there shortly."

Sugar slid her long legs off the bed, looked at him, and licked her lips.

Grant's adrenalin spiked, "Where?"

"He's in New Orleans."

Grant's elation turned to disappointment, "I thought you just said you had him?"

"We do. We know where he's been and where he's gone. Some faggot ticket puncher remembered him from his picture. Said he remembered how 'hunky' he looked."

"Can he be wrong?"

"Not likely. We threatened to come back and 'fix' him if he was lying to us. He started crying. He's tellin' the truth."

"What do we do now?"

"I've got to get to New Orleans. Not sure that I can fly out tonight. I haven't had a chance to check flights."

"Leave it to me. I'll find a plane that will get you there tonight. Let me make some calls."

"I'll hang out here and wait."

"Call me back in fifteen minutes."

1961

SAM GIANCANA AGAIN invited me to meet with him. This time I was summoned not to Las Vegas but to Chicago, Sam's hometown.

Chicago in early January was a cold, gray, and blustery place to be. The city was covered in about three inches of new snow when I arrived. Sam's brother, Chuck, met me at the airport. "Sam's got someone he wants you to meet. This guy could be useful to you in the future." Chuck's eyes betrayed his deep reservation as he spoke.

As we pulled up to a nondescript warehouse, its big garage door swung open to allow our Cadillac to pull inside. Two enormous thugs met our car as we rolled to a stop. Their girth seemed to strain the very seams of the cheap suits that they wore. They nodded knowingly to Chuck, looked me over deliberately and then rudely slapped my arms up into the air before starting to frisk me.

"Nuccio!" someone barked sternly. I turned and saw it was Sam Giancana. "Patrick is my guest. There's no need for that." It was evident Nuccio didn't agree by the withering stare he gave me as he moved out of my way.

Mr. Giancana shook my hand and quickly got down to business. "Patrick, I have to be able to trust the people I work with. My life and my livelihood depend upon it. The people I work with have to understand what happens if I ever lose my trust in them."

He glared at me—his eyes penetrated me with their cold cruelty. Unexpectedly intimidated, I nodded, "Yes, sir. I understand, sir."

"Fine," he said curtly. "Follow me."

We passed through another door into a brightly lit room that contained a small crowd of men. A fetid odor permeated the air. Some plain wooden chairs had been arranged around the room, and in one of the chairs sat an immense, profusely sweating man. His face was flushed; it appeared he had been crying because his eyes were bright red and running. His shirt and his suit were soaked in sweat, and it looked like he had just pissed his pants.

Standing nearby was a slender, sullen young man in his early twenties. Unlike all the other men in the room, he had stripped off his suit coat and shirt and stood before us in his white undershirt and suit pants. The powerful muscles in his arms bulged in anticipation of impending action. His shoes were immaculately polished, and his dark hair was carefully combed. He projected an aura of eminent danger.

Mr. Giancana led me into the middle of the room and addressed the men around him. "Gentlemen, this is Patrick McCarthy. Patrick comes to us courtesy of our friends in Washington." Mr. Giancana then walked right up to me and stood inches away from my face, studying my reaction. He was so close I could smell his toothpaste and his expensive cologne.

"Don't ever fuck me," he growled firmly and quietly. "Don't ever think you can get away with fucking me! I won't stand for it. Because if you ever fuck me, or betray me, not only will you live to regret it—your entire fucking family will live to regret it as well. I have taken you deep into my confidence because I've been told I can trust you. Don't ever give me a reason to believe I can't trust you. Do you understand?"

Hell yes, I understood! But I was too scared to croak a response, so I just nodded.

Giancana stared intently a while longer, and then he turned toward the obese sweating giant seated on the chair. "Patrick, this man is Mr. William Jackson. He likes to be called Action Jackson, don't you, William?"

The man was so visibly frightened his eyes bugged out of his head as he vigorously nodded his answer without a sound.

Then Giancana suddenly exploded in a white-hot rage of fury, "Mr. William 'Action' Jackson is here this evening because he forgot my simple rule—*HE FUCKED WITH ME!*"

Giancana's eyes steamed with hatred. He pointed at Jackson, "This fat fuck betrayed me! He talked to the Feds about me and my organization, and he thought he'd get away with it. But he got caught. And do you know why?" He screamed at the top of his lungs in Jackson's face, *"DO YOU KNOW HOW I FOUND OUT ABOUT YOUR FUCKIN' BETRAYAL, YOU GODDAMNED JUDAS? DO YOU KNOW HOW I KNOW? BECAUSE I HAVE FRIENDS IN WASHINGTON WHO GAVE ME THE FUCKING TRANSCRIPTS OF WHAT YOU TOLD THEM, YOU FUCKIN' COCKSUCKER!"* When he finished his tirade, he contemptuously spat right in Jackson's face.

I whistled silently under my breath. How in the hell did Sam Giancana ever get his hands on FBI wiretap transcripts? That's stuff that only the Attorney General, the Director of the FBI, and some very senior government people would have access to. Mr. Giancana was right—he was extremely well connected to *somebody* in D.C. Was he showing me the power of the Patriots?

Giancana stood over Jackson, angrily glaring and hyperventilating. He impatiently motioned to the sullen young man, who casually sauntered over to his side. Giancana motioned me over to join him as well. "Patrick, I want you to meet Derek Ruger. Derek, this is Patrick McCarthy of the CIA."

His handshake was a rock-hard vise grip. I tried not to flinch as I squeezed back just as hard. A sardonic smile slowly came over his face. He knew that I knew.

"Are we ready to begin?"

As soon as Mr. Giancana asked that question, Jackson began groveling, apologizing, and begging for a second chance. I was so fixated on the amount of emotional pleading that I didn't notice Ruger stepping in front of me brandishing the baseball bat.

I could hear a swoosh of air as he swung the bat, and the loud whack reverberated throughout the room as the bat smashed into Jackson's side and broke his ribs. The man, collapsing to the ground, howled in pain as Ruger backed away for a moment. He lifted the bat to swing once more; Jackson put his arm up to ward off the blow. With his next swing, Ruger shattered Jackson's arm; Jackson screamed even louder than before.

The sheer brutality of Ruger's attack caught me completely off guard. I had to stifle the feeling of revulsion welling up from inside me. I scanned the room and focused on a discarded paint can lying on some crumpled newspapers. The lid was rusted. The can was dented.

"Ya know what, Derek? I think this big side of beef needs some more tenderizing." Giancana cackled, "Why don't you tenderize him some more?"

Jackson looked up at Derek and pleaded, "Please, Ruger, don't do it. I'm begging you, please…"

WHAP! Ruger hit him in the ribs again.

"Goddamn it, Ruger, you fuckin' faggot fairy! When I get out of this, I'm gonna kill you, and then I'm gonna rape your momma before I kill her, too! You hear me, you fuckin' cocksucker?"

Ruger stood over him as if he were considering Jackson's request. He let the baseball bat slump down to his side. "What did you just say?" he asked quizzically.

Jackson screamed, "I said, when I get out of this, I'm gonna kill you and rape your momma before I kill her too, you fuckin' cocksucker!"

He glared at Ruger and then yelled at the top of his lungs, "What's the matter, you fuckin' faggot? You hard of hearing?"

Ruger's eyes noticeably darkened. Then in a voice tinged with feigned regret, he whispered, "I wish you hadn't said that."

Ruger's words were followed by a physical fury so intense, it was frightening. Jackson's teeth exploded all about the room as Ruger smashed him in the mouth with the bat as hard as he could hit him. I heard someone behind me snicker, "Well, I guess he ain't gonna be talking about his momma no more." A bunch of guys lining the wall behind me started laughing hysterically.

Giancana nodded at Jackson and ordered, "Don't kill him yet. I want that fat fuck to suffer as much as possible. Don't you dare let him off too soon."

"Yes sir," Ruger replied.

He walked over to the wall where one end of a chain from an overhead block-and-tackle was secured. A large six-inch meat hook was attached to the end. He grabbed the meat hook and walked back over to Jackson. Before anyone could grasp what they were seeing, he savagely swung the meat hook down into the side of Jackson's belly. The tangs of the meat hook disappeared into his soft side all the way up to the curve of the hook. Jackson's eyes instantly rolled back into his head. He let forth a blood-curdling scream. The agony must have been horrific. I silently made the sign of the cross, imagining myself touching my forehead, chest, and shoulders.

Ruger arrogantly sauntered back to the other end of the chain and then tugged so hard on the chain his feet momentarily left the ground. He hoisted Jackson off the floor as if he were a slab of beef. The three hundred-pound man dangled and twirled helplessly in the air as Ruger methodically secured the chain to the wall.

Even Sam Giancana appeared momentarily stunned by the absolute barbarism of Ruger's actions. I found myself holding my breath in the face of such monstrous evil. I intently studied the rafters above Jackson's head.

What happened next was three days of the most depraved violence that could ever be perpetrated by one man against another. For three days, Action Jackson dangled helplessly from that meat hook as Ruger ruthlessly worked him over. For three days, Jackson alternated between screaming in pain and total unconsciousness as Ruger flayed and filleted his skin. I was forced to watch Ruger use ice picks, razors, knives, wrenches, and even a blowtorch to inflict as much pain upon hapless Jackson as he possibly could. At one point, he even rammed an electric cattle prod up the poor man's rectum while cackling maniacally.

Derek Ruger metamorphosed into a monster more hideous than

any horror writer could imagine. He both frightened and sickened me tremendously. For three days, Ruger danced around that dying man as if he were a disciple of Satan himself. Eventually, even Giancana and his men appeared drained by the ferocity of Ruger's malevolence. A few of Sam's goons actually puked their guts out from the sheer horror of Ruger's unrelenting brutality.

I think everyone in the room was secretly thankful when Jackson's heart mercifully gave out and put him out of his misery. Derek Ruger scared the living shit out of me. I couldn't imagine the depths of Hell could possibly be any worse than that room in that abandoned meatpacking plant. I spent three days in a state of shocked physical and mental exhaustion. The screams—the sounds—the smells so horrifying in the light of day would rear up as gruesome phantasms in my unguarded sleep. I had to put this scene in a box in the back of my mind and keep the lid closed. I promised myself then and there to never, ever cross Sam Giancana, especially when Ruger looked directly at me as he wiped his brow with a clean white handkerchief, "Don't ever fuck with Sam." The message was explicit: *Mess with Sam and you'll have to deal with me.*

Derek Ruger was simply the most frightening human being I had ever encountered. I vowed that I never wanted to give him a reason to come after me.

ON FRIDAY, JANUARY 20, 1961, John Fitzgerald Kennedy was inaugurated as the youngest President of our United States of America. I went to the inauguration praying God would help us survive the next four years. America was at the most perilous Cold War point imaginable with the Soviet Union, and I knew Jack Kennedy was not up to the task of leading us effectively. I hoped for the best, but I prepared for the worst.

Maybe it was an omen of things to come that we awoke that morning to find our nation's capital paralyzed by a storm that dumped more than seven inches of snow on a city that had no snow removal equipment. The National Guard was activated to clear the D.C. streets of the hundreds of abandoned automobiles which had been stuck in icy ruts during rush hour the night before. Army combat engineers used flame-throwers to melt the ice and to clear the snowdrifts that had piled up on the steps of the Capitol Building.

Pam, Tim, and I struggled through the mounds of snow, unshoveled sidewalks, and almost impassable roads to arrive in plenty of time for the inauguration ceremony. We eventually found our assigned seats in front of the podium. Pam was seated where she could easily see Jackie who at the young age of thirty-one would become the First Lady of the United States of America in a matter of minutes.

As I made my way to my seat, I stopped to shake hands with various people who congratulated me on my new title, senior CIA liaison to the White House. Allen Dulles felt that my long association with Jack and Jackie Kennedy would make it easier for the Agency to look over Jack's shoulder and advise him on matters of national security. Minutes before the ceremonies were to commence, I bumped into Grant, who also had a new position in the administration as one of Vice President Lyndon Johnson's closest and most trusted advisors.

"Patrick, can you believe it? That's my son's godfather up there on the podium about to be sworn in as the next Vice President of the United States." Grant, who had named his son Lyndon in honor of his mentor, beamed with pride.

The morning was crisp and cold. The bright sun cast a slight shadow on Grant's face beneath his black fedora. "Did you see the military invasion of D.C. this morning?"

I wasn't sure I had heard him correctly. Grant had been making smart-ass comments for as long as I had known him.

"What did you just say?" Then, I added, "What do you mean by that?"

"Didn't you see all of the tanks, armored personnel carriers towing howitzer cannons, and heavy transport trucks filled with troops—how about the Pershing missile launchers that were brought in?"

Now that Grant mentioned it, I had to agree that it was an impressive display of military might. It reminded me of my first visit to Moscow.

"Lemnitzer is a crafty old general—he's conducting a war-game right here, and Kennedy doesn't even know it. He probably thinks that all the military hoopla is strictly for his Inaugural Parade."

I knew that General Lyman L. Lemnitzer was the chairman of the Joint Chiefs of Staff. But I didn't know why Grant would make such a preposterous claim. I asked him point-blank, "What's going on, Grant? What have you heard?"

He looked around to be sure no one was eavesdropping on our strange conversation. "Patrick, you should know the real soldiers in this country are extremely upset over the change of leadership."

He glanced around once more and lowered his voice, "Let me ask you a question: Do you have any idea how much the senior military leadership hates our new President? Mind you—I'm not talking about disliking him—I'm talking about strong visceral hatred," he whispered. "Word is that many high-ranking, senior military officers suspect that this new administration has been subverted by our enemies. And I'll tell you something else—they might do something about it."

I certainly didn't trust Jack Kennedy to be a good or a strong leader because he had never shown any inclination to be a good or strong leader in anything he had ever done. But Grant's revelation was astounding—I was staggered by his comments.

"Where did you hear this?" I hissed. "It sounds traitorous to me!"

He fixed me with a penetrating gaze. "It's not that outrageous. Do you have any idea what's been going on at various U.S. military bases around the world these past six months or so?"

I did not.

"On United States military bases all around the world, our senior military officers have been busy spreading the word that 'card-carrying Communists' are now in places of power throughout our entire federal government. We are at war with the Communists, yet our military leaders are not being consulted. Ever since Eisenhower began to prepare for this transition, the military chain of command has been edgy. They should be planning the upcoming Cuban invasion, not a bunch of civilian amateurs like the CIA."

Of course, the "civilian amateurs" he was referring to happened to include me.

"Don't you think General Lemnitzer must have been laughing out loud this morning when looked down on the streets of Washington lined with his own men? This whole Inauguration is strictly a military operation from start to finish. Our new President will be guarded by a military cordon of two dozen men and will be escorted to the White House by a phalanx of military vehicles. Think how easy it would be for this to be considered a dry-run for a future military *coup d-etat*?"

I finally sputtered my protest, "Jesus Christ, Grant. You're crazy. You're talking treason. Do you know that? Do you honestly believe our military thinks that way?"

"Pull your head out of your ass, Patrick. Quit acting like a goddamned ostrich."

I started to move forward, but Grant grabbed my forearm.

"Look around you at the past eight years of life in this country. Don't you think that the presence of a beloved general, a five-star general, like Eisenhower in the White House had a calming effect on the people of this country? After all, he led us to victory in World War II. He organized the D-Day invasion, the greatest successful military invasion the world has ever seen. He saved America from our enemies. For the past eight years, ordinary Americans went to sleep at night knowing that discipline reigned throughout their government. Everything was in order throughout the land—flags were saluted, shoes were spit-shined, and laws were obeyed."

Grant bent his head in a confidential manner, "Marital vows were considered sacred." He raised his head and looked toward the podium, "But now, our most experienced leader has retired to his farm at Gettysburg. He's been replaced by a pathetically mediocre Navy patrol boat skipper who narrowly avoided a court-marshal over the sinking of his own boat. It took both the grace of God and the intervention of his politically powerful father to prevent our new President from being drummed out of military service or even thrown in jail. Do you have any idea of how much our military hates the idea of Jack Kennedy assuming this new command?"

"No," I said grimly, "I don't."

"Then I'll tell you. Earlier this morning I ran into Admiral Arleigh A. Burke, the Chief of Naval Operations. He was quite scathing in his appraisal of his inexperienced commander in chief. He not only admitted that he didn't trust our new boy-president, he said he didn't trust any of Kennedy's people. He told me that 'nearly all of these people are ardent, enthusiastic people without any experience whatever in administering anything, including the President. He's always been in Congress. He's never had any job that required any administration. They don't understand ordinary administrative procedures, the necessity for having lines of communication and channels of command.' Now you tell me, does that sound like a ringing endorsement of good things to come?"

"No, it doesn't. But why are you telling me all of this?"

"Three reasons, actually. Number one: I know I can trust you to hear me out. Number two: I've worked hard to get Lyndon Johnson placed where he is now, and I would hate to see his future shot at the presidency possibly usurped by some head-strong, right-wing generals—who, remember, also took an oath to defend the Constitution of the United States."

"What's number three?"

He smiled waving to Pam and Tim who were working their way through the crowd toward us. "Number three? You are a Patriot. I want you to know you are not alone with some of your deepest thoughts, beliefs, doubts and fears."

And with that, he walked over to say hello to Pam and my son. He kissed Pam on the cheek, "You are looking beautiful as usual darlin'—save me a dance tonight, promise?"

Grant turned to me once more, "Talk to you later, buddy. Remember what I said."

INAUGURAL DAY WAS filled with the formal pomp and ceremony associated with the transition of power while the evening was filled with gala celebration. All of Washington had vied for invitations to the five Inaugural Balls set up around town. Pam and I received invitations to the official Inaugural Ball at the Washington Armory. The Armory ball, the most prestigious of the five, had a guest list of one thousand representing the cream of D.C.'s social and political elite. Even though we had tickets to the Armory Ball, I secured tickets to the celebration at the Statler Hilton Hotel where Frank Sinatra and the rest of the Rat Pack were waiting to greet their friend, President "Chicky Baby." While the President and the First Lady scheduled appearances at each of parties, I suspected this venue was more to Jack's liking.

Pam, dressed in a mint green gown, glowed. She wore the pearls that I had given her when Tim was born and the matching earrings that I gave her for our tenth anniversary. I loved her long slender neck—her blond hair was up in a simple twist, not in the bouffant style of most of the women present. To me, she was more beautiful than any of the actresses there.

Pam whispered excitedly, "Is that Angie Dickinson?"

I had seen Angie on the *Ocean's Eleven* movie set back in Vegas and at Frank Sinatra's suite at the Sands. I had noticed her in the reserved seats at the Inauguration with a close friend of Jack Kennedy's.

"I think I'm going to faint—Patrick, there's Frank Sinatra."

Pam was in awe of the celebrities at the party. Throughout the evening, she exclaimed that she couldn't believe she was actually rubbing elbows with such stars. Finally, Pam conceded that she was exhausted.

"One more dance," I said. "I want one more, slow dance with my beautiful wife."

I held Pam tight absorbing the moment—I smelled her hair and the Prell Shampoo that she used. I was incredibly fortunate. In the last moments of our dance, I caught sight of Angie Dickinson. She slipped through a service door, which I thought was odd, until I saw Jack go through the same door seconds later. Jackie, of course, was nowhere to be seen. I was astounded he could be so brazen and reckless.

Of course, I didn't breathe a word to Pam.

BOTH PAM AND I were beat the following day. Tim was spending the weekend with Pam's parents, so we planned on passing our day napping and relaxing. Pam was comfortably lying in my arms when the phone rang.

"Let it ring, Patrick," Pam pleaded.

"I can't do that, hon. I'll only be a minute—I promise."

It was my old friend, Connie, who was still serving as one of Dick Nixon's aides.

"Hey, I know it's Saturday, and I apologize for bothering you, but can you come meet me for a few minutes?" she asked. "There's something I've got to show you. I don't think you're going to like what you're going to see."

A couple of hours later, I was in the basement of the Securities and Exchange Annex on D Street, staring at the biggest mess I had ever seen in my life. The entire room was filled wall to wall in a pile of papers almost knee-deep, and standing right in the middle of it all was Dick Nixon, the former Vice President of the United States. Connie met me at the door.

"Connie, what's going on? What's all of this?" I innocently asked.

"I couldn't tell you on the phone," Connie said. "You wouldn't have believed me. This is something I had to have you see with your own eyes."

"Okay, I see it. It's a helluva mess. Now tell me: what am I looking at?"

"Patrick, you are looking at all of the important papers and personal effects belonging to Richard Nixon, the former Vice President of the United States of America." She paused to let me take it in, "Can you believe this? Can you believe that he could be treated like this?"

I looked at the unholy mess and shook my head. "So why is it just dumped in here like this?"

"This is a gift from those goddamned Kennedy brothers, those assholes! Do you believe this? This is an absolute insult to Dick. He's crushed at what they've done." Connie was in tears over the humiliation.

"Why did they dump it in here like this? It doesn't make any sense to me."

Connie stared at me with her hands on her hips in exasperation. "It's traditional that as the Inauguration is taking place at the Capitol Building, the ex-president's effects are moved out of the White House and the new president's effects are moved in. The same holds true for the vice president. It's the way it's always been handled."

Connie looked at the mess and suppressed a sob, "Except this time. It's not only petty and juvenile, it's demeaning to Dick—and it's demeaning to his staff."

"It's a mess. Are you going to tell anyone?"

"God—no! I don't want to cause a scene. We'll clean it up—I just don't know where to start. My staff and I have spent the past seven weeks carefully packing the Vice President's papers and file cabinets for the move. Everything was carefully labeled and sealed. The government assigned us this basement space for the transition."

Connie waded through the papers, "Then, the Kennedys ordered the movers to bring our stuff over here, open all of Dick's boxes and files, and then just dump them out of their boxes into the center of the room. It was a mean and spiteful."

"It was a shitty thing to do," I said.

"I'm mad as hell about it, and I had to tell somebody! I know there isn't anything you can do about it, but I wanted you to know what your new boss was really like."

I already knew what Jack and Bobby were like. I agreed with Connie—it was demeaning and spiteful. It was an example of the petty little tricks designed to let other people know where they stood with the Kennedys.

"Well, I've got a Kennedy story for you. Yesterday, at the Inaugural Ball, Pam and I went through the receiving line to congratulate Jack and Jackie. While Jackie was hugging and chatting with Pam, I kidded Jack, 'Gee, I don't know what to call you anymore.' He looked me in the eye and said, 'My friends call me Jack, and my family calls me Johnny. Since you're *neither*,' he said snidely, '*you* can call me Mr. President.' Bobby Kennedy was standing there. They both got a big laugh out of that. Pam and Jackie didn't hear what he said. But, that's the Jack Kennedy I've always known—once an asshole, always an asshole."

We both laughed at our similar plights, but deep down, I know we were saddened, ashamed, and amazed at such a display of brash immaturity on the part of the new President of the United States and his Attorney General.

ONE WEEK LATER, Mr. B and I met with President Kennedy on several national security issues. The Agency wanted the President to be fully aware of our activities. We began with a briefing on Operation Pluto. Unfortunately *The New York Times*, as well as *Time* magazine and many Miami newspapers, had already published stories and pictures about our planned invasion.

Mr. B explained that we had worked closely with President Eisenhower in planning every aspect of the operation. We drew upon Eisenhower's military experience, as well as our own previous success in Iran and Guatemala, to create a sophisticated invasion which would successfully overthrow the Castro regime. Mr. B described in detail our training program for Cuban exiles in Guatemala, parts of the Caribbean, and in the southern states and our strategy utilizing psychological warfare, military tactics, and covert intelligence to help stage the invasion. He outlined our plan to disguise sixteen B-26 bombers as Cuban Air Force deserters which would bomb Castro's air force while it sat on the ground. "This should assure us of complete air superiority throughout the attack." He further provided the details about the guerrilla army that we had supplied in the Escambray Mountains of Cuba and the plan for them to sweep down to the beachhead which would provide support for our invasion fleet when it came ashore.

Considering how thorough Richard Bissell's explanation had been, I was surprised when Jack raised an objection to our plan. He wanted to know how we hoped an invasion force of fourteen hundred men could expect to defeat the roughly two hundred thousand men in Castro's army.

Mr. B once again was very methodical and patient in his presentation. He explained we were employing the same strategy used to successfully drive Jacobo Arbenz from power in Guatemala in 1954. Just like our Voice of Liberation radio broadcasts in Guatemala, our media disinformation campaign would broadcast misleading reports of multiple invasion landings on the island—we would also broadcast massive uprisings among the local Cuban population who were helping the invaders oust Castro. Mr. B pointed out that our strategy, combined with the element of surprise, was designed to create mass confusion within the Cuban forces. With Fidel in Havana and all of his communications cut off, he would only know that a military invasion of unknown proportions had descended. We emphasized that President Eisenhower had committed extra air support to our operation in Guatemala—we hoped that President Kennedy would do the same—and that President Eisenhower had stressed "if you commit the American flag, you commit it to win!"

Jack's willingness to participate in the invasion briefing came as a pleasant surprise to me. While puffing thoughtfully on a Cuban cigar, he listened and then gave us his permission to proceed with our plan. Operation Pluto was a go.

Next, we updated the President on the current situation in Laos. It was a tiny country of striking poverty, landlocked in such a remote region that no one really knew how many people actually lived there. Best guess estimates put the number somewhere around two million, tops. Its only real significance was its long and unprotected border with China, North Vietnam, and South Vietnam which offered safe routes for Communist infiltrators to enter into non-Communist countries.

President Eisenhower had briefed Kennedy on the situation the day before the inauguration. "If Laos is lost to the free world, in the long run, we will lose all of Southeast Asia," he told Jack. He went on to say that Laos was a "bastion of freedom" in the region, and that it was the "the cork in the bottle of the Far East." He warned Jack that Laos was in imminent danger of falling to the Communists. The Joint Chiefs of Staff recommended the immediate insertion of 250,000 American troops to secure the borders. If Russia or China jumped in, nuclear weapons might be needed. Eisenhower tried to impress upon Jack how important Laos was for the security of the region.

Jack listened non-commitally. We left the meeting unsure whether he had fully grasped the situation in Laos. Of course, I was more focused on Cuba than Laos. We had invested a lot in the plan to overthrow Castro, and I had a nagging suspicion that our "best-laid plans" would hit a snag in the Kennedy administration. My concern grew with each new meeting we held with Jack. He insisted upon taking the lead role in planning for the invasion, a role for which he was completely unqualified. I could sense disaster on the horizon.

Just as Eisenhower had predicted, Jack was systematically dissolving many of the former President's carefully conceived checks and balances between the diplomats, the military, and his intelligence people. President Eisenhower's entire chain-of-command, which he had meticulously constructed over an eight-year period, was thrown in the trash, replaced by Jack's seat-of-the-pants "I'm-in-charge" style.

On March 11, the President reversed his approval of Operation Pluto and declared our final invasion plan unacceptable. Even though the Navy had originally studied and selected our site, Kennedy wanted Mr. B to find an alternative to our planned landing site at Trinidad Beach. Contrarily, Jack insisted that the site be selected in just two days—we had been working on the project for many months.

Mr. B found a new landing site at a place known on the maps as the Bay of Pigs, eighty miles from our previous site at Trinidad. On March 15, we presented our new Bay of Pigs plan to the President, code-named ZAPATA. This plan was more to his liking. But he then threw us another curve when he proposed a night landing, as opposed to a daylight invasion even though the United States had never carried out a major nighttime invasion. He also wanted us to reduce the "noise levels" of the invasion. Finally, on March 16, the President changed his mind on the nighttime landing requirement and formally ratified the new plan. I wondered if anyone in the White House realized that ZAPATA bore little resemblance to the plan we had spent the last year preparing.

Everything was in place to launch ZAPATA when on April 11 Jack almost exposed the entire operation in an interview on national television. We were only four days away from launching ZAPATA. Kennedy knew that the element of surprise was crucial for the success of our operation. Kennedy stated in the interview: "I think Latin America is in a most crucial period in its relation with us. Therefore, if we don't move now, Mr. Castro may become a greater danger than he is today." He might as well as have telephoned Castro to let him know we were on our way.

What in the hell was he thinking?

ABOUT FOURTEEN HUNDRED enthusiastic exiles packed themselves like sardines in a flotilla of five rusty freighters and two old World War II landing craft the day we set sail for Cuba. I was on the *Houston,* a ship once owned by the United Fruit Company. Rip Robertson, the Mad Bomber of Guatemala, was part of my team. Robertson was in charge of the frogmen who were supposed to go ashore first to clear a path through the coral reef for the rest of the *Brigade*. Derek Ruger, who was calling himself "Raoul," was also on board, ostensibly to look after the interests of our organized crime partners.

I had spent the past year training Cuban exiles to handle rifles and other weapons in a remote part of the Atchafalaya Bayou outside of New Orleans. This had put me in contact with Carlos Marcello and a former FBI special agent named Guy Banister who was our liaison between the Cuban exiles and the Agency. Ruger had joined us shortly after that nightmarish January Chicago meeting. He had quietly participated in all of the training drills. I found his presence unsettling, but at the same time, I knew that he was formidable in a fight.

Whether good or bad, Derek was my constant companion. His stony countenance intimidated everyone; his very presence bred discomfort. As a result, we found ourselves with more personal deck space than any other men on the ship. I was itching for a smoke, but no one was allowed to smoke on the ship because of the high explosives on board. I took to hanging over the railing and chewing tobacco instead.

Ruger ominously tagged along beside me. As we approached the battle zone, I turned to him and asked, "Do you ever think about dying?"

Ruger reached into his shirt pocket to pull out his pack of *Lucky Strikes*. Even though he was openly breaking a major rule on the ship against smoking, I felt reluctant to stop him. Once his cigarette was lit, he snapped his Zippo shut with a sharp click and sharply inhaled the harsh smoke. Then he said matter-of-factly, "I am not afraid to die."

"You're not afraid of death?"

He exhaled more smoke from his cigarette, never once breaking his gaze at the far horizon.

"There's nothing heroic about dying. It's not like the movies where some broad cries when you're gone. The movies always show death as something heroic, dramatic, and beautiful," he stopped a moment to spit over the railing. "It's not like that at all. It's mostly cowardly, stinking, and messy."

A horrible image of Action Jackson flashed through my mind. I shook it off.

Ruger elaborated, "Most men would kill their own mothers to save their own lousy skins. They'll cry like babies, and they'll whine like little girls, pleading for any last chance that just isn't gonna be there. Then, if that doesn't work, after they've given away every last shred of their dignity, they'll start pissing their pants or shitting their drawers. And if they don't do that *before* they die, they all do it *after* they're dead. Every single hole in their miserable body will start to leak and ooze like there's no tomorrow."

I shifted my weight uncomfortably.

"Do you know what it smells like when a corpse lets loose with about a gallon of rancid piss and five pounds of putrid shit? Try to imagine that. The fuckin' movies never show *that*, do they? Can you imagine how the popcorn sales out in the lobby would fall if they showed that shit on the screen?" He chuckled to himself. "People would never go back to the movies again." He paused and repeated, "Dying ain't heroic."

I don't know why I tried to have a conversation with this guy. He was capable of unbelievably monstrous acts, and here I was trying to make small talk with him just to calm my own nerves. I regretted opening my mouth. I really didn't want to know Derek Ruger's deepest thoughts. I didn't want to know what was in that dark abyss of his convoluted mind. He scared the crap out of me.

Ruger unleashed a stream of consciousness. "And don't believe all that shit about God. God won't save you from sufferin' or shittin' your pants."

He turned away from me to stare back over the railing at the endless expanse of water. "You probably lived in a house with a white picket fence, didn't you?" He had sensed my discomfort.

"Well, not quite."

"Yeah, but you had a father and a mother, right?"

He didn't wait for my answer. "I never knew who my old man was, and my mother was…" He flicked a bug off his arm. "I learned pretty goddamned early in life that if I didn't take care of myself, no one else was gonna do it for me."

He tossed his cigarette over the railing and turned toward me.

"You went to church as a kid, I can tell. I betcha you were an altar boy."

I didn't know how to respond—but Ruger didn't need a response.

He paused for several moments and then added, "If there was really a God, he wouldn't do to a little kid what he allowed to be done to me."

I swallowed hard.

"Did you ever stop to think: What if the world was really run by Satan? Did you ever think of that? I believe Satan really runs this world. And in a few hours, you're gonna come to the same conclusion. If you think that beach in Cuba is gonna be full of smiling Cubans, ready to welcome us with flowers and songs and not bullets, then you're fucked up."

He ran out of things to say after that, so we spent the rest of the way in silence.

HOURS BEFORE DAWN on Monday, April 17, the men began to prepare for the invasion's landing. Our men were a mixed bag of exiles. A few had once been professional soldiers under Batista or had fought as guerrillas under Fidel—a few were actually paid mercenaries. The vast majority were ordinary citizens, aged sixteen to sixty-nine, who had never held a gun prior to volunteering for the Brigade. At sundown the night before, they had proudly stood at attention and sung their national anthem—tears streamed down their cheeks. Now they looked like scared rabbits.

At 6:25 a.m., our five ships maneuvered into the Bay of Pigs positioning for assault on shore. A hundred and fifty yards from the shore, the ships got stuck on a coral reef, stranding our invasion force. Our men jumped out of the boats and waded through the chest-deep water to the beach while struggling to keep their weapons dry. They held everything from rifles to heavy mortars to cases of ammo over their heads.

Just as the men reached the shore, massive floodlights suddenly illuminated the shore as if the beach were a set of a movie. I could hear the men's confused cries and curses. I also heard the low rumble of a B-26 bomber in the sky above. Suddenly, the bomber appeared out of the morning sky, dropped in altitude, and began strafing our men as they struggled to reach the sand of the beach. The B-26 circled, then, returned dropping its bombs on the beachhead. Minutes later several of Castro's fighter jets took turns raking the beachhead, the boats, and our men with a barrage of bullets and bombs.

On board the *Houston*, Rip Robertson screamed for men to get off the ship and into their landing craft. "It's your war, you bastards! Get the hell off!" But the men were petrified with fear. I saw ten men scramble down the nets as he ordered. The rest cowered on deck.

It wasn't any safer on board the Houston because once we ran aground we became a prominent target for the planes overhead. We had no way to shoot down their fighters. Our plan had been to knock out all of Castro's planes prior to the start of the invasion—it was obvious that hadn't happened. We were a sitting duck.

One Cuban jet launched a missile ripping a hole through the ship's hull. A series of fires began below deck which panicked our men. An explosion blew a hole in the bottom of the ship; we began taking in water at an alarming rate.

Another Castro plane bombed our supply transport, the *Rio Escondido*. It was loaded with most of our crucial supplies: ammunition, medicine, all of our food, and two hundred barrels of aviation fuel. The resulting explosion literally lifted the *Rio Escondido* out of the water turning it into a blazing ball of fire.

I spotted a jet coming at us from out of the sun. It was only a matter of time before Castro's pilot dove in to finish us off. We were completely defenseless.

An explosive concussion blew me off the ship into the water. Stunned by the blast, I floated helplessly in the water. I slowly realized the water around me was turning red—I was bleeding from a wound in my left arm where either a bullet or shrapnel had shattered the bone in my upper arm. I tried to swim back to the ship, but found the pain so severe it almost knocked me out.

Meanwhile, men were jumping off the *Houston* into the water around me. They were trying to escape the fires on our doomed ship as well as the hail of gunfire from the fighter jets that circled overhead and repeatedly dove down upon us. I watched many men fighting to stay afloat only to sink and drown weighted down by their equipment and weapons. Others bobbed in the water around me, bleeding profusely like I was, and helpless to do anything about it.

I heard an anguished scream from a nearby man. The water began to roil around him. I couldn't comprehend what was happening until I heard the other men around me shouting.

"Shark! Shark!"

Several sharks, attracted by the blood, attacked the wounded men floating, pulling them under the surface of the water. Adrenaline coursed through me as I realized I had to get back to the safety of my ship. I could see other men frantically swimming to the climbing nets that hung down into the water from the deck of our burning ship. I struggled to swim along with them, but my shattered arm was too painful to move. The stronger men left me behind in the water along with the rest of the weak and dying.

A dark fin suddenly cut through the water in front of me then disappeared beneath the waves. A moment later, a nearby man screamed as he was taken under. My brain screamed at me to get moving, but my body physically could not respond.

A coarse weight bumped my right side. I swung around. A dark eye looked me over as another huge shark slid past me. To this day I don't know why it didn't grab my bleeding arm, but I also knew it wasn't going to ignore me much longer. I feared I was about to die, my body torn apart and eaten by sharks! An image of Pam and Tim flashed into my mind. Tim was holding Pam's hand saying "Mommy" as Pam lovingly brushed the hair out of his eyes with her other hand. I was convinced that I would never see them again. Time stood still.

A huge splash engulfed me, pulling me under water. I surfaced expecting to see a shark's gaping maw—instead Derek Ruger was inches from my face. I noticed a thin white scar under his eyebrow.

"I gotcha," he assured me as he treaded water at my side.

"My left arm…my arm is broken…it's bleeding. Get me out of this water!" I watched the sharks circling and screamed to Ruger, "Derek, get me out of here!"

Scanning the water left and right for signs of approaching sharks, he wrapped a powerful arm around my chest and began to do a swimmer's-crawl toward the ship. I could see other men hanging from the ship's nets, assisting the wounded as best they could.

I panicked as I felt something bump my legs.

Ruger said, "Hey, relax! That was just me kicking you. Come on, I'm not going to let anything happen to you."

I calmed down when we reached the safety of the nets. Hands struggled to grab me. Someone looped a rope around my chest and hoisted me onto the deck of our heavily listing vessel.

I said a silent prayer thanking God for rescuing me—I would think about the irony later. Ruger appeared at my side and shouted for a medic. I had lost a lot of blood and now, bleeding to death was a real possibility. I could vaguely make out Ruger grabbing a corpsman and dragging him over to me. The medic told me not to move as he strapped a tourniquet onto my arm and plunged a hypodermic needle into my shoulder.

In my growing haze, I heard cries for help from the men still left in the dangerous water. Blood-curdling screams cut the air—followed by heavy silence. Ruger sprang to his feet and ran back to the railing—without hesitation, he leaped back into the shark-infested water.

Drawn by the unfolding drama, I struggled to the railing. Ruger swam toward an exile who was laboring to keep his head above the water. Three fins encircled the man as Ruger approached. The churning water was red with blood. Other sharks cut through the water, waiting for their chance to strike.

Two fins disappeared under the water; the lone shark made its move at the two men—then swam past them. The other two fins popped up, making their move toward the men—and then unbelievably, pulled back.

I heard Rip say, "Holy Mary, Mother of God." My heart was in my throat as Ruger treaded water in front of the injured man. He anticipated the sharks' maneuvers managing to keep his body between the injured man and the circling sharks.

None of the sharks challenged Ruger. Gradually, their circles widened enabling Ruger to drag the injured man closer and closer to the safety of the nets where other rescuers hung precariously. Soon they were looping ropes around his chest pulling him to safety.

Only one man was left in the water near the boat and that was Derek Ruger. He was surrounded in the roiling water by agitated sharks. But rather than scrambling to safety on the nets, he stayed where he was slowly treading water, warily watching the sharks swim near him and then away again. At any moment, I expected him to be pulled under the bloody water in a feeding frenzy of sharks. Instead, a very strange thing happened. A single shark circled close to him, almost nudging him, then peeled off and slowly swam away. Ruger stayed until all the sharks had departed. He then swam to the nets and climbed up on the deck.

The stunned crowd, their faces displaying fear and reverence, parted nervously for Ruger. More than a few made it a point to bless themselves with the protection of the Sign of the Cross. I heard several whisper "El Diablo" as Ruger passed by. No one looked at him directly.

"How ya doin' McCarthy?"

"Another few minutes in the water with those sharks and I'm not sure I'd be talking with you now. I don't know what else to say except thanks for what you did."

He looked down at me—his eyes were expressionless. "You looked like you needed some help, and I saw none of these worthless cocksuckers looked like they were going to help, so I guess I had no choice."

"You know, that just might be true, Derek, but you still didn't have to jump into the water the way you did."

"Like I said, I didn't see anyone else rushing to help out. Just like any other shit job, this one was left up to me."

"You saved my life." I swallowed hard to suppress my emotions. "I owe you for that." I extended my right hand in a gesture of gratitude, but Ruger made no move to shake with me.

"It ain't anything you'll ever be able to repay," he said.

And with that, I mercifully blacked out.

I WOKE UP in a hospital bed at the U.S. Naval Base at Guantanamo. At first I was blinded by the intense sunlight, but I could make out the figure of someone sitting in a chair at the foot of my bed. I struggled to sit up.

"Hey—you're awake."

"Hey," I weakly responded.

Tracy Barnes asked, "How are you feeling? I heard we almost lost you out there."

I ached all over, but the searing pain in my shoulder and arm had been reduced to a much more bearable dull throb.

"Here's a sip of water. The morphine has probably made your throat dry."

He held a straw to my lips. I sucked down some ice-cold water marveling at how great it tasted.

"Don't drink too fast." He jerked the straw away from my lips, "You might throw it back up again."

I tried to speak, but my voice wouldn't cooperate. Finally, I managed to ask, "How'd we do?"

Tracy took a deep breath. "We got ass-fucked. The whole thing came apart on us."

"That's what I thought," I tried to say, but my words were only jumbled sounds.

"Patrick, it was a 'screw-the-pooch cluster-fuck.' Castro was waiting to ambush us on the beachhead. Our guys never had a chance."

"How many—did—we—lose?" I struggled to form the words. I must have been heavily drugged.

He paused before he answered, "All of them."

I felt my blood run cold. All of them? All fourteen hundred of them? I closed my eyes in disbelief.

"We lost all of them. We lost the entire *Brigade*. The ones not slaughtered were captured. There's no one left. They're all gone."

I thought back to all those men crowded on the deck of the *Houston* singing enthusiastically, waiting for the battle to begin—they were all dead?

"What happened?" I demanded weakly. "Tell me what happened, Tracy."

After a lengthy pause, he finally gave in. "Here's what we know. The paratroopers went in to the beachhead area first. The C-46 cargo planes dropped the heavy equipment into the swamp areas and every single piece promptly sank out of sight. The men were dropped next. Some of them landed in the swamp too. They drowned. Others somehow dropped behind Castro's lines and were promptly shot. The few that made it to the target landing area immediately dug in and started fighting, waiting for their reinforcements to arrive.

"Meanwhile, your invasion fleet came in and ran aground on some coral reefs our photo analysts thought were seaweed beds. The men of the *Brigade* took to the water to try to reach the beach. That's when the Cuban Air Force swooped in and cut you guys to shreds. Whatever men made it to the beach were surrounded by about ten to twenty thousand of Castro's elite troops.

They lit the beachhead with spotlights and then started attacking with tanks and heavy artillery bombardments."

"Back-up? Air support?" I managed to ask. I remember us taking heavy casualties.

Tracy snorted in disgust. "Listen to this. At the Tuesday 7:00 a.m. White House security briefing, Bissell told the President the *Brigade* was hopelessly trapped on the beachhead, and unless U.S. airpower was sent in immediately, this was going to turn into an American 'Dunkirk.' So guess what our Commander in Chief did?"

A nurse came in, so Tracy stopped talking. She checked my IV, then my pulse.

"Do you want to be propped up?"

I nodded. After a few moments, I was sitting up more comfortably. My head was clearing.

"Guess what our Commander in Chief did?"

"I hope he said: Send in the Marines."

"Don't we all. No, he merely walked over to the operations map of the theater of war, and he moved the small magnetic model of our destroyers to a spot that was over the horizon and out of sight of your beachhead. He then ordered our Navy vessels to retreat so they couldn't provide covering fire for your stranded guys on that beach."

"I can't believe that—he—what?"

"I know. Neither could anyone else in the room. You know Admiral Burke?"

"Arleigh Burke? Sure I do."

I recalled my conversation at the Inauguration with Grant Grantham about Admiral Burke who was Chief of Naval Operations.

"Admiral Burke tried his best to get the President to intercede, but the President wouldn't budge. He told the Admiral he did not 'want the United States involved in this.'"

Tracy recounted the conversation.

The Admiral challenged him, "Hell, Mr. President, but we *are* involved! Can I not send in an air strike?"

"No."

"Can we send in a few planes?"

"No, because they could be identified as United States."

"Can we paint out their numbers or any of this?"

"No."

"Can we get something in there?"

"No."

"If you'll let me have two destroyers, we'll give gunfire support and we can hold that beachhead with two ships forever."

"No."

"One destroyer, Mr. President?"

"No."

I lay there horrified. Tracy's description of Jack's stubbornness in the face of Admiral Burke's strong determination to do the right thing was mind-boggling. Unfortunately, once Jack Kennedy made his mind up, it was almost impossible to get him to change it again.

Tracy continued with his narrative. "Our aircraft carrier *Essex* launched F-4 fighters to help protect the men who were getting slaughtered, but the President refused to give them permission to engage the enemy. Our pilots could only circle helplessly and watch what was going on below them. They could plainly hear the *Brigade* begging for help over their walkie-talkies, and there was nothing they could do. When our pilots returned to the carrier, I was told they cussed a never-ending blue streak and smashed their helmets against the ship's bulkheads in frustration.

"Anyway, the *Brigade* managed to still hold out through Tuesday afternoon, all the while pleading for help—and our President kept refusing to send it. One radio message cried out 'Damn you, Yankees, come on! They're slaughtering our boys on the beaches!'"

I could feel a well of anger simmering within. My temples pulsed. I am sure my blood pressure went through the roof as I listened to Tracy.

"Finally, at 2:32 p.m. on Wednesday afternoon, we got a final radio message from the *Brigade* commander, Pepe San Roman. His last message was: 'Am destroying all equipment and communications. I have nothing left to fight with. Am taking to the swamps. I can't wait for you. And you, sir, are a son of a bitch.'"

"Who was he calling a son of a bitch?"

"Who do you think? The only son of a bitch I can think of was Kennedy."

"What's the mood back at headquarters?" I asked.

Tracy shook his head sighing heavily, "I'm not going to lie to you. It was bad. Most of the guys were crying, some were puking in their wastebaskets, and everyone was distraught about the whole thing. A general feeling of depression has descended over our entire Agency."

My head was pounding.

"This was a monumental failure, Patrick. What's especially hard to believe is that the President is furious with us. He's threatening to break us 'into a thousand pieces.' The Joint Chiefs know the real story of what happened, and they sympathize completely with our plight. General Lemnitzer told me he found the President's lack of action 'absolutely reprehensible, almost criminal.' He was furious at how this whole thing was mishandled by the White House."

I could feel my own anger rising—I felt like I could kill someone.

I exploded, "Why in the hell is the President pissed off? He's the one that turned this into a mess to begin with! We had a clear plan of action drawn up and rehearsed until Jack and his boys started to play 'general.' They should have gotten out of the way and allowed the real professionals to do their jobs. Kennedy's the one who screwed this up, not us."

"Well, I've got some more bad news. Allen Dulles is out as the head of the CIA, and Richard Bissell might be gone with him."

I needed to calm down. But I couldn't. I had never been so close to being in an uncontrollable rage as I was now. Jack had just fired the top two men in the Central Intelligence Agency? You can't do that in the middle of a war, especially when you have an inexperienced leader like Jack in the White House. This was devastating news.

"How do you know all this?"

"Bissell told me. He decided to 'seek an interview,' as he put it, with the President, and the President told him, 'In a parliamentary government, I'd have to resign. But in this government I can't, so you and Allen have to go.' Richard tried to reason with him, but he said the President remained 'affable, but firm.' He also told Richard, 'You always assume that the military and intelligence people have some secret skill not available to ordinary mortals.' He said he was surprised to find out they didn't. He said he 'felt sorry for Allen,' but that's the way it was going to be. He told Richard he was disappointed in him, and he blamed him for what happened."

"Who's going to take over?"

"I heard it would be Richard Helms. He never liked or got along with Bissell. He's thrilled to be rubbing his nose in it."

"What about us?"

"I'm probably gone, too. You might come out of this okay. I don't know. Anyway you look at it, the Agency, as we know it, is probably gone. The Kennedys are on the warpath, and now they've got plenty of people joining the war party to get rid of all of us."

This news was so depressing that all I wanted to do was shut my eyes and go back to sleep. It wasn't until after he left that I realized it hadn't even occurred to me to ask Tracy about my own family and whether or not they knew I was hurt but okay.

I SPENT A week in the hospital at Guantanamo before boarding a military flight for home. I asked Chase to pick me up. As he grabbed my duffel bag, he started lecturing me—no "How you doing buddy" or "Glad you're home."

"You want to know something, Patrick? It was a year ago that I recall asking you the question: 'What the hell were you guys thinking?' when Francis Gary Powers and that U-2 got shot down over Russia. Now I find out you were personally involved in the Bay of Pigs fiasco. I'm going to sound like a broken record, but I need to ask: What the hell were you guys thinking? Hell, what were *you* thinking? Or were you thinking at all?"

"God, Chase, you know I can't talk about this to you. You, of all people, understand that."

"Of course I do. But you better be prepared for what Pam will ask you. She's been calling me and crying ever since she found out you were hurt and almost killed. What are you going to say to her?"

"I don't have to say anything to her. She's an Agency wife. She knows the score."

Chase laughed and shook his head. "You don't understand women, do you? She'll pretend she supports you and your career, but when it comes to it affecting her family, then that crosses a line with her. The fact that you almost got yourself killed is also a mitigating factor. She's hurt, she's scared, she's angry, and she's not sure what she wants to do with you. She said she wants to hug you and then 'chug your head,' whatever that means."

I let out a long sigh. "It's a Southern saying her grandmother used."

"Well, all I can tell you is that your wife is very fragile right now. Remember that."

"Chase, I appreciate your concern, but my job is to keep America safe from her enemies. I do what I do so that my wife and son can be safe in their own home. I don't regret that. It's my patriotic duty, and Pam knows that."

"Man, you really are a knucklehead. Don't tell me you're going to tell Pam that your love for your country comes before your love for your family."

"It's my job, Chase."

Just then we pulled up in front of my house. Tim leaped off the porch and ran toward the car yelling and waving excitedly. Pam, forcing a smile, stood on the porch.

As I reached for the door handle, Chase grabbed my arm to momentarily stop me. "Do yourself a favor and keep your mouth shut. Don't tell Pam a thing. If she hears that nugget of truth out of your mouth right now, it'll kill her."

I got out of the car with my left arm in a cast and a sling, which impressed my son. He excitedly asked to sign the cast on my arm, but he never knew the extent of my other injuries, or even how I was hurt. I lied to him and told him I slipped and fell on the side of a swimming pool. I was careful to hide my other bandaged wounds from Timothy's eyes. I didn't want him to know that his father had been shot and almost killed.

Even though I had been on a secret mission, Pam knew everything, probably courtesy of Jackie. It was awful. She cried her eyes out almost every night for the first five days I was home. Chase was right. She was scared, hurt, and angry—she knew she couldn't ask me questions because I couldn't answer them even if I wanted to. So she imagined the worst and let it eat at her.

She finally told me Jackie was equally distressed with Jack and his behavior in the aftermath of the Bay of Pigs debacle. Jackie said that Jack "was so upset … and had practically been in tears…she had never seen him so depressed except once at the time of his operation." She said he spent time all by himself in the Rose Garden, and she suspected he had been out there crying by himself. She said he kept repeating, "How could I have been so stupid?" He also wanted to know something else. "I cannot understand how men like Dulles and Bissell, so intelligent and experienced, could have been so wrong." She told Pam that when Jack had called his father for some kind of solace, Old Joe became so exasperated with his son's sniveling he had yelled, "Hell, Jack, if that's the way you feel, give the fucking job to Lyndon!"

I shook my head and thought *so much for national security*. My wife had been debriefed by the First Lady. I couldn't let Pam know how I felt; I tried to consider her feelings in all of this. She had a right to be upset.

Jack did call former President Eisenhower to ask his opinion on how he should have handled the situation. Tracy Barnes told me Ike traveled to Camp David to listen to Jack's pitiful reasons for canceling the crucial air support when it was needed the most. Eisenhower told Tracy he was dumbfounded if Jack believed he could fool the world into thinking the United States was not behind the invasion. He then lectured the young new President: "I believe there is only one thing to do when you go into this kind of thing…It must be a success!" Later on, Eisenhower sarcastically told Mr. B that the botched Bay of Pigs operation "could be called a *Profile in Timidity and Indecision*."

Of course, the press was hot to find a scapegoat. I reluctantly read through clippings of important news articles that I received daily and braced myself. Surprisingly, the articles rightly focused squarely on Jack.

"Not much time remains for the education of John F. Kennedy. In his first great crisis, he bungled horribly," one southern newspaper angrily declared. The Republican Congressional Committee's newsletter claimed, "It is doubtful if any President had gotten the United States in so much trouble in so short a period of time." The May 5th edition of *Time* magazine was quoted as saying "Last week, as John Kennedy closed out the first 100 days of his administration, the U.S. suffered a month-long series of setbacks rare in the history of the Republic."

We held a postmortem with the key Agency figures that had helped plan ZAPATA. Allen had been told he could stay on until the new Agency head was appointed in September while Richard found himself shuttled into an undefined role where he could serve but not really do much of anything. Tracy Barnes was in the worst shape of all. He was bitter about what had happened and how Kennedy's meddling had gotten so many good men killed. It had been left to Tracy to settle the estates of the Alabama Air National Guard pilots who had been killed in the invasion. He was clearly shattered by that experience. I kept my job but I could see big changes coming. I worried whether I would still be used or whether I would be set out to pasture like my mentors.

Our analysis of the fiasco was unanimous: the President had "choked up" at the worst possible time by canceling the air support when it was needed the most. Our director of planning for ZAPATA, J.D. Esterline, summarized it the best when he observed, "As long as decisions by professionals can be set aside by people who know not whereof they speak, you won't succeed." He was exactly right.

The real reason for the failure of the Bay of Pigs essentially came down to the fact that Jack Kennedy refused to do what was necessary when the time came for him to act.

That had ominous implications for our nation's future safety.

I HAD LUNCH more and more frequently with Chase as I continued the rehabilitation from my injuries. When Grant couldn't join us, we would head over to Rosie O'Grady's, just like old times. Chase and I enjoyed the cool darkness of Rosie's because even though it was still May, summer's heat had already descended over Washington.

"So, how's the arm, buddy."

"Better. I don't have full mobility yet, but the exercises are helping. I've been back at work for a couple of weeks. In fact, I just returned from Canada. Jack met with Prime Minister Diefenbaker."

"How'd it go?" Chase asked.

"Typical Jack—it didn't take him long to alienate the Prime Minister. Diefenbaker was concerned with America's Cold War policies—he doesn't want Canada to be drawn into a conflict with Khrushchev."

"I read about it. I can understand Kennedy's viewpoint. We can't afford to let the Canadians weaken our North American alliance."

"I agree. But, Jack tried to force his hand with his speech before the Canadian Parliament. It was an embarrassment to Diefenbaker."

"I heard they exchanged a few choice words," Chase added.

"Somehow—I don't know how—Diefenbaker got his hands on a memo in Jack's own writing calling Diefenbaker an SOB. He threatened to publish the memo to embarrass Jack."

"That's not good for American-Canadian relations."

"Jack wasn't happy about it, but he wasn't about to issue an apology. Jack privately told a few of us: 'I didn't think Diefenbaker was a son of a bitch, I thought he was a prick! I couldn't have called him an SOB if I didn't know he was one at that time.' Bobby told me later that Jack hated Diefenbaker, that he had contempt for him."

"Sounds like another productive summit in international relations," Chase said sarcastically.

We stopped our conversation for a few moments while our waitress put down our order.

"Jackie also got pretty pissed off at her husband. Did you hear about that?"

Chase with a mouth full of burger shook his head.

"Jack and Jackie were in a reception line to say their farewells and thank all those who had helped with the trip. Jackie became furious and spun around to ream out Dave Powers in French…"

"Dave Powers and Kenny O'Donnell, the Irish Mafia," Chase sarcastically interrupted.

"Jackie was spitting nails. It seems that there was a woman, or should I say "blonde bimbo" who obviously was not part of either delegation standing in line to shake Jack's hand. Jackie put two-and-two together. I was standing next to a French Canadian embassy attaché who translated for me. Jackie screamed at Dave: 'Isn't it bad enough that you solicit this woman for my husband, but then you insult me by asking me to shake her hand?'"

"That was rude," Chase sardonically said.

"Jackie didn't say a word to Jack or any of his aides for the rest of the trip."

"Our President seems to lurch from disaster to blunder to disaster again," Chase observed.

"I think the Kennedy White House is taking on water and may be on the verge of sinking." I noticed that Chase had almost finished his lunch while I hadn't even begun to touch mine, "But enough about my work, how's your work been?" I asked.

"Well, Jack Kennedy's keeping us busy. The joke around the newsroom is that you spell *trouble*, K-E-N-N-E-D-Y. He's in a lot of trouble with the Negroes."

"The Canadians and now the Negroes?" I added my own bit of sarcasm.

"The Freedom Riders are just another black eye, no pun intended, for the fledgling Kennedy Administration. I'm on my way to Alabama later this afternoon."

"About the bus business? I've heard some radio headlines, but I'm not familiar with the whole story. What's happening?"

"The Negroes want the President to act on their grievances and the campaign promises he made. CORE sent thirteen black and white members from Washington, D.C. to New Orleans on Greyhound and Trailways buses."

I interrupted Chase, "What's CORE?"

"Congress for Racial Equality. They want to celebrate the seventh anniversary of the Supreme Court's school desegregation ruling by knocking down the racial barriers at the bus stations all across the South."

"How do they plan to do that?"

"By simply boarding buses and challenging segregated seating."

"Has it worked?"

"It's gotten a lot of publicity—too much publicity. It's sparked a strong backlash in the South." Chase explained, "It was well-covered by the Southern papers. By the time a Greyhound bus with six CORE riders on board left Anniston, Georgia, a small town halfway between Atlanta and Birmingham, Alabama, it was chased by up to fifty cars filled with angry white men carrying clubs, knives, and lead pipes. Before it left Anniston, the Greyhound's tires were slashed. And then, just outside Anniston, the bus was ambushed when a Molotov cocktail was hurled through an open window in the bus as it wobbled down the highway on its rapidly deflating tires. The Greyhound exploded in a huge fireball. When the CORE members bailed out of the bus, they were set upon by the carloads of whites and savagely beaten."

"Jesus."

"When the other bus, which was a Trailways bus with seven Freedom Riders aboard stopped in Birmingham, Alabama, the seven were pulled off the bus by a large angry white mob and badly beaten."

"They're lucky no one was killed."

"It's only a matter of time, and I think everyone knows it. Everyone is looking to the President for help."

"Well, good luck—you saw how he helped us in Cuba," I cynically replied.

"Yeah, well Jack is self-interested as always. He was hands-off until he realized that this could be another blow to his prestige, especially since he was traveling to Canada. I guess Jack called up Harris Wofford, his Special Assistant for Civil Rights, and exploded: 'Can't you get your goddamned friends off those buses? Tell them to call it off! Stop them!'"

"Did they listen?"

"Nope. The Negroes in the civil rights movement are fed up with Jack right now. He has refused to ask Congress for a civil rights law."

"Didn't he renege on his campaign promise too?"

"Yep, he's done nothing to desegregate federally financed housing. He knows it will cost him votes in the South in the next election. Jack privately complained to some of our mutual friends that he didn't see 'how in the world he had ever come to promise that one stroke of the pen.'"

Chase was always conscious of revealing his sources. I knew that "our mutual friends" meant Grant and LBJ.

"Jack would say anything to get elected, you know that," I commented.

"Sure I do, but I don't think he ever realized people might hold him to those promises. He offended Martin Luther King, Jr. by not inviting him to the Inauguration. He has gone out of his way to keep King as far away from the White House as he can. I interviewed Reverend King recently—he was plainly disgusted with the President. King predicted Jack would do no more than to reach 'aggressively' for 'the limited goal of token integration.' He went on to tell me that after observing Jack in office—Chase made quote marks again with his fingers—'I'm convinced that he has the understanding and the political skill but so far I'm afraid that the moral passion is missing.'"

"I'm not sure that Kennedy possesses political skill. He's an appeaser like his old man."

"I think James Forman, the head of the Student Nonviolent Coordinating Committee, might agree with you. Forman was much more blunt than King. He described Jack's efforts on the issue of civil rights as nothing more than 'quick-talking' and 'double-dealing.'"

"Do you think there's trouble brewing on the civil rights front?"

"No doubt in my mind. It's probably going to be a long, hot summer."

Chase was right, as usual.

AT THE CLOSE of our regular Monday morning briefing with the President and his advisors on the situation in Laos, Bobby announced, "There's been another bus."

Everyone around the conference table groaned.

"What have you heard?" the President asked.

"Some Negro students from Nashville have decided to resume the

Freedom Riders journey. They left Saturday, headed for Montgomery, Alabama."

Jack slammed his fist down on the table. "This goddamned civil rights mess has to stop. Bobby, you've got to get this mess under control."

The civil rights issues were drawing blood in the South. Jack had no idea how to handle the growing tensions created by the Freedom Riders.

ON MAY 20, the new Freedom Riders boarded a Greyhound bus to Montgomery, Alabama. The bus pulled into a deserted Montgomery Greyhound bus terminal, and as soon as the Freedom Riders stepped off the bus, a mob of attackers, who had been hiding and waiting, pounced on the helpless young people. They surrounded them, beating them with lead pipes and baseball bats. It was an ugly scene. Tensions mounted even further when Martin Luther King, Jr. appeared in Montgomery on Sunday night. He attended a service dedicated to the courage of the Anniston bus riders at First Baptist Church. Fifteen hundred people huddled in the sanctuary of the church, singing hymns and praying while two thousand angry whites milled around outside, screaming obscenities and threats. A buffer of one dozen U.S. Marshals armed only with nightsticks and armbands stood frightened to death in between the two groups, afraid of what was going to happen next.

Martin Luther King's people called the President from the church and asked him to declare a state of public disorder, which would allow the United States Army to be brought in to quell the unrest.

Unbeknownst to the White House, however, the telephone operators at Maxwell Air Force Base were relaying every single conversation between the church and the White House straight back to Alabama Governor Patterson. As soon as he heard that federal troops might be sent in, he quickly mobilized the Alabama National Guard and ordered them to go in ahead of any federal troops. The reservists, displaying only Confederate flags as they marched through the crowd with their bayonets unsheathed, surrounded the church. The U.S. Marshals quickly withdrew in U.S. Mail trucks as the National Guard pointed half of their weapons at the mob and the other half at the beleaguered churchgoers.

Now that the governor of Alabama had intervened, Jack really didn't care what happened next. It wasn't a federal problem anymore; it was an Alabama state problem—hence, it wasn't his problem.

Martin Luther King, Jr. was livid; he felt betrayed by Jack Kennedy. He screamed at Bobby Kennedy over the telephone, "You betrayed us! You shouldn't have withdrawn the marshals!" King and his supporters wanted the President of the United States to take a moral stand against segregation in favor of equal rights for all men. Jack, however, didn't want to take any risks with the voters of America.

King asked Jack to greet the Freedom Riders when they returned to Washington.

"No."

He asked Jack to declare a Second Emancipation Proclamation.

"No."

It was suggested that he go on television to say "a few stout words on this racial crisis."

"No!"

Jack was quick to respond that he was the one who felt betrayed when he found out a new group of fourteen students had bought tickets at the Greyhound terminal in Montgomery for Birmingham and Jackson, Mississippi. He complained around the White House about King and his requests. "What in the world does he think I should do? Doesn't he know that I've done more for civil rights than any president in American history? How could any man have done more than I've done?"

Bobby was pissed off as well. "The President is going abroad and this is all embarrassing for him."

Bobby tried to defuse the situation by appearing on television. He immediately diminished the courage of the Freedom Riders by declaring: "They performed a service bringing the problem to attention. Now it's before the courts...Are we going to let this be settled in the streets instead of the courts? I have no sympathy with segregationists, but segregation is far better than having it decided in the streets, with beatings."

Bobby further demeaned the efforts of the Freedom Riders by labeling them "curiosity seekers, publicity seekers." He and Jack wanted the Freedom Riders out of the South—the Kennedys were asking the Negroes and their supporters to quell the demonstrations for equal rights.

This wasn't appeasement—this was suppression. Maybe the Negroes only wanted the "inalienable rights" promised by our Founding Fathers.

THE UNITED STATES was facing the real prospect of a civil war breaking out in the South just as we were feeling the Cold War heating up with the Soviets. This latest civil rights situation could not have occurred at a worse time. Jack needed to concentrate on the upcoming Summit meeting with Premier Khrushchev, a meeting crucial to the success of his young administration. The President was scheduled to meet with French President Charles de Gaulle in Paris before flying on to Vienna to meet face-to-face with Soviet Premier Nikita Khrushchev.

Right away, I felt uneasy about the trip. I wasn't granted much time to adequately prepare Jack for this extremely important initial meeting with Khrushchev. Ted Sorensen and Arthur Schlesinger, two of Jack's closest long-time advisors, were busy pumping his head full of crap. They told him they expected the Vienna summit meeting to be very similar to Jack's initial debate with Richard Nixon. They were convinced that Khrushchev's dour personality would be completely eclipsed by Jack's handsome visage and his clever and witty repartee.

I thought they were both hopelessly naïve—they were actually doing the President a great disservice with such advice. Jack didn't like to hear from experts anyway, and now he was even less inclined to listen to me about properly preparing for his face-off with Khrushchev. I was the only one in the White House who had personally met Khrushchev and I knew him for what he was—a very shrewd, smart, and calculating man. He certainly wasn't going to be won over by Kennedy's boyish good looks and charm. Khrushchev would likely go into that summit meeting with a clear agenda. I was certain one of his primary objectives would be to get the measure of Jack's character. Sorensen and Schlesinger were setting up the President for disaster.

Even though Jack wouldn't listen to me, I hoped he would listen to the many experts who offered their opinion. The *International Herald Tribune* published a scathing column by Marguerite Higgins who feared the President "intends to act not only as his own foreign minister, but as his own Soviet expert, French expert, Berlin expert, Laotian expert, nuclear test ban expert, etc...." The French Foreign Minister, Couve de Murville, made the most humorous comment of all. Observing Jack's failures just prior to the summit, he dryly observed, "It's rather like fighting a championship bout after your last two sparring partners have knocked you out." Averill Harriman, who had been an advisor to Roosevelt and Truman, was desperate to give Jack some advice: "Don't let him frighten you. Remember he's just as scared as you are. Don't let him rattle you, he'll try and rattle you and frighten you, but don't pay any attention to that...His style will be to attack and then see if he can get away with it." I thought Harriman was mostly right, but I didn't think that Khrushchev was afraid of anyone, especially Jack Kennedy.

Jack and Bobby believed their biggest mistake in dealing with the Bay of Pigs was their reliance upon men whose titles were more impressive than their advice. Instead, they felt more confident relying on their own gut feelings. I tried repeatedly to get Jack to concentrate upon our briefing material, but he just couldn't be bothered to look at it. He told me he had decided to approach the Premier with a very simple agenda of his own. Following the advice of Sorenson and Schlesinger, he believed Khrushchev would find the famous Kennedy charm and wit too irresistible to argue with. His game plan was to carefully manipulate Khrushchev into an agreement that would mirror his own beliefs.

We arrived at the American Embassy in Vienna on the morning of June 3 around noon. The first meeting was scheduled to take place around a large coffee table set up in the music room. Each side had a half-dozen advisors and interpreters present to provide assistance and to take notes. Everyone in the American delegation was on pins and needles. As usual, Jack had discounted the importance of protocol and an agenda in meeting with Khrushchev. I thought having an informal discussion with Premier Khrushchev was not only foolhardy, it was dangerous—but they didn't listen to me.

Premier Khrushchev stormed into the room followed by his retinue of advisers. He walked in with a scowl on his face until he saw me standing in the American delegation; then, his scowl morphed into a big grin.

"It is my good friend, Comrade Patrick McCarthy! I missed seeing you when I was in America. I am glad you decided to come join us again here in Vienna. Perhaps we shall share some vodka and toast to old times together?"

"I would like that very much, sir," I said as the rest of the American delegation glared at me. They must have rules like Frank Sinatra's crowd, I mused—only Jack is supposed to be the witty one.

The conference began as soon as everyone settled around the room, and the President and Premier were comfortably seated around the conference table.

Jack started out with a basic message: "My ambition is to secure peace. If we fail in that effort, both our countries will lose…Our countries possess modern weapons…If our two countries should miscalculate, they will lose for a long time to come."

Khrushchev responded by angrily screaming at Jack.

"Miscalculations! Miscalculations! Miscalculations! All I ever hear from your people and your news correspondents and your friends in Europe and everywhere else is that damned word 'miscalculation'! You ought to take that word and bury it in cold storage and never use it again! I'm sick of it!"

He leaned forward across the table and shook his fist in Jack's face.

"Miscalculation is a very vague term, and it looks to me that what the United States wants is for the USSR to sit like a schoolboy with his hands on the desk…But the Soviet Union will defend its interests, even though the United States might regard some of its acts as 'miscalculation'!"

Jack sat in stunned disbelief. Khrushchev began a frightening tirade.

"The West and the United States as its leader must recognize one fact: Communism exists and has won its right to develop…Mr. Dulles based his policy on the premise of liquidation of the Communist system."

Jack weakly tried to rebut the Premier by claiming that just the opposite was true. Khrushchev yelled back that it was not only the Soviets but also the people of other countries who were the ones prepared to fight for change. He alleged that it was only the "capitalists," led by Kennedy, who wanted to preserve the status quo while the rest of the people of the world yearned to see their economies develop, too.

Khrushchev lectured Jack like he was an errant child who needed to be set straight. Because of protocol, none of the Americans could assist Jack. Each one of us waited anxiously for Kennedy to refute Khrushchev's statements; astonishingly, Jack Kennedy couldn't put up any defense of any kind. He passively sat there—meekly enduring Khrushchev's verbal beating.

Seeing that he could easily intimidate our young president, Khrushchev continued his tirade unabated. He insisted Communism would ultimately triumph over capitalism. "In order that there should not be any conflict between us, you wish that these ideas not be propagated beyond the already existing socialist countries. But I repeat, Mr. President, that idea cannot be stopped…The Spanish Inquisition burned people who disagreed with it but ideas did not burn and eventually came out as victors. Once an idea is born it cannot be chained or burned."

At this point, Jack finally found the courage to interrupt the Premier. He meekly pointed out, "Mao Tse-Tung says power is at the end of a rifle."

Khrushchev laughed in his face at his feeble retort and jammed it right back in Jack's face. "I do not believe Mao Tse-Tung could have said this. He is a Marxist, and Marxists have always been against war!"

I was astonished. Premier Khrushchev had just accused President Kennedy of lying to him. The other American advisors in the room grew restless as we waited for Kennedy's comeback. We were shocked when he said nothing at all. He simply sat there and took the insult without any rebuttal of his own. What in the world was going through his mind?

Emboldened, Khrushchev took Jack to task for lecturing him. "We have grown up," he said, indicating he believed the Soviet Union was the equal of the United States.

Jack was obviously befuddled and unable to mount any kind of a reasonable counter argument. Our glib and witty Harvard graduate and history major was tied in knots by this former Russian coal miner and pig farmer. It was embarrassingly painful to watch. Jack began to agree with Khrushchev on virtually every point the Premier made. In fact, Jack exhibited the same kind of weak debate style that Nixon had displayed in losing the 1960 presidential debate.

Thankfully, our scheduled 2:00 p.m. lunch break interrupted the Khrushchev's scornful tirade. Jack got up from the table looking pale. He had absorbed a considerable verbal punishment over the course of the past hour; it showed plainly and painfully on his face.

I was standing next to Ambassador Llwelyn Thompson as Jack walked out past us. His eyes conveyed a combination of fear and bewilderment. "Is it always like this?" the President asked us.

Ambassador Thompson was stoic in his response, "Par for the course, Mr. President." Privately, all of us had plenty to say about the President's performance. Those Americans who had been in the room nervously exchanged glances that told the same story. It had been an exceedingly bad meeting from Jack Kennedy's standpoint. We were alarmed as we watched the President take one verbal shot after another without putting up any defense. If this had been a prizefight, we would have been forced to throw a towel into the center of the ring to stop the bludgeoning blows.

The lunch break was a public affair, open to the press. Jack acted as if the earlier meeting had been nothing but cordial. He put on an impressive guise of smiling and talking—pretending to enjoy himself. The two leaders seemed to joke and frequently laugh together throughout their meal.

Before the afternoon meetings began, the Premier and the President took a brief stroll by themselves around the garden outside the meeting room. Khrushchev was shaking his finger in Jack's face while he circled around him snapping at him with heated facial contortions. Jack stood mute, absorbing the verbal whipping without a whimper.

The afternoon session started with Jack finally trying to take the offensive. He tried once again to turn on the vaunted Kennedy charm with some self-deprecating humor to clarify what he meant by miscalculation. He conceded he had made "certain misjudgments," and he included Cuba in that admission. "It was more than a mistake. It was a failure."

His admission opened him up to more of Khrushchev's taunts. The Premier claimed the United States propped up squalid little regimes around the world. The United States didn't stand for democracy, he asserted, otherwise the U.S. wouldn't support the Shah of Iran or Batista. In fact, he charged, it was the American support of those corrupt regimes that precipitated revolutions in the first place. To our horror, Jack agreed with him, claiming we shouldn't have supported Batista, and that if the Shah didn't improve the living conditions for the people in his country, then Iran would have to change as well. "I am for change!" he claimed.

Our State Department representative turned pale at Kennedy's assertion. I could only guess at how our ally, the Shah, would feel when the Russians leaked this particular comment to him.

Khrushchev laughed in Jack's face at his last remark. Sensing that he had the President of the United States on the ropes, Premier Khrushchev went straight for the jugular with his next threat. "If the United States supports old, moribund, reactionary regimes, then a precedent of intervention in internal affairs will be set, which might cause a clash between our two countries."

Instead of countering that threat with one of his own, Jack conceded and capitulated. He said, "We regard…Sino-Soviet forces and the forces of the United States and Western Europe as being more or less in balance."

Jack's ignorant declaration literally sent Khrushchev into a fit of ecstasy. I heard an audible groan emanate from one of our own military attachés seated next to me. He couldn't believe that the President declared the Russians were our equals—no president had every made that claim before. The Soviet Union was nowhere close to having parity with us on anything military; the Joint Chiefs would be furious. It was a huge strategic mistake to admit to the Russians that our two nations were at parity with each other in any way. Our nation's strength and security were based on the belief we were too militarily strong to be directly challenged by the Soviets anywhere in the world.

Our afternoon session broke up shortly afterwards. Jack emerged frustrated and exhausted. "He treated me like a little boy," Jack moaned. "Like a little boy."

Everyone at the summit took notice of Jack's haggard state. A British journalist thought the President looked dazed as he escorted Khrushchev to his car at the end of the afternoon. Chip Bohlen said he looked "a little depressed." Harriman declared he looked "shattered." The rest of us believed Jack had gotten "a little bit out of his depth" by being drawn into an ideological debate. Jack had studied at the London School of Economics, so he should have possessed at least a minimal understanding of communism, but it was readily apparent that he knew little about Marxism.

Jack and his advisors had grievously underestimated the Russian leader. Khrushchev, determined to test Kennedy's resolve and experience, visibly overwhelmed Jack. Jack miserably failed to prove his strength as a world leader.

I had tried repeatedly to warn Jack that Khrushchev would test his strength of character, just like he had tested Vice President Nixon's, by pushing, bullying, and belittling. "He does this with everyone," I emphasized, "and he won't stop until his opponent finally has had enough and starts pushing back. You are never going to win Khrushchev's respect unless you stand up to him. Once you do that, he will consider your side of the argument. Until that happens, he will unmercifully press his advantage."

I hoped it wasn't too late to salvage something.

THAT EVENING WE attended a formal dinner party at the Schonbrunn Palace, a seventeenth century estate the Hapsburgs had built outside of Vienna. The American delegation showed up wearing black tie, only to find the Soviet delegation wearing their simple business suits. It was the Soviets' way of pointing out Western imperial decadence, an effective public relations coup on their part. We felt overdressed and silly to have been so embarrassingly upstaged by the Soviets.

The meeting the next day took place this time at the Russian Embassy, where it was Premier Khrushchev's turn to play host. Khrushchev immediately wanted to talk about Berlin calling it "the bone in my throat."

Berlin was living proof to the rest of the world of the failure of Communism. Every single day hundreds of East Germans boarded trains, trams, buses, and subways bound for the west. They were defecting and taking with them a profound dislike of the Communist way of life, along with the technical skills and professional qualifications that East Germany so desperately needed for itself. That exodus had to be stopped, or the Soviet Union's precarious hold on Eastern Europe would be in jeopardy.

Khrushchev felt the current situation in Berlin was intolerable. There was still no official peace settlement for Germany, long after the end of World War II. More alarming to the Soviet Union was the fact that West Germany had rearmed itself and was now the leading European power in NATO. "This meant the threat of a third World War," Khrushchev stated.

Khrushchev wanted the Western powers to sign a treaty, effective immediately. If the West didn't agree to sign one, then Russia was prepared to take action on its own. "The USSR will sign a peace treaty unilaterally with East Germany, and all rights of access to Berlin will expire."

He was boldly testing the strength of our President's resolve over West Berlin.

"Would this peace treaty block access to Berlin?" the President demanded to know.

Khrushchev was brutally honest. "Yes."

Thankfully, our scheduled lunch break gave us time to cool off. Regrettably, the lunch break didn't cool anybody off. After lunch, Jack tried once more to impress upon Khrushchev his determination to be firm in the face of the Soviet threat. Unfortunately, Jack's bluff wasn't going to work on Khrushchev, now that Khrushchev had the full measure of his adversary.

Jack began by saying he hoped Khrushchev would not bring about a situation "so deeply involving our national interest... no one can predict what course it will take."

Khrushchev instantly became furious that Jack would now try to challenge him especially after Jack had not stood up to him at any point in the entire Summit. He slammed his hand down on the table and shouted, "I want peace! But if you want war, that is your problem!"

Jack tried once more to reason with him by saying, "It is you, and not I, who wants to force a change."

Khrushchev cut him off and yelled, "It is up to the U.S. to decide whether there will be war or peace." He stated that his decision to sign that peace treaty was "firm and irrevocable ….The Soviet Union will sign it in December if the U.S. refuses an interim agreement."

"Then, Mr. Chairman, there will be war. It will be a cold winter," Jack retorted.

I groaned—the President had verbally committed to a war with the Soviet Union over Berlin! I could not have been more discouraged or distressed. John F. Kennedy was not a strong enough leader to stand up to Nikita Khrushchev, and they both knew it. Kennedy ended his first summit meeting with the Russian leader by challenging Khrushchev to back up his words with action.

Our Cold War was now destined to turn hot.

OUR ENTIRE AMERICAN delegation was deeply distressed as the Vienna meeting broke up. Premier Nikita Khrushchev beamed for all the cameras, obviously happy the summit had gone so well for him. Kennedy who had gone into the meetings expecting to cajole Khrushchev stood grim and unsmiling for the cameras. Kennedy had been bullied and browbeaten into submission by Khrushchev's relentless and unyielding demands. Khrushchev had learned that Kennedy would collapse and fold under pressure. The encounter had been an unqualified disaster for the fledgling presidency of John Fitzgerald Kennedy.

General Maxwell Taylor told me his concern: "The meeting of Khrushchev with President Kennedy in Vienna had so impressed (Khrushchev) with the unreadiness of this young man to head a great country like the United States, plus the experience that he had seen in the Bay of Pigs, led him to believe that (Khrushchev) could shove this young man around any place he wants." It was evident that Jack repeatedly undercut his own arguments and was unable to defend the positions he had traveled to Vienna to protect. Jack Kennedy was not a decision-maker—especially a presidential decision-maker.

Afterward at the U.S. Embassy, Jack slouched on a couch with a "hat over his eyes like a beaten man" according to James Reston who described him to me later over dinner. Reston met with Jack in a darkened room with all of the shades pulled down and the lights turned off. He said Jack appeared to be in shock, repeating things over and over, and blurting out information that reporters should never have been privy to. Reston said that Jack didn't pull any punches when he asked Jack how things had gone.

KENNEDY MUST BE KILLED

"Worst thing in my life, he savaged me," he glumly admitted, very depressed. "I think I know why he treated me like this. He thinks because of the Bay of Pigs that I'm inexperienced. Probably thinks I'm stupid. Maybe most important, he thinks I have no guts."

By the time our presidential retinue stopped in London on the way home, the news of the Vienna disaster had preceded us. Jack held his own meeting with the British Prime Minister Harold Macmillan before we left. I later heard gossip from some of my friends in British Intelligence that the Prime Minister had written a note to Queen Elizabeth, summarizing the meeting for her. "The President was completely overwhelmed by the ruthlessness and barbarity of the Russian Chairman. It reminded me in a way of Lord Halifax or Neville Chamberlain trying to hold a conversation with Herr Hitler...For the first time in his life Kennedy met a man who was impervious to his charm."

When Jack got back to the White House, he was so mentally and physically exhausted that he literally collapsed into bed. Once there, he barely had the energy to leave its comfort for a week. I was told by one of the members of his Secret Service detail that he had suffered a mental breakdown and his personal physician had treated him with massive amounts of anti-psychotic drugs in order to get him back up on his feet and functioning.

Weeks later, Jack made a lame speech in which he informed the American people there had been "no threats or ultimatums by either side."

Of course, we all knew that was a bald-faced lie.

ON AUGUST 13, 1961, the consequences of Kennedy's ineptitude at the Vienna Summit began to manifest when Khrushchev sealed the borders between East and West Berlin. Nikita Khrushchev dared Jack to back up his threat concerning Berlin. East German police began to seal off the border between East and West Berlin. East Germans who attempted to cross into West Berlin were forcibly turned back into the East sector. More ominously, Soviet troops encircled Berlin to enforce the sealing of the border. Shortly thereafter, the East Germans and the Soviets began to construct a high concrete wall that split Berlin in two.

Anti-Communists in the United States screamed for Jack to challenge the Soviets and stop them from building that wall. Instead, he chose to announce the Soviets had every right to close off its zones—he permitted the construction of the Berlin Wall to proceed completely unchallenged.

On August 30, the Soviet Union abruptly resumed unannounced atmospheric tests of its thermonuclear weapons—specifically, powerful hydrogen bombs.

Jack's only reaction was simple and succinct: "Fucked again."

AFTER A SUMMER of frustration, Jack became alarmingly reckless with regard to his personal life. His devil-may-care behavior coincided with a marked increase in the number of visits from his personal physician, Dr. Max Jacobson. I was becoming quite concerned over the doctor's constant presence around the President and the First Lady. His vitamin injections had become daily White House occurrences.

Dr. Jacobson's hygienic standards were questionable. More than a few of Max's patients had contracted hepatitis because of the dirty needles he used. His medical bag was described by one patient as a "jumble of dirty, unmarked bottles and nameless chemical concoctions which he would just dump out on a table when he began to mix his injections." He was perpetually disheveled; his fingernails were permanently blackened from his exposure to his own proprietary chemical mixtures. He spooked a friend of Jack's named Chuck Spaulding with stories of his experiments with cells from elephant hearts and sheep placenta. As Spaulding told me, "He had obviously swallowed too many of his own pills."

Dr. Jacobson's concoctions turned Jack and Jackie into amphetamine addicts. Jack had no qualms about the injections and never asked what was in the injections. "I don't care if it's horse piss in there as long as it makes me feel good."

Now, Jack might not have cared, but I sure did. I adamantly believed that no President with his finger on the nuclear launch button had *any* business taking "vitamin injections."

I went into a livid rage when I discovered that Jackie had talked Pam into getting some of Jacobson's quack injections too. Pam had planned to go with Jackie to Camp David the day after a big dinner party at the White House. I volunteered to stay home with Tim for the weekend. Pam said that just before they left the family quarters of the White House, while all of Jack and Jackie's friends were busy sobering up from the previous night's party, Dr. Jacobson came in and casually started injecting everyone with drugs. "He just moved easily from person to person, chatting and sticking us with needles. He didn't even bother to change them."

She said Betty Spaulding, Chuck's wife, refused a shot because she had "a lot of allergies," but Jacobson persuaded both Betty and Pam to accept "a very light dose." Betty Spaulding later confessed to me "It was the damnedest performance I ever saw!" She told me she thought to herself, "These people are crazy to be doing this!" The end result was that the President and his First Lady took a retinue of their closest friends to Camp David while they were all high on "speed"—and my wife happened to be one of them.

Risky behavior of all kinds became more frequent in the Kennedy White House. Jack's womanizing was an open secret with the White House press corps and other D.C. insiders. Hugh Sidey of *Time* magazine even wrote a memo in which he began, "Not since the fall of Rome..." He described a wild New Year's Eve party in Palm Beach, Florida that involved the senior White House advisors. As a working member of the White House press corps, Sidey urgently needed an official comment by either Pierre Salinger or his assistant, Andrew Hatcher, on a brewing foreign policy matter. He described his shock when he discovered "Salinger was off someplace with a girl who was not related in any way by law or by blood to him. Hatcher had gone to Jamaica with a bunch of models. I went around. There was nobody available to talk with me. Everybody was partying. I have to say that I did sense it was excessive and probably not the way to run a presidency. He [Kennedy] was the leader of the free world and this was the height of the Cold War."

ON NOVEMBER 28, everyone at the Agency assembled in the McLean, Virginia, suburb of Langley, to dedicate the gleaming new headquarters of the CIA. Allen Dulles had been replaced by a wealthy California businessman named John McCone. Jack had graciously asked that Allen and his wife, Clover, attend the ceremony and sit on the dais as guests of honor. Allen had invested many years assisting in the planning of the new campus and was pleased to be back with us. In the middle of the carefully scripted dedication ceremony, Jack turned to the dais behind him and commanded Allen to step forward. He then pinned the National Security Medal on Allen Dulles' lapel.

Richard Bissell leaned over to me and whispered, "Short of a lordship or a knighthood, that's the highest honor in the United States government."

"He deserves it," I whispered back.

"You're damn right he does."

After the ceremony was over, Allen motioned me over to join him at his car. Mr. B was standing next to him.

"Clover, darling, could you please excuse us for a moment?"

"Sure, hon, but please remember, this car doesn't belong to you anymore. The government might not wait very long before they take it back."

"Then I guess I'll have to come home in a taxi tonight."

One of our Agency staffers overheard that remark and replied, "That limousine is yours for as long as you need it, Mr. Dulles. We'll find another car for Mr. McCone."

I climbed into the back seat ahead of Allen and Richard. We chatted making small talk about the ceremony and the medal Allen had received until Allen held his up his hand.

"Patrick, this day represents a milestone for all of us. I'm gone, Richard's almost gone, and the new Agency headquarters will almost surely be populated with Kennedy people from now on. You're going to find it mighty lonely at times."

"I know, sir. I'm going to miss you. We're all going to miss you."

Allen sadly shook his head. "I wish it were true, but we all know better. The gentlemen who were not part of the ZAPATA planning are having trouble concealing their happiness at our demise, aren't they Richard?"

"You mean Dickie Helms? You couldn't wipe the grin off his face if you tried. They've already started taking potshots at us, and we're not even gone yet."

"What do you mean?"

"Oh, the President had a review board set up. The Inspector General turned in a scathing critique of Allen and the rest of us. It makes us the official fall guys for the Bay of Pigs. The report was given to Director McCone just before he officially assumed office. It was so incendiary that he ordered the report immediately turned over to Allen while he was still in office."

"How bad was it?"

"It was chocked full of some ugly personal judgments and assessments," Mr. B snarled.

Allen was more circumspect. "You don't strike at one of your own when they are down. That's not the way we operate. It's not the way we were taught to respect our colleagues."

"Well, I don't like the fact that the report is being surreptitiously passed around the Agency and is being used as a mocking testimonial to our failures by those seeking to profit from our situation," Mr. B huffed.

Just then, Clover gently rapped on the window.

As I climbed out of the car, both Allen and Richard shook my hand. "Patrick, you're our legacy now. Do good things in our absence. We know you'll make us proud," Allen said kindly.

"You have always made us proud of you," Mr. B added. "But do yourself a favor and watch your back. You're on your own now. There's no one left at the Agency you can trust because of your long relationship with us. Be careful. They'll get rid of you just as fast as they got rid of us."

ON DECEMBER 19, Joseph Kennedy, old "Ambassador Asshole," suffered a debilitating stroke that came close to killing him. As it was, he was left permanently paralyzed on his right side. When his wife, Rose, heard the news of his near-fatal collapse, she was completely unfazed by it. Not wanting to upset her own daily routine, she left her house to play a round of golf and to go swimming at the Palm Beach Golf Club. After she had enjoyed her daily scheduled exercise, she leisurely proceeded to the hospital to see her critically ill husband.

I came home that afternoon to find my wife in jubilant mood. I couldn't begin to understand why she was so elated. She remarked she had heard something on the news that had made her exceedingly gratified. "I've been praying for this day since 1958," she said.

I didn't understand what she meant until years later.

"All events are secretly interrelated…the sweep of all we are doing reaches beyond the horizon of our comprehension."

— Abraham Joshua Heschel

"The events which we see, and which look like freaks of chance, are only the last steps in long lines of causation."

— Alfred North Whitehead

September 6, 1978
9:21 p.m.

Grant felt terrific. Patrick was in New Orleans, just a few hours away. It only took Grant a few minutes to arrange a flight for Ruger. As soon as he got off the phone, he was going to celebrate. Grant stood over the phone willing it to ring.

"Derek, I got you a charter flight leaving at 11:30 p.m. from Washington National. They'll have you down in New Orleans around 2:30 a.m. Is that quick enough for you?"

"It'll have to do."

"Should I arrange any help for you down there?" Grant asked breathlessly.

"Why, do you know some Girl Scouts wanting to do a good deed?"

Grant was momentarily taken aback by Ruger's humor. "I'm only trying to help," he weakly protested. Grant never let anyone talk to him the way Ruger did.

"You got me the fucking plane. That's the only help I needed. Tell me where the hangar is. I've got to get going."

Grant felt completely rattled by the time he hung up. Derek Ruger always teetered on the edge of being uncontrollable, and Grant didn't like that. Grant was used to yanking the strings of people who worked for him, not vice-versa.

"The water is getting cold," Sugar whined from the Jacuzzi. "And I need someone to keep me warm."

"I'll be there in just a second, Sugar. I'm gonna get us some champagne. Now you like champagne don't you?"

Ruger was a pit bull on a leash that could turn on him at any time. No use pissing him off right now. Maybe when this was all over, he would reconsider the employment tenure of Derek Ruger.

That thought gave him some small measure of comfort.

1962

MY RESOLUTION FOR the New Year was a simple one: I hoped we would all be alive when 1963 arrived.

Nineteen sixty-one had been a year of debacles. The year began with the President undermining our carefully crafted plans to invade Cuba with his mindless meddling. Escalating an already bad situation, he refused to authorize the military support which would have averted disaster. Finally, he compounded those errors by firing both Allen Dulles and Richard Bissell—the same mistake Truman made in 1952 when he fired General MacArthur during the Korean War. In one fell stroke, Jack decapitated the entire senior leadership of the Central Intelligence Agency when our country needed their expertise and knowledge the most.

The President's irresponsible foreign policies sparked a feud with Canada and her Prime Minister. Our Commander in Chief's complete capitulation to Chairman Khrushchev's thrashing at the Vienna Summit led directly to Khrushchev's decision to test America's resolve in Berlin. Later, the President's vacillation over the outlandish campaign promises made to Negro leaders ignited civil unrest throughout the South. Finally, Jack's reckless personal behavior and uncontrollable sex drive threatened to publicly destroy both his marriage and the nation's faith in his judgment and ability to lead.

I hoped the opening days of the New Year were not a harbinger of impending disaster—I thought the odds were 50/50.

KENNEDY MUST BE KILLED

I WAS URGENTLY summoned to an unscheduled meeting at the White House where I found Jack, Bobby, Ted Sorensen, Dean Rusk, and the president's military advisor, General Maxwell Taylor, waiting impatiently for me. It didn't take long for the ass-chewing to start.

Jack twirled an unlit cigar in his hand as his eyes burned holes in me. "Patrick, you guys over at the Agency have put me in a horrendous spot. I'm still royally pissed off about what you fucking wizards did with that Cuban invasion. Tell me, how could I have been so stupid to give you guys the go-ahead? God Almighty, it looked like the Three Stooges did the planning," Jack fumed.

"They did," Bobby promptly quipped, "Dulles, Bissell, and McCarthy."

Everyone laughed except me. I wanted to remind him it was his plan we tried to execute, not ours, but no one in the room cared. I decided to just sit there and keep my mouth shut.

Jack then ranted about how he was somehow duped by Richard Bissell. "You can't beat brains," he complained, "you always assume that the military and intelligence people have some secret skill not available to ordinary mortals, and I thought Richard Bissell embodied that completely. I think we were all fascinated by the working of Richard's superbly clear, organized, and articulate intelligence. As a result, this administration suffered a stunning defeat, and Allen lost his job."

He paused to briefly glance around the room to make sure everyone agreed with him. When no one said a word, he angrily added, "You want to know something? You're lucky you still have your job. You have Jackie and Pam to thank for that."

"I don't need my wife sticking up for me," I growled back. "I can take care of myself."

"No, you can't," Bobby smirked. "Anyway, your job is safe—at least for now."

Jack held up his hand with the cigar balanced between two fingers and shushed him. "It's a hell of a hard way to learn things, but I have learned one thing from this business. That is, that we will have to deal with the CIA. I've been so mad I wanted to break the Central Intelligence Agency into a thousand pieces and scatter it to the wind, but thankfully for all of us, cooler heads prevailed."

He once again looked around the table to make sure everyone was paying attention. "I will admit just one mistake on my part. I made a mistake putting Bobby in the Justice Department. Bobby should be in the CIA." He then motioned for his brother to slide an ashtray across the table and over to him.

Bobby leaned forward and pushed the ashtray within Jack's reach, but then he stayed there to make his own point. "Johnny, we talked about that. I'm more valuable to you at Justice. If I were named head of the Agency, you would completely lose your ability to plausibly deny Agency operations." He turned and pointed at me. "That's why we have Patrick here today. He's going to take on the project we discussed."

All eyes were on me as Bobby continued, "I chewed out Bissell a couple of months ago for sitting on his ass and not doing anything about getting rid of Castro and the Castro regime. We can't let him get away with his victory against us." He turned back to his brother, "You've got to act or be judged a paper tiger by Moscow. We need Patrick right now."

Bobby then eyed me as if challenging me to respond. I decided to hold my tongue until I knew what was going on.

Jack broke the silence, "OK, Patrick, goddamn it, it's this simple. We lost the first round; let's win the second! We've spent a lot of time discussing the next step we need to take and here it is. We're going to send more troops to Southeast Asia to do three things: show Khrushchev we're not going to abandon that part of the world to communism, show Moscow and Peking we're not as weak as we might look, and allow our Pentagon to blow off some steam after the failed Bay of Pigs fiasco. The Joint Chiefs want to show how efficiently they can run a war compared to the CIA. I told General Taylor we're going to let them do it. Do you understand?"

"Yes sir, I do."

Jack nodded to Bobby that it was his turn to speak.

"Here's what we want you to do. We are ordering you and the Agency to create a program to assassinate Fidel Castro. This time, however, I'm going to oversee it, and you're going to make sure my orders are carried out to the letter. I'm giving it the name Operation Mongoose. You're in charge. I've already drafted a memo to Richard Helms and John McCone to tell them I expect you to be left alone. They don't need the details, except to know that you are under direct orders from us. Understand?"

I didn't appear to have any choice. "Yes sir, I understand."

"You were chosen because of your extensive contacts with organized crime—Jack and I both know those guys trust you," he paused. "We also don't expect a repeat of the Bay of Pigs."

But just like the Bay of Pigs fiasco, Bobby and Jack then proceeded to give me their unqualified opinions and ideas about how to carry out the program.

Returning to Langley, I briefed Richard Helms and our new team about the Kennedys' order to assassinate Castro. It sounded to us that the Kennedy brothers got most of their far-fetched ideas from reading Ian Fleming's cheap dime novels about a British spy named James Bond. Nevertheless, because this executive action was a presidential order and because none of us wanted to be fired like Mr. Dulles and Mr. Bissell, we complied. We knew we couldn't do this alone—we would require the help of Sam Giancana and the mob to get at Castro in Cuba.

I was perplexed by Bobby's stance on organized crime. I never understood how Bobby could take on the mob on one hand and enlist the help of the mob in an Executive Action against Castro on the other—not to mention condoning his brother's association with known mobsters and their girlfriends.

Later that week, I was back at the White House meeting with Bobby to brief him about our ideas for Mongoose when Jack walked in on us.

"Did Bobby tell you what's going on?"

I didn't know what he was talking about.

Bobby let out an exasperated sigh, "Kenny O'Donnell received a hand-delivered memo from Hoover. The Director is trying to put us in our place."

O'Donnell was Bobby and Jack's closest personal advisor. I was momentarily confused. Why was Hoover sending O'Donnell a note? Before I could ask the question, Bobby answered it for me.

"It said the FBI had collected some interesting information from wiretaps, telephone intercepts, and physical surveillance of mob boss Sam Giancana. The main subject of Hoover's memo was to call attention to Judith Campbell's simultaneous relationship with Sam Giancana and the President. The memo precisely detailed the dates and times of the numerous calls Campbell has made to the White House switchboard. Now that's a problem. Since Operation Mongoose will be aggressively working with Sam Giancana to kill Fidel Castro, my brother's—our President's 'illicit and adulterous sex life' will be firmly linked to organized crime."

"Perhaps he's giving you a heads-up," I said.

I thought that Mr. Hoover had the memo hand-delivered for a reason—he was pointing out the consequences of Jack's risky personal behavior. That was a wily thing for the Director to do. Bobby, however, ignored my comment. I knew that Mr. Hoover and Bobby Kennedy were often at odds with each other. Mr. Hoover expected everyone to respect tradition. The Director was irritated that Bobby violated the established dress code by working in his shirtsleeves in the Attorney General's office. He thought that was disrespectful. He was also upset that Bobby played darts in the Attorney General's office, which permanently marred the wood paneling of the office. That also showed a juvenile disrespect for government property. Bobby knew all of that and kept it up just to irk Hoover.

Bobby reluctantly revealed another problem he was wrestling with, "My Justice Department lawyers are going after organized crime with a vengeance right now, Patrick, and they are highly offended that their President is associating with someone like Frank Sinatra. They feel Sinatra is just too heavily and visibly involved with organized crime—it makes the whole Justice Department feel uncomfortable."

"So that's why you reminded Jack in front of all of us that you were more valuable at Justice right now than at the Agency?"

Jack confirmed my allegation by simply nodding.

"Yes, that's why," Bobby added and then looked directly at Jack, "and the attorneys want me to tell you, Johnny, you can't associate with this guy."

"I don't want to hear that, Bobby. It's an unfair demand. Besides, I'm only looking out for our sister's best interests. You know that." Bobby grimaced as if to say they had argued over this point before.

Jack turned to me, "Everybody complains about my relationship with Sinatra, but he's the only guy who gives Peter Lawford work." I wondered if Jack was deliberately mocking Bobby or if he truly believed his own meager excuse. "The only way I can keep his marriage going is to see that Peter gets jobs. So I'm nice to Frank Sinatra."

Ha! And here I thought it was just because Frank always arranged for Jack to screw his brains out with Hollywood beauties when he went to California. Bobby and I both knew Jack only looked out for himself. I also knew Jack was scheduled to go to Frank's place in Palm Springs, California, in March and I could only guess what he was already thinking.

"Well, we've got to get some distance from Frank—he needs to get away from Sam Giancana and his influence," Bobby advised.

Jack looked crestfallen. He hung his head, "OK, I'll call Peter and tell him I can't stay there while you're handling the Giancana investigation. I'll see if he can't find some other place."

Jack ended up staying at Bing Crosby's house in Palm Springs. It turned out that as soon as he arrived, Peter Lawford joined him—with Marilyn Monroe on his arm.

THE PRESIDENT'S OFFICIAL birthday celebration was held at Madison Square Garden on May 19. It was a combination birthday party, political fund-raiser, and Hollywood extravaganza. Pam was very excited that Ella Fitzgerald, Peggy Lee, Jack Benny, Maria Callas, Bobby Darin, Harry Belafonte, and many other stars were there to entertain us and to wish the President a "Happy Birthday." Jackie had adamantly refused to attend the gala.

The highlight of the party—for every red-blooded male in the audience—

had to be when Marilyn Monroe wiggled up to the podium in a see-through glittery gown.

"She must have had that dress sewn on," said Pam indignantly.

Adlai Stevenson, who was seated at our table, agreed, "It appears to be flesh with sequins sewed on it."

"That is disgusting." Pam whispered in my ear, "You can see her nipples."

Indeed, you could see everything.

"I think she must be drunk," Pam said through her teeth.

Miss Monroe stood provocatively on the stage and sang the sexiest version of "Happy Birthday" I had ever heard in my life.

"Does she think that this is a bachelor party? This is a birthday party for the President of the United States. She should have some respect." Pam was livid.

As Marilyn began to sing, she closed her eyes, licked her lips, and suggestively ran her hands up and down her body. Every man in the audience was enthralled.

"Oh—my—God! I am glad that Jackie is not here. This would have been humiliating for her," Pam clenched her teeth making upper lip disappear.

Broadway columnist Dorothy Kilgallen described Marilyn's act as "making love to the President in the direct view of forty million Americans." Grant described it as one of the most lurid things he had ever publicly seen in his life—he loved it. He told me later that the President had taken Marilyn back to his suite at the Carlyle Hotel.

I hoped neither Pam nor Jackie ever found out about that marital betrayal.

ON MAY 29, Jack's actual forty-fifth birthday, the newspaper headlines reported the sharpest and steepest stock market drop since 1929. The pundits calculated $20 billion in stock market value was erased as the Dow fell from 611.78 to 563.24, before bouncing back twelve points just prior to the close. They called it "Blue Monday," and it was just the latest in a number of strong stock market sell-offs that reflected Wall Street's growing mistrust of Jack and his policies.

The stock market had fallen twenty-five percent over the past six months. The favorite joke on Wall Street was that when old Joe Kennedy heard about his tremendous stock market losses, he was suddenly able to speak for the first time since his stroke. The punch line claimed his first words were "To think I voted for that son of a bitch!"

SINCE I WAS at the White House on a daily basis, I became a silent witness to the President's insatiable sexual appetite. Jack held frequent sex parties in the White House swimming pool whenever Jackie wasn't home. Jack often encouraged Jackie to go out to their country house in Glen Ora, Virginia. Chase's cousin, Secret Service agent Larry Newman, told us "when Jackie was there, there was no fun. He just had headaches. You really saw him droop because he wasn't getting laid. He was like a rooster getting hit with a water hose."

Once Jackie was out of the White House, Jack ordered a chilled pitcher of daiquiris and scurried off to the pool for an hour or two of skinny-dipping and sexual intercourse in a small room off the pool area with two young White House employees nicknamed Fiddle and Faddle. Whenever the President was in the pool with Fiddle and Faddle, the waiters, household staff, and even the Secret Service were warned to stay away from the area.

Jack's sexual liaisons were common knowledge at the White House. I did my best to keep Pam in the dark, so it was a surprise when she brought up the topic as we were cleaning up after dinner one evening. I enjoyed completing this little domestic chore with Pam. It gave us some private time to discuss the day's events. Handing me a plate to dry, Pam said, "I ran into Mary Pinchot Meyer, Cord Meyer's wife, today."

"Ex-wife."

"I meant ex-wife. I didn't recognize her when she first approached me."

"You know something? Chase said the same thing, and he's known Mary for years."

"Well, she's changed—I enjoyed her company when we lived in Georgetown back when Tim was first born, but I was uncomfortable with her today."

"I always thought she was strange. There were a couple of cocktail parties where she wanted to talk about Agency projects—infiltration procedures, brainwashing techniques, drug experiments in mind control, especially LSD. All subjects that I would never have discussed for national security reasons, but Cord didn't seem to care."

"Well, I bet he'd care now. Mary made it a point to tell me that Cord was nothing but an alcoholic who openly cheated on her. Mary told me she felt justified in remaking herself in a radically new image. She said she had decided to become a 'blue-blooded aristocrat outlaw.' I told her I didn't understand what that meant and so she told me. Patrick, I must have turned beet red I was blushing so hard. She didn't care. I think she reveled in my discomfort."

"Well, Chase and I both used to joke that she was a dangerous woman because of her tendencies to say and do almost anything that came to her mind."

"Tell Chase it's a lot worse now. She even had the gall to brag that she was seeing Jack Kennedy when Jackie wasn't around. I wanted to slap her across the face."

"I'm glad you didn't," I joked. "Can you imagine the gossip?"

"*Can you imagine* the brazenness of that hussy? She knows I'm Jackie's best friend. Jack's not so stupid, so sexually reckless that he would risk an indiscreet affair with Mary Pinchot Meyer, is he?"

"Honey, I don't know," I lied.

Of course Jack would do such a thing. Jack Kennedy and Chase had known Mary since they were in school together. Jack told Chase he found the "new" Mary exciting to be around.

"She bragged that she goes to the Kennedy family quarters of the White House whenever Jackie is gone. She claims Jack even sends a White House limousine to her house to pick her up and take her home again when their little tryst is over. Can you imagine the nerve of her? I sure hope, for Jackie's sake, she's lying."

I put the last plate in the cabinet, walked behind Pam whose hands were still in the dishwater, and nuzzled her neck. Pam leaned back against me. "I'm the luckiest man on earth," I said.

The next day I examined the daily White House visitor logs. They showed that Mary wasn't lying—she was indeed a frequent and highly visible guest.

ON JUNE 13, Project Cocoon officially ended when Lee Harvey Oswald returned to the United States with his new Russian wife and daughter in tow. I had personally intervened with the FBI to make sure the authorities didn't arrest him for treason upon his return to the country. Technically, he was a traitor to the United States of America because of his defection.

I slipped into New Jersey to tell him how extremely proud I was of what we had accomplished with the project. Lee greeted me with a strong "Cossack" embrace. "This is my wife Marina and our baby daughter, June. They don't speak English."

Marina nodded politely and smiled toward their baby. It was a different Lee, in many ways, than the young idealistic immigrant who had said goodbye three years ago. His face looked older and thinner.

I looked around to make sure no one was paying attention to our meeting. "How difficult was it to get out of the Soviet Union?" I asked. We had managed to get him and his family exit visas to return to America.

"Easier than getting in—I didn't have to slit my wrists this time. I went to the U.S. Embassy in Moscow in February and recanted my earlier defection. I told the consulate that I had learned my lesson the hard way. I had been completely relieved of my illusions about the Soviet Union. They believed me."

"What did the Soviets say?"

"I think they were glad to be rid of me. They tried to turn me into a double agent, but I acted ignorant. They eventually gave up and let me go home. But here's the best part."

He stopped and looked for Marina and when he saw she was out of earshot, he whispered, "I brought back the daughter of a high-ranking KGB general. Marina's father is not happy with her. Not only did she leave the country, she took his granddaughter with her."

"Congratulations buddy." I looked at the suitcases sitting near by, "Any of that for me?"

"I brought you three suitcases filled with stuff I collected during my two and a half years behind the Iron Curtain. I'm going to leave them with you so I don't have to take them to Fort Worth to my brother's house."

That caught me by surprise. "You're going to stay with Ozzy's brother? Which one, John or Robert?"

"Robert. I got to know him in some of the letters we exchanged."

"Yeah, but why are you doing this? You don't have to be Lee Harvey Oswald anymore. You can go back to being Alek J. Hidell."

"I thought about that, but then I realized I might be valuable to you with the identity I now have. Maybe some other assignment will need my bona fides."

"I don't know how much work there is for a U.S. Marine who defected to the Soviet Union, especially in Texas."

Lee and I walked several feet behind Marina and the baby.

"I'll find some kind of work—I'm not worried."

"You did us a huge service, Lee. Your 'Marine defector' letters were invaluable. We learned that the Russian people would never rise up against their totalitarian government. The Russians don't trust anyone, even other Russians."

"Yeah, Russians are pretty strange ducks. They tend to view other Russians as enemies, with the exception of their own family and closest friends. The typical Russian citizen actually expects the government to protect them from their own neighbors. Everyone is suspicious of everyone else."

"When I conceived of Project Cocoon almost five years ago, I hoped it would give us some important insight into how much popular support the Kremlin leaders had from the Russian people."

"Patrick, you are looking at the concept of support with American eyes. The average man on the street doesn't have much influence over the government's policies or their leaders. Besides, they would be the first to tell you that the Kremlin doesn't care what they think. I drank a lot of vodka and had a lot of philosophical conversations about the government—the Russians understand the concept of democracy, but I don't think they understand what freedom really is."

"Why do you say that?"

"The Russian people feel that they are unique—different from the rest of the world. They feel surrounded on all sides by enemies they think are bent on their destruction. To them, government means order. The government is in place to preserve the order. The government's function is to be strong and effective."

"To protect them from their enemies," I asked.

"More than that—they see the world as trying to keep them in their place—to keep them from becoming a world leader. The Kremlin protects their world interests—they would never rise up against the Kremlin."

"Do you think that the Soviet Union is a dangerous enemy?"

"The Communist leaders can do anything they want—the people will never interfere with the government as long as it protects them. I guess it depends on the leadership within the Soviet Union. Do I think that Khrushchev is dangerous—hell yes."

"Lee, do you have any regrets? I am more than satisfied with your work—but I have to be honest here. I've worried that you would regret getting involved with this project."

"Nope. Not one. I got to see my parent's native country, and I'm glad I won't have to see my daughter grow up there. If anything, Patrick, this project has made me appreciate America more than I ever did before."

"I owe you and Ozzie a huge debt of gratitude. You bravely assumed another man's complete life history and risked your own life to voluntarily slip behind the Iron Curtain and live with our enemy for over two years. Your letters, journals and stories provided our Agency with invaluable insight into the closed society of the Soviet Union. You proved how invaluable human intelligence gathering can be. Electronic intelligence gathering will never replace it, as far as I'm concerned."

"I went into the project with my eyes open—you didn't force me."

"But you had to pretend to betray your own country in order to gain entry to the Soviet Union; you will be seen as a traitor in the eyes of most Americans, especially the ones who grew up with Ozzy."

"I did it because I love my country—and it was an adventure." Finally, I saw A.J.'s smile.

"You are truly an American hero—of the highest order, and Ozzy is too.

I can't tell anyone about your bravery until this Cold War is over. I hope I can make it up to you then."

Lee laughed in a self-deprecating way, "The real Lee Harvey Oswald is the hero. He has sacrificed everything—his name—his life story—to insure my safety."

Lee looked proudly at his wife and daughter. "How is Ozzie doing these days?"

"Ozzy lives under an assumed name with a whole new identity somewhere in the United States. I promised him I wouldn't reveal his identity to anyone, even you. I promised him that one day I'd restore his name. You know what he said?"

"What?"

"'I promised you I would never let you down, and you promised me the same thing. You've always been a man of your word.' That was the last time I talked to Ozzy."

"I hope I get a chance to shake his hand again one day."

"I do too."

IN JULY, SAM Giancana asked me to meet him at the Cal-Neva Lodge in Lake Tahoe rather than his casino in Las Vegas. I was somewhat apprehensive since the last time I had seen Giancana had been in Chicago.

When I arrived, Giancana himself genially escorted me out to a secluded patio that afforded us a maximum amount of privacy. He poured us a drink and offered me an expensive Cuban cigar. As I inhaled the rich tobacco, I began to relax. It appeared that this was a meeting just between Giancana and me.

We began by discussing Operation Mongoose. Johnny Roselli had been helping me run the program through his contacts in Cuba. Giancana wanted me to tell him how the Agency thought the program was going, and I assured him we were confident we would succeed in killing Castro and return Cuba to a democratic country. I also expressed my gratitude that Giancana had stuck with us even after Allen Dulles and Richard Bissell had been fired.

Giancana responded that he was satisfied with our Agency partnership. Through our combined efforts, Cuba was once again destined to be a country where people would be free to utilize the special talents of Giancana's whole organization, specifically gambling and prostitution.

"Patrick, this whole arrangement is working even better than I had hoped. Ya know, we've all invested millions in Cuba over the years. I think it's only natural we help each other out in solving this Castro problem together. You guys actually make good business partners, you know that?"

I smiled but did not acknowledge his comment. I didn't want to be a partner with him in any way, but this fight against the spread of Communism created some strange and unlikely alliances. I personally didn't care what he and his people did as long as it didn't involve any Communist influence. He assured me we were on the same page—I was as pragmatic about this as he was.

"But I do have to say I am concerned about the loss of both Dulles and Bissell. I knew those guys. I trusted their word. If they promised something, I knew I could count on it. I don't know the new guys that took their place. Because I don't know them, I don't trust them. I do, however, trust you. I trust you because I have put you through the test, and you passed. That counts for a lot as far as I am concerned. When you ask me to do things, I know that you'll protect my back, just as I will protect yours."

Giancana sat back in his chair and studied me for a moment.

"You know why I like you, Patrick? You got balls. Derek Ruger's been telling me all about you. I like what I'm hearing and I like what you're doing."

He paused to puff on his cigar. "You ever heard of *omerta*?"

"*Omerta*?"

"Yeah, *omerta*. Let me tell you a story," he said. "Back in the late 1920's, my kid brother, Chuckie, him and some friends stole thirty-five dollars from an old dago pie-man who used to earn his living around our neighborhood. The dumb wop had left his moneybag on the front seat of his truck, and Chuckie and his friends boosted it. Like stupid kids do, they went and spent the money on a bicycle and some roller skates—you know, kid's stuff. When I got home, I found him playin' with his new toys. The problem was, when I asked him where he had gotten them, he lied to me. He claimed he got 'em from some friends. Well, Patrick, that just fuckin' pissed me off. I picked that little liar up by the scruff of his neck, and I smacked him in the mouth a few times and yelled at him, 'Don't you *ever* lie to me! Understand?'

"He said he understood, and when I once again asked him how he got his new toys, the little shit lied to me once more! That just made me madder and madder. I smacked him around some more, and he still kept lying to me. Finally, after I kicked him in the ribs like you would a fuckin' dog, he finally told me the truth. So you know what I did next?"

I hesitated for another moment, "You praised him?"

He slouched back in his chair with a big grin on his face. "Fuck no, I beat the livin' shit out of him for being a goddamned stool pigeon! I screamed at him, 'Never, *ever*, be a stool pigeon, Chuckie. That'll get you killed!'"

Sam hit his fist into the palm of his hand making a smacking noise.

"I beat him up to teach him a lesson he would never forget. As I beat him, I kept repeating, 'This is for your own good.' I said, 'Chuckie! You ever heard of *omerta*? You keep your eyes and ears open and your fuckin' mouth *shut*! That's *omerta*!'"

He resumed puffing on his cigar, and then said with satisfaction, "*Omerta*."

He pointed at me with his cigar in order to reinforce his point. "Never forget that word, Patrick. Never rat out anybody. Especially me! Don't you ever rat me out! You got that?"

"Yes sir."

Fuck no—I didn't need a lesson on *omerta*—I vividly remembered what had happened to Action Jackson.

AFTER OUR MEETING, Giancana invited me to stay for dinner with him and "a few of his friends" who turned out to be none other than Frank Sinatra, Peter Lawford, and Marilyn Monroe. As I reflected on all of this later, I realized he had planned this particular evening very carefully. Everything was designed for a specific reason, from the people he invited to dine with me to the main subject of the evening—the Kennedys. Everyone had their own particular ax to grind with the President and his little brother, Bobby.

Giancana was a very cordial host who served us a terrific dinner with lots of good Italian food, wine, and other booze. He sat at the head of the table with Marilyn and me on his right, and Frank and Peter on his left. He was especially attentive to Marilyn's needs constantly refilling her wineglass and encouraging her to drink up. She was pretty well intoxicated by the time we got to dessert.

I complimented her performance at the President's birthday party—I told her she was the very epitome of a glamorous Hollywood movie star. She coyly whispered that she was sewn into the five thousand dollar see-through dress without any underwear so that she could sing "Happy Birthday" to Jack. I joked about how angry my wife was at the way she had flirted with the President.

This night, Marilyn wasn't a glamorous movie star. Instead, she was well on her way to becoming a completely besotted drunk. She listlessly picked at her food and drained glass after glass of wine while Giancana topped off her glass every time she drank from it. She either giggled inappropriately or stared zombie-like into space.

After dinner, the topic of conversation turned to the Kennedys. Giancana's jovial demeanor disappeared as he raged over how the Kennedys had double-crossed him.

"Jesus, if ever there was a crook, it's Joe Kennedy."

He regaled us with how Joe Kennedy had manipulated the stock market crash of 1929 and how Joe had personally made millions of dollars from short-selling stock during the crash. He told us that Joe Kennedy had *twice* begged the Chicago Outfit to protect him from being killed by other mobsters that he had angered. It seems that while bootlegging alcohol back in the 1920's, the Purple Gang in Detroit had placed a contract out for Kennedy because he had been bringing bootleg rum through their territory without asking their permission. Kennedy begged the Chicago bosses to intervene on his behalf. It had cost Old Joe a lot of money to save himself from the Purple Gang's hired killers.

"Now, you'd think any man in his right mind might learn a valuable lesson from that incident, but believe it or not, Kennedy didn't learn. He didn't learn, the SOB. He insulted Frank Costello in May of l956. Kennedy owed him some money, but he thought he could duck Frank. Costello finally put out a contract on him."

Giancana stopped in the middle of his story. He looked over at Marilyn, "You need some wine, doll?"

Marilyn drunkenly nodded.

Giancana filled her glass then resumed, "Frank was pissed. He called me and said, 'Who in the fuck does he think he is? We *made* that asshole millions of dollars, and I can un-make him, too.' I personally had to do a lot to straighten out the mess he got his sorry ass into."

The entire room was quiet as Giancana gave the details.

"Kennedy came to me and said he needed my help. I asked him why, and he said he had gotten himself into a misunderstanding with Frank Costello back in New York. I asked him what the nature of the misunderstanding was, and he told me that Frank wanted him to be the front man on a real estate deal that he was setting up. Joe said he refused to do it. I asked him 'Why?' You know what he said to me?"

"No, Sam," Sinatra answered, "What did he say?"

"He said, 'Look, I'm in a sensitive position given my son's political career.' Can you believe that? He went on to snivel, 'I can't afford the association right now. And my son, Jack, can't afford the association right now, either.' I couldn't fuckin' believe what I was hearing!"

Peter Lawford spoke up, "That sounds like something Joe would say."

"Well, it was the *wrong* thing to say. It was an insult to me, and it was an insult to Frank Costello. I started to get really mad at him when the old asshole whined: 'You don't understand…my son Jack is moving up in politics…I'm hoping he'll be President someday. Now, I can't jeopardize that, can I?' I remarked that his son had been making quite a name for himself and that old mick said, 'He has…and he'll continue to…as long as some ugly skeleton doesn't pop out of a closet. That, my friend, would be political suicide.'"

"Whadaya know about that!" Sinatra exclaimed. "He tried to sell out his own son to save his life. What a piece of shit."

Giancana puffed on a new cigar, "Oh, he didn't try to sell out his own son—he *did* sell him out! He whined and sobbed and whimpered, and I was getting sick of listening to him until he promised, 'Talk to Frank. If I live, I can help my son get to the White House. Isn't that what we've all wanted all along—a guy on the inside? You help me now, Sam, and I'll see to it that Chicago—that you—can sit in the goddamned Oval Office if you want. Then you'll have the President's ear. But I just need time. I get pushed, and I don't think my son has the experience, or the contacts, to see him through a presidential race. Do you understand now why I want you to talk to Costello?'"

"He really said that?" Marilyn asked in wide-eyed wonder, her voice slurred by alcohol. She struggled just to pay attention.

"Oh, he said a *lot* more," Giancana boasted. "He gave me his *word* that the day his son was elected, that's the day Sam Giancana is elected too. He promised, 'He'll be your man. I swear to that. My son—the President of the United States—will owe you his father's life. He won't refuse you, ever. You have my word!' Can you fuckin' believe that?"

"And we know how good Joe Kennedy's word is, don't we?" Sinatra bitterly observed. Everyone around the table nodded in agreement.

Giancana wasn't done, "I'll tell you all something else. From that day forward, whenever I had a gin, I made sure it was a *Gordon's Gin* because that's the brand that Old Joe imported. Whenever I had *Gordon's Gin*, it always reminded me that Joe Kennedy would sell anything to save his own skin. His liquor business, the Senate, the presidency, the White House, even his own son."

Sam Giancana was on a roll, enumerating all of the complaints he had amassed against the Kennedy family over the years. Peter Lawford suddenly became engrossed in moving the breadcrumbs from his side of the tablecloth into a tidy pile. Frank, on the other hand, sat as a silent observer occasionally nodding his head in agreement. At one point, he started to make a point of his own, but then stopped.

"I'm tellin' ya, when Joe Kennedy wanted our money for his kid's presidential campaign, did I say no? When he needed extra votes from Cook County, did I say no? Whenever the old man or his boys needed a dame, did I say no?" Giancana's voice escalated with each rhetorical question he asked. "And what about the time Jack stupidly got married without his old man's blessing…?"

"You mean his father didn't like Jackie?" Marilyn had suddenly awakened out of her stupor and interrupted his tirade.

He shot her a withering look and explained, "No, I don't mean Jackie. I meant that Durie Malcolm broad that he ran off with."

"I didn't know Jack had been married before," Marilyn struggled to get her words out. She had a drop of spittle in the corner of her mouth.

"No doll, I don't suppose he told you that. Nobody is supposed to know about that. That's because Johnny Roselli does such great work. The old man made Jack get an annulment, and he wanted it done without any publicity. It seems that such an *entanglement* might look bad to the voters." Giancana intentionally stressed the word entanglement to express his sarcasm over the whole mess. "So, the Catholic archdiocese removed the marriage from the Church registries, and Johnny Roselli removed the Church records from the Church offices."

Frank let out a slow whistle. He obviously had no idea that "Chicky Baby" had been married before. Peter's eyes met Frank's eyes silently imploring him not to ask him any questions.

"I'll tell you something else. You wanna know why Bobby was named Attorney General?" Giancana paused to look at me.

"The old man's got so many skeletons in his closet he could go into the funeral home business. He needed Bobby to keep the Justice Department from looking into the Kennedy family business dealings. At first, I was glad that Bobby could keep tabs on the Justice Department because it never hurts to have friends in high places. But I'm tellin' ya, that kid is a cocksucker just like his old man. He can't be trusted either."

Giancana's eyes conveyed a cold hatred for all the Kennedys. He claimed that Bobby Kennedy sent government agents to follow his brother Chuck. Thoroughly annoyed by the government surveillance, Chuck had gone to him and begged, "Can't you get Kennedy to lay off?"

Any control Giancana thought he had over the Kennedys had all but gone. It seemed the Kennedys were doing everything they could to weasel out of any obligations they owed to Giancana and his friends. He made it very clear that no one double-crossed Sam Giancana.

When Marilyn excused herself from the table to go to the bathroom, Giancana lowered his voice and bragged that he had wiretapped the Kennedys on Marilyn's telephone.

"That mick cocksucker, Bobby, we got him on the wire calling me a guinea greaseball! Can you believe that? My millions were good enough for 'em, weren't they? The votes I muscled for 'em were also good enough to get Jack elected. So now I'm not good enough for them? *I'm* a fuckin' greaseball, am I?"

His rage rose to a crescendo, "I even come to find out Bobby has called me a *dago scum*, and he plans to have the fuckin' FBI get rid of *me*! There's no fuckin' way I'll let that happen!"

Sinatra was a little shaken up. "Sam—man, how did you ever manage to wiretap Marilyn's phones? That's pretty heavy duty stuff!"

Giancana calmed down enough to scoff, "I had some help from some of my real friends in Washington."

He made it a point to look my way. "You know Bernie Spindel? They don't call him the 'King of the Wiremen' for nothing! Bernie's done work for Patrick's people, and now he does some work for me. I'll tell you something—I've had every one of Kennedy's play toys under surveillance for quite a while now. Marilyn, Angie Dickinson, Judith, that Meyer broad, they're all on tape and singing like songbirds. Shit, Marilyn's even been telling her friends she's 'in love with Bobby.'" He raised his voice in a mocking girlish tone, "Ain't that precious?"

Frank laughed heartily. Peter tucked his head sheepishly.

The relationships that Sam Giancana had nurtured were turning to ashes. The Kennedys, reneging on a number of promises, sought to erase any trace of their association with Giancana. Giancana's New Orleans associate, Carlos Marcello, was even kidnapped under orders from Bobby Kennedy, flown to Guatemala one night without money or I.D. or even a single change of clothes, and dropped off in the jungle. In essence, he was deported without due process—forced to hike through the jungles of Guatemala, wearing only his custom-made shoes and Italian suit, which further humiliated Marcello. He almost died before he eventually snuck back into the United States. He was a fugitive "in his own damned country."

Giancana fumed, "If I was gonna get fucked, at least it shoulda felt good!" Then he laughed, "Do you guys know that this place used to be a long-time hang-out of Joe Kennedy's? That old asshole would come out here all the time to place bets and bang my broads, and his sons are just like him. Hell, we used to have all kinds of working girls up here because those Kennedy boys all loved sex, and the kinkier, the better. They'd fuck 'em two or more at a time in the hallways, the closets, the bathtubs, the fuckin' floor—anywhere but the goddamned beds. They put on airs that they were better than everybody else. That always ate at me. Who the fuck do they think they are?"

Sinatra said that he was pissed off because he had effectively been blackballed from the President's list of friends. Frank made it a point to tell us he never forgot a friend, and he certainly didn't expect his friends to forget him.

"I'll tell ya, friends don't treat friends that way," he said, "After all I did for that prick—all the dames—all the dough."

Frank had raised enormous sums of money for Jack's presidential campaign with his Hollywood friends, not to mention his connections with the Outfit. Now that Jack was in the White House, he had expected "President Chicky Baby" to invite him to important state dinners and to entertain important visitors. None of those invitations had ever materialized. He said he had recently invited Jack to come and stay at his newly remodeled Palm Springs estate, but Jack had even spurned that invitation.

Peter Lawford was another mess. He moaned that even though he was married to a Kennedy sister, he was also shut out of the President's social circle now that Jack had access to the best pussy on the planet. Jack no longer needed Peter Lawford. Peter was an embarrassment. To make matters worse, Bobby Kennedy had a nineteen-page FBI report documenting Frank Sinatra's underworld connections. Jack humiliated Lawford by making Peter personally deliver the report to Sinatra.

Giancana looked around and finally noticed that Marilyn hadn't made it back from the bathroom yet.

"Hey Frank! Go and see where that fuckin' cunt is. She's probably passed out with her head in the toilet bowl." As Frank got up out of his chair and started for the hallway, Giancana hollered, "Make sure she ain't puking on my rugs! If she does, use her fuckin' hair to mop it up, ya hear me?"

Giancana boasted, "Ya know, when I bought this place, I had it wired from top to bottom. Frank would flip out if he knew that I knew what he did here."

Peter made a sickly noise and looked ashen. Giancana noticed and said mockingly, "Yeah, I got you on tape too with all of your nigger girls. You don't have much ability to satisfy a woman, do you? I heard they call you 'Peter Rabbit' behind your back. You're pretty much a one-shot wonder, aren't ya, a real sixty-second sprinter, huh?"

Lawford got up out of his chair. "I need a refill," he said in his haughty British accent. "Where are the drinks?"

Giancana replied with disdain as Lawford slunk out of the room, "You know where the fuck they are."

Giancana blew out a cloud of cigar smoke. "You know, I once bragged that we were all gonna be invited to the 'Greatest Show on Earth.' I said it would be well worth the price of admission—every goddamned dollar. Well, you wanna know something, Patrick? It ain't been worth it—not at all."

He sat pensively for a few moments. "I'm getting' tired of Frank's lame promises of intervention with the Kennedys. He's shot his wad with me."

Giancana was pissed off at Sinatra because Frank had been his middleman with the Kennedys. Sinatra had tried to play the "big shot" with Jack, and it had backfired on him, ruining his relationship with the President. But it had also ruined Giancana's access to Jack. He told me he had almost had Frank whacked for fucking up but had changed his mind.

"I guess I like the guy. Shit, it's not his fault that the Kennedys are assholes. But if I didn't like him, you can be goddamned sure he'd be a dead man!"

"Guess who we found?" Frank and Peter re-entered the room with Marilyn. Peter held onto her elbow, but she pushed him away. Her eyes were bloodshot, her lipstick was smeared around her mouth, and her hair was a mess. She shuffled slowly as she felt along the edge of the wall for support. Frank finally took her arms and guided her to her seat next to Giancana.

"How ya feelin', doll?" Giancana asked.

Bleary-eyed, she slowly shook her head and reached for a cigarette.

"She was passed out on the floor next to the shitter. She had her mouth against the side of the goddamned toilet," Frank said in disgust.

Giancana said, "That's OK. I know all the places that mouth has been. Believe me, my toilet's cleaner than most of them."

They all laughed as Marilyn silently struggled to light her smoke. Her hands shook as she tried to get the cigarette into the flame of her Zippo. Finally, Giancana reached over and gently steadied her hand.

"You want some more to drink, doll?" he softly cooed to her.

She shook her head "no." Her head hung down heavily.

"We were just talking about Jack and Bobby Kennedy," he delicately murmured to her. "You wanna add anything to the conversation?"

She perked up for a moment. "They're a couple of real bastards," she snarled. "I hate them both."

"You want some water, hon? Maybe that'll help ya to talk," Giancana gently asked.

Marilyn nodded her head, and he poured her some ice water from the pitcher on the table. After gulping down most of the glass, she came to life. She wiped her mouth on the sleeve of her blouse, smearing it with lipstick, and then she looked across the table at Frank and Peter, her eyes streaked with mascara.

"They're both assholes!" she spit out, "They used me, and now they won't even talk to me. You can't treat me like that." At first defiant, then silent, she grimaced in a torrent of pain.

She had been used by virtually every man that had ever touched her. Many of those men were mob connected. Johnny Roselli met Marilyn through his Hollywood connections with Joe Schenck, a powerful Hollywood producer, who as an aging seventy-year-old bedded Monroe. Marilyn knew that her fame and success would depend on bartering her body. Roselli introduced her to Giancana; the Chicago mob began to promote her career. Giancana introduced her to Harry Cohn, another powerful Hollywood producer, and Cohn and Schenck exchanged Marilyn's sexual favors for tiny parts in films. It was the classic story of the Hollywood casting couch.

Marilyn enumerated a long list of famous political figures from around the world that she had seduced. I had recently learned that our Agency had employed her services through Robert Maheu, our contact man in Las Vegas. Apparently, Marilyn used her charms to compromise world leaders from the Middle East to Asia. President Sukarno of Indonesia was just one of the names Marilyn mentioned.

She was now so drunk that any inhibitions she might have had were effectively gone. She described how she first went to bed with Jack back in Hollywood in the 1950's. She told us how she had been fucking both Jack and Bobby, and while she had been with the President strictly for sex, she had fallen in love with Bobby. In March, she started screwing Bobby and claimed they had formed a deep and meaningful relationship.

I looked over at Giancana. He smirked and didn't say a word.

But now, she sobbed, he wouldn't even take her phone calls. She told us that when she belittled him as the "Family Man of the Year," as he had recently been nationally named, he became violently angry with her, especially when she tried to call him at home one night in Virginia.

"I warned that motherfucker that I would blow the lid off the whole damn thing if he continued to shut me out. I think I finally got through to him that I mean business. I'm *not* going to let those two assholes treat me like nothing more than a piece of meat!"

She knocked over her empty wine glass in her fury. "They think they're such big shots! Well, let me tell you something—they're not that 'big' if you know what I mean." And to illustrate the point even further, she held her thumb and forefinger about two inches apart holding her hand up for all of us to see.

"Oh my *Gawd*," Peter exclaimed, surprised at the demeaning gesture. Frank, Giancana, and I laughed uproariously. Marilyn looked around the table seriously. When she saw the reaction her comment had elicited, she smiled a boozy smile, too. That old adage about "no fury like a woman scorned" was plainly on display.

After a while, her tirade ran out of steam as the alcohol completely took over. "I wanna go to bed now," she softly whined. Giancana said he would help her. The evening broke up at that point.

No one was in the mood for any more "F-U-N" tonight.

THE FIRST WEEK of August, Tracy Barnes stopped by my desk with a small package wrapped in brown paper.

"Patrick, we need to have you go back out to California and deliver this to your friend Giancana," he told me.

I looked at him quizzically as I surveyed its small size. "Why don't you just mail it?"

"We can't. It's too important. It's a special present from your old boss, Dr. Gottlieb. We can't afford to lose it in the mail."

I was surprised by the request, "Do you want to tell me about it?"

"Nope," he said simply. "Just take it to Giancana. He'll fill you in."

When I returned to California, Giancana cordially greeted me. I was surprised to see Derek Ruger there, along with two other men that I didn't know. They were introduced to me as Needles and Mugsy.

"We've cooked up a surprise for that cocksucking Attorney General. Our mutual friends want me to have you stick around and help us out," Giancana informed me.

I wondered what the little surprise was about. Uneasiness gnawed at me ever since I had delivered the package from Dr. Gottlieb, the mad scientist.

Late in the evening on Sunday, August 4, I joined Raoul—Ruger had me calling him that name ever since we trained together for the Bay of Pigs invasion—Needles, and Mugsy for a trip to Brentwood, a wealthy suburb of Los Angeles. Mugsy navigated our car through the shady tree-lined streets. He pulled up behind a utility truck parked at a curb in the dark, quiet neighborhood. Quickly dousing the lights and exiting the car, we climbed into the back of the darkened truck.

The truck was a cleverly disguised surveillance unit. One man was sitting at a console with a set of headphones on. He welcomed us in with a wave of his hand, told me his name was Bernie Spindel, and turned his attention back to the console. The small, lighted dials with jumping needles indicated something was going on.

Bernie looked at Needles, "He just arrived a little while ago. He's got someone else with him. He's gone into the back bedroom with her, alone."

Needles nodded and didn't say a word, and neither did Mugsy. It was clear to me that they knew what was going on. Ruger was also quiet, but he leaned toward me when I whispered, "What's going on?"

He looked at me with some degree of surprise. "What do you mean? You don't know what this is?"

I shook my head and he said indulgently, "Bernie here has Marilyn Monroe's house wired and…" His explanation was interrupted by a sharp glare and an urgent "Shhush!" from Needles.

Ruger gave him a bored smart-ass glance in return and leaned to whisper in my ear. "We've caught Bobby Kennedy in the house with her. We're here to create a major embarrassment for him." He didn't elaborate, and I didn't have the nerve to ask if this was some kind of set up to blackmail Bobby.

Bernie tried to hand Needles another set of headphones, but he waved his hand that he didn't want to listen in. Mugsy shrugged his shoulders and put the headphones on without comment. After a few minutes, he began to bob his head back and forth as if listening to music. Bernie turned and looked at Needles, a smirking leer on his face. Then he made a circle with his left hand's forefinger and thumb and proceeded to violate that circle with the stiffened forefinger of his right hand. It was a universal male signal.

Ruger saw that and immediately whispered "Hey!" at Bernie, and he pointed at his own ears. Bernie handed him another headset. Ruger quickly started grinning as he, too, eavesdropped on what was happening in the house. He then got Bernie's attention and pointed to me. Bernie produced yet another set of headphones and handed them to me. I slipped them on, unsure of what I was going to be hearing.

What I heard were the unmistakable sounds of two people making love. Marilyn's voice was every bit as distinctive as Bobby Kennedy's voice. Both of their voices were clearly identifiable.

The words, the exhortations, and the physical sounds mesmerized me. Ruger began to grab his crotch obscenely and act rather juvenile. I had never even imagined Ruger could have a playful side, but he was cutting-up for the benefit of amusing the three older men.

It was apparent that Needles was all business because he never acknowledged a single thing Ruger did—hell, he never even *blinked*. However, Mugsy smiled and Bernie nodded his head in agreement at Derek's antics.

After coitus, the mood completely changed. Marilyn's soft voice became strident. She yelled at Bobby for leading her on, for not being responsive to her needs. Surprisingly, he got just as angry in return. The two of them carried their argument out of the bedroom and back into the living room, where the other man had been waiting the entire time.

Marilyn's agitation and anger soon escalated into full-blown hysteria. She taunted Bobby about Jack, threatening to tell the public what the three of them had all been up to. Bobby was equally angry in return, telling her that it was over between them all and that neither he nor his brother would tolerate being threatened by her in any way.

Finally, in exasperation, he ordered the other man to give her a shot to "calm her down." Marilyn evidently allowed herself to be voluntarily sedated, for shortly afterward, we could hear Bobby and the other man leaving the house.

Soon we could only hear Marilyn snoring heavily through the hidden microphones. Needles held his hands palms up in a questioning fashion, and Bernie confirmed, "She's sound asleep."

"You got the stuff?" Needles asked Mugsy. Mugsy nodded and slipped out of the truck, returning a moment later with the small package Tracy Barnes had asked me to deliver to Giancana. Needles took the package and carefully opened it, revealing a small box containing what looked like four foil-wrapped capsules, all about the size of my thumb. He slipped the foil packets into his coat pocket. I suddenly felt cold. I ran my hand over my forehead and was surprised to find that I was perspiring.

"Let's go, fellas" he gruffly ordered. We followed Needles out of the truck and a very short distance to Marilyn's house. As Ruger slipped around the back of the house, he handed me a pair of rubber gloves. Needles and Mugsy were already putting theirs on. A minute later, the front door of the house swung open. Ruger beckoned us to join him inside.

He led us to a bedroom in the back where we found the most famous sex symbol in the world sprawled nude face-up across her bed. She never even had a chance to struggle before Ruger and Mugsy were upon her, holding her down.

Marilyn's eyes popped open in surprise and turned to stark terror when the two men jumped her. Before she could cry out, Needles had clamped his hand across her mouth.

"Don't scream—don't say a fuckin' word!" he hissed at her. He produced some heavy tape and applied it to her mouth to muffle any noise she might try and make.

Needles growled at me, "Hold her still," so I positioned myself at the head of the bed to hold her left wrist. A dim flicker of recognition swept across her face when she looked up and saw me. Mugsy held her right wrist while Ruger moved down and straddled her ankles so that she couldn't kick out at us.

"Ooooh, these are nice, aren't they, Mugsy?" I looked up and saw that Ruger was boldly running a free hand over her breasts.

I was bewildered about what was going on. What were we doing here? What in the hell was going on? They weren't going to rape her, were they? How was any of this going to teach Bobby Kennedy a lesson? A million thoughts and emotions swept through my mind in those first few seconds we held her down. I remembered those three days with Action Jackson, and I hoped I wasn't being tested again. I quickly discounted the idea. I knew this wasn't the time to start asking questions.

"Hey, Mugsy, you wanna see some Attorney General *love spooge?*" I looked down and Ruger had his hand between the frightened woman's legs.

"Hey, asshole, cut it out! You want me to tell Giancana what you're up to?" Needles threatened.

Chastised, Ruger quickly withdrew his hand.

"Let's get this over with," Needles said. "Flip her over."

They labored to turn Marilyn over onto her stomach. "Hey, McCarthy, you help too. Hold her still."

I helped hold her down although she really wasn't putting up any fight. I looked toward a large reddish brown dresser. It must have been from Mexico. It had an unusual pattern of rectangles carved on the side. I counted five large rectangles and four smaller ones.

Needles reached into his coat pocket and retrieved the foil packets he had placed there. He handed two of them to me and said, "Here. Hold these." Then he proceeded to remove the foil coverings from the other two and showed me the two gelatin capsules.

"These any good?" he asked me pointedly.

"I don't know. What are they?"

"What do you mean, 'What are they?' *You* brought 'em. You mean to say, you don't even know what the fuck they are?" he eyed me suspiciously.

"No, I don't," I truthfully replied.

Needles, Mugsy, and Ruger all exchanged worried looks. "If this doesn't work," Needles warned me, "you'll have to deal with Giancana. We're not gonna."

"Okay," I agreed, "but what's it supposed to be?"

Needles cut his eyes at me, "It's a special kind of sleepin' pill. Our little 'Sleepin' Beauty' here is gonna take it and go to sleep, only her 'Prince Charmin'' ain't gonna be able to wake her up—ever."

He laughed at his own joke, while looking at Mugsy and Ruger to see if they thought it was funny too. Whether they thought it was funny or not, they laughed anyway.

His admission struck me hard. All three men looked closely at me as I realized with horror what was about to happen. I was there to participate in the *murder* of Marilyn Monroe—I felt sick.

Satisfied that I wasn't going to try to stop them, or try to back out, Needles proceeded with the plan. He methodically pushed both capsules into Marilyn's rectum and held his thumb in her to keep her from expelling them. I looked toward the dresser again. There were rectangles within rectangles.

She was already so out of it from the other sedatives that Kennedy's friend had administered that she simply lay there docilely as the medicine began to take effect.

"What's in that stuff, Needles?" Mugsy asked.

Needles described it matter-of-factly, "It's supposed to be some kind of suppository filled with a lethal dose of sedatives." He nodded his head at me, "Our friends said that it would be too tough to make her to take this much stuff orally because she might puke it back up. We also might bruise her if we forced her to take it by her mouth. Plus, if she were somehow found in time, a hospital might be able to pump her stomach and save her. This way, it gets straight into her bloodstream. There won't be nothin' in her stomach to pump out, and no autopsy is gonna find this stuff either. No one is gonna think to look up her pooper for it."

As I looked down on poor Marilyn, I felt deeply sorry for her. I began to softly stroke her hair, trying my best to relax her as much as I could. Her breathing became more and more labored as the drugs invaded her system and did their deadly work. She was dying; I hoped it felt like a deeply satisfying sleep.

She was unconscious in only a matter of minutes. Needles sensed she was going fast. He lightly slapped the side of her face a few times to see if it would elicit a reaction, which it didn't. Satisfied she was quickly slipping beyond the range of help, he carefully removed the tape from her mouth and wiped her face clean with his handkerchief.

He then lifted his head toward the ceiling and said, "Hey, Bernie, come on in and get your stuff." He must have thought Bernie was still listening to his microphones.

"I'm already on it," a voice said from the hallway, which startled us because we didn't even know he was in the house. Bernie was feverishly working to remove his listening gear.

Needles turned to Ruger and noted, "The police will be crawling all over this place in a few hours. No sense in arousing any suspicions about what just went on here."

Still shocked by what I had just seen, I asked, "What the hell is going on?"

Mugsy looked at Needles as though I was retarded. Ruger turned his head away from me and chuckled almost self-consciously. Needles, however, didn't say a thing.

Mugsy chortled, "What's goin' on? What do you think's goin' on? We just killed the Attorney General's girlfriend. In a few hours, the world is gonna think that she killed herself because of him. The lying prick will be ruined and out of our lives. Him and his brother are both gonna have to resign because of this mess that they got themselves into."

Now it all made sense. Oh my God, would *this* ever produce a major scandal. The most famous movie star in the world commits suicide after her affair with Attorney General Robert F. Kennedy ended. Bobby's political career would be over, and his brother's whole administration would be crippled. If it was discovered that the Attorney General had administered sedatives to her just prior to her death, and her death was discovered to be due to an overdose of sedatives, people would believe that he killed her to keep their affair quiet. He might actually be accused of killing her. I could easily imagine the tabloid headlines: Attorney General Murders Marilyn Monroe.

At the very least, the mob would no longer have to worry about Bobby Kennedy coming after them anymore.

"This is truly Machiavellian," I murmured aloud.

"Yeah, ain't it?" Needles agreed. "Mooney's a fuckin' smart guy." At first, I didn't know who Mooney was, but then I remembered that "Mooney" was the nickname that Sam Giancana's family and friends used.

Giancana had tricked me into taking part in this plan without me even suspecting I was getting involved. He now owned me because I had just helped to murder Marilyn Monroe. He could blackmail me forever. I shook my head in disbelief—that explained why he had warned me about *omerta*. Here was one more item for my mental box.

I wondered how much the Agency, as well as others in D.C., were involved. Maybe even the Patriots were part of it. Tracy Barnes had told me, *"Patrick, we need to have you go back out to California and deliver this to your friend Sam…It's a very special present from your old boss, Dr. Gottlieb, and we can't afford to lose it in the mail…Giancana will fill you in."*

Was this some kind of sanctioned revenge for the firing of Allen Dulles and Richard Bissell? Frankly, I didn't know, but I did know that there were scores of people at the Agency who were still enraged over the way Jack had blamed them for the failure and the embarrassment of the Bay of Pigs fiasco. The Giancana people were riled enough to bring down the Kennedys any way they could. A scandal involving sex and suicide, or maybe even murder, could easily topple the Kennedy administration.

I was extremely distressed that Marilyn had to die, but if her death saved the lives of millions of Americans by removing Jack and Bobby from office before Khrushchev acted again, I could somewhat justify it in my own mind.

I snapped out of my daze when Needles barked, "Come on, let's get this wrapped up."

We climbed off Marilyn's almost lifeless body. Needles and Mugsy set about rearranging her on the bed.

"Bernie, ya' done yet?" Needles hollered.

"Yep," the answer came back.

"Then let's get the hell out of here." As we started for the bedroom door, Needles said, "Wait a sec! I almost forgot." He reached into another pocket of his coat and removed a piece of paper, which he carefully placed in plain sight on the nightstand. He saw me and simply explained, "Her suicide note."

We hurried out of the house and headed back to the utility truck.

Mugsy asked, "So now what?"

Bernie told him, "In a few hours, her housekeeper will come back to the house and find the body. She'll call the authorities and all hell will bust out. This place will be thick with cops in a little while."

"Did you get all your stuff out of the house?" Needles grilled him.

"Yeah, I did. I've still got some stuff on the lines, but they'll never find them. I'll be able to monitor what's going on when the police get there."

We got down to Palm Springs a few hours later and met up with Giancana. He was sitting by the telephone at his house when we walked in.

Needles knew that something was wrong. "What's up?" he asked.

Giancana had a dark scowl on his face. "That motherfuckin' cocksucker prick outfoxed us. That's what happened. The stupid cunt of a housekeeper found Monroe's body, but instead of calling the cops, she called somebody who called Kennedy instead. He immediately sent a team of G-men in there to clean the place up and remove the suicide note that you guys left. Peter Lawford and Fred Otash just got to the house to remove anything that they could find that would link that dead cunt to that little prick." He paused to let his frustration build up, and then he exploded, "GODDAMN IT!" at the top of his lungs. Sam Giancana wasn't accustomed to being outsmarted or out maneuvered.

He stood staring out the window, his back toward us. I noticed that his shirt was rumpled. Needles suddenly sneezed, and Giancana turned to face us.

"I called that fuckin' Lawford, and he told me that Bobby ordered him to pick up the bitch's diary and letters. He also said that Bobby ordered Hoover to cleanse the telephone records as well, so that nothing could ever be used to trace their little dead sex-pal back to the Kennedys."

His face darkened with rage. "GOD DAMNED MOTHERFUCKIN' SON OF A BITCH!"

Eager to avoid becoming a target of Giancana's uncontrollable fury, Needles and Mugsy quietly slipped out, dragging Ruger with them. I stayed there.

Giancana finally fixed his eyes on me and said testily, "His damn cover-up's gonna work. Everyone knows that cunt was mentally unstable, and she's tried to take her own life before. Shit, everyone in Hollywood knows she's mentally ill. Her career was in the toilet, and she's crazy as a loon. Everyone will easily believe the story that this was a suicide and nothing more. God damn it—we killed her for nothing."

Giancana was right. The papers made a big deal of her mental and drug problems. The world mourned the tragedy of her sad life.

I returned home shaken and somber. Tracy Barnes and some other people had known of Giancana's plans. It stood to reason that they approved of what went on. Someone had decided to make a move against the Kennedys, and I had been maneuvered into participating. On the airplane all the way back to D.C., I wondered who it was. I thought about poor Marilyn and the reason why I knew she had been sacrificed. Too bad it had all been in vain. And it was especially too bad that Jack and Bobby had gotten away with their treatment of her.

I realized that we had ended up doing the Kennedys a favor. No one would ever know the facts about their relationship with Marilyn Monroe—their secret went to the grave with her.

"Things are not what they seem; or, to be more accurate, they are not only what they seem, but very much else besides."

— Aldous Huxley

The Cuban Missile Crisis

SHORTLY AFTER I returned from California, I turned my attention to Cuba. I had a new office at Langley and an efficient assistant who had prioritized the many reports that I needed to review. I began with the smallest pile. I figured it would give me a feeling of accomplishment just to eliminate one of the piles from my desk.

I sorted through several intelligence reports and began reading one report from a Cuban refugee who had recently arrived in Miami. He told one of our undercover people about a long truck convoy that he had seen in the early morning hours of August fifth. The refugee said: "After about every third truck there was a long flatbed pulled by a tractor-like vehicle. On each vehicle there was a round object as tall as a palm tree and covered by a tarpaulin...I saw between 250 and 300 men, foreigners, standing near parked trucks...."

My heart stopped—this sounded like an eyewitness report of missiles being moved in Cuba. I immediately consulted our ballistic experts who agreed that the convoy had all the marks of missile transportation. I rushed the report to Director McCone's office; he reviewed it and immediately requested an emergency meeting with Secretary of State Dean Rusk and Secretary of Defense Robert McNamara. I accompanied McCone to the White House for the briefing.

I had no way of knowing at the time that the United States would soon be on the brink of nuclear annihilation.

THE REFUGEE'S REPORT was a harbinger of a dangerous situation for the United States. Director McCone forcefully made the case that suspicious military activity in Cuba should be taken as a serious threat to the United States.

"While we were on our way over, our top analysts have been pouring over this. This is not the only report we have received of unusual military activity on the island of Cuba. Our best Agency intelligence assessment strongly indicates the Russians are up to something in Cuba. This warrants serious and immediate consideration by the President."

McNamara and Rusk seemed annoyed with McCone. Their facial expressions betrayed their boredom. Rusk had his face propped up in his hands with his elbows on the table while McNamara slouched back in his chair, peering at us over the top of his glasses.

Patronizing McCone, McNamara spoke up first. "Tell us what you've got for us, Director. Then we'll decide if the President needs to see it."

Director McCone ignored the rebuke, "Our intelligence sources in Cuba are reporting that the Soviet military is actively working on various projects around the island. We believe that they may be placing intercontinental ballistic missiles in Cuba. If that is true, it poses an unprecedented risk to the safety and security of the United States."

I expected both men to sit up straight in their seats, but they didn't twitch a muscle. Rusk, his voice paternal, asked, "What proof do you have of this?"

The Director related the salient details of the various reports. After repeating the eyewitness testimony, he said, "It's becoming apparent to us that the Soviets are there to set up a network of SA-2 anti-aircraft missile batteries in order to protect something from the prying eyes of our U-2 cameras. Those sites could be the next phase of the installation of launch sites for medium range ballistic missiles, or even intercontinental ballistic missiles with nuclear warheads."

Director McCone and I were flabbergasted that Rusk and McNamara brushed us aside.

"That's highly unlikely." McNamara mused, "Why would they risk a confrontation with us?" He turned to Rusk, "Do you think they'd do that?"

"No, of course, not," parroting McNamara, Rusk continued, "That's highly unlikely. They have their hands full with Berlin. I seriously doubt they would also open up another Cold War front in Cuba."

"I agree," McNamara added. "I think it's our recommendation that these reports be dismissed until you have much more credible information in the way of proof of your allegations."

I quickly flashed back to Grant's conversation with me at the Inauguration: *"Did you know that a large number of our military's senior leadership believes* very strongly that their new civilian administration has been subverted by our enemies?....I ran into the Chief of Naval Operations, Admiral Arleigh A. Burke, and he was quite scathing in his appraisal of his inexperienced new boss...he didn't trust our new boy-president, he didn't trust <u>any</u> of Kennedy's people. He told me 'Nearly all of these people are ardent, enthusiastic people without any experience whatever....'"

Neither McNamara nor Rusk had experience in matters of national security. We had presented the White House with a very alarming report. Neither man took us seriously, simply dismissing us as an annoyance to their day.

Director McCone, however, understood the perilous ramifications of our discovery.

"Gentlemen, I'm afraid you might not grasp what is going on here. Khrushchev's simply copying our European strategy with NATO. We've got the Soviet Union surrounded in Europe and Turkey with MRBM's and ICBM's which can easily reach Moscow. We believe he's figured out he can employ that same strategy on us. By moving his own missiles into Cuba, it's just as easy for him to threaten to strike us as it has been for us to threaten to strike him. It's a damn brilliant tactical move."

Premier Khrushchev had always struck me as dangerously shrewd. The President's advisors had no experience with Khrushchev. They remained completely unconvinced of the pending threat.

"Excuse me, sir. May I have permission to add something?" I asked.

"Certainly, Patrick, please by all means." The Director motioned toward the two men seated across from us. They nodded okay—McNamara even gave a "what-can-I-do" palms-up motion with his hands.

"Khrushchev knows all of our early-warning detection systems are arrayed in the northern part of our hemisphere, pointed only toward the direction of the Soviet Union. So if any missiles were launched at the United States from Cuba, they could be upon us so quickly we wouldn't be able to react until it was too late. This, gentlemen, is a very, very serious threat."

Neither man so much as flinched, so I added some more information to our argument. "The very idea that offensive nuclear weapons could be in Cuba, ninety miles from U.S. soil, has caught us all completely by surprise. I did a fast calculation and found this out: medium-range ballistic missiles, which the Pentagon call MRBM's, have a range of about two hundred miles. They could easily reach Miami. ICBM's, or Intercontinental Ballistic Missiles, have a range of about fifteen hundred miles, which would easily put D.C. in range. If missiles could reach D.C., they could reach the Pentagon, which would then place my own house and my family—and your homes and your families—less than two miles from ground zero."

McNamara shrugged his shoulders and stood up from his chair. Rusk quickly followed suit, "Hearsay, gentlemen, hearsay. We would need much more in the way of facts to even consider taking this to the President."

Director McCone growled at me in frustration as the meeting abruptly ended, "Get me the proof I need, Patrick."

We ordered our Agency U-2's to immediately start conducting surveillance flights—they began to criss-cross the island at an altitude of 80,000 feet, snapping continuous photos as we had done over Russia back in the late 1950's.

We finally hit pay dirt on August 29. Our spy plane photographs finally gave us indisputable proof of construction sites containing what looked like long-range Russian SS-4 and SS-5 offensive missiles. SA-2 defensive missile batteries also protectively surrounded the various sites. This looked like a major Soviet military operation.

I returned to the White House with Tracy Barnes and another Agency delegation. We took our proof directly to the President this time; I was stunned at his reaction. Kennedy gave the photographs a cursory examination.

"These are very inconclusive," he said, pooh-poohing our evidence. "How do we know these sites are being manned?"

Tracy Barnes and a couple of other men in our little Agency delegation exchanged quizzical glances. I realized that I still had a picture in my folder that we hadn't shown the President. It was more or less a novelty photo, one that we had joked about in private, but at that particular moment I knew that it was powerful proof of our position.

"I believe this will prove that the sites are being manned," I stated confidently. I stepped forward and handed the picture to Deputy Director Barnes. He looked at it, smugly smiled, and handed it to the President without comment.

This particular picture of a finished missile site, taken by one of our U-2's from 72,000 feet, showed a Soviet soldier sitting on the toilet in an outdoor latrine. The photograph was so clear that you could read the Russian headlines on the newspaper he was reading.

The President looked at the picture, looked up at us, and laughed almost self-consciously. "You take damned good pictures," he sheepishly noted.

His tone became serious. "Put it back in the box and nail it shut," he ordered us. "How many people know about it?"

He wanted to strictly control the information himself. I guessed that he didn't want it passed around D.C. and discussed for fear of engendering even more criticism of his administration. After all, his administration's diplomatic failures of last year were still fresh in everyone's mind. To our amazement, he ordered us to halt the U-2 overflights.

When I got home that night, Pam jokingly remarked, "I don't think

Jackie's going to be able to invite you to dinner with Jack anytime soon—I think you are becoming *persona non grata* around there."

"Well, it's not the first time, and it probably won't be the last," I laughed as I kissed her on the cheek. "What did I do this time?"

She said that she had stopped by the White House in the late afternoon to visit with Jackie in the first family's private quarters. Jack had unexpectedly returned to the living quarters to catch a quick nap because of a long evening schedule ahead. Both she and Jackie tried to keep their voices down so as not to disturb him.

"It was rather difficult to have a private conversation with Jack around," Pam complained. "I know Jackie never feels comfortable saying what's on her mind when someone is within listening distance."

Pam said they heard a door slam, and then they heard Jack yell, "Those damn CIA bastards!"

"I pretended I didn't hear him because I knew he was talking about you guys. He was evidently pretty steamed about something because a few minutes later I overheard him swear, 'I'm going to get those bastards, if it's the last thing I ever do!'"

Pam put her arms around me. "Should I be worried? You're not going to get yourself fired, are you?"

"Sorry you had to hear that, hon," I replied. "You know Jack's had a hard-on for us ever since he took office. I think we're just a convenient whipping boy when things don't go his way. Don't worry about me. You know we would never deliberately do anything to piss Jack off."

Pam was smart enough to read between the lines. She smirked, "That's what I thought. I know that you, Patrick Sean McCarthy, would never do anything to deliberately upset the President."

ACTUALLY IN JACK Kennedy's eyes, maybe that was all we seemed to be doing. Cuban stories began to pop up in the news. On September 3, *The New York Times* alleged: "Mr. Kennedy is caught between Cuban charges that he is planning to invade the island and mounting congressional demands that he should do precisely that." *The New York Times* had been a frequent critic of the Kennedy White House, complaining again and again about the poor coordination of government under Kennedy. They referred to his procedures as a kind of "hit-or-miss" style.

I thought "hit or miss" was a very good description of Jack's management style. Jack had surrounded himself with many talented people who had no previous experience in the government, and to make matters worse, he second-guessed every single thing that they tried to do. We all remembered the results of his second-guessing at the Bay of Pigs.

Jack decided to fight the increasing allegations of incompetence by sending Arthur Schlesinger to talk to the *Times*. In an interview with the paper's editors, Schlesinger feebly tried to make a case to justify Jack's piddling around: "Orderly governments are very rarely creative," he maintained, "and creative governments are almost never orderly." He tried hard to make the world believe what he evidently believed. "Creative governments will always be 'out of channels'...[They] will always present aspects of 'confusion' and 'meddling'; [they] will always discomfit officials whose routine is being disturbed or whose security is being threatened. But all this is inseparable from the process by which new ideas and new institutions enable government to meet new challenges."

Like the challenge of the Soviets setting up nuclear missiles just ninety miles off our shore, Arthur? His quote became a running joke around numerous D.C. water coolers. Invariably, someone would push his glasses down past the bridge of his nose to mimic the Ivy League professor. In a faux New England accent, the prankster would haughtily clear his throat, and ask, "Mr. Schlesinger, are we dealing here with a *'bureaucratic mess,'* or are we dealing with *'constructive chaos?'* Perhaps Mr. Kennedy could elucidate for us." Another joke claimed that "constructive chaos" was Harvard-speak for SNAFU—Situation Normal All Fucked Up."

Democratic senators who were up for reelection in November told Majority Leader Mike Mansfield the President had to take stronger action and soon. They threatened they might "have to leave [him] on this matter" unless there were "at least a 'do-something' gesture of militancy." They demanded Jack consider everything from a simple congressional resolution to invade Cuba at one end to an all-out war with Russia at the other.

Wisconsin Senator Alexander Wiley was adamant something needed to be done. "What is our policy in relation to Cuba?" he asked. "I'm just back from the hinterland and everybody is inquiring about it.... (Is it) just to sit still and let Cuba carry on?" The criticism began to open up other concerns: If everyone outside of D.C. knew about the Soviet missiles in Cuba, how could our own President claim that he didn't know about them? New York Senator Kenneth Keating publicly referred to Jack in demeaning terms as our "Do-Nothing President."

On September 4, the President finally made his first feeble effort to publicly respond to these charges of ignorance and cowardice by releasing a statement which said: "There is no evidence of any organized combat force in Cuba from any Soviet bloc country...or of the presence of ground-to-ground missiles or of other significant offensive capability either in Cuban hands or under Soviet direction and guidance...." He went on to assert: "The major danger is the Soviet Union with missiles and nuclear warheads, not Cuba."

A growing number of Americans felt that Jack Kennedy had turned a blind eye to what they could see plainly. The President appeared unwilling to protect the country's safety and interests. Many began to draw parallels to Prime Minister Neville Chamberlain's 1939 policy of appeasement with Hitler, which ultimately led to World War II. Chamberlain had refused to acknowledge the reality of Hitler's annexation of Czechoslovakia for what it was. Chamberlain's staunch belief that he had achieved "peace in our time" was dramatically betrayed when Hitler invaded Poland. Later, Chamberlain sadly conceded that *he* had "painted himself into a corner" in 1939. Jack Kennedy was not ignorant of history—he (supposedly) had written an analysis on that subject entitled *Why England Slept.*

We were barely seventeen years past the end of World War II, but the bloody lessons of that conflict apparently had not registered with John F. Kennedy. I remembered what Chase had told me in 1947 about how Joseph P. Kennedy, while Ambassador to Great Britain, had been the highest ranking Nazi sympathizer in the American government and had forcefully argued for supporting Chamberlain's policy of appeasement in order to avoid confrontation. It appeared the Kennedys were out to prove that their father's strategy could still be a viable one when used with the Soviets.

I was profoundly worried.

ON THE EVENING of September 6, Chase phoned me at home. After exchanging pleasantries, Chase got to the point of his call.

"Guess who I ran into at Rosie O'Grady's at lunch today?"

I didn't have the faintest idea. "Bobby Kennedy?" I joked.

"Wow, that's pretty good. Close, but not correct. But close!"

"I give up."

"Georgi Bolshakov,"

I vaguely recognized the name, but I couldn't remember where. I guess my silence gave me away.

"You don't know who Georgi Bolshakov is? Patrick, you're CIA, for Christ's sake. You mean to tell me that you don't know who the KGB station agents are here in D.C.?"

"Hey, buddy, I only focus on the big picture around here. We've got lower level Agency peons to take care of stuff like that," I teased.

"Well, all I can say is, if you've never heard of Georgi, you'd better get some *higher* level peons to replace them. Listen to this little scoop he gave me: Did you know that Georgi happens to be best friends with Bobby Kennedy?"

Our Attorney General, the brother of the President of the United States and his closest political advisor, had a KGB agent as a friend? I didn't like the sound of that. It was either extremely stupid or extremely arrogant on Bobby's part.

Chase elaborated, "Did you know that the President's little brother is using Georgi to shuttle personal messages directly to Comrade Khrushchev?"

"Wait a minute," I protested. "You're not suggesting that Bobby is some kind of a Soviet mole, are you?"

"Nah, nothing quite that juicy," Chase laughed. "If I had proof he was a Soviet mole, I'd be writing the story for tomorrow's front page. But Georgi confided to me that he regularly passes diplomatic messages back and forth to Khrushchev from the Kennedys. They're deliberately bypassing all of the normal State Department diplomatic channels."

I stiffened at the information. "They're sending messages back and forth using back channels? They can't do that. That's utterly reckless and dangerous. What the hell?"

"Georgi told me it's because Jack and Bobby don't trust anybody in the State Department. But here's why I called you. Bobby invited Georgi to the White House to meet with him and the President today. Georgi said the President greeted him quite warmly saying, 'Hello Georgi. I know you are off to Moscow for a vacation, and I'd like you to communicate something to Premier Khrushchev.'"

Chase paused for effect.

"Don't leave me hanging, Chase." I tried not to sound as angry as I was. The Kennedys were playing with fire.

"Okay, okay—the message involved Kennedy's presidential assurance that the United States was going to *stop* all low-level surveillance flights by our military aircraft over Soviet cargo ships headed for Cuba. He said that our Ambassador to Moscow had informed him that Premier Khrushchev was personally unhappy and upset by this form of harassment, so Kennedy told Georgi: 'Tell him I've ordered those flights stopped today.'"

"The President's promised to stop all of our military planes from flying low over those Soviet freighters?" It was incomprehensible—why would Jack undermine our country by limiting our ability to gather intelligence?

I could almost see Chase smiling that sly grin of his over the telephone wires. "Yes, but that's not what I called to tell you."

"I don't know if I want to know anymore—I'm too pissed off as it is." I braced myself for the rest, "Go ahead."

"It's what Bobby *later* told Georgi in private that is so juicy. After the meeting with the President broke up, Bobby walked Georgi out to the private alley between the White House and the Executive Office Building. While out there alone with Georgi, he pleaded with him to ask the Russians not to embarrass his brother."

I interrupted him. "I think Jack's doing a good enough job of that all by himself."

"Let me finish," he said firmly, interrupting me in return. "This next part is almost verbatim, according to Georgi. He said Bobby told him: 'Goddamn it, Georgi, doesn't Premier Khrushchev realize the President's position? Doesn't the Premier know that the President has enemies as well as friends? Believe me, my brother really means what he says about American-Soviet relations. But every step he takes to meet Premier Khrushchev halfway costs…If the Premier just took the trouble to be, for a moment at least, in the President's shoes he would understand him.'"

I interrupted him again. "Does this story of yours have a point?"

"It's got a point, all right. Bobby shocked the living daylights out of Georgi with his next comment. Bobby admitted that he actually feared for his brother's life."

"What?"

"He said that he feared for his brother's life—Georgi was just as shocked as you are. He said that Bobby tried to explain: 'In a gust of blind hate, *they* may go to any length.…' Georgi said that he assumed Bobby was referring to American right-wingers or maybe even the military, but he didn't ask and Bobby didn't say. What do you think of that?"

I couldn't tell him what I thought. It was crazy. It wasn't any secret at all in D.C. that Jack had many enemies, but I had never heard of anyone suggesting Jack's life was in any danger. Bobby was being paranoid to even make the suggestion.

"Why did Georgi tell you this stuff?" I asked.

"I told you, we sometimes hang out at the same bar together. He likes to impress me and the women with how important he is, but sometimes I think he just needs to unburden himself and tell someone he trusts some of the things he knows about and can't tell anyone else."

"And he trusts you that much?"

"Many people do," Chase said slyly.

"What are you going to do with the story?" I inquired.

"Nothing, the only person I'm telling is you."

"Why me?"

"Same reason Georgi told me the story. It's too disturbing to me to hear this and to know this and not be able to tell someone. So I'm telling you. Listen, I gotta go! Give my love to Pam."

I was left to mull over what Chase had said. Jack and Bobby believed Jack's life could be in danger from within the United States. I thought about it for a long time, and then something jogged my memory to a Saturday sailing trip earlier this spring—it made a lot more sense to me now than it had at the time. I had tagged along with Pam to visit Jackie up in Hyannis Port. I ended up with Jack and his long-time friend, Red Faye—probably at Jackie's insistence—on their sailboat for a few hours on the waters off Cape Cod.

With me on board, Jack was guarded in his topics of conversation. Jack started out a discussion about recent books that we had all read—Jack wanted to talk about how much he had enjoyed two books in particular: the first was *The Guns of August* by Barbara Tuchman. It was a historical account of how much military and political miscalculation by kings and prime ministers, generals and marshals had inevitably led to the start of World War I in August 1914. The topic of the book fascinated Jack because it dealt with the reality of a war started over miscalculations. One of his favorite parts of the book was an exchange between two German leaders who asked themselves, "How did it all happen?" only to answer, "Ah, if we only knew."

Jack shared that he was haunted by nightmares that a similar such scenario could happen to him. He said the book should serve to educate all of his administration about how fragile peace can be, especially in the nuclear age. A wrong decision could end up annihilating the entire human race. He said he had issued orders that every commander in the military read the book, and he emphasized they were all informed that their Commander in Chief wanted it done sooner rather than later.

The other book that captivated him was a fictional thriller called *Seven Days in May* written by two veteran Washington newspapermen, Fletcher Knebel and Charles Bailey, about an attempted military coup against an American president.

I remember Red asking Jack, "Could it happen here?"

Jack had leaned back and smiled sardonically. "It's possible, but the conditions would have to be just right. If the country had a young President and he had a Bay of Pigs, there would be a certain uneasiness. Maybe the military would do a little criticizing behind his back."

"Then, if there were another Bay of Pigs, the reaction of the country would be, 'Is he too young and inexperienced?' The military would almost feel it was their patriotic obligation to stand ready to preserve the integrity of the nation and only God knows just what segment of Democracy they would be defending…" His voice trailed off for a moment as he turned his head away from us to look out at the vast emptiness of the Atlantic Ocean beyond our boat.

Jack was quiet for a few more moments, before telling us, "Then if there were a third Bay of Pigs, it could happen."

Red sat with his jaw open in disbelief. "So you're saying it could really happen here?"

Jack turned. For some reason, he fixed me with a long, hard glare and defiantly declared, "It could, but it won't happen on my watch!"

The memory of that May conversation with Jack and Red haunted me for hours after my conversation with Chase.

AT AN INTELLIGENCE briefing the day after Chase's call, we were handed a written copy of a conversation Interior Secretary Stewart Udall had with Premier Khrushchev on the sixth. The report said Khrushchev lectured Udall and claimed, "So when Castro comes to us for aid, we give him what he needs for defense. He hasn't much military equipment, so he asked us to supply some, but only for defense. However, if you attack Cuba, that would create an entirely different situation."

Khrushchev further told Udall he needed to know if Kennedy still had things under control. "As a President, he has understanding, but what he lacks is courage." Before Secretary Udall could stammer a response, Khrushchev threw out another threat. "It's been a long time since you could spank us like a little boy—now we can swat your ass! So let's not talk about force; we're equally strong."

On September 9, a story appeared in the press concerning Robert Frost's recent visit with Premier Khrushchev in Moscow. The eighty-eight-year-old poet told a New York press conference upon his return from that same trip with Secretary Udall that Khrushchev thought Americans were "too liberal to fight." Remarkably, Frost praised Khrushchev, who had charmed Frost completely. The poet was openly exhilarated by his visit with the Premier. "He's a great man.... rough and ready. He knows what power is and isn't afraid to take hold of it." Jack was pissed-off about Frost's comments and openly wondered why Frost made such comments. He felt betrayed.

At this same time, Jack began to take lot of heat from close friends about his personal life. Ben Bradlee at the *Washington Post* ran an article about the allegations that Jack had once been secretly married to a woman named Durie Malcolm before he met Jackie, the very same story that Sam Giancana had told me about. The Durie Malcolm story received quite a bit of media coverage all summer in a variety of newspapers and magazines—even in Jack's hometown newspaper.

I suspected Sam Gianacana had something to do with it, especially after the failure of his plan to link the Kennedys to Marilyn's death.

ON SEPTEMBER 26, *The New York Times* headlines read: "U.S. IS PREPARED TO SEND TROOPS AS MISSISSIPPI GOVERNOR DEFIES COURTS AND BARS NEGRO STUDENT"

"Isn't that a hell of a comment on this president?" Grant said disgustedly as he threw the paper down on the table in front of me and Chase one day at lunch. "He won't send troops to invade Cuba and remove the missiles that threaten our peace and safety, but he will send troops to Ole Miss just so a colored boy can enroll in class. What kind of a fucked-up set of priorities is that?"

"What's the matter, Grant? You don't think James Meredith is entitled to a college education?" Chase asked.

"Sure he is. There are plenty of colored colleges he can go to. He doesn't have to go to a white school, that's all we're saying."

Chase could barely contain his contempt at Grant's racism. "James Meredith is a young Air Force veteran who was so inspired by Jack's words in his Inaugural Address that he decided to become the first Negro to enroll at the all-white University of Mississippi. He's served his country, and I believe he deserves to go to a school of his choice."

"Yeah, well, he doesn't have to be so uppity about it. He bragged to the world he was going to drive up to school in Oxford, Mississippi in a new gold Thunderbird. That ain't gonna go over very well with the good ole boys down there, believe me."

"*Your* friends aren't going to like him going there."

"They're not necessarily my friends, Chase. You know that. But I know some things you don't know. I'm from the South, and you're not. You don't understand how it is down there right now."

"How is it? Enlighten me."

"Chase, I know how you are. You'll just take my words and twist them around so I'll look stupid. I'm not gonna play your game. So go back to nibbling on your watercress finger sandwich there and sip your chamomile tea like the good blue-blooded Northeastern elitist you are."

"Fine," Chase chuckled, "and you can go back to eating your black-eyed peas and sow belly with your knife and your fingers, you red-neck moron."

Grant spun toward me with a grin on his face. "See, what have I always told you! Every time we start to have a high-minded discussion on the issues, he always resorts to name-calling. What a prick."

I ignored Grant's last comment. For some reason, he and Chase got on each other's nerves these days. I tried to change the subject, "What's going on with the Kennedys on civil rights?" I asked Chase.

"The Negroes have finally grown sick and tired of Jack's apparent lack of interest in their civil rights. The President has been notably indifferent to the inhumanity of their plight, and prominent civil rights leaders have had enough. It looks to me that the civil rights movement is about to explode. It certainly threatens to rip the South apart, and perhaps the rest of the country with it."

"I know that Jack and Bobby don't want to support a voting rights law because they fear they'll lose their support in the South," I said.

"They don't have to fear it might happen. It will happen," Grant chirped. "They are very well aware of what it will cost them if they publicly come out and support any civil rights whatsoever. Jack and Bobby don't want to stir up any trouble in the South before the next presidential election in 1964. They are acutely aware of what happened with FDR—he never lost a single southern state in four elections because he wouldn't even address the issue. But the moment President Truman opened his big mouth advocating civil rights in 1948, he immediately lost five southern states and their electoral votes. Those two Kennedy boys have both calculated the political cost of taking such an unpopular stand. They're just not gonna do it."

"I don't know about that…" Chase started to say, but Grant interrupted him.

"Hey, he's tried to send us Southern guys a message. Take a look at all of the federal judges that he has appointed. Every single one of them is an avowed segregationist. Deep down, Jack Kennedy thinks just like we do."

"I've never heard him talk like that," I said.

"Actions speak louder than words some times," Grant added.

Chase jumped back in. "I hate to agree with the voice of reason over there, especially when he's dribbled tea on his silk tie…"

"Oh shit, did I do that? Damn it, I did. This is a twenty dollar tie, too!" Grant waved his napkin at a passing waitress to get her attention while Chase kept talking.

"Back in July, Martin Luther King Jr. publicly criticized Jack, trying to shame him into action. He said that our President 'could do more in the area of moral persuasion by occasionally speaking out against segregation and counseling the Nation on the moral aspects of this problem.' Jack's response was that he was committed to full constitutional rights for *all* Americans."

"That was a safe response," I said, "typical of Jack."

Grant said, "He just wasn't about to go out on a limb for the nigras, and they needed to know that." Grant carefully blotted his tie.

"They knew that—that's why they had to force Jack to act. Reverend King sent a telegram to Jack 'asking for Federal action against anti-Negro terrorism in the South.' Some other civil rights groups threatened to picket the White House unless the President did more to help them," Chase explained. "Hey, you still have a spot on your tie."

"I think they read the Kennedy administration the right way. Both Jack and Bobby are concerned about appearances remember? A picket line in front of the White House would be a public relations nightmare," I added. "Jack's civil rights strategy has been identical to his Cuban strategy—try to ignore it and hope it goes away."

"They're not ignoring it," Grant said, "Did either of you boys happen to read the memo circulating around the White House back in March?"

I hadn't read it.

Chase said, "I might have—remind me what it was about."

"Lyndon's working on the matter. Anyway the memo said: 'the proper groundwork has not been laid for [civil rights] legislation in Congress.... If legislation is submitted to Congress before the moral issue is clearly drawn, the result will be disaster. The country will be exposed to several weeks of divisive and inflammatory debate. The debate is likely to come to no real conclusion—thus disillusioning the Negroes...in their conclusion that the country is 'really with' them.'"

"How does he do that," I asked Chase, "remember things word for word?"

Grant ignored me, "Why then does he cater to those Negro activists? There's no way he'll pick up enough Negro votes to off-set all of the white votes that he's going to lose. He doesn't understand—we're never going to let them vote anyway."

"Is everyone down South a cretin like you?" Chase sneered.

"Hey, Chase, that's what happens when a family tree doesn't have any branches," I laughed.

Grant smiled and gave me the finger.

"Unfortunately for everybody involved," I said, "there exists a bigger problem that needs to be solved first. The civil rights leaders don't understand the Kennedy brothers, and the Kennedy brothers simply don't understand the Negroes. When you stop to think about it, how could they? The only Negroes that they have ever spent time around are their own servants. The Kennedy brothers are puzzled by the simplest of the Negro demands. Bobby, who's more sympathetic than Jack, even grumbled to me, 'Why couldn't the Negroes understand how much *he* has at stake?'"

"Well, I don't know what they know or don't know. But I know this. If he stirs up the nigras, he'll stir up a mess of trouble he might never calm down."

"Bobby knows that, Grant. I know how hard Bobby worked behind the scenes to delay the Civil Rights Commission hearings in Louisiana and Mississippi, and when the Commission's report was finally ready to be made public, he vigorously lobbied to suppress its findings from the public. I heard he bitterly complained to two of the Commissioners, 'You're making my life difficult.'"

"If the Kennedys think life is difficult now, they are about to find out just how difficult life can really be," Chase concluded.

MEANWHILE BACK IN Mississippi, things were getting stirred up—just as Chase had predicted. The stage was set for a huge confrontation on September 25, the first day of classes at the University of Mississippi. The United States Supreme Court had ruled that the state of Mississippi could not legally block James Meredith's admission, but Governor Ross Barnett and two thousand jeering white Mississippi citizens felt otherwise. Barnett vowed to personally block Meredith's admission and entrance.

Even though the odds were against him, Meredith stubbornly proceeded to enroll. Thankfully for Meredith, wiser heads at the Justice Department intervened and convinced Meredith to leave that gold Thunderbird at home. They also insisted that he accept a federal escort to the campus.

When Meredith and the federal authorities arrived at the doorstep of the university, a large and angry white mob blocked their progress. "Which one is Meredith?" Governor Barnett brayed to great laughter as he pretended to look past the only Negro in sight. For seven days, James Meredith tried to gain admittance to his classes; for seven days, an ever-increasing angry mob formed, threatening to prevent James Meredith from entering the university.

The Kennedys finally caved in to the growing pressure from throughout the rest of the country. They sent 23,000 U.S. Army soldiers to camp out on the Ole Miss campus; finally, James Meredith was admitted to class.

While I was glad that Meredith finally prevailed, my focus was on keeping all Americans alive by making sure Jack understood that if we didn't prevail in Cuba, the next sneak attack on the United States would render all of his other problems, personal and civil rights, moot.

ON OCTOBER 5, Director McCone forcefully argued for a resumption of U-2 overflights of Cuba in the face of the President's order. Director McCone was convinced that the existence of Soviet offensive missiles in Cuba was "a probability rather than a mere possibility." However, White House advisor McGeorge Bundy protected the President's position by arguing "the Soviets would not go that far."

Four days later, Jack, finally relenting to the growing pressure, authorized another U-2 overflight of Cuba. On October 10, Major Rudolf Anderson

Jr. flew over Cuba and took pictures which detailed Soviet-style troop encampments and newly constructed roads in remote areas. Then Hurricane Ella swept through the Caribbean and grounded all surveillance flights until the weather cleared on October 14.

This time, our U-2 came back from its six-minute flight over the island with 928 photographs, which distinctly and positively confirmed our worst suspicions. Our photographic experts identified what appeared to be forty medium-range missiles, many of them already in firing position and angled toward the United States. These missiles had a range of 1,200 miles and could easily reach Dallas, Houston, New Orleans, St. Louis, and D.C. If they were armed with one-megaton nuclear warheads, they would each possess fifty times more destructive power than the atomic bomb that we dropped on Hiroshima.

Even more horrifying was our discovery and expert confirmation that another six bases were being completed that could launch five-megaton nuclear warheads up to 2,500 miles, which would make all of America, from the Atlantic to the Pacific Oceans, vulnerable. We were further alarmed when we counted twenty-five twin-engine Ilyushin-28 bombers, all capable of carrying nuclear bombs as well.

When the film had been developed and thoroughly analyzed on October 15, we had incontrovertible proof. The only question was whether it was too late to do anything about it. We estimated that we only had about two weeks before all of the missiles were fully operational. We immediately alerted McGeorge Bundy that we had undeniable proof of the existence of the missiles—he told us that he would rather wait until the next morning to tell the President!

At 8:45 a.m. the next day, Bundy finally got around to telling Jack what he had found out the night before. Jack immediately called Bobby and told him, "We have some big trouble. I want you over here."

When I confronted one of the President's advisors, Abram Chayes, and asked why the White House hadn't believed our reports about the missiles, he told me, "I, for one, didn't believe the reports of offensive missiles because I didn't want to believe them. I didn't want to lie to senators when I reported on the Cuba situation, and I certainly wasn't inclined to take Senator Keating or Director McCone at face value because I didn't think they were reliable. I don't want to accuse anyone else of this, but it was very easy for me to disregard Keating and the other hotheads who were screaming about missiles in Cuba."

"So you simply believed whatever you wanted to believe?" I asked him.

He acknowledged that was the way the entire White House operated.

Later that day, I went back to the West Wing of the White House to convince the White House Chief of Staff, Kenny O'Donnell, of his need to intercede with the President to help change his mind when Jack wandered into O'Donnell's office and plopped all of our photos down on his desk. He had a glum expression on his face as he asked Kenny, "You still think the fuss about Cuba is unimportant?"

O'Donnell walked right into the wrong answer. "Absolutely!" he replied confidently. "The voters won't give a damn about Cuba!"

Jack gave him a disappointed look and said, "I want to show you something," pointing to the pictures he had just dropped on the desk. Confused, O'Donnell asked, "What's this?"

"It's the beginning of a launching site for a medium-range ballistic missile."

"I don't believe it!"

"You better believe it. Because of these pictures and this evidence, Ken Keating will probably be the next President of the United States," Jack said despondently. Then he gave me a searing look as he walked out without another word to either of us.

For the next three days, high-level discussions concentrated on an appropriate response to the Soviet aggression. The Pentagon wanted an all-out attack to destroy the missiles before they could be made operational. The State Department wanted to open talks. No one really knew what to do.

Finally, on Friday, October 19, Jack began leaning toward a blockade of Cuba because he said it would "allow the Soviets some room for maneuver to pull back from their over-extended position in Cuba." The problem was that a blockade would be perceived as an open act of war. Any military action was almost guaranteed to precipitate a Soviet military response.

On Saturday, Jack flew off to campaign in St. Louis, but by late afternoon, the decision had been made that he would have to address the American people. Claiming to have the flu, he cancelled the rest of the trip and flew back to D.C. "The campaign is over," he told Bobby. "*They* were right about Cuba."

I got a call at the office the night of Saturday, October 20. Pam called me to tell me Jack had called Jackie at Glen Ora in Virginia and had ordered her to return to the White House at once and to bring the children. "We are very, very close to war," he told her.

"Patrick, Jackie was frightened as hell. Could this possibly be true?"

"I can't talk about that, Pam. You know that."

"Patrick! I'm talking about your own family! I have a right to know. Is this true?"

My silence spoke volumes to her.

"We need to talk when you get home, Patrick. When will you be home?"

she demanded. "I'm sitting here absolutely terrified about what could happen to us all. I need you. Tim and I both need you. Please come home—now!"

I told her that I was sorry, but I couldn't tell her anything, and I couldn't be there with her. The sound of her slamming that telephone receiver down almost broke my eardrum…and my heart.

On Monday, October 22, Jack authorized the naval blockade of Cuba, but he was advised that he should call the idea "a quarantine." By using that specific word, the American public might not realize that such an action on the open seas was tantamount to an actual declaration of war against the Soviets.

Democratic Senator Richard Russell, chairman of the Senate Armed Forces Committee, expressed his annoyance at Jack's decision. "Why fuck around?" he challenged Jack in a White House briefing. He thought the idea of quarantine was a feeble response to the Soviet actions.

"It seems to me that we are at a crossroads. We're either a first-class power or we're not."

He told Jack he felt Khrushchev knew that nuclear warheads just off the coast of Florida were unacceptable to us. He believed that Khrushchev was once again testing the mettle of the young and inexperienced commander in chief—that it was Khrushchev's way of testing our nerve, and it was time for us to take a stand. The United States had to take the risk that the Russians were bluffing by fighting back. He concluded by saying that the United States was destined to war with Russia someday—and that we might as well do it now rather than later.

"The danger to this country is in the missiles already in place. If fired, they could destroy forty of our cities and inflict millions of casualties on our people. The quarantine will not remove that danger."

I watched Jack struggle to absorb Russell's arguments. Jack felt blindsided when others in that same meeting agreed with Russell's aggressive stance. Senator William Fulbright also favored an immediate invasion; he believed a quarantine to be the worst possible strategy. He argued that an invasion "would be less provocative and less inclined to precipitate a war with Russia." He lectured Jack that sinking or seizing a Russian ship in international waters was an outright act of war. "Remember, it is *not* an act of war against Russia to attack Cuba," he reminded him.

Other congressional leaders from both parties jumped into the fray to support Russell and Fulbright's beliefs, all arguing that the blockade was too slow and was not an adequate response to the inherent danger of this situation. They insisted that it be officially recorded in the meeting's minutes that they were "informed" by the President, but not "consulted" by the President. They collectively regarded Jack's plan as too weak to work.

The Senate Democratic leader, Mike Mansfield of Montana, held Jack directly accountable for the situation. He agreed with Senator Russell that Jack had never taken a strong stand against Khrushchev and the Russians. "None of us had anything to do with this mess—it was all Jack's fault," he said. He felt the meeting was a deliberate sham by Jack, an attempt of constructing a historical record, or more likely, a historical defense. Mansfield, the fourth-highest ranking official in the United States, knew he was helpless to prevent this crisis from turning into a war in which millions of American could die because of Jack's mistakes and miscalculations. He called his wife and asked her to meet him immediately at Washington National Airport. Together, they fled to their home in Billings, Montana.

The pressure on Jack mounted, not only from the military advisors, but also from politicians in the Democratic Party. Jack privately lamented his failure to support the Bay of Pigs invasion and grudgingly admitted that an American success in overthrowing Castro would have prevented the current missile crisis.

"That's why it shows that the Bay of Pigs was really right," he said, regretfully. "You and Dulles and Bissell were right after all."

A lot of good that did us now, I thought.

LIKE MANY OF my fellow Washingtonians, I headed home to be with my family to sit in front of the television that night. Dinner was bereft of conversation, filled instead with tension and a growing sense of doom. Pam and I sat on the sofa with Tim between us. We held each other in our arms as each of the television networks tuned into the White House for the President's speech.

As I hugged Tim, I asked, "How are you doing?"

"I'm scared, Daddy. Is there going to be a war?"

"I don't know, Tim. I sure hope not. That's what the President is going to tell us in a few minutes."

"The kids at school are all saying we're going to have a war. Greg's dad said so, too."

I didn't know who Greg was, but Pam said, "He's an officer at the Pentagon." I could see the worry on her face. Before I could answer, Pam added, "Our school has been showing Civil Defense films to the kids, like 'Duck and Cover.' The kids have also been hearing the Civil Defense sirens running their tests every Friday afternoon, and they're all spooked. Barb Moore told me that some of the first and second graders are having nightmares about what to do if 'the Bomb' falls when they are not at school. Those films have convinced them that the only safe place in the world is under their desk at school, and they don't know what to do if school isn't in session. A lot of the kids are scared to death."

Tim was upset. "I can't sleep, Daddy. What if something happens to you and Mommy?"

Pam stroked his hair. "We won't let anything happen to you—will we Dad?"

I lied and agreed, "Of course not."

At 7:00 p.m., President John F. Kennedy addressed the nation "on a matter of the highest national urgency." One hundred million Americans tuned in to hear the seventeen-minute speech that outlined the crisis and the gravity of the situation facing America. As his address began, I secretly knew that twenty-two United States Air Force planes, already circling in attack formation above Florida, turned and began flying directly toward Cuba. This was a precaution in case the Russians decided to launch a strike when they heard the President's message.

Of course, I also couldn't tell Pam that.

"Good evening, my fellow citizens," he began. "Cuba…Within the past week, unmistakable evidence has established the fact that a series of offensive missile sites is now in preparation on that imprisoned island. The purpose of these bases can be none other than to provide a nuclear strike capability against the Western Hemisphere." He told the public the medium-range missiles were operational and ready to fire—that they could fly far enough to destroy Washington D.C., Mexico City, the Panama Canal, and Cape Canaveral. The intermediate-range missiles, which were being installed and were not quite operational, had the ability to hit virtually every major city in the Western Hemisphere, from Lima, Peru, all the way up to Hudson Bay, Canada.

He appealed to Khrushchev to "eliminate this clandestine, reckless and provocative threat to world peace and to stable relations between our two nations." He pleaded with the Premier to "Abandon this course of world domination …and…move the world back from the abyss of destruction."

As a family, we all knew what this meant. We lived little more than a mile from the Pentagon and less than five miles from the White House. We were as close to being at ground zero for a nuclear strike as possible.

When the brief presidential address ended, Pam looked at me, "What are we going to do?"

"My job," I answered succinctly.

She eyed me with a combination of apprehension and helplessness. I told her about Mike Mansfield leaving town. I ventured a guess that he wouldn't be the only one headed for the hills. I had heard similar discussions throughout D.C. from people in the know.

"I talked to Jackie, and she is beside herself. She's scared for the kids. She wants to go back to Glen Ora, or even to Camp David, but Jack won't let her. He claims it would make him look bad," she said mournfully.

I tried to assuage her fears by telling Pam that I was sure the Russians would also target Camp David and Glen Ora if they launched against us. "Probably the safest place would be with some of the rest of the government up at the Greenbrier, in West Virginia."

Her face brightened with hope, "Is it safe there?"

I shrugged my shoulders, "I'm pretty sure it is. The Greenbrier is a Top Secret facility out in the middle of nowhere—away from any metropolitan centers that might be targeted."

"How do you know about it?" she asked.

"It's my job to know these things. We've done some simulated evacuations of high levels of government over the past few years. The Greenbrier's mostly where we have sent them. We have a secret government bomb shelter there that will supposedly handle a couple of thousand people. Nobody knows about it unless they need to know about it."

She suddenly got very excited at this new information, "Can *we* go, Patrick?"

"No, Pam, we can't go."

She sounded crushed at my answer, "Why not?"

"Because you're not cleared to go."

She looked at me, her eyes widening in surprise. "But *you* can go, can't you?"

I didn't answer her question.

She stared at me and asked again, "But you can go, can't you?"

I looked at her without speaking, but I finally nodded.

"God damn you, Patrick! You can go and we can't? Is that what you're saying? Tell me!"

"Pam, none of us is going anywhere. There's really no place for us to go. I don't possess the political clearance to be able to take my family. My government has decided that they can use *me*, but they don't have any use or room for my family. The families of higher-ranking officials get to go instead. Consequently, I'm not going either. I decided that if we all can't go together, then none of us are going."

Pam with tears in her eyes leaned over Tim to hug and kiss me. The tears welling up in my eyes as well, but I didn't want Tim to see his father crying.

The next day, Pam called me at work to tell me the faculty at Kate Waller Barrett Elementary School was practicing air raid evacuations of the entire student body. She said that as a member of the School Safety Patrol, Tim was helping to lead the students to a bomb shelter in the basement of an apartment complex about a block from the school.

"The children have been instructed to take positions on the floor covering their heads and to stay away from the tiny windows high up on the walls. The fall-out shelters have been pre-stocked with crackers and water, but we were also shown how to purify toilet water using household bleach."

"How long does it take to get everyone out of the school and down to the shelter?" I asked her.

She replied, "Twenty to thirty minutes."

"That's too long, honey. Those Russian missiles will be here faster than that. This is just an exercise to make the parents all feel better. Besides, everything within twenty-five miles of the Pentagon will be one gigantic smoking hole if this thing happens. Those are fall-out shelters, not blast shelters. They will protect you from the radiation fall-out, but not the explosion itself."

"I know," she admitted softly. "I saw the Smith family down the street packing their car. He works for the FBI, you know. As they left the neighborhood, they stopped and told me that they were headed for the safety of the Blue Ridge Mountains, out by the Luray Caverns."

I told Pam that there were probably a lot of other friends and families headed that same way this morning.

"Sure you won't change your mind? The McCarthy family can be packed and ready to go in an hour," she joked.

"It doesn't work that way, Pam," I said sadly.

"I know," she whispered.

ON OCTOBER 23, we tracked thirty Soviet ships steaming toward Cuba. The President had established a line for his quarantine that was eight hundred miles from Cuban soil, scheduled to go into effect on Wednesday, October 24. The eight hundred-mile radius was designed to be outside the fuel range of any Soviet MIG fighter that might be based on Cuba. The thirty Soviet ships showed no signs of either slowing down or turning around as they approached the imaginary demarcation. Jack wavered at the very last minute and hurriedly reduced the quarantine radius down to five hundred miles.

Experts at the Justice Department and State Department recommended using the Monroe Doctrine to legally force a solution to the crisis. The Monroe Doctrine, a unilateral declaration made in 1823 by President James Monroe, barred European nations from colonizing anywhere in the Americas. The President was advised that the Monroe Doctrine could be used as a legal justification to act against the Russians in Cuba. Inexplicably, Jack snapped, "What the hell is the Monroe Doctrine? Don't ever mention it again!"

At the Pentagon, Secretary of Defense Robert McNamara briefed reporters on the civil defense preparations the President had ordered. When he began to describe the President's plans for schoolchildren to dive under their desks and cover their heads with their hands and how families should stock up basements with cans of water, peas, and crackers, the room full of reporters exploded into hysterical laughter at the naiveté of the suggestions. They asked, "Surely the White House didn't believe that these ideas would do anyone any good, did they?"

Back at the White House, where things were going just as poorly, the laughter was bitter. Military aides went from office to office handing out envelopes marked "To Be Opened in Emergency." One jokester said it contained instructions to crawl under the nearest desk, cover your head, and kiss your ass goodbye. In actuality, the instructions were not even that helpful.

Secretary of State Dean Rusk had a similar reaction when he was given his evacuation instructions. He decided to go home to be with his wife. He told me that if there happened to be any survivors when this was finally over, the first thing the survivors would probably do would be to find him, McNamara, and the President and hang them all from the nearest tree for allowing this to happen.

I went to the White House that afternoon to meet Pam and Tim, who were spending the rest of the day with Jackie. I swung by the Oval Office as another meeting was breaking up. Jack and Bobby were alone in the office; both looked miserable.

"How are you two holding up?" I asked respectfully.

Jack shrugged his shoulders. Bobby glared at me and barked, "What do you want?"

"Hey, I'm sorry to interrupt," I apologized. "I just came by to pick up Pam. I thought I'd stop and see how you're doing, that's all."

"We don't need..." Bobby started to nastily add, but Jack put his hand up to stop him.

"Stop it, Bob. Come on in, Patrick. Pam will be down with Jackie in a minute or two."

He turned toward me, "Listen, I want you to know that I'm grateful Pam has been here for Jackie. She needs the support of her friends, and I haven't been able to spend the time with her that I should. I know she needs me right now, but I can't give her that kind of time. I want you to know that we appreciate what you and Pam are doing," he said kindly.

"How do you think it all looks?" I asked hopefully.

"How does it look?" Bobby irritably interrupted and snapped. "How do you think it looks?"

Jack was more gracious. "Ah, looks like hell—looks real mean, doesn't it?"

He crossed his arms and glanced out the window at the back lawn of the White House. "I'll tell you something," he confided. "If they get mean on this one, it's just a question of where they go about it next. No choice…" his voice trailed off a little bit. "I don't think there is a choice." He paused and added, "Our only choice is the quarantine."

"Well, there isn't any choice," Bobby told him. "You would have been impeached."

Jack remained looking out the window while Bobby's last remark sunk in. I saw him slowly nod his head in agreement. "That's what I think," he sadly agreed. "I would have been impeached."

Just then, one of his aides came in and announced Jackie and Pam were outside the office. I said my good-byes to the President and the Attorney General.

I headed home to Arlington with my family.

LATE THAT NIGHT, the phone ominously rang. Pam and I exchanged worried looks. It was after ten o'clock, much too late for a personal call. We expected the worse.

I was relieved to hear Chase's voice.

"Patrick, I've got some more info for you from my little Russian drinking buddy, Georgi Bolshakov. Did I wake you?"

"Chase? You scared the crap out me. No, you didn't wake me—I haven't slept in at least two weeks. What is it?"

"Bolshakov told me the White House wants to get a message to Khrushchev that they've got a possible diplomatic solution to this mess."

I could not fathom how diplomacy could work at this late stage.

"Want to know what it is?" he asked.

Of course I wanted to know.

"Bobby Kennedy told Georgi the United States would offer to close its missile bases in Turkey and Italy if Russia would do the same in Cuba."

"What! He can't do that! He doesn't have the authority to offer something like that without discussing it with the State Department, the Pentagon, and Congress. Bobby knows that. Hell, Jack certainly must know that, too. What kind of bullshit are you shoveling, Chase?"

"No bullshit, Patrick. I swear. Georgi was pretty shook up about the offer. Even he recognizes the implications of being a courier in unofficial back-channel negotiations—especially when a nuclear war is about to break out at any minute. You're putting a lowly journalist in a tough position when professional diplomats are not even consulted or involved. I don't have to tell you, Patrick, Georgi's scared shitless about this!"

"He should be."

"Well, he's in a dangerous situation. Think about it. He's been asked to help broker a solution to World War III. He doesn't know how much credibility he even has with Khrushchev. What if Khrushchev doesn't believe what he tells him? What if Khrushchev thinks the Kennedys are screwing around with these messages just to buy time for an attack on Russia? Georgi will be a dead man. The only thing he will earn for his efforts will be a bullet in the back of his head. This is serious stuff, Patrick."

"What's he going to do?" I asked.

"He told me that he told his KGB case officer about the offer—he told the Kremlin about the offer—and he told me about the offer. We're in the process of getting drunk together."

"Who have you told?" I inquired.

"No one but you," Chase replied. "I knew you might like to hear about it. I was hoping you could confirm or deny the info. Are the Kennedys acting on their own—without the knowledge of the Pentagon, or the Agency, or the Congress? Do you think they're selling out America to Khrushchev?"

"Jesus, Chase, I don't know. I hope not. But thanks for the call."

He hung up without saying goodbye.

I immediately got dressed to head back to the office. Back on October 20, our President had vowed that we would never, under any circumstances, abandon our NATO allies by removing our missiles from Turkey. That was solidly off the negotiating table. Now it sounded like that's what they were planning to do. What in the hell were Jack and Bobby really up to—a double-cross?

When I got to the office, we received word the president of Westinghouse Electric, who was in Moscow to discuss patent laws and procedures, had been summoned to the Kremlin. Khrushchev had apparently lectured the Westinghouse president that the root of the present crisis was simply due to the immaturity of President John F. Kennedy.

"My oldest son is older than Kennedy," Khrushchev was disdainful. "How can I deal with a man who is younger than my son?" He then added, "I'm not interested in destroying the world, but if we all want to meet in Hell, it is up to Kennedy."

HAVING MONITORED INTELLIGENCE reports for the rest of the night and into the morning, I finally intercepted some positive news. I interrupted Director McCone's presidential briefing to deliver a note based upon messages we had intercepted and decoded from Soviet signals intelligence. He read the note and announced, "Mr. President, I have a note just handed to me. It says we've received information through ONI (Office of Naval Intelligence) that all six Soviet naval ships currently identified in Cuban waters—and I don't know what that means—have either stopped or reversed course...."

Dean Rusk spoke up, "We're eyeball to eyeball, and I think the other fellow just blinked."

Later that afternoon, we received "An Urgent Appeal" from the Secretary-General of the United Nations, U Thant, who had sent identical letters to Khrushchev and Kennedy. He wanted both sides to agree to a voluntary halt of both the blockade and the military shipments to Cuba. He thought two or three weeks would be sufficient to reach an agreement that would be satisfactory to both sides.

Premier Khrushchev agreed, but President Kennedy refused. Jack reiterated, "The existing threat was created by the secret introduction of offensive weapons into Cuba, and the answer lies in the removal of such weapons."

Jack Kennedy now brought his own personal recklessness out into public for the first time. He was fully prepared to play a terrifying game of chicken in order to prove to his critics that he wasn't gutless. Here was a point where cooler heads should have prevailed, but instead Jack got a red-ass just to prove to Khrushchev that he could be tough, too.

THE NEXT MORNING, a Soviet cargo ship challenged the five hundred-mile quarantine line. It was an oil tanker named the *Bucharest*. Most members of the Ex-Com wanted that ship stopped so that Khrushchev would "make no mistake of our will and intent."

Inexplicably, Jack capitulated and refused to back up his earlier commands. He specifically ordered that the *Bucharest* be allowed through without a search. We later found out the Cubans held a huge celebration when it arrived in Havana.

Jack's mixed messages drove us crazy. All around D.C., people repeatedly asked: 'Does this President actually have the courage to do what he already publicly promised he was going to do?" It sure didn't look like it to most of us.

It only got worse when Jack intervened in our military operations and personally selected the first ship to be stopped and searched, a Lebanese cargo ship named *Marucla*. He arranged to radio the ship's captain the night before just to inform him that we would be boarding his vessel the next day. He reasoned that because it wasn't a Soviet-owned ship, it wouldn't represent an affront to the Russians. Jack claimed this action would demonstrate he was serious about enforcing the blockade although most of his advisors and critics were disgusted by his timidity.

At his Ex-Com meeting that morning, Jack came close to losing control of his own government. Undersecretary of State George Ball called for petroleum products to be added to the embargo list for Cuba. Secretary Dillon stepped up and declared that he was fed up with the current policy of stopping Soviet ships at sea. He called for an immediate air strike against the missile sites.

The quarantine was no longer the central issue. Jack admitted that "Even if the quarantine's 100 percent effective, it isn't any good because the missile sites go on being constructed." Even he conceded that time was rapidly running out on finding a peaceful solution to the situation. "We can't fuck around for two weeks and wait for them to finish." He seemed to pause to gather his thoughts and acknowledged what we all had been thinking. "If at the end of forty-eight hours we are getting no place, and the missile sites continue to be constructed, then we are going to be faced with some hard decisions."

On Friday evening at 6:00 p.m. sharp, the teletype at the State Department began receiving the transmission of a four-page letter that Premier Khrushchev delivered to our embassy in Moscow. It took over three hours for our equipment to print the letter to the President.

We were presented with Khrushchev's letter the next morning. The letter was a perfect reflection of Khrushchev's personality—part lecture to the young President, part history lesson, part negotiation, and finally, part bluster and part accommodation.

He started out by cordially saying, "Dear Mr. President: I have received your letter of October 25. From your letter I got the feeling that you have some understanding of the situation which has developed and a sense of responsibility. I appreciate this." That was the charmer at work. Then he snuck in a subtle put-down of Jack, reminding him of his utter failure at the Vienna summit in June 1961: "It is our discussion in Vienna that gives me the right to speak this way."

We had barely begun a discussion of the letter when Pierre Salinger came into the Cabinet Room holding a sheet of paper ripped from the Associated Press teletype. The headline blared, "Premier Khrushchev told President

Kennedy yesterday he would withdraw offensive missiles from Cuba if the United States withdrew its missiles from Turkey."

"Christ, he's got a point," I heard Jack moan. I saw him bury his head in his hands and then he said, "To any man at the United Nations or any other rational man, it will look like a very fair trade."

Nice touch, Jack, I thought cynically. I knew he was trying to stage-manage this moment because *he* was actually the one who had originally proposed this idea to Khrushchev. Now he wanted it to appear as if Khrushchev was proposing this as a rational idea for ending the crisis. I sat back to see if it would work.

McGeorge Bundy disagreed with the proposal, telling Jack it would look like we were "trying to sell out our allies for our interests." There was plenty of agreement with Bundy. It was also apparent that no one else in the room knew of the Bolshakov meeting and the back channel offer Jack and Bobby had proposed. Khrushchev was simply publicly asking for what he had been privately promised.

No sooner did we get that discussion out of the way than another problem immediately cropped up. FBI Director Hoover contacted the Attorney General and informed him that Soviet officials in New York City, which included KGB spies and accredited diplomats, were preparing to burn secret documents. Obviously, the Russians were preparing for a quick evacuation from America in case war did break out; apparently, they didn't expect a peaceful resolution to the problem either.

We had been backed into a corner. The quarantine had failed to force the Soviets to move the missiles from Cuba. Worse yet, trading our missiles in Turkey for Soviet missiles in Cuba would break the "policy of containment," the cornerstone of our foreign policy since the Truman Administration. The removal of our Turkish missiles, which were installed as a deterrent to the Soviets, would be harsh evidence to the entire world of America's shrinking power and complete lack of resolve. Such a settlement would certainly result in the break-up of NATO. No European leader would ever trust America again to risk our own national security in order to defend their freedom and their borders. Our final option, which was to invade Cuba and forcibly remove the missiles, would in all likelihood result in a nuclear war.

Then came the news we had all been dreading—a U-2 that had gone missing over Cuba was confirmed to have been shot down by a Soviet SAM missile. The Soviets had drawn first blood.

"Pilot killed?" Bobby Kennedy asked.

"Yes."

The pilot turned out to be Major Rudolf Anderson Jr., the same pilot that had photographed the Soviet missiles for us back in August.

We understood the gravity of the report and we all froze around the conference table. The President had vowed to bomb all of the SAM sites if one of our planes was shot down. Now it had happened. He would be forced to act. Or so we thought.

Once again, Jack waffled away his earlier commitment in a sort of mealy-mouthed attempt at justification. He said, "I think we ought to wait until tomorrow afternoon, to see if we get any answer....I think we ought to keep tomorrow clean, do the best we can with the surveillance. If they still fire, and we haven't got a satisfactory answer back from the Russians, then I think we ought to put a statement out tomorrow that we were fired upon, and we are therefore considering Cuba as an open territory and then take out all the SAM sites."

What the hell did "keep tomorrow clean" mean? That he was ready to consider supporting the planned attack on the same sites, so long as nothing was done until Monday? What kind of a feckless response was that? That evening, October 27, Jack told the White House staff, "Go home and see your wives and children. Tonight we decide whether to make war or not."

I was sitting next to Vice President Johnson when he turned to me and asked me about Khrushchev's actions. "Ask yourself, what made the greatest impression on you today, whether it was his letter last night or whether it was his letter this morning. Or whether it was shooting down the U-2?"

"The U-2," I declared.

"Exactly right," he agreed.

We had not responded in any way to the Soviet military act of aggression. I found out later that the President's order to call off the planned reprisal against the SAM sites was met with disbelief at the Pentagon. The American military felt it had to react swiftly and strongly to this provocation, but the President refused to act at all.

What would it take for us to respond? How far could we be pushed?

ON SUNDAY MORNING at 9:00 a.m., Radio Moscow broadcast a new letter from Premier Khrushchev. "In order to complete with greater speed the liquidation of the conflict dangerous to the cause of peace, to give confidence to all people longing for peace, and to calm the American people, who, I am certain, want peace as much as the people of the Soviet Union, the Soviet Government, in addition to previously issued instructions on the cessation of further work at building sites for the weapons, has issued a new order on the dismantling of the weapons which you describe as 'offensive' and their crating and return to the Soviet Union."

The letter concluded by saying, "I regard with respect and trust your statement in your message of October 27, 1962, that no attack will be made on Cuba—that no invasion will take place—not only by the United States, but also by other countries of the Western Hemisphere....Then the motives which prompted us to give aid of this nature to Cuba cease."

"What the hell happened?" We all were in a state of disbelief that the conflict ended so abruptly.

The Secretary of State called it, "Plain dumb luck," and many of the other advisors thought that Khrushchev had just lost his nerve. Everyone at the Agency knew otherwise. Vasily Kuznetsov, the deputy foreign minister of the Soviet Union, ominously warned John McCloy, an advisor to the President, "You got away with it this time, but you will never get away with it again."

I was never so eager to get home to my family as I was that afternoon. For the first time in weeks, Pam's brow was unfurrowed displaying her sheer relief—and Tim met me with a childish ebullience that I had not seen in a long time.

"Daddy, Daddy!" Tim rushed up and threw his arms around my waist almost knocking me down.

"We didn't know if we'd ever see you again when you left this morning." Pam searched my face for some assurance that the crisis had, indeed, ended. "Is it really over?"

It appeared to be resolved, but who really knew?

"It looks that way hon—it looks like everything is going to be all right."

That's all she wanted to hear.

THINGS WERE STARTING to get back to normal on Monday when a call from a former Arlington Forest neighbor, Stephen Soltz. His son used to swim with Tim at the Arlington Forest Swim Club.

"If you'll buy me lunch, I'll tell you a terrific story." Knowing his position with SIGINT, signals intelligence, I was quick to agree.

Soltz worked at the National Security Agency. The NSA was so super-secret, most Americans didn't even know of its existence. They were strictly an electronic intelligence gathering organization which monitored our enemies for possible threats to our national security.

We met at a quiet little greasy spoon restaurant on Glebe Road in Arlington. After some chitchat about our families, Soltz got to the point. "Did you guys over at the Agency happen to wonder why this crisis ended so abruptly?" he asked quietly.

I laughed. "Of course we did. So does everybody in D.C., if not the whole world. Why, what do you know?"

"Saturday night we intercepted a message from Soviet Ambassador

Dobrynin, which was being transmitted to Moscow. It was in the form of an enciphered cable, but we happened to know how to read it," he said matter-of-factly. Even though I possessed the highest security clearance possible, I really didn't need to know how they did what they did so I simply accepted it.

He lowered his voice almost to a whisper, "Ambassador Dobrynin sent a proposal to Khrushchev that apparently came from our Attorney General."

"What?" I hissed. "*Bobby* had been negotiating with Dobrynin? Where in the hell was the State Department? Or, for that matter, where was the President?"

"Don't ask me," Stephen said. "I'm only the messenger here. It appears that Bobby and the Ambassador went on to meet privately to discuss a resolution to the situation. Care to guess what was negotiated?"

"The removal of the missiles, I would guess."

"Well, technically, you're right," he smiled.

I waited for him to continue, but finally had to ask, "What is it, Stephen?"

"Listen to this," he leaned closer for me to hear him. "Dobrynin's message went like this: 'The most important thing for us, R. Kennedy stressed, is to get as soon as possible the agreement of the Soviet government to halt further work on the construction of the missile bases in Cuba and take measures under international control that will make it impossible to use these weapons. In exchange the government of the USA is ready, in addition to repealing all measures on the quarantine, to give assurances that there will not be any invasion of Cuba and that other countries of the Western Hemisphere are ready to give the same assurances—the US government is certain of this…'"

I interrupted him. "Did you memorize this message?" I asked. I knew Grant could quote word for word, but I was never quite sure if he was bullshitting me by making it up on the spot.

Soltz shrugged and blushed. "Actually," he admitted, "I was born with a photographic memory. I can recall virtually anything that I've read or heard."

"Jesus, Stephen, no wonder your bosses love you."

"Ahhh, Patrick, sometimes it's not a blessing. This just might be one of those times."

I could tell that he had more to get off his chest, so I urged him to continue.

"Ambassador Dobrynin went on to say: 'And what about Turkey? I asked R. Kennedy.'"

"He doesn't call him Robert, or Bobby?" I asked.

"Nope. He always calls him R. Kennedy. Anyway, here's what he says

Robert told him: 'If that is the only obstacle to achieving the regulation I mentioned earlier, then the President doesn't see any insurmountable difficulties in resolving this issue, replied R. Kennedy. The greatest difficulty for the President is the public discussion of the issue of Turkey. Formally the deployment of missile bases in Turkey was done by a special decision of the NATO Council. To announce now a unilateral decision by the president of the USA to withdraw missile bases from Turkey—this would damage the entire structure of NATO and the US position as the leader of NATO, where, as the Soviet government knows very well, there are many arguments. In short, if such a decision were announced now it would seriously tear apart NATO.'"

I held up my hand to temporarily stop Stephen's recitation. "I'm starting to get an uneasy feeling here from what you're telling me…"

"Then don't interrupt me again," Stephen protested, "because here comes the best part, or the worst part."

"Oh, no."

Stephen picked up where he left of, "Ambassador Dobrynin is still quoting our president's little brother. He next said, 'However, President Kennedy is ready to come to agree on that question with N.S. Khrushchev, too. I think that in order to withdraw these bases from Turkey, R. Kennedy said, we need 4-5 months.'"

"He said that Bobby actually offered that? What the fuck are Jack and Bobby up to? I thought we took that off the table."

Chase had been right after all. Georgi Bolshakov had actually been handling the negotiations with Bobby.

"Wait—there's still more. Bobby told him, 'However, the President can't say anything public in this regard about Turkey…only 2-3 people know about it in Washington.'"

"Oh my God," I whispered. A sudden realization hit me squarely in the stomach; I felt bile rising up into my throat. "He sold us up the river. Now it all makes sense. That's why this thing ended so abruptly. The President and his brother double-crossed the United States and our allies in NATO. Jack and Bobby not only caved in and gave Khrushchev everything he asked, they didn't have the fucking balls to let anyone else know what they had done."

Stephen could see my unease. "I know. I feel the same way. This isn't right, if you ask me. I think it comes close to treason, but I can't do anything about it on my own. It bothered me so badly that I decided to share this with someone, and I trust you."

"Thanks, Stephen. I appreciate it. I assume that I can call on you to repeat this story, if I need it?"

He nodded, "I can't put anything in writing. You understand, don't you?"

"It goes without saying, of course."

He crumpled his napkin and placed it on the table. "Well, I've got to get back to work. I have to arrange a delivery of radio vacuum tubes to Havana." He stated it so innocently I almost didn't understand what he said.

"You're what? Did you say you're sending radio vacuum tubes to Cuba? Stephen, you mean to tell me you're supplying our enemy with radio parts?"

He grinned, "Yeah, funny, isn't it? We're working to keep Castro's telecommunications system running so that we can keep monitoring what they're up to. Seems that our economic embargo has prevented the necessary electrical supplies from reaching the military—things that are critical to the Cubans, like vacuum tubes. Now these aren't small tubes, these are large tubes and components. Our problem is that the more their communications equipment breaks or burns out, the less we can intercept. So we devised a covert channel in order to supply those tubes to the Cuban government."

Soltz laughed and added, "Relax. We channel most of this stuff through Canada, so it can't be traced back to us. Pretty cool, huh?"

I was forced to admit it was.

IT TURNED OUT to be a busy week for lunch invitations. After the tensions of the last month, everyone seemed to be reaching out to friends whether to re-establish normalcy in their lives or to share their personal take on the crisis. I wasn't surprised to hear from Grant. Both of us had been in a powder keg for weeks. We met in a small dark bar in Rosslyn, just across the Key Bridge from Georgetown.

"It seems that after twenty-one months in the White House, our Kennedy brothers are not strangers to trouble, are they? Especially big trouble—let's see." Grant started to count, "The Bay of Pigs invasion, the Vienna Summit, the Berlin crisis, the Congo, Laos, Vietnam, racial unrest in the South, not to mention their threats against our own steel industry, and their dealings with organized crime. Let's add some other concerns such as sex orgies in the White House. What about adultery by both the President and the Attorney General? I've heard lurid stories about the use of illicit drugs in the White House, I mean truly horrifying rumors about our President experimenting with drugs and being under the influence of LSD, cocaine, hashish, marijuana, and who knows what else—while all the time having to be coherent to the ever impending threat of Soviet sneak attack. Jesus Christ, this man controls our nuclear arsenal. What the hell is he thinking? This is sheer recklessness—he's playing with the lives of millions of Americans. It's madness."

"I don't know, Grant," I admitted. "I don't know. It sure looks like both Kennedys are in way over their heads."

"You're damned right it does. How in the hell could he let nuclear weapons slip into the grasp of a nut like Fidel Castro? My God, he and Bobby have been trying to kill that guy for the past year and a half, and Fidel knows it. Don't you think that wily bastard is itching to get his paws on some atomic bombs? Damn, I sure would if I were in Castro's shoes."

I had to agree with him. "It's a frightening prospect—but how do you know about killing Castro. I thought it was classified."

"Operation Mongoose? We've got mutual friends remember? Buddy, I don't have to tell you, I was near shittin' my britches over what's been going on the last two weeks! And I've got a lot of friends who had to wash their britches out as well. This was too close for comfort, if you ask me."

"It was touch and go." I was uncomfortable with Grant's mention of Operation Mongoose, so I added, "We shouldn't be talking about this stuff."

Grant took a sip of his Scotch. He dropped his Texas twang and settled back into the calm and cool demeanor that everyone in D.C. knew him by.

"Just between you and me—you've been working to replace Fidel Castro in Cuba. Wouldn't you also like to replace Jack Kennedy in the White House?"

"Just between you and me? Of course I would. Jack almost got us all killed."

"Have you ever heard of something called the McCormack-Dickstein Committee?"

"Doesn't ring a bell," I responded.

"I'm not surprised, and yet I should be. I know you will be surprised when you research it. The McCormack-Dickstein Committee was the 1930's forerunner of the House Un-American Activities Committee of the 1940's. They were busy investigating Nazi and Communist activities in America, just as HUAC went after the Communists. That committee investigated something that happened in the summer of 1933 shrouded in such tight official silence that twenty-nine years later, those men that are still alive and know all of the facts, still refuse to talk about it. It doesn't appear anywhere in American history, even as a footnote. The official public documents pertaining to this event have been sanitized. You should have access to the secret and private report of the committee. Do yourself a favor and go look into it."

Grant had captured my curiosity. "Why don't you save me the trouble and just tell me what happened?" I joked.

He chuckled softly and then slowly stood up from the table. "I could do that, but it will carry much more weight with you if you do the research work yourself. It will be more credible that way." He drained the last sip of his scotch, "Your own actions will speak louder than words. If you love your country, track down that secret report and then go home. Hold your son and your wife in your arms while you decide whether to call me back."

I can't explain why, but Grant's cryptic instructions struck a chord with me. I did go up to Capitol Hill and though it took me far longer than I thought it would, I finally found the report. After I read it, I immediately knew why all references to it had been "lost" to history. It was a dangerous event that almost radically changed the history of the United States and our government as we know it.

I couldn't sleep that night because it gnawed at my mind.

JACK'S NEAR BRUSH with a nuclear holocaust didn't do anything to diminish his libido. On December 31, 1962, Chase's cousin, Secret Service Agent Newman was on duty during a raucous pool party at Bing Crosby's huge estate back in Palm Springs. Some of the women were stewardesses from a European airline whose names and identities were unknown to the Secret Service agents responsible for guarding the President.

Several California Highway Patrolmen mistook the shrieks and squeals of the partygoers for the nighttime calls of coyotes. Agent Newman received a radio call from the patrolmen on duty concerned that the coyotes might pose a threat to the President's safety. Agent Newman went poolside to take a look to be sure everyone was okay. He said he was embarrassed and upset when he saw Dave Powers "banging a girl on the edge of the pool. The President was sitting across the pool, having a drink and talking to some broads. Everybody was buckass naked." Just what the hell was going on here?

"You had to have some kind of a police squad room humor about the thing because here you are. You've got the Cold War going on. You're protecting the leader of the free world. And the highway patrol is going to come up and you're protecting him from getting caught naked. And you're carrying guns and you have all kinds of automatic weapons and you can't see in the desert, and the only thing you find is Peter Lawford out there, moaning in his beer because he can't get with the girl that he's just met that night."

I guess things were back to normal.

"The actions of men [are] the best interpreters of their thoughts."
— John Locke

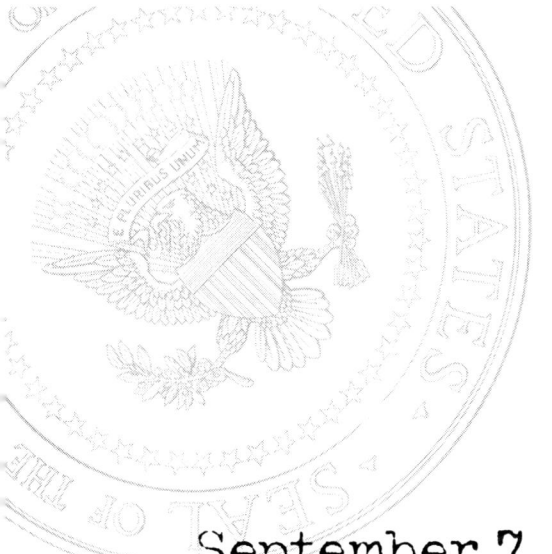

September 7, 1978
2:14 a.m.

The door to the Learjet cockpit clicked open, and the co-pilot twisted his way through the undersized opening. "Sir, we'll be landing in a few minutes. Did you want me to arrange a limo for you?"

Ruger smirked at the idea. "No, don't bother. I've made other arrangements. I won't need a limo."

The co-pilot didn't expect the sarcasm in the passenger's voice. *What a fucking asshole,* he thought. "Very well, sir. Make sure your seat belt is securely fastened." The co-pilot twisted his way back into the cockpit and closed the door.

Ruger was thinking the same thing as he watched the co-pilot return to the sanctity of his cockpit. *Why do these college-educated ass-wipes always act so smugly superior? In my younger days, I would have invited him to walk with me behind the hangar after we landed. I would have kicked his sorry ass all over the fuckin' airport just because of his my-shit-don't-stink attitude.*

Ruger gazed out the tiny window at the lights of New Orleans as they began their descent into the Crescent City. He had always had a hair trigger temper. He thought about how it bothered other people. If it wasn't for his temper, he'd probably be back in Chicago hustling stolen goods and scrounging a living on the fringes of society. *Ah hell, who am I kidding? I'd probably be dead or in prison.*

He gazed around at the luxurious appointments of the corporate Learjet that Grant Grantham had secured for him. His temper had earned this for him. His reputation for a hot temper and a sadistic streak that could scare other people had brought him to the attention of Sam Giancana, and Giancana had taken him under his wing. It only took a few short years for Giancana to promote him to be his number one enforcer. It was a continuation of the old Chicago mob traditions: Al Capone had Frank Nitti to do his dirty work, and Sam Giancana had Derek Ruger. He smiled to himself at the thought that he had become a legend like those famous names. Killing people was a far better profession than anyone had ever told him.

The jet shuddered and vibrated as the flaps and wheels came down to slow the plane and prepare for its landing. He grabbed the armrests and steadied himself as the plane prepared to touch down on the tarmac.

He peered out the window at the twinkling lights of the Big Easy and thought: *Where are you hiding, Patrick McCarthy?"*

"Come out, come out, wherever you are," he softly sang to himself.

1963

THE IMMEDIATE AFTERMATH of the Cuban Missile Crisis left me anxious and pessimistic. The United States had been taken to the brink of nuclear war by our young, inexperienced President and his even more callow, immature brother. Hailing them as heroes, the media effusively praised Jack and Bobby for bravely standing up to Khrushchev and Fidel using the force of their will to make Khrushchev back down.

The truth was that we only managed to avoid catastrophe through a deal our President covertly negotiated with Soviet Premier Khrushchev. Khrushchev had succeeded in getting our nuclear missiles in Turkey and Italy removed as a threat to Moscow. The secretly negotiated deal temporarily guaranteed the physical safety of the United States by betraying NATO and our European allies. The public believed the two Kennedy brothers had miraculously made the world a safer place.

Our State Department was embarrassed and angry at the extent of the President's betrayal. How could our foreign diplomacy experts have any confidence in their future negotiations with the Soviet Union? They knew the President and his brother could unilaterally decide to change any agreement—and never reveal what they had bargained away. Our policy of Soviet containment dating back to the late 1940's was history. Now, Soviet expansion into the Mediterranean and the oil-rich Middle East was a real and dangerous threat. Our country was in a vulnerable position in any future confrontations with either the Russians or the Chinese. To paraphrase Stephen Soltz, "This was a betrayal of national security bordering on treason."

I kept thinking back to that Atlantic sailing trip off Cape Cod when Jack,

Red Fay, and I had discussed *Seven Days in May*, a book about an attempted military coup against an American president. I remembered Red asking Jack if a military coup could happen here and Jack replied: *"It's possible but the conditions would have to be just right. If the country had a young President, and he had a Bay of Pigs, there would be a certain uneasiness. Maybe the military would do a little criticizing behind his back. Then, if there were another Bay of Pigs, the reaction of the country would be, 'Is he too young and inexperienced?' The military would almost feel that it was their patriotic obligation to stand ready to preserve the integrity of the nation...Then if there were a third Bay of Pigs—it could happen."*

Jack's words gnawed at me as I replayed the scene *ad nauseum* in my mind. The first *Bay of Pigs* he referred to obviously was the original invasion fiasco that he screwed up back April 1961. The next *Bay of Pigs* could encompass everything from the growing civil rights struggle that was inflaming the South to the calamitous Vienna Summit and the Berlin Wall crisis. *"Then if there were a third Bay of Pigs..."* obviously would have to be the Cuban Missile Crisis of October 1962.

The final part, which bothered me the most, was his assertion that *"...it could happen."*

Could it happen? I didn't know.

Should it happen? Maybe it should.

With barely two years into John F. Kennedy's first term, the administration had spent its time dodging calamity after calamity. In the aftermath of the most recent near-fatal debacle, I grew increasingly alarmed at the reckless behavior of the White House and its staff. Kennedy and his advisors had negligently discounted our intelligence by simply choosing not to believe the Agency's warnings. When the administration finally was convinced of the Russian duplicity, they refused to act. Once they were forced to act, the Kennedy brothers cowardly cut a deal behind everybody's back selling out our European allies and destroying NATO's security. Mr. Hoover had prophetically warned about a leader like Jack when he said, *"Can you even begin to imagine what would happen if we were betrayed by our own leaders? Our own President? We cannot afford to let down our guard—our constant vigil must be maintained at all costs."*

I thought back to a volatile discussion about Euripedes from a class called Early Civilizations that I had taken in college. The class vociferously debated Euripedes' premise that the sons would ultimately have to answer for the sins of their fathers. Euripedes' quote stuck with me all these years: "Visit the sins of the fathers upon their sons." As a young man, I believed that I alone was in charge of my destiny—not my father. It was a ridiculous supposition to me that my father's "sins" would direct the course of my life. Older now, I recognized the truth of Euripedes' words.

Old Joe Kennedy had been a truly despicable human being whose main goals in life were to push the Kennedy name and family as far as it could go, without regard for what was right and just. Old Joe bought his son the White House, just as he bought his son a congressional seat and a Pulitzer Prize. Because of Joe's ambitions, John F. Kennedy was now a threat to the lives of every single American. His actions, compounded by numerous mistakes in judgment, had almost resulted in millions of Americans being killed by Russian nuclear missiles.

I knew that I would worry about the impact of Jack Kennedy's mistakes and misjudgments every minute—for the rest of his term in office.

JACK KENNEDY'S DESTRUCTIVE influence was also evidenced by the number of marital casualties in his administration. Pam and I had grown increasingly concerned over the adulterous behavior of many in the Kennedy White House. Most of Jack's top advisors had openly and systematically destroyed their own marriages by imitating Jack's reckless behavior. Arthur Schlesinger, Pierre Salinger, Ted Sorensen, James Reed, and Charles Spaulding were just a few of the most prominent advisors whose marriages fell apart during that time, aided by their own indiscreet comportment.

A Georgetown psychiatrist friend of ours called it "White House Fever," which he claimed produced profound behavioral changes in the men. "I've diagnosed it before. Their close proximity to the power of the presidency brings out the very worst actions in people," he pointed out at dinner one night with our wives. He also said he thought that Jack reveled in the chaos that surrounded him—it made him appear stronger because he was the only person in his circle that could clearly handle it. "The whole thing is so irrational—it's like Louis XIV and his court."

"I think the whole world is spinning out of control," Pam said as we were getting ready for bed one evening. She pulled back the bedspread, folding it up and placing it on a chair in the corner of the room.

"I can't believe what people are doing. They don't seem to care if anyone knows. Even Jackie's sister Lee is having an affair."

"Oh yeah, with whom?" I hung up my pants and threw my shirt into the clothes basket.

"Aristotle Onassis, a toady little Greek," Pam laughed and simulated a gag. "He's so atrociously ugly! Lee said that he was alluring to her."

"It's his money that's alluring to her. You remember how Jackie's eyes always glazed over in the presence of wealth," I said while brushing my teeth.

"That is not so. Jackie could never be attracted to someone like Onassis, no matter how much money he has," Pam pretended to be indignant. "Lee said that she was attracted to him because he was such a powerful man."

Pam pulled her hair back with a headband, washed her face with Noxzema, and carefully patted it dry. "Oh, I almost forgot."

I got into bed. I propped the pillow against the headboard while Pam continued her conversation from the bathroom.

"I ran into Mary Pinchot Meyer again. She was openly bragging about," Pam stopped. "Patrick, I don't think I should tell you this just before we go to bed. Remind me, I'll tell you tomorrow morning."

"Tell me now, I'm listening." Pam always accused me of not listening while I accused her of not enunciating. "That is if you will enunciate," I teased.

"It's not that, you'll get too mad and won't be able to sleep."

Now she had my attention. Pam turned on the lamp on the nightstand and then climbed into bed. I pulled her close, "You can tell me." I kissed her neck, "If I can't sleep, then you'll just have to do something to make me sleep."

"She said that she and Jack have been smoking marijuana in the White House. She brought six joints, whatever that it is, and Jack smoked three."

"What!"

"At first, he didn't feel any effects, but then he closed his eyes and said: Suppose the Russians did something now—he laughed that he'd be too stoned to move."

Pam was right. She should have waited until morning to tell me.

Mary also boasted to Pam that she and Jack had sampled the hallucinogenic drug LSD while together one night in the White House. Neither of us had any reason to doubt her. We both knew Mary was a rabid disciple of Dr. Timothy Leary, the high priest of LSD; she loved to trumpet how brilliant she thought he was and how soothing the drug made you feel. Mary also said Jack confessed to her that pot "isn't like cocaine," and she said Jack promised her he would soon get her some to try.

Grant had relayed some similar gossip after the Cuban Missile Crisis—it now made sense to me. Pam and I were stunned at Jack's exceedingly imprudent behavior.

I remembered J. Edgar Hoover's words from fifteen years ago: *"A leader of men must especially be a moral man. Without a solid foundation in morality, that leader cannot lead. America cannot elect, nor can it follow, an immoral man as President. A man whose mind is clouded with sexual thoughts cannot be expected* to think clearly or rationally in times of crisis. This is especially important with the specter of atomic warfare hanging over our heads."

Something needed to be done—the only question was "What?"

PAM AND I were invited to attend the Emancipation Gala at the White House on February 12, Abraham Lincoln's birthday. A black tie event, the celebration paid tribute to the centennial anniversary of Lincoln's Emancipation Proclamation. Both Jackie and Pam were excited about it, discussing and planning what they would wear for weeks beforehand. Fortunately, they were blissfully ignorant of the firestorm of political controversy the gala was causing behind the scenes.

The Emancipation Gala was the brainchild of Louis Martin, a member of the Democratic National Committee, and one of two Negroes who had regular access to the Oval Office. On January 31, Martin sent a memo to the President and his advisory staff, reminding them of the unfulfilled campaign promises made to the Negroes of America. His memo warned that Negroes were on the edge of open revolt in our country. "The fact is the President cares more about Germany than about Negroes, he thinks it's more important." He said that young Negroes were tired of being told to wait their turn and that it was finally time for Jack Kennedy to do something about it.

Jack responded by telling Louis Martin to plan a reception at the White House for prominent Negro leaders on Lincoln's birthday. He left it up to Martin to make up the guest list which ultimately included eight hundred guests.

We, along with all of the invited guests, were thrilled to receive personal phone calls and telegrams from the White House the day before the event. We were directed to come to the Southwest Gate of the White House, instead of the more prestigious East Gate that had been specified on the invitations.

Pam, who meticulously chronicled all of these events in a scrapbook, was puzzled by the change. When I arrived home that evening, she told me she had called the White House for clarification.

"The operator told me the reason for the switch was so the President and the First Lady could personally greet everyone in the family quarters of the White House."

Pam was quite rightly suspicious of that rationale. "This doesn't sound right," she told me, "so I called Jackie to find out what was going on. Jackie was just as surprised when she found out about the last-minute change and said that she had not authorized the change."

"Knowing Jack and his advisors, maybe they don't want their Democratic supporters honoring the most popular Republican President of all time," I volunteered.

"That's not it. Jack's political advisors don't want the voting public to know that almost all of the guests are going to be Negroes. They don't want to offend anyone," Pam fumed. "Those same advisors told Louis Martin the White House would handle all of the publicity for the evening; then, they went out of their way to make sure there was absolutely *no* publicity or media coverage for the Gala."

"So the subterfuge about a change of gates is, in reality, a cheap ploy on their part to keep the invited guests—the Negroes—from being photographed in any part of the White House," I surmised. I had no doubt that Jack was behind this.

"I told Jackie she should talk to Jack immediately. But she said she had to wait because he was in such a foul mood over something that happened with the U.S. Civil Rights Commission. If I were Jackie, I would have marched right in there and gotten an answer," Pam had raised her voice at least two octaves.

"I agree with Jackie. It's better to let things cool down first," I added.

"Why is he having everyone go to the back entrance of the White House? Can't anyone see the horrible irony of this?" Pam calmed somewhat, "Jackie said that many of the guests are very distinguished Negro leaders who are seeing the inside of the White House for the first time. She said that she's not going to let Jack spoil it for them."

"I hope Jackie will be able to do something, but hon, there's nothing you can do about it," I said to soothe Pam.

"I know that Patrick! And that's the point. There's not a damn thing that I can do."

WHEN PAM AND I arrived, we were escorted to the Southwest Gate of the White House. Pam arched her eyebrow at me when she saw the well-dressed crowd excitedly waiting to enter the dinner and reception. Jackie had invited us upstairs to the family quarters for a drink before the dinner started. We were led into the living room where a cocktail table had been set with hors d'oeuvres. Jack and Jackie, still in their bedroom, were embroiled in a heated argument—which we uncomfortably overheard.

The one couple the President specifically didn't want to be seated was Sammy Davis, Jr. and his Caucasian wife, Swedish actress Mai Britt. Jack had obviously seen them when he looked out the window at the arriving crowd. He was apoplectic.

"What's he doing here?" the President hissed. "I personally removed

Sammy's name four times from the guest list, and four times Louis Martin added it back on."

"Everyone loves Sammy Davis, Jr.," Jackie said.

"Doesn't he understand that a picture of a black man in the White House with his white wife will be a political nightmare for me with the voters? I'll be crucified!"

I decided to make a drink. I asked Pam in a louder than normal voice what she wanted to drink, then noisily opened the ice bucket making sure to clink the glasses. Pam commented on the appetizers. We then engaged each other in small talk hoping that the First Couple would realize our nearby presence.

An aide suddenly appeared and knocked respectfully on the bedroom door. We overheard Jack whisper, "Get them out of here!"

Jack tried to impress upon Jackie the political consequences of seating the couple. Jackie would not budge so the President asked Jackie to personally greet Mai Britt and take her aside until all of the photographs were officially taken and the photographers gone.

"How dare you to even make the suggestion! These are *my* invited guests in *my* house."

"It doesn't matter. You've got to do this my way, Jackie."

"I won't, Jack. And don't you dare ask me again. The answer will still be 'No!'"

The more insistent Jack became, the more agitated Jackie became. Then, Jackie told Jack that she would not attend the Gala.

"You have to go. Everyone expects us to be there."

"That's too bad. You can explain to them why I'm not there."

"Jackie…," Jack started to whine.

"No, Jack! I mean it. I will not allow you to embarrass my guests like that. If you have that little regard for my feelings, then you can explain to the people I invited why I'm not going to be with them tonight."

There was a good bit of door slamming and heavy walking. Pam and I decided to quietly make our exit.

The reception began without the presence of either the President or the First Lady. No one seemed to notice the breach in protocol when Jack finally appeared alone to greet his enthusiastic guests. We were somewhat surprised when Jackie slipped through the crowd, graciously greeting everyone, to make her way next to her husband for a formal picture with Vice President Johnson and his wife Lady Bird, Ethel Kennedy, and eleven important Negro leaders. Then announcing that she didn't feel well, she left the room. Pam could tell she was fighting back tears and rose to follow her.

Since Pam and I knew everything that had been going on, I was tempted to go up to Jack and use my favorite line from the Laurel and Hardy movie, *Sons of the Desert*: "I had no idea that such a deplorable condition existed in your household."

I didn't think the President would have appreciated my humor. As Pam and I departed the White House that night, I found myself laughing and wondering which couch the President of the United States would sleep on that evening.

AT A PRESS CONFERENCE three weeks later, racial equality was once again a topic. Jack was asked about the quality of the judges that he had appointed in the South during his term. He coolly defended his appointees by saying, "I think that the men that have been appointed to judgeships in the South, sharing perhaps as they do the general outlook of the South, have done a remarkable job in fulfilling their oath of office."

I had to stifle a laugh the next day when Chase brought me an article about William Howard Cox, the man who was the President's first judicial appointment. Judge Cox happened to be an old college roommate of Senator James Eastland of Mississippi, who was the chairman of the Senate Judiciary Committee. In his first voting rights case from the Mississippi bench after being appointed, Judge Cox had branded some Negro plaintiffs as "A bunch of niggers….acting like a bunch of chimpanzees."

It was not jurisprudence's finest hour.

Grant had been right. Jack's federal court appointees were racists.

THE MONTH OF June began with a political sex scandal of near-epic proportions. The British Secretary of State for War, John Profumo, a highly respected Cabinet Minister, allegedly engaged in a sexual affair with a nineteen-year-old prostitute and showgirl named Christine Keeler. Gossip swirled around London—the juicy rumor that Keeler was also sleeping with a Soviet attaché from the Russian Embassy rocked Parliament.

The idea that a senior member of the British government shared a whore with a Russian spy was a devastating disclosure for Prime Minister Harold Macmillan. Profumo, standing before the House of Commons in March, vehemently proclaimed his innocence, stating there was "no impropriety whatever" in his relationship with Keeler. Nevertheless, he was forced to concede that his earlier admission to the House was a spectacular lie—he had indeed shared his mistress with a Soviet spy. Although he assured the public that he had not compromised national security in any way, the scandal almost toppled the entire British government.

The *New York Journal-American* linked Jack to the Profumo scandal by reporting that a "high elected American official" had been the paramour of Suzy Chang, another one of the girls caught up in the Profumo scandal. Suzy Chang freely admitted that she had been with Jack Kennedy numerous times; luckily for Jack, no one in the public believed her. Jack Kennedy's image as a good family man completely cloaked his private image as a sex-addicted serial adulterer.

Jack narrowly dodged the Profumo scandal but became embroiled in another eerily similar situation. Very few people outside of the White House knew the President had gone to bed numerous times with a woman involved with one of our nation's enemies. Ellen Rometsch, a high-priced call girl who worked for Bobby Baker in his Quorum club, was reputed to be an East German spy. Bobby Baker laughingly told me and Grant that Jack had boasted that Rometsch had performed "the best oral sex I ever had." Attorney General Bobby Kennedy quickly came to his brother's rescue by having Ellen Rometsch immediately deported without the benefit of any legal hearing or advice.

The Profumo scandal presented us with one of those "good news/bad news" moments around D.C. The good news was that Jack could have been forced from office by that scandal. The bad news was that Lyndon Johnson might also have been forced to resign since Bobby Baker was his protégé, and Baker was the one running the prostitution ring that employed Rometsch.

Meanwhile, Jack's right-hand man, Kenny O'Donnell, was embroiled in two growing scandals of his own. O'Donnell was on record for announcing in a drunken fit, that "the President was in fact rather stupid and that if it were not for [O'Donnell's] assistance, he would fall flat on his face." He also claimed he had received many offers from industry but was afraid to leave because he knew that "the administration would fall apart" without him. In addition to that, it was revealed that O'Donnell was being investigated for embezzling campaign money for his own use. The White House closed ranks around him; Attorney General Bobby Kennedy effectively shielded Kenny from much more than cursory scrutiny.

Old Joe Kennedy had certainly been shrewd when he forced Jack to name his younger brother Bobby Attorney General.

THE PRESIDENT'S SPEECH at American University in June was the last straw. Standing before the graduating class, Jack announced that the United States "had a deep interest in halting the arms race." Throughout his speech, he described the Soviet Union as a superpower of equal status to the United States boldly declaring that the United States would no longer "conduct nuclear tests in the atmosphere so long as other states do not do so." His goal was disarmament. He firmly asserted that he didn't care if the Russians agreed to do the same or not—the United States would "seek a relaxation of tensions."

Jack's speech blindsided the military. It went against everything we knew to be true about securing the safety of any nation. In *The Prince*, Niccolo Machiavelli said, "Without its arms, no principality is secure…That nothing is so infirm and unstable as the reputation of power not sustained by one's own force…Among the causes of evil that being unarmed brings you, it makes you contemptible, which is one of those infamies the prince should be on guard against…There has never been…a new prince who has disarmed his subjects…when you disarm them, you begin to offend them; you show that you distrust them either for cowardice or for lack of faith, both of which opinions generate hatred against you."

Sun Tzu was even more succinct in the *Art of War* when he wrote, "Invincibility lies in the defense." Kennedy announced to the world that the United States would unilaterally weaken our defense in the pursuit of peace. Sun Tzu also stated, "If ignorant both of your enemy and of yourself, you are certain in every battle to be in peril."

As a nation, our safety was in jeopardy. I soon discovered that others were as alarmed as I was. The next day, I received a call from Grant asking me to meet with him concerning a topic of great importance to us both.

"This isn't something I want to talk about over the telephone." He directed me to meet him in the theater of the Folger Library in D.C. the next day.

THE FOLGER LIBRARY is an independent research library located in a huge marble building almost across the street from the Capitol Building. I had been there a few times before with Pam who had tried to foster my interest in Shakespeare by encouraging me to attend several performances at the Folger's Elizabethan Theatre in our early years of courtship.

I entered the Folger at the west entrance, the American entrance which overlooks the Capitol and the mall. I meandered through the lobby and mingled with several tourists. I smiled at a couple, obviously grandparents, who were showing their grandson a sculpture of Puck from *A Midsummer Night's Dream*, and I thought that one day that would be Tim with Pam's parents. I entered the first room off the lobby entrance, a majestically paneled room. It was designed and built like a Great Hall from a medieval castle; its

35-foot ceiling and dark wooden walls dominated the interior space. The hall, 129 feet long, was reputed to be a good place for private conversations since it contained no alcoves or hidden spaces. I entered a curtained doorway and wound my way back through the reading room.

I finally found the entrance to the Elizabethan Theatre. The doors were closed. A sign hanging from a red velvet rope told casual visitors the theatre was closed, but I tried the door and found it to be unlocked. I could almost imagine myself transported into a world back in time as something akin to an Elizabethan courtyard loomed around me. Three-tiered wooden balconies, carved oak posts, and the ornately timbered and painted facade lent an imposing air to the setting.

I was so caught up admiring the surroundings that I didn't notice Grant sitting in a corner of the front row until he waved. I made my way down the short aisle to take a seat next to him. He motioned with an outstretched arm toward the stage and said, "It's pretty magnificent, isn't it?"

He paused to look around the room. "I love it here. I like to sneak over here and devote a little leisure time to my interest in Shakespeare. I often think that if my daddy hadn't made me go into politics, I might have been a simple scholar of Shakespeare. This whole building was a gift from its founders, Henry Clay Folger, and his wife, Emily Jordan Folger in 1932."

Grant paused for a moment to let me take it all in. I let him continue with his lecture.

"Its scholarly mission is to preserve as much as possible related to Shakespeare's writings as well as his life and times. This museum is home to the world's largest collection of Shakespearean printed works, manuscripts, playbills, costumes, artifacts, drawings, paintings, and musical instruments from Elizabethan times to the present. Scholars from all over the world travel here to study rare texts and other manuscripts that are archived here dating from the Renaissance. Can you imagine how much fun it would be to work here at this Library and produce Shakespearean research in books and papers?"

He stared wistfully at the empty stage for a few moments before his reverie was broken.

"Do you like Shakespeare, Patrick?"

I shrugged my shoulders, "I guess. We studied him in high school, but I spent more time making fun of my teacher trying to get the class to embrace the past than I did in actually studying the play. As a high school kid, it didn't seem very relevant." I suddenly remembered that I had enjoyed reading Shakespeare to pass the time when I was stationed at Groom Lake**,** but before I could add that, Professor Grantham resumed his discourse.

"That's too bad. I love the guy. I love his ability to explore the human experience in so many different ways. I find that intriguing. Love and war are his favorite themes, but deception and betrayal are his best. Experts admire the sheer genius of his plot construction. I think his ability to craft the English language in iambic pentameter is unmatched anywhere in the English language. Thankfully, it can be preserved in a place like this for future generations to discover and enjoy. I don't mind admitting that this good ol' Texas boy has spent many hours reading Shakespeare and memorizing his cadences. My daddy said that's how he was taught Shakespeare in school. It's a lost form of art, and we are all the worse off because of it."

Grant got up, straightened his pants, and peered up to the rafters as if he were looking for something.

"One of my favorite plays of all time is *Hamlet*. Have you ever heard the line: 'Something is rotten in the state of Denmark'?"

"Of course I have. That's a pretty famous quote."

Grant cautiously looked around the room—if he had wanted privacy, we should have met in the Great Hall. Satisfied that we were alone, he continued, "I am moved to observe something similar today: Something is rotten in the United States of America."

"Yeah, I think so, too. I think something *is* seriously wrong in this country."

"Patrick, this country is facing the gravest threat to its existence since the Civil War. We are facing the virtual annihilation of our nation in a nuclear war. One wrong move and we could be wiped off the face of this earth."

Grant had never impressed me as a deep-thinker; he had always been more of a self-interested cut-up. I had to remind myself that Grant had matured over the years and had actually become politically astute. I knew that he loved his country and was patriotic. It shouldn't come as a surprise that he would be concerned over the same things that I was.

"Grant, remember I was there in the Oval Office. I know how close we came to a nuclear war."

"You know, during the Cuban Missile Crisis, we Texans heard a lot of talk about Russian missiles landing in Washington, New York, and Miami. Well, I'm here to tell you that we were more than a little concerned those same missiles could as easily have hit the oilfields of Texas or even our homes and families in Dallas and Houston. Yet, we never heard a single word of concern out of the White House over the possibility of that targeting. There's a lot of money in Texas that was very upset about that."

"I can imagine so. If I were a Texan, I'd probably have been concerned as well. You know, my family lives less than two miles from the Pentagon. Believe me I know what living at Ground Zero feels like."

"I know you do. Well, my friends in Texas, as well as my friends here in

D.C. are also very concerned. My friends have all worked too hard all of their lives to consider living with a bulls-eye on their backs, if you know what I mean." Grant digressed, "Do you know the story of Hamlet?"

"I know the line: 'To be or not to be.' And I know that everybody dies at the end."

"Not entirely. Not everyone dies. Horatio is left to pick up the pieces. Basically, the story of Hamlet is about a King who gains his throne in an illegitimate manner. Hamlet, who is the rightful heir to the crown, is trying to reclaim the throne from Claudius, the King. There's one point when the conflict is at its peak, and the King has finally made the decision to get rid of Hamlet..."

Grant paused for dramatic effect. "It is Act Four, Scene Three when the King says: How dangerous is it that this man goes loose! Yet must not we put the strong law on him. He's loved of the distracted multitude, who like not in their judgment but their eyes."

"Interesting," I mused.

"Shakespeare could have been talking about John F. Kennedy."

"How?"

"Patrick, there are parallels here. We have a dangerous man on the loose that is loved by the public." Grant hesitated a few moments. "Do you think John Fitzgerald Kennedy is dangerous?"

"I personally think he's exceedingly dangerous."

"My friends do too. They look at this young President and see a leader who was voted in by 'the distracted multitudes.' He was elected to a job that has turned out to be way too difficult for him. Jack Kennedy was considered a political lightweight in Washington while he was a Senator and a Congressman. He's a lightweight President, too—a president who prefers to play and attend to his own needs rather than fully concentrating on his elected job."

Grant strolled over to the steps on the side of the stage and sat down. "He's managed to screw up every major foreign policy decision that has come his way."

"I know that Grant—the Bay of Pigs, the Vienna Summit, the Missile Crisis. He and Bobby have made one mistake after another. I pray to God to see us through to the next election."

"Not only that, Patrick, he's botched up our domestic policy by stirring up the damn Negroes. He has them believing that he'll soon be giving them 'equal rights' or some such nonsense. I'll tell you right now, the Soviets will jump all over us if they see the Negroes of our country rioting and causing internal dissent."

Grant let out a long tired sigh. He seemed to ponder how to phrase his next statement. "We are a nation in the midst of the greatest crisis it has ever known."

We both were silent for several moments. Grant was saying aloud everything that I had thought to myself.

"An antagonistic nuclear superpower threatens us with advanced weapons and a communistic way of life. Our Negro population is on the verge of civil unrest and disobedience. Our Commander in Chief won't listen to the advice of his generals—he's already fired the head of the CIA and his second-in-command."

"Dulles and Bissell should never have been fired. Allen Dulles devoted himself to this country," I said.

"I know he plans to fire the head of the FBI when he's re-elected."

"Mr. Hoover?" I was shocked.

"He also plans to dump his Vice President from the 1964 ticket."

"How do you know that?"

"I hear things. But the point is, Patrick, he won't listen to reason, and as a result, he has been absolutely wrong in every important decision he has been forced to make."

What Grant said was true. I was most troubled about Jack's recent decision toward disarmament.

Grant elaborated, "Look, we know he took us to the very brink of a nuclear war in Cuba last year. He ignored his military intelligence. As you know, he prevented war only by giving Khrushchev what he wanted which puts our country at risk. Kennedy doesn't understand the chain of command; he thinks that because he is Commander In Chief that he doesn't need to listen or even consider that there may be those more experienced who should be consulted. He's captain of the team, and he doesn't need a quarterback or a coach for that matter."

"Well, like father, like son," I said disgustedly. "I am haunted by the fact that our President's own father was the highest ranking Nazi sympathizer in the United States government prior to our entrance into World War II. It sticks in my craw that Ambassador Kennedy felt that appeasing Hitler was far more important than opposing him."

"Patrick, let me ask you something, is his son capable of doing the same thing? I look at that secret deal he made with Khrushchev to remove those NATO missiles, and I am forced to conclude that, yes, he would. He would act to appease any further aggression from Khrushchev in a New York minute."

I expected Grant to look at his watch soon. We had been in the theater for almost a half an hour.

"Let me ask you this: Do you think this country can survive another four years of John F. Kennedy as President?"

I firmly replied, "No." After a minute I said, "We can only hope that the country will elect a new President who will correct all of Kennedy's blunders."

Grant fixed me with a steely gaze. "What would you say if I told you there are other people both inside and outside of Washington who believe we may not survive another two years of John F. Kennedy in the White House? Would that surprise you?"

I stared back at Grant. "No, that wouldn't surprise me."

Once more, his gaze swept out over the empty theater as if to reassure himself we were alone. He took a deep breath. "Would you be surprised to learn that these individuals would do almost anything to insure that John F. Kennedy *didn't* serve another two years, let alone another full term in office?"

"No. That wouldn't surprise me either." This was serious territory, both legally and emotionally.

"Do you have any idea how much the military leadership of this country despises their Commander in Chief?"

"I've actually seen it first-hand."

"You have no idea," Grant snorted derisively. "Tell me truthfully, have you ever heard of something called Operation Northwoods?"

"Operation Northwoods? Doesn't ring a bell—I don't think it's one of our Agency programs."

"No, it's not. It's a program drawn up by the Joint Chiefs of Staff. It has the written approval of the Chairman of the Joint Chiefs and is ready to be implemented at any time by our Pentagon. It is both the *most secret* program that I have ever seen, as well as the most profoundly disturbing."

I had never heard of such a name, nor was I even aware that Grant had access to Top Secret classified government material. His high-level governmental and political connections never failed to mystify me. "What is it, Grant?"

Grant hesitated considering how to parse his words. "It lays the groundwork for a military takeover of the United States of America by our own generals. In short, it's a blueprint for an American military *coup d'etat*."

Shaken, I stammered, "Where did you hear that?"

Grant held his hand up to cut me off. "Just because you haven't heard about it doesn't mean it doesn't exist. This report really does exist. I've read it. In fact, I'm probably one of less than a dozen people outside of the Pentagon who has seen it. And after having read it, I can understand why everyone wishes to keep this thing buried. Its contents are absolutely explosive."

I began to put the facts together. Jack's own cryptic comments on that boat ride with Red Fay suddenly made a lot more sense to me now. Something was indeed going on. I had no idea that it had been formally written down, let alone given a name.

"As you may know, our senior military leadership campaigned quite openly against the President in the last election. It got so bad that immediately after taking office, Defense Secretary McNamara relieved Major General Edwin A. Walker of his command. He charged him with being a member of the John Birch Society and claimed he indoctrinated his troops with John Birch Society propaganda. Many people inside and outside of the military viewed this as a stifling of his right to free speech, as well as an attempt by the new administration to put a muzzle on anti-Communist activities. When Major General Walker went to Oxford, Mississippi in September of last year to protest against the admittance of James Meredith to the university, our Attorney General, Robert Kennedy, charged him with seditious conspiracy, insurrection, and rebellion. Bobby ordered the Major General jailed in a mental hospital for five days before finally turning him loose under tremendous political pressure from within the military itself. Well, that set the stage for a continuing escalation of tension between the military and this administration."

Grant lowered his voice nervously and continued with his story. "I heard reports that even at the National War College here in town, it's not at all uncommon for seminars to disintegrate into vitriolic diatribes against the Kennedys. A member of Secretary Robert McNamara's staff even wrote a report in which he cited how various meetings at the War College would turn into 'extreme right-wing, witch-hunting, mudslinging revivals' in which 'bigoted, one-sided presentations' were made 'advocating that the danger to our security is internal only.'"

I recalled something else that I had heard. "Didn't the Senate Foreign Relations Committee issue a report warning of this military unrest?" I asked Grant.

"Yes—yes they did. Their report warned of a considerable danger due to this so-called right-wing extremism in our military. Well, let me ask you something. What if it's not right-wing extremism? What if it is simply a patriotic concern by our military over how far left this country is turning? There's no doubt in the minds of many people that young Jack's domestic social program is Communistic in nature. Remember this fact: social legislation begets socialism itself, which in turn leads directly to Communism. Take a close look at this administration's domestic legislation. It's punishing the rich with a reduction of the oil depletion allowance and the graduated income tax. Social Security is now offering medical care. The federal government is getting involved with aid to education in order to dictate what is to be taught in our schools. They're also pushing disarmament negotiations with an enemy who cannot be trusted. This has grave implications."

"What about this Operation Northwoods? What's the significance of it?"

"That's what I'm trying to tell you. Everyone knows about the recent revolt of the army generals in France over the government's policies in Algers, do you remember?"

"Yes." It was all over the news here. De Gaulle's government barely survived. In fact, French generals tried to assassinate de Gaulle last year.

"Those French military leaders had expressed the exact same reservations about their government, only they took it a step farther. They actually revolted. Believe me, no one I know wants to see that happen here, but the concern is there. And it is very real—especially since the emergence of documents detailing Operation Northwoods."

"Go on, I'm listening."

He inhaled deeply then slowly exhaled. "In order to fight the growing spread of Communism, the Joint Chiefs proposed launching a very secret and bloody war of pure terrorism. It was to be waged against the United States itself in order to trick the American public into supporting a much more aggressive campaign of action against Fidel Castro."

"More aggressive even than Operation Mongoose?"

"This went way beyond that," Grant replied dismissively. "We're talking about innocent Americans being shot on American streets by fake terrorists. They were going to have a wave of public bombings kill people in Washington and Miami; boats carrying Cuban refugees would be sunk; commercial airliners would be hijacked and blown up; and even our space program would be deliberately sabotaged with the planned loss of life of our own astronauts."

"What the hell? That could easily lead to an all-out war!"

"Of course it could! That's exactly what the generals *want* to see happen! They hope to trick America into hating Cuba so much that our next invasion would not only be supported, it would be encouraged. World opinion would be on our side. If the Kennedy brothers continued their soft stance on this growing Communist menace, especially with American blood being spilled on American streets, then no one would fault the Joint Chiefs for taking more extreme and expedient action."

I couldn't believe what I was hearing. "This just isn't possible," I protested.

"Oh, it's quite possible, all right. I've seen it in writing. Remember the explosion of the U.S. battleship *Maine* in Havana harbor in 1898? That explosion killed 266 American sailors sparking so much public outrage the United States was forced to declare war with Spain. The entire Spanish-American War rallied the people of the United States to a patriotic cause and created a national hero out of Teddy Roosevelt. Operation Northwoods could have the very same effect. Can you imagine what the impact of a coordinated campaign of terror would be on our country? The military would step in and assume control. The citizens of America would demand it!"

"Jesus," I whispered.

"Listen, Patrick, here's what I know. On Tuesday, March 13, 1962, General Lyman Lemnitzer, head of the Joint Chiefs of Staff, signed the Northwoods document and took it into a special meeting with Secretary of Defense McNamara. Bizarre as it may sound, Lemnitzer actually presented it to the Kennedy administration, recommending that a national policy of early military intervention in Cuba be undertaken as soon as possible. I guess he believed in some strange way that because of what Bobby and Jack were doing with Operation Mongoose, the military's plan would be approved. He certainly didn't anticipate that his message would be rejected by any of his civilian leaders."

"Wait a minute, Grant. Slow down. You seem to know a lot about stuff you're not supposed to know about. Are you sure you've got all of the right information here?"

Grant gave me his old shit-eating grin, "Come on, Patrick, I know a lot of things I'm not supposed to know. You should know that by now. I knew about Operation Mongoose, didn't I?" Grant picked up where he left off, "Shortly after that meeting, Lemnitzer was denied a second term as the Chairman of the Joint Chiefs and was hurriedly transferred to Europe to become the new head of NATO instead. Operation Northwoods was quickly and officially shit-canned by all concerned."

"I would hope so…Operation Northwoods is crazy," I added.

"I agree. But in October, Jack and Bobby took us to the brink of a nuclear war. They cut the legs out from underneath Lemnitzer's NATO command with their secret agreement to withdraw our missiles from Turkey and Italy. In the aftermath of the Cuban Missile Crisis, Lemnitzer and his people got all worked up again, becoming even angrier and more maniacal. They are more convinced than ever about the need for preemptive action."

"Even if it involves the death of innocent Americans?" I stopped to consider the implications, "Well, that's clearly more than a problem."

"It really is. Concern has been growing in many circles around the country that a belligerent and hostile military leadership here in the United States could ultimately become as dangerous to our nation's welfare as an incompetent administration. We civilians simply cannot allow that to happen here."

"I couldn't agree more."

"I'm glad, Patrick. I'm very glad. You see, in order to solve this crisis, I believe that we have to look to history for guidance. Did you find that McCormack-Dickstein report I told you about?"

I nodded.

"What did you think?"

"I think I can easily understand why it is so 'hush-hush'. That's one of the most incredibly disturbing things I've ever read. How'd you find out about it?"

"Someone told me about it." Grant smiled and admitted, "Someone who was there and saw parallels to what's going on today called me up and talked to me. Back in 1933, we also had a weak new president in the White House, and certain powerful men felt they needed to save our nation from the communists who wanted to tear it down and wreck all that had been built in America. Their game plan even included using President Roosevelt's health as a pretext to taking action. By the way, that game plan could still be used today, don't you think?"

"I recall that prominent business people from DuPont, Goodyear, Bethlehem Steel, J.P. Morgan bank, and the American Legion joined forces with powerful members of both the Republican Party and Franklin Roosevelt's own Democratic Party to conspire to overthrow his government—which is almost too outlandish to believe."

Grant shrugged, "I know. But it actually did happen. Their only problem was the conspirators chose the wrong man to lead their *coup d-etat*. Just think—if that cabal of millionaire bankers and industrialists had chosen someone other than Major General Smedley Darlington Butler, they probably would have succeeded in changing American democracy by overthrowing an elected president."

"What amazes me is that no one was punished for it. People should have gone to jail, or even worse. That was treason, pure and simple."

Grant gave an authoritative smile. "The government couldn't afford to prosecute these industrial leaders during the height of the Depression, nor could the government afford to allow the masses to find out about what had almost happened. It was quietly swept underneath the rug. Everyone was forgiven and told to keep their mouths shut. The House Committee buried the McCormack-Dickstein records."

"I can understand why."

"But even though it failed, we can learn from that attempted coup. We learned that men of action have to take action." As he spoke, I could see the tension in Grant's face.

Grant got up from the step on which he was sitting. He stretched then straightened his pants. Ambling onto the stage, he seemed to survey an imaginary audience, facing first stage right and then stage left. Finally positioning himself center stage, Grant met my eyes and picked up his train of thought.

"As I see it, we have four options we need to consider. Do you want to know what they are?"

"Sure." Grant's demeanor conveyed a seriousness that I had never seen before in my former roommate.

"Let's go through them one at a time. The first option we can use is to try and defeat John F. Kennedy at the polls in 1964. Frankly, that won't be easy. He's a popular President with a very good approval rating. He also controls the ballot boxes extremely well, and as we saw in Chicago in 1960, he has the ability to manipulate the vote to get his way. The other problem is we don't yet have a presidential candidate that we feel could legitimately defeat him. No, we're afraid that if we have to rely upon the electoral process, we will surely lose, and John F. Kennedy will win once again. So we have ruled out beating him at the ballot box. Does that make sense to you?"

"Yes, it does."

"Good. The second option we could employ would be a scandal. If the nation learned about the President's disgustingly craven personal behavior, perhaps he could be forced to resign. Is that something that sounds plausible to you?"

"There has certainly been a great deal of recklessness in the White House."

Grant agreed, "If the American public knew the married President of the United States shared a girlfriend with a top American gangster, they would demand that he resign especially in light of the Profumo scandal. The similar behavior by our own President would strike most Americans as unforgivably reckless. I also think the nation would be horrified to learn of the President's adulterous behavior with Marilyn Monroe, not to mention all the other bimbos. This country absolutely adores Jackie and those two little kids. Americans would not tolerate Jack's repeated infidelity especially if some of it actually took place in the White House. Divorce involving a Catholic President would be a career killer."

"It's not just that," I said, "his reckless drug experimentation with Mary Pinchot Meyer would also shock the nation. We cannot have the President of the United States of America hallucinating on LSD while his finger is on the nation's nuclear launch button. That's just insane."

"Certainly the news that Bobby and his brother could be linked to the death of Marilyn Monroe would scandalize this presidency beyond its ability to govern, don't you think?"

I nodded once more and did not volunteer any information about my own knowledge of Marilyn's death. I fervently prayed Grant didn't know I was personally involved.

"Unfortunately, the nation will never know what we know," Grant continued. "I don't see Jack resigning his office even in the light of scandal. The Kennedys would probably do the dishonorable thing and fight to keep their place in office. Can you even begin to imagine the public uproar at a spectacle like that?"

I could, and then I couldn't.

"And what about our third option, which is the impeachment process? Could that legal procedure be used in this case?"

"I suppose it could," I admitted.

Grant slowly shook his head. "Sadly, I'm afraid a presidential impeachment, especially during the height of the Cold War, would create a monstrous Constitutional crisis. The Soviet Union would not hesitate to take advantage of that in an instant, especially if they thought there might be a period of time when no one legally had their fingers on the nuclear launch button in the White House. We certainly can't risk that."

"No, we can't."

"Then, what is our fourth option? What is the only other thing we could do to remove him from office and remove the threat that he represents? Can you tell me?"

I was silent. Of course there was only one other option: Executive Action. Kill him. Was that what Grant was proposing? I didn't know, but I thought I had better find out.

"*Coup d'etat?*" I asked, somewhat hesitantly.

Grant Grantham nodded grimly. He looked toward the ceiling as if it were the heavens, raised his arms, and in a majestic tone, he solemnly recited:

And therefore think him as a serpent's egg
Which hatched, would as his kind grow mischievous,
And kill him in the shell.

I think that Grant heard imaginary applause. I wouldn't indulge him though.

He finally said, "That's Brutus in *Julius Caesar*. He is advocating a preventive assassination. He is trying to convince Lucius that tyranny must be prevented at all costs, and one of those costs involves killing Julius Caesar. Some people, influential people, mind you, believe that John F. Kennedy must be removed for the same reason. He represents a threat to us all."

Grant saw the quizzical look on my face. He clarified, "Quite simply, we think Kennedy must be killed."

Kennedy must be killed. He had said it after all.

He paced back and forth for a few moments. Eventually he sat down, his legs hanging over the proscenium. "What if Adolph Hitler had been assassinated in 1932? Do you think the world would have been a safer place after that?"

I was momentarily offended by his comparison. "Oh come on, Grant! Surely you're not comparing Jack Kennedy to Adolph Hitler," I started to argue testily, but Grant held up his hand to interrupt me.

"No, no, no! Of course, I'm not. No person in his or her right mind would ever make that comparison. But I am hypothesizing an alternative historical track. What if Hitler had never been in a position to threaten the world with his ideas? What if all of those people that innocently died due to World War II never had to die at all? Wouldn't the world have been better off under those circumstances?"

When I didn't answer his questions, he pressed on. "Killing the President offers our nation the easiest way out of this growing crisis. We would get a clean transfer of power, we would get a man in the White House we can trust, and we would remove a 'problem child' from our political landscape. In their grief, the people of America will find courage and inspiration in his death, and they will be forever spared the gory details of his scandalous and treasonous behavior. Our nation's leaders would quickly act to convey great honors upon his memory by naming schools and airports and libraries after him. John Kennedy's moral turpitude could be covered up forever, and in death, he would attain the martyrdom of a great leader, sadly cut down in his prime. We could even elevate his memory to that of near-mythic proportions. What do you think?"

I was shaken by the enormity of Grant's proposal. "Are we talking theory here, or are we discussing actual treason?" I asked.

Grant stopped and stared at me once more. "This is what we believe."

His eyes bored into me waiting for me to respond, but I remained silent. Though I had been involved in planning Executive Actions in countries ruled by dictators, I never dreamed of implementing such an action in a democratic country, especially in America.

"Patrick, I promised you we could speak frankly, and that if you have any reservations about the nature of what I was going to ask, you'd be able to speak up loudly and clearly. Let me assure you, my promise still holds. After all, you are a Patriot. You have proven yourself to be a man of honor. I will respect your decision, whatever it may be. But please allow me to answer your question. Is this theory or treason? It's not theory, nor do we consider it to be treason. We consider ourselves true patriots, and we believe this to be the most patriotic test of our convictions."

Grant once again waited for my response. Finally, he asked, "But now I need to ask: What say you?"

I half expected Grant to dramatically produce some kind of a hidden dagger and demand I take a blood oath. Theatrics aside, I truly didn't know how I should answer. I did know this was going to be the most important decision of my life. "Who's in this with you?"

Grant slowly shook his head. "I'm sorry, but I can't divulge that right now. It protects the rest of us if you decide to decline our offer. But I can tell you this: 'Cowards die many times before their deaths, the valiant never taste of death but once.' That's also from *Julius Caesar*."

Grant reveled in the dramatic. "So let me ask you something: Are you *valiant*, Patrick? Or are you a *coward*?"

I stared at Grant. I wasn't going to be bullied by his passion though I agreed with everything he had said. I had spent hours and hours worrying about the constant onslaught of crises we were facing. I agreed that Jack Kennedy couldn't be allowed to serve another term in office, and I strongly believed it was highly probable he would end up getting us all killed. But did I really believe the needs of our nation warranted the death of our own leader by our own hands?

Could I really, in all honesty, condone killing my own President? I flashed back to a memory of my humanities class in high school. My teacher was trying to make a point about ethics. Was it morally permissible to kill one innocent life to save five? One girl in my class got so upset she cried, "You're wrong!" and stormed out of the classroom in tears. This ethics question was much larger. Did I believe it was okay to kill my president in order to save millions of innocent Americans?

Grant was a hell of a salesman. He knew whoever spoke next would be the loser in this deal, so he quietly sat and observed my squirming. I knew the next words were up to me. The wait must have seemed interminable, but my strong core of inner feelings ultimately guided me to give him my truthful response.

"We have to do something. We don't have any other choice," I stated at last. "Kennedy must be killed. Count me in. How can I help?"

A broad smile of relief broke Grant's pensive countenance as I pledged my support. He stood, lifted his face to the ceiling, and in a Shakespearean pose, raised a rich voice to the rafters:

...Stoop, Romans, stoop,
And let us bathe our hands in Caesar's blood
Up to the elbows, and besmear our swords.
Then walk we forth, even to the market place,
And waving our red weapons o'er our heads,
Let's all cry, 'Peace, freedom, and liberty!

He looked at me smugly, proudly boasting, "You know, I would have made a great thespian."

"Jesus Christ, Grant. What are you getting me into?" I stated, not really expecting an answer. I couldn't believe I had committed to join my long-time friend in a conspiracy involving treason and murder.

Grant was giddy. He laughed, sweeping out his arms in a wide gesture, "You know something, Patrick? William Shakespeare was an absolute genius. Who would have known in 1602 when he wrote Hamlet that his words would carry so much meaning for future generations? Or be the one line that you would remember?"

He bowed his head as if in reverence. Dramatically, he gravely recited the words of Hamlet's famous soliloquy on suicide:

To be, or not to be—that is the question.
Whether 'tis nobler in the mind to suffer
The slings and arrows of outrageous fortune,
Or to take arms against a sea of troubles
And by opposing...

He paused and with a subtle thrill in his voice shouted, *"...end them!"*

As we shook hands sealing our fate together, I glanced upward at a gilded canopy hanging over our heads.

Inscribed in gold thread for all to see was the sublime observation: "All the world's a stage."

TORMENTED BY SECOND thoughts, I called Grant one week later and asked him to meet with me at the Lincoln Memorial. I had questions that needed to be answered to my complete satisfaction before I could agree to go any further.

I arrived late in the afternoon as the commuters were heading home to Rosslyn, Arlington, Alexandria, and various points west. The Lincoln Memorial was filled with tourists when I got there. They were taking pictures and posing for pictures and organizing for the purpose of posing and taking pictures. Young boys and girls ran around the inside of the Memorial while their parents gazed silently upon the inspiring words of Lincoln carved in marble on the inside of the massive room.

I caught sight of Grant when he arrived a few minutes later, and without acknowledging each other's presence, he turned to the left, while I departed in the opposite direction and turned to the right. We ended up meeting each other halfway around the back of the huge monument. There were no tourists there to bother us or to overhear our conversation. The noise of the cars and buses going back and forth over the bridge below muffled our words.

"How are you today buddy?"

"Just fine, Grant. And you?"

He paused before answering my question. His head slowly turned from left to right as he took in the view. The Potomac River passed in front of us. Across the river I could see the majestic Custice-Lee Mansion, perched on top of the hill. The pillared mansion dominated the entrance to Arlington National Cemetery, hallowed ground for all Americans.

"This is another one of my favorite spots in D.C.," he said. "Do you realize that in 1861, just a little over one hundred years ago, Robert E. Lee lived in that very house that looks down upon the nation's capital? I'm told that back in those days, he could probably see the White House from there because the buildings were not as tall nor were the trees as mature or dense."

He reverently stood staring at the sight. "Can you imagine the emotions Lee must have been feeling as he prepared to give up his career in the United States Army in order to lead the Confederacy into war? He had been a commissioned officer in the Union Army, and he had sworn to uphold and protect the Constitution of the United States of America. With Virginia seceding from the Union, Lee made the momentous decision to do what he felt was right. It might have seemed treasonous to those other men who had taken the same oath but had stayed behind with the Union to enforce it. It had to have been a difficult decision."

"I'm sure it was," I responded. Grant was trying my patience with his history lessons.

"As a West Point officer, Lee loved the Union, but he loved his home state of Virginia more. Can you imagine the conflicted thoughts that must have gone through his mind as he stood upon that porch up there for the last time? He knew that if he successfully led the Confederate Army to victory over the Union, he would eventually be able to return to his beloved house, but his view below would be of a southern city that was no longer his nation's capital. If he failed and the Confederacy was defeated, he would never be able to return to his Virginia home."

Grant turned to me, tears welling up in his eyes. He looked away for a moment and then reached into his pocket for his handkerchief. I waited while he lightly swept at his eyes to compose himself. I wondered rather cynically if the tears were real or fake—knowing Grant, they were probably alligator tears.

"I'm sorry," he said, "but I get emotional whenever I recall the sacrifices great men have made throughout this nation's history for the love of their country." He turned to me after a few more moments, "Let's sit down, buddy."

We sat down on the broad steps. Grant continued to look at Arlington across the river. Staring straight ahead, he finally said, "Did you ask me here to tell me you had changed your mind?"

I looked at him, but he refused to look at me. "I have to be honest with you, Grant. Once I got outside the Folger and back into the strong light of day, I had nothing but second thoughts. Hell, I've had almost nothing but second thoughts since we last met. But in the end, I agree with everything you said. I just have a few questions that need to be answered."

Grant seemed startled by my answer. Now he turned to look me. For the very first time in our long friendship, I noticed the flecks of gold in his irises.

"Good!" He wrapped an arm around my shoulder and grabbed my other arm and squeezed it enthusiastically.

My first question involved Grant's boss, Vice President Lyndon Johnson. "I have to know if this has anything to do with the scandals involving Billie Sol Estes and Bobby Baker." Both men were rumored to be on the verge of federal indictments for various fraud allegations involving misuse and embezzlement of government money. Their legal troubles would certainly mean political, if not legal, troubles for Vice President Lyndon Baines Johnson, too.

Grant shook his head. "No. God, no! We have reached this decision because John F. Kennedy has to go. It's not because anyone felt we needed to protect Lyndon."

"But won't this, ah…action, conveniently get him off the hook?"

He shrugged his shoulders at me. "It might look that way, but that's not the reason why we're doing it."

"Yes, but if either Billie Sol or Bobby is convicted of anything, whether it be embezzlement or perjury or whatever, they're tied closely enough to Lyndon that he'll certainly be off the ticket in 1964."

Grant gave a deep sigh of disgust and disclosed, "He's going to be off the ticket anyway, Patrick. Those aren't rumors any more—they're fact. The President told Florida Senator George Smathers that Lyndon is going to be replaced on the ticket in 1964. The President intends to put his brother

Bobby on the ticket as the Vice President so he can groom him to succeed him in 1968. That Kennedy Dynasty that we're all so concerned about is already preordained."

"Where did you ever hear that rumor?"

He smiled, "I said, it's not a rumor. The President told Smathers and Smathers went back to his office and told this piece of juicy gossip to his secretary, a girl by the name of Mary Jo Kopechne. Miss Kopechne then went home that night and told *her* roommate the juicy gossip her boss had told her. Miss Kopechne's roommate happened to be Nancy Carole Tyler, and Nancy Carol Tyler just happens to be Bobby Baker's secretary. So when Kopechne told Tyler the news, Tyler immediately passed it on to her boss, and Bobby Baker unhesitatingly told Lyndon."

D.C.'s information grapevine was amazing—it made me wonder how many people knew about Grant's presidential-change proposal.

"Grant, you told me about rumors of a possible military coup at the inauguration in January 1961. That's no surprise to me. I learned from you that generals like Curtis LeMay have had no respect for Kennedy almost from the day he announced his candidacy. But your revelation about Operation Northwoods means that we have no choice but to act—if we don't, the generals certainly will. We will lose our democracy to the hardliners."

Grant nodded his head in agreement.

"Can you be sure that this action will prevent the hardliners from taking control?"

As thousands of cars and buses noisily swept past our feet, Grant methodically laid out the scheme. A great deal of planning had already been done before I was even approached and brought on board. This was not an amateur operation.

Because I had helped to edit the Agency field manual on assassination techniques, I shrewdly listened to the details of the plan. The plan was a "safe" plan—a "safe" assassination was one in which the assassin successfully escaped. Grant went to great lengths to assure me the killers would escape detection. No matter what happened, none of us could afford to have the killers end up alive in the hands of any authority. The planners, whoever they really were, knew what they were doing.

As our meeting ended, Grant urged me to travel to New Orleans to meet my contacts. In an effort to reassure me, Grant revealed that many of my contacts already had experience with the Agency—in fact, I had already worked with some of them on other projects.

The information did little to quell my discomfort.

WHILE I WRESTLED with the ethics and morality of killing Kennedy, Kennedy wrestled with the details of Operation Mongoose, the plot to kill Castro. Jack and Bobby blithely plotted to kill other foreign leaders as well—they showed absolutely no remorse, no pangs of conscience, in laying their schemes. It bothered me to the very core of my being.

The absurdity of my dilemma was spotlighted by the Kennedy brothers' amateurish, ludicrous directives. Bobby proposed that we invent some kind of chemical breakthrough using medicine or drugs as bio-weapons. Bobby wanted us to develop a neuro-toxin that could be sprinkled inside of a diving wetsuit which would either kill Castro or make his beard fall off. Bobby was earnest when he told me, "If he loses his beard, people will laugh at him and not take him seriously anymore."

Jack and Bobby also directed the Agency to pursue a number of outrageous ideas, like exploding cigars. At one point, I almost suggested that we consult Groucho Marx and his brothers for their ideas.

Instead, I kept my mouth shut and hoped the operation would not become a tragic farce.

BECAUSE OPERATION MONGOOSE secretly funded several scientific researchers located in New Orleans, I headed to the Crescent City. It would give me an opportunity to provide oversight to Operation Mongoose and to meet with the contacts Grant provided me.

Dr. Alton Ochsner and Dr. Mary Sherman were two doctors investigating the possibility of turning cancer into a bio-weapon. Dr. Ochsner's bona fides were gold-plated. Virulently anti-Communist, Ochsner was a long-time friend and associate of Allen Dulles. He had worked with Dulles during World War II in our Office of Strategic Services, known simply as the OSS. The OSS was the organizational model on which the CIA was based.

Ochsner had arranged for his associate, Dr. Mary Sherman, to run our clandestine cancer experiments out of her apartment. Her small apartment was crammed with cages upon cages of mice; the smell was stultifying in the August heat and humidity of New Orleans.

Dr. Sherman was assisted by a scientist named David Ferrie, a former Eastern Airlines pilot who had done some contract work for the Agency. Ferrie, one of Carlos Marcello's most trusted men in New Orleans, seemed excited and highly motivated to help create biological weapons to use against Castro and Communists in general.

David Ferrie reminded me of a character out of a cheesy science fiction horror movie directed by Ed Wood. His beady eyes conveyed a manic, frenetic energy. The most normal thing about Ferrie was the pallor of his skin which made him look pasty and unhealthy. He wore a dark wig cocked a little lopsided on his head, giving him an addled appearance. He had painted two broad slashes of brown for eyebrows, which didn't match the color of his wig. I tried not to stare at his freakish appearance.

Sherman and Ferrie were experimenting with creating a rapid growth tumor, using lung cancer cells. They were also working on a weaponized cancer virus that could knock out a man's entire immune system and render him susceptible to any disease. They thought this "anti-immune disease" had great potential for the future. To get the genetic material necessary for the anti-immune disease experiments, they used tissue scraped from the kidneys of sick monkeys.

Both Sherman and Ferrie were eccentric people. Sherman was businesslike as she explained the details of various experiments—she didn't seem bothered by Ferrie's frequent childlike interruptions: "Hey, Patrick! Wanna see something that will make you puke?" He cackled at my horrified reaction. As I was leaving, Ferrie said, "I'll see you later!" and broke into maniacal laughter.

I couldn't get out of that apartment fast enough; I wanted to take a hot shower to scrub away any germs I might have picked up.

FOREGOING A SHOWER, I went to meet Guy Banister, a former FBI agent working deep undercover in the New Orleans underworld. Grant told me that Banister was the most dependable of the New Orleans' contacts. I already knew Guy—he had helped me with training the Cuban exiles in Atchafalaya Bayou prior to the Bay of Pigs. He was a trustworthy associate with a long list of valuable contacts within the New Orleans community. He knew people in the anti-Castro Cuban exile community, he knew people in Carlos Marcello's crime family, and he knew people in the federal law enforcement and intelligence community.

Banister had arranged for Clay Shaw to assist us in New Orleans. I had never met Clay Shaw but knew he was the head of Permindex, an international trading company with a history of strong covert capabilities. The Agency had a long association with Permindex because of their ties to anti-Communist organizations throughout Europe.

Banister's office was located in a three-story building at the corner of Camp and Lafayette Streets. The U.S. Post Office Building, a huge marble edifice which held the regional office of U.S. Naval Intelligence, towered over Banister's office. Directly across from Banister's office was the regional office of the Federal Reserve, and surrounding the square were other federal office buildings that housed the CIA, the FBI, and other organizations central to the security of our country. All these buildings fronted a lushly wooded city park that offered a cool respite from the unrelenting summer heat and humidity. Park benches beneath live oaks draped in Spanish moss allowed secretive men to meet openly and yet privately, away from their respective offices or branches of government.

I asked Banister how he managed to get an office location in such a convenient spot. He grinned, "I've got friends in high places," and pointed toward the top floors of the post office across the street. Guy had worked for U.S. Naval Intelligence during the war. Setting up shop across the street from his old friends proved mutually advantageous—they provided contacts for Banister's Caribbean gunrunning operations while Banister could be counted on to provide them with solid information.

Banister had once been the special-agent-in-charge of the FBI office in Chicago in the 1940's. He left the Chicago FBI in the 1950's to go to New Orleans as the city's chief of police. After Banister threatened a waiter at Old Absinthe House with a gun during a heated argument in 1957, he "retired" from the force. Shortly thereafter, he began a new career as a private investigator doing far more work for the Agency than he ever did chasing philandering husbands and their bimbos.

A large man with a ruddy complexion, Banister had a fetish for neatness in his personal grooming. His hair, which was once dark, was now mostly gray, but he kept it Brylcreamed in place. Banister demanded that his agents be well groomed—I am sure he was influenced by Mr. Hoover who was a stickler for appearances—and he demanded that they wear a hat, even in the tropical heat of New Orleans. Guy Banister was a FBI agent at heart, and he dressed the part.

While Guy Banister's personal appearance was impeccable, his office was a crowded maze of loose papers, files, and boxes. Empty and half-empty coffee cups, napkins, discarded food containers, handguns, rifles, sub-machine guns, even a few bazookas were piled wherever there happened to be space. Boxes marked "Ammo" were stacked alongside reams of paper for the mimeograph machine. I had to turn sideways to walk through the narrow confines between the boxes and the rest of the clutter. I wondered how a big man like Banister managed to squeeze through his own office to work.

"I've got the kooks and the clowns locked away upstairs where I can keep my eye on them," he told me. When I asked who he was referring to, he informed me that he had a bunch of revolutionary groups as tenants in his building. "I've got your Cuban Revolutionary Council here..." he started to say before I interrupted him.

"What do you mean '*my*' Cuban Revolutionary Council?"

"Oh, you know what I mean—it's run by some of your CIA buddies."

The Newman building was known locally as Cuban Grand Central Station—its front door address was 544 Camp Street. Two virulently anti-Castro Cuban groups worked out of the building but each used a different mailing address. Guy set up his offices on the first floor, but he only used the side door of the building, which had a mailing address of 531 Lafayette Street. Unless you physically visited the building, you would never have known that these different groups worked together underneath the same roof.

Banister had helped to organize the Cuban Revolutionary Democratic Front and the Friends of a Democratic Cuba, anti-Castro groups operating out of New Orleans and south Louisiana. He ran a network of informants on the college campuses of Tulane and Louisiana State University who reported back to him on the student groups there. He bragged that he had the largest file of anti-Communist intelligence in the entire South.

"Come on, we're gonna meet some of my boys for drinks."

Navigating a short distance through the French Quarter, we stopped on Burgundy Street at a small two-story bar called Cosimo's. Nestled in the heart of a residential section, it felt secluded from the hustle and bustle of the city. Guy waved to the bartender and headed for a table up in the front corner where three men were seated.

"Hey boys, we're here!" boomed Banister. "How many do I have to drink to catch up with you?"

My eyes slowly adjusted from the bright sunlight of the street to the dark, poorly lit room. I could make out the figure of a tall man—he immediately stood up respectfully as we approached the table. The other men pushed their chairs back standing up as well. Guy moved over to the older gentleman and shook his hand vigorously. "Hi, Clay, how are you?"

Guy turned and shook hands with the second man. I realized that the third man was David Ferrie.

"Surprised to see me? I told you I'd see you later! Didn't I tell you that?" He turned to the others at the table and repeated, "I told him I'd see him later and he didn't believe me!"

"You're right. I didn't believe you."

"Here, shake my hand!" he offered.

"I wouldn't touch him or anything he touched," Shaw sagely counseled. "Hello, I'm Clay Shaw. I assume you're Patrick. I've heard a lot about you from mutual friends. It's nice to meet you. Welcome to New Orleans."

"Thank you, Clay. It's nice to meet you as well."

I immediately recognized Jack Ruby. "I already know you," I grinned and shook his hand. "How are you, Jack?"

Guy stood next to Ferrie. "David is our resident pilot and expert in everything from chemicals to biology. He's written numerous papers about cancer research—he's been published in important medical journals around the world." Guy seemed proud of Ferrie. I wondered about the extent of their connection.

"It's a fact!" he replied. "Anyway, me and Patrick are already buddies, aren't we?"

"Oh, God," Clay sniffed in haughty disapproval.

"Actually, we met earlier this morning," I said.

"Here, shake," Ferrie extended his hand once more.

"Stop it, David. Calm down," Guy snapped.

I knew Jack Ruby from our work together running guns and money into Cuba, both before and after Castro took power. Jack had also worked in Chicago for Sam Giancana before moving to Dallas to help New Orleans' mob boss, Carlos Marcello, run the vice rackets in Dallas. Ruby owned a strip club in Dallas, and also ran some illegal gambling operations for Marcello there, along with prostitution.

"So, Jack, how are you doing?"

"I'm doin' just fine, Patrick. How are you? I'll bet you're glad to be out of Washington on a day like this, aren't you?"

I assumed he was talking about the weather, but New Orleans was just as hot if not hotter than D.C.

David Ferrie sniggered, "Yeah, we've been sitting here watching the television coverage of all them niggers congregating up in Washington at the Lincoln Memorial. You tell me how they're ever gonna get that white marble cleaned from those dirty nigger bodies that been sitting and leaning and shittin' on it!"

I had forgotten that the Civil Rights movement had scheduled a "March on Washington" to further press the issue of equal rights with the Kennedy administration. When I had telephoned Pam last night, she told me the federal government had ordered all non-essential workers to stay home because of a fear of potential violence. Major league baseball had pressed the Washington Senators to cancel their scheduled game, and the National Guard had been put on alert. The crowd was expected to be the largest one to ever congregate inside of D.C. The White House had even prepared an executive order to declare martial law if the Negroes started rioting or causing trouble.

A small television up on the bar was on. Reverend Martin Luther King, Jr. was addressing a huge crowd gathered around the Reflecting Pool in front of the Lincoln Memorial.

"How many people did they say are there?" I asked.

"People? None! Niggers? Hundreds of thousands of 'em!" Ferrie bellowed. "If the Russians are ever gonna drop a nuclear bomb on Washington, D.C., then today would be the ideal day to do it! They'd actually be doing all of us white folks a favor!"

There was a murmur of agreement.

Guy Banister asked, "Hey, did you guys hear about what happened to George Lincoln Rockwell this morning?"

"Who's George Lincoln Rockwell?" Jack asked.

"Who's George Lincoln Rockwell? How could you not know who George Lincoln Rockwell is?" Banister challenged him.

"I don't know. I don't get to read as much as you do," Ruby replied, somewhat defensively.

I knew who George Lincoln Rockwell was. Everyone who lived in Arlington knew Rockwell was the head of the American Nazi Party. He had a small house in Arlington with a huge billboard up on top of the roof that exhorted: WHITE MAN *FIGHT!* STOP THE BLACK REVOLUTION *NOW!*

Guy looked around the table to make sure that everyone was paying attention to his explanation. "George Lincoln Rockwell got arrested this morning for trying to drive a steamroller across a bridge into Washington. When the police asked him what he was planning to do with the steamroller, Rockwell replied, 'Isn't it obvious? I'm planning to blacktop the road today!'"

Ferrie laughed so hard he had to readjust his wig. Both Ruby and Banister reveled in Rockwell's quick wit. Ruby repeated "blacktop the road" several times before he finally exhausted himself. Shaw joined the others, but his laughter was tinged with arrogance. I personally found the joke distasteful, but I pretended to laugh along in order to create some credibility with these men. If I hoped to work with these people, I had to make sure I fit in with them.

"Why do those niggers think they can push our government around like that?" whined Ferrie. "I just don't understand it."

"You don't have to understand it. No one can understand it. The Negro doesn't think like the Caucasian. His brain is different. Negroes are a baser form of humanity—a much more primitive form," sniffed Clay. His Southern accent oozed wealth and sophistication, along with the cut of his suit and his manicured hands. That's probably why I found his comments to be so disturbing.

Ferrie chimed back in, "Ya know, you're right about that! I heard some screwed-up people on the radio the other day discussing evolution. Some brainiac scientist claimed man descended from apes, and that the story of Adam and Eve was a myth. I was so mad, I wanted to go down there and wring his neck! Everybody that's got half a brain knows the real story." He looked suspiciously at me and said, "Do you know the real story of evolution?"

I didn't have a clue as to what was safe to say or how I should answer, so I just shook my head.

"Ah, it's easy," he gloated. "The *white* man descended from Adam and Eve," he informed me. "It's the *niggers* that descended from monkeys!"

Once again the table exploded in bawdy laughter as Clay Shaw turned to Ferrie and observed, "You really are a moron, aren't you?"

"What?" he protested. "You didn't know that?"

"You really are a miserable human being, you know that?" Shaw said.

"All I can say is, I know what I know," Ferrie adamantly maintained.

Guy said, "There could be some truth to that theory."

Ferrie poked Shaw's elbow and retorted, "See? What did I tell ya?"

"Please don't touch me," Shaw responded.

Banister wasn't done. "What I don't understand is why they think they should have the same rights that white people do. That just ain't gonna ever happen," he stated emphatically.

"Oh, it could happen. It sure could happen with the Kennedys in the White House," Shaw reminded everyone.

"Man, I hate the Kennedys!" Ferrie spit out. "I feel like taking a gun and blowing their fuckin' heads off! What makes them think they have the right to bring their nigger-lovin', Harvard-educated ideas down here and force them on us? Huh? What gives them that right? That's what I want to know!"

"Nothing gives them the right," Banister exclaimed. "But they think they've got to force their beliefs on the rest of us. Do any of you want to see a country where the niggers take over? Can you imagine having to take orders from them? Where your daughter is forced by law to marry one? No sir, not me."

Suddenly David challenged me, "Hey Patrick! Do you think that could happen?"

I was momentarily startled at being dragged into this hateful discussion. "Do I think it could ever happen?" I asked rhetorically. I was stalling for time while I tried to figure out how not to piss off this table with what I really believed. I was saved by Clay's intervention.

"It will never happen. The Negro will never get equal rights with the white man. You want to know why?" he asked us.

When no one answered, he stated, "Because they are a non-progressive race, that's why. They were bred to be told what to do. For hundreds of years, our ancestors bred them to be docile, just like cattle. They are not equipped to be leaders because they do not possess the ability to lead. It has been bred out of them. They are a non-progressive race. They have always been a non-progressive race, and they will always be a non-progressive race."

David Ferrie jumped in, "There's a lot of scientific fact in that! I think you're right!"

"Of course I'm right. Everyone in the South knows that because we've grown up around the Negro. I don't know why those Kennedy boys don't understand that. All their servants are Negro. I doubt they went to school with any Negroes at Harvard. I certainly doubt they grew up playing with any pickaninnies."

The whole table brayed at that idea.

"So why do they think they can order us to integrate our schools and our businesses? That takes a lot of nerve, if you ask me!" Ferrie was getting worked up.

Guy voiced his views. "But you want to know what this is all about? It's about a bunch of northern, nigger-lovin' white men tryin' to manage a problem rather than trying to solve the problem, that's what."

"So what's the solution?" I asked.

"Tell them they can't vote and prevent them from doing so. They're a non-progressive race," Shaw replied.

"President Kennedy is a nigger lover! He wants to give the niggers the right to vote so that they'll all vote for him in the next election," Ferrie bellyached.

"Well, he's gonna need them, because all the white people are gonna vote for whoever is running against him!" Guy stated. More raucous laughter ensued.

I had never been exposed to such virulent racism and hatred. David Ferrie made my skin crawl, but Clay Shaw's arrogance was just as repulsive. For the first time in my life, I realized that the Civil War wasn't over even if it ended about 100 years ago.

I had led a sheltered life growing up in Minnesota. I worked with Ivy League graduates and blue bloods in D.C. I had often seen water fountains and restrooms labeled Colored Only, but I had never paid attention to them. The civil unrest shown on television news broadcasts failed to show the depth of hatred and animosity the South felt on the subject of equal rights for Negroes. The deep-seated hatred of the Kennedys exceeded any level of hatred I had encountered in and around D.C. This was a visceral hatred brought on by Southern racial bigotry. The South didn't like Washington telling them how to run their lives.

I tried to keep a low profile at the table until this particular topic eventually ran out of steam. It was difficult to shake off my emotions. I concentrated on drinking my beer, and for a moment I thought about getting drunk. I held onto the hope that not all people in the South felt the way these men did. I wondered if Banister was putting on an act, but there was no way to know. I had to remind myself that their mutual hatred of Kennedy was important for the successful completion of our plan.

I would work directly with Clay Shaw, Guy Banister, David Ferrie—all on the Agency's payroll—and Jack Ruby, who had worked extensively on our anti-Castro operations. Clay Shaw's company, Permindex, was an Agency-supported firm operating in Canada and Europe. He would provide carefully laundered financing for the entire operation, as well as access to certain European assets needed to complete the mission. Our OAS contacts in Algeria were willing to provide us with as many expert snipers as we needed. Permindex would provide a swift means of getting them out of the country as soon as the job was done—the gunmen could never be traced.

Guy Banister was in charge of the weapons and a secure training location in a secluded portion of the Atchafalaya Bayou in Louisiana. We would use an abandoned facility, previously utilized for staging some of the operations for the Bay of Pigs invasion plan. It was private, out-of-the-way, and afforded us the secrecy we absolutely needed to get our training done.

David Ferrie would coordinate our transportation needs from New Orleans to Dallas and back. It was his job to provide cars and planes for our immediate exit from the scene of the planned ambush.

Jack Ruby was our local liaison with the Dallas Police Department. Ruby would also act with the Giancana crime syndicate while Banister and Ferrie were very well connected with Carlos Marcello and his crime network.

I explained that Dallas had been strategically selected because the Patriots controlled the entire state political machine. Our backers in this plan controlled the governor's seat and the legislature. They virtually owned the entire city of Dallas. We could count on more help in Dallas than any other place in the country.

"Because the murder of the President is not a federal crime, there isn't going to be a single issue raised about federal jurisdiction or intervention. That means the whole investigation will be local and will be handled by local people. Since our backers control the police department, we will control the investigation," I confidently assured them.

"So Jack," Clay said, "you know quite a few members of the Dallas police force?"

"Oh, yeah, probably half of them—the other half are born-again Christians, or I'd probably know them too," Ruby bragged. "Hell, most of the guys I know are John Birchers!"

I saw the corner of Shaw's mouth turn up into a sly smile, "John Birchers?"

"Hell, yes, John Birchers. Easily half the Dallas force are John Birchers. We love America. We're not gonna stand by and see it torn down by anyone."

Banister turned to Shaw and asked, "Who are the shooters? Pro's?"

"Pro's," he confirmed. "People that have done this before and can keep their mouths shut about it."

"Who's the patsy going to be?" Ruby innocently asked. "Don't you think we should have a patsy take the fall for this?"

I saw both Banister and Shaw shoot a look at him.

"There's not going to be a patsy," I explained. "This is being carried out as a safe plan, which means the assassin successfully escapes. We're going to make certain our mechanics don't end up in the hands of any authorities."

No one said a word; I was left with the impression that they agreed with me although Clay Shaw did add, "I've got a contact in Dallas named George de Mohrenschildt. He's available to provide additional help if we need it." He seemed to be addressing the other men at the table.

"Well, when do you want to get this done?" Ruby wanted to know.

The table fell silent as it waited for my response.

I hadn't been told that yet. "Before the New Year," I replied.

"Hey! Then it will be a Happy New Year," David giggled, "Oh, yeah, except for a certain poor fucker!"

AS THE SUMMER gave way to autumn, anti-Kennedy sentiment steadily spread throughout the country. The radical left reviled Kennedy for approving the original invasion plans to overthrow Castro while the radical right vilified him for not wiping Castro off the face of the earth when he had the chance. Both were outraged at how close we had come to nuclear war because of the Cuban Missile Crisis.

Jack was on his way to becoming the most hated president since FDR. American sociologist and author of *The Power Elite* in 1956, C. Wright Mills, said on his deathbed that he was "ashamed to be an American, ashamed to have John F. Kennedy as his President." Bertrand Russell said, "We used to call Hitler wicked for killing off the Jews, but Kennedy and Macmillan are much more wicked than Hitler. They are the wickedest people who ever lived in the history of man and it is our duty to do what we can against them."

The Boston-based right-wing organization known as the John Birch Society saw its membership ranks swell with businessmen, management executives, physicians, lawyers, and other solid members of society. They may have been viewed as a joke in New York, but in cities like Tampa, Houston, Shreveport, and Dallas, the memberships in the local John Birch Society chapters increased weekly.

A sign on a theater marquee in Georgia advertised the movie *PT-109* with the bold assertion: "See How the Japs Almost Got Kennedy."

A popular riddle making the rounds of the Agency asked, "If Jack, Bobby, and Teddy were all on a sinking boat, who would be saved?" The popular answer, "The country."

Pam even brought home a mimeographed leaflet one day from school that jokingly described the elaborate plans for a John F. Kennedy monument in Washington: "It was thought unwise to place it beside that of George Washington, who never told a lie, nor beside that of Franklin Delano Roosevelt, who never told the truth, since John cannot tell the difference."

When I read it, I laughed over the part which joked, "Five thousand years ago, Moses said to the children of Israel, 'Pick up thy shovels, mount thy asses and camels, and I will lead you to the Promised Land.' Nearly five thousand years later, Roosevelt said, 'Lay down your shovels, sit on your asses, and light up a Camel; this is the Promised Land.' Now, Kennedy is stealing your shovels, kicking your asses, raising the price of Camels, and taking over the Promised Land."

Throughout the South, the talk of presidential treason wasn't so funny. Texas was especially incensed by all manner of Kennedy behavior. The chairman of the board of the *Dallas Morning News*, E.M. Dealey, even directly accosted Jack at a White House luncheon for some of the nation's newspaper publishers. Calling Jack a weakling to his face, he further heckled, "We need a man on horseback to lead this nation, and many in Texas and the Southwest think you are riding Caroline's bicycle."

Dallas millionaire oilman H.L. Hunt went even farther when he openly exclaimed there was "no way to get these traitors out of government except by shooting them out."

Machiavelli would have recognized the warning signs of what was to come. He had said in his writings, "Princes cannot fail to be hated by someone, they are at first forced not to be hated by the people generally, and when they cannot continue this, they have to contrive with all industry to avoid the hatred of those communities which are the most powerful…A prince should take little account of conspiracies if the people show good will to him; but if they are hostile and bear hatred for him, he should fear everything and everyone."

Sun Tzu was equally prescient. "When the general is morally weak and his discipline not strict, when his instructions and guidance are not enlightened, when there are no consistent rules to guide the officers and men and when formations are slovenly the army is in disorder… Know the enemy, know yourself."

Kennedy, who was so conscious of the slightest censure, had no power to stop the public condemnation.

THE DEATH IN August of newborn Patrick Kennedy drove yet another wedge between Jack and Jackie. Poor Jackie fled to Europe in late September to take a cruise with Aristotle Onassis, even though the impropriety of her actions was politically damaging to Jack. She told Pam before she left that she didn't care anymore, nor did she give a damn what anyone thought. She said Jack's affair with Mary Pinchot Meyer was the final straw. She said it was about time he found out what she felt like when he cheated on her.

The White House was extremely upset with Jackie's decision to go on the cruise. They clearly didn't need to have the First Lady sailing around the Greek Islands with her sister and her sister's lover in a photo op for the scandal sheets. Jack's popularity had already reached a new low in that week's Gallup Poll. Now the *Boston Globe* even ran an editorial questioning what was going on behind the scenes in D.C. "Does this sort of behavior seem fitting for a woman in mourning?" it asked. Someone in Congress made headlines asking whether it was proper for the First Lady to accept the "lavish hospitality of a man who has defrauded the American public."

When Jackie returned home, she confessed to Pam that she had accepted more than Onassis' hospitality. She had also accepted a gift of a gold and ruby bracelet worth $80,000. Pam later told me she too thought her behavior was becoming increasingly reckless.

"She didn't come out and say so, in so many words, but I know that she slept with Onassis," Pam told me. Then she added, "The way that marriage is going, it wouldn't surprise me that after the November election, we'll see the first divorce in the history of the White House."

I sympathetically murmured that I hoped it wasn't true.

"I hope it's not true, either, but you and I both know the hell Jack has put poor Jackie through. She would have divorced Jack a long time ago if it hadn't been for Joe Kennedy's payments to her. This whole Kennedy thing has been perfectly awful for her."

> "To ignore evil is to become an accomplice to it."
> — Martin Luther King, Jr.

The Assassination

WITH THE presidential motorcade plan provided by the Patriots in my pocket, I headed to Dallas in late October to analyze various sniper vantage points. The President, arriving at an airport called Love Field, would proceed to the International Trade Mart where he was scheduled to speak at noon. I needed to evaluate the possibilities of setting our trap against the odds of escaping successfully at each point along the motorcade route.

I liked the openness of Love Field, but the very openness which made a shooting easy made spotting a gunman easy as well. The gunman would have little chance of a successful escape. That I didn't like.

I roamed around the International Trade Mart. Maybe the President could be ambushed in the kitchen area as he headed for the dais before the speech or as he left the dais after the speech. Unfortunately, that would put the Secret Service in close proximity to the shooter. The gunmen would have a high chance of success, but a low chance of getting away alive. A shoot-out would be a certainty. Controlling the outcome of the event would be difficult.

As I both walked and drove the planned motorcade route, I became smitten by one particular spot, a small open plaza near the expressway. I envisioned the potential of Dealey Plaza as I sat at various points then strolled around its perimeter. The presidential motorcade would have to drive directly beneath a railroad overpass—perhaps I could put a gunman there. My shooter would be able to escape either up or down the tracks, or he could slip away across the overpass to a freeway and city streets beyond.

I walked the area around the overpass, along a wooden fence that at first ran parallel to the street then broke off at a ninety-degree angle toward a large red brick building. The fence had some bushes and trees that obscured portions of its length and offered plenty of opportunity for hiding. At one point, the distance from the fence to the center of the street was no more than ninety feet. That looked promising. A large parking lot opened up behind the fence and was not visible from the street. A railroad yard bordered the back of the lot, again offering multiple escape routes by foot, by car, or even possibly by train.

I surveyed the red brick building perched on the corner of the plaza. I wondered if I could get a man onto the roof. I circled back around into the plaza and found myself on a concrete walkway, with some kind of a pergola behind me. The pergola was too exposed for my liking, but it was close to the street where the motorcade would pass.

I sat down on the concrete wall and tried to imagine the presidential limousine crawling slowly in front of me. There were other tall buildings in the background which appeared to be affiliated with some government entity. I thought one of them was the county jail, but I wasn't sure. The Dal-Tex Building was another building that I considered. The street down which the parade might conceivably travel was Elm Street; the Dal-Tex Building looked straight down Elm all the way to the railroad overpass. The sightlines from the roof of the building held excellent potential.

I liked the vantage point from the Texas School Book Depository, a red brick, warehouse-like building, located at the corner of Houston and Elm Streets. As the presidential parade turned off Main Street, it would lumber down a short city block on Houston and then make a slow, sharp turn to the left onto Elm. Coming down Houston, it would travel directly toward the Dal-Tex Building and the Texas School Book Depository. A shooter on either roof would have an easy shot, aiming either head-on or at the sharp left turn. However, a gunman positioned on the roof would be clearly visible to the police and the Secret Service. As soon as a sniper became visible, the President would become invisible beneath the protection of the Secret Service. It would be problematic to shoot and escape without being seen.

Standing on the corner of Elm and Houston, I thought about two other scenarios. Maybe a gunman could sit on the curb with a pistol—a scenario reminiscent of the pre-World War I assassination of Archduke Ferdinand. As the presidential limousine slowed to make the sharp left turn, a man could step out of the crowd and shoot the President with a pistol. He could then run for the cover of the fence and the parking lot beyond. His chances of getting safely to the cover of the fence and parking lot were slight. The killer would have to be willing to sacrifice his life to carry out the mission. Probably could not be done.

Next I considered a scenario with the sniper shooting behind the President. What if the limo turned onto Elm Street and the shooter popped up on the roof from behind? Chances were the Secret Service would be watching the President in the car ahead of them and not paying attention to what was behind them. This idea was intriguing.

The Dal-Tex Building was still a better option because the angle from the Texas School Book Depository became too sharp and was partially blocked by trees and a Stemmons Freeway sign at the most opportune times. If the limo was traveling too fast, the shot would be difficult logistically. To make the shot viable, the President's limo would have to be creeping. The road dropped down a little hill and twisted toward the right making it easy to misjudge the distance. A sure hit of the target would be too challenging from that angle.

Lt. Col. Harris had taught me to use the environment to disguise the location of a sniper. *"If you use the terrain as your ally, it can help to confuse the enemy and to further conceal and protect you. An obstacle of any kind—a tree, a large boulder, a deep ditch, a creek, a building of some kind, can all be used to make that rifle shot appear to originate from there instead of from its true location."*

Sitting in Dealey Plaza, I mulled over the rest of Lt. Col. Harris' lesson. I sat for hours, assessing the possibilities and probabilities—just like playing poker. The poker games with General Eisenhower came to mind; he taught me the odds of assessing a winning poker hand. After surveying the trees, signs, and buildings around the plaza, I knew I had found the ideal spot. The direction of our bullets would be easily concealed by the terrain. Even a trained observer would be confused by the echoes and the baffling of the sounds.

By the end of the day, I felt confident we could pull this off successfully. I submitted my recommendations to Grant. One week later, the senior members of the group approved Dealey Plaza. They had reviewed it with their gun experts, and their experts liked it.

Dealey Plaza in Dallas was now officially a "go."

ON NOVEMBER 2, South Vietnamese President Ngo Dinh Diem was assassinated in Saigon under orders given to the Asian sector of our Agency. Once again, I found it ironic that while I plotted the murder of Jack Kennedy, he and Bobby were plotting the murders of two other leaders, Fidel Castro and President Diem of South Vietnam. Regime change by murder had become an acceptable foreign policy option for Jack and Bobby.

U Thant, the Secretary General of the United Nations, had recently declared the South Vietnamese government to be the most corrupt government in the world. Diem and his brother, Nhu, had radically inflamed the populace by firing into a crowd of Buddhist monks whose only crime was flying religious banners. In protest of the Diem regime, Buddhist monks throughout the country burned themselves to death by dousing themselves with gasoline. The worldwide pictures horrified the world, and yet Diem and his family were oblivious to the revolting impact of the pictures. Diem's sister-in-law even infamously joked that she would willingly bring the mustard to enjoy the next barbecued monk.

Jack Kennedy had been spending one million dollars a day of American taxpayer money to keep the Catholic Diem brothers in power—all he got in return was a growing public relations debacle in Saigon. Jack and Bobby ordered Diem to admit responsibility for the Buddhist uprising, pay compensation to the families of the monks, and guarantee future religious equality and tolerance. Diem refused. In an effort to humiliate the President, Diem opened secret talks with the communist North Vietnamese, defiantly negotiating a peace agreement without the input of the United States government. All of Saigon knew that peace negotiations would be on North Vietnam's terms.

Jack and Bobby now had a problem. North Vietnam would demand that the United States' sixteen thousand military advisors be kicked out of the country. Another foreign policy defeat for the Kennedy administration just prior to the 1964 presidential election would be devastating. Having lost all confidence in Diem, Jack and Bobby implemented a plan of action—regime change.

In a bizarre turn of events, the day before the coup the White House lost its nerve and ordered our local Agency contacts in Saigon to shelve the plan. Bobby Kennedy, who had no qualms about the morality of coup, was concerned about deniability and blowback. He told the Agency, "I mean it's different from a coup in Iraq or South American country. We are so intimately involved in this...."

But it was far too late to stop what was already in motion. South Vietnamese General Minh's men arrested President Diem and his brother, Nhu. According to news reports, a pistol had accidentally been left in the back of the government-armored vehicle in which the brothers were detained. Humiliated over their arrest, the two brothers found the pistol and committed suicide.

Since both men were devout Catholics, their suicide was dubious. Two weeks later, photos of the bodies surfaced. Both men had their hands bound behind their backs, their bodies riddled with gunshot and stab wounds.

Diem was dead; now Castro was in the Kennedy sights. The Kennedy brothers were moving quickly to knock off their rivals in a very bloody fashion.

THE DATE OF our regime change had been officially set for November 22. I traveled to our old Agency training camp in a remote portion of the Atchafalaya Bayou to prepare the practice site for our professionals. It was important to keep personnel to a minimum in order to maintain complete secrecy. I had enlisted the aid of Guy Banister and David Ferrie to help with the maneuvers. I was uneasy when Derek Ruger surprisingly showed up. But I was engaged in nasty business—if there was any trouble, it was better to have Ruger on my side.

Based upon my prior reconnaissance, I formulated a plan for triangulated firing positions in Dealey Plaza. Derek and I set about constructing three practice gun towers along an abandoned roadway, miles from any prying eyes. I situated our gun platforms precisely where the buildings would be located along the motorcade route.

A big old Caddy limousine was procured, its roof cut off with a cutting torch. Our new convertible was filled with mannequins and hitched to a tractor outfitted with protective armor for the driver.

David Ferrie and another man named Mac Wallace arrived on Monday, November 18, with our three professional hired guns, loaned to us by the OAS and transported through Permindex. For security reasons, they were identified only as Lucien, Jean-Paul, and Marcel.

Guy Banister delivered a box of six Italian Mannlicher-Carcano rifles that were to be used in the plan. Upon seeing the inferior weapons, Lucien and his men lost their tempers.

"These rifles are terrible—they are pure shit!" Lucien spit out. "We cannot possibly use these."

Banister swore back, "You have to use them—that's what the plan calls for."

"I don't care what the plan calls for! We cannot use these! They are shit!"

Banister screamed at them—they yelled in return. Tempers flared into a volley of French expletives and hand gestures, which bridged any language barrier.

The commotion attracted the attention of David Ferrie and Derek Ruger. A wild-eyed Ferrie pushed past Ruger, who immediately pushed him back. I had an explosive situation on my hands.

Putting my fingers to my lips, I let out the most ear-piercing whistle I could muster. Temporarily silenced, everyone paused in their furor long enough for me to ask, "What the fuck is going on?"

Lucien petulantly kicked at the box of rifles; Jean-Paul made a show of spitting on them to make his point. That got Banister all riled up again and once he started yelling, everyone started yelling.

Once again, I whistled.

"Everybody! Shut up! Shut the fuck up!"

Everyone froze. Once I had their attention, I asked Lucien, "What's wrong with these rifles?"

"They are crap, that's what's wrong with them. They don't work. My Italian friends call these rifles 'Humanitarian Rifles' because you can't kill anyone with them. That's why Italy says they lost the war—they were forced to use these shitty rifles."

I hadn't bothered to look at them before, so I walked over and picked one up out of the box. It looked like a simple bolt-action rifle to me, nothing complex at all.

"Okay," I said, "what's wrong with it?"

Lucien said, "Look through the scope. Tell me what you see."

I raised the rifle to my shoulder and located one of our three towers. I tried to sight in the front corner of the tower with the rifle's telescopic sight.

"Oh my God," I gasped. "Why didn't anybody notice this before?"

Instead of the crystal-clear image of a high quality riflescope, this scope distorted the view—its optics were like the peephole in a hotel room door. The scope's optics were so bad the rifle was virtually unusable with the scope in place.

I turned to Banister, "Did you know about this?"

He shook his head, "I was just told to bring you guys these specific rifles. No one asked me to check them out."

"Lucien is right—we can't use these. They are crap."

Lucien gave Banister a triumphant glare.

I immediately called Clay Shaw to see about getting different rifles delivered. When Shaw finally called me back, he said, "Those are the rifles the plan calls for. You have to use them."

"They're not going to work, Clay. We need better guns."

"Patrick, the plan specifically calls for using Mannlicher Carcanos. It's too late to change. I've been told you'll have to make them work. There's nothing else that can be done."

Lucien cursed and kicked his feet in the dirt when I told him he had to use the Carcanos. He turned to leave, I thought permanently, but instead he walked over to the Cadillac and leaned against it. He smoked several cigarettes, picked up his butts, and came back.

"We can use sabots," he informed me.

I didn't know what he was talking about.

"A sabot, a tiny sleeve, lets us use smaller size ammunition in a bigger bore gun barrel. We can then use a better rifle with more precision accuracy than these Italian pieces of crap. The sabot helps the bullet to stay on track as it accelerates down the long barrel of the rifle. Once it exits the barrel, the bullet sheds the sabot sleeve, and continues on its way."

"Is there any chance someone can tell a different rifle was used?" I asked.

He shook his head. "Not possible. But there is also one trick we can use. We take a jeweler's saw—we can cut a tiny 'x' in the bullet's tip—it fragments upon hitting its target. All you have will be fragments and pieces of bullets—no whole bullets left for ballistics."

"So it would be like a dum-dum bullet?" Ruger asked.

"Yes, exactly, a dum-dum bullet like your American gangsters use—a frangible bullet."

"Okay, but what's a jeweler's saw and where do I find one?"

"I always carry one with me."

Lucien produced a small hand-held saw that looked like a coping saw, except its blade was as fine as a human hair. I gently ran it across my fingertip and could immediately appreciate the sharpness of its tiny teeth.

"We'll use our own Mauser rifles and scopes. We'll load the bullets into sabots so that we can fire them accurately. We'll criss-cross the tips of each bullet with the jeweler's saw. They will shatter as they penetrate our target. The wounds will be massive and devastating—I know from experience."

ON TUESDAY, NOVEMBER 19, Jean-Paul slipped while climbing down from his gun tower, falling about twenty feet to the ground. Luckily, the fall didn't kill him, but he suffered a concussion, a broken arm, and a separated shoulder. We were down to two shooters—we needed three.

I faced the distinct possibility of being forced to call off the mission, which was less than three days away. I was on my way to make a call when Ruger came to me, "Give me the damn rifle. I'll take his place."

"Derek, I don't think we can do that. These guys are going overseas the minute this is over. You'd have to go with them. You wouldn't be able to stay here."

He shrugged his shoulders, "Don't matter to me. This gig pays well. I'll just eat food I can't pronounce and screw poontang I can't understand. Don't matter to me at all."

I sent word to Grant—to my surprise, he gave me the go-ahead to use Ruger in place of Jean-Paul. "Derek Ruger's expendable, so's Mac Wallace."

We spent the next twenty-four hours giving Ruger as much practice as possible. We towed the Cadillac in front of the three gun towers over and over again until it was bullet-riddled.

I remembered Lt. Col. Harris' advice about taking our time to sight and shoot. "Don't hurry your shots! Hurrying will only increase your chances of missing altogether." The OAS gunmen thanked me for the reminder by giving me the finger.

On Wednesday evening, Ruger was ready. I instructed the team to head back to New Orleans for the night while I headed to Dallas.

I ordered Banister to dispose of the bullet-riddled Caddy in the bayou and burn the three wooden gun towers before he left.

ONCE I ARRIVED in Dallas on Thursday, I met with Jack Ruby at his Carousel Club—his preparations were complete as well. According to the plan I was given, Ruby would make sure that the Secret Service detail that traveled with and protected the President was thoroughly hung over for their motorcade detail on Friday. Ruby had arranged for the agents to hang out at the Fort Worth Press Club after the President went to bed. Their entire evening would feature lots of booze and lots of admiring female attention. On Friday, Ruby would go to the hospital after the motorcade departed to make sure that the President was dead. His final assignment was to slip a bullet to a morgue technician. The tech had been hired to plant our evidence to insure a Mannlicher Carcano rifle we had concealed in the Texas School Book Depository would be identified as the presidential murder weapon.

Ruby assured me, "They'll find the rifle, but they'll never find the shooter of that rifle. It's an untraceable gun."

My team was expected to arrive from Louisiana that evening. They would stay at a safe house in Dallas near Jack Ruby's apartment.

Later that night, I made my way alone to a wealthy neighborhood in Dallas where I planned to meet Grant who was attending a dinner party at Texas oil multimillionaire Clint Murchison's house. There were quite a few Cadillacs parked in the driveway and out front in the street. I nervously checked my watch. It was nearly midnight, but I was right on time.

I felt the same butterflies in my stomach that I would get back in high school before our football games. It was a combination of fear and excitement, coupled with a sense of eagerness to get going and put our hours and hours of preparation to the test. I felt ready, and I knew my team felt ready. But, were my Patriot friends ready as well? Would I receive the final go-ahead that we needed? It was time to find out.

A servant let me into the foyer and directed me to a study off the back of the house. I turned an ornate brass doorknob. Feeling the weight of the heavy mahogany door, I entered the room. Two small Tiffany lamps cast a fractured light over a massive hand-carved desk. My eyes moved around the room. I thought it was empty until I heard Grant say, "Over here." I turned to my left where a wing back chair loomed in the shadows. Grant stood to greet me, "Hey, there you are—punctual as ever. Did you have any trouble finding the place?"

"No, I didn't. Your directions were just fine. All the cars out front kind of gave it away though," I joked.

"Yeah, I know. This is a big evening, and everyone wanted to get together...," his voice trailed off. I think he was embarrassed that I might think they were celebrating prematurely. He shifted to his host mode. "Hey, can I get you a drink?"

A crystal decanter filled with bourbon sat on the side table. I guessed that Grant was at least on his second glass when I arrived.

"No thanks, not tonight. I've...I've still got things to do."

"Well, then, sit down. I've got a few things to tell you," he motioned to a leather wing chair directly across from his. The entire room was enveloped in a dark air of privacy.

Grant's posture conveyed a subtle nervousness. "This country is going to be a lot safer this time tomorrow, thanks to you. We've planned this as the perfect crime, and as long as you follow your part of the script, everything will be fine. I promise."

I thought Grant might be overextending himself a bit with his promise. I wasn't worried about carrying out my role tomorrow, but a part of me wanted to say friend to friend that we didn't know what the outcome would be. Neither of us had talked about what would happen after tomorrow's events. I hadn't given serious thought to where I would be or what I would be doing the day after tomorrow.

Grant was waiting for me to accept his promise.

"Of course" was all I could muster.

He seemed satisfied with my answer. "Good! Patrick, you wouldn't believe who's sitting in the next room even if I were to throw open the door. Only a wall separates us from some of the wealthiest and most powerful men in the United States today—oil men, business tycoons, media owners, military leaders, as well as two Vice Presidents of the United States and the Director of the FBI. Every single one of them is here to support you, you know that?"

I should have felt comforted by that news.

"As long as we all keep our mouths shut, and I mean *shut*, we can carry this off. Everyone involved in this has too much to lose by opening their mouths. The Patriots, the group in that room, are truly heroic men who will alter the shape of American history forever—with your help, of course. It will make this country a safer place for us all. Our children and grandchildren and great-grandchildren will get to grow up in peace because of what we are doing here today. I firmly believe this will ultimately be as important as the signing of the Declaration of Independence proved to be, don't you think?"

Once again, I waited for him to elaborate.

"Back in 1776, those were brave men who faced certain death as traitors to the British crown if they didn't stand together. We face similar consequences if our beliefs and actions are ever discovered. I am reminded of what Benjamin Franklin said at the signing of the Declaration of Independence back in 1776. As the Declaration was about to be voted upon, someone emphasized the necessity for all of the delegates in the room to hang together. Franklin, God bless him, wryly added, 'Or surely we shall hang separately!' Patrick, I can assure you that the lesson of 1776 is as vital now as it was then."

Grant peered into his almost empty glass and tinkled the ice cubes. "Follow the plan and everything will be all right. Understand?"

"I understand."

"Good. You know, as I was getting ready for tonight's meeting, I remembered a favorite quote of mine from many years ago. It's by the noted Cambridge historian, Lord Acton, who quite succinctly said, 'Power tends to corrupt, and absolute power corrupts absolutely.'"

He paused to take a sip of his drink. "The administration of our current President, John Fitzgerald Kennedy, is testimony to that. Not only has his power corrupted him, but his judgment has repeatedly been shown to be highly suspect in virtually all matters of serious consequence. His arrogance and his inexperience in governing have already resulted in a nearly catastrophic nuclear clash with the Soviet Union. I like to believe that our Lord God Almighty stepped in at the last possible moment to spare us from Armageddon. He expects us to have learned from that lesson and to do something to prevent it from happening again. President John F. Kennedy is inexorably marching us all down a path to nuclear annihilation. It is up to us to put a stop to it before it's too late. If we don't do this, the military is liable to do it for us."

Grant fixed me with an unblinking stare, as if to discern any disagreement on my part. Grant was no longer the brash young man that I met in 1947. He was a man who had the ear of many other powerful men—he was confident in his power and in his access to power.

"John Fitzgerald Kennedy must be stopped before it is too late. I think we all know that. The future fate of our families, our friends, and our country may very well ride upon what we do tomorrow."

I nodded.

Grant stood indicating our meeting was over. "I would like to say a prayer, if you don't mind. I think it's only appropriate that we ask for the Lord's blessing and guidance."

He didn't wait for my answer. "Let us bow our heads. Dear Heavenly Father, we praise your power and ask for your protection in our actions to insure that this country will always be a God-fearing nation. We ask that you smite our enemies as we humbly endeavor to free this nation from a sinful ruler. Please guide Patrick McCarthy. Grant unto him the steadiness and patience necessary to carry out his job tomorrow. If it be your will, return him to the safety of his family and friends. Guide our wounded nation out of the darkness and into the light of the Holy Ghost. Thy will be done."

Grant paused after saying his prayer. "I forgot you and Pam are Catholics. Do you want to say *The Lord's Prayer* with me? I'm sorry," and then he began: "Our Father, who art in heaven, hallowed be thy name. Thy kingdom come, thy will be done, on earth as it is in Heaven. Give us this day our daily bread, and forgive our trespasses, as we forgive those who trespass against us. Lead us not into temptation but deliver us from evil, for thine is the kingdom, and the power, and the glory, forever. Amen."

I softly added, "Amen."

Grant's eyes glistened with tears. Once more, I silently wondered if his tears were real or fake. I hoped they were real.

"You're one hell of a man, Patrick. No one will ever forget how much we all owe you for doing this. I give you my word. We'll take care of you forever."

He hugged me tightly. "I can't wait to see Lyndon's face when I tell him that after tomorrow, the Kennedys won't be able to kick him around anymore!"

On my way back to our safe house, I swung by the Fort Worth Press Club. Nine members of the President's Secret Service detail were there having arrived after the President and the First Lady had retired for the evening. They had left a single unarmed volunteer fireman on a folding chair in the hotel hallway to guard the sleeping couple. The bartender tipped me off to the fact that the men were drinking beer and mixed drinks.

"Here's something to keep the party going," I said placing five twenty dollar bills on the bar.

"Keep the drinks going until the money runs out. I admire the job that the Secret Service does. It's just my way of saying 'Thanks' to all of them." I took out another bill, "This is for you. You take care of them now," I said in my best good ole boy imitation.

Satisfied that everything was in place, I finally fell into bed, utterly exhausted.

FRIDAY, NOVEMBER 22, was a rainy, dreary morning in Fort Worth and Dallas. A line of violent thunderstorms raced through the Dallas Fort Worth area earlier that morning, but the local weather forecast called for clearing by noon. I woke up around eight a.m. and was showered and dressed when Ruger rapped on my door.

"The Secret Service detail left the Fort Worth Press Club to go to a coffee house called *The Cellar*. They took their own booze, and I made sure the coffeehouse provided the set-ups for them. Ruby sent several of his strippers over to the party. His broads made sure everybody was having too good a time to go to bed early. I stuck around—most left between 1:30 and 3:00. One guy was so drunk that he didn't leave until 5:00 a.m."

I was relieved that Jack Ruby's part in this had worked as planned.

"They're all sporting hangovers this morning—and they've been assigned protective duties in the presidential detail. So far, all reported for duty—even the guy who was out until five this morning. They looked green around the gills," Ruger added sarcastically, "I'm sure they are in top form."

"What about the duty roster," I asked.

"One will be at Love Field to provide security, four have been assigned to the Trade Mart, and the other four will be in the follow-up car behind the Presidential limousine in the motorcade."

Ruger added confidently, "These guys won't get in our way today. They'll have a hard enough time just standing up. None of them will be where they're not expected to be. Dealey Plaza will be free of Feds this morning."

I accepted his assessment. Secret Service regulations absolutely forbid the consumption of any alcohol any time that a president was traveling. All Secret Service agents were considered to be "on call" during a presidential trip. The agents would want to keep a low profile after a night of drinking.

Ruger had set out various identification badges on the dining room table. Each badge had been scrupulously manufactured for each of the different roles our team members might have to play during the day. Dallas police had been given samples of the color-coded lapel pins worn by the Secret Service, White House staff, and White House communications personnel. They passed those color codes on to our people, who furnished us with carefully made counterfeit copies. We also had the necessary documents to get us in and out of areas of trouble, without evoking suspicion.

As we made our final preparations, Lucien appeared. He was late, and my first instinct was to jump on him. But the worried look on his face signaled that something was wrong.

"Marcel is in bad shape. He's been sick all night long—vomiting and shaking. He thinks he has food poisoning."

"How bad is he?" This was the last thing I needed.

"Marcel is too sick to get out of bed."

We were four hours from our deadline. The logistics of replacing Marcel would be too risky.

"What do you want to do? Call it off?" Lucien asked.

"That's not possible." I was left with no other option. "I'll have to take Marcel's place."

I looked at Ruger, but his face didn't show a single sign that he either agreed or disagreed with my decision. He asked, "What about Mac Wallace? He's done this stuff before."

"We can't risk it. Mac's got his own assignment. I can't have someone else do it. I'll do it."

Lucien looked at me questioningly, but he didn't say anything either.

"It's got to get done. He's got the easiest shot of the three. I'll do it," I said once again, looking for some assurance that I was making the right decision. I was met instead by an ominous silence.

It was settled. I was now a gunman. "I'll take the grassy knoll."

AT 9:30 A.M., I reviewed the logistics one more time with the men, but this time I added my new role as a shooter into the mix. I would go out to Love Field and report back to the team on the arrangement of the motorcade, including Jack's seat location. I expected him to be seated on the right-hand side of the car, but we had to be sure ahead of time. I would then make my way through Dallas to the Texas School Book Depository, where I would find a parking spot reserved behind a plain picket fence on a small hill next to the motorcade route. We had designed our ambush to include "triangulation of fire" angles which Dealey Plaza easily provided.

Ruger would be positioned on the rooftop of the Dal-Tex building underneath a huge Hertz rental sign. Lucien would be in a building across the street. Both men had a clear shot straight down the street at the back of the motorcade. Since the Secret Service would be watching what was coming up ahead, the shots from behind would take them by surprise. Mac Wallace was to construct a fake sniper's nest in the sixth floor of the Texas School Book Depository warehouse and hide our untraceable Mannlicher-Carcano rifle there. We wanted the authorities to believe that they had discovered the assassin's lair, thereby allowing our trail to grow cold.

The acoustics of Dealey Plaza would mask our locations. As Ruger and Lucien's bullets whizzed by the trees and the other buildings in Dealey Plaza, the noises and echoes would confuse even the best experts in pinpointing the origins of the shots. Ruger's bullets would whiz right past that sixth floor window of the Texas School Book Depository where most eyewitnesses were bound to look first.

Each sniper had been assigned a spotter. The spotter's job was to watch the shooter's back so he could concentrate on his job without interference.

I positioned a spotter on the curb on Elm in the kill zone. His sole job was to tell us when the President was dead. He would pump a black umbrella up and down as long as Kennedy was still alive. We wore earpieces, part of a state-of-the art miniature radio system, to stay connected with each other. Either way, by sight or by sound, we would know when we were successful.

Our plan called for someone to fake an epileptic seizure on the street corner of Houston and Elm just before the motorcade's arrival in order to distract the crowd from the movement of my people into their assigned positions. As the ambulance, with its sirens blaring, attended to the poor helpless epileptic, our men would sneak into their spots. The less time they actually spent in position, the less chance they would have of being spotted. The ambulance, removed from Dealey Plaza, would be unable to render assistance to our stricken president.

We had three more men positioned as hoboes behind the Texas School Book Depository to provide further distractions if necessary. One of my old acquaintances, E. Howard Hunt, had volunteered to masquerade as one of them. David Atlee Phillips was also in Fort Worth helping out behind the scenes.

"He's calling himself Maurice Bishop. The guy never stops acting." I found it funny that Howard would complain about David's acting when Howard was the biggest and most obnoxious guy I had ever worked with. Our Guatemala group was at it again.

Everyone assembled around me for the last time—I gave them one last reminder. I spoke directly to Lucien and Derek, "The most important thing is to 'gun and run.' Once you're done—run. Get the hell out of there as fast as you can. You only have a minute, maybe less to make your getaway. Move as fast as you can to the collection points, and we'll all get out of there safely. You understand?"

Everyone nodded.

"You guys know what you have to do," I finally said. "Let's get going. I'll see you back here immediately afterward."

Everyone checked his weapon one last time, along with the spurious credentials. We headed out, one by one, so we wouldn't draw attention to ourselves in the neighborhood. It was smart precaution to take even in a working class neighborhood where most people had left for work hours ago.

The sky began to lighten up and the clouds began to break apart as I headed out to Love Field. It looked like it was going to be a perfect day weather-wise. I had worried that if the stormy weather continued, the plastic bubbletop would be placed on the presidential limousine, shielding the President from the weather and our snipers.

The official order of the motorcade had been rearranged as promised. Normally, the presidential limousine was preceded by various local dignitaries and police. The press caravan, usually in front of the President's car so that the press could arrive at the next venue to cover the President's arrival, was buried at least eight vehicles back in the motorcade. They wouldn't be able to witness a thing.

We had managed to strip away most of the security normally in place for a presidential visit. No motorcycle escorts were allowed to be alongside the President. Secret Service was not allowed to ride on the rear bumper of his limo on this particular trip. We also instructed the local office of military intelligence to stand down during the President's visit.

We had everything under control.

I BEGAN TO worry when I picked up the local newspaper. The second page of the *Dallas Morning News* carried a disturbing full-page anti-Kennedy ad full of vitriol against the President. Surrounded by a black border, it said: "Welcome Mr. Kennedy to Dallas…A CITY that rejected your philosophy and politics in 1960 and will do so again in 1964—even more emphatically than before."

At the same time, five thousand handbills had been passed out on the streets of Dallas to further inflame passions. The headline read WANTED FOR TREASON. It featured a full-face picture of Jack, along with a side photo of his head that mimicked a police mug shot. The leaflet declared, "This man is wanted for treasonous activities against the United States," and it offered seven reasons to back up the allegation. Among them, Jack Kennedy was accused of betraying the Constitution by "turning the sovereignty of the U.S. over to the Communist controlled United Nations," having "been wrong on innumerable issues," which included Cuba, and encouraging racial riots. "He has been caught in fantastic LIES to the American people (including personal ones like his previous marriage and divorce)."

In short, most people in Texas didn't like the President. I only hoped that these items didn't increase the vigilance of his Secret Service detail. I was counting on their late-night escapades to dull their attention to their surroundings and their reaction time during the ensuing commotion.

AT 12:10 P.M., I pulled into the parking lot behind the Texas School Book Depository. I backed into a parking spot by the corner of the fence positioning the car so that the trunk with my rifle was up against the fence, leaving me a few feet of space in which to stand. My spotter, Roscoe, wore his Dallas Police Force uniform and appeared to be part of security for the parade. As I looked through the trees and bushes that surrounded the fence line, I could see a small crowd of about forty people milling around in Dealey Plaza; most were too far away to cause a problem. I noticed a family setting up next to fence, so I flashed my credentials and asked them politely to move on.

"How are we doing?" I asked Roscoe.

"Everybody's ready to go. The umbrella guy is down on the curb where everyone can see him. Y'all keep shooting until he says to stop."

I inserted the radio earpiece into my left ear—I heard our umbrella man talking down on the curb in front of me. I turned to check the parking lot behind me and saw E. Howard Hunt with two of our other men dressed as hoboes. It was their job to make sure that no one would come up behind me and that we got out of the parking lot safely.

I noticed a few people in the crowd carrying various kinds of cameras. I knew that could pose a problem. "Roscoe," I whispered. "Keep an eye on those camera buffs. If you think they snapped pictures of us, go flash your badge and confiscate their film when this is over."

He grinned and nodded, "Gotcha."

I was alone with my thoughts in those last few minutes. I cleared my mind and focused on the task at hand. Roscoe pulled out a smoke, but I motioned for him to put it back.

Just before the motorcade arrived, the ambulance at the corner of Houston and Elm Streets left the area, lights and sirens blaring—the epileptic seizure must have worked as planned, I mused. I checked my watch.

The bottom of the hour approached. The crowd began to get restless until they saw the first vehicles at the beginning of the motorcade making the right turn from Main Street onto Houston.

"Roscoe, here we go."

I waited for the procession to make the slow left turn onto Elm and begin its descent down the slight incline in front of me. There it was—right where it should be. The dark blue Presidential Lincoln limousine made the turn behind two motorcycles and a lead police car. I checked the crowd around me. No one seemed to notice us behind the picket fence. All eyes were on the approach of the President of the United States of America.

I raised my rifle and steadied it on the top of the fence. Checking the telescopic sight, I zeroed in on Jack's head. The angle of my particular shot was relatively simple. I heard the first shots fired by my men on my left.

I knew the moment I squeezed the trigger that something had gone wrong. The recoil of the rifle didn't deliver the customary hard, crisp jolt to my shoulder. The sound was dirty and muffled.

A fraction of a second later, I saw what I had just felt.

The voice in my radio earpiece screamed, "Green light! Green light!" Out of the lower left corner of my non-shooting eye, I could see the motion down on the curb. The open, black umbrella mechanically pumped up and down in our prearranged signal.

He was still alive.

Through my telescopic sight, I saw both of Jack's hands turn into fists as his arms flew up to protect his throat—my bullet's errant trajectory apparently caught him in the Adam's apple. A range of emotions swept over his face—Jack didn't know what the hell had hit him. His survival instinct kicked into motion. He was having trouble breathing. He was alive for now, but he was doomed.

I calmly and quickly racked another round into the bolt-action chamber of my rifle. I again reacquired my target through the precision gun-sight. The head of the man sitting in front briefly blocked my view when he turned toward the commotion in the backseat. But instantly, a fusillade of bullets from Lucien and Ruger cut down the momentary obstruction—flinging him into his wife's lap and out of my way.

I heard the anxious "Green light! Green light!" as I searched to place Jack's face in the middle of my crosshairs. I felt a reassuring pat on my shoulder by my spotter, who kept his eyes pealed for anyone who might have observed us. He undoubtedly felt time was running out, but for me, time was standing still. Jack was still alive—I had a job to finish.

The first shot I squeezed off had to have been a misfire. It wasn't my aim; I knew that. The sabot must have had a bad powder charge or had been incorrectly loaded in its firing sleeve. The second bullet in my chamber was a full-charge cartridge without a sabot.

I had meticulously used Lucien's jeweler's saw to cut a small 'x' into the tip of all my bullets to insure that the bullets would fragment immediately—resulting in a devastating wound just as Lucien predicted.

I watched through the optical precision of the expensive Zeiss gun-sight as the big 1961 Lincoln convertible parade limousine came to a halt directly in front of me. I brought my crosshairs to bear, centering upon his right eye in my sight. He was barely ninety feet away—so close that I felt I could reach out and touch him.

I paused to study the familiar face in my sight. Fear had taken hold of him.

He knew that he was helpless—sheer panic enveloped his face. I had prepared myself for any possible equipment failure or operational disruption—but I had never thought about how I would feel as I completed my assigned task.

"Green light! Green light!" It was an annoying reminder of my team's combined failure up to this point.

Roscoe's breath panted in my ear, "Come on, Patrick. You can do it." His voice rose with coiled tension. The crowd below had begun to panic. But I was completely at ease.

Jack's eyes wildly swept his surroundings; then, they locked onto mine through the telescopic gun-sight. I felt my adrenaline surge. Experienced shooters had warned me that seeing the eyes of my victim would shock the hell out of me. I knew that Jack really couldn't see my eyes, but I sure couldn't miss his. His eyes frantically searched for answers.

"Goodbye, Jack!" I whispered, squeezing the trigger smoothly a second time. This time the rifle's recoil felt crisp and firm as it kicked back into my braced right shoulder. I saw my bullet's impact instantly. I was so close to where he sat—upright, wounded, vulnerable, and frozen in shock.

The full force of my shot took off the top of his head. It exploded in a pink cloud of blood, brain matter, scalp, vaporized skull bone, and gristle. He was dead now.

The voice in my earpiece shouted, "Red Light! Red Light! Red Light! Red Light! Red…" I tore the annoyance out of my ear. The umbrella man on the sidewalk signaled that the President was dead. I withdrew the rifle from the top of the slats of the white picket fencing and handed it to Roscoe. He threw it into the open trunk of the sedan parked directly behind me.

I suddenly noticed Jackie—it hadn't registered with me that she had been sitting next to Jack the entire time. I saw her desperately try to crawl across the Lincoln's broad trunk only to be shoved back down her seat by a leaping Secret Service agent. He threw himself on top of her to protect her as he was trained to do.

I solemnly watched the big presidential limousine accelerate out of Dealey Plaza—its wounded occupants slumped in their seats. I turned away as the rest of the presidential motorcade raced underneath the triple underpass in a panicked pursuit of the President's car.

Roscoe adjusted his Dallas police uniform and drew his service revolver out of his holster while I pulled my fake Secret Service credentials out of my pocket and held them in my clenched fist, ready for display.

We planned to use the chaos of the moment to slip away. We would descend into the horrified crowd, pretending to be just as shocked and alarmed. It was hard, however, not to be too elated—our plan had worked perfectly.

President John Fitzgerald Kennedy was dead.

AS I MADE my getaway from behind the fence, my heart started racing. Goose bumps covered my arms. I felt a metallic taste in my mouth—my salivary glands ached. My face felt cold and clammy. My body was rapidly shifting from locate-and-shoot mode to let's-get-the-hell-out-of-here mode.

I sprinted around the picket fence and walked purposefully toward the front of the Book Depository. I remembered Lt. Col. Harris' advice: "*Remember, the hunter suddenly becomes the hunted—Gun and run!*" Several men already scrambled up the grassy knoll toward the fence.

My inner voice implored me to stay calm. Slow down; stay calm. Slow down; stay calm. I joined the crowd on the sidewalk and began to survey the area. Everyone was either running toward the front door of the Book Depository, the grassy knoll, or the street to follow the departing motorcade. I needed to locate the spotters. I searched the rooflines for Ruger and Lucien. I hoped they had stuck to the plan and disappeared. I ignored all the bystanders dazed by what they had witnessed. I ran headlong into a man and immediately muttered my apologies.

The man grabbed my arm, and I started to shake him loose.

"Patrick, hold on."

It was A. J. Hidell! What the hell was he doing in Dallas?

"I thought I recognized you, Patrick," he cried. "What's going on?"

I didn't know what to say. I tried to appear less harried, "A.J., what are you doing here?" I asked.

"I work here," he nonchalantly pointed to the Book Depository. "I was out front watching the parade. I thought I got a glimpse of you in the crowd. Then all this shooting started, and I ran down here to see what was going on. Did you see anything?"

I was speechless. I couldn't afford to have him begin to question me. "A.J., I don't have time...," I started to say. Suddenly, I saw Ruger in a dead run, pistol in hand, headed toward A.J.

Time slowed down to a stop—A.J. was at the cusp of making a connection between the shooting he had witnessed and my coincidental appearance. Ruger was rapidly approaching and drawing his pistol with a silencer. His eyes were centered on A.J.

"Oswald!" he yelled. "I've been looking for you. You were supposed to stay inside."

A.J. spun around.

I saw Ruger raise the pistol. Just as he fired, another voice shouted, "Look!"

At that very moment, one of the spotters moved between us pointing out the crowd heading toward the grassy knoll. The trajectory of Ruger's bullet caught the poor guy in the side of his stomach catapulting him to the pavement. Ruger, surprised that he hit the wrong man, froze for a moment.

A.J. met my eyes—then he bolted like a sprinter around the back of the building and quickly disappeared from view.

"What are you doing?" I screamed at Ruger. "Why'd you shoot him?"

"I wasn't aiming at *him*," he said, pointing to the bleeding man lying on the sidewalk. "I was aiming at Oswald."

I was confused. Oswald? How did he know Oswald? How did Ruger know Alek Hidell's agency cover name? What the hell was going on?

Before I could verbalize my thoughts, Ruger said, "He was supposed to die inside the building trying to escape."

I was even more confused, "That wasn't part of our plan. What are you talking about? That guy Oswald wasn't part of this!"

Ruger looked at me like I was stupid. "Yes he was. He was our patsy."

"We don't have a patsy! We're all supposed to get away cleanly."

He looked at me in exasperation. "The only way we are going to get away with this is if everyone thinks they caught the real killer. That's why this guy Lee Harvey Oswald works here. That's why we planted his mail-order rifle up there. He was framed. It was all set—he was going to get plugged tryin' to resist arrest. Dumb fuck!"

The bleeding man on the ground groaned in agony. A man in a plaid shirt and horn-rimmed glasses came running over, "Is he okay? Who is he?"

"He's a Secret Service agent," I lied.

"Is he okay?" he repeated as he looked at the growing puddle of blood on the pavement.

"He might be dead," Ruger interjected. "Get out of here!" he barked at the on-looker.

"We've got to get him out of here!" I ordered. "Help me move him."

One of our guys ran to a getaway car and quickly brought it around. We dumped the wounded man into the back seat. "Get moving!" I yelled.

The man in the plaid shirt stared, unable to move.

"I told you, get the fuck out of here!" Ruger raised his gun in his direction. The man ran backwards, stumbled, crawled to get his balance, and fled the scene.

"Get your gun out of sight. We don't need to attract any more attention."

Ruger threw me a menacing glare, "We've got to find Oswald," he growled. "We're both dead men if we don't!"

I didn't know who was pulling Ruger's strings. He obviously had received different instructions than I had. I didn't have time to think about it.

Ruger yelled, "Come on!"

Ruger spotted a cab down the street and motioned to the driver to pick us up. Ruger shouted out an address as he opened the door. "Get going, now!"

The driver nervously pulled away from the curb. "Step on it!" Ruger ordered.

We headed away from the downtown area across a long, low bridge. As soon as we crossed the bridge, he yelled at the driver to drop us off. Pointing to a small house across the street, he jumped out of the taxi. I pulled a couple of dollars out of my pocket and handed it to the cabbie. The driver peeled away before I barely got my door shut.

"Stay here!" Ruger barked as he ran over to look in the windows.

He peeked in the front windows and crouched down to run around the back and out of sight. Moments later, he ran back across the street.

"He's already gone!" he yelled in frustration.

Ruger was a hunter on the trail of his prey. His eyes had a look of deadly determination—the same as they did when he tortured and killed Action Jackson.

"He's probably headed to Ruby's apartment."

"How does he know Ruby?" I asked incredulously.

"They're friends—that's how we recruited him," his voice tinged with annoyance.

Ruger was focused, angry, and deadly. He raced down the middle of the neighborhood streets with the stamina of a long distance runner. I tore along behind him. I was growing concerned we would attract unnecessary attention to ourselves. We ran for almost a mile before we reached Ruby's apartment in the same neighborhood. I doubled over, gasping for breath, while Ruger ran up to and in the front door.

Seconds later, he was back. "He's been here and gone. Come on."

My heart was pounding, and my head was throbbing as we took off running in a different direction. Ruger seemed to know where he was going. I was too winded to ask; I puffed and gasped as I ran behind him. After a few blocks, Ruger spotted and flagged down a Dallas police car. I trailed Ruger by a modest distance.

Ruger was arguing with the officer as I approached. The officer got out of the car and walked around to face Ruger. In one smooth motion, Ruger raised his revolver and fired four shots point blank. The officer collapsed on the ground as Ruger yelled, "Let's get out of here!"

He dashed ahead. I never looked back to see what happened to the officer.

Ruger ducked beside a garage waiting for me to catch up to him.

"That officer back there, Tippit, he was supposed to keep an eye on

Ruby's house. He said he saw Oswald at the house but didn't detain him. When I demanded to know why, he told me he had changed his mind about getting involved once he heard the President had been shot. It's too late for that. I shot the cowardly bastard." He caught his breath, "We can't afford to have people changing their minds."

As we fled the neighborhood on foot, Ruger's eyes continuously swept every intersection we crossed for some sign of A.J. Hidell. I was running on pure adrenaline—I worried that if I didn't stop soon my heart would explode. Minutes later we heard sirens heading in the direction of Ruby's house.

After a frantic hour of fruitless searching, it was apparent we needed help. Ruger stopped at a payphone outside of a gas station and placed a call while I listened to the sound of sirens screaming in different directions blocks away from us. By the sound of it, the entire Dallas Police Department was out in force.

My train of thought was broken when I heard Ruger loudly swear into the phone. "Jesus Christ! You've got to be fuckin' kiddin' me!"

He slammed the receiver down so hard I thought it was going to break. He turned to me in an absolute rage and screamed, "Oswald's been arrested already! That little shit's in police custody, and he's alive and talking! Jesus Christ!"

This was bad news for all of us. I didn't know if I should call him A.J. Hidell or Lee Harvey Oswald. It didn't matter—he had recognized me outside the book warehouse. If he talked, I would be identified. Not too long after that, the entire country would know of our secret operation. I felt my stomach start to churn. I fought to suppress the bile rising up in the back of my throat.

"Damn it, Ruger, what are we going to do? We can't let him talk…"

"Shut the fuck up!" he cut me off. "We're gonna have to go in after him."

We're gonna have to go in after him? Was he insane? "Derek, he's in police custody! No one's going to get anywhere near…"

"I said, shut the fuck up! We don't have a choice. Our only chance of staying alive is to kill him. The people that gave us our orders aren't going to let him rat us out. If we don't shut that guy up, then you and me are dead men. Come on—let's get out of here!"

Ruger glared at me. It was apparent I was no longer in control of the operation. I laughed at my own stupidity.

We grabbed another cab and had the driver drop us off two blocks past our safe house. Satisfied that it wasn't being watched, we doubled back and went around the block once just to be sure. Once we slipped inside through the back door, Ruger headed for the phone, but I beat him to it.

I dialed my home number back in Arlington, but the phone never rang. The operator eventually told me the entire phone system in the Washington, D.C. area was out of operation. I slammed down the phone in frustration.

Ruger didn't say a word. He picked up the phone and dialed his call while I collapsed in a chair in front of the television. My whole world had turned completely upside down in the past few hours. I was in a suffocating nightmare. I sat in numbed silence with my chest pounding and my heart racing, struggling to make sense of what had happened. None of this was part of the plan I had been given.

"Hey," Ruger called out. "He wants to talk to you," he said holding the phone out to me.

I took it from him. I immediately recognized the voice on the other end.

"What the hell happened?" Grant screamed at me. "What's going on? Ruger said our patsy got away alive!"

I battled to control my own temper. "You tell *me* what happened! No one told me there was going to be a patsy! I was under the assumption that the killers would never be found. Why was I double-crossed?"

There was a long period of silence before Grant replied. He brought the tone of his voice back under control. "It was on a need-to-know."

"You mean you didn't want me to know!"

My head was throbbing. Grant was silent on the other end, waiting for me to continue ranting. When I didn't, he placidly said, "His background was too good not to use. He was a nut with a gun—a defector and a traitor who hated his country and decided to kill the President of the United States."

"Oh hell, Grant, no one will ever believe that line of bullshit. Why would a defector want to kill his President? It doesn't make sense."

"It will make sense by the time we're done. But if he talks, all bets are off. I heard he recognized you. Is that true?"

I flashed back to my unexpected run-in with A.J. "Yeah, it's true."

"How does he know you?"

"He worked for me. He was an employee of the Agency."

"What?" he screamed. "Why didn't I know this?"

"Probably because you didn't tell me what you were going to do in the first place. If you had, I would have told you why you couldn't use Lee—or A.J.—or whatever the hell his name is today. He can be directly linked to the Agency. It's going to look like the Agency killed the President. The shit will hit the fan—it will be all over all of us."

"Then we've got a massive problem on our hands. Let me talk to Ruger."

I handed the phone to Ruger and walked out of the room—more enraged than I've ever been in my life.

Half an hour later, he hung up and came to get me. "Let's go find Ruby."

We headed back out onto the streets of Dallas. It was late afternoon. All of Dallas had come to a complete standstill. Everywhere we went, people huddled around radios and television sets in groups large and small—men, women, children, Negro and white alike, all gaunt with grief.

We found Jack Ruby at his Carousel Club. Even his club was closed. He was inside with a few employees. The girls in various states of undress held onto each other sobbing. "Go on home," he cried wiping his eyes with his handkerchief, "be with your families."

As the last one left, he closed and locked the door to give us some privacy. His mood abruptly changed.

"Well, we did it," he beamed broadly. "It worked like a charm!"

"Guess you ain't heard the news," Ruger said dryly.

Ruby's face fell. "No, what happened?"

"Oswald got away."

Jack Ruby stood mute. He knew what that news meant. "Do we know where he's at?"

"Yep," Ruger snapped. "The cops have got him."

Jack's jaw dropped stupefied at the news. "You've got to be fuckin' kiddin' me! How'd that happen?"

Ruger shrugged his shoulders. "Don't know. Just did."

"What are we going to do about it?" Jack asked apprehensively.

"We're gonna figure out how to get in there and shut him up before he talks."

"How are we going to do that?"

"You're gonna go scout things out," Ruger told him.

"Me? Why me?"

"Because the cops know you and trust you. They won't suspect you. If you get the chance, then you can pop him for us."

Jack's face lost its color. "I can't do that."

"You don't have a choice," Ruger replied.

Jack turned to me and started to plead, "Patrick…"

I held up my hand to stop him. "Jack—it's got to be done, and you've got to do it."

"But I can't," he whined.

Ruger snapped at him, "Quit sniveling! If you can't do it, then go check the place out for me and let me know how I can get in there."

A few minutes later, Ruger sent Ruby on his way, pale-faced and shaken.

"This better work," he growled, "or we're screwed." Ruger helped himself to a shot of whiskey. He closed his eyes as he downed it in one gulp. It was the only time that I saw a chink in his armor.

Meanwhile, when we got back to the safe house, I was finally able to reach Pam on the telephone back in Virginia. I needed to hear her voice to put some normalcy back into my life. I wasn't emotionally prepared for Pam's state of mind when she answered the phone.

"Patrick, is that you?" she cried. "Did you hear what happened to Jack? He's dead, Patrick! It's horrible! They killed him, oh my God, they killed him," she broke into gut-wrenching sobs.

It was only at that very moment that I finally stopped to consider the impact our actions had on my family, and by extension, on the rest of the nation. Ruger turned on the television. The news of the assassination had pre-empted all programs.

Pam shrieked, "It's so horrible! It's so horrible!" over and over again, in between crying fits. "What's Jackie going to do?—oh those poor kids—oh, Patrick, this is killing me—I can't breathe."

I could hear her coughing and crying at the same time. My heart broke at the sound of her misery.

Tim picked up the phone. His voice was frail and needy, "Daddy, come home," he pleaded. "Mommy's so sad. Come home Daddy, please."

The magnitude of my actions staggered me as I listened to Pam in one ear and the television in the other. I had ignored the suffering displayed by the people of Dallas when we were out, but my own family's pain was something I couldn't possibly ignore. I was barraged with Pam's intense grief.

It had never, ever occurred to me to consider how America would react to the loss of their President. I was so caught up in doing what I thought was right, I didn't even stop to think about how other people would feel. A shroud of gloom, sadness, and mourning rapidly descended across the country. The sorrow was palpable, so heavy it was oppressive.

"Where…where are you?" she sobbed. "I need you. Tim needs you… when are you coming home?"

I labored to keep the emotion out of my voice. "I've…I've got to go to Dallas," I lied. "We don't know if there is a plot of some kind or what," I lamely contrived an excuse that I hoped would satisfy her curiosity.

"Tell them to send someone else, Patrick. Tim and I need you home—now," she begged.

"Pam…I can't do that, honey. My country needs me right now…."

"Your family needs you right now, Patrick! Your *family*! Please....*come home*!"

There was nothing else I could do or say. "Hon, I'm sorry...I've got to go."

"Patrick..." she wailed as I hung up on her.

For hours and hours after that, I sat numbly in front of the television as the rest of the world hung onto every piece of news about the shooting. Events in every community around the world were canceled out of respect for the loss of the President.

My paralysis was broken when I heard the news that Officer J.D. Tippitt, a Dallas policeman, had been gunned down and killed in a neighborhood not too far from where the alleged assassin was arrested. The police were convinced the man they had in custody, Lee Harvey Oswald, was responsible for not only the murder of the President and the wounding of the Governor, but also for killing Officer Tippitt.

The local news station reported that a Secret Service agent had also died in Dealey Plaza; I knew they must have been referring to the guy that Ruger accidentally shot. Jerry Coley, a thirty-year old employee of the *Dallas Morning News* reported he and his friend, Charlie Mulkey, noticed a pool of red liquid on the steps leading down to Elm Street from the side of the Texas School Book Depository. Charlie touched the liquid with his finger, tasted it, and exclaimed, "My God, Jerry, that's blood!"

They hurried to the *Morning News* building and got photographer Jim Hood to return to the scene with them, where he snapped a picture of the pool of blood from different angles. They reported it was more than a pint's worth. It was too far from the street to belong to either President Kennedy or Governor Connally.

Dan Rather of CBS News reported the FBI released information that the suspect in custody was Lee Harvey Oswald, a one-time Marine sharpshooter who had betrayed his country and had defected to the Soviet Union, only to return with an obvious chip on his shoulder. For some unknown reason, he was carrying identification at the time of his arrest in the name of Alek James Hidell.

Shit! The world would soon know Lee Harvey Oswald was really Alek J. Hidell. It probably wouldn't take long for authorities to make the connection to the Agency after that. Most of the Patriots were still in town. Would Grant advise them that Alek was associated with the Agency? I couldn't imagine that Dulles would let the name of the Agency be besmirched. My only hope was that the Patriots would intercede before it was too late.

I was relieved when news reports began to claim that the assassination was the work of a lone gunman and that there was no evidence of a conspiracy.

I felt the tightness in my chest loosen. In the midst of all the confusion, I remembered I was supposed to call David Ferrie to get us out of Dallas, but with A.J. still alive and in police custody, there was no way I could even think about leaving. Ferrie would just have to wait.

AROUND 7:20 P.M., NBC broadcast a live shot of a press conference at police headquarters, and there was Oswald on the screen. He was wearing a dark shirt over a white t-shirt. His hands were handcuffed in front of him as two plainclothes officers steered him through the crowd of waiting reporters. He had a cut on his forehead, and his left eye was noticeably swollen. A cacophony of reporters yelled, "Did you shoot the President?" He calmly replied, "I really don't know what this is about." When asked if he had a lawyer, he said, "No, sir, I don't." Then, when asked again, he said, "I didn't shoot anybody, no sir."

The next six or seven hours became a gut-wrenching blur. We waited for Ruby to tell us what was going on. Television news completely took over and began wall-to-wall coverage of everything having to do with the President's murder.

It was impossible not to become emotional when I saw pictures of Jackie arriving in D.C. in a blood-splattered pink suit, looking dazed and confused. I put my elbows on my knees and buried my face in my hands. My thoughts kept going back to Pam and how hard she was taking all of this.

I was dumbstruck by the outpouring of grief from around the country and around the world. Never in my wildest dreams did I ever imagine that Jack's death would provoke such a reaction. It left me with an uneasy feeling, a feeling that maybe things were spiraling out of control for all of us.

Ruger and I sat in the safe house, silent in each other's presence. Ruger sat at the kitchen table, playing solitaire.

I slumped exhausted and catatonic in a worn overstuffed chair in front of the television.

SOMETIME AFTER MIDNIGHT, the Dallas police again paraded Oswald in front of the reporters and television cameras at the Dallas Police station. Oswald told the reporters, "They're taking me in because of the fact that I lived in the Soviet Union." As he was pushed through the mob, I heard him say, "I'm just a patsy."

Early in the morning, Ruby finally returned to the safe house.

"I don't see how you can get in there," Ruby explained to Ruger. "There's cops and reporters all over the place. They'd see you coming and arrest you before you ever got near him."

"I didn't ask you to tell me how I couldn't get in—I told you to find a way that I could get in," Ruger gave Ruby a withering stare. "Get the fuck out-a-here."

I was glued to the television, watching the coverage of the funeral preparations and waiting for the phone to ring. Ruger, dressed in an undershirt and dress slacks, paced back and forth almost unceasingly. I could see the veins in his arms pop as he clenched and unclenched his fists. We knew that every minute Oswald was alive represented another minute closer to the time our plot would be uncovered. The long Saturday drew to a close and passed into Sunday.

Finally, the phone rang. Ruger answered. He barely spoke, listening to whatever was being said. When he hung up, his eyes were dark and menacing. "Get Ruby over here."

Jack showed up about twenty minutes after I called him. He looked nervous. I noticed that he had buttoned his white shirt crookedly. "What's up?"

"You are," Ruger replied. "Here's the story. This Oswald guy's gonna talk any time now. When he does, it will blow the lid off this whole thing. You've already proved to us that there is no way I can get near him. So we're left with one option—you're gonna have to do it."

"Oh, hell no! No fuckin' way am I goin'…"

"SHUT THE FUCK UP!" Ruger screamed.

Ruby's eyes almost bulged out of his head. A bead of sweat trickled down his forehead.

"It's not your decision. You do this, or I'll have to hurt you until you agree to do it." Ruger turned toward me and smiled, "Tell him how persuasive I can be. Remember Jackson?"

Oh my God did I remember Jackson! I couldn't watch another scene like that. Jack could see the horror in my eyes, "Jack, you'd better do what he says…"

"But Patrick, I can't! I'm tellin' ya—really—I just can't do this!"

Ruger glared at me. "Talk to him," he growled and angrily stalked out of the room.

I looked at Jack—he kept blowing air out over his lips. I could see how scared he was—I was scared, too. This could turn into a grisly nightmare.

"Jack, listen to me. You've got to do this—not for us—for yourself. You've got to do what Ruger says. The alternative is—there is no alternative for you."

Jack began weaving drunkenly though I knew he was sober. "I can't. I don't know. I can't."

"You have to—I've seen what Ruger will do to you. Listen! Jack—listen!" I grabbed him his upper arms as if to shake him. "Do this for us, and I'm sure that we can get you out of jail after a very brief time. Hell, you'll probably be a hero when you get out."

"Hero? You think so?"

"I know so. Hey, four years after President Lincoln was assassinated, President Andrew Johnson gave a presidential pardon to all of the conspirators, and they were released from jail. I'll bet that we can do the same thing for you."

Jack grasped for a strand of hope, "Really? You think I might be a hero and get a pardon?"

"It wouldn't surprise me at all," I lied. "Just don't let us down." Then I remembered the lesson Sam Giancana taught me one night. "Jack, you know what *omerta* means?"

Jack stiffened at the mere mention of the word *omerta*. "Of course I do."

"Well, so do all of our friends. Do this right, keep your mouth shut, and everything will work out."

Less than twelve hours later, Jack strolled into the Dallas Police Headquarters and shot Oswald as he was being transferred to the more secure County Jail—and he managed to do it on live TV. The entire nation witnessed the execution.

He walked up to Oswald, stuck a gun in his gut, and pulled the trigger. Oswald doubled over in pain. The image was seared in my brain.

For the first time in three days, I saw Derek Ruger smile.

ONCE LEE HARVEY Oswald was dead, there was no longer any reason for me to stick around Dallas. I caught the first plane back to D.C. landing at Washington National Airport by suppertime.

The house was dark and empty when I arrived. All the shades were pulled down tight, a chill in the air. I walked into the kitchen to look for some kind of note. Finding none, I opened the icebox instead—nothing appealing there. I walked into the bedroom. The closet door stood open, the bed usually neatly made was in disarray, and Pam's robe was on the floor. I grabbed a hot shower and collapsed into bed, totally exhausted.

I was awakened around midnight by the sounds of Pam coming home. My presence at home evidently surprised her.

"I heard the son of a bitch is dead. Is that why you're home?" she said testily.

"Yes, that's exactly why I'm home. Where have you been? Where's Tim?"

"Tim's down the street with the neighbors. I've been at the White House all weekend with Jackie."

"How's she doing?"

"How do you think she's doing? Someone blew her husband's head off while he was sitting next to her. She's traumatized. She's totally in shock. I don't know how she's even able to function."

"I know, hon. She's lucky she has a friend like you. How are you doing?" I asked.

"Oh, Patrick," she wailed. Her anger disappeared as she flung herself onto the bed and on top of me. We lay like that the rest of the night while she cried and cried, her poor body shaking and sobbing as the pent-up grief poured out of her.

I was as emotionally drained as Pam. I wasn't in the clear—my whole life was on the verge of destruction. And worst of all, I harbored a horrible secret that I could never share with my wife.

I could only hold Pam and tell her I loved her.

IMMEDIATELY AFTER THE death of Oswald, most of us considered the case safely closed. The accused presidential assassin was dead; more than enough circumstantial evidence ascertained his guilt. But it wasn't that easy—the rest of the nation suspected things weren't on the up-and-up in Dallas; a cry began to build for a national investigation. Americans didn't trust the Dallas authorities to give them the truth regarding the details of the shooting. Their young President had been brutally murdered while in the arms of his young wife. Americans needed to blame someone—Dallas and Texas became the scapegoats for the nation's rage.

We had been concerned that details of the crime scene might point an accusing finger our way. But Grant assured me that prosecuting the case would prove virtually impossible. The customary rigid standards of the chain of evidence were either broken or wholly ignored all weekend in Dallas. America was so hungry for information that reporters were given *carte blanche*. This worked in our favor.

For example, take the way the suspect "Lee Harvey Oswald" had been handled. Ever since the first radio broadcast on Friday afternoon, the Dallas police had fallen all over each other to release evidence to the growing press corps substantiating that they had indeed arrested the right man for the President's murder. They even went so far as to arrange an actual press conference featuring the most compelling piece of evidence in their possession—the suspect himself. A.J. was trotted in and out of various offices and holding cells—paraded in front of the reporters and cameras so that everyone in the world could get a good look at a presidential assassin. The grieving public satisfied their curiosity at the carnival freak show that ensued.

Reporters were allowed into the book warehouse to see the sniper's lair—they even were allowed into Jack Ruby's apartment within hours of Jack's arrest. The press was given unprecedented access to suspects, witnesses, crime scenes and evidence—enough to taint a trial.

The federal government, or the Patriots, stepped in to protect our plot right from the beginning. When Dr. Earl Rose, the Dallas County Coroner, refused to allow the President's body to be removed from the hospital, the Secret Service brushed him aside with guns drawn, physically removing the body. The federal government had absolutely no jurisdiction in the proceedings because the murder of the President of the United States was not a federal crime. The coroner acted within his authority under Texas law because a homicide in Texas required an autopsy.

While Lyndon Johnson was being sworn in as President, Jack's body was secretly removed from his big bronze casket and placed on Air Force Two for a faster return to Andrews Air Force Base in D.C. His body was taken by helicopter to Walter Reed Army Hospital where a quick examination was performed to remove any of the most obvious pieces of ballistic evidence. His body was then swiftly shuttled to Bethesda Naval Hospital in a simple body bag and casket for the "official" autopsy. It arrived just before the ambulance bearing Jackie and the decoy casket from Air Force One.

None of the doctors at Bethesda assigned to do the presidential autopsy had any experience in conducting autopsies, nor did they have any experience in ballistic wounds and gunshot deaths. They had been selected as men most likely to be ignorant of the significance of certain important details.

Director Hoover assigned two of his agents to stand in with the doctors as they performed the President's autopsy. They took immediate possession of all of the bullet fragments collected, as well as a "missile removed" and recorded on the autopsy receipt. We were told later that it was a bullet which had been retrieved intact from what was left of the President's brain—and it didn't match the ballistics of the Oswald murder weapon. That "missile" mysteriously disappeared.

The official autopsy was conducted under the supervision of the same military officers that had professed their dissatisfaction with JFK from the very beginning of his term in office. Some of them had also been privy to the details of Operation Northwoods. I was later told General Curtis LeMay sat watching the full autopsy for every minute of the eight hours, smoking a cigar and seemingly smug about what had happened to his Commander in Chief. Not a single general shed a tear.

The autopsy officially confirmed that all of the President's wounds had come from a single gun. We had proof that Lee Harvey Oswald was a lone gunman. Case closed. Unfortunately, the rest of America, and the rest of the world, didn't believe the story. Eyewitnesses testified to any reporter willing to listen that they had seen other gunmen.

The government would have to deal with the incriminating fact that some lucky bystander had captured the entire ambush on his home movie camera.

A DAY AFTER the impressive state funeral for President John F. Kennedy, I received a phone call from Grant. He asked me to meet him at Mount Vernon, George Washington's stately mansion on the Potomac River about fourteen miles south of D.C. I arrived at noon and found the grounds almost devoid of the customary tourists. Grant gave me a slight wave. We bypassed the mansion to take a walk through the garden and down the path toward Washington's gravesite. Once there, we were alone and unlikely to be overheard by anyone that we didn't spot approaching us first.

It was a crisp fall day, but the sun was warm and the wind off the Potomac was gentle enough the leaves still left on the trees barely rustled. The beauty of the day belied the reality of our discussion. Nothing about it was sunny.

"We've got a problem," Grant grimly told me. I figured as much. The newspapers had been filled with letters from people of all walks of life, imploring that someone do something about investigating the President's death. I had been nervously following the growing drumbeats, and I didn't like the momentum they were generating.

"The President's under a lot of pressure to allow an independent investigation of all of the facts pertaining to what happened in Dallas. Congress is talking, the Texas Attorney General is talking—hell, anybody who has any kind of political clout is talking about what should be done. It's a real mess."

My stomach was in knots. "What's he going to do?"

Grant looked at me in surprise. "What's he going to do? What the hell do you think he's going to do? He's gonna circle the wagons and try to ride this out, that's what he's going to do. Hoover is already frantically working to finish the FBI's own investigation into what happened."

"How's he going to do that? There wasn't any jurisdiction in this case at the federal level," I pointed out.

"That's why I'm glad we've got him on our side," Grant grinned. "Do you know what that wily old bastard did for us? He found an obscure technicality in federal law that enabled him to declare jurisdictional control over all of the investigation from the Texas authorities. He said that because federal property had been damaged when the assassin's bullet struck the windshield of the president's limousine, he was entitled and legally empowered to wrest control from the Secret Service."

My anxiety ratcheted down a notch. I had hoped that under Hoover's oversight, we'd be protected. "He'll make sure some areas of investigation are excluded and some clues are ignored?" I ventured.

"Oh hell, he'll do better than that," Grant laughed. "Hoover's assigned the murder investigation to the FBI division that handles bank robberies and the theft and destruction of federal property. The guys that normally look for missing and stolen typewriters will be the one's handling this investigation. The Director's making sure that his two most qualified Bureau divisions, the ones that handle organized crime and the ones that handle domestic and foreign conspiracies and national security will not be working on this investigation. Hoover expects to have this wrapped up in a day or so."

"What if it doesn't work?"

"Then we go to Plan B. I advised the President to set up a Presidential Commission by executive order. That will allow him to handpick the blue ribbon panel that will essentially rubber-stamp the FBI report. We'll string it out until just before the November election and then release it to great fanfare. The papers will endorse it, and the whole thing will be over."

"Why do you think the papers will buy it? Aren't you afraid of Freedom of the Press and their tendency to poke their noses into a story?"

Grant smiled and glanced around, just to be sure no one ambled up on us without us knowing about it. When he saw we were still alone, he said, "Freedom of the Press is B.S. The press might be free, but the presses don't run without government approval. All those news organizations are regulated businesses, subject to scrutiny by the IRS, the SEC, the FCC, and whomever else we can think of. Believe me, they'll toe the line and publish any viewpoint we give them to publish. No television network news organization, no radio outlet, no newspaper, no publishing house of any kind is going to risk incurring the wrath of the President, the White House, or the Justice Department and the FBI by saying something that doesn't toe the official line. Nope, don't worry about it. Believe me, we're covered."

We both lit a Marlboro and sat quietly puffing our cigarettes as we tried to both put our anxieties to rest. This meeting was as much to calm Grant as it was to inform me of what was going on behind the scenes. I had taken the week off to help my own family deal with their grief. Pam was still shattered by the event, and Tim was having nightmares that the assassins were coming to get him, too. I tried to hold them both and reassure them that the worst was over.

Finally Grant asked me the question that had been gnawing at him. He needed to know if my men could be counted on to keep our mouths shut.

"That shouldn't be a problem," I assured him. "They're familiar with *omerta*. I'm just worried about our OAS contractors."

"Well, don't be. First of all, our European guests had an unfortunate accident on the 22nd when they left Dallas. The small plane they used to fly out of Red Bird Airport suffered a mechanical problem over the Gulf of Mexico. It crashed—they're all dead."

"I didn't know that. When were you planning to tell me?" I bristled.

Grant's eyes flared at the insinuation. "Don't you trust me? I told you we would take care of you," he chuckled. "That plane crash was good news for us, but too bad for them. What about your local guys?"

"Banister, Shaw, and Ferrie won't talk. Ruger scares the shit out of them. Ruger won't talk either. Giancana will keep an eye on him. Jack Ruby's got his orders and his assurance of a presidential pardon in the future. He's also scared to death of Ruger. He won't talk. The rest are all professionals and will keep their mouths shut."

Grant nodded, "I know Mac Wallace personally. I can vouch for the fact he won't talk."

Then he stung me with his last question, "What about you?"

"Oh, Jesus Christ, Grant! How can you even ask me that? I'm sure as hell not planning on talking about this, ever! First of all, I could never face my wife ever again if she found out that I was the one who killed her best friend's husband, who also happened to be the President. Second, I could never allow my own son to go through life stigmatized as the son of a presidential assassin. Third, there's no statute of limitation on murder. I would never want to have to stand trial. The infamy would destroy my family and friends. No, you can count on one thing in this world—Patrick Sean McCarthy will never say a word about what he did. Count on it."

Grant studied every nuance of my face as I spoke. He evidently believed me, "That's great, buddy. I told my friends we could count on you forever. Look's like I'm right."

A partner in crime, he offered me his hand. "Let's get through this and get on with our lives. There's a new sheriff in town and the Soviets know it. We don't have to worry about getting pushed around any more."

After we left, it occurred to me that I was the one who made the assurances to Grant. He never once assured me that he could keep his mouth shut.

CIRCLING THE WAGONS didn't work so the White House had to implement Plan B. The political pressure was too much for President Johnson to ignore.

The people of the United States wanted answers and expected justice to be served. The American people didn't trust the Dallas Police Department to conduct an impartial and objective inquiry. Initially, President Johnson objected to reopening any investigation of the assassination: "Now we can't be checking up on every shooting scrape in the country...." In an attempt to quiet the uproar, Johnson agreed to convene an outside, independent investigation into the murder. The public outcry was temporarily quelled with the announcement that the Warren Commission would conduct a complete investigation into the death of President Kennedy.

I was satisfied that this particular investigation would find nothing amiss and support the notion that Lee Harvey Oswald was a lone assassin.

> "When it comes to conspiracy, anything is permissible."
>
> — Napoleon

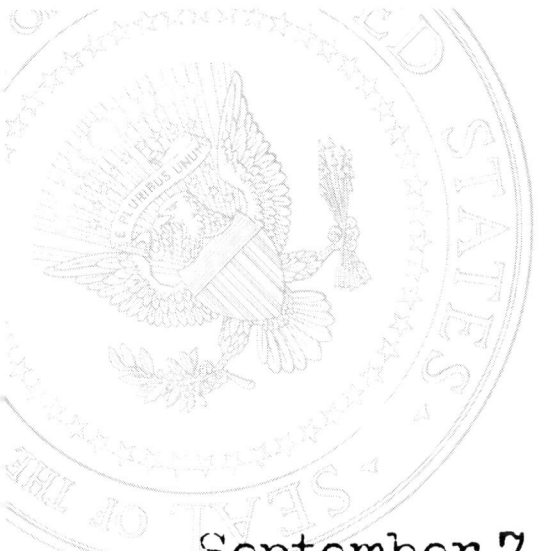

September 7, 1978
3:57 a.m.

The ringing phone startled Grant out of his sleep. He'd booted Sugar out around midnight. He didn't like to share his bed anymore. He settled between the soft sheets, fluffed up his down pillows, and stretched full length in the very middle of the bed. But he was restless and found himself checking the clock at one, two, and three. He must have dozed off. He was wide-awake as he grabbed the receiver.

"I've found him," Ruger said, dispensing with civilities.

Grant didn't care to chitchat anyway. "Give me the short-and-sweet."

"Got to the taxi stand and started showing his picture around. Finally found some fruitcake remembered picking him up around eight hours ago. Said he thought it was strange that a guy from out of town would want to go straight to a flophouse."

"You sure it's him?"

"Told him his name was Patrick McCarthy."

Grant was momentarily confused. "Why would he go there? That doesn't make sense."

"It makes perfect sense. He can't check into a hotel because they'd want his name, address, and credit card. He can't pay cash because he'd look like he was waiting for a hooker."

"But a flophouse? That's not Patrick."

"Don't matter. He's there. A flophouse wants the dough. They don't ask questions."

"Do you believe the cab driver steered you right? Maybe Patrick paid him to say that."

"The guy's not lying. He knows it's not in his best interests."

Ruger had far more street smarts than Grant would ever have. "When will you have him?"

"The fruitcake's taking me there now. I checked in so you wouldn't worry."

"I don't worry about you, Ruger."

He laughed as if it was a stupid joke. "I didn't mean me. You're worried about your own skin."

The line went dead.

1964

NEW YEAR'S EVE 1963 was subdued. No showers of confetti or raucous whistles from noisemakers greeted the New Year. The few revelers who did celebrate the New Year choked back tears when they sang *Auld Lang Syne.*

My own household was enveloped in sadness as well. It killed me that my son found no joy in opening his Christmas presents. There was no running down the stairs on Christmas morning with shrieks of excitement. He had waited patiently on the sofa for us to awake. Pam and I put on our best looks of surprise and excitement about the presents that Santa had left, but Tim merely went through the motions of opening each present. "Thanks Mom—thanks Dad," Tim politely said as he indulgently smiled.

One wintry afternoon he asked me, "Is this hurt ever going to go away?" Tim often experienced sudden fits of crying. No longer seeking solace in Pam's comforting arms, he withdrew into himself.

I searched for words to console him. I tousled his hair and drew him to me. "One day, buddy, it will be gone. Sometimes, we have to just live through it. I think it helps to pretend that you're happy—even if it is only for a few seconds. If you do that each day, you will find that you can pretend longer and longer. Soon you can pretend for an hour without thinking about it. And then one day, you will find that you can pretend for two hours and then three hours. That's what I try do."

Pam's grief left deep circles under her eyes. Her skin, once soft and supple, took on the pallor of her sorrow. She spent many days with Jackie, trying to comfort her. Jackie was able to draw upon the support of her family while Pam felt isolated with her grief. We both thought it was ironic that our Jackie, who had once been so fragile and flighty as a young woman, now seemed to bear the weight of the nation on her shoulders. She was only thirty-four years old, but the entire world openly admired her courage and strength in the face of this tragedy.

Jackie confided to Pam that she actually hoped Lee Harvey Oswald was part of a larger conspiracy. Shocked, Pam asked her to explain. She said it would help her to accept that Jack's death was inevitable and that he was killed because of his ideas—not because some nobody with a gun wanted to make a name for himself.

I think it was probably that feeling that led Jackie to create the myth of Camelot in Jack's honor. Camelot was a popular Broadway musical written by a former classmate of Jack's. Jackie thought the idea of the Camelot romance and tragedy played right into our grieving nation's image of the Kennedy White House. Knowing Jack, I think he would have simply laughed off such an analogy as mawkish and stupid. I'm sure he would have been uncomfortable with such a schmaltzy and sickeningly sentimental comparison to his administration and his life. After all, the story deals with an older man marrying a much younger woman. The younger woman enters into the marriage but doesn't love him. She then betrays her husband when she finds true love in another man—a younger and braver man. Their illicit affair destroys her marriage. Camelot dissolves into ruin.

Jackie, however, was drawn to the tale. She made up a little fib about how Jack loved to listen to the Camelot record at night before he went to bed. She said he was captivated by the whole myth of Camelot and had been since he was a little boy—just the hook the nation needed to help deal with its own sorrow. Jack and Jackie Kennedy became the living embodiment of the Camelot myth from that moment on.

As Grant had predicted, our nation rushed to pay tribute to our fallen leader. Airports, schools, streets, and parks were renamed for JFK. Even Cape Canaveral, our nation's space center in Florida, became Cape Kennedy.

The image of Jackie, Caroline, and John-John standing bravely during the funeral haunted me. I would be working at my desk or shoveling snow or reading the evening paper when the image would flash through my mind. I became crippled by my secret guilt. I felt duplicitous in every single action of every single moment of the day. I turned to Shakespeare, and like Macbeth, I lived the words: "Away, and mock the time with fairest show/False face must hide what the false heart doth know."

Pam tried to comfort me, but often, I am ashamed to say, I lashed out at her with a harshness that she didn't deserve. Our nightly bedtime conversations withered and died. My guilt was raw; I was undeserving of love and affection. I pushed Pam away when she needed me the most. I cloaked myself in an armor of numbness—if I could not feel, I would not hurt.

I could not fathom the pain that millions of Americans felt around the country. My anger and exasperation with Jack's behavior and conduct had blinded me to the vast degree of hope he represented in the minds of people throughout the United States and around the globe. I had been completely unprepared for the vast blowback of emotion.

I had been hoodwinked by my own zealotry—I was protecting the best interests of my country. Unlike the American people, I had been oblivious to the attributes of the First Family. The Kennedys were the embodiment of the American family. They were outdoorsy, always playing touch football or sailing or tennis or horseback riding. They were cultured and cultivated an affinity for the arts to which most Americans had never been exposed. Many Americans had never heard of Pablo Casals until he played at a White House dinner. After his performance, sales of his recordings shot up almost overnight; he was in constant demand for concert appearances.

Once America learned that Jack could read 1200 words a minute, speed-reading courses increased ten-fold. Jack's reluctance to wear a hat or button-down shirts almost single-handedly destroyed the hat industry, and men's haberdashery underwent a monumental change.

The pulp fiction writer, Ian Fleming, saw the success of his fictional character James Bond grow into a string of popular books and movies as a result of Jack's interest in the British secret agent. Fleming became a millionaire as a result. Vaughn Meader, an unknown comic before the sixties, spoofed the Kennedy family in a series of popular comedy acts and records that created an international audience for his humorous view of their lives.

Jackie's own impact on America was equally hard to ignore. Interest in Parisian couture and bouffant hairstyles grew almost overnight. Her loving commitment to her children was universally admired.

The Kennedys permeated the culture and the imagination of America. Caught up in my obsession over Communism, I had been completely oblivious to the Kennedy influence.

I found it hard to admit and even harder to accept, but I was directly responsible for plunging my family and my country into that deep chasm of despair. Overnight, the newspapers and reporters who had reviled Kennedy and the Kennedy White House tempered their criticisms in respect to our fallen leader.

All of Jack's shortcomings were duly erased from the American psyche in one fell swoop.

PRESIDENT JOHNSON'S MAIN concern in 1964 was to be legitimately elected to the White House in November. However, he had to surmount the hurdle of being a Texan first. After the assassination, the city of

Dallas, as well as the state of Texas, was roundly excoriated, condemned and ostracized—in short, no one wanted to be identified with Dallas or Texas. The nation punished all of Texas for being host to the assassination.

President Johnson himself wasn't above suspicion in many quarters, especially in the eyes of many of the old Kennedy loyalists. There were too many convenient coincidences for them to ignore. Many loyal Kennedy supporters thought LBJ did have something to do with the murder. When Lyndon took the oath of office from Judge Sarah T. Hughes on Air Force One, the photos showed a grief-stricken Jackie standing numbly at a very solemn Johnson's side while he was being sworn in. Unfortunately, the last photo in the series of pictures by the same photographer showed Congressman Albert Thomas of Texas smiling and winking at LBJ—LBJ appeared to return a smile of his own and later bragged, "I never felt better." Even Lady Bird had a huge smile on her face.

On November 29, 1963, LBJ summoned Chief Justice Earl Warren to the White House. The President explained the gravity of the situation—wild rumors were rampant about Cuban and Russian involvement in JFK's assassination. LBJ suggested that should the public sentiment escalate against Khrushchev and Castro, we might be drawn into an action that could imperil the lives of millions of Americans. The head of the Atomic Energy Commission had recently briefed the President on how many Americans would be killed in a nuclear war with the Soviet Union.

Grant said the President told the Chief Justice that the only way to dispel all of these wild rumors was to have an independent investigation headed by the highest-ranking judicial official in the country. Then he twisted Warren's arm. "You've been in uniform before, and if I asked you, you would put on the uniform again for your country."

"Yes sir, Mr. President," Warren replied, "Of course."

"This is more important than that," the President emphasized.

"If you're putting it like that, I can't say no."

Chief Justice Earl Warren took the job. Hours later, President Johnson signed *Executive Order 11130*, appointing six other members to the President's Commission on the Assassination of John F. Kennedy. Their orders were to evaluate all FBI investigative material, make further investigations of their own if warranted, and to appraise "all the facts and circumstances surrounding" the murder of the President and his assassin.

The political appointees were all men who were not political or personal friends of John F. Kennedy, but were instead political and personal friends of Lyndon Johnson. The other figurehead members included two southern senators, John Cooper of Kentucky and Richard Russell of Louisiana (a frequent critic of the Kennedy administration's civil rights moves, as well as Jack's conduct during the Cuban Missile Crisis), Louisiana Representative

Hale Boggs, Representative Gerald Ford of Michigan (a highly supportive fan of J. Edgar Hoover), and international banker John J. McCloy.

The name of the seventh member appointed to the Commission gave me a profound sense of serenity over what that Commission would ultimately find. I felt confident that my part in all of this would remain secret. I knew that because I knew this man as well as I knew anyone else in D.C. He was my former boss, my mentor, and the man unjustly blamed by Jack Kennedy for the failure of the Bay of Pigs invasion. He was also a man who had been publicly fired and humiliated by young Jack Kennedy. That man was Allen J. Dulles.

Some of those seven members of the Warren Commission also shared another common bond that the public was never to know about. Just like President Johnson and FBI Director Hoover, they were all Patriots.

This could have been a risky venture for LBJ—but he was too cagey a politician to ask questions to which he didn't already know the answers. After appointing a Commission composed of friends and colleagues, he put Grant in charge of oversight. Grant moved expeditiously to have me appointed to the investigation to provide "technical assistance"—technically, I was to keep a close eye on every aspect of the investigation. If the Commission got too close to the truth, I would subtly re-direct their course. During our first full staff meeting on January 20, 1964, Chief Justice Warren solemnly told us "our only client was the truth."

Grant was confident that we could pull off the ruse. "So far, so good," he boasted. I had a gut feeling that it was only a matter of time before the jig was up.

ON FEBRUARY 3, the Warren Commission formally convened to investigate the "facts" behind the murder of the president. The first order of business was to turn over the grunt work to a roster of minor legal talent specifically recruited by the members of the Commission. The Commission had been flooded with unsolicited resumes from lawyers all across the country volunteering their services—not one of the unsolicited applications landed a single job, much less an interview. The selection of the Commission staff was especially important and tightly controlled.

I met with Grant in his new White House office to plan the structure of the staff. Grant was cavalier about the entire procedure.

"Patrick, all seven Commission members have made it clear to the President that they can't devote much day to day time to this inquest. Chief Justice Warren said that he would have to delegate most of his responsibilities on this Commission, or he would be unable to head the Commission. In fact, the main criteria he had for accepting the appointment from the President was that it could not interfere with his job running the Supreme Court."

Grant put his feet up on his desk and leaned back in his chair.

"He claims every single brief submitted to the Supreme Court has be read and reviewed by every single Justice before any work can even be delegated to their law clerks."

"He sounds like a busy man."

"He's also a whiner. Warren really doesn't want the job of heading this investigation. In fact, when the other six Commission members heard Warren's excuse, they all tried to use it, too. All of the other Commission members declared the same terrible constraints upon their time as well. So, it is absolutely imperative for the Commission to have a competent staff."

Grant walked over to a credenza and pulled out a large legal-sized box.

"The Patriots and my boss have entrusted both of us with oversight. Here's the organizational chart that I've cooked up. Take a look at this."

He handed me a legal pad on which he had drawn a bunch of boxes with names in the boxes and lines connecting the boxes.

"Chief Justice Warren nominated J. Lee Rankin as the general counsel for the Commission. Mr. Rankin is a former Solicitor General of the United States; it is supposed to be his job to assemble a staff to handle the investigation. That staff reports to Mr. Rankin, and Mr. Rankin reports directly to the Commission itself. Rankin will be the buffer, or the filter, for everything between the junior staff and the seven commissioners."

"Can he be trusted?"

"Don't worry. We'll handle him."

He pointed to the chart and continued. "Lee Rankin has hired two main aides, Norman Redlich and Howard Willens, to help him. Redlich has been put in charge of the investigation and Willens will run the day-to-day operations. They, in turn, have surveyed their friends and acquaintances for some young lawyers to assist them."

"This seems pretty complex for an organization chart," I said.

"That's the point," Grant smiled. "Once they get done setting this up, it will be a cluster-fuck of confusion. No one's going to know what anyone else is really doing. See here. Willens and Redlich hired five senior lawyers to work directly beneath them, and each of those senior lawyers assigned junior counsels to work for them. Look at this mess."

Grant pushed the chart toward me so that I could see what he meant. The organizational chart looked something like this:

- Chief Justice Earl Warren
- Six Commission members

- Lee Rankin
- Norman Redlich and Howard Willens
- Five senior attorneys
- Junior counsels

"What do you think?" Grant asked.

"Well, I think we can probably exploit the junior counsels the easiest."

"I agree. I think we take advantage of the junior counsels the most; they are going to be the most pliable and the most easily influenced. After all, they're assigned to do the grunt work."

"They are the least competent to conduct this inquiry."

"Believe me, because of their inexperience, they will turn out to be the easiest ones for me to manipulate. These junior counsels will be selected mostly for their work ethic and their ability to follow instructions, not their expertise. Howard Willens told me he wants junior counsels who can work sixteen hours a day. Now I'm guessing that requirement was really Redlich's criteria because he often boasts he can work from 8 a.m. to 3 a.m. seven days a week, and he wants people who can keep up with him. His ridiculous work ethic will only result in sloppy work, which is fine with me."

"And me. But what kind of legal backgrounds do these guys have?"

Grant grinned again. "You're gonna love this, too. The junior counsels have a variety of legal backgrounds; however, only a few of them have ever been involved in criminal law. Specifically, we have a co-editor of the Yale Law Review who has worked with Howard Willens. We've got two Wall Street corporate lawyers, a former assistant U.S. attorney from northern Ohio, a former law clerk of Chief Justice Warren, a trial lawyer from Denver, and, get this—an estate-planning tax attorney from Iowa."

"What's the estate-planning attorney going to do? Jack's already dead."

"Hell, I don't know. I think it would be funny to put him in charge of ballistics."

I couldn't help but laugh. Grant had the sickest sense of humor of anyone I knew.

"So basically," I cynically observed, "this is a carefully controlled 'old boys network' at work."

"Yep, and I have a feeling it's going to work magnificently. The Warren Commission is actually made up of seven prominent friends of President Johnson who don't like to go to meetings. They have decided to delegate their work to one lawyer who has appointed two more lawyers to oversee five more lawyers who also don't do any work but simply push their work off onto seven or eight young and inexperienced staff lawyers, many of whom have no criminal forensics background. It's perfect!"

GRANT'S ORGANIZATION CHART did just what we wanted it to do: obfuscate, confuse, and mislead. Howard Willens paired each of his senior counsels up with a junior counsel. He then divided their inquiry into five major areas: one, the basic facts of the assassination; two, the identity of the assassin, Lee Harvey Oswald; three, the background and motive for Oswald's actions; four, possible conspiratorial relationships with Oswald; and five, Oswald's death. Later, at the request of the commissioners, a sixth area on presidential protection was added.

The senior and junior counsels examined any minor problems and inconsistencies in their assigned areas. They passed on major problems to Rankin who then passed them on to the seven head commissioners for further examination.

Once all of the facts were ascertained, the six teams drafted a chapter of their findings for the final report. That organizational chart kept all the members of the lower Commission staff brilliantly compartmentalized. There was little or no sharing of ideas—or discussion of areas of concern—among the junior counsels.

We convinced the Commission they needed to work in private; the Commission members agreed with us. They also decided that no evidence would be released publicly before the final publication of the Commission's report. They felt piece-meal news releases would only confuse the public and perhaps lead to unsubstantiated and irresponsible rumors, which in turn would mean more work for them to follow up on.

Existing Federal agencies like the Federal Bureau of Investigation would conduct the basic investigation, and the facts they uncovered would then be turned over to the junior staff to evaluate. Lack of time and money made it impractical for the Commission to consider hiring its own investigative force. Allen Dulles agreed with the notion and added that independent investigators might cause unnecessary friction with government agencies and officials, but he was more concerned that it would be difficult to control security leaks with non-government investigators. He concluded that since the Commission had been promised the full cooperation of all federal agencies in the investigation, it would be unnecessary to use anyone else. The rest of the Commission, not knowing any better, eagerly agreed with him.

J. Edgar Hoover also figured prominently in controlling the direction of the Commission's investigation. Hoover assigned the FBI assassination probe to the bureau division that handled the destruction of federal property and bank robberies—based upon the premise that federal property was destroyed when one of the bullets struck the presidential limousine's windshield. Hoover deliberately kept the more highly qualified FBI divisions away from any part of the investigations.

Of course, that made our cover-up easier. If the government did its own investigation, and the junior counsels were only given facts that the various federal agencies had selectively fed to them, how could the Commission be sure that they were getting all of the facts—and not just the ones most biased to the conclusion we wanted them to find?

The answer—they couldn't.

"YOU DO KNOW that there isn't adequate time for the Commission to do everything that needs to be done, don't you?" I rhetorically asked Grant one day.

"Of course I know that. We all know that. That's what the Patriots are counting on. Our government has a tremendous capacity to generate information. Its greatest problem lies in the ability to analyze and process what it generates. Typically, that job goes to lowly paid and unqualified people. None of the staffers have the necessary experience to analyze classified material such as CIA reports."

"They better not ever see a classified CIA report," I warned.

"Relax. They won't. Dulles and Hoover will see to that. Besides, we've deliberately given them too much other information to sift through. We've inundated them with over 300 cubic feet of paper—reports from twenty-eight different government agencies. Director Hoover, the wily old bastard, made sure the FBI sent over 25,000 different reports—all them unindexed, unsummarized, and uncollated. The junior staff, already overworked, will have to assess all of that before they can compile and analyze anything else."

"That sounds damn near impossible."

"I think it is," Grant chortled. "But to their credit, they dug right into it with the enthusiasm of the truly dedicated and inspired."

"They must be working around the clock."

"They are—which is to our advantage." Grant added, "It's an endless task—once they compile the data, they'll need help analyzing it. I've made sure that they will get help from only the most trustworthy of people."

"Like me, you mean?"

"That's exactly what I mean."

"Jesus, Grant. You're like a puppet master, aren't you? You're just sitting back and pulling strings and making people dance."

He smiled, "More than you'll ever know, Patrick. More than you'll ever know."

HIDDEN DEEP WITHIN the mass of data needing to be sorted and analyzed was a home movie taken by Abraham Zapruder, a manufacturer of ladies dresses who worked in one of the buildings along the parade route. Zapruder hadn't even intended to film the motorcade that day because of the morning rains and his heavy workload. In fact, he wasn't sure he'd even have a chance to see the President. But his secretary urged him to make use of his new camera, which was a Bell & Howell 8 millimeter with a telephoto lens.

Zapruder positioned himself just to the left of my shooting position on a concrete wall. He hadn't seen me hidden behind the picket fence to his right, and I hadn't noticed him because of the foliage that provided my cover. Unfortunately, Zapruder successfully captured the whole shooting on his film; fortunately, his camera angle wasn't sharp enough to capture anything of value behind the fence where I had been concealed.

In hindsight, our team had been foolish not to have foreseen the number of cameras that would be present in Dealey Plaza that day. Unlike still photos, the Zapruder film provided a chronology of events—events which disputed the reports of a lone gunman. The film irrefutably showed Jack taking hits, along with Connally. It even captured Jack's head snapping violently backward when my second and fatal shot hit him.

I was sure that the Zapruder film would be our eventual undoing. The film was a highly incriminating piece of evidence which easily disputed reports that Oswald was the assassin. When I consulted Grant, he convinced me to relax. "The public sensitivity to the feelings of Jackie and the children will certainly insure that film will never see the light of day on any network television set or in any theater."

"Are you sure?"

"Of course I'm sure. Besides, we can tamper with any film to make it show what we want it to show. We're the government. We've got experts that can do that and get away with it."

"What if people notice the splices?"

"Hell, tell them the film was accidentally damaged while it was being developed. Blame the damage on a lab technician who mixed the chemicals wrong or something."

That hadn't even occurred to me because I had allowed my guilt to cloud my thinking. I took Grant's advice and had the film modified so the order of frames 312 and 313 were reversed. Now Kennedy's head snapped forward, substantiating our claims.

The film also showed a brief spark where one shot hit the ground behind the car, and another that showed a shot striking the windshield of the limo. We edited and spliced the film until the telltale signs of the other gunmen were removed. When I was sure no one was paying attention, I surreptitiously slipped the un-cut original Zapruder into my own pocket.

Life Magazine had acquired an uncut copy of the film. They intended to run still photos of selected frames of the movie in an upcoming issue. After contacting their editors, we convinced them to cooperate with the Commission by printing only "authorized" photos. We had successfully put out a brushfire which could have erupted into a full-fledged inferno. Unluckily, a number of curious people who knew of the existence of the Zapruder film and wanted to see it fanned the embers—Abraham Zapruder had given television and newspaper interviews within hours of the assassination claiming he had captured it all on film.

Grant proposed that we release our edited version to the American public. The Patriots arranged for Dan Rather, a young television reporter from Dallas, to view the Zapruder film for CBS News and to narrate what he saw for the public. Sensing a career opportunity, he eagerly agreed.

He did a magnificent job of describing the fatal shot: "…the third shot hit the President, and…his head went forward with considerable violence." Grant was so delighted with Rather that he recommended that the Patriots help his budding television career. Rather was exactly the type of media asset that could prove valuable to all of us in the future.

I was still apprehensive about the photographic evidence collected and confiscated. Photographs confirmed eyewitness accounts about activity on the grassy knoll which contradicted the official findings. Additionally, the Zapruder film provided a time clock for the assassination. When subjected to a stopwatch, the junior counsels discovered that Oswald could not have fired three shots as quickly as he did. They knew the rifle had only been fired three times because only three empty shell casings were found on the floor underneath the sixth floor window. They also knew that one shot had missed the limousine entirely and had wounded a bystander by the name of James Teague a short distance up the street. One shot had clearly hit Jack in the head and had killed him. That left at least seven wounds that had to be accounted for by only one shot: Jack Kennedy's back wound, Jack Kennedy's throat wound, John Connally's back wound, John Connally's chest wound, John Connally's wrist wounds, and John Connally's leg wound, not to mention the damage caused to the limousine by flying bullets.

Either all of those seven wounds had to be made by the same bullet, or it meant other gunmen were involved, which would mean a conspiracy existed. The Zapruder film was pure trouble. But it wasn't the only film that gave us fits. A woman named Beverly Oliver took a home movie of the shooting with a Super-8 Yashica movie camera. She had been standing by the curb almost next to the presidential limousine when our ambush took place. Her camera pointed toward my place of concealment behind the fence on the grassy knoll.

It took our team three frantic days after the assassination to identify her and to track her down. On November 25, we found her working at the Colony Club, of all places, which was right next door to Jack Ruby's Carousel Club. Derek Ruger and I approached her, pretending to be government agents. When we told her we knew about the film, and we needed it for evidence, she nonchalantly handed it over. She hadn't made a copy or shown it to anyone else. I was amazed when I viewed it because she actually had a much better film than that damned Zapruder movie. She had managed to capture not only the muzzle flash from my rifle but also a fairly good picture of my face. I managed to keep the Oliver film out of the chain of evidence. Only Ruger knew about it, and he didn't seem at all curious about what happened to it. I carefully hid it away with my Zapruder original.

Another problem film was from a guy named Gordon Arnold. He was almost directly in front of me when I took my shots. I remembered flashing my badge at a guy and his family when I arrived at the grassy knoll parking lot; Arnold had simply moved down in front of the fence to take his pictures. Roscoe pursued him immediately after the shooting and had to kick the guy to forcibly remove the film from his camera. I still had his processed film in my possession—I wasn't about to let any Commission staffers see it.

Yet another incriminating Polaroid photo was taken by a woman named Mary Ann Moorman while standing on the curb next to the presidential limousine. She got a picture of my shape behind the fence, but I didn't think the picture was clear enough to identify me. However, another picture taken only moments earlier clearly showed Lee Harvey Oswald on the steps in front of the Texas School Book Depository just as the President's car passed. I quickly suppressed the picture. When Moorman later questioned what had happened to her film, she was told by our staffers that the picture "had no value."

The staffers never knew the picture in question was one they had never seen.

THE JUNIOR STAFFERS had no real world experience investigating a homicide—they didn't know what they didn't know. The pivotal ballistics theory, upon which the entire case against alleged assassin Lee Harvey Oswald rested, literally was dreamed up by a junior counsel whose expertise was in estate plans, trusts, and wills. Grant and I laughed that the guy who came up with the single bullet theory had no experience in forensics or ballistics.

The most delicious fact about the crucial "single bullet theory" was that it he claimed it came to him in a dream when he slept one night.

I was interrupted at the Commission offices one day by a young staff attorney named Len Specter. He had encountered a problem making all the pieces fit and wanted my assistance.

"Hey, Patrick, do you have a minute? I need your help with something."

Len plopped in the chair next to my desk and set down a huge manila envelope on top of the desk.

"What do you have?"

"I just spent eight days interviewing 28 doctors and other medical personnel at Parkland Hospital. All of the doctors in Dallas identified the throat wound as an entry wound. That's not possible if Oswald was firing from behind the President."

I tried to remain cool as he fidgeted in his chair.

"What if Kennedy had turned and was temporarily facing the Texas School Book Depository when the shot hit him? Would that explain it?" I asked.

"I already thought about that. The Stemmons Freeway sign blocks our view of President Kennedy for a few seconds. He's fine when he disappears behind the sign and he has been shot when he emerges."

"Well, there you go. He turned and was shot when we couldn't see him."

"I thought about that, but I don't think it will work. But I have another idea that might work really well. David Belin has been working on the ballistics, and he dreamed up a solution last night."

I paused to let that statement sink in. "What do you mean he dreamed up a solution last night? You mean he literally dreamed it while he was asleep?"

"I know it might sound crazy, but I've thought it over. I'm now convinced it will work. Hear me out."

I wasn't going to argue with Specter. I wanted him to find a reason why it appeared Kennedy had an entrance wound in his throat.

"OK, Len. What is it?"

"We know one shot missed the President and hit a spectator in the crowd. We know a separate shot killed the President. We also know Oswald only had time to fire three shots from his rifle in the time the Zapruder film clocks. So get this: What if one bullet ricocheted and caused all of the other wounds."

I played the devil's advocate. "A ricochet? Is that even possible? It sounds crazy to me. How can you prove that?"

"When David first told me about it, I was skeptical, but the more I thought it over, the more I realized it could be just the answer we need. This single-bullet theory just might work if we massage it enough."

"I like your enthusiasm even if your premise is pretty far-fetched," I said.

"No, listen. Hear me out. I've given this a lot of thought. I'm going to make sure this works. This report is essentially nothing more than a prosecutor's brief. Oswald is dead, and there will never be any trial. That also means there will never be any cross-examination. Ergo, we're free to accept as *fact* any point that we want to make—right?"

"Well, I'm not a lawyer, so I will have accept your word for it," I answered.

"Suppose I could get the Parkland doctors to agree that it was theoretically possible that President Kennedy's throat wound could have conceivably been either an entrance wound or an exit wound?"

"Yes, theoretically, it is possible. It's probably not probable, but it's possible."

"Good! I'm glad you agree! Now if it's theoretically either an entrance wound or an exit wound, then it has to be an entrance wound—because that's the conclusion of the Commission. Simple as that."

He seemed quite self-satisfied with the logic of "if it walks like a duck, and talks like a duck, it must be a duck" claim. I thought he was taking syllogistic logic to the extreme, but hey that's his job.

"So you're saying you can prove all seven wounds were caused by the same bullet?" I asked.

"Absolutely! It's brilliantly clever and logical."

I'm sure my face conveyed my utter discombobulation at his confabulation—I tried to keep a serious look on my face. As much as I wanted his findings to clear us, I had to convince him that this train of thought was ridiculous—no one would buy it.

"Look at it like an attorney does. I can ask you: Was it likely that both men were hit by the same bullet? And you could say: No, not likely. However, if I asked: Was it theoretically possible for both men to have been hit by the same bullet?—you must respond: Yes, it was theoretically possible. In that case, that is exactly what must have happened. Both men *must* have been hit by the same bullet."

"I like your enthusiasm, Len. But was it likely that a single bullet could pass through two different human bodies, smashing, breaking, and ricocheting off hard, dense human bone and not even be so much as scratched, let alone mangled?" I asked.

"No, of course not, that is extremely unlikely. However, is it theoretically possible for a single bullet to pulverize a man's rib and shatter his wrist without suffering any damage, even though the lead of the bullet is softer than the human cartilage or the human bone it destroyed? Well, yes, it theoretically might be possible."

"OK, but let me try another approach. Was it likely that a bullet could pass through the President's body, lodge in the Governor's body, and then later be found *back* on the President's hospital stretcher—even though at no time did the two men ever share the use of the same stretcher in question?"

"No, it isn't likely. However, is it theoretically possible for that bullet to be there? Yes it is! That has to be what happened. There's not another possible explanation."

He sounded like a broken record. I wanted to ask him if it was *theoretically possible* for there to be another explanation. I happened to know the actual explanation—Jack Ruby had screwed up and tossed the planted evidence onto the wrong stretcher. Of course, I couldn't say that to Len.

Specter's approach to solving this tremendous dilemma of the so-called Magic Bullet certainly would never stand up in any court under cross-examination. Expert witnesses would testify that such a theory defied the physical laws of nature. The fact that junior staffers were uneasy with the theory did not deter Specter—or the Commission, who accepted Specter's Magic Bullet as theoretically possible.

We now set out to validate our ballistics tests by recreating the shooting; we incorporated the Magic Bullet theory in all of our recreations. I persuaded the junior counsels to use an older model Cadillac as a stand-in for the actual Presidential Lincoln, which was conveniently "unavailable" for analysis. The 1956 Cadillac had been built using a chassis-on-frame construction, which was typical of older cars from the fifties. Jack's presidential limousine had been a 1961 Lincoln Continental. It didn't use a chassis-on-frame construction—it used a new uni-body construction which allowed for a lower, wider, and longer passenger compartment.

Our use of the older model Cadillac enabled us to change the angles of the bullet trajectories because the stand-ins we used for the victims were seated more upright and much closer together. The ballistics geometry could thus be fudged to within the tolerances we needed to prove our single-bullet theory. Even though pictures were widely published which showed Arlen Specter using the wrong kind of car, no one challenged the results of his recreations. We also filmed all of the assassination re-creations with the most modern Zeiss and Unertl telescopic gunsights, rather than the almost opaque telescopic sight of that awful $20 Mannlicher Carcano rifle. Again no one mentioned our subterfuge.

The public accepted our re-creations without question—only a true gun expert would have recognized our slight-of-hand.

AS THE COMMISSION'S investigation drew to a close, we acted to suppress any and all information damaging to the FBI or the CIA by either withholding it or discounting it. There were public rumors that Oswald had been assigned an FBI informant number. Director Hoover quickly stepped up and declared that "any and every informant" was known to FBI Headquarters, and no record of Oswald ever being paid by the FBI existed.

I literally sweated bullets as numerous discrepancies in Oswald's life were examined. If anyone pulled any one thread too far, the whole bogus story I had constructed would unravel.

The disparities were serious, too. A.J.'s height didn't match Ozzie's real height. Ozzie had undergone a mastoid operation when he was young and had a visible scar; A.J. didn't have a mastoid scar, and none was seen in the numerous photos taken after his arrest, nor did the mastoid scar and surgery show up in the autopsy and its photos. A.J. had all of his teeth, but pictures popped up of young Ozzie at about age fifteen showing a missing front tooth. Commission attorneys interviewed Ozzie's best friend at the time, Edward Voebel, who told how two bullies knocked out Ozzie's tooth when they were kids. The autopsy of the alleged assassin showed no missing teeth.

The Commission never questioned other contradictions in any of their briefs or interviews. Ozzie's letters and writings reflected that he was severely dyslexic. Ozzie had done quite poorly all through school—his grades were terrible and his truancy was a constant problem. A.J., however, was well-educated and fluent in Russian. One woman who had met and spoken with Lee Harvey Oswald just as he was trying to defect said he spoke perfect Russian. Another woman described to the Commission attorneys that she thought Lee Harvey Oswald was a native-born Russian because his speech patterns were perfect. Marguerite Oswald, Lee's mother, claimed the man police arrested wasn't her real son and claimed he was an imposter. I think Lee's brother, Robert, suspected as much when he visited Lee in the Dallas jail—the visit was over in minutes.

There were also multiple sightings of Lee Harvey Oswald at different locations during the same periods of time. According to numerous eyewitness accounts, Oswald was seen traveling to Mexico, meeting with the Soviet consulate at the Russian embassy in Mexico City, and generally attracting attention while at the same time other witnesses placed him in the Dallas area trying to buy cars and shooting guns at a local rifle range. The witnesses said it was as if he wanted people to notice him and his strange behavior.

THE MOST TROUBLING of evidence was the April 10, 1963 assassination attempt on Major General Edwin Walker at his Dallas home.

Walker had been sitting at his kitchen table and wasn't even moving when a gunman, allegedly Oswald, fired a Mannlicher-Carcano rifle at him from a distance of fifty yards and missed. But just seven months later, Oswald supposedly pulled off a world-class feat of accuracy. Using the same shoddy rifle and defective scope, he somehow managed to hit a moving target the size of a man's head in a car traveling down a hill and around a bend from a sixth floor window whose sight lines were partially obscured by tree branches.

I was worried that the two shootings could not be reconciled in a believable fashion. Oswald's service records clearly showed he was a horrible shot, barely qualifying as a Marine "marksman." That fact could be reinforced by the unsuccessful attempt on General Walker's life, which was essentially a very easy shot. The mail-order Mannlicher-Carcano rifle was notoriously inaccurate and the scope was poorly made and ineffectively mounted. Again, the results of using such a poor weapon were clearly on display in the Walker shooting.

A search of Lee Harvey Oswald's possessions after his arrest turned up three photos of the alley behind General Walker's home in a fashionable area of Dallas. These photos enabled the Commission to link Oswald to the shooting by showing he had been engaged in reconnoitering the site. The attorneys didn't mention the hole in the photo, nor did they mention Marina Oswald's testimony that the hole hadn't been there in the picture when Lee was alive. The attorneys calmly linked the attempted murder of Major General Walker to Oswald.

Any rational person should have doubted that the same gunman was involved in both shootings. I thought the jig was up at that point, but not one single person stepped forward to question any part of that scenario.

Amazing.

ALL IN ALL, the junior counsels proved invaluable in the cover-up. The senior counsels rarely showed up for work, and when they occasionally graced us with their presence, they only managed to get in the way. The junior staffers were the ones who did all the work of the investigation: they lined up the witnesses, interviewed the witnesses, reviewed and analyzed the evidence, solved all the problems—and finally wrote the report. The seven named members of the Commission rubber stamped their findings and walked away with the credit and recognition.

Arlen Specter was the most valuable of the junior counsels. I went out of my way to put in a good word for him telling Grant, "If he ever decides to run for office, he could be a great recruit for the Patriots." Grant heartily agreed with my assessment and promised to help advance his career.

Finally on September 24, the Commission delivered its report to President Johnson in time for the November election. The Warren Commission Report declared Lee Harvey Oswald, a demented Marine defector recently back from the Soviet Union, had acted alone in killing President John F. Kennedy. No evidence of any conspiracy could be found.

This inquiry was nothing more than a prosecutor's brief on Oswald's guilt. Our Commission made no attempt to do anything other than to paint Oswald's guilt as plainly as they could. Satisfied with our work, Johnson closed the investigation.

We presumed that only the occasional scholar would ever look at the report or its twenty-six volumes of evidence.

I HAD DELIBERATELY stayed away from Chase during the investigation. But once the Warren Commission submitted its report, I agreed to meet him at Rosie O'Grady's one night. Investigative journalism was Chase's forte, and I knew he wanted to pick my brain about the Commission's findings. I would have to play my cards close to my vest—I put on my best poker face.

We made short work of the niceties; I wasn't anxious to volunteer much about my home life since it was almost non-existent. Chase, as far as I knew, had no home life.

After a few sips of his drink, Chase directed the conversation to the Johnson administration. "Lyndon Johnson scares me. The more I look deep into his background, the more concerned I become."

"That's how I felt about Jack. All presidents have skeletons in their closets," I responded.

"I don't like the implications of what I am uncovering. Johnson is a frightening man."

I stubbed out my cigarette in the ashtray. I was nervous—Chase was one of the best in his business at ferreting out a story.

"What's got you so upset?"

"There apparently is a whole "nother way" of doing business in Texas that has nothing to do with ethics. Our new president has become very wealthy over the past fifteen years by acting almost like a Mafia don. I've found evidence of massive bribes—lots of money changing hands."

This was shaky ground. I didn't want Chase to delve too deeply.

"Well, look at Old Joe Kennedy—he was in bed with the mob."

"It's more than that, Patrick. There's more disturbing shit."

"Like what," I asked. I needed to know how much Chase had found out.

"I'm beginning to wonder if Kennedy's assassination involved deeper issues than we've been led to believe."

He paused to light a cigarette. He'd dangled the bait; he wanted me to confirm or deny.

"That's pretty serious." Now I lit a cigarette, not because I wanted it so much as I wanted to buy some time. "I didn't see any evidence pointing that direction, Chase. We were pretty thorough in our investigation."

He flashed me a look which momentarily betrayed his doubt. "It was a government investigation," Chase started to make a point then changed his mind.

"Patrick, I've grappled with this. All the facts point to something heinous, and it's tied to Johnson. The implications are monumentally disturbing. Believe me, I've lost a lot of sleep over this in the past few weeks."

"Chase, listen to me," I began. But Chase waved me away.

"In all my years as a newsman, this might be the most important story I've ever covered. I can't even fathom the impact if the story turns out to be true. It could bring down the entire Johnson administration."

"Yeah, but how will you get the story into print? No one in his right mind will want to go out on the limb for you over this. This type of stuff can ruin careers, reputations, and cost people their jobs, their savings—hell, maybe even their lives. Is it worth it? Did you ask yourself that?"

"I've already encountered that resistance," he admitted. "My editor has warned me to drop this crap and get back to work."

"That sounds like good advice. Take it."

I thought that the years had not been kind to my dear friend. Chase no longer had a youthful appearance; his brow was creased with furrows and his eyes were almost lost between deep crow's feet.

"I can't. Listen to just some of what I've found out. Johnson's been taking bribes from organized crime since 1955. He stole the 1948 senatorial election by illegally stuffing a ballot box. He owns the only television station in Austin, as well as other media monopoly stations throughout Texas. Those alone have made him rich, well beyond anything he could have saved on his congressional salary."

"There must be dozens of congressmen who have gotten rich just because of their positions, Chase. There's no story in that."

"Shit, Patrick…," Chase stopped then lowered his voice. "I can even point to a least six men who have been murdered as a result of Johnson's actions."

"Stop it, Chase. You're my friend, and I think it is dangerous to say these things even to me. The laws against libel and slander won't protect you against allegations like that if you go public."

I wasn't worried about Chase getting sued—I was worried about Chase getting a late-night visit from someone like Derek Ruger or Mac Wallace. Texans were not to be messed with.

"Just listen to me, Patrick. I have to tell someone what I've found, and you're the only person I trust. I certainly can't talk to Grant about this."

No shit! If Grant knew what Chase was poking around in, I hated to think of the consequences. When I didn't answer, Chase seemed to think it was a signal for him to continue.

"I discovered that in 1960, Johnson was loaned an airplane by Texas oilman John Mecom for use in the 1960 election. In order to hide this campaign irregularity, a false lease was scribbled together for $300,000 under the airplane's true worth. After the election, when Mecom asked for his plane back, Johnson claimed he was exercising his option to buy the plane at the deeply discounted valuation. Mecom pressed Lyndon to return the plane, but Lyndon refused. On Friday, February 17, 1961, in the midst of a terrible bit of weather, Johnson ordered that plane flown to his ranch to pick him up. The two pilots, along with the air traffic controllers in Austin, said it was too dangerous to fly that day. Johnson apparently let loose a string of profanities and ordered the flight crew to get airborne immediately. They crashed in the storm, killing both men and destroying the plane."

"Jesus, Chase, you're not implying Johnson deliberately created the storm, are you?" I tried to joke.

Chase ignored me and continued with his story. "Johnson had insured the airplane and the two pilots for a total of $700,000—even though he technically didn't own the plane. He pocketed the entire $700,000 without paying either Mecom or the families of the two dead men."

"So he is ruthless, many rich men are. Chase, that doesn't prove anything."

"I'm not done. Remember Billy Sol Estes?"

"Of course I do. Everyone in D.C. knows about Billy and his troubles. Hell, you and I know him."

"Yes, but did you know that a U.S. Agricultural agent by the name of Henry Marshall was hot on Billy's trail, which involved a multi-million dollar swindle of the U.S. Agricultural Department?"

I did not.

"Listen to this: June 3, 1961, Agent Marshall was found dead next to his pickup truck in rural Texas. Found next to his body was a single-shot bolt-action rifle. The coroner certified the death as a suicide. But the autopsy showed that Agent Marshall died of five gunshot wounds to the head. The coroner maintained that Agent Marshall killed himself by loading a bullet into his rifle and firing it into his head. He repeated this procedure, according to the coroner's report, four more times until he finally succeeded in succumbing to his wounds. I've already thought of a great headline to get the readers' attention: MAN SHOOTS HIMSELF IN THE HEAD FOUR TIMES AND LIVES!"

I immediately thought of Arlen Specter's defense about the theoretical versus the possible, but I couldn't tell Chase that. I simply agreed with him. "OK, that sounds pretty unlikely."

"I thought so too. On March 29, 1962, Billy Sol Estes and three of his associates were charged with fraud. On April 2, 1962, Billy's chief accountant was found dead with a hose attached to the exhaust pipe of his truck. The coroner ruled that a suicide as well, even though an El Paso pathologist did an autopsy and found that the guy didn't die from carbon monoxide poisoning after all. He found a large, ugly bruise on the accountant's forehead, which the coroner had somehow missed seeing. Oh, and the other two men indicted with Billy Sol also turned up as suicides in Chicago and Amarillo. That's six suspicious deaths that can all be traced directly back to Johnson in some way."

He leaned back in his seat and waited for my reaction.

My reaction was shit, shit, shit! Chase was getting way in over his head with people that played for keeps. If he kept poking around, he could become a suicide victim himself. I picked up my glass of bourbon, but my hand betrayed me. It shook visibly.

"Chase, I don't know what to tell you. Are you sure you really want to pursue this? I'd be nervous about it, if I were you."

Chase's eyes flickered in surprise and instant insight. He looked at my hand and then looked me straight in the eye. I did my best to meet his penetrating stare, but I couldn't pull it off.

"I...I think you're probably right after all. That's probably good advice, Patrick."

He had a look of sadness as he stared into the depths of my soul. I silently stared back. Neither of us had to add another word.

"Listen, I've got to get back to the office. Say hello to Pam and Tim for me." He threw down a ten-dollar bill and gave me one last look of disappointment.

I decided to have one more drink; I certainly wasn't in a hurry to get home.

I lost count seven drinks later.

LYNDON BAINES JOHNSON swept the election with over 61% of the popular vote in November 1964. His challenger, Senator Barry

Goldwater, received over 27 million votes, a paltry showing to Johnson's 43 million votes.

This time Johnson truly did win an election in a landslide.

ON AN UNSEASONABLY warm November afternoon, Grant invited me on a private dinner cruise down the Potomac River on Jack Kennedy's old presidential yacht, the *Sequoia*. After a sumptuous meal of sixteen-ounce T-bone steaks, baked potatoes, salad, and Baked Alaska for dessert, we retired to the seats back on the stern of the boat to enjoy cigars and brandy. The scenery slowly slid by as we relaxed chatting about life, family, and fate.

I felt relaxed for the first time in a very long time.

"Hey, buddy, could you ever imagine that back in 1948 when we were Capitol Hill errand boys that just sixteen years later we would both be on top of the world?" Grant asked.

"We were flat-bellied kids," I mused remembering our youth.

"Look at you! You're at the highest level of the Central Intelligence Agency. Hell, you're practically running the show. I wouldn't be surprised if Lyndon named you as the next director when McCone steps down."

I knew that Grant was a very powerful voice in the Johnson administration. I didn't respond to his comment. I leaned back, inhaling the rich tobacco of the cigar and tried to enjoy the moment.

"And just look at me! Here I am, the right-hand man to the President of the United States of America. I'm telling ya, it doesn't get any better in life than this, does it?"

Again, I kept my thoughts to myself. My life had been better than this. I wished that I could return to the old days when all I worried about were the Communists.

As if he had read my thoughts, "Hey—wasn't that too bad about Khrushchev? Who could have ever guessed that tough old bird would be overthrown? I guess those Commie hardliners in the Kremlin didn't think he was tough enough to stand up to Lyndon, don't you think? I'm tellin' you, we all got a big kick out of that!"

"At least Chairman Khrushchev was a known entity. We don't know anything about Brezhnev."

Grant grinned, "Ah hell, that doesn't matter. There's a new sheriff in town these days, and he's not gonna put up with any of the shit that those two weak-assed Kennedy boys did. If those Kremlin boys get too cocky, ole Lyndon will just rip Brezhnev's head off and shit down the hole in his neck."

Grant sounded dangerously cocky to me. "Grant you've got to understand, this is a different ballgame now. Your actions and comments not only represent the President, they also represent the United States of America. You've got to learn to be a lot more circumspect with your opinions."

Grant looked at me and laughed. He sat back and holding his cigar at an angle as if to contemplate its form. He made a deliberate sucking sound on his teeth.

"Patrick, you don't have any right to chastise me." His eyes squinted as he glared, "Who do you think you are?"

"I'm your friend…"

"Bullshit!"

As if a switch had been flipped, Grant's mood turned mean and ugly, "Who the fuck do you think *you are* telling *me* to watch my mouth?"

Grant's outburst blindsided me. I had a brief flashback to an encounter with Sam Giancana a few years ago. It was eerily the same. "Hey, all I'm saying…."

"Fuck you!" A vein next to his eye popped rhythmically. I could see some members of the crew and the staff glancing discreetly in our direction. Grant, oblivious to the scene he was making, screamed even louder, "Just who *the fuck* do you think you are talking to *me* like that? You're nobody, that's who you are! Nobody! Listen, I made you who you are—don't you ever forget that! *I* made you and *I* can unmake you!"

His face flushed as he threw down his brandy in one big gulp.

"You know something, Patrick? You are right. We do owe you a lot. You got rid of a problem for us and, by doing so, many of our other problems magically disappeared. Hell, you probably single-handedly kept us all out of jail. But don't you *ever* think that enables you to run your mouth off like that ever again."

I was stunned—I got rid of a problem for them…kept them out of jail?

"I don't understand what you just said, Grant. Just what do you mean by that?"

Grant stopped in his tracks. He realized that he had let something slip that I wasn't supposed to be privy to. His attitude completely changed. He smiled that shit-eating grin of his and admitted, "Ah, shit, you got me. I'm sorry for being such a red-ass."

I wasn't going to let him off the hook. "What did you mean I *single-handedly* kept you out of jail?"

"You weren't supposed to know that," Grant gave me an "oops" smile like a kid caught in a lie.

"What—wasn't I—supposed—to know?" I pointedly asked.

Grant slumped back deep into the cushions of his chair and stared into the distance. I could see that he was trying to think of a way to get out of his predicament.

"Come on, Grant. What wasn't I supposed to know?"

Grant stared into the air looking for an answer. "You weren't supposed to know the real reason we needed Kennedy killed."

I felt like I had been sucker-punched in the stomach. I had a hard time breathing—I doubled over, put my head below my knees, and then rose up taking in a deep breath.

Grant studied me for a moment, looked me squarely in the eye, and delivered a verbal knockout punch. "We conned you, old buddy. We got you good. All of us were too chicken-shit to do the deed. But we knew that if we got you all riled up, we could talk you into doing what needed to be done. Everyone else was skeptical, but I convinced them that you were our man. And you were our man. You turned out to be perfect—just like I knew you would be."

I felt my stomach turning over and turning sour. I could actually taste the bile in the back of my throat just before I vomited all over the teak wood deck at my feet.

"Hey, buddy, take it easy," Grant patted me on the back. "You're letting some good T-bone steak go to waste."

My heart was palpitating, and my skin had turned clammy. The realization of Grant's monstrous betrayal literally knocked me off my feet. I staggered back onto a chair. I had been the real patsy all along—not Oswald—me!

"Hey, don't worry! Nothing's gonna happen to you. Everyone knows you and likes you. You're gonna be just fine as long as you keep your mouth shut." His voice grew low, tinged with concern, "You will keep your mouth shut, won't you?"

A second gut-wrenching wave of vomit came spewing out again.

He helped me to my feet. "Let's get you over to the railing so that you don't ruin the varnish on the deck."

"Hey, boys! Bring a bucket and a mop! My buddy's getting seasick over here!"

He steadied me and led me over to the railing. We were slowly passing by Mount Vernon and the grave of George Washington.

"Come on, Buddy. Get hold of yourself."

I had to catch my breath before I could answer him. I flashed back to my first reading of Othello, when Othello just having killed Desdemona realizes Iago's ultimate betrayal. I had merely read over Othello's "O! O! O!" and thought what a lame response it was. But now, I understood the impassioned agony of Othello. I was in shock at the realization of Grant's villainy.

"Hey, how are you feeling?" he asked.

"Jesus Christ, Grant." I doubled over once more. I thought I might pass out.

"Say something, Buddy."

I could only state the facts, "I committed an act of treason and murder. I ruined Jackie's life, I caused my wife incredible heartache, I traumatized my son, I took this country to hell and back—and I find out I was being manipulated by one of my best friends the entire time. How do you think I should feel?"

"You're looking at this all wrong..."

"Oh, yeah? Well, how should I be looking at this? It turns out you're telling me that I assassinated the most popular president of the twentieth century for nothing."

"It wasn't for nothing. It was for something..."

"Oh, bull*shit*, Grant."

"Listen—you know yourself you didn't want John Kennedy running this country. You saw what he did to the security of our nation with his unfortunate, immature, and ill-starred decisions. The Pentagon wasn't going to sit still much longer. The military was fully prepared to act if we didn't. We also couldn't just sit by and watch Bobby groomed to eventually take over for John. That family was intent upon forming a family dynasty that would have finally led to Teddy's elevation to the presidency. Our nation could not possibly allow that to happen, especially if we were fortunate enough to survive John's first term."

"That's what I believed. That's why I acted."

"I know that. But John and Bobby were also determined to dump Lyndon from the ticket this year. You know that Lyndon deserved to be President, not John. Lyndon was much more qualified anyway. The nation needed Lyndon's steadying influence in the White House. We couldn't allow the Kennedys to summarily dismiss him."

"Grant, I know that. But now you're revealing that other reasons were also present and deliberately concealed from me. I don't like that one bit."

"I know you don't. But we had to do that."

"No, you didn't. This was never really about fighting Communism. It was about greed. It was about power...your quest for power. Fuck you, Grant! Fuck you for what you have done to me and to the country! I trusted you and you used me!"

"We had to. We had no other choice. Lyndon was in trouble. This Billy Sol Estes thing stood to ruin his career...and I might add the careers of a lot of other powerful men."

My head was pounding. The realization that I had been a mere stepping-stone to further Grant's career overpowered me.

"Patrick, you performed a service to many, many people. And they won't forget that. By the time Lyndon is out of office, he will be a very rich man. Hell, I'll be a rich man. We can pass some of that on to you too, buddy.

Pam deserves more in her life. She could give up her job. Tim's future will be secure. You owe it to your family."

"Leave my family out of this, Grant. I've allowed you to destroy me, and I'm not about to allow you to destroy my family too."

"Patrick, you're not talking any sense. Turn down the money if you want; that's your prerogative."

Grant must have seen the furor in my eyes because his arguments suddenly changed course. "Patrick, you saved the country. Hey, you might not believe it, but you probably averted a race war with what you did."

"That's the stupidest thing I've ever heard." I felt literally hollow inside.

"No, it's not. It's the truth. Look, if Jack Kennedy had gone on giving hope to the nigras the way he was, blood was going to be spilled. And I'm talking about a lot of blood, too. Civil war would have broken out."

Now what the hell was he talking about? "Grant…"

"No—listen to me. The South isn't ready for the Negro to be treated as an equal to the white man. Remember George Lincoln Rockwell's slogan? *White Man Fight! Stop the Black Revolution Now!* Well, we're going to prevent all that from happening. You helped us here. You've helped the country avoid massive unrest and violence."

Grant was grasping for anything that would convince me that I was a hero after all. "I've already got it all planned out. You want to know how we're gonna do it?"

"No, I don't," I was shaking with anger. "I don't want to be a party to any of your plans. Besides, Lyndon already has a civil rights bill up on Capitol Hill. It's going to pass, and everybody knows it. You can't deny the Negro what's morally right. The Negro will have equal rights under the law very soon."

"No, he won't. Lyndon's Great Society program is a sham. Hell, Lyndon entrusted me to draft the program. That's what's great about being the man behind the power. I can protect Lyndon and at the same time further the agenda. He doesn't have to know or get his hands dirty." Grant gloated as he relied on his cleverness to cajole me.

"I've designed a program that is essentially a plantation strategy, Patrick."

Thinking he had my full attention, Grant continued, "Instead of offering equal opportunity for work and pay, my program will pay the Negro NOT to work! We'll give him a government check that will remove any incentive that he might have. I'm also going to set up government-subsidized housing projects so that we can keep all the nigras corralled in one place in every town. Think of it! We'll give them money *not* to work, AND we'll give them housing that's segregated in every town and city far from decent white folks, schools, and businesses. And that's not all—we'll make money with the government contracts that will be needed to run those same programs."

The depths of Grant's duplicity and villainy shocked me. His plan for racial harmony was not only abhorrent, it smacked of a bastardized form of communism designed to suppress the Negro in the greatest democracy of the world. I had only myself to blame. I had been suckered and duped. I felt my skin crawl. The man standing next to me was a total stranger in terms of what I thought I knew about him. "Do you really think you're going to get away with this?"

He turned to me in disbelief. "Are you kidding me? Not only are we going to get away with it, this will change the face of America for the next fifty years. And it's all thanks to you, Patrick."

"You're not pinning this on me, Grant. I won't accept responsibility for any of this."

He laughed in my face. "Hey, old buddy, you don't have a choice." He smiled villainously adding, "After all, there's no statute of limitations on murder."

The threat had just been delivered. I felt my knees start to buckle. I willed myself to stand.

"That's right, Patrick. We've got you over a barrel and you know it. What do you think would happen to your son if the word ever got out that his father was the guy who shot and killed President Kennedy? Can you imagine how difficult life would be for him after that? Or your wife? What would Pam do if she ever found out that it was her husband who shot and killed her best friend's husband and took away the father of her two kids? Do you really think your marriage could survive that? I kind of doubt it."

His voice took on a deeply menacing tone. "I love Shakespeare's line: 'Cry havoc! And let slip the dogs of war!'"

He paused to let his words sink in. "You even think of ruining us, and I'll let those same dogs loose on you. I'll bring all of Hell down upon you and your family. You understand?"

Grant smiled with obvious satisfaction at my silence. "Good. You know, Lyndon's favorite saying is: 'In Washington, the key question is: who is doing the fucking and who is getting fucked?' Well, guess what, buddy? You're not fucking anybody anymore. Got that?"

I got it.

"He who controls the past controls the future; and he who controls the present, controls the past."

— George Orwell

September 7, 1978
4:42 a.m.

Grant picked up the phone before it could finish its first ring.

"Getting a little anxious, are we?" the voice taunted.

Grant didn't care for the mocking tone of Ruger's voice, but he was in no position to piss him off. "What do you have?"

"That fruitcake cabbie took me to the fleabag joint where he dropped off McCarthy. It's called the *Little Rose Perpetual Mission and Salvation Hall,* according to the sign out front. The place looks pretty quiet. There's a couple of lights on and not much movement. Cabbie said the streets are mostly quiet by now. It looks like all of the drunks have bedded down for the night."

"Where are you now?"

"I'm at a phone booth on the corner. I can see the front door from here. I'm gonna take a little walk around the joint and see if I can find where McCarthy might be."

Grant stood in front of his antique chiffarobe and glanced at himself in the mirror. He looked like hell. There were deep circles under his eyes. His face was puffy. He didn't recognize himself anymore. He turned away from the mirror and spoke into the phone,

"Are you sure you've got him?"

"I'm as sure as I can be. The cabbie recognized his picture right away. I'll call you back when I've taken care of him."

Grant sensed an anxiousness in Ruger's voice. He hoped his own voice hadn't sounded too eager to the killer on the other end of the phone. He was actually very sad.

But now was not the time for weakness: it was either kill or be killed.

September 7, 1978
4:43 a.m.

My neck muscles were knotted, and my eyes were strained as I closed the dirty green notebook cover on my journal. The French Quarter of New Orleans had become peaceful and quiet outside my window. I was exhausted from reading all night in the poor light of the room, but I was also satisfied with my story. No one's reputation would survive the revelations contained in this journal if it were ever made public. But then again, I hadn't written this story with the intent of ever publicly revealing it. I had named names and provided dates, times, and places where the facts of my story could be verified. I wrote it as a life insurance policy hoping it would keep me alive.

I felt a serenity and a peace I hadn't felt in a long, long time because I had finally decided what I wanted to do. Now it was time for me to act.

One thing I was sure of—I couldn't answer the subpoena from the House committee. Johnny Roselli had talked to the committee, and he was dead. George de Mohrenschildt had been asked to talk to the committee, and he was dead. Sam Giancana had not only been asked to speak to the committee, but he had been under professional protection by three different agencies—he had been killed right under their noses. It didn't take a genius to figure out my life expectancy if I decided to cooperate and testify. I would be dead, too.

But then again, I was probably a dead man anyway. Grant Grantham had grown too rich and too powerful to allow me to say something that might bring him down. I had foolishly trusted Grant once, but trusting him now would be a death sentence—probably at the hands of someone like Derek Ruger.

I had just reopened my journal and laid it next to me on the bed open to the last page when I heard a soft rapping on my door.

"Patrick?" The Preacher whispered, "Are you still up?"

I covered my journal and a small cardboard box with the bedcover. I jumped up, stiffer than I realized, and opened the door for my friend. He was standing in the narrow hallway clutching two Lone Star long-necked beers in each hand.

"Yeah, I'm still up. I can't sleep." I held the door open and motioned for him to come in.

"*Bon homme*, it's well past 4 a.m. You need your sleep. Here, have a beer."

He slipped past me, looked around the tiny room, and grimaced. "This room is a pigsty. I'm sorry. I should have given you a better room." Then he grinned, "Of course, all my rooms are pigsties. You're lucky. At least you've got a window."

"It doesn't help much." The bottle was cold and wet—I ran it over my forehead.

The Preacher sniffed and wrinkled up his nose, "Poo-yee, it smells as bad inside as it does outside. Oh well, that's the Crescent City for you. Some good—some bad."

He sidled over to a rickety wooden chair placing the other two beers at his feet.

"Feel like talking?"

"I have told you too much already."

"I couldn't sleep thinking about what you said earlier."

"I'm sorry about that."

He smiled and took a swig of beer. "Something wicked this way comes," he philosophically muttered.

"Quoting Shakespeare now? That's one of Grant Grantham's favorite little sayings. Whenever the Washington Senators loaded the bases and had to bring in a relief pitcher, he always mumbled, 'Something wicked this way comes.' It's from *Macbeth*."

"Shakespeare? I thought it was the title of a Ray Bradbury book."

"And he got it from Shakespeare."

"No kidding? Huh? I thought he had just come up with a catchy name. Are you sure?"

"Go pick up *Macbeth*."

I plopped down on the edge of the bed and guzzled down some of the cold beer. "I thought you were dyslexic and couldn't read."

"I never said I actually *read* the book. Somebody might could have read it to me, you know."

When I gave him a skeptical look, he was quick to add, "One of my lady friends likes to read to me in bed. She thinks it's very romantic. You should try it sometime."

"I don't think romance is in my future."

"You're *never* too old," the Preacher quipped. "You can still put the pizzazz back in your marriage."

"I don't have a marriage anymore," I admitted. For the first time, the words didn't rip open the hole in my heart.

After a long pensive pause, the Preacher said, "I'm a good listener if you want to talk about it. I can't offer you absolution for your sins or bathe you in the blood of the Lamb, but I can listen. Sometimes it helps to tell your story."

I leaned back against the headboard of the bed and looked up at a moth desperately fluttering around the bare light bulb in the ceiling.

"I fucked up—I was fucked up. You know that."

"That I do, my friend. The last time I saw you, you were pretty messed up. When was that?"

"Six years ago. I had just returned from 'Nam."

The Preacher cradled his half-empty bottle in his arms. "You sure were messed up. If I didn't know you better, I would have been scared of you. You were crazy back then."

"It was that damned Operation Phoenix. It screwed me up. To tell you the truth, I'm surprised I even survived it myself."

"You did what you had to do to win that war. I understand that."

I shook my head in disagreement. "No, we went well beyond the terms of human decency. I was over there with a bunch of psychopaths who enjoyed killing and torturing gooks. I got caught up in their collective attitude and went along for the ride. By the time I saw you, I didn't know right from wrong. Hell, maybe I still don't."

"Then why did you do it?"

I shrugged my shoulders and grunted. "I thought it was my job."

"Your job? What kind of god-awful job did you have?"

"A hellish one. The Agency was so heavily involved in the conduct of the war that I began spending more and more time on assignments in Vietnam myself. By 1969, I was on the front lines. I volunteered to help supervise and run our Phoenix program, which was an operation to eliminate by assassination, various Vietnamese who might be providing aid and comfort to our enemies. We had fifty Agency officers in Saigon who could call upon six hundred American military men to help with our assignment. We were actually given a quota of eighteen hundred 'neutralizations' a month. A quota! Can you believe that?"

"Sounds like the government to me."

"Yeah, it was asinine. In 1969 alone, our Phoenix program neutralized almost 20,000 South Vietnamese insurgents. At least I was in charge of the sniper program—other departments were involved in kidnapping and torture. I had one intelligence liaison officer, a guy named Okamoto, who used to complain about the combination of false reports, bad intelligence, and psychotic behavior in his men. He said his guys would get a tip about a Viet Cong living in a certain village. The boys would march into a village looking for 'Nyugen So-and-So.' Of course the villagers were frightened to death of the huge American soldiers, so they wouldn't say a word. Okamoto said that didn't deter his guys. They'd just grab some poor son of a bitch off the street and torture him to reveal where 'Nyugen So-and-So' was really living."

"Chooh," the Preacher sighed.

"Okamoto told me his guys would then slip an empty sandbag over the frightened villager's head, poke two eyeholes in the sack, slip a length of barbed wire around his neck and then lead him through the village like a dog on a leash. 'Scratch your ass, Fido, when we pass Nyugen's house, that way we'll know where he lives.' Later that night, the Phoenix boys would return to that house, knock on the door, and when someone answered, they would shout out, 'April Fool's, motherfucker!' and proceed to kill everyone in the house. As far as they were concerned, everyone that lived there must have been Viet Cong sympathizers."

"What about women and children?"

"Okamoto said it didn't matter. If they lived there, they were all obliterated."

"That's pretty sick."

"Oh, it was worse than sick. Okamoto reported that his loonies even brought back human ears to prove they had met their quotas. By the end of the war, the Vietnamese estimated our program had killed over forty thousand people."

The Preacher looked at me with empathy, "You know, I have had a lot of conversations with guys who came back from Vietnam. You can't do the stuff you did and come out of it any way but fucked up. You know that, don't you?"

"I know that now. I didn't know it then. But remember, I ran the sniper program. I didn't have close contact with my victims."

"Your victims? Did you actually go out into the field?"

"Of course I did. I didn't want to be considered a REMF—Rear Echelon Mother Fucker—by my own men, so I routinely went out in the field and took on assignments myself. I got used to the adrenaline rush I got from shooting my target and returning safely to base...." I closed my eyes tightly in a grimace. This was the first time I had ever talked about what I did in Vietnam.

"That's fucked up, man."

"I know that now. I told you, I didn't want to acknowledge it then. I remember getting dropped off miles behind enemy lines where my spotter and I would spend hours inching our way into position for my shot. 'One shot, one kill' was our proud motto. I had that sniper's ritual down pat."

"Sniper's ritual? You snipers had a ritual?" He sounded astonished by my revelation.

"Of course we did. You had to have a ritual. Every sniper has the same ritual—it's how he prepares to kill a man."

"So, what was this ritual? What did you do?"

The Preacher patiently waited for me to go on with my story. I had a sudden flashback of crawling through a field of elephant grass and spotting a cobra a few feet ahead—I had to lie absolutely still until the cobra left its lair.

"Well, we would hunt these targets for days. We used the jungle as camouflage, crouching behind the foliage in absolute stillness. Any movement, no matter how small could put you in extreme danger—you had to ignore all sensations. The moment I had my Viet Cong target in my sights, I would begin the sniper's ritual. I would calmly take two breaths. On the second one, I let half out. When you've got nothing left in your lungs, your body responds with an almost imperceptible tremor. At the top of your breath, when your lungs are full of air and just before you start to exhale, there is another almost imperceptible tremor. The most stable part of your breathing cycle is halfway between breaths. That's when you gently squeeze the trigger. An imperceptible tremor when you are shooting at a target two hundred meters away can easily cause the bullet to miss its target entirely. Hence, the need for that pre-shot ritual."

The Preacher wiped his eyes with his forearm. "Just sweat," he said, but I knew better.

"I told you I was crazy. I started to get more and more reckless about the missions I took. I craved only the most dangerous and did everything I could to make them more dangerous. I would sneak up far closer than needed to take my shot, which enhanced my ability to confirm the kill, but it also made it much harder to escape afterward. I enjoyed the excitement of running away with bullets whizzing after me. Unfortunately, it scared the hell out of my spotters, who genuinely wanted to get home safely. After a while, my reputation got so bad no one wanted to go out on a mission with me. So

I started going out as a lone wolf, which was even more incredibly stupid and dangerous."

"You had a real death wish, didn't you?"

"I sure did. Some of the stuff I learned there didn't help either. While I was in Vietnam, I discovered another covert operation going on. The U.S. Mafia was smuggling billions of dollars of heroin out of Southeast Asia into Europe into the United States. The CIA was actually helping them. My own Agency actively helped the operation because it provided additional funding for critical black budget operations out of the view of congressional oversight committees. Can you believe it?"

"Yeah, I can. It's all about money in the end."

"I saw things going on between the U.S. mob, the French Mafia of Marseilles, the government of South Vietnam, and my own Agency that curdled my blood. But you want to know something? I was too tired to do anything about it, so I kept my head down and my mouth shut. I originally fled to Vietnam thinking I was safe from the Patriots, only to find out I was in just as much danger, if not more. After all, it would be very easy for me to die in Vietnam without raising anyone's suspicions. That's when I added marijuana and occasionally even heroin in combination with alcohol to numb myself to the world. I didn't care what became of me."

There was pain in the Preacher's eyes. I now understood why so many down and out came to his mission. There was no judgment, no recriminations. He listened. "I've seen guys in here that I thought had hit rock bottom. You were in the abyss."

"I was in hell. But I didn't hit rock bottom until…," I couldn't finish my sentence. I swallowed hard. As much as I had come to terms with my life, there were some memories which still gave me pause. I took a swallow of beer and savored its taste for a moment before I resumed my story.

"My son, Tim, joined the Navy and became a Navy Seal. He did two tours in Nam. I'm sure he did it just to spite me, but I'll bet he didn't realize how much his mother worried about him the whole time he was gone. When he finally got back home safely, Pam and Tim sold our house in Arlington. They moved to Ypsilanti, Michigan, where Pam got a job as an elementary teacher while she was working on her graduate degree in education at Eastern Michigan University. They lived for a year or two in Ypsi, and then they got a house in nearby Ann Arbor while Tim went back to college and finally graduated from school. Pam said she chose Michigan because she needed to get away from D.C. and all of its bad memories."

"Bad memories, huh?"

"Oh yeah, I forgot to add that she also divorced me. The divorce should have shocked me, but to be honest, I viewed it as just another part of my punishment in life. I knew I couldn't ever let Pam know that I was the gunman on the grassy knoll that sickening day in Dallas. It took her a long time before she finally got fed up with my self-destructive behavior, but when she did, she packed up and moved taking Tim with her. She never asked me for a penny—that's how finished she was with me."

"You were bent on self-destruction, my friend. Are you still?"

"I don't know. I have nothing left anymore—except the secrets."

"What were you guys in the CIA up to? Didn't it occur to you to come back home and try to stop that madness?"

"I didn't have much of a hand in anything by that time. I tried hard to stay focused on my job and my responsibilities. When Director McCone left the Agency in 1965 and was replaced by Bill Raborn, I was devastated. Raborn was a former Navy officer with no previous intelligence background or experience. What did he know that I didn't?"

"You were robbed," the Preacher observed.

"I guess I was. I thought President Johnson's decision to pass me over had all the earmarks of another Grant Grantham screw job."

"Grantham couldn't give you more power than he had."

"Probably not, but it was a mistake. It didn't take long for Bill Raborn to become one of the worst DCI's the Agency ever had."

"How so?"

"During the Dominican Republic crisis of 1965, I watched Raborn contribute to the chaos by rushing every single piece of paper the Agency received to the President's desk for his review and approval. He didn't possess the ability to analyze a single piece of intelligence information."

"Did you really think you were going to be running Langley?" he mused.

"You wanna know something? I did. I had served my country and the Agency. I had sacrificed a lot. I felt I deserved to be rewarded. But like Frank Wisner before me, I was slowly losing control of myself. I'm quite sure my colleagues knew about my drinking, though I thought I was still in control."

"So what happened?"

"In 1966, I got passed over once again for the position in favor of Richard Helms. This time, I had to agree that Helms was a good choice, a much better choice than Bill Raborn had certainly been. Hell, in my opinion, Helms should probably have been promoted years ago instead of Bissell. But by now it was clear to me that my career path was blocked, and I was not going to advance any farther within the Agency. I started to drink morning, noon, and night after that."

"You must have been a lot of fun to be around," he sarcastically joked.

"Oh yeah.

I looked at my open duffel bag on the floor. "I'm leaving this morning."

"I figured as much. Are you running away for good?"

I didn't have an answer—I shrugged my shoulders and took another sip of beer.

"You still miss Pam and Tim?" he asked gently.

"Of course I do. I miss them tremendously. I always will. But I also have a duty to protect them," I thought about the danger I was in and added, "to try and keep them alive."

He looked at me quizzically. "Who would want to hurt them?"

"My former associates. They can shut me up by keeping my family in harm's way. Just like those Phoenix operatives who used to go in and slaughter an entire family of innocent people, these guys would kill my family if they had to in order to stop me."

"Who are those guys you're so afraid of?"

"They call themselves the Patriots."

The Preacher asked, "Who are they really? Are they really that powerful?"

"They are the people that truly run this country, my friend. They're a shadow government. They're always there and mostly out of sight. They are businessmen, government bureaucrats and elected officials, military officers, and mobsters. Our visible governments may change due to elections, but the Patriots are always around. When some of them move out of elected power, they hang around on various special interest groups until they get back into another position of power in the government."

"Which special interest groups?"

"They've got a lot of different names: the Council of Foreign Relations, the Trilateral Commission, the Bilderberg Group; they all have different names, but the same people are in all of them. Follow a few of them, and you'll see the same patterns. They never really leave. They never go away."

"Do you know them all—these Patriots?"

"No, of course not. Even though I was entrusted with one of the most dangerous secrets imaginable, I was never part of the innermost sanctum at the highest levels. They're kind of like the Masons but without the fancy rituals."

"My friends have talked about the same kind of stuff—but they're on the lunatic fringe." He paused and added, "Makes you wonder though, doesn't it? What else?"

"They've got lots and lots of secrets that they must protect at all costs."

The Preacher sat up a little straighter in his chair. "What kind of secrets?"

"The darkest of secrets—secrets that would destroy the public's faith in its own government. These Patriots would lose everything they have amassed in their lives and would go to jail for a very, very long time. They're not about to let that happen."

He nodded and sat in silence for a few moments, as if contemplating how to phrase his next question. "So tell me why you're here."

"I already did."

"No, you told me what you thought I needed to know. Now tell me the rest."

The Preacher's eyes were clear and vibrant. We stared at each other. Then he broke the silence, "You know I need to know it. You also know why I need to know it. So, quit the bull-shitting and tell me."

I took a deep breath, "Back in 1975, a new government investigation got underway in Washington. The Senate Select Committee to Study Government Operations with Respect to Intelligence Activities was formed and run by Idaho Senator Frank Church. The Church Committee was charged with examining how the CIA and the FBI had abused their powers for years."

"I remember that one. Didn't they find that the government was working with the Mafia? We laughed here in New Orleans—we know everything is run by the mob."

"Yeah, but it went deeper than that. They linked the CIA, FBI, and the Mafia to the assassinations of foreign officials."

"I thought it was common knowledge that the CIA, the Kennedys, and the mob tried to kill Castro? Why were those senators so surprised?"

"It's all a control issue. As Grant Grantham once told me, its all about who's doing the fucking and who's getting fucked."

I patted my pocket, "I need a cigarette. You want to go out on the roof?"

"Nahh—I'm comfortable where I'm at."

I pulled a crushed package of Marlboros from my shirt pocket. I had three smokes left. "You want one?" I motioned.

"Nope—I'm good. Go on with your story."

"Richard Schweiker from Pennsylvania was one of the senators shocked by the disclosures. I remember laughing about something he said—I think he said that 'I did a backflip on a number of things' that he thought had been true. One of those things happened to be the Warren Commission Report."

"That's not so good," the Preacher said. "Is he the one who set up the subcommittee to investigate the assassination?"

"He is. My old CIA friends and co-workers are now anxious to publicly cooperate with the Schweiker probe so they can prove they have nothing to hide. They know and I know they have plenty to hide."

"And the Patriots know it too," he looked to me for confirmation. "I think I know what happens next."

"I'll bet you do. Back on September 17, 1976, the U.S. House of Representatives passed House Resolution 1540 which established the House Select Committee on Assassinations. The government decided to re-open the investigations into the murders of President John F. Kennedy, Senator Robert F. Kennedy, and the Reverend Martin Luther King, Jr."

"I thought you told me the Patriots controlled everything."

"I said they controlled everything. I didn't say they controlled everyone. There's a big difference. Not everyone in government is a member of the Patriots, and not everyone agrees with what the Patriots do. Or, for that matter, how they do it."

"So this Schweiker guy isn't a Patriot?"

"Doesn't appear to be," I answered. "I spoke with Chase Newman, my former roommate, and he said that in the aftermath of the Watergate investigation, he was confident the truth would finally come out. I spoke with my other former roommate who is a Patriot, Grant Grantham. He was equally confident the loose ends would be tied up well before the truth could be discovered."

"That makes me nervous," the Preacher whispered. "How many loose ends are there?"

"Makes me nervous, too. Do the math. The number of people still alive that know the real truth about the assassination of JFK is rapidly dwindling."

The Preacher leaned back in his chair and squinted. "Are you saying that people have been murdered?"

"I'm not the only one saying it. Others have noticed it, too. The *London Sunday Times* actually hired an insurance company actuary to examine some rather bizarre coincidences. The article reported that in a three-year period following the murders of President Kennedy and Lee Harvey Oswald, eighteen material witnesses died. By material witness, they meant people who had actual knowledge of various events surrounding the two deaths."

"So what? People die all the time."

"Perhaps. But listen to how they died: Five may have died from natural causes, but six were killed by guns, three died in car accidents, two by suicide, one from a cut throat, and one from a karate chop to the neck. That actuary concluded that, based upon their different ages and backgrounds, the odds were one hundred thousand trillion to one that these eighteen people who witnessed something unusual on November 22, 1963, would all be dead by February 1967."

The Preacher's jaw dropped open, "Did you say one hundred thousand trillion to one odds?"

"I did."

"Damn."

"I told you these guys mean business. And those odds don't even count all the other people who have died."

"Like who?"

"Let's start with three New Orleans residents. Remember Guy Banister?"

"Sure. He's our former police chief. When did he die?"

"During the Warren Commission investigation, June of 1964, supposedly, he had a heart attack."

"Was it?"

"I don't really know. I think it was. At least, I did then. Now I'm not sure at all."

"Why?"

"Remember when your local district attorney, Jim Garrison, decided to open his own investigation into the murder of President Kennedy?"

"You'd think Garrison was a coon-ass, he was so crazy. He knew how things worked down here. He should have known it was dangerous to go rooting around."

"Yes, but most troubling of all was that Garrison had the names of David Ferrie, Guy Banister, and Clay Shaw as participants in what he alleged was the actual assassination conspiracy. When I called Grant to find out what we were going to do, he claimed it was all being handled as we spoke. He told me since Guy Banister was already dead, pretty soon any other troublemaker would be dead, too."

"He really told you that?"

He sensed my hesitancy. "Don't stop now," he prompted, "You've gotten this far, you might as well finish the story. I can handle it," he assured me.

I paused for a minute or two. I hadn't planned to go into all of this with the Preacher. I wanted some answers, some salvation for myself. I found that telling everything that I had kept bottled up for so long was cathartic.

"All of a sudden, people in the know started dying at dizzying rates. On January 3, 1967, Jack Ruby died in his prison cell, the victim of the same cancer bio-weapon that Dr. Mary Sherman and David Ferrie had been working on for Operation Mongoose. David Ferrie died mysteriously in his apartment February 22, 1967. The coroner said it could have been a heart attack or a brain aneurysm—he couldn't really be sure. Clay Shaw's was the best. Even I had to marvel at how badly it was botched and not discovered."

"What happened?"

I chuckled darkly, "An ambulance pulled up to Shaw's house not too far from here in New Orleans. A neighbor said she saw two ambulance attendants jump out of the ambulance, open the rear door, and remove a stretcher…"

"What's wrong with that? That's what they're supposed to do."

"You interrupted me. Their stretcher already had a body on it. It was covered by a sheet. They carried it into the house and then came out a few minutes later with the empty stretcher. A few hours later, it was reported that Clay Shaw was found dead in his home *alone*. Of course he was alone."

The Preacher let out a low whistle. "What did he die of?"

"Who knows? He was buried without an autopsy. The medical coroner protested, but our media friends kicked up a stink, and he eventually backed off."

"Dr. Mary Sherman, the cancer researcher, was murdered—no doubt about that. She was shot, stabbed, and her body was set on fire in the bedroom of her apartment in New Orleans shortly after David Ferrie was discovered dead. Other important witnesses began to die unexpectedly early too."

"Man, these guys don't mess around, do they?"

"No, they don't. They actually got even more brazen. Now the murder victims were getting closer and closer to me. Sam Giancana was executed gangland style in his own house back on June 19, 1975 while he was supposed to be under round the clock police protection. Coincidentally, it happened the very night before he was to be questioned by Senate committee investigators looking into the CIA/mob ventures in Cuba. Giancana had been under constant vigilance by the Oak Park Illinois police, the FBI and the CIA. There were always three cars parked in front of Sam's Illinois home, keeping a close eye on him. Whenever one group took a food or bathroom break, the other two cars remained to keep the silent vigil in front of his house. When the first car returned, the next car would leave to take a break. But generally there were three cars present in front of that house. But not that night. That night, around 11 p.m., both Sam and his caretaker looked out the window and noticed all three cars driving away at the same time. Sam's housekeeper said Sam's last words were 'What the hell?'"

"This is giving me the heeby-jeebies," the Preacher confessed.

"Sam went down to the basement kitchen to fix a late-night snack while the housekeeper stayed up on the top floor with his wife, watching TV. An intruder somehow slipped in the back door, crept up behind Sam, and shot him in the back of the head with a .22. The assassin then nudged him over onto his back and fired a second bullet into the front of Sam's neck, a third into his lower lip, and a fourth, fifth, sixth, and seventh shot into a circle pattern around his mouth. I'm told it was the Mafia sign that a snitch had been silenced."

"That was overkill."

"It was. But listen to this. Shortly after the gunman slipped out of the house unnoticed, the housekeeper noticed the same three surveillance cars had returned and had taken up their previous station out in front of the house. The .22 used in Sam's murder was later traced to Miami. Sam once gave me a piece of advice that I never forgot. He said, 'Find out who's still alive and you'll find the killer.' I knew who was still alive and who was behind the killings. I also knew who the killer probably was."

"The Patriots?"

I nodded and continued with my list. "One month after that, Jimmy Hoffa disappeared and was never seen again. He knew about the hit on Kennedy and had bragged about knowing who was behind it. One year later, in July 1976, my dapper friend, Johnny Roselli, was found dead in Miami. Two weeks before he was murdered, Johnny had secretly testified before the Senate committee. His legless body was found floating in an oil drum in Dumfoundling Bay in North Miami. The mutilation and torture he obviously endured before he was strangled meant he had also violated the oath of *omerta*."

"They thought he was a snitch, too, right?"

"Yes, and on March 29, 1977, George de Mohrenschildt was found dead, this time just an hour before he was to meet with a House Committee investigator. The news reports said he died of a shotgun blast to his mouth. They said it was a suicide. I knew better."

"Who's he?"

"He was a White Russian émigré who had also helped us behind the scenes in Dallas. George de Mohrenshchildt was the head of the Russian ex-patriate community in Dallas and had strong connections to Permindex and Clay Shaw."

"What's a white Russian?"

"They're the Russians who were Czar Loyalists—they opposed the Bolsheviks." I blew a lazy smoke ring above my head. "Jim Garrison claimed he found evidence that George deMohrenschildt had been the Dallas 'babysitter' assigned to keep an eye on Lee Harvey Oswald."

I picked a piece of tobacco off my tongue. "You want to hear something ironic, though?"

"What's that?"

"It was also weirdly coincidental that George de Mohrenschildt was a close friend not only with both Lee Harvey Oswald but also with Jackie Kennedy's mother, Janet Auchincloss."

"No kidding? Imagine that. I wonder what the odds are?"

I laughed, "I don't know. Anyway, the House Select Committee wanted to question him about that Oswald relationship under oath, and the Patriots obviously didn't want him to appear."

"Just as they don't want you to appear," the Preacher wrapped his arms around his body as if he was cold. "Damn, Patrick, you gave me the freesôns with that story."

"Oh, I'm not done. I know the list of victims is much, much longer. You'll be astounded at these other names."

The Preacher cocked his head as if to listen better. "Try me."

"How about J. Edgar Hoover?"

"They killed Hoover, too?"

"I think they did and I'll tell you how. On May 1, 1972, J. Edgar Hoover died at his home in Georgetown. I later heard a rumor of a special powder that might have been administered to his hairbrush in order to facilitate a heart attack in the old man. I found the rumor credible because Hoover's annual health check-up showed a blood pressure reading 'a man of fifty would envy.' It sounded like my old colleague, Dr. Gottlieb, was up to his tricks. The Agency loved stuff like that."

"The CIA killed J. Edgar Hoover? Wow!"

"It wasn't the Agency. It probably was the Patriots, though."

"Why?"

"Frank Donner, one of Hoover's closest associates, said afterward that 'something chilling happened to the Director in the course of the last decade of his life.' He described Hoover's paranoid descent into madness in which he claimed he saw enemies and threats coming at him from all directions. I knew the Nixon administration had been trying hard to get Hoover to resign—they couldn't bring themselves to fire him."

"I never liked Hoover."

"He saved your skin."

"Maybe. Maybe not. Who else?"

"There was another, really big problem brewing. Lyndon Johnson's days out of office slowly drove him into madness as well. He saw his life transition from jobs that were all time consuming to suddenly having nothing to do. Grant Grantham said that LBJ fell into an almost life threatening depression. LBJ let his hair grow long just like the hippies he despised, and he stopped grooming himself. Grant revealed that Lyndon had become so psychotic he needed psychiatric help—the Patriots didn't want any doctors near LBJ because he was so unpredictable and uncontrollable. The Patriots needed iron-clad assurances that whatever Johnson divulged would be permanently protected by both attorney-client privilege and the physician's duty to privacy."

"He actually went cuckoo? I hope the SOB was tormented until his last breath," the Preacher added, "That's the best news you've told me so far."

"It wasn't good news for me or the other Patriots. The rigorous psychotherapy brought out a terrible sense of guilt in LBJ, and he had a growing compulsion to confess. His inner demons caused a major heart attack in 1972. At least I *think* it was a natural heart attack. He died January 22, 1973."

"You think they got to him the way they got to Hoover?"

"What do you think?"

"I think you're probably right."

"LBJ was under a tremendous amount of pressure. His dream of being President didn't bring him the happiness he thought it would. Remember the Gulf of Tonkin incident?" I asked.

"The Gulf of Tonkin? That was a long time ago—that's when we got attacked by the North Vietnamese navy, right?"

"That's what the Johnson administration wanted the world to believe. The real facts are quite a bit different."

The Preacher leaned back in his chair with a knitted brow. "So it didn't happen the way they said it did? Wasn't LBJ a dove back then? I heard a rumor he was really an anti-war dove."

"Yes, he was, but by the summer of 1964, LBJ was looking for a way to appear more hawkish on the threat of Communism since his likely Republican opponent in the November election was Senator Barry Goldwater who was about as conservative as they come."

"I gotta tell you, Goldwater scared me. I didn't want him in control."

"Oh, bull. It was all an act to intimidate the Russians. He claimed he was going to be even more of a hardliner than they expected. At least, that was his bluff."

"Not much of a bluff. It worked on me. I believed him."

"It worked on a lot of Americans. Goldwater didn't fool me. But I've got to tell you, I loved his campaign motto: Extremism in defense of liberty is no vice! You know, it's too bad that motto wasn't around for the Agency to use in our earlier days. It would have made for a great public relations campaign," I joked.

"You guys didn't need a motto. You lived that motto."

"Yeah, you're right. We did."

"You started to tell me something. Why did Johnson cook up that bullshit about the Gulf of Tonkin attack?"

"He needed to appease the militant generals in the Pentagon who were still spoiling for a fight. The generals wanted to go after the Communists, preferably in Cuba. But since that couldn't be done, Johnson realized that

Pentagon pressure cooker was liable to blow unless a lot of that steam could be let off. So he gave them the Vietnam war, by proxy."

"We lost a lot of good men in Vietnam. Are you telling me that war could have been avoided?" the Preacher bristled.

"I don't know—I fought in that hellhole too. You can make up your own mind."

The Preacher slapped his knee and reached for his cigarettes. I took another swallow of beer. He blew a haze of smoke into the air and said, "Go on."

"On August 2, 1964, LBJ got the opportunity he was looking for. One of our American destroyers, the USS *Maddox*, had reportedly been attacked in international waters sixteen miles off the coast of Vietnam by three North Vietnamese torpedo boats. The *Maddox* claimed it sunk one and damaged another of the North Vietnamese boats. Two nights later, the *Maddox* reported it was under attack once more. This time LBJ authorized US warplanes to retaliate by bombing North Vietnam. We learned the next morning that American forces had damaged or destroyed thirty-five North Vietnamese torpedo boats and 90% of an adjacent oil depot. But what the public wasn't told was that the second attack on the *Maddox* might not have actually occurred. The Maddox captain had radioed to his headquarters: 'Review of action makes recorded contacts and torpedoes fired appear doubtful.'"

"You're shittin' me. They lied to us?"

"Yep—the public was told that American naval vessels had been the target of a second unprovoked attack well outside of North Vietnamese territorial waters."

"That attack never happened? Are you fucking kidding me? Those air strikes started a war that led to the deaths of over one million Vietnamese and about 58,000 American troops. Not to mention all of the poor sorry souls who were so damaged that they couldn't live a normal life. I can't even count the number of fucked up 'Nam vets that have shown up on my doorstep. And now you're telling me it might not have really happened? That's bullshit, Patrick."

"LBJ actually laughed when he told me, 'For all I know our Navy was shooting at whales out there.'"

The Preacher let out a sardonic laugh, "You guys shot the wrong goddamned bastard, you know that?"

"I do now," I laughed uneasily along with him.

"What did LBJ hope to gain?"

"It's easy. Lyndon wanted permission from Congress to take a free hand in dealing with the North Vietnamese without actually having to ask Congress to declare war. What he got was the Gulf of Tonkin Resolution. Remember, the Constitution clearly states that only Congress can declare war."

"Sounds like these guys really don't give a rat's ass about the Constitution or the concept of legality," he grumbled.

"Seems that way, doesn't it?"

He shook his head in disgust. "What happened next?"

"Because of that damned resolution, our nation's commitment to a war in Vietnam was virtually assured. The studies that Robert McNamara made all came to the conclusion that by the end of 1965, the North Vietnamese would have sustained heavy casualties and been defeated without having achieved any major gains. LBJ's military advisors convinced him the war could be over by 1966 if we went ahead and did this. So by the time October 1965, rolled around, we had 200,000 U.S. troops deployed to Vietnam. Our generals were as happy as could be."

"I'll bet they were," the Preacher remarked sullenly.

"Johnson and his advisors increased our U.S. military presence in Southeast Asia. The war kept growing, right along with its Pentagon budget."

I stopped for a moment remembering a smart-ass comment Grant had made to me when I got home from Vietnam. "While you got fucked in Nam, I got fuckin' rich." I took the last swig of beer left in the bottle, and then continued, "Companies controlled by various members of the Patriots made money hand over fist."

"War is good for business. It's just not good for all other living things," the Preacher solemnly stated.

"Were you a hippie?" I asked attempting to lighten the conversation and my memories. "Is there something in your past I don't know about?"

"I was a 'head.' I smoked a lot of good dope in those years. You could walk down Bourbon Street and get a contact high," he laughed. "This town toked up a storm. I'd take pot over booze anyday—it's just that now if you get caught, it ain't so cool."

"If you say so."

"You mean you like booze better than dope?"

"Didn't say that."

I didn't like to remember my pot-smoking years. It was a dark time for me—I was out of control. I tried to put myself in a box to forget about the past, but I realized that eventually, you had to open the lid. You either got out of the box or you died.

"All those pot smoking friends of yours sparked a lot of dissent on campuses around the country protesting the war."

"They weren't 'my friends.' You forget I was a Marine?" the Preacher curtly replied. "Almost 17,000 American soldiers died in the jungles of Vietnam in 1968 alone."

"That's my point—it wasn't good news for LBJ. Remember how Senator Eugene McCarthy challenged Johnson's candidacy in 1968? LBJ faced a humiliating campaign and a possible defeat in November especially when Bobby announced his candidacy in March of sixty-eight. And that was the opposition from his own party—the Democrats."

"I hated that prick—him and McNamara. Hey Patrick, remember that old anti-war chant? 'Hey, hey, LBJ, how many kids did you kill today?' I supported our soldiers, but I sure as hell found it hard to support LBJ," the Preacher shook his head, "God, that was a bad time."

"What if I told you there was another, much more terrifying reason Johnson abruptly announced he didn't want to be president anymore?"

The Preacher in the midst of stubbing out his cigarette in an ashtray that overflowed with butts said, "Shit. Nothing is simple for you is it?"

"What if I told you it wasn't the war—the racial unrest—the student demonstrations. What if it was something else infinitely more terrifying? Would you believe me?"

"Depends on what it is. Try me."

I took a deep breath. "It's classified Top Secret—Eyes Only."

"Then why are you telling me?"

"Because I don't care anymore, I'm fucked anyway."

He gave me the one-finger salute, "So you want me to be fucked too? I want to hear it now. You've piqued my interest. Go on and tell me."

"Listen to this. On March 7, 1968, a rogue Soviet nuclear submarine, commandeered by some really hard-core KGB agents, and with the tacit approval of hardliners in the Kremlin, snuck to within 360 miles of Hawaii to launch a surprise nuclear attack against Pearl Harbor. Fortunately for the world, something went wrong during the launch and the missile accidentally blew up the Russian submarine instead."

"No shit?"

"Our Pacific SOSUS system picked up the explosion with their undersea microphones. We initially had no idea what it was, but when the Soviet navy quickly began to mass in the Pacific and conduct a search hundreds of miles from where we knew the explosion had occurred, we got really curious really fast. Fortunately, we were able to triangulate the exact location of the explosion.

"Our Navy immediately set out to discover what the heck was going on. We knew from underwater noise analysis that a Russian submarine had most likely been lost. Analysis of the Russian codes indicated they were frantically searching for their lost missile submarine K-129. Because of ongoing Cold

War hostilities between the Soviets and our military, we couldn't tell them we knew they were looking in the wrong spot without revealing our own intelligence capabilities.

"After we realized the Russians were searching hundreds of miles from the right place, we decided this could actually work in our favor. We had an opportunity to examine an important Soviet submarine-bearing ballistic missile up close and without interference."

"Did you find it?"

"Of course, I said we knew exactly where to look. It's what we found that was so menacing and terrifying in its implications."

Recounting the story still gave me a sick feeling in the pit of my stomach. I thought about the people who would never hear this story. The communist menace was real, but there were those who wanted to believe that such a menace existed only in the minds of a few hotheaded generals.

"So, what did you find?"

"Our underwater photos of the wreckage of Soviet submarine K-129 showed one missile launch tube hatch opened. It was evident from the pattern of damage the sub sustained that they actually tried to launch that particular nuclear warhead when the accident occurred. It wasn't long before our intelligence people figured out the Kremlin plotters had attempted a surprise attack against the United States—but—they were trying to shift the blame to Mao Tse-Tung and Red China instead."

He spit the last of his beer across the tiny room, spraying the side of my bed. "Are you shitting me? Is this for real? They really tried to do this?"

"We almost lost Pearl Harbor all over again, but this time to a nuclear warhead."

"God, Patrick. How did they think they would ever get away with that?"

"Easy. The close proximity to Pearl Harbor for their cowardly launch would have pointed the finger of blame at the much cruder Red Chinese submarines since a Russian sub could have launched at Pearl from outside eight hundred miles. The Soviets figured our surveillance systems would have detected the launch from inside four hundred miles, and the conclusion would have easily made the Chinese the most likely culprits. Our angry and automatic response would have embroiled the two biggest threats to the Soviet Union—the United States and Communist China—in a nuclear war between each other. The only winner would have been the Kremlin. Luckily for the United States, a Soviet built-in fail-safe destruction system must have activated to both disarm and destroy the missile during the unauthorized launch, which in turn destroyed the rogue submarine as well."

"So that's why LBJ dropped out of the race?"

"I'm convinced of it. Remember, Jack Kennedy had taken a lot of heat for almost getting millions of Americans killed in the Cuban Missile Crisis. He averted that disaster at the very last minute. I think LBJ was frightened to death that a similar nuclear disaster had almost befallen him."

The Preacher wouldn't let me stop. "What did he do about that?"

"He didn't know what the hell to do. No one really did. LBJ couldn't let the American public know how close we had just come to a surprise nuclear attack. He certainly didn't want to take responsibility for deciding upon a response to this Kremlin ambush. Besides, LBJ had his head barely above water. Remember, the Vietnam War and race riots were tearing America apart by 1968. Negroes rioted in frustration with the injustices they had endured for far too long. Watts, Newark, Detroit, cities large and small bristled with racial tension. The whole nation was on the edge of coming apart."

"I remember it well—the whole Black Panthers crap—it wasn't a good scene."

"I think all of that is the real reason he decided to bail out of the White House. Remember how he stunned the nation a few days later when he announced…"

"…I shall not seek, and I will not accept, the nomination of my party for another term as your President.' I remember that as if it was yesterday," the Preacher grinned. "So, he decided to let Bobby Kennedy deal with it?"

"It was a no-win situation."

"I'll say. But Bobby never even got the chance."

"No, he didn't. The Patriots couldn't let him near the White House."

"Too much of a risk?"

"Bobby left the Justice Department less than a year after Johnson was elected. He couldn't function without his older brother around."

"Why did Bobby run for the Senate?"

"He went after New York Senator Kenneth Keating's seat in 1966. Keating had been a vehement critic of Jack Kennedy. It was simply Bobby's way of getting back at his brother's enemies."

I started to take another swallow of beer and then realized the bottle was empty. Changing the subject, I asked, "You going to open those other two bottles?"

"Yeah, sure." He pulled a bottle opener out of his pocket and popped the tops. "You know, I always liked Bobby. He should have stayed put. He might be alive today, like Teddy, if he had just stayed put."

"Bobby knew that it was dangerous to run. He even told my wife, Pam: 'There are guns between me and the White House.' He was absolutely right—the Patriots were not about to allow another Kennedy back into the White House."

"Do you think Bobby wanted to expose his brother's killers?"

"Could be. Probably. In 1964, Bobby publicly supported the Warren Commission and its findings, but privately he told others the Warren Commission Report was a sham and a fraud. He said he knew Lee Harvey Oswald had not acted alone, if he had indeed acted at all. In fact, Bobby secretly commissioned his own private investigation into his brother's murder and had the results published in a European book called *Farewell America* by James Hepburn."

"So why didn't this Hepburn fellow just come forward and have the book printed in the United States?"

"Hepburn didn't exist."

"The dude didn't exist?"

"We researched it. When we looked into the author's background, we discovered James Hepburn didn't exist. He wasn't a real person. We found out it was the work of a number of sources tied to French intelligence and Interpol, along with other well-informed sources that even included OAS."

"Weren't those the same guys you hired?"

I sat up straight, "How did you know about the OAS and the shooters?"

The Preacher waved his hand in a supplicating motion, "The Clay Shaw trial. It's The Big Easy. People talk. I have a buddy that's a bartender over Cosimo's in the French Quarter where Shaw used to drink."

"Yeah, the OAS are the people who supplied our three original shooters," I conceded. I shouldn't have been so surprised that the Preacher knew more than I gave him credit for. The story was out there even if it was in bits and pieces. His response only confirmed my decision not to testify for the House investigation.

"It also looked like the Soviet KGB was in on the story's creation," I continued. "The book was published in France as *L'Amerique Brule*, which is French for 'America Burns.' It became a huge bestseller overseas—the publisher rushed German and Italian translations to the market."

"I don't understand why we never heard of it here in the States."

"Easy—the Patriots used their substantial media influence and clout to get the book suppressed in the United States. They weren't about to let anyone in the United States read about Bobby's suspicions regarding who really killed Jack."

"That's hard to believe. They actually stopped its publication here? Isn't that censorship?"

"Yes, but the Patriots will do anything to stay in power. Here's something you probably didn't know. The Patriots also used their influence to have CBS News present a four part report on the Warren Commission which consisted of carefully edited interviews conducted by Walter Cronkite."

"If Walter Cronkite says it's so, it must be so," the Preacher interjected. "I remember watching it. When was it? 1967? During Garrison's investigation of Clay Shaw?"

"Good memory—June 1967. The entire program was designed to bolster support for the conclusions of our Warren Commission and to discredit Garrison's allegations."

"Disinformation?"

"Exactly. It was a powerful piece of propaganda. The Patriots made sure that the CBS script found Lee Harvey Oswald just as guilty as we had proved he was. Everything was expertly slanted to leave the viewer with no doubt that Walter Cronkite and CBS supported the Commission's findings 100% and that absolutely no evidence of a conspiracy existed."

"It caused a stink around here, especially with Garrison's investigation going on. But, I have to tell you that as convincing as the show was on the surface, I smelled a rat."

"Then you are more astute than the average viewer," I said. "It was slick—ridiculous statements backed up by carefully edited opinions by experts with dubious qualifications. CBS followed Arlen Specter's line of reasoning: if it was *theoretically possible,* it *must* have happened that way."

"Garrison's case fell apart after that."

"It sure did. By the time Jim Garrison finally sent the Clay Shaw case to the jury, his entire case had been reduced to shambles. The jury quickly found Shaw innocent of all charges. We thought the matter of a conspiracy had finally been put to rest."

"Hey, I've got a question for you. Why did everybody get so worked up over Jim Garrison? Everyone in New Orleans knew he was a nut job. Why didn't the rest of you?"

"It was all of those damned books that started to come out around that time."

"What books?"

"A bunch of books started getting published that threatened to let the shit hit the fan. Back in 1966, a number of books questioned the conclusions of the Warren Commission."

"And you were surprised? That magic bullet theory was bullshit. Hell, everybody I know questioned the Warren Commission report."

"Even so, I was on the front lines because I had helped the Warren Commission reach its conclusions."

"You did? I didn't know that."

"Most people don't know that. I don't advertise it. Anyway, we had orchestrated the conclusions of the report. So, I am sure you can understand how I began to feel uneasy about our secrets being exposed. *Rush to Judgment* by Mark Lane was a very perceptive critique of our Warren Commission."

"I think I remember that. He was some New York lawyer."

"He was a defense attorney. He easily picked apart the prosecutor's brief that the Warren Commission Report embodied. He interviewed all the witnesses that we had pointedly chosen to ignore because their testimony didn't fit our storyline."

"So, what happened?"

"Two more books hit the market shortly after that, *Six Seconds in Dallas* by Josiah Thompson and *Accessories After the Fact* by Sylvia Meagher. They expertly expanded upon some more of the flaws of our investigation. What's worse was that the American public was beginning to respond to the message that perhaps a lone gunman had not murdered Kennedy after all."

"Never underestimate the populace. Patrick, your Warren Commission story stunk. Most people are realists. American people are smarter than you give them credit for."

"I know that now," I replied. "I came from a generation that believed everything the government told us. I guess I thought if the government said it, people wouldn't question it—it would be unpatriotic. And if the government had to lie—like we did with the U-2, it was because we were protecting America."

"So, those books gave the evidence of a conspiracy and a cover-up?" the Preacher rubbed his fingers of his left hand. It was then that I noticed that he had arthritis. "They figure out who was behind it all?"

"Garrison thought he had. In fact, I'll bet he did. He certainly had most of the important names and facts."

"Wouldn't his life have been in danger, too?

"Maybe so, but I think he thought he was protected if he got enough publicity. Everybody in the media was in on the story. I got a call from Chase Newman, a buddy who was a reporter with the *Washington Post*, just before he headed to New Orleans to cover the story. He said he was convinced that this was the big break everyone who suspected a conspiracy had been hoping for." I finished the last warm sips of beer in the bottle. "I think Chase was one of a few reporters that took Garrison seriously."

"They did a good job making it sound like it was all a Garrison hoax."

"You, of all people, knew it wasn't a hoax," I reminded him.

"Well, of course I knew it. But nobody else knew it, did they?"

"If it would have been left up to Chase they would have. Chase began to follow and verify the same leads Garrison was investigating. He found out that Dallas Mayor Earle Cabell was the brother of General Charles Cabell. General Cabell had been another one of Allen Dulles' closest Agency advisors who JFK had sacked after the failure of the Bay of Pigs. That helped explain how we had been able to so easily manipulate the police presence in Dallas that day. Mayor Earl Cabell wanted revenge for what Jack had unfairly done to his brother, Charles. All of Mayor Cabell's Texas friends cooperated to help us achieve that revenge."

"Why didn't he prove that?"

"How could anyone prove that? They couldn't. Chase knew it, too. But there was a lot of stuff Garrison could prove."

"Like what?"

"Garrison's investigation pointed out that three rifles were found in the Texas School Book Depository on November 22. Two of them were found on the same floor—the sixth floor. That was the floor that the assassin supposedly fired from."

"Two rifles on the same floor? I never heard that before."

"A German Mauser 7.65 rifle was found on the sixth floor and was identified by two gun experts as a Mauser. It even had the word "Mauser" stamped on it. Yet the gun experts our Commission used had said it had to have been misidentified as a Mauser because three Mannlicher-Carcano 6.5 rifle cartridges were found beneath the supposed sniper's nest window. Garrison explained there was a significant difference between a highly accurate first-class German Mauser and a cheap mail order Italian Mannlicher-Carcano. Neither rifle could fire the shells of the other gun—they didn't match caliber-wise. Garrison also found television footage of the third rifle being removed by police officers from the roof above the sixth floor. This rifle was also identified as 'The Assassin's Rifle' on the news broadcasts, but it didn't have a telescopic sight mounted on it."

"No scope?"

"No scope."

"Oops! Somebody messed up."

"Yes, somebody did—but once again we got away with it. No one caught the problem. Anyway, the murder weapon also presented a huge problem. The Mannlicher Carcano rifle found on the sixth floor had been mail ordered by someone using the name Alek J. Hidell."

The Preacher sat up at attention. He was startled, "A.J. used his real name?"

"Of course not, somebody framed him. That's why we were forced to use that rifle in the first place. Someone had already ordered one in the name of Alek J. Hidell. The higher-ups knew it would be connected to the guy they had arrested. Remember, A.J. hadn't stopped using the name Lee Harvey Oswald since we gave it to him. The police claimed they found the same name on an identification card in the wallet of Lee Harvey Oswald when he was arrested and booked by the Dallas police. That proved to be the ironclad link to the murder weapon. Fortunately, no one in the media followed up on that name discrepancy, or our whole plot might have unraveled."

"You mean to tell me nobody was at all curious about that name?"

"That's the only name they claimed they found on him. Of course, his wife identified him as Lee Harvey Oswald."

"That's pretty weird." He puffed on his cigarette and stared out the window in silence. "What was A.J. doing carrying identification with his own name on it?"

"I wondered about that too. But you know what I think it was? If it's true, then I think it was A.J.'s own form of personal insurance. Sure, he was known by the name Lee Harvey Oswald, but my guess is that he was confident he could also prove he was actually Alek James Hidell if he ever needed to."

"Yeah, but it didn't work. Nobody even cared about that name, did they?"

"Nope. I thought we could have major problems with that discrepancy, but the media was too lazy to pursue it. Even when our Commission claimed Oswald shot the President in order to validate his life and to become famous, I thought someone might bring up Alek's name."

"What I don't understand is how anybody could believe that. Once he was arrested, he kept denying that he had anything to do with it. If he did shoot Kennedy to become famous, he should have been crowing to the world about what he had done. That didn't make any sense."

We sat quietly for a few moments. "Why do you think Ruby shot him?"

I couldn't tell him that I helped convince Jack Ruby to kill A.J. in order to keep my own role secret. I was still too ashamed to admit to that heinous betrayal, so I let him continue.

"Poor bastard," he muttered. "I watched the whole thing go down—all the talk about 'Lee Harvey Oswald *this*' and 'Lee Harvey Oswald *that*' messed me up for a while. I was worried that people might notice we looked like each other. You think he was really in on it?"

I shook my head, "He was set up as the patsy. My associates deliberately kept me from finding out he even had a role until it was too late for me to stop it. I was just as surprised as you were."

"That's what I thought. I knew A.J. Hidell pretty damn well. That stuff about A.J. being a crazy ex-patriot and pulling the trigger that killed Kennedy is complete bull crap," he erupted.

I could see the Preacher getting worked up over something that had happened fifteen years ago. "Hey, take it easy and keep your voice down."

"Sorry," he nodded his head knowingly. "That's what I figured. I didn't think you could let us down like that. Not after all we did for you."

I felt my guilt surge up. "Yeah, but I did let you two guys down." I thought back to how naïve I had been. "I got A.J. killed. I turned your name into a national villain like John Wilkes Booth."

"But my name will live forever in infamy in American history books," he weakly joked.

I moved over to the edge of the bed next to my journal and the box I had hidden under the covers. I glanced at my watch. I brushed off a strange feeling of anxiety.

The Preacher stared up at the ceiling then turned his head slightly as if listening for something out on the street. "Yeah, the fact is, my name will live forever. But don't forget that John Wilkes Booth was eventually forgiven by many Americans. Besides, I'm secure in the personal knowledge that Lee Harvey Oswald is actually 100% innocent. Maybe that fact will finally come out one day."

He had a peculiar look on his face as he sat facing me.

I could read his mind. "I've never told anyone who or where you are, not even A.J. when he asked."

He dismissed my concern with a wave of his hand. "I know that. I'm not worried that you ever will. I was just remembering that I wanted to be like Philbrick that FBI agent who led three lives for his country. That was my favorite TV show when I was a kid. You gave me a chance to do something for my country even though I didn't get to meet any real Commies. Hey, remember the first time we met?"

"I'll never forget that. I couldn't believe you weren't A.J. Hidell. Even when I went to see the base commander, and he told me your name was Lee Harvey Oswald, I was still convinced it was some kind of a weird test by the Agency."

"I guess my life worked out better than A.J.'s," he murmured. "Everybody knows me as the Preacher and that's fine with me. I just tell people I was a skid row bum for years before I got my act together and decided to set up this Little Rose Perpetual Mission to help other lost souls like myself. Everybody loves a story with a happy ending, so they don't question me too much about my life. That's cool with me."

"What about your mom and your brothers? Don't you ever want to see them again?"

The Preacher shook his head without any hesitation whatsoever. "Why? What's the point? They've had a big enough burden to bear. My mother was pretty fucked up most of her life, and the media attention has probably been a mixed blessing for her. My brothers have kept out of sight. I'm sure they want to keep it that way. Besides, what would I say to them? Apologize for lying to them and allowing a stranger to pass himself off as me? Allowing them to think he really was me? No, I've thought about it, and I'm convinced that nothing good can come of the fact that anyone but you and me know that Lee Harvey Oswald is really still alive."

We heard a cat cry out on the street below. I could see the light coming up in the window. Gray dawn was moving into early morning softness; I hoped this wasn't the last dawn I would witness.

"Alley cats. This is actually the quietest it gets here in the Big Easy—just before dawn. Everyone's either passed out or gone on home."

There was a rustling sound, followed by a sound of someone brushing up against the building outside the window. "Probably a drunk getting rolled or some guy finally getting lucky," the Preacher said but making no move to look out the window next to him.

He finished his beer in one long gulp. He suppressed a belch as he asked, "You said the murder rifle was a problem. Why?"

Our conversation had veered off course, but the Preacher's question reminded me of a point I wanted to make.

"Oh, yeah," I went on, "that bullet Jack Ruby planted at Parkland Hospital became Arlen Specter's 'magic bullet.' A medical technician found the bullet planted on Kennedy's bloody gurney in a Parkland Hospital corridor—it was directly linked to that same mail-order gun."

"That's suspicious."

"Wasn't there also something about a handgun?"

I looked at him with a skeptical eye. "What did you do, attend the Clay Shaw trial?"

"Hell no, I'm not that stupid. But I heard stuff."

"Did you waste your money on those conspiracy books I just mentioned?"

"Maybe."

"You are unbelievable," I moaned.

The Preacher held up his hands in mock surrender, shrugged and said, "Hey, maybe I'm just intellectually curious."

"Well, whatever you are, you're right. Garrison pointed out that when Oswald was arrested, he was carrying a revolver in his pocket. Our Warren Commission stated Oswald also shot and killed Officer J.D. Tippitt. The problem was Tippitt was shot with an automatic pistol which ejects its spent cartridges. That's why four cartridges were found at the scene of Tippitt's murder."

"But Oswald's gun was a pistol, and pistols don't work that way."

"Right. Used cartridges from a pistol stay in the revolving cylinder of the gun until they are manually removed. The eyewitnesses reported they didn't see the gunman stand over the fallen officer and reload his gun. In fact, eyewitnesses testified they noticed two men approach and kill Tippitt, and neither one matched the description of Oswald. But they couldn't identify the men they witnessed fleeing the scene."

"You were lucky, *bon homme*."

"I know. Anyway, Garrison also pointed out that paraffin tests on Oswald's cheeks showed Oswald had not fired a rifle, and his fingerprints could not be found anywhere on the surface of the murder weapon. Garrison's timeline showed that someone saw Oswald downstairs at the Texas School Book Depository at the time of the assassination which would make it unlikely he was on the sixth floor at all."

"That would have been another big problem?"

"Yes it would have been."

"Anyway, Chase called me to tell me Garrison was facing tremendous political pressure in New Orleans to drop his investigation. Garrison was a stubborn guy, and Chase felt he probably wouldn't back down. The Patriots exerted pressure on Garrison's investigation by hustling subpoenaed witnesses out of town and not allowing the governors of other states to have the witnesses extradited back to New Orleans for the trial. The Patriots actually had a member of our Agency planted deep within Garrison's inner staff who tipped us off to everything Garrison knew and was planning to do."

"So Garrison's investigation didn't have a chance?"

"That was the plan—to discredit Garrison."

"But it didn't completely work, did it?"

"No, it didn't—it wasn't going to rest. Bobby Kennedy made sure of that."

"So it killed him in the end—the investigation?"

"Him and a lot of other people too."

The Preacher looked tired; he had deep circles under his eyes. He closed his eyes for a moment and became very still. I thought he was falling asleep, but he said, "Lyndon Baines Johnson's decision not to run for re-election. Was that the end of the Patriots' power?"

"Absolutely not. Neither his decision nor his later death was the end of the story, or even the end of the deaths associated with our crime. Four days after LBJ announced he didn't intend to run again in 1968, Martin Luther King, Jr. was gunned down in Memphis. At first I didn't think much of it, other than how sad his death was. But when I heard the details of the hunt for the assassin, it caught my attention."

"James Earl Ray," the Preacher grunted, "he was a sorry son of a bitch."

"He was named as the prime suspect almost immediately, yet he somehow managed to elude a worldwide manhunt for almost two months."

"Didn't they finally catch the guy in England? I seem to recall they caught him at Heathrow Airport, didn't they? How in the hell did he manage to get out of the country so easily?" the Preacher frowned, "I read that the guy was a red-neck and a small-time crook. There's no way he was smart enough or rich enough to do that on his own."

"I thought that maybe my old friends at Permindex might have had something to do with it. He fled the country through Montreal, Quebec, and they had extensive resources in Montreal. It sure sounded suspiciously like some of the things Clay Shaw had originally planned for our own escape routes after Dallas." I reached behind my head to massage my neck the best I could. I stretched my arms over my head.

"Well, did they have something to do with it?"

"I don't know. Ray claimed he was a patsy and that he didn't kill King."

"There goes that old patsy excuse again."

"I don't know if he did it or not. But I'll tell you this: when the authorities told James Earl Ray they had the rifle with his fingerprints on it, his answer made my hair stand on end. He claimed a mysterious man he knew only as Raol had given him the rifle."

"Maybe I'm getting tired—or just old," he yawned, "but I don't see the connection."

"You wouldn't see it. I saw it, however. The name *Raoul* happened to be Derek Ruger's nickname for himself. Ray spelled the name R-A-O-L. Ruger spelled it spelled R-A-O-U-L. Close enough. I was dumbfounded when I heard it."

"So was Ray's *Raol* the same as this Derek Ruger's *Raoul?*"

"My question exactly—if the answer was yes, it meant that the Patriots were behind Martin Luther King's assassination."

The Preacher whistled long and low, "That's some heavy shit."

"It only gets worse. Two months after King was killed, Bobby Kennedy was assassinated in the kitchen of the Ambassador Hotel in Los Angeles after his campaign rally. Even though the alleged assassin was caught on the spot, numerous pieces of evidence and eyewitness testimony indicated he had certainly not acted alone. Quite a few witnesses saw other gunmen in the crowd, and the number of bullets and bullet holes in the room indicated more than one shooter had to have been present. In 1968, it was not a federal crime to shoot a presidential candidate, so the local authorities handled the case and the questions raised were never adequately answered or explored."

"Did your guys do that one too?"

"They're not *my guys* anymore. But, I suspect so. The police claimed Sirhan Sirhan was the lone gunman. Sirhan claimed someone else did it."

"Do you believe him?"

"Well, I found out something concerning Bobby Kennedy's assassination that is almost too bizarre to be believed. My information came from a reliable source in the Middle East."

"You mean none of this other stuff is bizarre? *Bon homme*, everything you've told me so far is bizarre."

I shot a look at him.

"OK. How bizarre?"

"The money to pay for the Sirhan Sirhan job came out of a Palestinian freedom group in the Middle East. Guess who provided the money to them?"

He shrugged his shoulders. "I give up."

"Aristotle Onassis."

His eyes bugged out of his head in surprise. "Oh man. So you think Onassis had something to do with Bobby Kennedy's murder?"

"I can't say for sure. There was bad blood between the two that went back to the late forties. I looked into the story and it checked out. Onassis had a connection to Bobby's murder. Did he actually know what the Palestinians were going to do? Who knows? Would he have stopped them if he had?" I just shrugged my shoulders.

"Didn't Jackie move to Greece pretty soon after Bobby's funeral?"

"She shocked everyone worldwide by marrying Aristotle Onassis. She was this country's version of royalty, and she fled her own country."

"A lot of people were angry about that."

"She told Pam that her children had lost their father and their favorite uncle to violent deaths less than five years apart. She didn't feel safe raising her children in America anymore."

"Hey, she was right. She had to protect her kids."

"It was Jackie's way of saying, I've had enough. Both Pam and Jack's old friend George Smathers said it was Jackie's way of finally humbling the Kennedy women who had always flaunted their money and power. Pam said that Jackie finally had the chance to rub it in their faces and say, 'Okay, what are you going to say now that I can buy and sell you?'"

"Ouch. That's harsh."

"Jackie needed to get away from everyone. I doubt she knew the rumor about her new husband. If she did, I'm sure she wouldn't have married Onassis. Remember, when Jackie finally left D.C. after Jack's funeral and moved to New York. Bobby quickly followed her there."

"You think Bobby was boinking Jackie?"

"Who knows? They were close, always had been." I recalled how Bobby had always been there for Jackie, even when her own husband wasn't.

My back had begun to ache from leaning against the headboard so long. When I moved to stand, a burning tingle ran through my foot.

"That's some heavy shit, Patrick." He leaned back and looked at me as if he was afraid of what else I would disclose. "The country was sick of LBJ, and Bobby was dead, and nobody was going to elect Hubert Humphrey as president. So that's how Nixon got in?"

"That's how. In November, Richard Nixon finally attained his goal of becoming president. And the Patriots retained their control of the White House as well."

"Yeah, but he was as bad as LBJ, except for the trail of dead bodies LBJ left behind. Remember the "enemies list"? He wiretapped anyone he didn't like—with a little help from Hoover—and he used the IRS as a hammer against anyone who tried to stand up to him."

The Preacher wiped his forehead on his arm, "Damn humidity." He continued with his vitriol, "Nixon claimed he had a secret plan for ending the war in Vietnam. Yet he sent more and more young men to Southeast Asia to fight. Just empty promises! He was a bastard."

I knew the real Dick Nixon, and my friend didn't. "Hey, he wasn't really that bad. Dick was basically a good guy, deep down."

"Bullshit. He was a lying bastard. I don't know who I hated more—LBJ or Tricky Dick. Look how he escalated the war in Vietnam."

I winced. I couldn't agree with him, but I couldn't disagree with him either.

"You know, if I hadn't done what I did in Dallas, maybe things would have been different. Thousands of American soldiers were dying needlessly, and I blamed myself."

"But you didn't act alone, my friend."

"I acted to save my country from the threat of Jack's inexperience, and all the country received was Lyndon Johnson' calculated betrayals instead. Nixon really wasn't able to do any better, and Hoover was out of control."

"You are right about that," the Preacher commiserated.

"I'll tell you, I lived a miserable existence in Vietnam, but I kept up with events back home. Nixon's re-election in 1972 was no surprise, but what was a surprise was the Watergate break-in the summer of '72. I was astonished to see my old acquaintance, E. Howard Hunt, arrested as one of the burglars. I later found out from sources that Nixon and the Patriots thought the offices of the Democratic National Committee might have contained some evidence of that fateful meeting at Clint Murchison's house in Dallas on November 21, 1963, linking them all to the plot to kill Jack Kennedy. Paranoid that such information might prove to be true, they felt they had no choice but to go in and get it."

"Slow down a minute. You think Watergate was really about the assassination?"

"I do."

"I never understood Watergate. Nixon was hiding something. I always wondered what was so important that he would sacrifice himself rather than tell the truth."

"You remember the infamous thirteen-minute gap on the Nixon White House tapes?" I asked.

"Yeah, again that never made sense to me."

"Maybe now it will. It contained a discussion of that evidence and what it could mean for all involved. They had no other choice but to go to great lengths to protect themselves from having such information revealed. The resulting cover-up led to Nixon's speech on August 8, 1974. Nixon felt it was his duty to finish his term and said that it had 'become evident that I no longer have a strong enough political base in Congress to justify continuing that effort…I have never been a quitter. To leave office before my term is completed is opposed to every instinct in my body. But as President I must put the interests of America first.…Therefore, I shall resign the Presidency effective at noon tomorrow.' And that's exactly what he did."

"I can tell that you admired something about Nixon."

"I did. I understood him. He was vilified by our nation when he only had the nation's best interests at heart. On November 22, 1963, we set some wheels in motion that couldn't be stopped. They came back to run him over later in life."

"So did the Patriots lose power when Nixon resigned?"

"Nope. Our new President just happened to be an old Warren Commission accomplice, Gerald Ford. Ford had been the snitch who fed inside information about the Warren Commission directly to Director Hoover in order to make sure the FBI's investigation was steered away from problems. The Patriots retained control of the White House—they managed to do it in a bloodless coup this time."

"This is unbelievable shit," the Preacher gasped.

"It is, but not all of the strange events were due to the Patriots. The Patriots were out of control, but they weren't responsible for all of them. For example, Mary Jo Kopechne was one of the most unfortunate victims of Dallas."

"Wasn't she the girl that drowned in Teddy Kennedy's car in 1969?"

"One and the same. She had been Senator George Smather's secretary. She was the hapless girl who told her roommate, Nancy Carole Tyler, that she had heard some juicy gossip about how Jack Kennedy intended to drop LBJ off the ticket in 1964. Tyler died in a mysterious plane crash in the Atlantic Ocean near Ocean City, Maryland back in 1965."

"I remember it was a suspicious accident."

"The evidence showed Kopechne may have been deliberately left to drown in the backseat of Senator Kennedy's car. Some investigators thought she had been murdered. I've always wondered if Teddy directly blamed her for causing his brother's death and decided to take out his anger and frustration on her one night in a drunken rage."

"Wow! That's heavy. Can you prove it?"

"Of course not. But no one seems able to disprove it, either."

"Let me ask you a question. You have mentioned Ruger several times. At first, I thought he was part of the Agency. Who is this guy?"

"Derek Ruger is a stone-cold killer—the scariest man I have ever met." I hesitated, "He was part of Sam Giancana's organization when I first met him. He's not CIA, he's mob, or he was mob. Now, he's a tool of the Patriots." I thought twice before I revealed, "He's the real reason I'm here."

"Jesus Christ, Patrick! You've got a hired killer after you? Are you shittin' me?"

"Wish I was."

"Shit."

"I covered my tracks. He's on a wild goose chase right now."

"The Patriots send him?"

I nodded. "Trust me," I assured him. "No one knows about you. If he ever finds my trail, and I highly doubt he will, I'll be long gone."

The Preacher's face was suffused in worry.

"Listen," I said, "if he shows up here, you tell him what he wants to know. Don't try to protect me. Tell him you met me in the Marine Corps and that you were surprised to see me. Tell him I said something about going to Brazil. Don't lie. Don't elaborate."

"Jesus, I hope you're right," he said as he stood up. "I've got to go get something stronger than beer, I'll be right back."

I took the time to repack my duffel bag. I kept my journal and small cardboard box where they were. I packed up the stuff on the nightstand and put it in my shaving kit. I ran my hand over my chin; I needed a shave. I felt for my pistol—it was safely stowed with an extra box of bullets. I pulled back the sheets on the bed just to make sure that I had not accidentally left something of importance. I looked under the bed to see a cockroach scurry away.

I heard the creak of the Preacher's steps outside my door. "I've brought us a friend," he said, "Let me introduce you to Mr. Jack Daniels." He held out the bottle and two small glasses. Handing me a finger-smudged glass, he poured us both a couple of inches of booze.

He held up his glass in a melancholy toast, "To your safety, Patrick."

The Preacher slumped back in his chair while I lit up another cigarette. I had long since finished my drink and poured myself another. I slugged down a couple of swallows. I looked at my watch. I had been talking far too long. It was almost daybreak.

"Have the Patriots won?"

"Not yet. That's what the subpoena is all about," I motioned over to my duffel bag. "They want me to tell them who was behind it."

"You mean to tell me, I might still have a chance to become famous?" the Preacher kidded.

"I did make you famous. Don't you remember?"

"Yeah, I remember. But I should have told you I wanted to be *famous*, not *infamous*. You made my name infamous but thankfully not my face."

I laughed at his sense of humor. Then his tone turned serious. "What does all of this mean for you?"

"It means that one of the last conspirators still alive, outside of Derek Ruger and Grant Grantham, is me."

"You mentioned Grant Grantham before. He is…?"

"The man the Patriots have put in charge. He used to be my roommate and best friend. Now he apparently wants to see me dead. I'm pretty sure Grantham is looking for me." I put down the empty glass. "Let me ask you something—something philosophical."

"I thought you said you're leaving this morning. If you get me started on philosophy, it might take all day," he replied.

"I just want to know what you believe."

The Preacher leaned back on the chair, lifting its front legs off the floor.

"That's a heavy question in and of itself," he said, "What do you believe?"

"I've tried to make sense out of everything that has happened, and I think I've got it boiled down to two things: fate and free will."

"The question of the ages: how much of life is fate, and how much of life is free will. Or is there a divine plan?"

"I've lost my faith—I don't know if I believe in a higher power so I can't talk about a divine plan. But when I look over my life, I wonder if I was destined to do what I did or did I make a wrong turn somewhere?"

"Go on," the Preacher urged.

"I was betrayed by my long time friend—I was the real patsy the whole time. The people I trusted deliberately duped and manipulated me."

"Life can be ruthless," the Preacher commented, "but I think you always have a choice in some way over what befalls you."

"Chase Newman, my old roommate, tried to warn me. Even in the very beginning, he warned me about Grantham. He told me about the ruthlessness of Lyndon Johnson and the people that surrounded him once LBJ became president. But it was already too late for me—I think I had already sealed my fate. When I honestly opened my eyes and looked around me, I could see ruthlessness everywhere I looked."

"How so?"

"The Warren Commission and the successful cover-up—I was heavily involved in that. I justified it to myself."

"Self-preservation is a strong emotion—you did what you thought you had to do. It was wrong, but I understand your motives." The Preacher sat silently for a moment and then asked, "So, Patrick, was it free will or was it fate that brought you to this place in your life."

"It was a lot of things. It was poor judgment. It was a blinding patriotism. It was naiveté, ambivalence, you name it. I am a very flawed man."

"But for the grace of God, go I. We are all flawed creatures, Patrick. That is the nature of being human."

"It is, isn't it?"

He stretched his arms out and yawned. "It's way past my bedtime, my friend. We both need to get our sleep."

The Preacher stood and hugged me instead of shaking my hand. As he held me in a tight embrace, I realized it was the first time in a long time that I felt a faint glimmer of hope.

"I will pray for you, my friend," he said earnestly.

"I would like that," I whispered back softly.

As the Preacher quietly exited the room and closed the door behind him, I moved the bedcover out of the way and glanced at my journal which was open to the last page. I was struck by the quote I had written down:

Men at some time are masters of their fates.
The fault, dear Brutus, is not in our stars,
But in ourselves, that we are underlings.

— Shakespeare (Julius Caesar)

September 7, 1978
5:01 a.m.

Derek Ruger lit up a Camel. Patrick McCarthy was in a room on the upper floor in the back of the mission. He was sure of it. When he walked around the building, he could hear snoring from most areas except in the back. There was a light on. He heard two voices—one of them was McCarthy's.

Ruger's senses were fully alert. He felt wired whenever he came in for the kill. He was the predator. Damn it felt good.

He smoked his cigarette, savoring the kill-memories. Action Jackson—his favorite—he made the fat fuck suffer. Three days to kill the asshole—better than any sex he had ever had. But Sam didn't like it. He said he wanted the fucker to suffer, but when he did what Sam wanted, Sam told him, "You enjoy it too much, Derek. Just kill 'em and get it over with."

Ruger blew smoke through his nostrils. That stool pigeon Johnny Roselli had pleaded for his life. He should have suffered longer than he did.

Miss Marilyn Monroe—what a waste of pussy. But it wasn't his call. Sam wanted her dead to pin it on the Kennedys. Ruger grinned. It didn't work out quite the way Sam wanted it to. Sam should have left it to him to handle.

He flicked the ash from his cigarette. He strained to hear the conversation in McCarthy's room.

That nosy newspaper columnist, what was her name? Oh yeah, Dorothy Kilgallen. She was on that TV show "What's My Line?" The Patriots said the dumb bitch interviewed Jack Ruby in prison and bragged about what she found out. She was gonna blow off the lid to the whole Kennedy assassination. After he killed the old bat, he got a call that her best friend was holding onto Kilgallen's notes—Mrs. Earl E.T. Smith, the wife of the former ambassador

KENNEDY MUST BE KILLED 597

to Cuba. He could have lived years in Bangkok on what he had been paid for both jobs.

He took another drag on his cigarette and recalled the Mary Pinchot Meyer job. That one was a CIA rush job. She was a jogger—easy to ambush on her morning run along the Chesapeake & Ohio canal in Georgetown. He felt a flicker of excitement in his groin. Yeah, he would have liked to have spent some more time with her. He could have had some real fun. A brief flicker in her eyes told him that she was a broad that thought she liked pain—but it didn't take much to convince her to tell him where she kept her diary.

He smiled, thinking of Martin Luther King and James Earl Ray—two famous names for his mental trophy wall. Uppity nigger. And that stupid fuck, Ray, almost got him caught when he spilled his guts about the mysterious "Raoul." The Patriots paid him well to get James Earl Ray into Canada and then into England.

He took another puff and thought about the Kennedys. He and Mac Wallace still argued over whether it was their shot or McCarthy's little punk-ass shot that killed JFK.

Ruger took pride in bagging Bobby Kennedy. A matched pair, he had joked to Wallace, just to piss Wallace off. He managed to shoot Bobby just a foot behind him and no one was the wiser. That sand nigger, Sirhan Sirhan, said he was coerced. He had to hand it to the Patriots. That lone gunman bullshit worked.

Ruger smiled when he thought of the night of sex he had with that girl... Sharon? She had gotten him the Kennedy campaign credentials to be in the crowd off the podium at the Ambassador Hotel. She helped him push his way into the kitchen area and then helped him get out during all the confusion. The only problem was that the dumb broad kept screaming, "We've shot him! We've shot him!" He had to take her back to their motel for a quick kill. He stripped off that polka-dot dress and found the sexy black crotchless panties. She did everything he wanted her to do. The best part was when he strangled her—as big a thrill as killing that punk Kennedy.

He botched the Oswald kill. Shit, some numbnuts got in the way. That was a real fuck-up. He should have killed Patrick then, too. Maybe none of this other shit would have happpened. No Warren Commission, no Garrison investigation, no Church Committee, no House Select Committee on Assassinations. And no Grant Grantham constantly whining and wetting his pants to keep all this shit quiet. He couldn't count all the people he had killed because of those fucking investigations. But, hey, he was rich. He could stop anytime he wanted to.

He felt strangely nostalgic for his mentor, Sam Giancana, whenever he remembered one piece of advice the crazy old dago had given him: "As long as corruption and greed exists in men with power, your services will be needed. Count on it. The Patriots will always need to keep some things secret—and you'll be able to name your price."

He had been right. The Patriots were excellent employers. Sam never tried to jack him around. When he went to kill Sam, he snuck up behind him in the basement and softly whispered, "This'll be quick." He shot him in the back of the head before Sam could even turn around. Then he kicked his body over onto its back and placed five more shots around his mouth to signify he had been a stool pigeon. After all, it was all about *omerta*. Sam would have understood that. Yeah, Sam Giancana was a good man. Too bad he fucked up.

He became very still. He stopped his breathing and listened. The conversation had stopped—McCarthy was alone now. McCarthy was fucked from the get-go. Too bad he had to kill him especially since he saved him from the sharks during the Bay of Pigs clusterfuck. Crazy spics called him El Diablo. He knew the sharks wouldn't attack him. Sharks are opportunistic—it's their nature to take out the weak and wounded.

He took one final drag, tossed the cigarette butt aside, checked his watch, and glanced toward the flophouse mission.

He caressed the cold muzzle of his pistol.

Time to go to work.

September 7, 1978
5:17 a.m.

I reached for the cardboard box sitting next to my journal. I tipped the box over and dumped its contents next to me on the bed. This was the physical evidence I had kept hidden ever since 1963. It would backup the claims I had made in my journal. If I could manage to stay alive, I hoped the combination of my written history and these few indisputable artifacts would be all I would need to keep Grant and the Patriots from publicly railroading me.

Strewn on the bed lay five extra 6.5 mm bullets we had test-fired from the Oswald rifle. I marveled at how these tiny little pieces of lead had changed the course of American history. Fifteen years after the assassination, the media still guarded and fiercely protected our myth of the "Magic Bullet." God bless them for that.

I placed the bullets in the cardboard box and reached for the film packet with the Gordon Arnold and Mary Ann Moorman photos. The Moorman photo still amazed me; the picture of Oswald standing in front of the Texas School Book Depository with the President's limo passing right in front was tangible proof of his innocence. The Arnold photos showed me and Roscoe walking behind the fence just before the motorcade got to Dealey Plaza, indisputable evidence of our guilt.

I laid the photos down inside the box and picked the small tin off the bed that held the Beverly Oliver Super-8 movie film. Oliver's little home movie showed the whole grassy knoll, the muzzle flash, the smoke from my rifle—and my face as I aimed and fired the fatal head shot from the Grassy Knoll. No one would doubt the presence of a second gunman in Dallas that day if they ever saw this film.

Setting the Oliver film tin down in the box next to the other items, I protectively picked up the crown jewel of my little collection. The lid on the small film canister read: Original negative (uncut—ZapruderFilm). The Warren Commission had relied heavily upon the Zapruder film to support their case against Lee Harvey Oswald. I had pulled a fast one on my fellow conspirators when I told everyone concerned I had returned the original negative to Abraham Zapruder. No one questioned me about it, and Zapruder never noticed the switch. It would take quite an expert to notice how subtly the Zapruder film had been altered, but those alterations would be very easy to see if it was compared to the crystal-clear original that I had in my possession.

I pulled my last cigarette out of my jacket and snapped open my Zippo lighter. I had been so obsessed with the idea of serving and protecting my country that I had ended up betraying my country. I leaned back against the headboard, puffed my cigarette, and thought of my tattered career and the shambles it had made of me.

Jack Kennedy was dead. Bobby Kennedy was dead. Lyndon Johnson was dead. J. Edgar Hoover was dead. Richard Nixon was disgraced. The tensions with the Soviet Union were still at a boiling point. The Vietnam War and the race riots had happened anyway. The country was in a bigger mess now than ever before.

My marriage was gone, and my life was in danger. I couldn't even begin to count the number of lives I had ruined and the number of people I had let down. And in the end, it was all for nothing.

What a waste. What a goddamned waste it had all turned out to be.

My cigarette burned down. I extinguished it in the overflowing ashtray on the nightstand. I swung my feet off the bed and dug into my duffel bag for some packing tape and my penknife. I then carefully removed my film and bullets from the cardboard box and gently laid the green notebook in the bottom of the box. I placed the two tins of film on their sides next to the notebook and positioned the photo envelope on top of the notebook. I wrapped the five "magic" bullets in my handkerchief and placed it atop the notebook, too.

After double-checking to be sure everything was where it should be, I crumpled up some newspaper using it to wedge the contents of the box in place so they wouldn't slide around and possibly get damaged once they were shipped. I closed the flaps of the box and secured it shut with the packing tape while saying a brief prayer and goodbye to the contents.

Satisfied with my handiwork, I sat back and stared at the address on the box top. I was confident the box and its contents would be self-explanatory if they were ever opened and examined. The box contained my ironclad piece of personal protection. My little cardboard box full of evidence would shred all of the Warren Commission lies and expose the Patriots' twisted conspiracy.

I had conceived a simple plan to conceal my evidence with my trusted friend. I would leave explicit instructions with the Preacher to immediately mail the box to a special destination if anything were to ever happen to me. I prayed that wouldn't be necessary.

I slipped on my shoes and opened the door to the hallway. The corridor was completely deserted. I tiptoed down the corridor and descended the stairs to the Preacher's apartment on the ground floor. I lightly rapped at the door. I could hear him wake up and start cussing whoever had awakened him. A moment later, he opened the door in his dingy underwear.

"Oh, it's you," he griped. "I had just gotten to sleep, *bon homme*."

"I'm sorry, old friend, but I have to get going."

He gave me an empathetic look. We had already said our good-byes; this was just a formality.

I pulled the box out and handed it to him. "I forgot to give this to you when you were upstairs. I need you to hold this for me. I might come get it one day, or I might have you mail it for me to the address on the top."

He looked at the address and nodded knowingly. "I can do that." He paused and then said, "You're very worried about all this. I could see it in your eyes when you showed up yesterday."

"No you couldn't. That's bullshit. I've been too good a liar all my life."

He shook his head sadly. "You might think so, but you're wrong. The people close to you know better."

I couldn't argue with him because he was right. "Believe what you want to believe," I bravely replied. I stood mutely as he took my box and slid it underneath his sofa.

"I'll move it to a much more secure spot once you leave. If it's as valuable as I think it is, I don't even want you to know what I've done with it."

"Good idea," I agreed. "Listen, we need to agree on a password or phrase that will indicate you need to destroy this package for me. The day might come when I won't need it anymore. The rest of the world won't need to see it either."

"Okay, what do you have in mind?"

"Something simple. I'll identify myself as 'Watchdog.' If you ever get the message that 'Watchdog' is calling, that password will verify the authenticity of my call. Got it?"

"Got it. Watchdog."

"Don't forget it."

"I won't."

I held out my hand, and he brushed it aside to hug me. "Good luck, *bon homme*. And if you ever need a place to stay, Patrick, you're always welcome back here. Remember that."

"Thanks." His basic decency touched me immensely. "I better get going."

The old wooden floor of the hallway creaked with every step I took as I returned to my room to retrieve my duffel bag. I tried to be as quiet as I could as I made my way back to my room. I was finally starting to relax a little bit. A feeling of well-being washed over me.

I checked my watch as my thoughts moved on to my next course of action. In about four hours, I planned to catch a tramp steamer to Morocco that was leaving out of New Orleans. Once in Morocco, I thought I would head either to Europe, Africa, or the Middle East. I might even head to South America. I had a lot of time to make that decision.

I wondered what Tim was doing right now. I was so proud of him. I heard he was wandering wherever the road took him on his motorcycle. It was a shame I couldn't take him to Morocco with me. We could have had a great adventure together.

My dear Pam was in Michigan. By mutual agreement, we had not spoken in a couple of years. I still loved her with all my heart, and I think she still loved me. But in the last fifteen years, I had deliberately caused her a tremendous amount of hurt and pain. As far as she was concerned, I wasn't worth the heartache. *Pam, please forgive me and take me back again.* I desperately wanted to go to Michigan. But it was too dangerous—and I was too much of a coward. Maybe all of this would be over one day, and I could safely see her again. Wouldn't that be wonderful?

I finally reached my third-floor door and slipped quietly back inside. I meticulously scanned the tiny room one last time to make sure I had all of my belongings stuffed back into my canvas duffel. My bag felt noticeably lighter without the weight of the journal and the box.

I was startled by a gentle knocking at the door. My only thought was the Preacher must have wanted to tell me one last thing before I left. I grabbed the doorknob and joked, "Hey, we have to stop meeting like this."

It was not the Preacher who greeted me—it was the glint of a gun pointed at my stomach.

I recognized the frighteningly hollow eyes of the one man I had hoped to never, ever see again.

Derek Ruger softly whispered, "I've been looking for you."

Acknowledgements

This story could not have been told without the help, guidance, and encouragement of some very special people.

Vali Helppie, my wife and personal editor, who believed in my story from the very beginning. She corrected all of my many, many mistakes and tightened up a dull narrative with suggestions which transformed it into a compelling story with an overarching theme, literary touches, and a broad historical context. I lovingly dedicate this book to her.

Diane Pittaway, whose editorial input helped us tremendously with her insightful recommendations regarding dialogue and character development. I can't thank her enough for the many, many hours she spent reading the manuscript. Thank you very much, Diane.

Kathy Haskins, Candace Terhune-Flannery, and Marge Swager who read the early drafts of the story and gave us much needed feedback. We tightened up the story with their help. We needed their positive feedback and appreciated their encouragement. Thank you very much, ladies.

My uncle, Dennis Helppie, who read the very first draft (in its roughest form) in two days and said he couldn't put it down, and my cousin, Richard Helppie, who bolstered my confidence by assuring me it was exactly the kind of book he loved to read and recommend to others. Thanks, guys.

Finally, I want to express my considerable appreciation to the community of researchers into the JFK assassination who never let the story die. Their unwavering dedication to discovering and uncovering the truth motivated me no end to craft my own story, based upon the thousands and thousands of pages of information they published which revealed facts ignored and overlooked by the Warren Commission. Thank you for all you have done to educate the American public.